FLAM-FLAM-FLAM-FLAM.

Nathaniel's eyes popped open. What was that sound? He rubbed the sleep from his eyes and strained to see through the darkness. Across the room Basil snorted, still slumbering.

Rat-a-tat-tat. Rat-a-tat-tat. FLAM-FLAM-FLAM-FLAM.

Nathaniel sat up. Those were drums! He jumped out of bed and ran to the window. In the waning moonlight, he saw men running down the street toward Market Square.

"The redcoats! The redcoats!"

Rat-a-tat-tat. More drums, more shouts.

Nathaniel scrambled to pull on his stockings and breeches. "Master!" he called. "Master Basil, something is amiss. Get up."

He pushed on Basil's turned back. "Master, I think we've been attacked! Master, you must get up!"

FLAM-FLAM-FLAM-FLAM. To arms, Williamsburg! To the magazine! Alarm! Alarm!

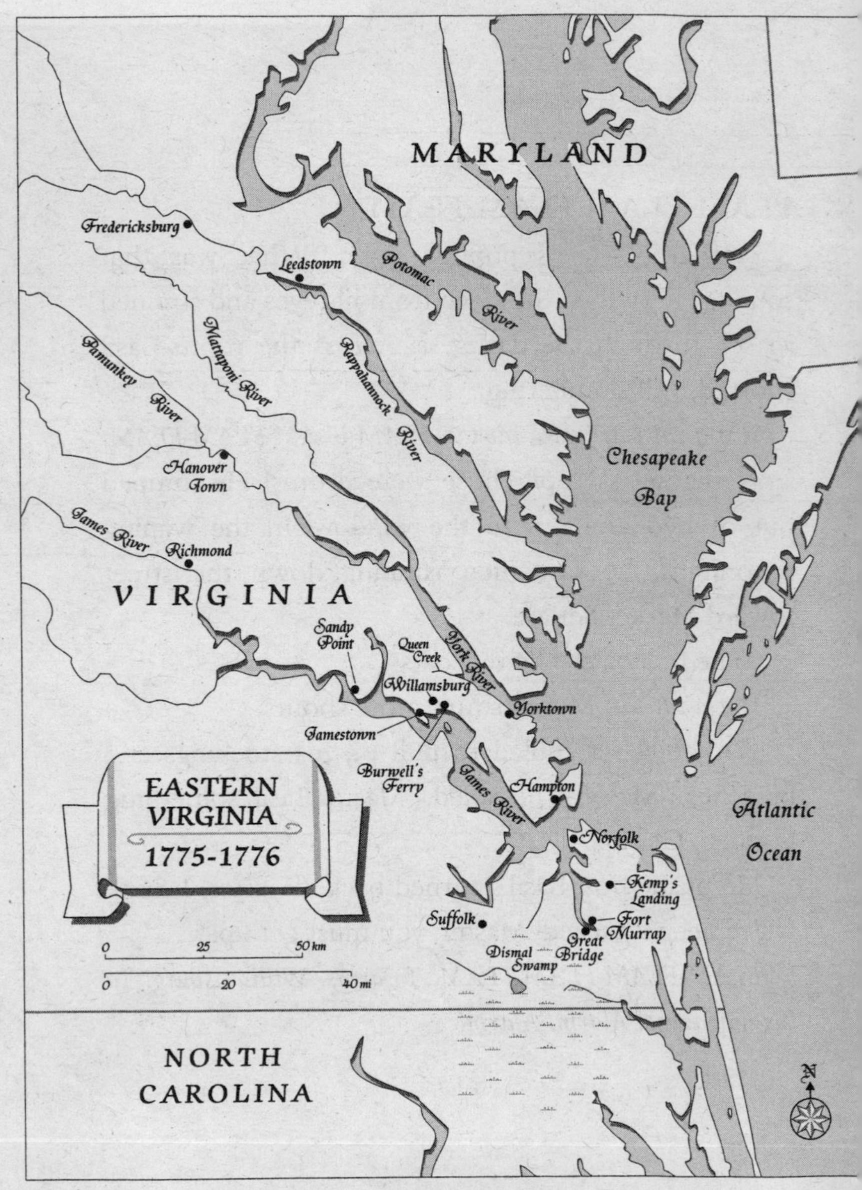
MARYLAND
Fredericksburg
Leedstown
Potomac River
Pamunkey River
Mattaponi River
Rappahannock River
Chesapeake Bay
Hanover Town
James River
Richmond
VIRGINIA
Sandy Point
Queen Creek
York River
Willamsburg
Yorktown
Jamestown
Burwell's Ferry
EASTERN VIRGINIA
1775-1776
James River
Hampton
Atlantic Ocean
Norfolk
Kemp's Landing
Suffolk
Fort Murray
Great Bridge
Dismal Swamp
0 25 50 km
0 20 40 mi
NORTH CAROLINA
N

GIVE ME LIBERTY

L. M. Elliott

Katherine Tegen Books
HarperTrophy®
An Imprint of HarperCollins*Publishers*

To the memory of Diane Granat Yalowitz,
extraordinary writer, friend, mother, and humanitarian

Harper Trophy® is a registered trademark of HarperCollins Publishers.

Epigraph from *Books I Read When I Was Young: The Favorite Books of Famous People*, edited by M. Jerry Weiss and Bernice E. Cullinan, National Council of Teachers of English, 1980. Reprinted with permission.

Give Me Liberty
 For information address HarperCollins Children's Books, a division of HarperCollins Publishers, 1350 Avenue of the Americas, New York, NY 10019.
www.harpercollinschildrens.com

Library of Congress catalog card number: 2006018166

ISBN 978-0-06-074423-6

Typography by Joel Tippie

❖

First Harper Trophy edition, 2008

All the changes in the world, for good or evil, were first brought about by words.

—Jacqueline Kennedy Onassis

PART ONE

May 1774

Oh, that I was where I would be,
Then I would be where I am not,
Here I am where I must be,
Go where I would, I can not,
Oh, diddle, lully day,
Oh, de little lioday.

—"Katy Cruel," eighteenth-century ballad

Chapter One

NATHANIEL PRESSED HIS nose against the coarse linsey-woolsey of his sleeve. He breathed in deeply. It was the first time in almost a year that it hadn't stunk of horsehair, dirt, straw, and leftover grease from wiping dinner off his lips. He kept his face buried in the fabric. It smelled instead of lye soap, of clean, of the warm sun that had dried it. The smell was wonderful.

Nathaniel dropped his arm to look across the York River, swollen and muddy from May rains. His mother had made him the shirt two years ago, right before they left England for the New World. Now it was barely long enough to protect his backside from the scratch of his breeches. It was well made, though, twenty tiny stitches to an inch in the seams. And it was clean. Silly, he knew, but somehow the feeling of clean gave Nathaniel a sense of rebirth.

Standing atop a bluff overlooking the Virginia river,

Nathaniel watched gulls drop out of the sky into the slow-moving waters. He assessed the horizon for a good omen. Blue skies would promise fortune, surely. But the heavens were coy about their thoughts. Wispy clouds fogged the sky, coloring it a shy white-blue. It was, in fact, just the color of Nathaniel's eyes—a veiled, barely-there blue.

His father had hated the paleness of Nathaniel's eyes. When irritated, he'd curse them as bewitched and lily-livered. Nathaniel could judge the souls of strangers by their reaction to his eyes. Those with meanness inside smirked. Those afraid of devils looked away. Kindness smiled.

His mother had said, "They're the color of sky and mist mixed together, as the world's waking up to the day, my son. Those be your eyes—the promise of a new day."

She was like that, his mother. Her own eyes had been the brilliant hue of bluebells, abloom with springlike hope, always believing in possibilities. Even during their six-week voyage across the Atlantic Ocean to Virginia—while they and seventy other passengers clung to the below-deck posts of the merchant ship lurching through storm after storm during the winter of 1772—she held fast to his father's promise of the faraway colonies being a place of dreams to be had for the taking. She believed even as she lay dying of ship fever.

"'Love *hopes* all things,'" she quoted Corinthians from the Bible, the one book Nathaniel's family possessed.

A breeze brushed Nathaniel's face and ruffled his blond hair, lifting it to dance in the air—another unfamiliar feeling of clean. He'd been startled after scrubbing himself with the lye to look down into the barrel of water and to see the reflection of such fair skin and hair, bleached by the Virginia sun. Grimy for so long, he'd forgotten what he really looked like.

Nathaniel took another deep breath, this time pulling in the sweet smells of new bloom, of greening grasses. There had been a wild hailstorm earlier in the month that destroyed all the peach blossoms and sent the plantation's owner into a fit about the loss of peach brandy for the year. But now the earth was in full blossom, joyfully shaking itself awake, spewing out millions of flowers in field and trees. Nathaniel looked back up to the gulls. He wondered if they rejoiced in the festival of color beneath them.

When the breeze rustled his hair and shirt again, Nathaniel felt a hesitant happiness creep through him. He closed his eyes and held his arms out, imagining, just as he had when he was a small boy. The wind picked up a bit, flapping his billowy sleeves. He willed his feet to lift up off the ground, his arms to sprout feathers. He could almost feel himself float on the pale blue air of soft breezes, delicious new-life smells, and fledgling possibilities.

Today was a day that would change his circumstances. Perhaps today, he could brave hoping for his own spring.

"All right, sir, let's see what you have to offer," spoke a voice behind Nathaniel.

Nathaniel dropped his gaze to his bare feet, waiting. Two long shadows slid across the clover toward him. A well-polished set of boots came into view alongside a set of fat, cracked shoes with tarnished buckles.

"What? This? This here? This be nothing but a runt of a lad."

Nathaniel lost the scent of new bloom in the stench of rum, garlic, and sweat the men carried. His heart began to pound.

One of them rattled papers as he spoke: "He's thirteen years of age, Mr. Owen. He'll grow into your needs. Remember he has eight years more on his indenture until he turns twenty-one. If you purchase a grown man's time, you only have him four years. Price is eleven pounds, his cost of passage from London. If you want a strong slave, like that one, it'll cost you upwards of sixty pounds." The man pointed to Nathaniel's friend, Moses, who stood nearby amongst a group of slaves. He was sixteen but tall and strong, and could handle a hogshead of tobacco on his own.

"Hmmm . . ." Owen growled. He grabbed Nathaniel's arms and squeezed, looking for muscle. "Blacksmithing is hard work, boy. I need someone to stoke my fires, carry water, sort scraps of iron. You've no meat on you." He began testing Nathaniel's legs.

Nathaniel tried to keep from recoiling from the bruising, sausage-thick fingers. It'd been like this at Leedstown, when their ship had finally docked in the Rappahannock River—people checking him over as they might an ox, assessing strength and the amount of feed the animal required to pull a plow for as many seasons as possible. He'd been purchased then by the plantation owner, who'd seemed kind enough. But the planter turned out to be a gambler. He lost most of his tobacco fortune on horse races held in Fredericksburg. The rest evaporated when an unusually large tobacco crop in Virginia caused the prices England would pay for it to plummet.

As the planter became poorer, he'd starved his servants—twenty-some slaves and a dozen indentured servants. Since winter, Nathaniel hadn't eaten anything much but corn and hoecakes. The only kindness done them had been the recent laundering to make them presentable, because all of them, along with everything in the estate—the house, the acres, the hogs, plows, featherbeds, pots, pans, and hoes—were up for sale to pay off the master's debts.

"Any pestilence about him?"

"No. He's fit. They say he is exceedingly good with horses. Useful for a blacksmith, I thought." The man holding the papers was clearly an auctioneer, assigned to market the plantation's human merchandise.

Owen grunted. He seized Nathaniel's jaw and twisted it around so that sunlight fell full on his face. Prying Nathaniel's mouth open, Owen stuck a filthy finger in and counted his teeth, lingering over the one in the back that had just finished growing in.

"Well, they look sound." He shoved Nathaniel aside and wiped his hand on his jacket. "If nothing else, if I work him to death, I can sell those teeth. There's a surgeon in Norfolk giving forty shillings a tooth. I'd make a profit." Owen jabbed the auctioneer with an elbow and guffawed.

The auctioneer straightened his waistcoat and asked coldly, "Do you want him?"

"Aye, he'll do for something. But I'll only pay seven pound for him."

Nathaniel's heart sank. This man seemed worse than the planter. *No! Say it's not enough coin. Make him go away.*

The auctioneer thought a moment. "Nine."

"Eight and ten shilling."

"Agreed." The auctioneer made a note in his papers.

Nathaniel fought off fainting.

"Right then," said Owen. "Let me see what horseflesh you have. Come, boy." He shoved Nathaniel to walk abreast of him.

Hopes all things?

Only fools hoped. Hope made life's disappointments hurt the more. Hope is what had brought him to bondage.

Owen hadn't even asked Nathaniel's name. And he certainly hadn't looked him in the eye. That was the other kind of reaction to Nathaniel's eyes—none—born of such indifference to his existence as a human being that a person never saw them because they never bothered to look Nathaniel in the face.

Chapter Two

MISERABLE, NATHANIEL TRUDGED toward the stable, listening to the heavy, grunting breathing of his new master. From sideways glances, he saw that Owen was a massive man, with a lot of weight to pull along on gout-inflamed legs. He dared a backward look toward Moses. His friend was being questioned by a man in a fine frock coat with silver braiding and lace sleeves dangling beneath the cuffs. Moses would be all right, then. Such a richly dressed gentleman had to be a merchant or such. It was sure to be better than the circumstances to which he was headed.

Nathaniel swallowed hard. It'd been Moses who'd convinced him to eat, to breathe when he'd nearly died of grief at first coming to the plantation. Moses had a large goodness about him. The smaller slave boys used to skip along behind him, like devoted puppies. Remarkably tall, Moses had a long, odd scar like a crescent moon across his forehead. It came from his mother having to work the fields with him on her back when he was a baby. One day her hands were full with tobacco leaves, and he'd fallen. But Moses liked the moon shape of it. He claimed it was an omen, a mark showing that he was destined to travel. He loved to hear Nathaniel's stories of England and the sea. Nathaniel had just started to teach Moses the alphabet, scratching letters in the sand down by the river after their chores were completed. Nathaniel would miss him sorely.

The two of them had discussed the possibility of being separated this day. Moses seemed resigned to it. Many years before, he had been sold away from his family. All Moses remembered of his father—who'd been a "saltwater slave," stolen directly from West Africa—were his gold earrings and face tattoos.

"It's the way of it," Moses had said. "But it won't be forever, Nathaniel. We hear about good men talking on liberty, breaking with the king. If they be arguing against their master, they see it wrong to use us the way they do."

Nathaniel, Owen, and the auctioneer passed the manor house, a rectangular, brick building of two stories and long windows, with a commander's view of the river.

In front of the door was a crowd of people as if it were a market day. A man waddled down the stone steps, bracing a huge basket filled with china against his legs. In the drive, a wagon was being filled with delicately made chairs. Several slaves balanced rolled-up Persian carpets atop their heads, following a gentleman whose arms gleamed with a mass of silver candlesticks.

An older, gawky man struggled to toss a sack stuffed with leather-bound books up into a two-wheel, bright green riding chair. Nathaniel noticed that the carriage horse fretted and shied away from the man, who foolishly flapped his arms and grabbed at the harness, further flustering the horse.

That one would be fortunate to make it home in one piece, thought Nathaniel. *He knows naught about horses.*

In the past year, Nathaniel had come to know almost everything about horses. He'd fed them, brushed them, soothed them when the farrier hammered in their shoes, soaked their sore spots after races, walked them to health when their guts twisted up in colic. He'd happily slept in the hayloft of the finely built stables. Even in the winter, it wasn't so bad. He'd burrow into the straw like a field mouse and sleep just fine, listening to the comforting sounds of the horses munching their hay. Sometimes he crept into the stalls and curled up against mares that had just had their foals taken from them for training. He seemed to calm their anxiety at losing their offspring, as if they regarded him as just another colt in need of care.

The head groom often commented on Nathaniel's way with the animals. Nathaniel didn't know from where the instinct came. He never had had a horse of his own. That was far too much of a blessing for his poor family. But back in England, his father had worked for a saddler and harness maker. Nathaniel steadied the horses being fitted, even when he was so young his head had barely reached the horse's chest.

That'd been his father's dream—to serve his indentureship with a saddler and then set up his own shop.

But it hadn't worked out that way at Leedstown. A planter who had depleted his rich, Tidewater soil with years of tobacco crops had bought new land on the frontier, past Richmond, toward the wild Indian country of the Blue Ridge Mountains. He came looking for strong men to clear fields. He'd taken Nathaniel's father and several other skilled tradesmen, who'd cried out against the change in their hopes. But Thomas Hodge, the Leedstown merchant in charge of selling their time, hadn't listened, didn't care. Money was money. Unlike most planters who used tobacco as currency, this one had actual coin to pay.

Nathaniel's father hadn't bargained to include

Nathaniel in the deal as other fathers did their sons. He'd said nothing when Nathaniel was taken from him. He'd said next to nothing, in fact, since the horrible night halfway across the Atlantic Ocean when they had wrapped Nathaniel's mother in a hammock and buried her at sea, a victim of the fever coursing through the servants crowded in the putrid cargo hull. It was as if he had died too, along with his wife. She had been the heart and soul, the light and joy of their small family. All his father had done before walking away to the West and out of Nathaniel's life was to hand Nathaniel a German flute. "That be your grandfather's," he said, and turned away.

"You know the horses well, lad, do you not?" the auctioneer asked, startling Nathaniel from his thoughts.

"Aye," he answered, barely above a whisper.

"Speak up, boy," Owen barked, and cuffed Nathaniel's ear. "Know you the horses?"

"Aye, sir, I know them," Nathaniel spoke, keeping his head bowed. He figured the smaller and meeker he appeared, the less trouble would come to him.

Owen shoved him again. "Be off with you, then. Bring back a good mare. One that will pull a cart and breed. No lameness. Hear? If you bring me a horse that goes lame next month, your hide will pay for it."

"Aye, sir." Nathaniel shuffled off. It wasn't until he

was many yards away that he raised a hand to rub his throbbing ear.

No lameness next month? There was no way to guarantee that! Canter on a stone the wrong way, trip over a tree root in the road, and a horse could limp for days. The demand would just turn into an excuse to beat him. Nathaniel could tell that Owen struck out in foul temper as readily as he breathed.

The coolness of the stable greeted Nathaniel. So did the horses. One after another they raised their heads to whinny, hoping for dinner. At least the bankrupted planter hadn't starved them in the last months. Nathaniel gently touched them as he passed, letting them know he carried no treats. Snorting their disappointment, they turned back to their hay.

Nathaniel lingered at the end stall, that of Warrior. He was a tall, muscular, dappled gray, a son of the legendary Dotterell, an English blooded horse that had been imported by the Lee family. Warrior had won many a fifty-pound purse for Nathaniel's master. But Warrior's days of glory were over. Greedy for money, the planter had over-raced him. Finally one of Warrior's tendons had bowed, leaving his right front leg swollen and slow. What would happen to the magnificent horse now? Once he might have commanded five hundred pounds in price, now more like fifty. Still a fortune to Nathaniel, but not a price that would guarantee he be treated as the treasure he was. Nathaniel rubbed his hand down Warrior's neck and scratched along his mane, a trick he'd learned by watching the horses affectionately nibble on one another in greeting.

A rage began to boil up in him. God forbid that someone like Owen get a hold of Warrior. How was it that he, Moses, and this beautiful horse were subject to such unknowns? Nathaniel's hands balled into fists. His feet begin to trot, then run toward the mares' stable.

He knew exactly which horse he was going to present to Owen to consider. And if she were in her usual temper, Owen would receive a thrashing he deserved. Nathaniel knew he'd be beaten for it. But he didn't care. It'd be worth the price to just once hand back what he was given.

Chapter Three

HER NAME WAS River Fox, because of her reddish coloring, but everyone about the stable called her Vixen. They didn't mean it kindly. She'd kicked every last one of them at least once. Even with gentle currying and handfuls of tender clover, she didn't tame. The plantation master kept her because she birthed beautiful foals.

Nathaniel figured she acted the way she did out of anger. Vixen was a gorgeous, rounded animal, but she didn't hold up in Virginia's subscription races that required a horse to win two out of three heats. After running and losing and being whipped for the failure, Vixen was given to the plantation mistress as a pleasure horse. But she threw the lady off onto hard ground. So Vixen was hitched to a lightweight chaise like a common farm mare. Nathaniel just knew the noble-blooded mare felt her new job was humiliating.

Nathaniel crept along the wall of the stall to avoid a

bolt from those brutal back hoofs. "Here, girl," he crooned, and ran his hand along her chestnut coat before attaching her halter to a line. He led her out into the lukewarm sunshine. Dancing along behind him, her eyes wide and her nostrils flared, she snapped her head to and fro, alarmed by the crowd. Nathaniel felt her quiver with agitation.

Good, he thought to himself. *She's in fine fettle, ready to throw a fit.*

He couldn't believe what he was planning. He was so careful to hang in corners, to remain unremarkable. This was asking for trouble. But Nathaniel didn't care. He was so unhappy about the day's twist in fate, he wouldn't care if Owen beat him senseless. He'd almost prefer death to yet another unknown. Maybe that's what he was really after. He kept his head low, his grip tight on the line, and walked on, like a condemned man happy for the gallows.

"What's this, boy?" Owen snapped. "I cannot afford the likes of her. And she'd be worthless hauling iron."

"She pulls a two-wheel chair, master. She can pull a cart." Nathaniel didn't add that she'd nearly kicked the small carriage apart. He was counting on a vanity that he could sense in Owen—a desire to climb up in social class. A fine-looking mare could help. Virginians set a store on their horses.

"What's her price?"

The auctioneer began to sift through his list. "What's her name, lad?"

"River Fox," murmured Nathaniel, hoping she was recorded as Vixen, buying him time as the auctioneer looked for her information.

He positioned Vixen so that Owen was several strides away from her backside. Nathaniel knew that horses hated being approached from their hindquarters, where their vision was blocked and from where predators such as wolves attacked. Stupidly, Owen walked straight toward her rump. *That's it,* Nathaniel thought, watching Owen approach for his inspection. Vixen began to flinch aside and crane her neck to see what was coming.

"Hold her steady, fool," Owen grumbled. He was looking at her silky, flowing tail that cascaded to the ground. How many times had Nathaniel been knocked over trying to comb it out to keep it so attractive?

"I'd have to dock this," Owen said, referring to the practice of bobbing horses' tails. It was a cruel doing in Nathaniel's mind—for fashion's sake, denying a horse his ability to switch away biting flies. "Docking's the macaroni in Williamsburg. No horse has a long tail. A pity, though. Fullest tail I've ever seen. Maybe I can sell that horsehair for surgeon's thread."

Yes, pleaded Nathaniel silently. *Take hold her tail. That'll do it, sure.*

Owen lifted his meaty hand and grabbed up Vixen's tail. He might as well have slapped her with a thorn-studded crop.

Vixen's eyes rolled back. Whinnying in alarm, she pawed the earth with her front hooves, threw her head down, and kicked back with a force that catapulted Owen and all his bulk several feet. He landed with a thud and a curse, in mud.

Nathaniel felt a small, sly smile of triumph slide across his face. It felt good to embarrass someone who'd cuffed his ears. A strange, hot vengeance overcame him. Nathaniel knew that given the chance, Vixen wasn't done with Owen. Oh no. He should have held on to her, as she thrashed and kicked, to prevent her doing further mischief. But Nathaniel didn't. He let go of the line.

Vixen wheeled around, snorting like a dragon, high tailed, murder in her look. Owen had been lying and shouting curses. Seeing Vixen turn, he stopped mid-blasphemy and struggled to get up. But he couldn't right his heft. Instead, he rolled onto his hands and knees and crawled.

Vixen reared onto her back legs, pumped her front legs in the air, screamed shrilly, and then came down, hard, missing Owen's body by inches as he rolled to the side.

She reared again, landed again, missing only because Owen rolled the opposite direction. It was the way horses killed snakes—Nathaniel had seen it—rearing and pounding until the serpent was sliced apart.

"Help, ho!" Owen cried out in despair.

Vixen was in more of a rage than Nathaniel had planned. She really might kill Owen. This is not what Nathaniel had meant to happen. He just wanted Owen humiliated, as he'd been over and over again since setting foot on this accursed shore.

Nathaniel waved his arms. "Hey, hey, Vixen! Off with you now! Hey!" Once more, she reared up. Owen seemed rooted to the ground.

Nathaniel scooted between them. For a moment Vixen balanced herself on her hind legs, as if considering. If she came down straight now, she'd hit Nathaniel. But he held his ground. Her eyes seemed to meet Nathaniel's. She twisted, landed to the side and took off, running the fastest race she'd ever given, straight for the big house.

Feeling like he might throw up, Nathaniel doubled over, all his anger spent. But in the distance came the sound of cries and crashes. Now he'd be responsible for the price of Vixen if she escaped.

Nathaniel straightened. He'd have to try to catch her. Nathaniel struck off as Owen crawled toward him like a crocodile and just missed latching on to him by the ankle.

Chapter Four

IT WASN'T HARD to track Vixen. Nathaniel simply followed the trail of dropped baskets, scattered papers, and startled people, all staring in the same direction. He heard a whinny, a terrified "Great God!", a clattering and crashing, and the sound of dozens of items hitting the road—*plop . . . plop . . . plop, plop, plop, plop*. . . . "Oh my! They'll all be ruined. Ruined! Someone shoot it. Shoot it!"

Nathaniel sprinted. He didn't care that the crushed oyster shells in the house's pristine lane were cutting open his bare feet. If someone shot Vixen, Nathaniel would be indentured for the rest of his life for sure.

More people scattered, parting the crowd. Now Nathaniel could see that Vixen's victim was the old man with the book-filled carriage. Vixen was nipping and driving the carriage's horse, in play more than anything else, to assert her dominance. But by Vixen's herding the poor weaker mare, the riding chair was going round and round like a whirligig, spewing out books as it spun. The old man had dropped the harness reins and was clinging to a long, ornate box, crying, "The spinet! Not the spinet!"

None dressed in finery were willing to approach the wild Vixen, churning up clods of mud as she danced the carriage horse around. The scene, in fact, was so ridiculous, the spindly man so silly looking, that a few of the merchants standing about were laughing. But Nathaniel was not amused. The reins were slithering along the ground, beginning to wrap about the carriage horse's hoofs. A few more loops around her front legs and the horse would go down, overturning the riding chair and perhaps crushing the man underneath.

Nathaniel inched his way toward Vixen and the other horse with his arms outstretched. "Whoa, now, girl. Easy, Vixen, easy." The reins, more than Nathaniel, saved them. With the leather wrapped around her, the carriage horse finally refused to move, and Vixen, satisfied that the mare was completely under her control, stopped too. Nose to nose, the horses snorted into each other's nostrils, completing the negotiation between them.

Carefully, Nathaniel took hold of Vixen's halter. He held the carriage horse's as well. Vixen even nudged

Nathaniel in a friendly manner, as if to say the chaos she'd caused had been a fine joke between them.

With a hearty laugh, a man approached Nathaniel. Head bent, Nathaniel got his usual chest-down view of a person. The man's tall boots were polished but well worn, and his plain breeches had rub marks along the thighs from the saddle, telling Nathaniel the man spent many hours riding horses. "Quite a horse, lad," he said in a young, friendly voice. "Is this her usual behavior?"

Nathaniel hesitated. Not exactly, but close enough. "Aye," he mumbled.

"What say you, lad? Would she be good for the steeplechase in Williamsburg? A rare fast mover, she seems."

The man actually laid a gentle hand upon Nathaniel's shoulders. Nathaniel almost gasped in surprise. For the kindness, Nathaniel spoke up honestly. "She does not finish well, sir. But she does have beautiful foals."

"Yes? Hmmm." The man stroked Vixen's neck. She seemed pleased with the touch. "Know you her price?"

"No, sir. But she's caused enough trouble, she'd deserve being bought for shillings."

The man laughed. "That will be useful information when I bargain for her." He called to his servant, "Abel, take this horse, please. Let us see what we can have her for." He patted Nathaniel on the shoulder and turned to walk away.

Oh, why should a devilish-maker horse be treated to such a fine owner, when a hero like Warrior was left? Nathaniel braved to speak. "Sir," he called out.

The man stopped. "Yes, lad?"

Nathaniel was afraid to step forward, afraid to let go the carriage horse, afraid to speak loudly enough for others to hear. The man came back to him with light and athletic strides. He leaned over to be nearer Nathaniel's head. "Yes, lad. Have you a secret to tell me?"

"There is a fine stallion in the stable, my lord," Nathaniel fell back to using Yorkshire's titles for noblemen. "His name is Warrior. He's a gray. You may not recognize him from the track. My master sometimes had us paint him a horse of a different color to get larger odds on him. He oft won disguised as a dark horse. He hasn't run, my lord, for almost a year, because they bowed his tendon. But he'd make a proud riding horse, my lord, and would father fine racers. He and Vix—River Fox"—Nathaniel nodded toward Vixen—"would have comely foals."

"Indeed?"

"One other thing, my lord. Don't put her under carriage. She doesn't like it," he finished in a whisper.

The young man laughed once more. It was a good, deep laugh, no checks, no hesitation about it, the laugh of a free man. "I wager not, lad! Thank you. And you needn't call me 'my lord.' There are no lords here in Virginia, just citizens, with all the rights afforded Englishmen that God granted us. Here in Virginia, lad, a man can accomplish anything when guided by reason and self-reliance. So my father and his friends claim at least." He reached into his pocket, pulled out a coin, and placed it into Nathaniel's hand. "Godspeed, lad."

The young man walked away as others called to him, "John! John Henry! Here's the jolly fellow! Come tell us about the latest trouble your father is causing! Think you Virginians will stop drinking tea and merchants will cast aside their fortunes to forego British imports? On the oratory of that obstinate firebrand Patrick Henry? And does he really think that will convince Britain and the king to change their ways? Is he mad?"

"Indeed, friends, he is. But to listen to him is to embrace what he says. He has the preacher's way about him. He's certainly convinced me of things, when I full planned to disagree with him! I believe if he could have an audience with His Majesty, he could convince King George to pay *us* taxes!"

The men walked out of earshot.

Nathaniel looked into his hand. A shilling! A whole shilling! He furtively bit the coin to test its strength—real, all right—before thrusting it into his pocket. As an indentured servant, he had to carry a pass, a legal permission slip, to run errands for the master off the plantation. He didn't know if he were allowed to have coin of his own. Nathaniel glanced about to make sure that no one saw him pocket the precious money, afraid they might take it away. It was only then that he realized that the old fellow remained frozen to the carriage seat, still clutching the wooden box to his chest, breathing heavily, as if dazed.

Threading the reins back through the harness rigging along the horse's rump, Nathaniel attached them to the front of the carriage. He stooped to pick up the books, dusting them off. *Gu-ll-i-ver's Tra-tra-vels,* he sounded out in his mind. *Ro-bi-bin-son Cru-soe, The Whole Du-ty of Man, The Art of Th-thi-thin-king.*

He gathered up a dozen leather-bound volumes and packed them into the carriage. Still more littered the ground. He paused a moment, worried that the old man was ill, since he remained silent and completely still. Nathaniel came around to touch his shoe, about to ask if he could help him out of the riding chair.

But before Nathaniel could speak, he felt himself lifted and twisted around to confront Owen's bloodred face, snarling in anger.

"You! You saucy whelp! You'll learn to trick me so!"

Chapter Five

OWEN'S FIRST BLOW caught Nathaniel full in the right eye, sending a concussion of pain through his skull. The second split his lip. By the third, Nathaniel had managed to hold his hands up to protect his face. Owen switched to pounding Nathaniel's back. It felt as if he were being stoned.

"That's enough, man. Hold!" Through hits, Nathaniel heard the alarmed voice of the old man in the carriage chair. "Stop, I say!"

"He's my property," shouted Owen. "I'm going to beat the trouble out of him."

Another blow and Nathaniel crumpled to the ground. Owen gave him a kick. "There, brat. Now get up and find me another horse."

The world was rocking, the feet in front of his eyes spinning around and around. Nathaniel couldn't move.

"Get up!" Owen hauled Nathaniel to his feet. Nathaniel hung limp.

"I insist! Let go the lad!" came the same reedy voice. The riding chair lurched a bit, and delicate but determined hands managed to pry Nathaniel loose and prop him up against its huge wheel. Nathaniel noticed the hands were stained heavily with ink before he slowly slid down the wheel to the ground.

Now came the clatter of running feet. Shoes seemed to dance around him. Nathaniel blinked to clear his blurred vision.

"What's the matter, man?"

"He nearly killed the boy."

"No need to beat him so, blacksmith; you'll lose your investment."

"He's mine to do with as I want," Owen roared.

Another set of feet walked up, boots Nathaniel had seen before. They belonged to the auctioneer. "We haven't signed the indentureship papers yet, Mr. Owen. Seems to me the lad might not be what you need after all. Perhaps you'd like to consider one of the stronger slaves."

"This one will do, I tell you. He just needs forging, like a piece of iron that must be beaten into shape."

"How much is the boy's price?" asked the old man's thin voice.

"Eleven pounds, sir, his cost of passage. Mr. Owen offered eight and ten for him."

There was a momentary silence.

"I'll pay ten for him."

"What?" shouted Owen. "I'll not be outbid for a cur like this."

"The bidding stands at ten pounds, Mr. Owen. Would you care to top it?" asked the auctioneer.

There was another silence. Nathaniel fought to remain conscious.

"Fine," Owen spluttered. "Take the devil child. He'll rob you in your sleep for your pains, mark my word."

One after another, the feet began to move off. After watching the fat, cracked shoes of Owen stomp away, Nathaniel let the world go black.

He awoke in the shade, propped up against a tree. Pulling a wet rag from his eyes, Nathaniel saw the carriage horse tethered beside him, still attached to the riding chair but calm and eating grass. He heard the same voice that had saved him from Owen: "Tsk, tsk, tsk, such a pity. I suppose I have to give up this book on surveying. I won't really use that. And I don't need the *Poor Planters' Physician*. I have Ainsworth's dictionary already, so I suppose I don't need Samuel Johnson's, although I did so covet it for its wit. Truly I did."

Nathaniel watched the old man, sitting in the riding chair, sorting through his books. He could tell his right eye was badly swollen from the beating, as each blink stung horribly.

The fellow continued talking to himself. "That brings the tally to four pounds, ten shillings. What other books should I give back to make up the rest of the boy's cost?" He sighed plaintively and crossed his arms. "A pity it is. But it can't be helped. After all, Aesop said that no act of kindness, no matter how small, is ever wasted. The lad may become the mouse that saves this poor old lion one day. Yes, perhaps."

He eyed the pile of books on the seat next to him. "I will not give up Pope's *Essay on Man*. I have wanted that too long. Hmmm . . . I'll just have to forego Ovid's *Metamorphoses*. That makes six pounds. Four more pounds to make up. Three more books to choose. I'll even get back ten shillings—there's a happy thing."

He was an angular, older man, all elbows and knees it seemed, like a grasshopper. He wore his own gray hair, tied back with black ribbon, bow akimbo. His face was lean, with pronounced cheekbones, and his eyebrows were hairy and a bit wild, sticking almost straight up. He needed a shave. Nathaniel tried to puzzle out the man's circumstances. His English frock coat was simple, dark, with wooden buttons, no shine about him. He was no merchant, clearly, or he was one who had fallen on hard times. A tradesman didn't usually wear a coat like that. A middling planter, perhaps? Why so consumed with books, then? He wouldn't have time from his fields to read that many.

While Nathaniel was looking him over, the old man glanced his way. Instantly Nathaniel dropped his gaze.

"There, boy, feeling better?" The riding chair squeaked as the man climbed out of it. "Let me see that eye."

Nathaniel turned his head away.

"You needn't fear me, child." He knelt and reached out to gently lift Nathaniel's chin. Their eyes met. The man's were hazel, a mixture of green with golden brown, surrounded by laugh lines. There was merriment in them. Nathaniel held his breath. The old fellow smiled. "That's better. It looks as if that swelling will not completely close up your eye. It'd be a tragedy to shut off that, ah . . . unique blue." He let go Nathaniel's chin and extended his hand. "We should introduce ourselves in proper fashion. I am Basil Wilkinson, schoolmaster and music teacher, sometime clerk. And you?"

In disbelief that the man had asked his name, he took Basil's hand. "Nathaniel Dunn, servant, sir," he mumbled.

"What ship brought you here, Nathaniel?"

"The Planter."

"Ah. I came over on the *Justitia*. Was schoolmaster for the children of this household for four years before the sons went off to Harvard and the girls were sent to England to find husbands. It was a happier era for this family then. My time was much easier than I warrant yours has been. Now I make my way as best I can in Williamsburg. When I read in the *Virginia Gazette* this estate was for sale, I came back to purchase the books I used to teach these children. I'm sentimental. Cannot help myself. Besides, I can well use the books to tutor others." He stood. "Can you walk?"

"Aye, sir." Nathaniel lifted himself, head throbbing.

"Good. We'll leave in a moment. I wish to make it across the York River before dark. I just have to settle accounts first. The auctioneer said I could turn in seven books to make up your price." Absorbed in the thought, Basil turned. "Oh yes . . . a slave brought a sack he said belonged to you. He's the one who carried you to this tree."

Nathaniel knew that must have been Moses. "Did . . . did . . ." Nathaniel choked on the words. Was he not to have the chance, then, to say farewell?

Basil waited.

Nathaniel tried again. "Did . . . did he say where he was to go?"

"No, lad. He left with a number of slaves. The man taking them spoke kindly to them. That's all I can tell you."

Just like that. Gone. With no knowledge of where Moses had been taken. *That's the way of it.* Nathaniel took a deep breath and squelched his sorrow. Well, if that were the way of it, 'twas better to feel nothing at all. Nathaniel vowed to lock his heart closed.

Basil turned back to sorting. "Perhaps I can keep this book of botany and sell it to Mr. Wythe. A fine man of learning, Nathaniel, who lives next door to the house in which I lodge. Interested in natural sciences as well as the law he teaches. An enlightened man, to be sure. He even has a reverse kind of telescope that allows a man to see tiny things like ants up close and larger."

Basil stopped a moment and stared off into space, then shook his head. "Amazing, truly amazing, what man can invent. We are in such an age, my friend, such an age of discovery and new thought. . . . Well . . . If I sell this volume to him, perhaps he'll let me borrow it. That's a plan. We'll keep the botany, then. But what to sacrifice? I need Wise's *Arithmetic* and Salmon's *Geography and Grammar*. Here: Mercer's *Abridgement of Law.* This one can be left behind. Oh, I've forgotten the count. That would bring me to . . . to . . ."

Nathaniel knew. The way Basil had been tallying

before, each book was priced at thirty shillings. Twenty shillings made up a pound. That meant Basil had now accounted for seven pounds, ten shillings of Nathaniel's price. "That leaves you two and one half pounds to make up, master." Nathaniel spoke with shame. He felt horrible that this man was giving up things he clearly wanted to save Nathaniel from Owen.

Basil looked at him in surprise. "Can you cipher, lad?"

"Aye, sir. A little."

"Read?"

Nathaniel nodded again. "Poorly, sir, but I can."

"This is excellent good news, Nathaniel! I had no idea what I was to do with you in Williamsburg. I have no need of a servant. I barely feed myself by teaching grammar and Latin, violin and flute. But I rent an upstairs room from Mrs. Maguire, and her husband, Edan, runs a profitable carriage-making shop. He just advertised for apprentices. He wants them, let's see how he put it—'genteelly brought up and tolerably educated.' If you can read, well . . . Now, normally, he would expect a boy's family to pay an apprentice fee. Then Edan would keep the boy seven years, teaching him the trade in exchange for his labor. But Edan has little patience for teaching. I came to know him by teaching one of his apprentices to write."

Basil rubbed his face, his beard stubble bristling. "Perhaps we can bargain this way: The spinet is for Mrs. Maguire. She wishes me to teach her to play like ladies of fashion. When she heard that the daughter of Silversmith Geddy, across Palace Green, was being taught harpsichord, she was determined to learn herself. Mr. Maguire lent me this riding chair to bring home that spinet. He bade me promise to tell everyone I met that he had made it. It's a fine one, don't you think? Oh dear, I do hope I have hawked it enough for him. . . . Mmmm . . . Edan sees the value of creative arrangements, yes, yes."

Basil reflected a moment. "He can be harsh with his help, though." He squinted his eyes as if trying to see a memory. "But truth be told, I have never seen him lay more than a slap on his servants. It's more Mrs. Maguire whom he constantly berates. . . . Perhaps in exchange for lessons . . . that way you'd stay under my care mostly. . . . Hmmm . . . I think it would be all right."

It was hard for Nathaniel to follow Basil's meandering thoughts, but it sounded as if he would stay with Basil and be hired out to work for this carriage maker—a common enough arrangement with servants.

Certainly the riding chair was well made. It was a good trade to learn. Still an unknown, but it was a far more promising one than going with Owen. When he saw Basil pick up a transverse German flute and hold it, weighing its value, Nathaniel knew what he should do. He opened his sack as Basil prattled on to himself. "I have an English flute already. It's just that these transverse flutes seem to handle livelier music better than my recorder can. They have a brighter, fuller tone. But its cost is three pound. . . . If I give it up, that would finish Nathaniel's price and give me coin for the ferry crossing as well. Ohhhhh . . ." He sighed deeply.

"Here, master." Nathaniel held up the flute his father had given him. "You may have this." He didn't know how to play it. His father had deserted him. The only thing Nathaniel felt truly precious was his mother's Bible. That and the other pair of breeches and shirt she had made him would remain as treasure in his otherwise empty sack.

Basil took the long, thin instrument and placed it to his lips to test it. A sweet, melancholy tune came out. "Lovely," murmured Basil. "Do you play, Nathaniel?"

"No, sir."

"How did you come by it, then?"

"My father gave it me."

"Where is he now?"

Nathaniel shrugged and looked to his feet.

There was a long pause before Basil played the plaintive melody again. When done, he asked, "Know you the words, Nathaniel?"

Shaking his head, Nathaniel kept looking to the ground.

"It was one of the first songs I learned in this land. A fellow indentured servant taught me. These are some of the words to it." In a quavery voice he sang:

"Five years served I, under Master Guy,
In the land of Virgin-ny-o,
Which made me for to know sorrow, grief, and woe,
When that I was weary, weary, weary-o. . . .

"I have played my part, both at plow and cart,
In the land of Virgin-ny-o,
Billets from the wood upon my back they load,
When that I was weary, weary, weary-o."

Nathaniel fought off tears. Did this man understand what the last two years had been like? The terror and pain of becoming a piece of property, of being left among strangers who cared nothing about him? A beloved parent dead, the other essentially so. He could feel Basil watching him closely, and he could barely stand it.

When Basil finally spoke, it was in a solemn, pact-making voice. "Let us do this, Nathaniel Dunn. I will borrow this flute from you. And I will teach you to play it as well, so that we may entertain ourselves and the Maguires with music. Will that suit?"

Nathaniel was being asked? *"Hopes all things?"* Nathaniel pushed aside the hope that bubbled up within him. *Careful. There's no telling what might happen in Williamsburg and who's to say this old man will keep his promises.*

"Aye, master, it suits," Nathaniel muttered, keeping his voice clean of emotion.

"Let us be on our way, then."

PART TWO

June 1774

You gentlemen of England,
Who live at home at ease,
How little do you think upon
The dangers of the seas.
Give ear unto the mariners,
And they will plainly show,
All the cares, and the fears,
When the stormy winds do blow.

—"You Gentlemen of England,"
eighteenth-century mariner song

Chapter Six

"I HATE RIVER crossings," moaned Basil.

They stood beside a small dock, watching a single-masted sloop bob its way across the York, the boat's sails full in winds that brushed up occasional whitecaps.

"A music master drowned on one of these ferries, Nathaniel. He rode from plantation to plantation, staying several days at each. With all the rivers and marshes cutting up this region, he had to use a ferry at least once a week. When he died, I gave up traveling to teach. Too many risks with rivers, so unpredictable. And with horses. Beastly, temperamental animals, really."

Nathaniel could almost feel a smile inside himself. The day had been a quick and full education into Mr. Basil Wilkinson. He was, indeed, no horseman. Basil had so worried the horse with jerking the reins that

Nathaniel had walked alongside the poor creature to steady it. Now it rested its head against Nathaniel's shoulder, almost as if trying to hide.

Nathaniel had never before met such a talkative person. He felt sure he already knew all his new master's history. A Scotsman, Basil was trained in religion and music, but was unable to find work. Times were bad in Scotland—that Nathaniel knew—ever since the British had defeated Bonnie Prince Charlie. In the Highland clearances that followed, British landlords evicted Scottish farmers and placed sheep on their lands. Many had fled to the cities, only to starve or fall into debtors' prison. Basil supported himself by teaching children to read and write, bookkeeping, chimney sweeping, and occasional music lessons. Eventually, Basil boarded a ship for America, looking for a better life. He paid for the trip by selling himself into temporary bondage as a schoolmaster.

Since leaving the plantation, he'd been a field school instructor, a private tutor, a music teacher riding a circuit, a clerk in one of Williamsburg's many shops. Sometimes he played flute for the visiting opera companies. He adapted himself to people's changeable needs for "the gentleman's arts," as learning was considered. "Williamsburg is a very nice town, Nathaniel, but it is not a city like Philadelphia or Charlestown, where music and education are in high demand. Virginia has no major port cities because these cursed rivers are so wide and deep. Merchant ships come straight from England to a planter's private wharf, making little need for town trade."

Basil interrupted himself: "Oh, I would hate to drown. How deep do you suppose this is?"

Nathaniel had already learned that Basil often did not really want an answer to a question. It was more a pause in his monologue.

"I don't mind working so hard," continued Basil. "He that will eat the fruit must climb the tree, after all. Here in Virginia, musicians must be jacks-of-all-trades. Even Peter Pelham, the organist for Bruton Parish, doesn't make enough money to feed his huge brood of children. He also runs the jail."

As crew members lowered the sails to slide the sloop safely into dock, Nathaniel heard waves splashing along its board, the wind rattling the riggings. It was a pretty sound. Nathaniel looked forward to the crossing.

Two gentlemen with horses and another three on foot got off. The boat dipped wildly as each stepped out onto the dock. "That's not sturdy," muttered Basil. "Let us go another way." He jiggled the reins. The horse remained glued to Nathaniel.

A squat, sunburned man called from the deck:

"Passage to Capahosick side, four shilling for you, seven for the chair and horse."

"I . . . I think perhaps we best ride around," Basil answered.

"Where are you going?" asked the boatman.

"To Williamsburg."

"I take you within eight miles of the capital, sir. My ferry saves eighteen riding miles. That's four hours' time."

Still Basil hesitated. "Such a small boat."

Nathaniel had seen smaller, more weather-beaten vessels load tobacco and head out to open sea. Basil's timidity confused Nathaniel. Basil had been so brave in stopping Owen from beating Nathaniel. How could he be so fearful of water? And why now? They had already dallied two hours, waiting for the ferry to show up.

The boatman jumped lightly off the sloop. "This boat is as good as any in the colony," he said. "It will carry nine horses to the other side. With your small weight, we'll fair skip along the water. Once over, you will find our public house. My wife made pigeon pies today. Stay the night. The way to Williamsburg is swampy. Best take it in full light when you can see the bogs. Nice carriage chair like that might snap an axle if the wheels sank in the mud."

Pigeon pie? The last time Nathaniel had tasted pigeon pie was in England. He longed to beg Basil to take the ferry to the pie, yet he knew he could not ask for more charity. Besides, he chided himself, what made him think he'd be allowed to sit at table?

In the end, the thought of harming the chair persuaded Basil. During the twenty-minute crossing, he was silent, hunkered down to withstand the boat's rocking.

Nathaniel delighted in the smell of brine in the wind, the taste of salt when water sprayed into his face, even though it made his split lip burn. He tracked the flight of a huge blue-gray heron, its long legs held straight out behind its wide wings, making the bird look like a crossbow. Black waterfowl dove into the waters to emerge yards away with thrashing fish in their red beaks. The sky still clouded, the water was a dark emerald. No matter how far over the side Nathaniel leaned, he could not see into its depths, but he knew crabs and oysters aplenty were below.

When they landed on the opposite shore, near a vast swath of salt marshes, Nathaniel was disappointed for the voyage to end.

Basil harumphed: "There. What folly. Foolish of you to be fearful, Nathaniel."

"Me, sir?"

Basil hurriedly changed the subject. "Look there, boy." He pointed to a large black-and-white woodpecker darting among the sycamores. "Isn't it beautiful? The

Indians use their ivory bills for necklaces. Magnificent beings, the Algonquians, the Iroquois, the Cherokee. We used to see their canoes on the rivers all the time when I first came. A rare few come into Williamsburg still to trade. Mostly they stay to Kentucky and Ohio now, since Parliament denies our settling there."

Nathaniel had never seen an Indian. He imagined them to be gigantic and painted with blood. The plantation slaves had told him terrible stories about scalpings and demon doings in the night by the tribes. And recently a half-French Mingo had led raids against settlements along the Appalachian Mountains, saying Virginians had murdered his family. Shawnee were attacking there too—right in the area Nathaniel figured his father to be.

Unnerved thinking about Indians, Nathaniel noted how long the shadows were across the marsh path, how eerily the grapevines twisted up the trees in the thinning light. The peepers and bullfrogs were almost deafening in their chant, their song to greet twilight, as insistent as birds at sunrise. Night was coming fast.

"Two hours at a goodly pace to Williamsburg," Basil answered Nathaniel's thoughts. He stretched. "Let us rest. I must admit that pigeon pie sounded fine. Shall we have some, Nathaniel?"

Chapter Seven

Basil had consumed his pie before Nathaniel even took his first bite. Nathaniel had crept away from the table, holding his precious slice against his chest. At the large fireplace in the one-room tavern, he sat upon the hobnob metal on its edge, warming his back and savoring the anticipation of biting into the flaky crust. He caught the scent of roasted onion and clove as he bit into the sweet, buttery meat inside the crisp pastry. He closed his eyes and rolled the delicious morsel around and around in his mouth. Finally, he swallowed. The pie was as good as his mother's had been. He took twenty wondrous mouthfuls to consume the four-inch slice, remembering.

Nathaniel sat back to watch the scene before him. The tavern was loud, filled with smoke from the men's long clay pipes. They all seemed slightly drunk and dangerous. Men bet on dice, argued about cards, knocked over their mugs of ale and jumped up to yell at one another. Two men holding caged roosters planned a cockfight, calling each other scurrilous names.

A pasty-faced man in frilly clothes rose unsteadily. His powdered wig was sliding back off his head. Waving a huge handkerchief, he raised a glass, and shouted, "To the glory of his Majesty, King George of England, may his reign be long."

It was as if he had fired a musket. Abruptly, the entire tavern silenced. A few chairs scraped along the floorboards as several well-dressed men rose shakily to their slippered feet and raised their glasses. "Indeed, sir," one of them added, "and to all his loyal subjects, here and in our good mother country, England."

"Hear, hear." The men smiled at one another in a late-night, ale-drenched stupor, a swaying circle of silks and lace and brocade. They didn't seem to notice that most of the inn's revelers stayed seated, either glaring at them or looking down into their cups, studiously ignoring the prompt to praise the king.

But an elegant man who'd been quietly reading would have none of the crowd's silence. He rose, held up a glass of garnet-red wine, and with a high-court English accent, said, "Come, gentlemen all. Raise your glass. 'Tis treason not to toast our sovereign."

Up shot a man with scars thick across his sun-roasted face. He wore buckskin breeches, a leather shirt, and a raccoon tail sticking out of his round hat. "Treason to ye, but not to me and me friends," he barked. He held up his own wooden cup and turned a circle speaking to the crowd: "I give you the people of Boston. Here's to their steeping the king's tea where it belongs—in the harbor. May we all have such backbone when it comes to it."

"Aye!" A dozen men stood and downed the remains of their drinks, slamming the empty mugs onto the table.

The rest of the inn's patrons seemed to slide down into their chairs even further, refusing to look up.

"In Boston, men who speak thus are to be arrested and sent back to England for trial on charges of sedition." The elegant man put his hand atop the hilt of a sword that hung at his side.

"We aren't in Boston." The rough-clad man pulled a thick hunting knife from his belt. "This here is Virginia."

The two swaggered toward each other.

Seeing the trouble he had caused, the man in frills sat down with a gasp, mopping his brow with his lace handkerchief. One of his friends pointed a huge flintlock pistol. The others cowered behind him.

A knot of brawny farmers and woodsmen, grabbing up their table knives, gathered behind the frontiersman. Others scattered to the walls to be out of trouble. The caged roosters crowed as if delighted that their scrap was to be postponed by a human one.

The tavern keeper looked as if he would cry. "Sirs, please, mine's a respectable establishment."

Just as the two antagonists reached one another, toe to toe—the elegant man calm and disdainful, the buckskin ruffian snarling like a hound—a familiar voice cried out, "Stop! Hold, sirs."

All eyes turned. Basil stood atop a table with a glass in one hand and his pocket fiddle in another. His gray hair floated about his head, and his face was flushed. "Let us use a toast I have heard the learned Mr. Wythe bespeak: Here's to the king—may His Majesty long and gloriously reign—"

"Fie, old fool, get down off the table with ye, or I'll be knocking ye down meself," growled the frontiersman.

"Peace," the refined gentleman held up his hand. "We must respect age. Continue, old sir, and then we will proceed with our argument!" He bowed to his opponent and smiled, bringing on a ripple of relieved laughter.

Basil nodded, ". . . may His Majesty reign in the hearts of his *free* American subjects, and to our friends in Boston *and* London, and to a speedy, honorable, and happy reconciliation between Great Britain and America, which will preserve the liberties of all mankind." He took a deep breath. Before the inebriated crowd could think through his long sentence, he sung out, "And let us seal the peace between us with a song. Gentlemen, I give you the *Devil's Dream* to chase the devil out of us!"

Basil gulped his wine, put down his glass, and began playing.

It was a fast, whirling jig, up and down from high to low. Basil's fingers flew along the fiddle's neck. His bow sawed the strings. He almost looked like a flapping chicken. But there was nothing funny about the effect Basil had on them all. First there was simply a pause in the growing trouble, then silence, then one by one people sat back down. As they began clapping to the merry tune, the frontiersman disappeared out into the night and the swordsman took up his book again.

The sigh the tavern keeper breathed was large enough for Nathaniel to feel across the room.

For an hour Basil played, finding melodies to please and to pull out singing. Some were sad, some about heroes, some celebrated poor men's pranks on the mighty. Finally he came to a song from the comic opera *High Life Below Stairs*. The words made fun of the rich and what they were slave to. The tavern crowd needed little prompting to sing along with gusto after the night's earlier clash:

"Come here, fellow Servant, and listen to me,
I'll show you how those of superior degree
Are only dependents, no better than we.
Both high and low in this do agree. . . .

"See yonder fine spark, in embroidery dress'd
Who bows to the great, and, if they smile, is blest;
Who is he? i'faith, but a servant at best."

Chapter Eight

THE NEXT MORNING Basil climbed into the riding chair with a wide smile that lit his thin face with a sunburst of wrinkles. He held up several coins before putting them into his waistcoat pocket. "Never underestimate the power of music to soothe or pay the rent, Nathaniel," he chirped. "That innkeeper was very grateful for the help of my fiddle last night. He gave me back the cost of our passage and our board in thanks. Ho ho!"

Basil picked up the reins and slapped the poor horse, causing her to prance nervously along the path. Nathaniel jogged along behind. He admired Basil's self-motivated cleverness. He himself never thought quickly enough to bring on good fortune. And bravery, or defiance—as he found out yesterday—only brought on trouble. He could still barely see out of his swollen and bruised eye. He knew he'd carry the embarrassing mark of being beaten for days.

Nathaniel did long to ask what the tavern brawl had been about. How did men dare to speak ill of the king, and why would such rich men care a wit about what commoners had to say? And what was "sedition"?

When they entered the edges of Williamsburg, a little past ten o'clock, Nathaniel received his answers.

He was already agog at the multistoried brick buildings at the edge of town. Basil had explained they were part of the College of William and Mary, a place dozens of scholars came to study together—philosophy, history, ancient languages.

Fancy that, Nathaniel had thought. He hadn't before realized that there was much to learn beyond adding sums or reading words.

Then he spotted two long rows of elegant gentlemen. Gravely, silently, they followed a man in purple robes, who carried a silver mace. Hundreds of people—some in silk and wigs, some in workmen's frocks and leather aprons—lined the street. No matter their dress, none made a sound. Only a tolling church bell accompanied their march.

Instinctively, Nathaniel lowered his voice to a church-service whisper. "What is this, master?"

Basil watched a moment, before answering in a somber voice, "These men are members of the House of Burgesses. Know you what that is, Nathaniel?"

Nathaniel shook his head, not taking his eyes off the strange and silent parade.

"It is like Parliament in England. They are elected by Virginia freeholders to represent our needs. The royal governor, Lord Dunmore, represents the king. The House of Burgesses passes laws about roads, the militia, fees the ferries can charge, even taxes. The burgesses have been meeting since 1619, starting in Jamestown.

"This procession is in support of the people of Boston. Know you what has happened in Boston?"

Again Nathaniel shook his head. All he knew of Boston was what the frontiersman had shouted the previous night. Little news of the outside world had traveled to the plantation other than word there was new trouble with Britain.

Basil took a deep breath before beginning, as if to give a speech: "For more than a hundred years, colonial legislators, like our burgesses, governed without Parliament's meddling. The burgesses had been responsible for levying taxes in ways that were well considered and fair, putting the money to use here, to run Virginia to the benefit of both the colony and Britain.

"But the French and Indian War cost the king a pretty penny. Parliament decided to pay off England's debts by taxing us. First came the Sugar Act taxes;

then the Stamp Act, which imposed a fee on all printed paper—newspapers, legal documents, even playing cards.

"We have no members of Parliament elected here, speaking for us in London. It's taxation without representation. Most unjust, completely against the British constitution.

"If Parliament forces us to pay taxes, without our agreeing to it first, what arbitrary rule might come next? Besides, it was through our sweat and tears that the colonies grew. No member of Parliament I know has braved the ocean, Indian attacks, unknown disease, and a wilderness to build this new world. Why should they profit from work they have not done?

"The latest insult is to force us to pay an import fee on tea and to purchase it solely from the British East India Company. The tax itself is not much—but it's the principle of the matter, Nathaniel, the principle! Boatloads of that unwanted tea sailed into Boston. The people of Boston refused to unload it. Men calling themselves the Sons of Liberty dressed up as Mohawk Indians and dumped out every bit of that tea—ninety thousand pounds into the harbor.

"Now England is going to blockade Boston's port until the town agrees to pay for the tea. Nothing—no foods, no goods—will be able to come in or out of the city. The people could starve. British troops control the city. Anyone caught promoting protest—engaging in sedition, as is the legal term—will be sent to England for trial. That's a passage to the hangman, if ever there was.

"When our Virginia burgesses heard of these Coercive Acts, they called for this day of fasting and prayer. It is to show that an attack on one of our sister colonies is an attack on all British Americans. These men are on their way to say prayers. That's all. But Governor Dunmore sees our standing by our Boston brethren as a challenge to the king's authority. So Dunmore dissolved the House. He banned their meeting.

"See that man there?" Basil pointed to a dignified, heavyset gentleman in front of the procession. "That is Peyton Randolph, Speaker of the House. Well, I suppose I should say 'was' speaker. When the governor dissolved the House, Mr. Randolph led the burgesses straight to the Raleigh Tavern and kept right on meeting. They have called on Virginians to give up tea and to not buy anything shipped here from England. They've suggested a congress of all the colonies, so that representatives from Georgia to New Hampshire can unite, making our voice stronger. Very clever, that move is.

"The burgesses may even urge us to stop selling

our tobacco to England. The thought is that completely cutting off trade would pressure the king to stop this madness.

"Breaking off trade altogether could ruin planters and merchants, the people who hire me to teach their children. . . ." Basil wrung his hands in worry. "Well . . . such methods worked once before to push Parliament into repealing the Stamp Act. Hopefully they will again. Everyone is trying to keep the disagreement polite so that reconciliation can come quickly."

Basil watched a moment longer before adding, "Still, I fear this business will tear friends and families apart. Evidently it was Mr. Randolph's brother, John, who advised the governor that a quiet day of prayer and fasting was a prelude to more dangerous defiance. He is the attorney general to the governor. Some say it was on John's word that the governor dissolved the House. I wonder what those two brothers have to say to each other today."

An extremely tall, very serious, and very strong-looking man, who dwarfed all the other burgesses, caught Nathaniel's eye. "Who is that, master?"

"Who?"

Nathaniel pointed.

"Oh, that's only George Washington. A surveyor and planter. Now, let me see if I can find Patrick Henry.

That's the voice stirring up patriotic zeal." Basil stood up in the riding chair and scanned the crowd.

Nathaniel recognized the name as that of the father of the youth who'd purchased Vixen. He waited with curiosity.

"Odd. Unlike Henry to not be in the middle of this," Basil muttered. "A most controversial man who argues the most radical of points. Why, he's even defended Baptists!"

Basil nearly fell out of the carriage with looking. Nathaniel stroked the horse to keep her still. "He'd be dressed almost like a parson, Nathaniel. He's a rather plain fellow in appearance, really. No one can argue his affect on people, however, or his bravery. It was Mr. Henry who convinced the burgesses to resist the Stamp Act. He insisted we have the same constitutional rights as Englishmen, despite our living in the colonies. He even hinted that the king was becoming a tyrant. Some of the burgesses shouted that Mr. Henry was speaking treason. He is said to have answered: 'If this be treason, make the most of it.'"

"Make the most of it, indeed, Mr. Basil!" A lean, dark-haired youth appeared behind the riding carriage. He grinned merrily. "Another of your lessons, Mr. Basil? Do you ever tire of preaching? At least this lecture is worth the having!" The youth winked at

Nathaniel. He was freckled and dimpled, with huge, chestnut-brown eyes, and there was a good-natured light touch about his teasing. Basil did not seem offended.

"Fie, Ben," Basil matched his banter, "had your lessons equaled your revolutionary rhetoric, you would be a master craftsman in your own right much sooner."

"And miss the delight of bedeviling you, sir? No indeed, reading and ciphering are for old men."

Basil smiled at Nathaniel. "Listen not to this wastrel, lad. This is the very apprentice I told you of, who introduced me to Edan Maguire. Edan had despaired of teaching him his catechism, and so he hired me. The atrociousness of his spelling is equaled only by his lackluster addition!"

"Awww, Mr. Basil, why would anyone be concerned about spelling and adding when we are in the midst of such times! There are so many more important things to be concerned about."

"But Ben, we are trying to redefine our relationship with the crown, to safeguard the rights of Englishmen around the globe, whether colonists or Londoners. 'Twill be accomplished through rational, legal, *learned* arguments."

Ben rolled his eyes and hit upon a way to stop Basil's lecture. "Mr. Basil, for shame, methinks you've forgotten your manners." He nodded toward Nathaniel.

"Oh dear, so I have. Ben, this is Nathaniel Dunn. He comes to join our household, hopefully as an apprentice. Junior to you, of course."

"Huzzah!" Ben threw up his arms in celebration. "That means you get kindling duty, Nathaniel!" He walked around the chair to shake hands. Nathaniel nodded and looked down shyly. "I like the looks of that eye, Nathaniel." Ben lowered his head to inspect Nathaniel's black eye. "Got you that in defense of our liberty?"

Not understanding his meaning, Nathaniel remained mute.

"A silent one, then?" Ben asked. "Not allowed in these times, my friend. Be you Whig or Tory?"

Nathaniel was still perplexed.

"Patriot or loyalist?"

Nathaniel didn't know what the labels Ben was using meant, but he knew he planned to stay out of trouble. He would keep his head down and get by. Choices only brought on abuse from those who didn't agree—especially choices that put one at odds with people in power.

"Leave off, Ben," Basil said gently. "The lad's just

arrived. He knows naught of politics."

"But he best learn, master tutor. Choices must be made. Those who stick by Parliament will not be popular. But those who try to straddle the fence between both, or claim to be neutral, will only be suspected and hated by both sides."

PART THREE

November 1774

Rouse every generous thoughtful mind,
The rising danger flee,
If you would lasting freedom find,
Now then abandon tea. . . .

Shall we our freedom give away,
And all our comfort place
In drinking of outlandish tea,
Only to please our taste?

Forbid it Heaven, let us be wise,
And seek our country's good:
Nor ever let a thought arise,
That tea should be our food.

Since we so great a plenty have,
Of all that's for our health;
Shall we that blasted herb receive,
Impoverishing our wealth? . . .

Adieu! Away, oh tea! Begone!
Salute our taste no more:
Though thou art coveted by some
Who're destined to be poor.

—"India Tea," a colonial protest song

Chapter Nine

"GOD'S TEETH! I will not drink sassafras! Does she think me a savage?"

Edan Maguire shoved a cup of the Indian herb drink at Nathaniel. Nathaniel managed to bobble the cup and saucer and save it from crashing to the floor. But hot liquid drenched his new waistcoat and spilled onto Edan's table, just missing a design page of heraldry for a carriage. He winced as the heat soaked to his skin.

"Baaah," Edan waved his hand impatiently. "Clumsy fool! Mop that up. Then go and tell that wench of a wife of mine that I'll have none of this substitute. I don't care that there's a three pence tax per pound. I don't care what these ruffians say about protesting British doings in Boston. I want real tea. Where is the liberty they speak of, when I can't even choose for myself what to drink of a morning?"

Nathaniel hurriedly mopped up the spill, ducking to

avoid being smacked as Edan threw his hands about in indignation. Edan's temper was poker hot when it flared. This morning it was as scorching as the embers in the blacksmith's forge where Edan's smithy made nails for carriage wheels.

Shaking out a copy of the *Virginia Gazette*, Edan went on: "Listen to the Association Resolves of this so-called Continental Congress. They call themselves most dutiful, loyal subjects of the king while calling on us to defy him. Do they really think that by our not drinking tea or refusing to buy English goods the greatest empire in the world is going to bow down and change? They obviously know naught of the lobsterbacks. They ought to talk to my Irish countrymen to know what comes of challenging the British crown and its soldiers. I came to this land to be free of such suicidal argument."

He threw the broadsheet newspaper to the ground. "Where am I to purchase the gold leaf I need to guild my carriages if not from British merchants? I will be ruined! These madmen want us to make our own homespun cloth and . . . and . . ." he spluttered, and picked up the paper to find the exact wording. He read with heavy sarcasm, "And 'to engage in frugality, economy, and industry, discouraging any display of extravagance.' Why, that could include my magnificent work, since riding in one of my carriages makes a man appear an earl. . . . And look here. Next summer, if the British don't do our bidding, we will stop exporting our goods to them—everything but rice. That means every tobacco planter in Virginia could end up in the poorhouse. My business will die!" He slammed the paper to the table.

Sticking out his lower lip, he glared at Nathaniel. "Then you'll be out in the streets, boy, back where you came from. And you and you and you as well." Edan pointed at Ben, then at John Hunter, an indentured servant, and finally at Obadjah Puryer, a journeyman in the trade. The two men worked in Edan's shop in the many stages required to complete a carriage. Ben helped them finish projects, actually doing some of the work under their watchful eyes. Nathaniel had inherited all Ben's grunt labor—sweeping, stoking fires, sharpening tools, and caring for the horses and chickens.

Nathaniel stood silently, never quite sure when Edan's tirades were over and he should go about his commands. Walk away too soon, and Edan would grab him by the collar.

"Well?" Edan roared, throwing up his hands. "What are you waiting for?" He stood up from his chair. "Return straightaways. I need you to crank the wheel for the lathe. We need to carve this piece of elm into a hub today. I've an order for a phaeton from a well-off gentleman, whom I trust will pay speedily." Grumbling, he picked up the slab of wood. "Nobody can do anything around here without my telling them. When I was a journeyman in Dublin—now there's a city—I was grateful to work. I used to . . ."

Nathaniel scrambled for the door. As he passed, Ben crossed his eyes and pulled down his mouth with his fingers to make a grotesque face at Edan's turned back. Nathaniel couldn't believe how reckless Ben was.

But even John was rebellious in mood that morning and whispered to Nathaniel, "Don't worry, lad. They don't call him the Palace Street Puffer for nothing."

"What? What did you say, scurvy scoundrel?" Edan shouted, turning around. He slammed the hunk of wood down. "I'll not tolerate any gossiping among you rabble!"

"We just told him to a-hurry, master!" answered John in a singsong voice.

"Baaah!" barked Edan.

Nathaniel bolted for the safety of the kitchen before he could be questioned. If Edan really pushed him to know what John had said, Nathaniel would have to tell. If he didn't tell, Edan would shake it out of him. He'd hate to get John into trouble. Nathaniel liked John. But better it be John than Nathaniel. Being in trouble with Edan was a deep and wide chasm that Nathaniel would do anything to avoid. So Nathaniel ran, clutching the teacup and spilling more tea all over his waistcoat.

Inside the warm outbuilding he found the most revered servant of the household, Sally, the slave cook. Her status came partly from her formidable bearing, partly from her close relationship with Edan's wife, but mainly from the delicious foods she created and her frank wisdom. She was plucking a chicken, making a little pile of downy feathers. Mrs. Elizabeth Maguire stood beside, holding a book titled *The Compleat Housewife*. Before he could say anything, she spoke with a sigh: "I know, I know. I heard him."

Mrs. Maguire shook her head. "Everyone this side of the governor's palace could probably hear him, more's the pity. Here we are among the gentles he hopes to befriend, and there he is sounding like a fishmonger. What must our neighbors think?" She put her hand to her cheek, flushed with dismay. "Well . . . it's not as if that Mr. Wythe isn't a bit odd himself, now is it? Taking a bath daily? Imagine!"

She checked a small kettle hanging over the fire. "I've already started a pot of chocolate for him, Nathaniel, to replace the sassafras." She stirred something else in the fireplace and took a sip of it from the ladle, wrinkling her nose. "The sack whey is ready for

Mr. Wilkinson, though. All it needs is hartshorn spirits." She added a few drops from a small vial and stirred. "This should cure that cold."

Nathaniel knew Basil would not be happy to receive Mrs. Maguire's sack whey. The elixir of wine, watery milk, and distilled slices of deer antler was disgusting. But she'd read in her book that the way to stop a cold was to lie much in bed and drink such concoctions. She was determined to get him well quickly, and Basil wanted to avoid being bled by a surgeon.

"I can't stand being cut," he had moaned. "Last time they took a whole cup of my blood to balance my humors. So I'll try her remedies. Besides, I'd not hurt Mistress Maguire's feelings for the world. She is very kind."

She was that. A tiny woman, not much taller than Nathaniel, Mrs. Maguire was quiet and thoughtful. She wasn't exactly pretty or dignified. There were too many worries etched into her face for that. Underneath her mob cap, her graying hair was thin and stringy. But she watched to see what people needed and then silently provided it—a matter-of-fact kindness that bred beauty of a sort. A few weeks after Nathaniel arrived at her house, a set of clothes and a pair of shoes appeared beside the rolled-up straw mattress he used in the stable's hayloft.

She'd recently given him the waistcoat as protection against the November chill. He looked down at the striped wool and was relieved to see that the wet spots were drying. He'd hate for her to think he was careless with her gifts. He glanced up shyly at her, but her back was turned. After six months in her household, Nathaniel had come to recognize that her generosity was not born of an outgoing personality, or the beginnings of affection. It was more the simple decency someone might show in taking in a stray dog. Starved for care, it was enough for Nathaniel. Had she been more warm and loving, like his mother, it would have torn his heart out.

Mrs. Maguire pulled the chocolate off the fire. "Basil . . . Mr. Wilkinson . . . has asked me about your sleeping on the floor in his room now that the weather is turning. I told him that is acceptable. The nights will soon be frigid. But you must keep to your morning stable chores, Nathaniel, without fail."

She turned and caught him watching her. As always, Nathaniel averted his eyes. "Look at me, lad. I want to make sure you hear me well." She smiled when he obeyed, but she said pointedly, "Mr. Maguire will not like it if you are late with the horses' oats."

"Aye, mistress. I will not fail."

Sleep in the house? Yet another privilege he had not

dreamed of. He was so afraid that it would all disappear or reveal itself to be a trap of some kind. He tasted meat—mutton, bacon, beef—or salted fish several times a week. He had a pair of shoes and bedding to sleep on. Nathaniel distrusted it all. He couldn't help it.

He was almost glad of Edan's temper, which kept his life rooted to what he had known the past two years—unending labor and unpredictable punishment.

"Please take this upstairs to Mr. Wilkinson." Mrs. Maguire handed the sack whey to Nathaniel. "I'll take this cup of chocolate out to my husband. I need talk with him about this Non-importation Agreement. There is much pressure for Williamsburg's merchants and shopkeepers to sign their names to it. We must do so as well. County committees will check merchants' books to make sure we stick to the ban on imports. The threat is if we purchase or sell any British goods, they will print an ad in the *Gazette* telling townsfolk to break off all dealings with us.

"We cannot afford to be shunned." She turned to Sally and confided, perhaps forgetting Nathaniel's presence. "Mr. Maguire's debt is large. We owe seven hundred pounds for this house. He thought our fortune would be made by following Lord Dunmore to Williamsburg from New York City when the king made Dunmore royal governor here. Edan was convinced that Virginians would be so impressed by the coaches he made for Lord Dunmore that they would flock to our workshop. He insisted on moving us to Palace Street to make our association with the governor clear. We had no need for such a large house."

Clucking in sympathy, Sally kept at her work.

Mrs. Maguire rubbed her forehead. "He is a fine carriage maker. That he is. He is right to take pride in himself. But . . ." She looked out the door toward the shop in back of the garden. "But things have not worked out as planned. And now our Williamsburg neighbors might not like the fact he has done so much work for Lord Dunmore. Edan must come to understand that. Otherwise we could lose everything." She picked up the tray with the pot of chocolate and squared her shoulders.

Sally stopped plucking to warn, "Have a care, mistress."

"Aye," Mrs. Maguire quietly replied. "That I will."

Chapter Ten

NATHANIEL PUSHED OPEN the door to Basil's bedchamber, carefully holding the steaming and smelly sack whey. Basil was sitting cross-legged under the window, his gray hair down upon his shoulders, nightcap askew, reading a book in the sunlight. When he heard the door creak, he scrambled to his feet in a comical bolt of bare legs and flapping pages. He might be old, but he was spry. He was on his feet and running for the bed in an instant.

But he stopped with an embarrassed snort. "Oh, 'tis only you, Nathaniel. Methought it was Mistress Maguire. She has disciplined me severely when she found me out of bed. But I simply cannot resist *Gulliver's Travels*. I've come to the part where Gulliver is about to—" Basil breathlessly pointed to a passage, when he stopped himself abruptly. "Oh, forgive me, lad. I have read ahead of where you and I are. I shan't spoil it for you." He looked a bit ashamed. "But just wait, Nathaniel. It is so exciting. We'll read again tonight, shall we? Imagine creating a whole universe of little people and naming the nation Lilliput. Where in the world did Swift get that name? Where does a writer come up with such wonderful nonsense?" Basil sighed with delight.

Back in the hot nights of August, when the air felt as if it could sear Nathaniel's lungs, Basil had sat on the back steps to read in the long summer twilight. He'd called Nathaniel out of the stable and read aloud *Robinson Crusoe*. The novel was about a spoiled young man who'd been stranded on a desert island for twenty-eight years, only to find a remarkable courage and resourcefulness inside himself. Nathaniel had never before heard stories other than those in the Bible. He would close his eyes and could almost see Crusoe being swept to shore by the raging sea; teaching his parrot, Poll, to talk; saving the man Friday. The words made such powerful pictures. As Basil read, a door opened to a world Nathaniel had not known existed.

But perhaps the most amazing new universe had been the music. The music! Basil was gone most days, tallying numbers for storekeepers, teaching in homes about the city, repairing musical instruments. But he had still found time to keep his promise to teach Nathaniel to play the German flute.

Nathaniel had surprised himself by learning quickly. The fingerings were easy. All fingers went down over the flute's holes for low C and then the player basically walked up the instrument to go up the scale, lifting one finger at a time, starting with the right pinkie. But balancing it was awkward. The German flute's mouthpiece was held underneath the lips, and then the length of it went up and out to the right. The real difficulty was blowing strongly enough down into the mouthpiece hole to make a note sound. It took a huge amount of air. Countless times, Nathaniel had almost swooned.

But now Nathaniel was actually making melody. So far Basil had taught him three tunes. Basil played and Nathaniel mimicked. When Basil said, "You have an amazing ear, lad, to learn these songs so quickly," Nathaniel had bloomed with pride. He couldn't remember how long it had been since he had taken pleasure in a task. When nightmares about the voyage over the Atlantic or the treatment at the plantation haunted him, Nathaniel simply replayed those melodies in his mind to chase away the ghosts of fear.

Nathaniel knew that was why Mrs. Maguire was fussing so over Basil's cold. He had given her the same gift with the spinet. Through open windows, Nathaniel had heard her playing the small harpsichord that Basil had brought back from the plantation. She'd stumbled and banged through the summer, but now she was working on a hornpipe, where the melody was clear and delicate. He'd heard Basil encourage, "Yes, my dear. That is excellent."

Afterward Mrs. Maguire had come to the workshop with a radiant smile. "Come hear what I have learned, Mr. Maguire."

"I've not time for idle entertainment, mistress," he'd snarled. "You browbeat me into buying that spinet for you. I did so. I've taken this puny boy in exchange for your lessons. Need I do more?"

Her smile had disappeared. So had she. Mrs. Maguire walked back into the house and played and played and played.

Nathaniel shook his head to toss off his daydreaming. *Too close*. You are getting too fond of this old man, Nathaniel warned himself. Your own father deserted you. This old man can, too. He squelched his burning desire to ask what was happening to Gulliver in the land of Lilliputians. Instead, he held out the cup of sack whey.

The stench of it wafted toward Basil. His face fell. "Oh, must I, lad? It is so wretched. I drank the whole lot of it yesterday." He pouted and kept his hands to his side.

Nathaniel pushed the cup at Basil.

"Ah me," Basil took it, held his nose, and swallowed. "Oh, horrible." He took another gulp. "Oh, could hemlock be any worse?" He managed a third swig, his face contorted like a gargoyle's. Gagging and coughing, he spluttered, "That's enough. Enough, I say." He lifted the lid of his chamber pot, releasing another stench into the air, to pour the remainder in. "That's where that belongs." He closed it back up and turned to Nathaniel.

"Nathaniel, lad, may you never be so blessed with a woman's good intentions." He sank onto the bed, his face pale from the ordeal of taking his medicine.

Nathaniel made for the door.

"Lad?" Basil held up his hand to stop him.

"Aye, master?"

"I wish to speak to you about Ben."

Nathaniel waited.

"He reports you avoid his company."

Nathaniel frowned, but said nothing. He didn't avoid him exactly. But when Ben asked him to travel at twilight to meet his friends, Nathaniel did hang back. Ben was very likeable, but he was such a risk taker. Edan had whipped Ben more than once for smelling of ale. Two years older than Nathaniel and tall for his age, Ben at fifteen could slip into the taverns and talk protest. As much as he was drawn to Ben's playful personality, Nathaniel wasn't about to join in those dangerous doings.

"I know he is a bit of a roustabout, but he has a good soul, lad," Basil coaxed, seeming to read Nathaniel's thoughts. "Ben's circumstances are confusing for him. He has several childhood friends at the College of William and Mary. His family was middling gentry. They owned a small farm, and his father made additional money as a joiner, building houses, fences, cabinets. But his father died. Without the income of his father's craft, Ben's mother was unable to keep their family together. Thinking carriage-making would be a steady industry, she apprenticed Ben to Edan. But Ben clearly chafes at the assignment. Although he is a mediocre student at best, I think he longs to be talking patriot philosophy with college scholars."

Nathaniel nodded. "Aye, master, I understand." He had sensed Ben's frustration.

Basil pushed a little harder. "'Twould do you good, Nathaniel, to have a friend."

Nathaniel froze. He had had a friend. Moses. And Moses had been ripped away from him. Since coming to Williamsburg, he'd searched every African face that passed by—it seemed half the city's residents were black. He kept hoping to find Moses somewhere. He'd even slipped away to the market square to see if one of the carts coming in from outlying plantations carried him. But he'd never found him. It made his heart ache thinking of it.

Nathaniel's silence discouraged Basil from further prodding. "Well . . ." he murmured, clearly disappointed. "We shall read on tonight, after your chores, yes?"

Nathaniel nodded, keeping his eyes down and his face blank. But inside, as much as he hated to admit it, he could hardly wait for sundown to visit the Lilliputians.

Chapter Eleven

A WEEK LATER, Edan Maguire stood on the lawn of the Capitol, arguing with the most revered man of Williamsburg, Speaker Peyton Randolph. Even Nathaniel could see that Edan was making a fool of himself.

One of the richest and best-educated men in the colony, Randolph had just come home from Philadelphia, where he had been chosen president of the Continental Congress. Calm, tactful, and cautious, Randolph listened to radicals like Patrick Henry and his own cousin Thomas Jefferson. But he kept Virginia's official protests polite, designed to bring about repeal of British taxes and to restore good relations with the king. Williamsburg newspapers were calling him the Father of American Liberty.

Randolph was at the Capitol that cool November day along with hundreds of merchants and planters promising to not sell or use any British goods. While Edan ranted, a dozen townspeople stood nearby, waiting to talk with Randolph. A short distance away was a table to which man after man stepped, took up a pen, and signed the Association Resolves. A gentleman overseeing the process shook the hand of each man as he signed. Observers clapped him on the back in congratulations. The crowd inside the high brick walls of the Capitol yard was growing and getting louder each minute.

Not heeding how many people were listening, Edan blundered on: "But how can the people of Williamsburg so abuse Lord Dunmore when he's just won a war against the Shawnee Indians and claimed all of the territory south of the Ohio River for Virginians to settle?" Edan's face was red. He leaned way too close to Randolph.

Taking a slight step back, Randolph pulled a lace handkerchief from the wide sleeve of his floral frock coat and held it to his nose. Even by the city's standards, Edan's odor was strong. Nathaniel had seen many a lady hold a nosegay up to her face when he passed.

"These resolves have nothing to do with Governor Dunmore," Randolph replied evenly. "They are directed to Parliament to convince it to stop this unconstitutional taxation of us. They do not tax Englishmen at home without representation. Nor should they us. We have made humble and reasonable petitions to the crown. Our letters have been treated with contempt by His Majesty's ministers. We cannot sit idly. Participating in our government, protesting actions we do not like, are fundamental rights of Englishmen. And we are Englishmen, even though we live in the colonies. And so . . ."

"Peaceably?" Edan interrupted. "Do you find boarding the ship of a man who has long been good to the planters of this colony and dumping his cargo into the York River peaceable, sir?" He referred to a "tea party" two days earlier. Following the example of Boston, about twenty men boarded a merchant ship docked in nearby Yorktown. They threw two half-chests of tea from England overboard. The ship's merchant, John Prentis, had printed a groveling apology on the same day the local committee of safety issued a statement that anyone who broke the embargo should "be made to feel the resentment of the publick."

Pointing his thumb toward the Duke of Gloucester Street, Edan went on, "Someone has put a 'liberty pole' outside the Raleigh Tavern. On it hangs a bag of feathers, and beneath it is a barrel of tar. Is that to frighten me into signing this association? Aren't you, sir, being just as coercive as you claim Parliament to be?"

"Hear, hear!" applauded one of those awaiting Randolph, a portly man in a plush, burgundy coat, an obvious loyalist.

"Fie, man, for shame!" cried another. "Such talk makes you an enemy of American liberty."

Two other men took steps forward, one growling, "Perhaps Mr. Maguire should be the first to taste of tar and feathering."

"Peace, gentlemen, peace." Randolph held up his hand. "We must not argue among ourselves. It is important that we make a united stand. That way we will convince His Majesty to repeal these offensive acts. We did the same to protest the Stamp Act, and it worked."

"Aye, that and a little bit of fright put to the stamp collector," whispered one listener to another, who laughed.

Randolph continued: "Mr. Maguire, these resolves call for non-importation, non-consumption, non-exportation—in short, shutting down trade between us and England, getting them in their purse. It is the most speedy, effective, and *peaceable* way to show Parliament we mean what we say. When they see how determined we are, they will have to repeal these oppressive acts. Then we can return to a calm and loving state with our sovereign king. Representatives you elected agreed to these resolves for you. We are bound by honor and love of our country to follow them. Good day, sir." He bowed his head in courtly fashion and turned away.

The knot of men followed, save one, who hissed, "Be forewarned, Maguire. Those who are not with us will definitely be seen as against us." He left, looking over his shoulder threateningly.

Edan stayed rooted, breathing hard in anger. But after a few moments, his coloring changed from red to chalky white. He hung his head. Mumbling about bankruptcy and backwater tyranny, he shuffled off to join the line of signers.

Basil, Ben, and Nathaniel had watched the scene. "Mistress Maguire will not be happy to hear of her husband's tantrum," said Basil. "That made him at least ten enemies."

"Not that he doesn't already have a host of them," quipped Ben. "I've been asked to keep an eye on him and report any disloyal acts of consuming British goods."

Alarmed, Basil turned to Ben. "Report him? To whom?"

"To a few patriot gentlemen who have taken an interest in our ill-tempered carriage maker," answered

Ben. "They are like to be on the committee of inspection to be elected next month."

"Ben, lad." Basil shook his head. "He who asks you to pry into your master's doings and spread gossip is no gentleman."

Ben grinned. "I didn't say I was planning on fulfilling the request, master tutor, but"—he looked at Nathaniel meaningfully—"it would feel good, wouldn't it, to stick it to the old curmudgeon? A little payback for those whippings."

"Ben!"

"Oh, don't worry! You taught me better than that, old sir. I am no Brutus." A passing youth caught Ben's eye. "Oh look, if I'm not mistaken, there goes James Monroe. I knew him at home. I heard he was coming to the college. Nice lad." He darted off, calling, "James! James!"

Basil watched him go. "I worry about that boy," he muttered. But he brightened suddenly. "He remembered about Caesar and Brutus. A miracle! Mayhap I did teach him something. Now there's a story of conceit and betrayal I must tell you, Nathaniel. Back in the time of Rome . . ." A gust of cold wind rattled the trees and shook out the remaining autumn leaves in a tumble of crimson and gold. Basil began to cough violently. Nathaniel wanted to tell him to return home to bed.

"Mistress Maguire's remedies are foul and only so effective," Basil gasped through his coughs.

A girl touched Basil's sleeve. "Posset drink might help that cough," she said. "You curdle milk and ale and flavor it with sugar and spices. That's what Mother gave us."

Basil straightened up. "Ah, Miss Rind." He bowed his head and made formal introduction. "Nathaniel, this is Miss Maria Rind, daughter of the publishers of the *Virginia Gazette*, first her father, and then her mother, Clementina. I have oft placed advertisements in their broadside about my teaching. Maria, this is Nathaniel Dunn, my . . . my . . ." He paused, considered, and said, "A fellow musician."

Maria put her feet into a V and curtseyed at the knee.

Nathaniel had no idea what to do.

"Like this, Nathaniel," Basil whispered. He placed one foot in front of the other, bent with the back knee, and bowed his body over his right arm. "It's to show the young lady what a well-muscled leg you have," he teased.

Maria giggled.

Awkwardly, his face flaming in embarrassment, Nathaniel made the formal greeting.

"Don't worry," Maria told him. "There are lots of things I am supposed to know how to do that I do not." She paused a moment to think. "My penmanship is awful," she offered.

Grateful, Nathaniel nodded.

"Mother simply did not have the time to teach me after Father died and she took up the press."

"I am sorry for the recent loss of your mother," said Basil. "She was a brave lady. Look around you, Maria. Much of today's patriotism is a result of what your mother was courageous enough to print."

Maria's smile was a mix of pride and sadness. "Yes, she was very strong."

Basil explained to Nathaniel, who burned with new embarrassment that he knew nothing of this obviously important printer. "Burgess Thomas Jefferson wrote an eloquent defense of our rights in August, called *A Summary View of the Rights of British America*. Mr. Randolph presented it to the House of Burgesses to adopt, but it was too revolutionary for its members.

"It said that because we had established these colonies through our own hard work, we had the right to make our own laws without Parliament's interference. Mr. Jefferson said that government must be honest, and that it exists only through the consent of the people. He wrote that God gave us liberty at the same time he gave us life. Stirring words, yes?

"But then he went on to say—and this is what many felt bordered on treason—that the king was no more than a chief officer of the people, obligated to serve *our* best interests. Therefore, he was subject to *our* will. Most people were afraid of those words. But not Mrs. Rind. She printed them. And because she did, Thomas Jefferson's ideas traveled throughout the colonies. They were reprinted in cities as far away as Philadelphia. The resolves that these merchants are signing today bear the mark of Mr. Jefferson's belief in our ability and right to govern ourselves.

"It is strange, is it not, that a man who so stumbles when he speaks can write so beautifully. I hear it was the same with his courtship of Mrs. Jefferson, completely tongue-tied but won her heart through his violin playing." Basil put his hand over his heart. "I never had the opportunity to play with Mr. Jefferson; he was a student of Francis Alberti. He and his cousin John Randolph are the best violinists in the city. I wish. . . ."

Basil was about to wander off into one of his stories, but Maria interrupted: "Thank you for your kind words, Mr. Wilkinson. Mother would be pleased by them. Although a woman, she was a bold believer in liberty." Maria sighed. "I wish I could stay to hear them read the resolves, but I best collect my younger brothers before they get into trouble. They left the house without asking. The littlest is only four years old. I hope you will do us the favor of more advertisements, sir. My cousin, John Pinkney, will continue printing our paper. We children are to stay with him."

She curtseyed once more to Nathaniel. "I hope we meet again," she said shyly.

Pale, with solemn dark eyes, Maria was pretty, probably a year younger than his thirteen years. Nathaniel hesitated. Basil elbowed him, and Nathaniel clumsily bowed again as she left.

Nathaniel hadn't managed to speak one word. Maria was a recent orphan. Yet she had the graciousness to be kind to both Basil and him. He began to feel ashamed of the way he always held himself in.

On the walk home, Nathaniel decided to do something he knew would please Basil. "Master, can you explain more about what Thomas Jefferson wrote?"

Basil lit up like a firefly in summer. "Oh, Jefferson was undoubtedly influenced by John Locke and Alexander Pope. These are English philosophers who believe that by nature, man is born free and good, with the right and the ability to choose his own course. And rather than being afraid that we will blunder, Locke and Pope believe man has a sense of reason that will guide him to make the right moral decisions. We are not in need of higher authorities. In fact, those higher authorities—kings, the Church—are often corrupt and foolish. Man's God-given common sense is the best ruler of our actions. Each man is capable of learning and directing his own destiny. Laws of the land should be tailored to allow him to do so.

"This concept of man's capabilities is new, revolutionary, dignifying all of us with an inborn intelligence before only thought to belong to kings, lords, priests, and the mighty." Basil stopped walking and put his hand on Nathaniel's shoulder. "It includes you, Nathaniel."

Nathaniel looked at the old tutor blankly.

Basil patted his shoulder and repeated: "That includes you, lad. Believe it."

No, he had spent so much time being directed by others that he had no faith in himself or in any promise of freedom. Basil's words rung like a distant bell in Nathaniel's head, but he couldn't yet heed its call.

Chapter Twelve

"THERE, GIRL. THAT'LL feel better." Nathaniel straightened up to pet the carriage mare.

He'd been packing a poultice into her hoof. With the weather turning cold, the ground had stiffened to rock hard. Edan had taken her out to pull one of his finest chairs up and down the streets of Williamsburg, hoping to spark some interest in purchasing it. Keeping the horse at a smart trot to show how light and fast the carriage was, the pounding against the road had chipped up her hoof and made her limp.

The horse nudged Nathaniel, her hot breath warming his face. He smiled and held still, enjoying the horse's gentle affection. Ever since he had protected her against Basil's bad driving, she had been attached to him.

"I wager the Indians have names for people like you. He-who-speaks-not-to-people-but-charms-animals."

Ben's voice made Nathaniel jump. He hadn't noticed Ben standing in the stable door.

"Or Basil probably knows some old fable by what's-his-name—Aslop?—about a lowly stable boy who takes such good care of a donkey that the king makes him a duke or whatever they became back in Greece." Ben clapped Nathaniel on the back and laughed good-naturedly. "Now if this old mare can get you to talk, surely I can as well. Hmmm? What say you, Nathaniel?"

Ben's humor eked a smile from Nathaniel.

"Aha!" Ben put his hands on his hips as if to crow. "The lad dost smile!"

Nathaniel blushed.

Ben eased his teasing. "I mean nothing by it, you know, Nathaniel. Let us be friends. I can use all the allies I can find in Edan's shop. In these changeable days, all we colonists are in need of friends." He put his hand on Nathaniel's shoulder and Nathaniel did not pull back—like an easily spooked horse grateful for a sure-handed trainer. "There's a bit of fun I want you to see in town, Nat. Come along."

It was early evening. Nathaniel's chores were done. Basil was late coming home from his rounds, so it was unlikely there would be music or reading that night. But in town? "I . . . I don't like taverns, Ben," Nathaniel murmured, thinking of the trouble he'd witnessed in the ferryman's inn and of the thrashings Ben had taken for frequenting Williamsburg's.

"No taverns tonight, lad. This is a bonfire—a bonfire celebrating the triumph of King James over Catholic rebels. A company of boys I know have organized it."

"You mean Gunpowder Plot Day?"

"Aye, Nat. The very same! Basil will be so pleased that you know your English history." Ben sobered abruptly. "I'm sorry, Nathaniel. Of course, you know that. You just came over the sea, didn't you? Did they celebrate gunpowder day at home?"

Nathaniel nodded. Commemorating the defeat of Guy Fawkes and his Catholic lord conspirators had been an annual event in Yorkshire. Each November there had been a bonfire and dancing in the village. His mother had always held tight to his hand and taken him home when the revelers began enjoying their ale a bit too much, burning a huge stuffed straw doll—an effigy of the plot's leader. That's about the time the celebration turned nasty and almost superstitious prejudices against people with different religious beliefs flared.

"Then you must come for certain. You will be our expert." Ben put his arm around Nathaniel's shoulders and propelled him out of the stable, through the back of the Maguires' small orchard, onto Nassau Street. "I must admit, Nat, that I know little of the thinking behind the holiday. Just that it celebrates foiling a plot to destroy the English constitution."

"Well," Nathaniel hesitated, trying to remember the historical reason for the festivities. Like so many annual revels, the initial reason for the event had been overtaken by the party itself. "It had something to do with religion."

Ben snorted. "Didn't all England's troubles have something to do with religion? Let us hope that is something we can change here in America. Freedom to worship God as each person sees fit. I heard Burgess Jefferson talk on it at the Raleigh Tavern."

"But can't people do that already in Virginia?"

"They can. Still, they are required to attend service in an Anglican Church established by the Church of England—like Bruton Parish—at least once a month or pay a large fine. And Baptists, Methodists, Catholics, and Jews are not exactly in the center of things in Virginia, are they? But go back to the gunpowder plot."

Nathaniel searched his memory. "There were Catholic lords who wanted to overthrow King James, I think—the Scottish king after Elizabeth. I think he had been lenient toward Catholic practices at first. His mother, Mary of Scots, had been Catholic. But then he changed his mind. Catholic nobles rented a house in

London that had cellars directly beneath Parliament's House of Lords. They filled it with barrels of gunpowder and were planning to ignite it at the same time they captured King James's son and daughter. The idea was to kill the king, his advisors, and the Protestant members of Parliament all at once. But one of the conspirators realized they'd also kill lords sympathetic to Catholics. He warned one of them to stay away. So the king found out about the plot and arrested all of them."

Ben nodded. "I see. I warrant those involved were treated to the executioner."

"Aye," Nathaniel answered, shuddering at the practice of cutting a traitor open—drawing and quartering—*before* hanging him.

"Somebody should have lit that powder sooner then!" Ben said in a strange mix of laughter and grim seriousness.

Nathaniel was shocked. There was nothing funny about such a joke. Was Ben really so violent? He felt himself begin to recoil from the older boy when Ben sung out, "Here we are!"

They'd come to the edge of town, past the main lawn of the college, where the land spread out in grassy fields. There was a good-sized fire blazing and a large crowd of youths jumping and skipping around it. "Come on." Ben started trotting, and Nathaniel dutifully jogged behind.

"There you are, Ben!" cried out several boys, circling around them.

Night's darkness had come. In the crackling light thrown from the fire, Nathaniel could only see half their faces; the rest were cast in shadows, making their expressions look slightly devilish. They were sweaty from dancing close to the flames. Ben introduced them. "Nathaniel, this is Beverly Dixon, son of the postmaster. This is Robert Greenhow, of the store. Methinks Basil does books for your father sometimes. Am I right, Robert?"

The boy nodded.

"And this is Henry Nicholson and this"—Ben patted the shoulder of a hulking, sour-faced boy—"this is Jeremiah Nowland. Do not let his jolly countenance fool you," Ben teased. "Underneath this friendly exterior beats the heart of a beast." The other boys laughed. Jeremiah shoved Ben off.

"Brought you some tea?" he snapped. "If you didn't, you can't join us."

"I did," Ben answered stoutly, not at all shaken by the youth's threatening voice.

"Prove it. We're all free men's sons. You're just an apprentice. You have no money of your own. Where would you get tea?"

Ben drew himself up tall but didn't respond to the taunt other than to pull a sack from his waistcoat. "I have tea," he answered calmly. But there was a cold anger in his voice.

Nathaniel gasped. He knew where that tea had come from—it belonged to Edan.

"Huzzah!" The boy named Beverly cheered, breaking the tension. "Your turn then, Ben. Come throw it into the fire." He pulled Ben close to the flames and held up his hand to still the group. They stopped and listened.

Mimicking older men, Beverly held onto the lapels of his coat and planted his feet wide apart. He cleared his throat dramatically and took on a deep, pompous voice: "Gentlemen, herein we accept into our association of Protestant schoolboys, the presence of one, Benjamin Blyth, who will proclaim his loyalty to Virginia's resolve to not consume tea subject to tax by the crown. By throwing said tea into the fire, we show our allegiance to American liberty as well as to the good old English constitution! Huzzah!"

The boys picked up the chant: "Huzzah! Huzzah!"

Ben threw handfuls of tea into the fire, creating

little flares and sizzles in the flames. The boys began dancing round the bonfire, chanting an old rhyme Nathaniel recognized:

"Remember, remember the fifth of November,
Gunpowder, treason, and plot.
I see no reason why gunpowder treason,
Should ever be forgot!

"Guy Fawkes, guy, t'was his intent
To blow up the king and the parliament.
Three score barrels were laid below
To prove old England's overthrow

"By God's mercy he was catch'd
With a darkened lantern and burning match.
So, holler, boys, holler boys,
Let the bells ring.
Holler, boys, holler boys,
God save the king!"

Only Jeremiah stood, watching Ben with a smoldering malice to match the fire's. He turned on Nathaniel. "Got you tea?"

Nathaniel vehemently shook his head no.

"Then back out of the circle. You don't belong."

Nathaniel retreated. He watched from the shadows, confused. It made no sense to him that the boys would protest England's tea tax by celebrating a past king's victory over a man who was protesting oppression of Catholics. Nathaniel thought on the distrust still held against Catholics back home in England. They weren't allowed to vote or inherit property. The few Catholic families he knew of in Yorkshire disappeared from view around Guy Fawkes Day. Wasn't that even more unfair than a tax on tea?

No, none of it made sense. He resolved to keep clear of it, despite the fact the boys were obviously having great fun.

On the way home, Ben was flushed and excited.

Nathaniel did like Ben. He worried for him. If Ben had stolen that tea, he was in for it. "Ben?"

Ben stopped. "The lad speaks! Huzzah!"

His loud merriment embarrassed Nathaniel. He fell silent again.

"Oh Nat. I am sorry." Ben stopped short. Nathaniel couldn't see his face in the gloom, but he knew Ben meant the apology. "My teasing gets me into trouble all the time with people, like that arrogant boy Jeremiah. My own fault with him, really. This summer I was in town for Edan and passed through market square. The boys were playing cricket. I stopped to watch for a while. Jeremiah was playing in the field. He kept trying to hit the wicket from way out there. He should have thrown it to a player closer in. He was just showing off. So they asked if I knew how to play. I answered that I did, having watched how that lad had fumbled things. A joke. But he didn't take it that way. He's been an enemy every since. . . . What did you want to say, Nat?"

Nathaniel hesitated then blurted: "Ben, where did you get that tea? Did you steal it from Master Maguire?" He didn't explain that his concern was for Ben's safety.

In the darkness, Ben's voice came back offended. "I may be only an apprentice, Nathaniel, but I am no thief. All the boys went about town asking citizens to donate their tea to our bonfire to show their resolve to abstain from British goods. I convinced Mistress Maguire to give it to me when I told her we'd be having a gunpowder plot bonfire. I told her 'twould be better for her to face the ire of her husband than the ill-will of the town."

"Ben!" Nathaniel knew just what giving away Edan's remaining tea supply would cost her in his foul temper and curt language.

"'Tis true," Ben said defensively. He began walking in quick strides. "The Maguires are being watched. They are disliked because of his close bond with

Governor Dunmore. She needed to show support for our cause." He walked even faster. "Besides," he muttered, "it was the only way I could join up with the boys tonight. They're going to start a company of boy volunteers and drill on the green like the militia does. I can't miss it, Nathaniel. I can't. I want to be part of the fight. For a fight is coming, no matter how much they talk on reconciliation and goodwill for the king. Right now in Boston, British lobsterbacks occupy the city and crush the people. It's a pot waiting to boil over. It'll come, mark my words. And I am going to be in it. All Americans who have any self-respect should be."

Nathaniel had been almost running to keep up with Ben's long-legged stride. But he slowed and let Ben stalk off ahead, realizing that given time, with his dimpled smile and genuine, easy manner, Ben could probably charm the fur off a bear. He'd get the wool off a lamb—like Mrs. Maguire or himself—in a minute. Nathaniel was going to be very careful of what he allowed Ben to talk him into doing.

PART FOUR

January 1775

Goody Bull and her daughter together fell out.
Both squabbled and wrangled and made a great roul. . . .

The old lady, it seems, took a freak in her head,
That her daughter, grown woman, might earn her own bread. . . .

The daughter was sulky and wouldn't come to,
And pray what in this case could the old woman do?

In vain did the matron hold forth in the cause,
That the young one was able; her duty, the laws;

Ingratitude, vile, disobedience far worse;
But she might e'en as well sung psalms to a horse.

Young, forward, and sullen, and vain of her beauty,
She tartly replied that she knew well her duty,
That other folks' children were kept by their friends,
And that some folks love people but for their own ends. . . .

Hello Goody, what ails you? Wake woman, I say,
I am come to make peace in this desperate fray.

Adzooks, ope thine eyes, what a pother is here!
You've no right to compel her, you have not, I swear. . . .

Come, kiss the poor child, there come kiss and be friends!
There, kiss your poor daughter, and make her amends.

—Colonial political words set to "The World Turned Upside Down"

Chapter Thirteen

"THE TIMES AND this town completely perplex me, Nathaniel. Here, lad, hold that mirror higher. I cannot see to tie this cravat. Aargh!" Basil tore the long linen tie from his throat, nearly choking himself as he did so. He began again to wrap it around his shirt collar. "Isn't it odd that all Williamsburg's leaders—many who are defying Parliament and harassing anyone drinking tea—are heading to the Governor's Palace tonight for a ball honoring *the queen's* birthday? My students have talked of nothing else all week long. Their households have been uproars of preparation. All the ladies have pulled out the silk dresses they are supposed to give up in favor of homespun cloth. How quickly principle gives way for a party!

"But I do suppose the ball will ease tension. No sane person wants this disagreement between us and Britain to grow. Look how easily the British bottled up Boston.

"Aargh!" He ripped the tie from his throat again. "I have to tie this wretched thing correctly or I won't be able to breathe to play." He closed his eyes and took a deep breath, exhaling slowly to calm himself.

This time he managed to thread and weave the long tie correctly as he spoke. "Of course, the evening is advantageous to me. This is the first time in years that Mr. Pelham has invited me to play flute to his harpsichord for dancing. There is to be an oboe, a French horn, and two violins as well. It will be thrilling to play in a real ensemble again! And it is a happy occasion, after all, since Governor Dunmore is also celebrating the christening of his daughter. Clever of him to name her Virginia, don't you think? That certainly charmed the city. That and his parading back into town last month as conqueror of the Shawnee. I hear he might even have some of his Indian captives there in native dress to entertain his guests. The man is wily. All these displays make citizens forgive what a disagreeable braggart he is.

"Hold the mirror up again, lad, so I can see to this hair. I suppose I should have a wig, but then I would have needed the barber to shave my head. It does make one so cold in the winter."

Basil had washed his hair. Now strands of it stood out every which way as he brushed. He rolled his eyes.

"I am not made for court, Nathaniel. In appearance or conversation. I find it too confusing—our leaders calling the members of Parliament villains at the same time praising Lady Dunmore for her beauty and wit. It is hard to know what opinion is safe."

Nathaniel nodded, agreeing with Basil. It was hard to know what was safe to say or do these days. No matter what the choice, you were sure to offend someone. Conversations with Ben, for instance, were nearly impossible since Ben saw everything in black-and-white absolutes. Anything short of revolution was cowardice or betrayal to him.

Basil put down the brush with a snort, giving up. "Of course, it's not likely that any of the guests would speak to me tonight in any case. Tonight I am simply one of the household servants and slaves."

Out of a box he pulled a gray queue, a long, thick braid of hair, neatly finished with two large black ribbons, a cheaper alternative to a wig. Basil tied the hairpiece on his head with a string. "This cost me a month's wages. It's made of yak hair from Tibet. Goodness knows what human hair would have cost." He stroked it a moment. "Soft, though. Now powder to hide the string."

With a large puff, Basil dusted his head, making a snowstorm of white powder.

"*Kerrrrr-ccchoo*! Oh dear, we will have to get this powder off the floor . . . *kerchoo* . . . hand me that rag, Nathaniel . . . *kerchoo* . . . *kerchoo* . . . *kerchoo*." The queue nearly fell off Basil's head as he wheezed.

Nathaniel watched in astonishment. He'd seen fine gentleman thus dressed and powdered, but he'd never before seen the process.

Finally free of sneezes, Basil laughed at himself. "Who needs snuff when one has powder, eh, lad? Know you the song 'The World Turned Upside Down'? They've changed the words to politics recently, but the original words went . . ." He thought a moment, then sang, "'*If boats were on land, churches on sea, if ponies rode men and if grass ate the cows . . . if summer were spring and the other way round, then all the world would be upside down*.' That's how I feel all dandified—completely out of sorts. But, my music will make me a place of belonging. They won't be able to dance without me!"

Basil took a blue wool coat from the bedstead and shook it out before putting it on. It was pleated and long, down to his knees. "There, how do I look?" he asked Nathaniel.

Still like a grasshopper, all arms and legs, thought Nathaniel, but he answered, "Very comely, master."

Basil smiled. "Aye?"

"Aye, sir."

There was a large crash downstairs and the sound of something rolling along the floor. Basil sighed. "Mistress Maguire has been so upset. She's been dropping things all day. She is disappointed not to be invited to the ball. You would think the governor could invite the Maguires since there is only one house between this and his palace gate. Even though the Maguires are from the middling class, this house is as fine as many belonging to the landed gentry.

"But Lord Dunmore obviously follows the European code—only those *born* to privilege may enjoy it. He forgets that America was founded as the land of opportunity, a new world where everyone has the chance to pursue a better life. Work hard and prosper and welcome to the upper class. But tonight, all those ideas seem to have been put away. Tonight, we revert to the old ways."

Another crash and clatter.

Basil sighed. "I had better make my way to the palace, lad. I think my preparations make her feel worse." He picked up the satchel in which he carried his recorder and Nathaniel's German flute. "Wish me good fortune, Nathaniel. Tonight I play for the mighty. And with your flute, I will play all the better." He made a flourishing bow to Nathaniel, as if he were governor, only to catch one of his pleats on the door handle, yanking the door to *thwack* his backside.

"Ah me," mumbled Basil as he made a more humble exit.

Nathaniel almost laughed out loud.

Through the bedroom window, Nathaniel watched Basil walk up the green to the governor's palace. To see Basil go all the way through the ornate gates—with its lion and unicorn statues and royal seal—past the liveried footmen awaiting carriages, Nathaniel pressed his nose to the windowpane. The coldness of the glass startled him into pulling back. Seeing he'd left a nose print, Nathaniel hurriedly polished it away with his shirt sleeve.

Nathaniel stepped back to marvel for the hundredth time at the huge windows, six panes tall and three panes wide. As awe-inspiring as the governor's mansion was, the Maguires' two-story clapboard house had seemed a king's castle to him. With plaster and paint on the inner walls and glass in the windows, the Maguires' home was beyond anything Nathaniel had ever imagined living in. His own cottage in Yorkshire had been cozy, warmed with firelight and his mother's love, but it had been just one large room with a loft. There was nothing to decorate the stone walls. They were the same on the inside as the outside. The floor was dirt; the windows merely open holes, closed up with shutters against the cold.

Night was falling, darkening the room quickly. Nathaniel lit a tallow candle by the small fire flickering in the bedroom's hearth. Resting the pewter candle-holder beside the pitcher basin on the table, he pulled a trundle bed out from underneath Basil's. Having it, too, was an unaccustomed treat. In Yorkshire his mother had stuffed a bedding tick with goose down and sweet-smelling lavender for him, but it lay upon the cold, dirt floor.

He paused, remembering how once, when he was about five years old, a garden snake had crawled into the house and his very bed for warmth. His father had snored through the invasion, refusing to wake. It'd been his delicate mother who'd beaten the snake to death with a fire tong. Then, with her usual calm, she'd rocked Nathaniel back to sleep, singing. He'd never told his mother that she had so astonished him with her sudden ferociousness that for a while he'd been quite afraid of her!

He took off his stockings and breeches, folded them carefully to place on the closet shelf, and quickly slid under the blanket in his shirt and bare feet. Snuggling in, he pulled his mother's Bible out from under his pillow and hugged it to his chest. They might have been poor, subject to garden snakes, damp cold, and hunger, but his childhood cottage still seemed a safer place to

Nathaniel. There he had his mother's love and his parents to make decisions. He knew what to expect. Here the world indeed seemed upside down, on the brink of such upheaval—an upheaval that could swallow up people like Ben and tear apart the little bit of stability Nathaniel knew. What would Basil do if fighting came as Ben predicted and longed for?

Nathaniel closed his eyes against his fear. He imagined playing his flute while his mother listened, her bright blue eyes dancing with joy. He slipped into peaceful Yorkshire dreams.

Chapter Fourteen

"NATHANIEL?" A HAND shook his arm gently.

Dreaming of home, Nathaniel put his own hand over it and sleepily murmured, "A little longer, Mother, please. Sit you awhile beside me."

"Poor lad," said the voice. "It's me—Basil." He cleared his throat and said more loudly: "Nathaniel, I need you to arise."

Nathaniel's eyes popped open. Waking and realizing that it was Basil, not his mother, Nathaniel pushed Basil's hand away. He saw the hurt expression on Basil's face, but he couldn't help the rage he felt that the old man stood where he wanted his mother to be. Even his dreams had to be interrupted—even asleep he wasn't allowed to stay at home where he wanted to be. He bit his tongue to keep from shouting at Basil, at the world: "Why did she have to die? Why did I have to come here?" For a moment his ice-blue eyes glinted with hatred.

Basil sat on his heels. "I understand that look, lad," he said softly. "Someday, perhaps I will explain why." He then spoke in a more matter-of-fact tone. "Never look at Edan that way, Nathaniel. It will earn you a whipping." He stood. "Now, we must do something for Mistress Maguire. Get up and dress quickly. Come down to the parlor."

Dawn was seeping into the house as Nathaniel hesitantly entered the parlor. He'd never before been in the formal room with its painted floor covering of black-and-white checks and its blue-gray chair rails. Beside the polished walnut spinet sat Mrs. Maguire in a high-backed chair. Her eyes were red and puffy. She'd obviously been crying. "I just wanted to hear the music and to see what the ladies wore," she was lamenting to Basil.

"Yes, my dear, I understand. We can play a piece right now, though, as if we were royalty ourselves. And you are a far lovelier person than any of those grand dames in their white lead makeup and paste-on beauty marks. There was one lady whose wig was so big and so weighted down with feathers and jewels that it fell right off during a country dance."

"Oh no, Mr. Wilkinson, you make up stories to make me feel better."

"No, mistress, 'tis true, very. We musicians had a

hard time playing through our laughter. At that point, I'm afraid that all the gentles had had a bit too much rum punch."

He spotted Nathaniel. "Come in, lad. It's all right. Mistress Maguire and I have been practicing this piece by Handel, but it wants a flute and violin to her keyboard. I will play violin and you your flute."

"Nay, master!" Nathaniel cried. "I know not the work."

"Aye, but you read music now. You've worked through all the songs in my flute tutor. We will play the adagio movement, which is slow and simple in melody." He put his arm around Nathaniel's shoulder and drew him out of Mrs. Maguire's hearing. "She plays only so well herself, Nathaniel. This way she will have company in her mistakes. 'Twill make her feel better to help you through it. Understand, lad?"

"But could we not play the Stamitz duet we've learned already for her to hear?"

Basil shook his head. "'Tis one thing to listen to music being performed—a wondrous experience, yes. But it's quite another to brave playing it yourself. It is far better medicine for the soul. Let us do that for her, yes?"

Nervously, Nathaniel blew an A note for Basil to tune his violin. The three instruments only matched intonation so well, but Basil did his best to blend with both the spinet and flute before nodding at Nathaniel to begin. Nathaniel looked at the sheet of lines and black notes before him. When he realized that he was the lead instrument, the first melody voice instead of Basil, the little dots of notes swam before his eyes. Four times Mrs. Maguire played the opening chord that Nathaniel was to follow while he stood dumb, staring at what suddenly seemed a foreign language.

"It's all right, lad," coaxed Basil. "Concentrate."

Nathaniel swallowed and glanced over at Mrs. Maguire. She was staring hard at her music as well, just as unsure. Nathaniel very much wished to please her. She had been so kind. But why was Basil pushing him to try this—performing this piece without practice? This was too hard, too big, too sudden a leap.

"Let us begin again, Nathaniel," Basil said reassuringly. "After all, nothing ventured, nothing gained, eh?"

Nathaniel considered. A person couldn't do something if he didn't even try. Basil was right about that. Nathaniel's recent change in fortune had shown him that even when things seemed hopeless—set like stone in sorrow—there might be a way out, a possibility of change. Still, Nathaniel didn't trust change or braving to hope that it would last. Instead, he expected failure or betrayal—it safeguarded him from disappointment.

But surely this sheet of music was a small enough challenge, wasn't it? One to his head and fingers, not his heart. Couldn't he manage to drum up the courage to play this simple string of notes? Suddenly impatient with himself, Nathaniel felt a desire to shake off his shield of timidity.

He put the flute back to his lips. "Aye, sir." Nathaniel nodded. "I'll try."

Pleased, Basil smiled. "I will count a measure of preparation . . . one, two, three . . ."

Mrs. Maguire rolled out the notes of the chord. This time Nathaniel stepped in with his melody—only five notes in the first phrase, held out long, then trilled, then turned to momentary dissonance, then neatly resolved. Pause, and again. He and Mrs. Maguire's notes circled one another in a slow, dignified turn of song. A measure of rest and then Basil joined in, his line echoing and following Nathaniel's, like birds calling to one another: *answer me, answer me*. The music was an incantation to speak, to express, without having to find the right words, without having to brave eye-to-eye conversation. Even the most shy, the most timid, could take flight—soaring in independent voice, blending together in harmony, then out again in solo. It was a dialogue of sound, of emotions that could remain undefined, and it unlocked something in Nathaniel.

When the adagio ended, Mrs. Maguire had a glow about her as alive and warm as the rose-colored sunrise filling the room. Nathaniel felt bathed in light as well, as a glimmer of confidence dawned inside him.

They played on—a sonata for violin and keyboard by Corelli, another for flute and keyboard by Abel. Now more sure of herself, Mrs. Maguire picked the composer Henry Purcell. It was only when Basil and Nathaniel put down their instruments to listen to her that they realized Edan had slipped into the room in his robe and nightcap. He was sitting in a corner chair. His usual scowl was missing and his eyes were half closed in pleasure. He was even tapping his foot in time with the lively rigadoon his wife was playing.

Tugging on Nathaniel's sleeve, Basil motioned for them to leave. They tiptoed out of the room. The Maguires seemed not to notice.

"A moment of harmony like that," Basil whispered, "is a sacred thing to be relished. Would that it could last. Or that the colonies and England could find the same."

"Perhaps the king and Mr. Randolph should play duets together," Nathaniel murmured.

Both Basil and Nathaniel were startled by Nathaniel's attempt at political wit. They stopped short in the hallway and gazed at each other in surprise. Nathaniel smiled shyly. Basil absolutely beamed.

Chapter Fifteen

THE REST OF January passed quickly and quietly. The excitement of the governor's ball vanished. Williamsburg residents disappeared into their burgundy, green, and mustard-colored houses against the cold. Smoke drifted up from their hearths into the pepper-gray skies, the backyard gardens lay barren, winds rattled through the leafless orchards, making a hollow, haunted moan. Those who did walk the mile-long Duke of Gloucester Street did so in businesslike hurry, their woolen capes wrapped snugly around them, their faces so bundled they could take little notice of passersby. Darkness flooded the streets by the late afternoon, and the nights dragged by, lit by tiny, scattered dots of candlelight. There was an air of waiting throughout the town—waiting for spring, waiting to see what would happen next between the king and his colonists.

Mornings dawned icy. When Nathaniel scurried to the stable to feed Edan's horses, milk cow, chickens, and hogs, he often skidded along the path, white with thick-glazed frost or sprinklings of snow. He liked being out as the sun rose, though, to hear the rooster's crow echo through the silence of Palace Green, answered by one, then another neighbor rooster making his own audacious cry to the world. Prodded by these small, arrogant bundles of bright feathers, the town stirred and woke itself. Cows lowed; horses nickered and snorted to clear themselves of sleep. Here and there a door opened and shut as someone came out to feed them. These sounds punctured the crisp air and carried far, a reveille of town life.

By the time he'd finished feeding the livestock and pulling up water from the well for them and the household, Nathaniel's face and hands were red from the cold. He'd gratefully race to the workshop and stir the embers of the great fireplace there to reawaken the warmth of the previous day's fire and feed it with new kindling. His next job was to sweep up the wood shavings that littered the shop's floor and gave the place a wonderful smell of freshly cut wood. Only then would he venture into the kitchen to collect his breakfast of cold ham and corn bread from Sally.

Usually Nathaniel would sit by the shop's hearth to

eat and be long finished before John and Obadjah, Edan's indentured servant and journeyman, came sleepily stumbling down the stairs with Ben. The three shared the room above. But toward the end of the month, Nathaniel discovered them already up and arguing. Obadjah was telling John that he was a fool. John was saying something about the town of Richmond. Ben was babbling about change and begging John to wait for it. They snapped silent when they saw Nathaniel.

Obadjah scowled and brushed past Nathaniel to go to the kitchen. Ben trotted behind, promising to bring back a biscuit for John.

John grinned at Nathaniel. "Morning, lad. Frozen your fingers off yet feeding the swine?" He reached over to count Nathaniel's fingers, purposefully omitting one. "Good God, only nine. Let me count again. Eleven. My oh my. Where did you pick up the extra?" He held up one of his hands, with the thumb tucked behind his palm, making it appear missing. "Hey, give back me thumb!" John joked.

It was a game you might play with a younger child to great effect. Most boys Nathaniel's age would find it quite stupid. But Nathaniel liked John in spite of his resolve to not become attached to anyone in the Maguire household. John had a jolly insolence about him. Along with Ben, he was constantly mimicking Edan's fussy bustle when the master's back was turned. John was a small man, and his thick hair naturally stood up in spikes, much like the hedgehog wigs that gentlemen paid good money for. With such a sassy wit and physical appearance, John had an elflike quality about him. Nathaniel marveled that in his bondage he could be so lighthearted. He wouldn't exactly call him friend—as he had Moses and was beginning to call Basil and Ben—and yet Nathaniel enjoyed John's company.

Moses. With Basil, the flute and books, decent food and clothes, Nathaniel hadn't thought much about Moses recently. He felt a twinge of guilt. He had stopped searching the faces of Williamsburg for Moses. Where Moses had ended up was a mystery. Nathaniel prayed that his situation had improved as much as his own had.

"Hand me one of the spoke shaves, eh, lad?" John settled onto a stool behind the long, thick worktable. Nathaniel went to the back wall where tools were hung—saws, chisels, clamps, files, and felloes, thin curved pieces of wood that served as patterns for portions of the wheel rim. He picked the shaver he knew John preferred.

Each worker—except Nathaniel, who answered anyone's needs—had a specific task within the shop. Back home in London, John had been a wheelwright. It was his job to chisel the wheels, their spokes, and the hub or nave. The hardest part was then putting the three together. John had to carefully cut a mortise, or hole, into the wheel section or hub, then whittle a tenon in the spoke end to make it fit snugly into that hole. He was clever and fast.

Edan's blacksmith then fired the iron hoop to encircle the wooden wheel to protect it against the bumps of Virginia's dirt roads. The blacksmith also produced iron axles that held the wheels together, steel springs, the risers and steps. Obadjah's job was creating the body of the carriage, the delicate Windsor chairs or the wooden and leather closets for closed chariots and coaches.

As the master craftsman, Edan did little hand labor. He drew designs, created the paintings that might decorate the fancier products of the shop, critiqued work, helped tighten joists or finish hubs, and pushed for speed. It had been a long and impressive climb from his own apprenticeship in Dublin. As a result, Edan expected the same kind of drive and focus in his workers that he had had in his youth. He saw no need for compliments to motivate. And having created his own wealth in his own lifetime, Edan was desperately afraid of losing it.

Nathaniel was watching John shave away transparently thin slices of oak to fashion a spoke. "Look here, lad." John pointed to a bump in the wood. "Hardest thing there is . . . to make wood flat. Its natural state as a tree is to bulge and grow as sunlight directs it—not what we tell it."

Once more he pulled the shaver down along the length of the stick of wood, popping his wrists up a bit at the bump to try to nick it out. He ran his finger over the smooth surface and considered a moment. "Well, that's close to perfect. Good enough to stop." He added it to his growing pile of finished spokes.

"That's really the trick of it, Nathaniel, coming to understand when we are close enough to perfection to stop whittling. If we don't recognize when something has become as good as our human hands can make it, and keep fussing over it, we're like to ruin it completely by our meddling. Carve too long and the wood becomes so thin it snaps, worthless. It's the same with life—at some point we have to decide whether a situation is good enough to accept or if we must risk all in the hopes we can hone it better." John drifted off in thought and said more to himself than Nathaniel: "Just like making a spoke . . . "

Nathaniel could sense John was trying to tell him something. He started to press for more when the door to the shop flew open. There stood Edan, swaying, holding a large green bottle.

Glancing up, John's face changed to caution and then to the expressionless mask all servants knew how to put on when their master was in foul mood. "And then, lad," John muttered, "there are times to break that spoke and completely start anew."

Chapter Sixteen

UNSTEADILY, EDAN STEPPED through the door and stomped to his desk. He sat down with a thump, crashing the bottle to the tabletop. He turned to stare out the window with a loud sniff, rubbing his nose with his coat sleeve.

"Keep your head down, lad," John whispered, "and get to work."

Grabbing the broom, Nathaniel began sweeping the shavings John had made. He picked up tools that had been left lying about and hung them. He brought in and stacked kindling, making as little noise as possible to avoid attracting attention.

Not knowing he was there, Obadjah and Ben made the mistake of reentering the shop, calling out to John that there was trouble afoot. John shook his head at them, but it was too late. Edan swung around and fixed his temper on them. "What say you, curs? Trouble? Whose trouble?"

Obadjah hesitated, his mind obviously racing to find something to claim as trouble other than the obvious—Edan himself.

Ben came up with a ruse first: "I . . . I . . . I . . . I hear that the *Virginia Gazette* . . . yes, the *Gazette* . . . the *Gazette* printed a letter from Parliament that forbids our importing gunpowder. . . . The redcoats clearly fear our arming ourselves. . . ." Then he couldn't help himself: "It's outrageous, sir, that's what it is. How can we continue to tolerate such tyranny?"

John and Obadjah rushed to interrupt Ben, knowing his patriot indignation would infuriate Edan.

"What will happen if savages attack Williamsburg and we have no gunpowder?" John moaned, throwing his hands up dramatically. He made a face at Obadjah to prompt him to chime in with something.

Obadjah looked confused, then babbled, "Or . . . or . . . or pirates. That's right—pirates! Pirates could make their way up from North Carolina and kill us all in our sleep!"

For a moment, Edan looked baffled. The news of Parliament forbidding powder imports was two weeks old. Some people had been in an uproar over it, but most Williamsburg residents were unruffled, knowing that the brick octagonal magazine in Market Square was loaded full of gunpowder and several thousand Brown Bess muskets.

"I know that!" roared Edan. He squinted at Ben. "You will not be one of these idiot patriots. Hear me? If I find you participating in treasonous activities or standing about talking trouble, I will . . . I will," he blustered, "I will do such things to you that you'll wish you'd never been born."

He shouted at all of them: "I am trying to stay neutral in this mess so that anyone—loyalist, patriot, innocent bystander like me—who wants a carriage will still come to me. If politics prevent business, I'm done for. I may have signed that Non-importation Agreement, but I did so under unjust pressure, I tell you."

Nathaniel held his breath, watching Ben, fearing he would argue. Ben looked down, but his face flamed red with hatred. Obadjah nodded obediently. John's grip tightened on the tool he still held.

"Get to work!"

"Aye, master," they all muttered.

Obadjah set to mixing paint. Ben helped. Obadjah had recently completed a chair to sit atop a riding platform. With ten delicately rounded spindles in the back and curved arms, the Windsor chair could easily grace a house, much less a carriage. Obadjah had painstakingly painted the chair a deep forest green. Now he was about to add a yellow trim stripe to accentuate the bit of paneling he had carved at the base of the chair.

As a journeyman, Obadjah had completed his apprenticeship and was almost a free man. Within a year, his labor for Edan would be done. Then he could set up his own shop. He had been saving money toward that day, wearing threadbare clothes and broken-open shoes that exposed his blue woolen stockings. Unlike John, who was owned by Edan during his indentureship, Obadjah received a small commission for his work. As he'd fashioned the chair, he'd talked constantly about the four pounds that Edan would owe him upon its completion.

Obadjah carefully measured golden lumps into a bowl and crushed them into powder with an apothecary mortar and pestle. Ben poured in thick, sticky oil while Obadjah stirred.

"Have a care not to waste that," barked Edan, taking a sip from his bottle.

"Yes, sir."

Edan swung back around to look out the window. It was sooty from the fire's smoke. "Clean that," he shouted at Nathaniel.

Nathaniel found a clean cloth and water. As he passed Edan, he caught the strong, sweet scent of cherry brandy. Nathaniel knew that the Maguires had a large supply of brandy, gin, rum, and cordials for sale. He had often been sent down into the cool, dark cellar to retrieve bottles for customers. There was nothing unusual in it. Many Williamsburg tradesmen sold things from their homes that were completely different from their main craft. The organist and jailer Peter Pelham, for instance, sold ivory combs, buttons, and shoe buckles. Mrs. Maguire also took ladies' measurements for a New York City stay maker.

But Nathaniel had never seen Edan drink any of that liquor before. Many a person consumed ale at midday meal, but certainly no God-fearing person was drinking at this early hour. Something must be terribly wrong. He wished he could escape to the house and find Basil. Basil always seemed to know what was afoot.

Edan continued to mutter: "Have to sell them cheap. And for cash only. That's all there is for it. A pox upon that man. All dressed in his finery and wanting the fastest carriage possible. How can he order a phaeton worth seventy-five pounds and then once I've built it say he can't pay?"

Nathaniel gasped. That phaeton had taken them weeks to complete and was a gorgeous thing. The two-man seat was leathered and soft, perched atop the front two wheels. With larger back wheels, the phaeton could move like lightning when drawn by four good horses. Edan had carefully painted the wheels and body in burgundy and gold, giving it a rich appearance. It was not something that an ordinary townsperson would just walk in and purchase. It was meant for show and the rich.

Edan looked over to John and Obadjah. "What have we in the storage house?" he asked.

"Excuse me, sir?" Obadjah answered.

"What carriages have we completed and are awaiting purchase?"

"The new post chariot, and a number of chairs, single and double. And, of course, the phaeton," John spoke up. "That be our best work this year, sir."

"Aye," Edan said with self-pity. "Aye, some of the best work I've ever done." He took another drink and sniffled again. "The *gentleman*"—he spat out the word—"won't pay. He says the coming embargo of tobacco will bankrupt him. He can no longer afford the phaeton. Two others who owed me more than a hundred pounds between them have sailed for England without warning, saying they fear for their property and their lives among these blackheart rebels. And I doubt that Norfolk shipping merchant will pay me for his chair, either, since he deals mostly in English goods that now no one will buy.

"That's near three hundred pound I'm owed, never to be had thanks to these accursed patriots. I might as well burn the shop for all the good my hard work does me." He looked as if he might cry.

Silence hung like the tools on the wall—sharp, potentially dangerous—as Edan sniffed and swigged.

Finally, anxious about his own future, Obadjah couldn't stand the suspense. "Master, you will still pay me for this chair I've just done? My time with you is up this summer. I have plans to set up my own shop and I—"

"Plans to set up shop, eh? Steal my business, eh?" Edan heaved himself up. "Like that ungrateful Canadian living near the madhouse who left my employ then besmirched my name whenever he had a chance? Must I deal with yet another dog I've trained nipping at my heels?"

Enraged, Edan reached for an axe hanging on the wall.

Safe in a corner by the window, Nathaniel froze in terror. John jumped back from his stool, knocking it over. "Look out, Obadjah," he shouted. "Run, Ben!"

Ben bolted toward the door, but Obadjah stood rooted by his precious chair, paintbrush in hand.

In six long, staggering strides, Edan reached him.

Heaving up the axe, he brought it down with a crash, splitting the beautiful Windsor seat in half, splinters flying.

"That's what it feels like to work hard and be cheated." He swung the blade again and cracked the chair back down the middle.

"Betrayed!" He sliced a chair arm in two.

"Promises broken!" He hacked at the legs. "Dreams destroyed!"

"Stop!" Obadjah finally screamed. "Stop it!"

Edan kept swinging the axe. John rushed to pull Obadjah back. With a brave lurch, he pushed Edan so that he stumbled and fell into the table. "Go to, sir. Enough!" he shouted.

Stunned, breathing hard, still clutching the blade, Edan suddenly seemed to sober. He looked at the axe in his hand, frowned, shook his head, and then slowly took in the scene of the room, as if seeing it for the first time. The chair, its wreckage, John, Ben, Obadjah. When he turned to look at Nathaniel, Edan dropped the axe to the floor and covered his face. "Don't look at me with those eyes!"

After a moment, he lifted his head. He seemed ashamed, disgusted, confused. In a hoarse voice, he croaked, "I . . . I am sorry. . . . I don't know what came over me. . . . I . . . " With a sob, Edan rushed from the shop.

That night, John Hunter ran away.

PART FIVE

February 1775

When Britons first by Heaven's command,
Arose from out the azure main,
This was the charter of the land,
And guardian angels sung this strain:
Rule Britannia, rule the waves
Britons never will be slaves.

To spread bright freedom's gentle sway,
Your isle too narrow for its bound,
We trac'd wild ocean's trackless way,
And here a safe asylum found.
Rule Britannia, rule the waves,
But rule us justly, not like slaves.

While we were simple, you grew great;
Now swell'd with luxury and pride.
You pierce our peaceful, fine retreat,
And haste t'enslave us with great stride.
Rule Britannia, rule the waves,
But rule us justly, not like slaves.

With justice and with wisdom reign,
We then with thee will firmly join,
To make thee mistress of the main,
And every shore it circles thine.
Rule Britannia, rule the waves
But ne'er degrade your sons to slaves.

For thee we'll toil with cheerful heart.
We'll labour but we will be free.
Our growth and strength to thee impart,
And all our treasures bring to thee.
Rule Britannia, rule the waves.
We're subjects, but we're not your slaves.

—American words to British patriot song
"Rule Britannia"

Chapter Seventeen

"HERE, LAD." Mrs. Maguire handed Nathaniel a scrap of paper. "Go to the *Gazette* office. Ask that they publish this notice." She started to give him a coin to pay for the advertisement, but held it back to her chest, looking at him pointedly. "There will be change. Bring it straight back to me."

"Yes, mistress. That I will," Nathaniel reassured her.

Her eyebrow arched, she placed the coin in his hand and closed his fingers around it. "Straight back."

"Aye." He nodded and scurried out into the street.

The household had been in an uproar since John's running off. Every servant was viewed with suspicion. After witnessing how violent Edan could become, all of them were trying to avoid being interrogated by Edan about John's whereabouts.

Nathaniel had found the charred remains of a note in the shop's fireplace the morning John disappeared.

It read: "Edan Maguire, carriage maker, has authorized John Hunter to travel to Richmond to deliver a chaise." The ink was blotted and smeared. John obviously had been trying to forge a pass to get through the slave patrols that kept watch for runaways. He must have thrown this one out to make another, cleaner one.

Nathaniel was staring at the note, wondering what to do with it, when Ben came up from behind. Ben snatched it away. "Not thinking of handing that over to Master Maguire, were you?" he'd snapped, without any of his usual good-natured jests.

"N-n-no." Nathaniel was no telltale. "But what if master questions me? What am I to say? If he thinks I know something—like about this pass—he might beat me to know it."

With disgust, Ben took a step back from Nathaniel. "Then let him beat you. Are you really that weak? I thought you were just shy and mightily abused in your past, Nathaniel. I didn't figure you for a plain and simple coward." He crumpled the paper in his fist. "If you tell Edan about this, he'll know exactly where to find John. If John's caught, for each day he's run, a month is added to his indentureship. Captured after a fortnight out, and there's a year more on his bondage. If you tell about this pass, you're locking chains on John. You must stand by friends. Would you also betray me so easily for fear of a harsh word?" Ben's voice was full of contempt, his expression the same he might have when tossing kitchen slops to the pigs.

Nathaniel hung his head. He just wanted to stay out of trouble, that's all. Why should he stand up for someone else? His own father hadn't protected him. But still, seeing Ben's reaction, he was ashamed. Nathaniel knew his mother would never have placed her own welfare above someone else's, especially someone she cared for. "'Love bears all things . . .'" she'd have said. And Basil had stepped in to save him from the blacksmith without even knowing Nathaniel.

Nathaniel looked up at Ben with his eyes full of self-hatred and sorrow. What had he allowed himself to become?

For a long, withering minute, Ben glared at him. Then, slowly, as Nathaniel held his gaze, Ben softened. He sighed with impatience. "You must learn to stand by your friends, Nat. We must all steel ourselves. After the Continental Congress met, someone drew a picture of a snake cut up into segments. Each segment was named for a colony—Virginia, New York, Pennsylvania. Underneath it there was a caption: 'United we stand, divided we fall.' It's true. We have to stick together in Edan's shop just as sure as the colonies need to bind fast. John could no longer endure Edan's moods and tyranny—just like the people of Boston. Someday soon they are going to crack under the lobsterbacks and fight back. When they do, Virginia will follow.

"I had hoped that John would stay to join in our fight. But he chose to run now to secure his own freedom instead. That's all right. Liberty called to him in a different voice than it does me." He was quiet, as if convincing himself not to be disappointed.

After a moment Ben continued, "Ten years ago, before he died, my father helped lead Virginians against the Stamp Act. Patrick Henry and Spencer Monroe—the father of my friend James—wrote out a petition protesting the tax's violation of our rights. My father helped them collect signatures to it. He also convinced our neighbors to not purchase anything that carried the British stamp. I was only six at the time, but I remember my father risked jail doing so. But it was worth it. By banding together, we forced Parliament to repeal the Stamp Act.

"My father would never run away from trouble. So I won't either. I'm going to stand right here and demand that we be treated justly. We are in the right no matter how hard the redcoats bear down on us. That's the real mistake the British have made—trying to force us."

He closed his eyes and recited: "'The God who gave us

life gave us liberty at the same time. The hand of force may destroy but cannot disjoin them.' That's what Mr. Jefferson said. I memorized it. Don't you feel it, Nat?"

Ben seemed very tall suddenly.

Nathaniel felt like a worm. The thought of escaping or demanding his release from indentureship had never occurred to Nathaniel. He hated to admit it, but once . . . no, twice . . . he'd thought of freeing himself a completely different way. He'd thought of throwing himself into the York River to end his misery at the plantation. It was Moses who had seen him on the cliff and called him back. After all the good fortune that had befallen Nathaniel since, that thought now did seem gutless and foolish.

Seeing Nathaniel so thoughtful, Ben patted his shoulder. "There's a good lad." Ben threw the forged pass into the fire and waited until it turned into a blackened ash that drifted up and out the chimney.

As the paper disappeared in flames, Nathaniel resolved to burn the information it held from his mind as well, making it impossible for him to reveal it no matter what Edan did to him.

Ben continued to stare into the flames. "That reminds me to visit James at the college. When his father died, James's uncle was able to send him to William and Mary. When my father died, I was sent here to labor for Edan Maguire." He picked up the tongs and began jabbing at the fire. "I'll prove that I'm just as good as those who can still afford frilled shirts and new boots. I may only be an apprentice, but I can do my part."

Outside on the street, Nathaniel realized he now held another piece of paper that could endanger John. His walk to the *Gazette*, published by Maria Rind's family, would be a short one—right onto Palace Green, left at Bruton Parish Church, and then just past the courthouse, the magazine, and Mr. Chowning's Tavern. The wintry day was bone-chilling, yet Nathaniel slowed to read the notice:

> *Run away from the subscriber, in Williamsburg, an indented servant man, named John Hunter, a native of London, about five feet high, speaks very quick, and has a comical, sly, squinting look, and a bushy head of hair; had on, when he went away, a dark, drab short coat. Whoever secures the said servant in any of his majesty's gaols, so that I may have him again, shall have ten shillings, or twenty shillings for bringing him home.*
>
> *I suspect he may be lurking somewhere about Richmond."*
>
> *E. Maguire*

Twenty shillings! There'd be many a man who'd hunt John down for twenty shillings. Oh, how Nathaniel wished he could simply lose the note on his way to the newspaper.

He stopped abruptly in the middle of the street. Several carts nearly ran over him. If Nathaniel could only purchase John some time, John could lose himself on the frontier. West beyond Richmond rolled the Blue Ridge's mysterious wilds. That's clearly why John was heading that way. There was little need for wheelwrights in the outpost of Richmond.

What would Ben do with this advertisement?

He certainly would not stand by idly as Nathaniel would like to. Would he throw it out? Rewrite it? He'd likely do something bold and stupid that would only land them all into a cauldron of trouble. What about Basil? Basil's courage seemed to come out in the face of unkindness. Bringing John back was unkind, wasn't it? Certainly. But how could Nathaniel betray Mistress Maguire, who had been nothing but kind to him?

Nathaniel rubbed his forehead with frustration. This was precisely the kind of daunting and dangerous choice he had never, *ever* wanted to make.

He stood agonizing over what to do, quivering with cold and confusion. There was no way that he could avoid delivering the advertisement. If he did, the

Maguires would simply write a new one and take it themselves, more than like, no longer trusting Nathaniel with the errand. But—Nathaniel finally felt a solution hit him like the February wind—he could at least stop potential bounty hunters from knowing to look for John in Richmond.

Breathing hard with nervousness, Nathaniel tore off the bottom of the notice and Edan's suspicion that John was "lurking about Richmond." This way people might start looking for him at Norfolk wharfs or even the borders of North Carolina—giving John enough time to vanish into the mountains.

Nathaniel would just pray that Edan wouldn't notice the omission. He refused to think about what would happen if he did. Nathaniel walked on. Feeling both strong and absolutely terrified, he had the vague recognition that the decision to help John completely changed the way he navigated the world. Like Gulliver, Nathaniel had stepped onto a foreign land with no familiar compass to guide him.

Chapter Eighteen

THE RIND-PINKNEY VIRGINIA GAZETTE was printed in an impressive, two-story brick home. Like many of the houses in Williamsburg, it was rented by the owner to tradesmen who lived and worked their craft in the same building. As he knocked on the door, Nathaniel heard voices and the thumps and bumps of business being done inside. Maria opened the door. She blushed when she saw Nathaniel, who stood gawky and silent, letting the cold air rush through the door to rattle Maria's skirts.

When he realized she was shivering from the frigid blast, Nathaniel reached up to tip his round hat as he'd seen gentlemen do in respect to ladies in town. But instead he knocked it off his head to her feet. Terrified it would blow away, he dove for it, nearly tackling her. When he popped back up, hat in hand, they almost cracked heads.

A brood of children saved him from his embarrassment by suddenly emerging from inside, crying, "Who is it, who is it?"

"A . . . a . . . subscriber?" Maria provided Nathaniel's answer.

"Yes, miss. I have brought a notice from the Maguires. One of their servants has run off."

"Goody!" The littlest one clapped his hands and danced about.

Maria shushed him and reddened again. Nathaniel guessed that her family was having money difficulties as well. With five young orphaned children to care for, Maria's cousin, John Pinkney, had his hands full. Nathaniel knew that a number of people rented rooms in the house to cut some of the family's housing costs. He wondered too if the paper's strong voice for freedom was losing them readers.

"Come in," said Maria. "There is still time to set type for this issue."

Nathaniel followed Maria into a room crammed with tall, wide printing presses and stacks of paper. There, her cousin Pinkney, an apprentice a few years older than Nathaniel, and a slave were preparing the Thursday broadsheet.

Pinkney was pulling out individual letters from rows and rows of tiny lead squares in a compartmented wooden box. One by one he placed them along a long iron ruler. He squinted as he worked. When Nathaniel drew closer, he could see why. The letters were no bigger than a black carpenter ant, and backward!

Seeing how puzzled Nathaniel looked, Pinkney laughed. "It is confusing having words in reverse. I must lay out the entire sentence like that—backward—spelling a word like 'the' as 'eht.' That's because when we press the paper down onto the galley, the printing reverses the image. I really have to mind my *p*s and *q*s because they appear almost identical reversed."

He wiped his inky hands on his apron and reached for Nathaniel's note, obviously glad for a break. "Ah, perfect! I had a hole in this column. I'll place your notice in between the one about a strayed horse and the one about a found slave."

Pinkney counted up the letters and spaces in the notice. "Maria, can you take care of payment, please?"

"Yes, of course." She gestured for Nathaniel to follow her into the next room, which was filled with books and pamphlets for sale. "That will come to three bits, Nathaniel." She caught herself and blushed again. "Is it all right if I call you Nathaniel?"

Maria's dark, soulful eyes met Nathaniel's. "Oh my," she whispered, probably not realizing she spoke aloud, "what beautiful eyes."

Nathaniel felt like telling her she could call him by whatever name she wanted. But instead he cleared his throat and stammered out, "Y-y-y-yes."

Her smile was sweet. "You may call me Maria then."

Nathaniel ducked his head and stuck out his hand with the coin, hot and sweaty from his nervousness. Maria weighed it and cut the coin in quarters, giving back one triangle slice to Nathaniel.

"Thank you, miss, ah, Maria." Nathaniel began to back out of the room, squishing the brim of his hat.

"Would you like to see your notice laid out?" Maria stalled his departure.

Nathaniel nodded. They entered the pressroom again. By now one of the pages was completely composed in a frame. The apprentice was applying ink to the type by "beating" the laid-out letters with leather balls stuffed with wool on sticks that he had smeared with black ink.

Pinkney wasn't quite finished laying out Edan's notice. "Your master always writes long," he commented. "A year or two ago he had quite a battle with an old journeyman of his in our newspaper. I remember a lot of name-calling and a challenge between them to each make a carriage and then let the public pick the best. A contest to decide who was the better artisan. But nothing came of it, as I recall. A bit of a hothead, is he not?"

Nathaniel didn't know what to say. Criticize his master in public? He might risk punishment to help John, but gossiping about Edan was simply foolhardy.

Maria frowned at her cousin and changed the subject. "Here, Nathaniel, I have learned to read backward. I can tell you what this notice says, if you like?"

Nathaniel nodded, grateful to avoid answering about Edan.

"Let's see." She puzzled a moment. "'*d-e-t-t-i-m-m-o-c.* Committed . . . to the public jail, a . . . y-a-w-a-n-u-r . . . runaway . . .' Wait a moment. Watch this, it's like magic." She reached under the counter on which Pinkney worked and pulled out a small mirror. She positioned it to reflect the type, now reading forward in the mirror. Slowly, for she was not a fluid reader, she spoke: "'Committed to the public jail, a runaway slave named Moses, says he belongs—'"

"Wait, did you say Moses?" Nathaniel's heart started to beat wildly. In America, there were many Africans named Moses, he knew. But could this be his friend? He fought the desire to grab the mirror from Maria.

"Yes." She nodded.

"Please," he urged her, "please read the rest."

"'A runaway slave named Moses, says he belongs to a plantation in Surry County on the James River, but will tell no more. He is unusually tall, close to six feet, very muscular and strong. . . .'"

Yes, that's right, thought Nathaniel. *Incredibly strong.*

"'On his forehead is a scar shaped like a crescent moon. . . .'"

Nathaniel gasped. It had to be Moses. He snatched the mirror from Maria to finish: "'. . . a scar shaped like a crescent moon; had on when he was taken up a mint-colored broadcloth coat, double-breasted scarlet waist-coat, and a pair of buckskin breeches.'" Nathaniel remembered those clothes. They were Moses's Sunday clothes. "'His owner is desired to apply for him, pay charges, and take him away. Peter Pelham.'"

Peter Pelham. That meant Moses was in the Williamsburg jail!

Nathaniel managed to shove the mirror back into Maria's hand before he was out the door, running.

Chapter Nineteen

THE WILLIAMSBURG JAIL was a grim place. On the opposite side of town from the Maguires' home, just north of the Capitol, the prison was surrounded by a tall brick wall. Within the exercise yard behind it, pirates, thieves, murderers, debtors, and runaways might be let out of their cells to walk for a few minutes—their view limited to the red bricks holding them in, the filth and dirt at their feet, and the sky above. Until recently the insane had been housed there, too. Their screams and pleas for mercy or to the phantoms that plagued them pierced Nicholson Street, strangely mixing in with the everyday sounds of passing carts, cows, gardening, and conversation among neighbors.

Attached to the prison was a two-story house. There lived the jailer—the acclaimed organist of Bruton Parish Church, Peter Pelham—with his wife and their flock of children. Pelham regularly took a prisoner to church to pump the bellows that operated the organ while he played. It was to his front door that Nathaniel ran. A sour smell of sewage, trampled mud, and rotting garbage hung about the place. Mrs. Pelham answered Nathaniel's knock, balancing a baby on her hip and soothing a sniffling toddler clinging to her apron.

"Please, ma'am," Nathaniel asked, panting from his run. "You hold a slave, named Moses. May I speak to him, please?"

With a weary face, Mrs. Pelham looked him over. "Have you come from his owner to claim him? You'll want more strength than is in you, child, to get him back to his master. He put up quite a fight when the sheriff brought him in."

"No, ma'am. I'm just a . . . a . . . a friend," he blurted out the word.

Mrs. Pelham frowned. Nathaniel realized too late that whites were not supposed to be "friends" with slaves, especially one who had run away and caused trouble for the jailer. But he sensed compassion in her. "I used to work with him before. We . . . we were . . . we spent a great deal of time together then."

"Where do you belong now?"

"To Basil . . ." He corrected himself. "I work in Edan Maguire's shop."

"The governor's carriage maker?"

Nathaniel hesitated, not knowing whether that bit of information would help or harm his hope to see Moses. But there was no way around the answer. "The carriage maker, aye, mistress," he muttered.

Mrs. Pelham nodded, seemingly impressed.

"Up . . . want up," the small child whined, holding his hands toward her. She sighed and somehow managed to gather him up and balance him on her other hip. "I'm not sure that Mr. Pelham would allow this, but he's at the church right now. Come. I will leave you with him for a few minutes. I've my young ones to tend to. When I come back, though, you must leave straightaways."

Nathaniel followed her out of the wintry sunlight, through a large room, down stairs into darkness. He put his hand along the wall to steady himself and felt dampness and moss growing along it.

"Here the rascal is." Mrs. Pelham put down her children, who both began wailing, to pull a large key off the wall. She unlocked a heavy wooden door.

Nathaniel gasped. Inside, lying facedown on straw was Moses, chained to the wall by leg irons.

"He is too strong," Mrs. Pelham said softly. "He needed to be contained." She handed Nathaniel a bowl filled with a nasty-smelling salve of turpentine oil. "His face and arms are bruised. I was afeared to try putting it on his cuts. Mayhap he'll let you." She disappeared, carrying her infants, their cries escorting her retreat.

Nathaniel tiptoed in, more out of fear of the place than of making noise. "Moses," he whispered. "It's Nathaniel. Wake up, Moses."

Moses lifted his head. Nathaniel bit his lip to keep from crying out in dismay. Moses's eyes were nearly swollen shut they were so bruised. His mouth was split open on one side. There was no recognition in his bloodshot eyes.

"Moses, don't you know me? It's Nathaniel, from the York River."

Moses looked at him blankly.

"Let me put this balm on that cut, Moses. It wants physick to heal." Nathaniel scrapped up a dollop of the sticky salve and spread it on Moses's chin.

"Nathaniel?" Moses finally spoke in a raspy voice.

"Aye, Moses. What happened? Why did you run away?"

"I could stand bondage no more, Nathaniel. I could not. My new master teach me to pilot boats, up and down the James River and into the Chesapeake Bay. He were kind enough, but the hours on the tides, they spoke to me. You feel so free on the waters, Nathaniel. That river comes and goes, pulling, going the way it wants. And on the bay I could see to the ocean and the way to my homeland. If the waters have their own mind, why can I not?"

Moses was sitting up straight now, his voice growing stronger as he spoke. "There was a good woman among us, name of Lucy. She finished what you start. She taught me to read, Nathaniel. She's a slave, too, but she lived in Williamsburg when she were young. Her master sent her to the Bray School, where they learned black children, free and slave, to read. So, she been teaching me. She used the good book to learn me, Nathaniel. I learn about Moses, the man my mama call me for. I learn how he show up the pharaoh and set his people free. Why didn't you tell me about Moses, Nathaniel?"

Nathaniel hadn't even connected his friend with the biblical hero. Perhaps in those days, when Nathaniel was so sad, so beaten down, he couldn't contemplate the Old Testament story of escape and salvation. "I'm sorry," Nathaniel said, although as he looked at Moses in chains, he wondered if his friend had been well served by the knowledge.

"Moses"—Nathaniel choked out the words—"did

your master do this to you?"

"Nay, Nathaniel. It was the slave hunter. A foul man I pray God punishes."

Nathaniel looked about the cell. All it held beside the chains and the straw was a bucket of water. A barred, open window let in a trickle of sunlight and an ocean of cold. He began to shiver, a chill washing into his bones and heart.

"Cold, boy?" Moses asked. "You never was hardy enough." He tried to reach out to rub circulation back into Nathaniel's arms, but his chains clattered and stopped him. "But you look better than when we was parted, Nathaniel. Where you be?"

In ease and luxury by comparison, Nathaniel thought. He was suddenly flooded with unchecked gratitude toward Basil. And wasn't it just like Moses, as he lay locked in prison, to worry over Nathaniel. He told Moses about Basil and Edan. Moses nodded, pleased. "Near the governor palace, you said?"

"Yes."

"How close?"

"One house down. Before you reach the brick house belonging to Mr. Wythe."

Moses thought a moment, as if memorizing the location.

"Moses, what will happen to you now?"

"They take me back."

"What then?"

Moses shrugged. "Twenty lashes for the last man what run. That's all."

"That's all?" Nathaniel gasped.

Moses smiled and then winced, holding a hand up to his battered mouth. "A lash may cut my skin, but it can't hurt me no more, boy. Not now my mind be free."

Footsteps approached. Mrs. Pelham appeared. "I've just been told that his master is sending for him tomorrow. Best say your good-byes."

Nathaniel fought off sudden, childlike tears. He struggled to ask: "Can I do something for you, Moses?" But he knew there was no helping Moses here, today. But in the tomorrows ahead? Surely those calling for liberty for themselves would think to include slaves like Moses in their cause—if patriots took up the fight, if Moses could stand bondage until then.

Moses shook his head. He gestured to Nathaniel to come closer and whispered into his ear. "The Lord will show us the way to the promised land. I'm going to follow. You do, too."

That night without warning, without quite realizing

what he was doing, Nathaniel caught up to Basil and hugged him around the waist from behind, darting away again, out the door to the horses before he could see the old man's joy.

PART SIX

April 1775

Come, join hand in hand, brave Americans all,
And rouse your bold hearts at fair Liberty's call;
No tyrannous acts shall suppress your just claim,
Or stain with dishonor America's name.

Our worthy forefathers, let's give them a cheer,
To climates unknown did courageously steer;
Thro' oceans to deserts for Freedom they came,
And dying, bequeath'd us their freedom and fame.

The tree their own hands had to Liberty rear'd.
They lived to behold growing strong and revered;
With transport they cried, Now our wishes we gain,
For our children shall gather the fruits of our pain.

Then join hand in hand, brave Americans all,
By uniting we stand, by dividing we fall;
In so righteous a cause let us hope to succeed,
For heaven approves of each generous deed.

—"The Liberty Song," words set by patriot John Dickinson as a parody of the English song "Heart of Oak"

Chapter Twenty

"OH, TO HAVE been there, Nathaniel!" Basil sighed. "To have heard him! His words were so stirring that one of the men leaning through the window of the church to listen has requested to be buried underneath that window when he dies."

Basil had wandered out to the stable to find Nathaniel to talk about Patrick Henry for about the hundredth time. For the past weeks, the town had discussed little else than Henry's March twenty-third speech to the Virginia Convention. The fiery Henry had demanded that the colony raise troops to defend itself in case Britain used military force to stop their protests. At first he was dismissed. Despite the harsh occupation of Boston, despite the British warship anchored at Burwell's Landing just outside Williamsburg, leaders like Peyton Randolph stubbornly held on to the belief that reasonable legal arguments plus the trade embargo would convince the king to recognize American rights.

But Henry wouldn't give up. He thundered that the colonists had done all they could to avoid fighting. They had "petitioned, remonstrated, and prostrated themselves before the throne." Still, Parliament refused to listen and only sent navies and armies to suppress them. "If we wish to be free . . . we must fight!" he'd shouted.

Basil had been to the Raleigh Tavern and heard bits and pieces of Henry's already legendary speech.

"They say no one stirred as Mr. Henry spoke, they hardly breathed, listening to him. Can you imagine having that kind of effect? It's the power of words, Nathaniel, the power of words! Never forget it."

Nathaniel smiled as he brushed to pull away the horse's itchy, hot winter fur. Although his back was turned to Basil, he knew the old tutor's eyes were glossy with an awed rapture. Basil was like that about words.

"A man who'd witnessed it acted out Mr. Henry's speech. Mr. Henry said we must replace 'the illusion of hope' with 'the lamp of experience.' He went on: 'Gentlemen may cry peace, peace, but there is no peace. The next gale that sweeps from the north will bring to our ears the clash of resounding arms! Our brethren are already in the field.'

"'Then Mr. Henry slumped, with his hands crossed before him as if shackled, and cried out, 'Why stand we here idle? Is life so dear, or peace so sweet, as to be purchased at the price of chains and slavery? Forbid it, Almighty God!'

"Mr. Henry held his arms up toward heaven like this"—Basil reached for the sky—"and ended: 'I know not what course others may take; but as for me, give me liberty, or give me death.'" Basil pulled out each word of the last sentence like a drumbeat.

He dropped his hands. "Oh Nathaniel, what a man! What a mind! What a speech!"

Somewhere during the course of Basil's description Nathaniel had turned, currycomb quiet, himself spellbound by Patrick Henry's dramatic call for action, just as Virginia's lawmakers had been. In the end, Henry's impassioned words pushed the Virginia Convention to muster two regiments of infantry. Everywhere men were beginning to gather rifles, muskets, even Indian tomahawks to join up.

Flushed with inspiration, Basil remained motionless, staring off into air. "The recruits will wear hunting shirts as uniforms at first. On those shirts, men are embroidering Henry's words: 'Liberty or death.' Think Nathaniel! Those words will march straight into battle and be the banner that steadies men under fire. Those words may create a new nation—a nation of hope, of fairness, of equality!"

He lapsed into silence. Nathaniel turned back to the horse but he, too, was lost in thought—about the choice Patrick Henry was calling for. About the choice Moses and John Hunter had made.

A chance that Obadjah had taken as well, on the very day that Patrick Henry stirred so many souls. Perhaps encouraged by John's escape, Obadjah decided he also had had enough of Edan's tirades.

Absentmindedly, Nathaniel laid the currycomb on the horse's neck. It stamped its hoof impatiently, waiting.

Liberty or death. Is life so dear as to be purchased at the price of chains?

What had happened to Moses when he was returned to his owner? Had John made it to liberty? There had been no word of him. Hopefully escape would be easier for him and for Obadjah, men of the same skin color as European noblemen. When poor Moses had fled, it had been easy to spot him. There were freed Africans in Virginia, yes, but they were few. Moses must have stood out like a comet in the night sky.

Nathaniel began to brush the horse again.

Basil broke into Nathaniel's musing. His voice was changed, the enthusiasm over Henry's oratory gone. "How old are you now, lad?"

Nathaniel stopped his combing. He hadn't thought about that in the longest time. If it were April . . . "What month is it, master?" he asked.

"April, mid-through."

"Aye?" Nathaniel suddenly remembered small celebrations of his birthday—his mother finding honey to make sweet cakes, her hugging him and whispering that the day of his birth had been the most glorious of her life. Even his father had managed a few compliments that day, led by her example. He had always wanted to please her.

A new thought came to Nathaniel about his father—a thought that made him freeze mid-stroke. Would his father ever consider running from his indentureship as John and Obadjah had? If he did, would he come take Nathaniel?

In a torrent of confusion, Nathaniel looked at Basil. Would such liberty be worth the price of leaving Basil, his books, his music?

Basil's voice barely came to Nathaniel through the storm suddenly raging in his mind. "How old are you, lad?"

Nathaniel merely stared.

"Nathaniel?" Basil prompted.

His father would never come. Never. Why would he? Nathaniel shook off the idea and tried to focus on

Basil. "Excuse me, sir?"

"I asked how old you are."

"Oh! Fourteen, master. Just. On the fourth of this month." The day had passed without Nathaniel even recognizing it.

"Why, happy birthday, lad!" Basil said happily. Then in hushed voice, he added, "I am glad you are so young."

"Why, master?"

"We may be washed in blood, lad, if it comes to war. King George has thousands of well-trained troops, plus Hessians he purchased from German princes. Those mercenary soldiers are ruthless. We have but a handful of militia, only a few of them experienced, and that in the French and Indian War, mostly under British commanders.

"There was a great deal of discussion about this last night at the Raleigh Tavern. No one knows who we'd have to command an army against the British. Take George Washington, for instance. He's the Virginian with the most battle experience. He fought in the French and Indian War, but he has never led more than a regiment. The British Army thought so little of him that they refused to give him an officer's commission.

"But," Basil added, "there were several men there

last night who said that Washington has a calm courage about him that they would follow straight into Hades."

Basil sighed. "Most of our fighters will be farmers and yeomen. You, thank the Lord, will be too young to bear a gun. The one to worry on is Ben. If I know that hothead, he's already plotting how to get his hands on a musket."

Ben had, in fact, discussed the very same several nights back with some of the boys from the bonfire. Ben had gathered them in the stable, including Nathaniel, as if he were sure to want to join in. Ben had said the gunpowder magazine housed plenty of muskets and that no one would notice if they took a few. He joked about dressing up like Indians—as they had in the Boston Tea Party—to raid the magazine, which the boys laughed about excitedly. That's when Nathaniel left with the excuse of feeding the chickens. He didn't want any part of stealing muskets.

Basil shook his head in disapproval of Ben. "You keep an eye on our young friend, Nathaniel. He is too impetuous. He knows naught what war means. As rousing as Mr. Henry's words are, as just as is our cause, I do wish . . . mayhap . . . let us hope that Mr. Henry has been premature in his warnings."

* * *

But Patrick Henry was not. At that very moment, riders were galloping south from Massachusetts, spreading the news of a deadly skirmish between American minutemen and British troops at Lexington and Concord.

That night, Lord Dunmore and twenty royal marines struck against the people of Williamsburg.

Chapter Twenty-one

FLAM-FLAM-FLAM-FLAM.

Nathaniel's eyes popped open. What was that sound? He rubbed the sleep from his eyes and strained to see through the darkness. Across the room Basil snorted, still slumbering.

He must have been dreaming. Or Basil's snores had awoken him as they so often had during the winter. He turned over.

Rat-a-tat-tat. Rat-a-tat-tat. FLAM-FLAM-FLAM-FLAM.

Nathaniel sat up. Those were drums! He jumped out of bed and ran to the window. In the waning moonlight, he saw men running down the street toward Market Square.

"Alarm! Alarm!"

Scanning the rooftops, Nathaniel looked for flames. When a house caught fire, townspeople rushed to pass buckets of water to prevent flames from spreading and burning down entire blocks of buildings. But he saw none.

"The redcoats! The redcoats!"

Rat-a-tat-tat. More drums, more shouts.

Nathaniel scrambled to pull on his stockings and breeches. "Master!" he called. "Master Basil, something is amiss. Get up."

"Eh? What's the matter, lad? Go back to sleep." Basil groaned and stretched and rolled over with another snort.

Nathaniel could hear Edan and Mrs. Maguire stirring downstairs. He'd have to hurry the old man so that he could get out of the house before Edan might prevent it. He pushed on Basil's turned back. "Master, I think we've been attacked! Master, you must get up!"

FLAM-FLAM-FLAM-FLAM. To arms, Williamsburg! To the magazine! Alarm! Alarm!

"Master Basil!" Nathaniel pleaded.

Basil propped himself up. "What is it?"

Rolling drums answered before Nathaniel could.

"Good Lord!" Basil tumbled out of bed. "Grab my coat, lad!"

The two of them clattered out the door, down the stairs and onto the green as Basil pulled on his clothes. His long gray hair flew about his head as they trotted. Other men dashed by them, stuffing their shirttails into their breeches as they rushed. Women in nightcaps, wrapped in shawls or blankets, peered out from behind their open front doors.

The entire town was up, running, afraid.

Nathaniel and Basil joined a crushing crowd in the Duke of Gloucester Street between the magazine and courthouse. Jostling one another, trying to hear, people shouted questions and answers, anxiety and anger bubbling, building to a boil.

"What's the matter? What's happened?"

"They've emptied the magazine of our gunpowder!"

"Who?"

"British marines! They came to town in the night and stole more than fifteen barrels of the colony's gunpowder!"

The man with that information was quickly engulfed, illuminated by dozens of lanterns. He tried to shield his eyes.

"What? Say again, man."

He repeated the news. It rippled through a hundred people, passed by indignant bellows.

"But that's ours!"

" . . . to defend ourselves against Indian attacks and slave uprisings . . ."

"And takeover by the Royal British Army!"

"That's right!"

"Let's after them!"

"Aye! Aye!" The crowd erupted into a guttural chant. Many in the mob carried muskets, gardening hoes, workmen's axes—whatever they had been able to grab as they raced to the alarm. They held them in the air and shook them threateningly, knocking one another about in their excitement. Nathaniel was nearly squashed by a bull of a man beside him. He instinctively grabbed for Basil's coat sleeve, but Basil had been washed aside in the storm surge of infuriated people pushing roughly to be on the move.

A shrill voice kept calling until finally it stilled the mob. "Wait! Wait! It's too late!"

It was the same man. Again he became the center of a swarm. "They've already made it back to the *Magdalen* at Burwell's Landing."

"How say you?"

Frustrated calls of "We can't hear!" "What did he say?" echoed through the multitude.

He held his hands up imploringly and the crowd gradually silenced. "This was a well-planned theft, lads! He knew our watchmen had gone home to their beds, the lazy sots. He had the schooner and the marines waiting."

"He? Who?"

"Lord Dunmore! He must have ordered it. He has

the key to the magazine gate. They used his wagon and came from the palace stable yard. Mayhap he had the marines there for days waiting for the right opportunity. It's obviously to prevent us from arming as Patrick Henry called for."

At this, the crowd roared. Dawn was breaking, and its gentle light fell on faces clouded with disbelief and disappointment, faces twisted in rage and vengeance. "Treacherous villain!" "To the palace!" "Dunmore will answer for this." "We'll hold him hostage until he orders the powder's return." "Aye. Let's to it."

Reignited, the mob bumped and shoved and turned itself to march toward the palace. Gathering on the green, with muskets in hand, was Williamsburg's company of volunteers, organized the previous year to fight with Dunmore against the Shawnee. Shouldering their muskets, they too, moved forward to join up against the man who so recently led them.

"Nathaniel! Come here, boy!" Basil and Nathaniel swam toward each other, elbowed and pushed. They fell together, and Basil dragged them out of the tide of rushing people.

"Good God," murmured Basil. "I think we might witness an assassination. If this gets any more out of hand, we must back out of it, lad. Who's to say that Dunmore hasn't fortified himself with armed marines?

From behind his wall, they could shoot into the crowd and slaughter dozens."

Just as Basil spoke, Nathaniel spotted Ben at the mob's tail end. Pointing, he called out to him, "Ben! Come back!"

Ben waved before he squirmed his way further into the crowd, his excited grin plain to see.

As the feverish horde began to gain direction and speed, a refined voice called out, "Peace! Hold! Stand down, gentlemen."

Voices echoed the call to "hold" and the crowd paused, looking back toward the courthouse. On its brick steps stood three men.

"Shsssh. It's Peyton Randolph. Quiet, lads. Listen to Mr. Randolph." The crowd slowly shushed itself.

Basil and Nathaniel inched to the crowd's perimeter.

"Who are the other two gentlemen, master?" Nathaniel whispered.

Basil stood on his tiptoes to see. "Mayor John Dixon and the colony's treasurer, Robert Carter Nicholas. Cool heads, both. Let us listen."

" . . . write a petition, asking for return of the gunpowder," Randolph was saying.

"Nay. We've petitioned enough!" a man with a musket shouted. "Patrick Henry is right. Parliament never listens! Look how they hold down Boston. Parliament has already declared Massachusetts in rebellion and clearly plans to crush it. Virginia might be next. Maybe that's what this gunpowder theft is leading up to!"

"Aye, aye," murmured many. "Maybe." "Yes, maybe so." "Maybe more marines are marching toward us right now to occupy our city!" Panic crackled through the mob, like heat lightning through a summer sky.

Peyton Randolph held his ground. "This is not Massachusetts and this petition is not going to Parliament." Accustomed to unruly debate in the House of Burgesses, Peyton remained composed despite the heckling. "This is to a governor many of you know personally. . . ."

"That we do! We know him as a scurrilous drinker and boor!"

A few men laughed. Randolph ignored them. "Give us leave to write a petition and deliver it to the governor immediately."

"Never mind more paper and polite niceties," countered another man. "Let us take the governor before he slips away to a ship as well."

"He will not desert his wife and children," answered Mayor Dixon, playing off the popularity of Lady Dunmore.

The crowd mumbled and argued among itself until

finally one man shouted, "Gentlemen, Mr. Randolph is about to leave for the Second Continental Congress in Philadelphia as our representative. That august body of leaders from all thirteen colonies has elected him their president. I think we can trust Mr. Randolph and our town counselors to pen a persuasive petition to Governor Dunmore."

Randolph and the man bowed at each other.

"What say you?"

For a moment, there was silence. Then several seconded the motion, persuading the rest. Randolph and Dixon withdrew into the courthouse to write hastily. The crowd remained rooted, watching the courthouse doors like a cat at a mousehole.

Chapter Twenty-two

"I CAN'T BELIEVE they are writing yet another petition!" Ben found his way through the mob to Basil and Nathaniel. He was trailed by four boys, including the foul-tempered Jeremiah. They were impatient and itchy. Like horses denied their morning feed, thought Nathaniel. He nervously realized that Edan's carriage horse was probably twitching about in her stall wondering where he was with her oats.

"Haven't they figured out that their petitions and arguments only give the redcoats more time to plot?" Ben fussed. "Words are the weak weapons of fat, old men."

His friends laughed. The boy named Beverly chimed in, "They probably are in there napping for all the courage they have."

Frowning, Basil turned on Ben and spoke with

uncharacteristic vehemence. "For shame, Ben. For shame, Beverly. Is not your father inside as well?"

Beverly hung his head, but Ben sighed and rolled his eyes. His reaction infuriated Basil. He caught Ben up by a buttonhole of his coat.

"These men have risked the hangman for years with their words. And it is their words that have inspired all of us to believe enough in our rights as human beings to speak up and demand justice. For generations, nay centuries, mankind has held that we must do the bidding of a king, no matter how idiotic, how tyrannous he was. Words have taught us that he is—how did Mr. Jefferson put it?" Basil hesitated a moment and then went on, "'That kings are the *servants* not the *proprietors* of the people.' This crowd is born of such words, ennobled by such words. I am no longer just a poor musician, a lowly servant, because of words. I am a man guaranteed by my very nature to have rights, to have dignity. I stand tall because of words."

Basil stopped abruptly, realizing that he had raised a fist and was shaking it at Ben. Ben's chin was lifted, his eyes rebellious. He was grinding his teeth so hard as Basil spoke that his dimples appeared and disappeared repeatedly. He was obviously aware that whoever was near enough to hear was listening to Basil chastise him.

Basil dropped his hand but ended forcefully: "If Mr.

Randolph wants to pen a few more words, I am for it. We owe him that respect, Ben."

At that moment, Randolph, Dixon, Nicholas, and several other town aldermen emerged. Ben had opened his mouth to make some retort, but upon seeing them turned expectantly toward the steps of the courthouse. So did everyone in the crowd.

Mr. Dixon began to read, and it was immediately obvious that the mob's reaction would be a mixture of Basil's and Ben's.

We, His Majesty's dutiful and loyal subjects . . .

"I'm not feeling the might bit dutiful meself right now," sneered a listener.

"Shhhhhh, listen." His neighbor elbowed him.

. . . humbly beg leave to represent to your Excellency . . .

"Excellency of what—deceit?" heckled another.

. . . that the inhabitants of this city were this morning exceedingly alarmed . . .

"Now there is a fact!"

. . . that a large quantity of gunpowder was, while they were sleeping in their beds, removed from the public magazine and conveyed on board one of His Majesty's armed vessels . . .

"Yes, that's right." "Well said." Heads began to nod.

. . . we therefore humbly desire to be informed by your Excellency, upon what motives, and for what particular

purpose, the powder has been carried off in such manner . . .

"If that's not an act of war, what is?"

. . . and we earnestly request your Excellency to order it to be immediately returned to this magazine.

Dixon ended, looking up and squinting into the now bright morning sunshine. "Come, friends," Mr. Randolph called. Without waiting for a response, he and the other officials began walking to the palace. The independent company of volunteers fell in behind them. Silenced by their belief in Randolph, the crowd followed dutifully. It came to a halt in front of the Wythe and Maguire houses. The town officials went on alone to the palace gate and disappeared inside.

Nathaniel saw Edan and Mrs. Maguire standing on their front stoop, and slipped behind Basil to hide from view. He knew from Edan's scowl that he would punish Nathaniel for being part of this march if spotted. He looked for Ben to forewarn him. But Ben had disappeared with his friends.

"That petition should have had a little more teeth to it," grumbled a well-dressed man, standing beside Basil.

"Remember the proverb, sir: Civility costs nothing," Basil murmured.

"True." The gentleman tipped his hat to Basil. "But here's another one: 'Blessed is he who expects nothing, for he shall never be disappointed.' Dunmore will not return the gunpowder. I've hunted with him and gamed with him. He stops at nothing to win. I would not be surprised to learn he cheats at cards. He also has a terrible temper. If anything he will see this mildly worded petition as an insult. 'Twould be better to grab him by the throat and shake the powder out of him."

The man turned out to be right.

Acting almost as if it was beneath him to answer, Lord Dunmore stated he had taken the gunpowder to protect it from being stolen by slaves. Dunmore claimed there was a slave uprising brewing in nearby Chesterfield, Prince Edward, and Surry counties. His action was merely one of concern for the well-being of the colonists. He continued that the magazine was ill guarded by the colonists, vulnerable to seizure, and that there had been sightings of slaves around it after dark—that was why he had chosen the middle of the night to clean it out of powder.

Dunmore promised—if an emergency arose—that he could return the gunpowder to Williamsburg within half an hour's time. However, for the time being, he said, it would remain aboard ship. Given the fact the townspeople were so upset, Dunmore did not think it wise to put gunpowder into their hands.

With that, he dismissed Dixon and his council.

It was with some difficulty that Peyton Randolph and Mayor Dixon persuaded the crowd to go home and go about their jobs. But disperse they finally did. Perhaps their anger had been cooled by the wait, their lack of breakfast, and the realization that their only other option was to go ahead and seize the palace and the governor. Despite the company of armed volunteers standing before them, and their indignation, the crowd of Williamsburg citizens wasn't quite ready to storm the home of the king's man.

But tempers remained hot. That night another crowd gathered when rumors coursed through the town that the marines from the *Magdalen* were coming again. Again, when no actual redcoats were seen, the city elders and Mr. Randolph convinced the townspeople to go home.

The next morning, Dr. Pasteur made a call to the palace. Enraged with what he called the city's insolent response to his rightful taking of the powder, Dunmore told the doctor that if the town insulted him any more, he would declare freedom to the slaves, arm them, and "reduce the city of Williamsburg to ashes." He commanded the doctor to give that message to Peyton Randolph and the town council: "I have once fought *for* the Virginians, and by God I will let them see that I can fight *against* them."

Within hours, most everyone knew of the governor's threat.

It was also reported from house to house, from person to person, from shop to shop that Patrick Henry had collected one hundred fifty marksmen and was marching to the Capitol from Hanover to recapture the stolen gunpowder.

"See," Ben had said excitedly. "A man of action. When he says 'liberty or death,' he means it!"

Dunmore was completely game for giving Patrick Henry exactly what he asked for if liberty was not to be had. He renewed his threat to destroy Williamsburg if Henry came any closer than Ruffin's Ferry, thirty miles to the west.

No one doubted that the defiant Henry would stick to his word. Likewise, no one doubted that the wrathful Dunmore meant what he said as well. Anxiously, Williamsburg awaited their head-to-head clash. A number of prominent families fled the city.

Then, on April twenty-seventh, an exhausted rider careened into the city, carrying the report of Lexington and Concord.

There, in Massachusetts, eight days earlier, British general Thomas Gage had ordered seven hundred redcoats stationed in Boston to march into the countryside to capture colonial stockpiles of weapons. A silversmith named Paul Revere learned of the plot and spread the word that the redcoats were coming. Seventy minutemen flocked to Lexington Green to face off with ten times their number. Someone fired a shot. After a confused volley, eight Americans lay dead, ten wounded.

The British continued to Concord, where they destroyed the colonists' depot of weapons and supplies. On their march back to Boston, however, New England patriots dogged them, shooting from behind trees and boulders. Two hundred and fifty British regulars were killed or wounded.

The argument between the parent and its child now was sealed with blood.

The timing of Dunmore's theft of Virginia's gunpowder with Gage's destruction of Massachusetts's weapons seemed too coordinated to be coincidental. Virginians could no longer deny the inevitable. The war of words was giving way to a war of bullets.

The *Virginia Gazette* summed it up: "The sword is now drawn and God knows when it will be sheathed."

Chapter Twenty-three

AT DAWN A few days later, Nathaniel lingered over haying the horses, slowly shaking the dried grass to separate it into airy mounds. It was so peaceful in the gray-lit barn. He hated to leave it. The whole town was on edge, awaiting the showdown between Patrick Henry and his militia and the governor and his marines. The tension within Edan's workshop was nearly unbearable as well. With only Ben and Nathaniel left, Edan's paranoia festered. His tirades about the colonists and their conspiracies were filled with more and more curses.

Ben's attitude worsened Nathaniel's jitters. He'd become blatantly reckless. Nathaniel had found him standing in the street, scribbling on a paper, right in front of the Maguires' house.

"How do you spell 'guard'?" he asked Nathaniel when he approached.

"I don't know," Nathaniel answered. "*G-a-r-d*? What are you doing?" He peered at Ben's messy writing. It was hard to decipher, but Nathaniel could make out "Shawnee" and "musket." He gasped. "Are Indians coming?"

"Nay," Ben answered without looking at Nathaniel. He kept writing. "The governor is arming the palace with them."

"But the Shawnee are his hostages. Basil says he shows them only to his dinner guests."

Ben smirked. "Basil doesn't know anything. Look up at that window." He pointed to a second-story corner window of the governor's palace.

Nathaniel looked. "I don't see anything, Ben."

Ben glanced up and frowned. "Well, he was there a minute ago. A great huge savage holding a musket. Look there." He gestured to another window. "See that slave?"

This time Nathaniel could indeed see an African servant looking out the window. But what of it?

"They're keeping guard," Ben spoke impatiently, reading Nathaniel's thoughts. "I followed one of Dunmore's maids to the market and asked her how things were inside the palace. She told me that the governor had dozens of muskets loaded and he had shown all the men servants how to fire them."

"Why are you writing that down, Ben?"

"To give this information to the right people. We're watching to see what Dunmore will try next."

Nathaniel couldn't believe how foolhardy Ben was being, acting as spy for the very people Edan raged about. He was like a flint that could set off a wildfire with one strike. "You better stop, Ben. What if Master Maguire sees you?"

"So what if he does?" Ben dismissed Nathaniel. "What Master Maguire thinks or does is of little consequence in what is about to happen. Besides, I've given a report on him as well that should silence him soon enough." And with that, Ben stalked away.

Worrying over that conversation, Nathaniel had nearly jumped a foot when a swallow shot out the barn door just above his head. Normally the swifts' darting flight in and out of the eaves never startled him. Now a rustling in the hayloft sent a tingle along the back of his neck. He paused in his work, cocked his head, and listened. Nothing. He must have been imagining it. He shook his head to steady himself.

He poured fresh water into the trough. Wait. There it was again. Louder. Too large a sound for mice or birds. Nathaniel's hands began to shake a bit. He listened. Once more it came.

Slowly, Nathaniel reached for the pitchfork. It probably was a mother raccoon trying to nest in the straw, a dry, warm place for her young. But that could be dangerous. Raccoons loved to pick up bits of oats dropped from the horse's feed bin. And a mother raccoon was very aggressive. It could bite a horse and sever tendons. Nathaniel would have to run it off.

Holding the pitchfork, he climbed the ladder. Somehow in a flash of shadow and movement, up and out of the straw, a huge, strong body arose and pinned Nathaniel to the floor, pressing the fork's prongs against his throat. Gasping, Nathaniel stared into the eyes of a very angry African.

"Please," he whispered. "Let go."

"Not a word, boy, or I'll push this fork right through you."

"Aye," Nathaniel whimpered, fighting off a wrenching cough from the pressure of the pitchfork and the man's arm across his chest.

"Wake up," the man hissed. There was more rustling in the hay. "Hurry. The household is up. I've got one here."

Another figure rose behind the man atop Nathaniel. He was enormous too. Wait a minute. Nathaniel focused through the gloom. Wasn't that . . .

"No, no, no. That's Nathaniel. Get off." With two easy lifts, Moses pulled the man away and Nathaniel to his feet.

"Sorry, boy." Moses brushed him off.

His companion glanced nervously over his shoulder and said, "How'd we fall asleep? We best move on. Fast."

Moses took Nathaniel by the shoulders. "You got money?"

Nathaniel nodded. He had his one precious shilling that Patrick Henry's son had given him. "Why? What are you doing here, Moses? Did you run off again? Oh Moses, what will they do if they catch you this time?"

"That's why I need money."

"But why did you come back into Williamsburg, Moses? There are slave patrols all over town. And they're really watching because Lord Dunmore said there was an uprising."

Moses rubbed his forehead and sighed heavily. His companion sneered and spat. "We came because we hear the governor promise to free the slaves. And that Williamsburg folk were after him. So me and Robin and a couple others left the farms to help. Went straight to the palace last night to say we stand with him. His men turned us away and locked the gate." Bitter disappointment and confusion puckered his face.

Roosters began to crow.

"We gots to go, Moses." His friend tugged urgently on Moses's sleeve. "I told you this was a fool idea.

This boy ain't got money."

Moses spoke in a tumble. "Since the governor turned us away, we heading to the Chesapeake, Nathaniel. Last month we was delivering and picking up at the Norfolk docks. I met a Captain Collins. He say the British navy was looking for men what know the Virginia waters. My master was right there, so there was naught I could do then. But word all along the river is now's the time to run.

"There's a boatman say he sail me right up to the *Magdalen*, what the captain command. But I gots to pay him, Nathaniel. A whole pound. A pound for me and a pound for Robin, here. You know where we can find two pounds, boy?"

Nathaniel took off his shoe and pulled the shilling out of it.

"I need more than that, boy." Moses looked at him hard. "I was glad to do it, Nathaniel, but I save your skin onct or twice, didn't I?"

Nathaniel hung his head. "More than once or twice, Moses," he whispered. He stuck the shilling back into his shoe.

"I need you now, Nathaniel. I need your help. There must be money somewhere about this house. Please." For the first time Nathaniel could remember, Moses looked frightened and vulnerable. He had to help.

Full light was coming on strong. He'd have to hurry. There was only one place Nathaniel knew he could get his hands on money quickly, without getting caught. That was the small tin box Basil kept under the foot of his mattress.

Changing the ad about John's whereabouts had given Nathaniel new pluck. And God knew Moses was a true friend who deserved his loyalty. He didn't stop to consider or to worry about consequences. Within five minutes, Nathaniel had slipped into the house, fished out two pounds from Basil's meager savings while he snored, and sent Moses out into the growing light of day.

Patrick Henry did not halt his march at Ruffin's Ferry, as Lord Dunmore ordered.

Enraged, Dunmore sent his wife and children to safety aboard the HMS *Fowey*, a warship just off Yorktown. The captain of the *Fowey* announced that he would bombard Yorktown if any harm came to Lord Dunmore.

Under those threats to the populace, Henry finally halted at Duncastle's Ordinary, about fifteen miles west of Williamsburg. But he sent some of his men to kidnap the governor's receiver general to force payment for the stolen gunpowder. Retaliating, Dunmore promised to spread devastation as far as he could reach. With several British warships and marines at his command,

Dunmore could certainly do it.

Once again, Peyton Randolph and other moderates scrambled to reach a compromise. Under pressure from them, Henry accepted 330 pounds for the gunpowder. He vowed to use the money to buy replacement gunpowder. Warning his troops to remain vigilant, he sent them home. Henry himself turned northward toward Philadelphia, to take his seat at the Continental Congress, already in session.

Firing a parting shot at Henry, Dunmore declared him an outlaw. He warned Virginians "not to aid, abet, or give countenance to the said Patrick Henry."

But Henry was too popular, too much the symbol of eloquent, steel-hard bravery, too much the voice of liberty. People turned out in legions to cheer and protect him from arrest. One after another, their fifes and drums playing, county volunteer troops escorted Henry across their borders on his trip north to Philadephia. When Henry reached the Potomac River, separating Virginia and Maryland, the ferryman fed him and rowed him over for free. Only a few Virginians accompanied Henry across since it was easy to see the flags and bright colored jackets of the Maryland volunteers awaiting him on the other side.

Once Henry was gone, calm somehow returned. It was the homecoming of the beloved Lady Dunmore that seemed to reassure Williamsburg the most. She would talk sense to her belligerent husband, said townspeople. And surely Dunmore would not recall his family if he planned more treachery.

Dunmore even reinstated the House of Burgesses and called it to reconvene in June. Although some feared it was merely a trap to arrest colonial leaders, others hoped it meant Henry's daring had convinced Dunmore to cooperate. A kind of wary optimism hung about the city and quieted its streets.

That was when Nathaniel's life erupted.

"Nathaniel," Basil called to him one evening about the time they typically played flutes together.

"Yes, master?" Nathaniel sensed from Basil's stern tone that what he had been dreading was about to happen.

"I am missing money, Nathaniel. Know you of it?"

Nathaniel swallowed hard and lied: "Nay, master."

Basil stood silent, watching him carefully. Nathaniel tried to keep his eyes steadily on Basil's. But he began to squirm, and his gaze dropped.

Basil sighed heavily. Then he spoke in hoarse sadness. "I think the weather is warm enough for you to resume sleeping in the stable."

Nathaniel felt a stab in his heart that made him dizzy. But he managed a feeble, "Aye, master."

Tell him! Nathaniel's mind screamed. *Tell him why.* But Nathaniel didn't trust Basil to protect Moses. Didn't trust him to understand. Still, didn't know how to trust.

He picked up his few possessions and made for the door.

"Wait," Basil spoke.

Oh please, thought Nathaniel. *Please don't banish me this way*. But still he did not speak, did not offer the old man any explanation.

Basil handed him something wrapped in a linen cloth. "Happy birthday, Nathaniel," he said, and turned away.

Alone, up in the hayloft, Nathaniel unwrapped the package. Inside were two gifts: a book, *The American Instructor or Young Man's Best Companion*, and a wooden fife. Flipping through the book, he found exercises in reading and arithmetic, ways to improve himself and his opportunities. Ways to groom his God-given reason and intellect to make his own destiny, just as Basil had told him. Tearfully, Nathaniel put it aside.

With shaking hands, he held the fife to his lips and blew a high-pitched note, a sound he knew called soldiers to duty, a sound that sang of liberty. He knew Basil had meant it to be a symbolic as well as musical gift.

Nathaniel dropped his face into his hands and sobbed. Basil would never feel the same about him, now that he thought Nathaniel was a thief and liar. Oh, if only he had explained. The sorrow he felt was almost unbearable. Because this time Nathaniel knew that his trouble, his loss were his own fault. He could not blame it on an unjust fate, or the brutality of his masters. His situation was born of his own actions, his own choices. *He* was responsible.

If that's what liberty meant, it was a cruel and hard price to pay for it.

PART SEVEN

June 1775

Come join hand in hand all ye true, loyal souls,
'Tis Liberty calls, let's fill up our bowls,
We'll toast all the lovers of Freedom's good cause;
America's sons will support all our laws.
Our firelocks are good:
Let fair freedom ne'er yield.
We're always ready,
Steady, boys, steady,
By Jove we'll be free
Or we'll die in the field.
Though the lords and the commons may rail in the House,
At our patriot assembles, we don't care a souse;

We'll keep cheerful spirits, nor mind their commands
The sun of fair liberty will shine o'er our lands.

—A liberty song composed at a town meeting in Chester

Chapter Twenty-four

"If master sees you doing that, you'll catch it, you know."

Nathaniel glanced up at Ben. For the past week, Nathaniel had been slipping into the shop even earlier than usual to use the pen and ink on Edan's desk. "Do you see him coming?"

"No, but it's well past his time," Ben answered. He watched Nathaniel finish a capital *D*, with an elaborate curlicue at its top and a perfect backstroke at its bottom. "Very nice, Nat," he murmured. "You could be an excellent secretary or bookkeeper with that penmanship."

"Really?"

"In fact"—Ben puffed himself up and jokingly threw out his chest and lower lip—"you can be my secretary when I am elected to the Continental Congress. Or mayhap when I am governor of Virginia." He grinned.

"Yes. I like the sound of that. You and me running Virginia, Nat. What say you?"

Nathaniel blew on the letter to dry the ink, ignoring Ben's fantasies. The older boy was so full of himself these days. But he did linger on one thing—being a secretary or bookkeeper. Nathaniel hadn't really given a thought to the advantage good cursive might give him for a trade once he was free of his indenture. He was simply trying to win back Basil's friendship with it.

When Basil had sent him to live again in the stable, Nathaniel thought he might die of the ache in his heart. Basil had not sought him out to play music at night or to read from his novels ever since. Nathaniel had lain in the hay in the stable's loft and listened to Basil playing his violin or his flute, all alone. There were no jaunty jigs or quick-paced allegros with their dazzling run of notes or bravado of trills. Basil played melancholy tunes, one after another.

Selfishly, Nathaniel took hope in their sad sound that Basil was missing his company, too. But he knew that part of it was Basil's deep disappointment in him. Unwittingly, Nathaniel had fulfilled the prophecy of the abusive blacksmith, from whom Basil had saved him—Nathaniel had indeed robbed Basil as he slept. So in the stable Nathaniel hid, despairing, until the evening light of May lasted long enough to prompt him to pick up the book Basil had given him. Nathaniel wound his way through its words.

In Basil's gift, he had found an idea. Perhaps if he completed the spelling and arithmetic exercises in the book, Basil would be proud of Nathaniel's effort. Mayhap it would rekindle Basil's interest in him as a student. Basil loved to teach—to teach anybody who would listen, really. Nathaniel realized it was his best chance.

The problem, of course, was how to record his work. Most pupils used chalk on slate hornbooks, erasing their work after their tutor approved it. Nathaniel had none. And certainly he could not afford the purchase of paper, pen, and ink. But one night he came up with a solution. The loft's floor could be his tablet! Nathaniel took a piece of chalk from Edan's desk, justifying that bit of thievery by the end result and the hard work he did about the place.

Hour after hour Nathaniel lay on his stomach, scratching spelling words and math problems onto the planed pinewood. He covered them all with hay, to keep them from smearing away and to keep his project secret from Ben, who came up at night sometimes to tell Nathaniel about his gallivanting about town. Nathaniel didn't want anything ruining his surprise for Basil.

What Nathaniel was writing now was a thank-you note for the book and fife. With it, Nathaniel could approach Basil to start a conversation. Then he would invite the old tutor to the stable to see his work.

For that note, he had taken a sheet of Edan's paper and was using his ink and quill pen. He knew it was dangerous. But he was almost finished. The *D* he had just completed was part of his signature. Only three more letters—*u*, *n*, *n*—to write.

But today was not the time. Edan would come into the shop any minute; Ben was right. Nathaniel carefully folded the paper along creases he'd made the previous days and tucked it into his waistcoat.

"You should have come with me to the illumination last night," Ben chided Nathaniel. "There's no use sulking in the loft."

"What was it for?" Nathaniel had heard the church bells and seen that every household window glowed with candlelight.

"It was to honor Peyton Randolph. He's back from Philadelphia for the session of the House that Governor Dunmore called. But nobody trusts that Scottish snake. General Gage has authorized the lobsterbacks to arrest and execute rebel leaders. There's a wanted list, and Mr. Randolph is on it. Williamsburg's militia escorted Mr. Randolph to the safety of his house last night, fearing Dunmore might try to arrest him on the road. We boy volunteers were there, too, to greet him."

So that was the commotion Nathaniel had heard. The Randolph home was two blocks away from Edan's house. In the loft, as he puzzled over a long set of sums, Nathaniel had heard a low roar of huzzahs. But that was not such an unusual sound in Williamsburg these days. Ever since Dunmore and his British marines had emptied the magazine of its gunpowder, volunteer militiamen had been drilling on the open ground of market square.

More and more out-of-town frontier marksmen were arriving too, clad in homespun hunting shirts that fell to their knees and covered leather leggings. They were weather-beaten and hardy, crude in their language and manners. One had terrified Mrs. Maguire the other morning when she'd tripped over him, sleeping in their orchard.

"You should have seen us, Nat, oh, we were so grand! Robert Greenhow got a copy of *The Manual of Military Exercise as Ordered by His Majesty* from his father. We've been practicing all its drills. We marched right up to Mr. Randolph's front door and everyone there said—"

At that moment Edan stomped through the door. He was breathing hard and holding a hand up to his chest, rubbing it, as if trying to push something away from his heart. He shuffled to his desk, sat down with a thump, and took up his pen. Ben and Nathaniel pretended to be busy.

After much scribbling and muttering, Edan grunted to Nathaniel, "Take this notice to the *Gazette*. All the high and mighty burgesses are in town. Several owe me money. This should scare them into paying me." He shoved the slip of paper at Nathaniel and barked at Ben, "About work, boy."

"What would you have me do?" Ben's question was earnest, and for once free of sass. "We've no order, sir."

Indeed, new work had ground to a halt. And it wasn't just due to the disappearance of John and Obadjah. With the embargo hurting everyone's purse and the Continental Congress cautioning against frivolous purchases, nobody was buying large items such as carriages. Edan's finances were decaying rapidly.

Edan threw his head back and laughed a guttural crazed sound. "No work?" He grabbed at his chest again, bending over and coughing. "Dreams will ruin you. Customers will misuse you. People will turn on you." His unnatural laugh continued. "What can you expect from a pig but a grunt?" Edan stumbled out of the shop toward the house, chanting, "A grunt, a grunt, a grunt."

Ben stared after him. He held his hand out toward Nathaniel. "Let us read that notice."

I request those gentlemen that are indebted to me pay me immediately that I may thereby support my credit and be enabled to carry on my business. The many disappointments I have met force me to let those gentlemen know that unless they discharge their respective balances this meeting, their names will be inserted very shortly in all the Williamsburg papers, that the world may know how tradesmen are treated in Virginia.

E. Maguire

Ben let out a long whistle. "That'll get some backs up." He grinned and added, "That might spur the committee to finally take action they speak of, which in turn should push Edan to go home to Ireland. Then we'll be free, Nat! Free!" He did a little jig.

Nathaniel was completely baffled. "What are you talking about, Ben?" The apprentice was acting as crazed as Edan.

"Oh, nothing," Ben answered mysteriously. "You know, if there's no work, I think I'll just meander down to the store to see when the Greenhows think we'll drill again. Hop to the *Gazette*, boy," he teased Nathaniel, snapping his fingers, once again imaging himself the congressman.

Not knowing what else to do, Nathaniel put on his round hat and followed orders.

Chapter Twenty-five

ROUNDING THE CORNER of Edan's house, Nathaniel emerged to a commotion on Palace Green.

"Get control of them, confound you!"

Two perfectly white horses attached to a luxurious, open carriage were rearing, jostling the gentlemen inside about wildly—enough for one's powdered wig to be down over his eyes and the other to be dumped to the carriage floor, his feet straight up in the air. A shoe went flying.

"I'm trying, my lord," the liveried slave on the driver's seat said apologetically, but his urgent shushing was doing nothing to calm the horses. Harnessed together, they had to quiet together. But as the two animals knocked each other about in agitation, their panic only rose. Simultaneously Nathaniel and the driver recognized that the horses were about to bolt. "Lord save us," the driver prayed.

Holding out his arms, Nathaniel stepped in front of the horses. "Whoooooa, boys . . . bea-u-ti-ful boys."

One horse reared, the other lunged out as if to strike Nathaniel. He jumped to the side, but kept talking. "Eeeeeasy, beauties. No need to run off, boys. Eeeeeeaaa-sy." The horse nearer Nathaniel paused in its flailing.

The driver echoed Nathaniel's crooning. "That's right, fellas, eeeeeasy." He pulled back on their reins hard and firm, all the while his voice a chant of calming.

The horses settled down to simply snorting and quivering and tossing their heads. The danger was past. The slave tipped his hat in thanks. Nathaniel nodded back. "What set them off?" he asked.

The driver pointed down Prince George's Street, the small lane that ran between the Maguire and Wythe houses. In the distance was a cloud of dust. "Runaway horse," he muttered. "Chestnut demon, saddle still on, stirrups flapping, making it wild." He leaned over and added in a softer voice: "Musta dumped some fine gentleman on his rear end."

He grinned. Nathaniel did too.

"Enough idle chatter! If you can't control these horses better, I'll sell you to a West Indies rice plantation!" shouted one of the passengers.

"Wouldn't make no never mind to me," muttered the driver under his breath. He faced forward and became a statue of servitude.

The man with the wig askew resumed his seat and straightened his appearance. "You there. Boy."

Nathaniel pointed to himself. "Me, sir?"

The man spoke contemptuously: "All these colonials are idiots, I swear. Yes, you. Hand me that shoe."

Nathaniel picked up a huge slipper that looked very like a lady's shoe. With a bow, he handed it up to the man. The man snatched it, not bothering to look at Nathaniel, much less thank him. "Drive on," he shouted.

As the carriage rolled away, Nathaniel heard: "What do you think the response of those provincials will be to my speech? I nearly choked when I said, 'the king has no object nearer his heart than the peace and prosperity of his subjects in every part of the dominion.' A good lashing is rather what they all need in my opinion. . . ."

The carriage rolled out of hearing. Nathaniel resumed his walk.

"You just saved Governor Dunmore's neck, lad," said a passerby. He winked. "Next time leave well enough alone!"

★ ★ ★

The Duke of Gloucester Street was packed with horses and people, as it always was at public times, when the House convened or the courts were open. Overnight the town became a crowded city, with all the self-importance and bustle of a place that changed people's lives and fortunes. Nathaniel was bumped aside by many a well-heeled gentleman until he arrived at the *Gazette*. One of Maria's brothers let him in and took him to the little office where she was writing as a lanky, freckled, red-haired man dictated.

She was flushed. So, too, was the gentleman, who was trying unsuccessfully to dust himself clean. His rumpled but well-cut blue coat and pants were caked with mud and filth. He smelled a bit of manure. He was a tumble of thoughts, as if his mind raced too fast for his tongue to keep up.

"I have never been thrown like that. Unseated in front of all those people. The conservatives will make hay of it, I warrant. Please don't accept any tale of it, Miss Rind, if someone tries to print a ridicule. . . . And what of my saddle and all that is in my saddlebag? My clothes, my papers, my . . . Oh, no . . . my kit! My pocket fiddle! The one with which I wooed Mrs. Jefferson. I always travel with it to remind me of her when we are apart. . . . How will I ever . . . Oh, it cannot be. . . ." The man flopped down into a chair, his long legs stretching across the room, it seemed, he was so tall. In anguish he concluded, "I am undone." He hung his head.

"Oh Mr. Jefferson, someone will find your horse. You'll see. But we need finish your notice, sir, so that my cousin can set the type."

"Yes, yes. That is all we can do, I suppose. Where were we, lass?"

Maria read: "Strayed, from the city of Williamsburg, a chestnut mare, about fifteen hands high. She has the head of an Arabian and . . ."

"And the disposition of a harpy," Mr. Jefferson muttered. "What possessed me to purchase her from Mr. Henry, I will never know. His silver tongue, I'd say, that convinces a man to do anything!"

Nathaniel's ears pricked. Could it be? Could the horse be Vixen? Surely Mr. Jefferson's runaway horse was the one that set off the governor's carriage horses. And surely the description and behavior fit the wild Vixen.

Mr. Jefferson was mourning: "How will I explain the loss of my violin to my beloved? She will chide me, sure. . . ."

"Yes, sir," Maria murmured. "What else shall we say, sir?"

Still slumped over, Jefferson continued to dictate:

"all-over red, with a thick flowing tail, slightly ash in color. The contents of the saddlebag are not expensive, but precious to the owner. . . ."

Maria was scribbling madly to keep up.

Mr. Jefferson rose. "Ah me. Is that how I wish it to read? Is admitting the contents are important to me a mistake? Let me read over the text, please, Miss Rind, to collect my thoughts."

Hesitantly, Maria handed him the paper. He bowed formally as he took it. "I thank you." Looking down, he squinted, and then frowned. "Child," he said gently. "I am afraid I cannot read this."

It was Maria's turn to hang her head.

Nathaniel startled himself by stepping forward. "I can transcribe your words, sir. May I?"

Tears of embarrassment in her eyes, Maria looked at Nathaniel gratefully. Jefferson caught the exchange and smiled slightly. "Yes, lad. I would be beholden to you."

Nathaniel picked up the pen, ready.

"Whosoever returns the mare to me shall have as reward fifty shillings."

Nathaniel's head popped up. "Fifty shillings!" he couldn't help exclaiming.

"Hmmm. Perhaps you are right, lad. In for a penny, in for a pound. I should offer more given how desperate I am to secure the return of my saddlebag. Hang the horse. Let us add this: 'Return of the saddlebag and its full contents intact shall bring an additional thirty shillings.' There. Think you that will spur people to look for her?"

Nathaniel forced himself to concentrate on writing down the words he was so excited. Spur people to look for Vixen? Rather! Eighty shillings was four pounds. With four pounds, he could replace the money he'd taken from Basil and still have extra. A fortune!

Hands shaking in impatience, he handed the slip of paper to Jefferson. The tall man smiled and nodded. "Well written, lad. The spelling is exact. Well done." He looked down looked at Nathaniel, clearly assessing his modest clothes. "Who has taught you?"

Nathaniel hesitated. "I have been teaching myself of late, sir."

Jefferson's eyebrows went up. "Then you are the very kind of citizen in whom I am putting my faith, lad. The Greek philosopher Epictetus said that only the educated are free. I firmly believe that if we enlighten the populace, tyranny will die. Because the people will know they deserve better."

"Thank you, sir," Nathaniel answered hurriedly, not really taking in Mr. Jefferson's words. His mind was consumed with the promise of four pounds.

Without waiting another moment, he was out the

door and dashing, hurtling down the street as fast as he could. Nathaniel would find Vixen before anyone else knew about the reward for her. If he did, he could right his world.

He completely forgot the advertisement he was supposed to place in the *Gazette* for Edan.

Chapter Twenty-six

VIXEN HAD BEEN heading west toward the College of William and Mary. Darting around people and carts, Nathaniel calculated where she would finally stop to graze. She could run full speed for at least half a mile, and canter the rest of it. After that she might trot another. That would get her far past the college, thankfully, out from the clutches of robed students who might catch her, out to the beginnings of farms and swamplands.

It was about a half mile from the *Gazette* offices to the college's Wren Building. Winded by then, Nathaniel slowed to a jog, noting the clock in the cupola of the beautifully symmetrical brick building. It was half past twelve already. Nathaniel knew there would be the devil to pay for not returning to Edan's shop. But he was determined.

In the sandy road he saw dozens of hoofprints and

wagon ruts, nothing to really help him track Vixen. No, wait. A few yards ahead were deep hoof marks, far apart, darker in color, not yet bleached by the sun or sifted with the tread of passersby. Some horse had recently taken this path at a racing pace. He prayed that it was Vixen and not one of the governor's messengers.

He trotted on, looking from side to side to see if she had detoured off the road for a morsel of grass.

Fifteen minutes later he climbed up onto a split-rail fence and scanned a horizon of knee-high corn, tobacco beginning to unfurl its voluminous leaves, watermelon vines spreading into carpets. No horse in sight.

He walked on, passing muddy streams and overgrown woods. From tangled, thick bushes he plucked honeysuckle blossoms, their sugary nectar easing his thirst.

Twenty minutes more. He came across an orchard, a pen of hogs happily sunning themselves, a ramshackle hut of a farmhouse.

Another fifteen minutes. At a neater farm, a pair of fat plow horses rolled to rid themselves of the itch left from their harnesses. Nathaniel checked the newly turned garden, scanned the hay fields beyond. Nothing.

Dejected, Nathaniel flopped onto the roadside. He'd searched for an hour. That meant he'd covered around four miles. He couldn't imagine a horse not stopping by now to find water or clover—no matter how crazy it was. He'd missed Vixen somehow.

He backtracked, zigzagging along the road.

By the time Nathaniel neared Williamsburg enough to see the Wren Building's white cupola in the distance, he was almost crying in frustration. Gauging time by the sun, it was around four o'clock. The midday meal was over. Edan would definitely be in the shop. Nathaniel's hard work would earn him nothing save a whipping. Maybe he should just turn tail right here and run to the frontier rather than face what surely awaited him in Williamsburg. With all the trouble brewing in the colonies, no one would care about a runaway boy. Given Nathaniel's mistakes, Basil wouldn't. Would he?

Nathaniel sighed. The truth was he cared, even if Basil might no longer. Basil was the closest thing he had to a guardian and friend. He had to go back.

Please, please, please, Nathaniel thought. *Please let me find her.*

A piece of white paper fluttered across the road, rattling and turning somersaults. Another tripped along behind. A third wrapped itself around Nathaniel's ankle. He reached down.

"We must consider alternatives to the frenzy of revenge spawned by the news of Lexington and

Concord. I beg you to write a petition of peace. Your eloquence would convince . . ."

Nathaniel flipped the page over. *"To Thomas Jefferson, esquire."* Huzzah! On the other side of the fence a book lay open on the ground. Stuffing the letter pages into his pocket, he picked up the book by Sir Isaac Newton. Down the hill, a silk stocking hung from a wild rose. One of the pockets of the saddlebag had obviously opened and was spilling as Vixen moved. The litter should lead him to her. Gratefully he scampered, picking up bits and pieces of Mr. Jefferson's belongings.

Nathaniel found himself on the edges of a vast reserve of rolling hills and groves of trees. A herd of cattle milled about, some curled up under shade trees, others dealing with frolicking calves. In the distance, atop a hill, cresting the tree line, were the massive, tall chimneys and the gilded weather vane of the governor's palace. Nathaniel recognized that he was trespassing on the sixty-acre park belonging to Lord Dunmore. Of course, Vixen would choose to graze in a place that could bring a jail sentence to him if caught.

He crept from tree to tree until he spotted her. She was lathered in sweat. Her saddle hung akimbo. Cautiously, Nathaniel inched toward the mare. Her head snapped up and her nostrils flared at his approach, but she was too weary, and too happy in meadow grass, to run off. Nathaniel caught her easily.

Coaxing her to a stand of redbud trees to hide them from view, Nathaniel repacked Mr. Jefferson's things. He was relieved to find the fiddle case safe inside the bag. He sat down to await twilight. To get out of the governor's park undetected and down Palace Green to the tavern where Mr. Jefferson was lodging, he'd need darkness and the distraction of people hurrying to their dinner. He tried to keep his mind off the retribution that would await him for his day-long absence.

Four pounds, four pounds, four whole pounds, he repeated to himself over and over.

"May I speak with Mr. Jefferson, please?" Nathaniel stood at the door of the tavern, holding onto Vixen tightly. Inside, he could hear men talking and laughing and the shuffle of chairs being pulled about as dinner was being set.

Within a few moments Jefferson appeared, sleeves rolled up, carrying a pen and a sheet of paper in the other hand. He dropped both with an exclamation of joy upon seeing Nathaniel.

"You found her!" Reaching for the saddlebag, Jefferson startled Vixen and set her to dancing and snorting. Nathaniel held on to her as best he could and calmed the horse and man, saying, "The violin is inside, sir. She had scattered many of your belongings, but the fiddle stayed safe. I think I found everything else."

Jefferson stepped back. "Lad, you are an interesting case. Did you teach yourself to handle such horses as well as write?"

Nathaniel puzzled a moment. Who could teach someone else to calm a horse? But he answered, "I suppose so, sir."

"There, you see. Just my point," said Jefferson. "The nobility of the common man. Completely able to rule himself."

"Sir?"

"Ah, forgive me, lad. My head is full of philosophy and argument. I am in the throes of writing a reply to the governor's welcoming address for the burgesses. Hard work, writing. It is so important these words be diplomatic yet firm, guarded yet concise. . . . Nothing I have scribbled thus far suffices. . . . Hmmm." He thought a moment. "I help myself think by playing violin. Now that you have returned it, I shall be able to concentrate far better."

Carefully he undid the saddlebags and called for the tavern keeper to take Vixen to the stable. "Thank you, lad. I have a fine stable at home, at Monticello. My best mare, Allycroker, has just foaled a colt by Young Fearnought, one of the greatest blooded stallions of Virginia. I purchased this willful chestnut from Patrick Henry, hoping she'd mother good colts as well. What say you to coming to Monticello to help train her, lad?"

"I . . . I cannot, sir," Nathaniel spoke hesitantly. "My time is already purchased."

"I can match the fee, lad. Who owns your time?"

No, no, no, thought Nathaniel. *I don't want to be taken away again, even by as great a gentleman as this.* But he didn't know how to say it. He looked up at the tall, imposing man, shadowed by the tavern's lanterns. Perhaps he could simply change the subject. "Please, sir," he said awkwardly, "may . . . may I, please, have those four pounds you offered for the horse's return?"

"Oh yes! Quite so," said Jefferson, shaking his head as if waking himself. From his pocket, he pulled the treasured pounds and counted them out into Nathaniel's outstretched hands.

"Thank you, sir!"

"No, the thanks are to you, lad." He patted the case of his violin. "I am grateful beyond words." He paused and sighed. "I do wish I could leave the noise of this tavern and go to my cousin's house. John and I always played duets together when I was in town. But his politics are my enemy these days, I am afraid. Know you my cousin John Randolph, the governor's attorney general? A staunch loyalist. After all we've shared and all the affection we bear each other, it is almost impossible for us now to share an evening. It saddens me greatly. Of course, it must be far worse for his brother, Peyton. . . . Well, I am indebted to you." He bowed formally. "I think it would have broken Mrs. Jefferson's heart had I lost the violin which first won it. Your name, lad?"

"Nathaniel Dunn."

"Godspeed, Nathaniel." Jefferson bowed again and then added with a smile, "By the way, Nathaniel. I surmise the lovely Miss Rind is a bit fond of you. My advice is to think of what she loves and play to it, as I did to Mrs. Jefferson's passion for music."

Nathaniel turned as red as Vixen's coat.

"Ah me." Jefferson turned to go back inside. "I can put off my task no longer."

"Sir," Nathaniel stammered, for the idea of an enormous gift to Basil had suddenly come to Nathaniel.

"Yes, lad?"

"Sir, if you truly yearn for a duet, my master, Basil Wilkinson, is an excellent violinist. Lodging at the Maguire house, sir, next to Mr. Wythe's." He pointed down the street. "He is a great admirer of your writings. He is a fine musician, he has played at . . ." Nathaniel paused, unsure if the credential would bring favor or rejection. "He has played at . . . at . . . at the palace."

Jefferson nodded. "I myself played at the palace with Governor Fauquier. Quite a fine musician and educated man. Those were easier times. Thank you, Nathaniel. I know the house. Mr. Wythe was my law professor. Good night."

"Good night, sir." Nathaniel tipped his hat and ran for home, keeping his hand over the waistcoat pocket that held his fortune.

Chapter Twenty-seven

NATHANIEL'S LUCK HELD. Edan had gone to bed earlier in the day with an ache in his chest. Mrs. Maguire had hovered over him all afternoon, mixing an elixir from the leaves of foxglove flowers and coaxing him to swallow it. She even called the surgeon, who charged her five shillings to tell her what she already knew—something was strangling Edan's heart.

Thus occupied, no one noticed Nathaniel's absence. Only Sally mentioned it as she handed him his breakfast corn bread the next morning. "Best save night walking for evening time, child," she said kindly, referring to the evening visits more liberal owners allowed their slaves to make to family members at neighboring plantations. She didn't know where Nathaniel had really been.

It was quiet in the shop. Ben whittled and whistled. Nathaniel glowed with the presence of four pounds in his waistcoat. He also, at dawn, had finished his thank-you note for Basil. Following Mr. Jefferson's advice, he had begun a new project, copying a poem on penmanship from the *Young Man's Best Companion* to give Maria.

Hold your Pen lightly, grip it not too hard,
And with due care your Copy well regard.
Join every Letter to its next with Care,
And let the Stroke be admirably fair. . . .

Quit yourself nobly with prudent Care,
Of clumsy Writing and of Blots beware.
Remember strictly what the Art enjoins,
Equal siz'd Letters, and as equal Lines.

Nathaniel smiled as he copied, thinking how Maria might profit from the directions of the poem. Not that he was fond of her, as Mr. Jefferson, had put it. Oh no. It simply was a kindness. His heart felt so light, he actually began to hum as he wrote, a tune his mother had sung, "'Are you going to Scarborough Fair? Parsley, sage, rosemary, and thyme. Remember me to the one who lives there; she once was a true love of mine. . . .'"

Nathaniel's only worry was how to slip the two pounds into Basil's tin box without being seen. His plan was to simply return the money without comment, since he had never admitted to taking it to begin with. Somehow it seemed best to Nathaniel to leave it all unspoken. Easier, certain. But that would require stealth and opportunity.

That evening, he had his chance. It was a delicious June twilight, the air full of sweet smells and gentle breezes. The kind of rejuvenating night Tidewater people tried to remember during August's firestorm of heat. He had just finished watering the livestock when Nathaniel heard the clear, vibrant notes of two violins tuning.

Nathaniel ran to the open window of the parlor and peeped in over the sill. Mr. Jefferson had come! There he stood with Basil, all flustered and grinning. Mrs. Maguire sat in the corner, smoothing her skirt and gracefully fluttering a fan before her face. She looked completely different from the woman fussing over cold remedies in the hot backyard kitchen. Startled, Nathaniel realized that once upon a time, she probably had been rather pretty.

Nathaniel inched around the house. Once they started playing, he could sneak up the staircase to Basil's room and deposit the money without being noticed. The trick would be getting past Edan's room on the first floor, where the carriage maker was still abed. He took off his shoes and left them under a bush near the back door. He'd have to be very quiet and quick, moving during louder music. It wouldn't do to try during a smooth, delicate adagio, which the creak of a floorboard would interrupt like cannon fire.

Nathaniel waited until the violins were chasing each other in song. Each instrument raced up and down in pitch, whirling about each other like the small white butterflies that spiraled around in the garden. Nathaniel slipped through the door, wincing at its slight squeak, and crept up the edge of the stairs. He stuck to the wall's edge, tiptoeing where the stair plank was nailed and less likely to groan under his weight.

Halfway up, still safe. Round the landing, up three more stairs. He was there!

Breathing hard, Nathaniel fished out Basil's tin box. He pulled from his pocket the money Jefferson had given him. Counting out two pounds, Nathaniel dropped that amount into the meager collection of coins inside and closed the lid. He started to shove the box back under Basil's mattress.

For several long moments Nathaniel hesitated, looking down at the tin box, listening to the jaunty allegro below. Finally, he reached into his pocket and pulled out his remaining money. He dropped all of it into Basil's savings.

Perhaps now Basil could purchase the books he'd

sacrificed to free Nathaniel from the blacksmith one year before. He only wished he hadn't taken off his shoes and could retrieve the shilling he kept there to add to the trove. Nathaniel owed Basil everything. It was only right.

Nathaniel pushed the lid shut with a snap and tucked it back under the mattress. Now he faced trying to retreat out of the house undetected. But he wasn't worried. He suddenly felt strong and free, no longer shackled by indebtedness or deceit. He turned for the door.

There stood Mistress Maguire.

Nathaniel gasped. *Oh no! She'll think I'm stealing.* Nathaniel's mouth popped open to explain, but nothing came out. Mrs. Maguire stepped into the room and closed the door.

"What are you about, boy?" she whispered.

What could he say? How could he explain? The violin music downstairs rose in a crescendo of sixteenth-note runs and Nathaniel felt his own heart race with it.

"I saw you," she said.

Oh, he was lost, done for. Who would believe his story?

"I saw you," she repeated. "I saw you putting money

into Mr. Wilkinson's tin. From whence did you get it?"

Nathaniel shook his head, still silent, feeling himself falling, falling.

"I think you'd rather explain to me than to Mr. Maguire."

There was something about her voice that saved Nathaniel. Something akin to his mother, something that reminded him of the time he'd managed to break every egg they'd collected and spill the precious bucket of fresh milk. "Tell me, my love, what happened," his mother had said. "We mustn't grieve over what we cannot change."

In a torrent of words, Nathaniel told. Told about Moses, told about taking Basil's money, told about tracking Vixen, told about Jefferson and Nathaniel suggesting he find Basil to play violin. Told how his father had not seemed to care about their being sold apart. How Basil had saved him from sure abuse at the hands of the blacksmith. How Basil was building his mind with books and music. Flushed, breathless, he ended and waited, immediately kicking himself for his honesty. Now he was completely exposed, stripped to his soul. And worse, without thinking, he had betrayed Moses.

Mrs. Maguire was quiet for an eternity, it seemed.

Nathaniel's head spun.

Finally she patted his shoulder. "My, that is a tale, lad. Mr. Wilkinson had never explained exactly how you came to be with him. And he never told me that he was missing money. He is a generous man, indeed." She crossed her arms and looked out the window. Below stairs, Jefferson and Basil began the andante section of their sonata, a beautiful lilting melody. She held up a finger and said, "Listen. Isn't it wondrous that man can make such harmony?"

She sighed and then continued softly, "One of the greatest challenges of life, Nathaniel, is deciding to move forward. To live as if each day presents a new, hopeful possibility. To make the decision to leave the past there, in the past. That is the only way to be free of its pain. We must not let past sadness or tragedy or mistreatment rule the way we act today. It takes courage to do so, yes, but we must. I . . . I myself have lost three children. I thought I could never have affection for anyone ever again. And yet, as of late, I have rediscovered that ability."

She turned to him and smiled. "You must learn to trust people who care about you, like Mr. Wilkinson. Go back outside, boy. I will not tell your story. But someday, you should tell Mr. Wilkinson the truth."

Grateful beyond words, Nathaniel inched toward

the door. "Mistress," he whispered, knowing that he was pushing her. "Mistress, please, you will not tell about Moses?"

Mrs. Maguire frowned. "I know naught what is right on that, Nathaniel. Helping a slave run is a crime that could send you to the gallows. I do not want that to happen. And yet, the slave should be pursued. He is valuable property. If we sold Sally, for instance, as Mr. Maguire is suggesting, we could clear a large portion of our debts." She shook her head. "Can you imagine? Selling Sally," she murmured.

For a moment she was silent as the music danced on below. "I must think on what I should do with that information, lad. My instinct is to do nothing. But still, I must consider it a bit. Go on, now."

Nathaniel slipped back down the stairs and out to his loft, feeling free and chained at the same time. He couldn't know that soon events would so rattle the Maguire household that Mistress Maguire would forget completely about Moses.

Chapter Twenty-eight

NATHANIEL DIDN'T NOTICE when paper dropped out of his pocket the next morning. But Ben did. And it would have been far better if he hadn't.

"Pssst, Nat." Ben pointed to the floor behind Nathaniel.

Edan was at his desk, scribbling a design for a carriage they had no order to make. Ben was sharpening chisels and axes, making a piercing, scraping squeal each time he held a blade to the grindstone that Nathaniel was pumping. He thought Edan was paying no attention to them. But he was wrong.

"What is that?" Edan growled, heaving his massive self up.

Nathaniel looked down and gasped. It was Edan's demand for payment that he had forgotten to give to the *Gazette* to publish. Underneath it was the poem he was copying for Maria.

Terrified instinct took over. He snatched up the papers. He bolted for the door.

But Edan pounced. Nathaniel felt himself yanked back by his collar and pinned against the wall. Edan ripped the papers out of his hand.

As he skimmed the top one—his own advertisement—Nathaniel whimpered: "Please, sir, please, I am so sorry. I forgot to give it to the *Gazette*. I . . . I . . ." He couldn't think of any excuse, any story to hide what he had actually done. He wasn't about to confess about Thomas Jefferson, Vixen, and his four pounds.

But it was the way Edan turned over the next page with such calm—as if he were suddenly coming to a vital recognition—that was the most bone-chilling.

In a cold, amazed voice, he said, "I was unaware that you could write. So . . . you must be the one . . . the one to betray me."

Still held against the wall by Edan's meaty hand, Nathaniel shook his head fervently. "Master, I don't know what you mean. I just forgot. Please forgive me. I just forgot to deliver it."

Edan leaned so close that his bulbous nose almost touched Nathaniel's. His putrid breath blasted his face. Keeping his bloodshot eyes fixed on Nathaniel's, he crumpled up the papers and threw them to the ground. He slipped his free hand into his waistcoat and pulled out a letter. "You claim to know nothing of this?" Edan snarled, holding the crackling thick paper up almost as if he were going to ram it down Nathaniel's throat.

"No . . . no sir . . . I know naught."

Edan cackled. "It's a summons—a summons to appear before the committee of inspection. They have demanded to see my accounting books. They want to know if I made the cart that carried off the magazine gunpowder and, if so, when I delivered it. They say they suspect me of being in league with the British Marines because they received a letter claiming I have oft spoken ill of the burgesses and the Non-importation Agreement. Two scurrilous hooligans, so-called patriots, threatened me last evening with tar and feathering as I passed the tavern. All this stems from a letter, a slander.

"I have done nothing wrong. Nothing! I gave up my tea. I haven't ordered items from England. I have stuck by their agreements that I do not like, that can bankrupt me. All I have done is to have an opinion different from theirs. I've taken no action against them. All I want is to be left alone."

He shook Nathaniel, banging him so hard against the wall that pain burst like fireworks through his head and set his ears ringing. "I do all that is asked, and then a letter—a letter from an unidentified assassin—brings me down!" he howled in rage. "It must have been you. I've fed you, clothed you. Why?"

"Master, I don't know what you are talking about. Please, I don't know."

He shook Nathaniel again. "Don't lie to me. I knew when I saw those devil-ghost eyes of yours that you were a viper. It was you!" he screamed. "You! You!" Edan punctuated each "you" by slamming Nathaniel against the wall.

With a crazed, murderous leer, Edan looked over to the tool table, where lay the sharpened axes. His thoughts were clear.

"No!" Finally, Ben reacted. "Mistress Maguire! Sally!" he screamed. He leaped for Edan and landed on his back like a cat. He hung there, while Nathaniel squirmed and kicked, finally breaking free.

Frantically Nathaniel crawled away as Edan shook off Ben and grabbed up a block of wood. He hurled it at Nathaniel. It hit the table with such force that chisels went flying. Nathaniel covered his head against the falling blades and cried, "Please, master!"

Edan seized a turned spoke and rushed for Nathaniel. Nathaniel skidded under the table, darting away from Edan's powerful swings.

"Master! Stop! You kill that boy!" Sally was in the door. She shrieked back toward the house, "Mistress Maguire, come quick!"

With a forceful lunge, Edan caught Nathaniel's foot. Nathaniel desperately scratched at the floor as Edan dragged him out from under the table. Edan pulled him up and held him by the throat.

"Now I have you."

Nathaniel started to close his eyes and turn his head to brace for the blows to follow. He'd been in this position countless times before. But this time something kept him staring at Edan, his head held high, defiant. He prepared himself to hurt, but he did not look away.

Startled perhaps by Nathaniel's boldness, Edan hesitated just long enough for Ben to tackle him, latching onto his knees. Edan let go of Nathaniel to pound Ben with the spoke. But Ben held tight, gasping, "Run, Nathaniel, run for the mistress!"

Nathaniel scrambled for the door, nearly colliding with Mrs. Maguire, who was already darting in. The look on her face was one of horror and disgust. "Edan!"

Edan wavered just enough that Ben broke loose. But Edan reacted swiftly and gripped Ben's arm. He raised the spoke again.

"Edan, stop! Stop at once! You may bully me, but you'll not harm these boys. Stop! Or I will find some way to have you put in the stocks for all our sakes." She was shaking, but she stood firm.

Sally stared at her mistress in disbelief. So did Ben and Nathaniel. It was the first time any of them had heard her stand up to her husband. So astounding was her courage that Edan did stop. He dropped the spoke. They all froze, suspended in surprise, only their frightened, winded breathing breaking the silence.

Then suddenly, Edan screamed. He fell to the ground, writhing and clutching his chest, fighting for each breath. "Elizabeth," he gasped. "Make it stop! Please! Make the pain stop."

For a moment she delayed—a strange mixture of rebellion and relief on her face. A look of something seeing a gate open, a chance at liberty, thought Nathaniel with surprise. Could that really be what he saw in her expression? But it passed, and a resigned sadness, a studied businesslike air, settled over Mistress Maguire. She took a deep breath, knelt beside her husband, and tended to him.

Chapter Twenty-nine

THAT NIGHT NATHANIEL was so sore and bruised he could barely climb up into the loft. He ached too much to sleep. He lay awake wondering what ailed Edan and marveling at Mistress Maguire. He didn't have to wonder who reported Edan's oaths against the trade embargo and the burgesses. He knew it was Ben. That must have been what Ben meant when he'd said he'd done something to make Edan want to return to Ireland.

Around midnight Ben's voice called up the ladder. "Nathaniel? You there?"

"Aye," he replied. Where else would he be? he thought irritably.

Ben swung up the ladder and sat in the hay. The moonlight coming through the manger's open door provided scant illumination. Nathaniel could not see Ben's face, only the dark shadow of his presence.

"I'm sorry, Nat. I was the one who reported Edan."

"I know," answered Nathaniel.

"You do?" He paused and then asked guiltily, "Are you mad at me?"

Of course he was! But should he answer honestly? Nathaniel hesitated. "A little, yes. Master Maguire could have killed me."

"I know, I know." Ben pulled his legs up, wrapped his arms around them, and dropped his head onto his knees. His voice became muffled. "I . . . I . . . I am ashamed that I didn't stop him sooner, Nat. I should have said it was me what sent the letter. I was . . . I was afraid." He sighed and ran his hand through the hay. "I can't believe I was so afraid. What use am I?"

Ben seemed so sad that Nathaniel took pity on him. "Well . . . you were brave enough to get him off me, Ben. Thank you."

There was a long silence until Ben lifted his head. "I suppose that's right. You're welcome, Nat." He was quiet again. "You know, Nat, I think what slapped me into acting finally was seeing you steel yourself for a beating. It made me ashamed of myself. You are very strong, Nat. I just followed your example."

Strong? Nathaniel shook his head. He wasn't strong. He'd taken countless whippings like a dog, tail between his legs. He felt his face turn red, and it was his turn to feel ashamed. "I'm not strong, Ben."

"You're wrong, Nat. You've changed. I've seen it. It was in your face and the way you glared at him."

Maybe. Maybe it was just the sheer unfairness of Edan's wrath that had given Nathaniel strength this time. Perhaps Basil's lectures about his having rights and an inborn intellect and dignity had sunk in without his realizing it. Now he understood what the patriots were all about—fighting against a power that used them unfairly, ruled them with force. Yes, he saw it all better now. He felt it himself. His world of the carriage shop mirrored the struggle between the colonists and the British king.

But there was still one thing that he had to ask—Ben's reporting of Edan seemed, well, spiteful. Of course Nathaniel sympathized with the desire to get back at Edan. Hadn't he loosed Vixen on the blacksmith for hitting him? But if Edan got in trouble, Mistress Maguire was hurt too. And she had been too kind to them for that.

"Ben, why did you report Master Maguire?"

"Because!" Ben's voice was defensive and abrupt. "Because he's a tyrant and a bully!"

"Aye, that he is. I'd be glad to put him in chains in a cargo hull and set him adrift in the seas. He deserves it!" Nathaniel, in fact, quite liked the sound of that.

"But"—he tried to keep his own feelings of vengeance in check—"but that means Mistress Maguire. . . ."

"I know!" Ben nearly shouted. Nathaniel heard the sound of handfuls of hay being thrown. "I know. I'm going to go to the committee tomorrow and tell them I was mistaken.

"I had just wanted a way to be free of him, Nat. That was all. I didn't think anyone would tar and feather him, just make him mad enough to go back to Ireland. So many loyalists and merchants are fleeing Virginia, returning to England. Mrs. Rathell just sold off her store's Irish muslins and English silks for a song and sailed back home. She had the sense to know no one would buy her goods in these times. Why do the Maguires have to be so stubborn?" he asked in exasperation.

"I guess they feel America is their home, too," Nathaniel said quietly, recognizing it himself for the first time.

Ben sighed. "Well, I've found another way to liberty. I'm sixteen now. I'm old enough to join one of the Virginia regiments that are forming. Patrick Henry is going to head them. I know that out of loyalty to my father, he'll make sure that I can stay in it even if Edan protests that I am breaking my apprenticeship. Who is going to care about apprenticeships during a revolution? I just need a musket. In fact"—he stood up and brushed off hay—"the boys and I are going to get some tonight."

"What? You're not going to steal it, are you, Ben, because—"

"No, we're going to the magazine. Nobody is guarding it now that the powder's gone. The guns inside belong to the colonists. I'm a colonist. I've a right to one." He moved to the ladder. "I best go. I'm supposed to meet up outside Mr. Greenhow's store. I just wanted to make sure you were all right." Ben swung his leg onto the ladder, then paused. "Nat?"

"Aye?"

"Come with me?" Ben's voice was uncharacteristically vulnerable. "We could use a good man like you. Please?"

Asked like that, Nathaniel could not refuse. He couldn't sleep anyway. Plus, he suddenly had a new interest in the colonists' demand for liberty. He arose stiffly and followed Ben into the eerie, dark streets of a Williamsburg asleep.

The morning would dawn Whitsunday, so there had been the usual celebrations of it in town that afternoon—cudgeling, wrestling matches, pig chasing, and footraces. The boys had been smart to wait until the deep hours of the night to approach the magazine, to allow all the celebrants to go home and be snoring off their ale. Still, the boys tiptoed, guided only by moonlight. Their boastful whispers gave way to unnerved grumblings when they stumbled into one another or tripped over unseen roots and manure.

Nathaniel kept to the tail end of the group, following Ben's back, unable to see exactly how many boys were participating in the raid. A dozen ahead of him, he thought, including Ben's usual cohorts—Beverly, Robert, and Jeremiah.

Ever surly, Jeremiah had tried to run off Nathaniel, complaining that it was enough to suffer Ben's presence, but did they have to associate with an indentured servant as well? "What will you bring next?" Jeremiah sneered. "A slave?"

But Ben had insisted Nathaniel come, bragging on his cool head. "Why, he just stood down Edan Maguire, boys!" Ben boasted. "That's more than you could do, Jeremiah! If I had to choose between you and Nat to be in our company, I'd choose Nat twenty times over. He'll take on a brigade of Hessians for us someday."

Nathaniel protested Ben's boast, but Ben shushed him. "Nat's just being overly modest," he said. "I witnessed the whole thing."

Nathaniel was beginning to get a very bad feeling about this jaunt.

It was a short distance from Greenhow's storefront to the magazine. When they reached the tall brick wall surrounding the octagonal arsenal, the boys grew silent, although the energy of their nervousness could have lit lanterns.

"Anybody in the guardhouse?" one of them whispered.

"No. Home with a bottle, most like," another answered.

"How are we going to get in?" The wall was sealed with a huge double wooden door that was locked.

"I've the key," someone hissed.

"Where'd you get that?"

"Never you mind," Beverly hushed him, taking command. "Give me the key."

The large, heavy key passed from hand to hand until Beverly inserted it in the lock. With a resounding click and groan, the massive doors drifted open.

A few of the boys laughed nervously. They slipped in quickly, as if their break-in was an innocent game of hide-and-seek.

Nathaniel paused, about to turn back—this was insanity—but Ben pulled him inside the magazine yard.

He pushed the huge door closed behind them.

"Come on," Beverly ordered. The boys fell in line. But at the door of the magazine building, they all paused, suddenly skittish.

"Well, here we are, boys." Beverly took in a deep breath. "I hear there are hundreds of blue-painted stock guns and Brown Bess flintlocks inside. Plenty for each of us to have one. They'll never be missed. Then we'll show the militia we're just as good as they, shan't we, boys? Here's to liberty!" Beverly put his hand on the latch.

"Aye!" "That's right!" "Give us liberty!"

All of them save Nathaniel joined in the whispered crowing.

Jeremiah noticed his silence and jeered: "This one's afraid. You lie about him, Ben, just like you lie about everything—your family, your father. I say if this servant is going to join us and taint the integrity of our company, he has to go in first."

All eyes turned to Nathaniel. Before he could shake his head and back away, Ben spoke up. "Shut up, Jeremiah. You're just afraid yourself. I'll go first."

And with that, Ben pulled Nathaniel behind him and opened the door to the magazine.

There was a blinding flash of light and a thunderous *BANG!*

Nathaniel felt himself blown backward, his arms stung by something hot and vicious. Bashing his head against the ground, it took several moments for him to come to consciousness.

When he did, his ears were ringing from the blast. The only sound he could make out was Ben screaming.

Chapter Thirty

"HOLD ON, LAD, I've almost got it."

Nathaniel gritted his teeth as the surgeon dug in his flesh to find a small piece of lead. He thought he might vomit. He was lying in the hayloft, unsure how he'd gotten there. Although, if he thought hard enough about it, he remembered being lifted and carried, an uproar of shouting and a flood of lantern light. All he could figure was that the blast had awoken the town and someone had brought him home.

Basil was there. Nathaniel turned away from the surgeon and his prying needle pinchers to Basil. Basil looked like he was about to cry. But he smiled at Nathaniel. "Brave lad," he whispered.

"There. I've got it. It wasn't embedded far at all." The searing pain stopped.

The surgeon held up a tiny black ball and examined it in the lantern light. "Swan shot," he muttered. "The redcoats must have rammed two handfuls of balls into that spring gun. Diabolical wretches rigged a gun to go off when someone opened the door. I think this time the townspeople really will riot. Lord Dunmore best watch his back."

He began to pack up his things. "You're lucky, boy. You were just nicked. It didn't touch bone. You'll be back to work in a few days. The others weren't so lucky. That boy Beverly still has two balls in his shoulder and one in his wrist."

Trembling from pain and anxiety, Nathaniel lifted his head. "Ben?"

The surgeon didn't answer. He looked to Basil. Haltingly, Basil answered. "Two of his fingers were shot off. He lost a lot of blood. The surgeon did what he could, and now Mistress Maguire is nursing him."

Nathaniel sobbed—hot, bitter tears of regret. Oh, if only he could reverse time. How could they have been so stupid?

Awkwardly, Basil patted him on the head. "I will return, lad. I must see the surgeon away."

Nathaniel fought to stay awake, but he sank into blackness as he heard the surgeon tell Basil that his fee was five pounds. He wanted the money now. He was leaving town. He feared what might happen next. "There's rumor," he said, "that there is powder buried in the magazine yard linked by an underground fuse to the palace. Dunmore could blow up the town in an instant without leaving his dining room. God knows the town is full of panic and false rumors. But if this one is true, Dunmore is probably vengeful enough to do it!"

When Nathaniel awoke, it was late afternoon the next day. Basil was sitting beside him, reading.

He blinked and lifted himself, feeling enormously hungry. But his movement caused a jab of ache in his arm. He flopped back down, groaning.

"There, there, lad, don't try to move yet." Basil stood. "Let me get some porridge for you. Sally has been up here twenty times in the past hour, I think, to tell me that the instant you awake, I am to get some hot gruel for you."

He reappeared with a steaming bowl. He helped Nathaniel sit and watched to make sure he could spoon the liquid himself.

"She's put honey in it to sweeten and no medicine, I promise." Basil grinned. "No one else warrants such treats. You must be her favorite."

As Nathaniel ate, blowing on the scalding liquid before sipping it out of his spoon, Basil's expression of relief changed.

"Lad," Basil cleared his throat. "When I went

to pay the surgeon . . ."

Nathaniel looked up at him with guilt. Oh, to have cost Basil money yet again. He started to apologize, but Basil held up his hand, "Nathaniel, I think I might have misjudged you. I thought you took something when perhaps I just miscounted. I don't know what to think. I . . . is there something you wish to tell me?"

Nathaniel froze, spoon midair, unsure what to say. In the wake of what had happened to Ben, stealing Basil's money for Moses now seemed so long ago. But Basil's sudden surprise made his answering unnecessary.

"Oh, my goodness!" Basil jumped up as if swarmed by ants. He stared at the floor. "What in the world? Nathaniel, what is that?" He dropped to his knees and excitedly began flinging hay aside, like a groundhog throwing dirt as he dug a den.

Nathaniel laughed in spite of his pain, laughed in joy and pride and hope and affection for an old man who could become enthusiastic so easily. "Aye, master. I've been using your gift." Wincing, Nathaniel raised himself up and found the thank-you letter to Basil that he had hidden inside his mother's Bible.

Basil's eyes filled with tears as he read. Embarrassed, he cleared his throat loudly and turned instructor. "Show me, lad, what you have done here."

They sat for an hour, cross-legged, checking

Nathaniel's sums, his spelling. "Oh, well done, lad, well done! I am so pleased. You are a glorious example of all that Mr. Jefferson talked about the night he came—the inborn nobility of the common man, his ability to educate and govern himself. If Mr. Jefferson has his way, we will raise an aristocracy built not on family ancestry but on merit, on intellect, on hard work. If that becomes the measuring stick, lad, then you will be a great man, indeed."

With a catch in his throat, Nathaniel remembered Ben's boast of someday being elected to the Continental Congress. He braved the question that he had been dreading to ask. "Master, what will become of Ben?"

Basil's face clouded. "His right hand may be useless now. Mistress Maguire will keep him here until he is better and then probably send him home."

"But what about the time he owes for his apprenticeship?" Nathaniel asked.

"He won't be able to learn the trade now, with his hand mangled so."

"But . . . but what is to become of him?" Nathaniel asked in horror.

Basil looked out the manger door. "What indeed, lad?" he murmured sorrowfully. "What indeed."

Rage began to boil up inside Nathaniel. But it was Basil who leaped to his feet in a fury.

"I cannot stomach the cruelty, the cunning, the barbarity of the British setting a spring gun like that!" He paced. He thumped his chest. "Such man-made traps are used to kill poachers who might disturb a lord's storehouses. Like rat traps. As if people were annoying vermin to exterminate. Such treachery! Such arrogance! Do the redcoats think we'll sit still while they lay such murderous inventions to maim our sons?" Breathing hard, flushed with ardor, Basil raised his fist and quoted Patrick Henry's cry: "'Forbid it, Almighty God. Give me liberty! Give me liberty against such callous disregard for life, for rights!'"

He turned to Nathaniel with a new idea shining on his face. "Nathaniel"—he straightened his back—"I am going to join the infantry."

"What?" Nathaniel was still agape at Basil's passionate speech.

"Yes, that's it. I am going to join up." The gangly old tutor was lit up from inside. "When we see a wrong that we know we have the ability to correct, we have the responsibility to do so. If men of principle don't fight for an idea they started, who will? I worry that all my lectures set Ben to his reckless acts. I must do as I say. Old men must not send the young to settle their arguments while they sit at home in comfort." He stuck his lower lip out and nodded. "Yes, that's what I shall do. I am going to volunteer."

He stopped and looked at Nathaniel hard. When he spoke again, his voice was quiet, reflective, sad. "I cannot afford to take you with me, Nathaniel. And I would not have you in harm's way. And if I am to fight for liberty, I will hold no one in bondage. I release you—with affection, lad—from the time you owe me. Perhaps I can recommend you to Mr. Greenhow as bookkeeper." He turned to look down at the floor and trailed off in thought. "These sums you have tallied are impressive."

Nathaniel felt as if he had been shot again. Basil was going to leave him?

No, no, no. Nathaniel stood, shrugging off the discomfort in his arm, shrugging off his old ways of simply accepting whatever fate others decreed for him. He felt as if he were shedding a skin he'd long outgrown, that had bound him tight and kept him from growing. It felt wonderful. "Master, haven't you said that as a human being I am completely capable of understanding and determining my own fate?"

"Aye, lad, that is what Pope and Locke have written. I believe it."

"And you are now telling me that I am free of my indenture?"

"Aye."

"Free to make my own choices? Free to make my

own coming and going?"

"Aye, I will write it out and sign it," Basil answered.

The choice was simple. "I am going with you, then," Nathaniel said stoutly. "I want to get back at the British for Ben too." He almost, almost confessed that he couldn't bear the thought of losing Basil.

"Lad, you are too young."

Nathaniel thought a moment about the companies of volunteers he had seen marching on the market green. They didn't move until the fife major and drummer played. The musicians' calls directed the troops. "How old must you be to be a fifer?"

A slow smile spread across Basil's face. "Fourteen."

Nathaniel grinned back.

"Where is your fife, lad?"

Nathaniel pointed to his thin sack of precious belongings.

Basil nodded. "I think you need to learn a few drill calls, then. I saw that Mr. Greenhow had a fife tutor in his store. I will borrow it. We'll begin lessons tomorrow."

PART EIGHT

September 1775

With fife and drum he marched away.
He would not heed what I did say.
He'll not come back for many a day.
Johnny has gone for a soldier.

Chorus: Shule, shule, shule agra
Sure, ah sure, and he loves me.
When he comes back we'll married be.
Johnny has gone for a soldier.

I'll go up on Portland Hill,
And there I'll sit and cry my fill
And every tear should turn a mill.
Johnny has gone for a soldier.

Chorus

I'll sell my rock, I'll sell my reel,
I'll sell my flax and spinning wheel,
To buy my love a sword of steel.
Johnny has gone for a soldier.

—"Johnny Has Gone for a Soldier," American adaptation of a seventeenth-century Irish tune

Chapter Thirty-one

"**Read that to** me again, lad." Basil sat on a thick oak tree, downed in a storm that had howled inland up the Chesapeake Bay, stirring the James and York Rivers into raging tempests.

Nathaniel straightened the *Gazette* and repeated: "'Lord Dunmore, it seems, fared but poorly in this hurricane, as, by some accident or other, occasioned by the confusion in which the sailors were, his lordship fell overboard, and was severely dunked. But according to the old saying, those who are born to be hanged will never be drowned.'"

"Oh, well said, well said," laughed Basil, his mouth full of thread and needle. He was sewing—not very well. On his lap was the cutout of a large, blousy shirt. He was trying to stitch together the seams of the sleeves, fumbling with the coarse, Oznabrig linen. "And the next section?"

Nathaniel continued: "'Dunmore has received twenty to thirty more men from British troops in Florida, and soon expects to bring his army to five hundred; with which, we hear, he intends taking possession of his palace in this city that he lately abandoned—if not prevented by those he terms *rebels*.'"

"*Rebels!* Ho ho! That's us!" Basil said gleefully. "Doesn't that make us sound like renegades of legend?" The old man grinned, looking silly and youthful. "Now let's see. I think I have it." He stood to shake out the hunting shirt. But Basil had managed to thread his needle through the sleeve and his pants leg at the same time, sewing them together. The shirt stuck fast to his thigh.

"Oh dear." Basil sat down with a thump, rattling the darkening leaves that still clung to the uprooted oak. He leaned back over his task.

Nathaniel fought off a laugh. So far Basil's career as a soldier hadn't been particularly glorious. He couldn't even sew the frontiersman-like uniform required of Patrick Henry's shirtmen!

The two of them had joined the 2nd Virginia Regiment. They belonged to a company captained by George Nicholas, a young Williamsburg man who had led William and Mary students on a raid for arms into the governor's palace. Shortly after the spring-gun blast in the magazine, Dunmore and his family had fled to the HMS *Fowey*. Fearing Dunmore would soon lead an invasion by marines, Nicholas and his friends emptied the palace of two hundred muskets and three hundred swords. James Monroe, Ben's friend from home, had taken part. When he came to visit Ben and heard Basil rail against the boy's misfortune, Monroe had given one of the seized guns to Basil.

With it, Basil passed muster. With his fife, Nathaniel did, too.

Now they sat in a crowded encampment on fields behind the college, waiting, waiting.

Nathaniel looked around at the men clustered nearby. Many worked on their own purple-dyed shirts, cutting fringe in the shoulder-wide, capelike collar to allow rain to drip off. Others labored over the blue wool "half-thicks" they'd been given to sew gaiters to cover their legs up their thighs, to where the long hunting shirt dropped. They joked and bragged as they worked.

Despite the blustery confidence of the men, Nathaniel knew trouble was coming—real trouble—just like the hurricane that had roared up the rivers bringing destruction and death. Dunmore may have fallen off his boat, and some of the tender ships that followed his larger warships may have run aground in the storm, but the truth was that Dunmore was gaining momentum.

In addition to his well-trained and well-equipped British troops, Dunmore was building a powerful fleet. He had the fourteen-gun *Otter* and the *King's Fisher*, an eighteen-gun sloop. He had also confiscated two merchant ships, the *William*, with thirteen guns, and the *Eilbeck*, with seven. Their tender ships—small boats that carried cargo and passengers back and forth between the shore and the main vessel—were equipped with swivel guns and four-pound cannon. Dunmore was harassing fishing vessels and threatening to bombard riverside plantations and the town of Norfolk.

Plus, in Nathaniel's mind, Dunmore had another secret and potent weapon. For in the *Gazette* was also the news that British naval officers were using Africans as navigators and guides. Nathaniel just knew that Moses was one of the escaped slaves helping the redcoats find their way in the marshy back streams of the Tidewater. His courage and strength would serve the king's forces well. If Moses was fighting for the British to secure his liberty, something wasn't quite right with the patriot cause.

Nathaniel tried to not think about Moses being with the British. Dunmore and the marines he commanded were not to be trusted. Whatever promises they had made Moses, Nathaniel doubted they'd keep.

However, he did think constantly on Ben and his horrible wound. His hand was still bandaged when he came to say good-bye. Mistress Maguire was sending him home. She had contacted Ben's mother, who thought him old enough to try to run their farm and reclaim the family's financial equilibrium. With one good hand and a strong back, he could still manage to do many of the farm's tasks.

"I don't want to be a farmer," Ben complained.

Putting his hand on Ben's shoulder, Basil had spoken gently: "You didn't want to be a carriage maker either, did you?"

"I wanted . . . I wanted . . ." Ben hesitated.

"I know what you wanted, lad. But wanting glory shouldn't be what drives a man to take up arms against others."

Ben frowned. "I do believe in our cause, too, Basil. It wasn't just vanity. I believe in our right to stand up against tyranny."

"I know, lad. Let that be your driving force now. Patience. I have a feeling that this fight may last awhile. Heal. Perhaps one day your hand can hold a musket to defend us. Or better yet, raise your heartfelt thoughts in legislature. Study, Ben. There's the way. Refine your mind with books. You don't need a strong hand to think or speak out to lead others."

Ben stood a little taller. "I'll try, master tutor."

"Oh, oh, let me lend you something, Ben." Basil darted off to his tent.

Ben and Nathaniel grinned at each other, sharing their fond amusement at Basil. Then Ben grew serious. "You keep an eye on the old fool, Nat. He's no soldier."

"No, he's not," agreed Nathaniel.

They stood in awkward silence, not knowing what else to say. Nathaniel had come to care about Ben, there was no denying it. He would miss Ben's jocund humor, his confidence in him, his prodding. He opened his mouth to speak and then closed it. Opened it again, but could only manage, "Take care, Ben."

Ben took a step closer to Nathaniel and looked him firmly in the eye. "You're stronger than you think, Nat. I've learned"—he held up his wrapped hand—"that steady men make better leaders."

Skipping back, holding a book aloft, Basil interrupted. Seeing him coming, Ben adopted a little of his old swagger and concluded loudly for Basil to hear well. "Steady and slow, just like that old tortoise in his race against the hare. Just don't retreat back into your shell, eh, Nat?" He winked at Nathaniel. "Boil some lobsterbacks for me, lad."

Then he turned toward Basil and covered his face in mock horror. "What, old tutor? Not a grammar book!"

Basil ignored the banter. "Not quite, lad. It's Locke's *Two Treatises of Government.*"

Nathaniel gasped. He knew how precious that book was to Basil.

Ben did, too. "I can't take that, Master Basil," he whispered.

"Yes, lad, you can. I've probably memorized every line. I shan't miss it. Learn some philosophy to support your zeal. An argument backed with reason, with eloquence, will prove too strong to deny." He put the book in Ben's good hand. "If we win this fight, it may mean we break away from England altogether. Then we must devise a new social contract, a new way of governing. We will need men of thought to create one. Go on home, now, lad. Read. Think."

Ben nodded, turned, and left, looking down at the book as he walked.

Nathaniel had been straining to watch Ben disappear into Williamsburg's bustle when their company sergeant interrupted with astounding news.

"Pay," he grunted.

With hands trembling in surprise, Nathaniel took the first payment he'd ever received for his labor: seven and one-third dollars for the month. He was even more amazed when he found out that Basil, as a private, received less—six and two-thirds dollars! He was so happy, he didn't even mind when the fife major, in charge of teaching all the lower musicians the important camp calls, took half Nathaniel's money as fee for his instruction.

Chapter Thirty-two

In his sleep, Nathaniel nodded: "a sixteenth run up G-A-B-C to eighth notes D-D-B-G. Skip up to hold the E long . . . I have it. Keep the tempo with the drummer; don't rush." He rolled over, bumping his head against Basil's feet.

His eyes popped open. He stared into dark, now completely awakened by the smell of damp straw and feet and the snores of five other bodies crammed into a six-and-a-half-foot square tent. The tune he had been practicing in his sleep was still sounding. How was that possible? He rubbed his eyes. Outside the tent flap, something *bump-bumped* and a voice hissed through the tent flap, "Be up, Nathaniel. It's the drummers call. Be quick!"

Nathaniel jumped up, knocking into the sloping canvas of the tent. His tent mates grunted, complained, and went back to snoring.

Of course! That was the duty drummer and fifer playing the call to assemble the musicians. He hurled himself out the tent's flap. Skidding along the dewy grass, he caught up with Ben's enemy, Jeremiah, who by a stroke of ill luck was Nathaniel's company drummer.

"You'll get us in trouble for your laziness," Jeremiah sniped, his drum bumping against his legs as he ran.

Jeremiah had escaped injury at the magazine. But he was Nathaniel's age, still unable to join as a soldier. Almost a foot taller, hefty and mean, drumming seemed a perfect role for him. Yet, he was slow to learn. He blamed his fumblings on Nathaniel playing wrong notes—lies, but ones that Jeremiah made with such vehemence that the drum major often corrected Nathaniel. Nathaniel dared not protest. The major teaching them tolerated no interruptions. He had served in the French and Indian War and believed in the harsh discipline practiced by the British officers. Talking back brought a beating.

Also, Nathaniel was permanently paired with Jeremiah. Each company of sixty-eight foot soldiers had its own set of officers—a captain, first and second lieutenant, and junior ensign—plus one fifer and one drummer. That meant that altogether the 1st and 2nd Regiments had about a dozen pairs of fife and drummers. But they were not rotated. There was no escaping Jeremiah, as a result. If Nathaniel got Jeremiah into trouble, Jeremiah would make Nathaniel pay dearly for it, and have ample opportunity to do so.

In the dim glow of a lantern, the on-duty fifer and drummer stood in front of the commanding officer's tent. There had been frost in the night—the first of the season—and Nathaniel could see puffs of vapor hanging about the fifer's mouth as he blew. Nathaniel knew it would be hard to play his tiny wooden instrument in such cold. He tucked his hands under his armpits to warm his fingers.

Quickly the camp musicians gathered. Together they struck up reveille, telling the soldiers to rise, comb their hair, clean their hands and face, and be ready for the day's duties. It was a quick-tempo walk down the scale from *g* with a few sixteenth-note embellishments. Nathaniel was still working on those runs, and often substituted a single quarter note in the run's place. Still, his fife's voice pierced the air, much like a rooster's crow, creating a ripple of stirring in the camp.

Within minutes, several hundred men were up and about, scratching, stretching, shouting, stumbling into things. Cooking fires were stirred and rekindled. Men heated up biscuits and coffee. Children darted about, playing soldiers, cared for by the women who'd followed their husbands and did laundry, mending, and nursing. Sutlers opened their wagons for business, offering rum, soap, thread, fruit. Crammed together behind the campus of William and Mary, the encampment had the same bustle and almost the same number of people as the town of Williamsburg.

Nathaniel skipped back through the two long parallel rows of tents. As cramped as it was, he was grateful to be housed in one. The new army was still scrambling to outfit its men. Many were sleeping out in the open. Only those who had brought all their own equipment had shot pouches to carry cartridges or horns to hold gunpowder. Oxen around the area were being shorn of their horns as quickly as possible to supply the rest.

Nathaniel squatted beside Basil and their campfire. They gobbled up the last ham biscuits that Mrs. Maguire had sent them through Sally. They hid what they ate, knowing the other soldiers might make a grab at the tender ham. Already they were all sick of the charred food each tent mess prepared out of the raw meat, dried beans, flour, and vinegar that the army gave them every few days.

Before she'd left, Sally had elbowed Basil and announced, "Master Maguire done died."

Basil had just looked at her, blinking.

"Had a fit. Died. Doctor said it was his heart." She'd leaned close to Basil and whispered, "But iffen you ask me, I don't think he had one." She tapped him on the arm. "You ought to go see Mistress Maguire."

Basil had turned red. Nathaniel thought back on their leaving the Maguire house, when Basil had gently taken Mistress Maguire's hand, bowed, and kissed it as a knight would a lady's. Nathaniel wondered if perhaps Basil would one day court her.

Basil interrupted Nathaniel's musings. "What are you about today, lad? The same?"

"Aye." Nathaniel would have music practice, and then an hour of demonstrating tunes so the troops could memorize the sound and instruction of each call. It was rather important, for instance, that soldiers know the difference between reveille and "To Arms," the emergency alarm to be up and armed against a surprise attack!

"I have fatigue duty," mourned Basil.

That meant Basil would spend most of his day gathering firewood, digging new necessaries, cleaning up the camp. Nathaniel pitied him. None of the men liked it when Nathaniel and Jeremiah played the "Pioneers' March" around 9 A.M. to signal fatigue duty. It was hard and disgusting work. The camp was filthy. Many of the men already had lice and were trying to soothe the horrendous itch brought by the tiny vermin by smearing their bodies with lard. "Well, at least it will get you out of drilling," Nathaniel said sympathetically.

Basil sighed. Nathaniel worried that the tutor's spindly body was too old for such labor. But Basil actually seemed to be growing stronger with the strain rather than weaker. He was particularly thriving in nightfall's camaraderie, when he and Nathaniel entertained their company with music. Basil might start off with more refined fiddling, but by the end the men were singing and joking—adding their own words to songs like "Old King Cole" from the opera *Achilles*: "Old King Cole was a merry old soul, and a merry old soul was he; and he called for his pipe, and he called for his bowl, and"—here the men merrily shouted out words they'd added—"he called for a CUP OF TEA!"

Basil delighted in the patriotic excitement around camp. The only thing missing was his hero, Patrick Henry, who had recently returned to take command of Virginia's regiments.

Despite his complete lack of military experience, Henry had been given the Virginia command because George Washington was in charge of the Continental Army up north, trying desperately to hold off the British in Massachusetts and New York. Many worried that Henry's impatient, fiery tongue—while it did wonders to inspire—might be dangerous with an army behind it. But they could not deny that it had been his words that had stirred so many recruits to join Virginia's forces. Henry wanted a command, and so Virginia gave him one.

Later that day, Basil would finally have the thrill of hearing Henry. But it was not exactly the oratory he expected.

It started off right enough: "Gentlemen, we are now in the service of our people, in the service of justice, in the service of liberty." Patrick Henry stood on a makeshift stage of board and barrels. "Each day dawns with hope. I feel the sun shines brighter as it sees us below ready and determined. My brave people, the very heavens are inspired by our resolve."

Rapt, the thousand men stood hushed, eyes fixed on the small man with the long nose and stern appearance, the man with a voice that seemed to vault to heaven. Henry could probably tell the men they needed to swim across the Atlantic Ocean to fight the British and some might have tried. They leaned forward with anticipation.

"I would expect soldiers in such a noble endeavor to conduct themselves with dignity. Yet . . ." He paused, letting the "yet" resound. "It has come to my saddened attention that some of you are not behaving with the decorum and discipline befitting our cause. The town of Williamsburg complains bitterly of men carousing in the taverns, drinking and sporting with women, haranguing the good townspeople in the streets. Some have torn down fences to fuel fires, stripped the town's gardens and orchards. I have even been told that men practice throwing their tomahawks by hurling them at citizens' doors."

Henry scowled and boomed: "This riotous behavior is to stop at once!"

Looking uncomfortable, the men shifted their weight from foot to foot. Some glanced at one another in surprise and embarrassment.

"There will be no more gambling about the camp. Rolling of dice will bring arrest. No soldier will leave camp without orders to do so. Henceforth, every noncommissioned officer and soldier shall retire to his tent at the beating of retreat, in default of which he will be punished." He paused and added, "Furthermore, men are to stop easing themselves except in the necessary holes!"

That was the end of the inspiring orator's speech. The men were dismissed for three hours of drilling in "woods fighting."

Hugely disappointed, Basil lingered a moment, watching Henry talk with his junior officers. "Ah me," he finally murmured, sighing. "I suppose even an army of ideas has rules and day-to-day chores to attend to."

PART NINE

November 1775

Hark! 'Tis freedom that calls, come patriots awake!
To arms, my brave boys, and away;
'Tis Honor, 'tis virtue, 'tis Liberty calls,
And unbraids the too tedious delay.
What pleasures we find pursuing our foes
Thro' blood and thro' carnage we'll fly,
Then follow, we'll soon overtake them, huzzah!
The tyrants are seiz'd on, they die. . . .

'Tis freedom alone gives a relish to mirth,
But oppression all happiness sours.
'Twill smooth life's dull passage, 'twill slope the descent,
and strew the way over with flowers.

—American words set to British tune
"The Echoing Horn"

Chapter Thirty-three

"THINK YOU THE regiment will march soon?" Maria reached down and picked up a maple leaf from the sea of autumn leaves swirling about their ankles.

"Aye. That's the word of it, soon." Nathaniel scooped up a leaf as well and twirled the five-pointed, bloodred fan to hide his shyness. "Dunmore is causing trouble on the rivers and around Norfolk. We must stop him."

"Yes, I know. Our newspaper is full of the accounts of his plundering."

During October, guided by loyalists, Dunmore had raided up and down the Tidewater area, capturing almost all the cannons and gunpowder patriots had hidden in homes and warehouses. He'd also torched several riverside plantations and villages.

Most recently, Dunmore's ships attacked Hampton, a town overlooking the Chesapeake Bay. The British burned several houses on its outskirts. But they were unable to bombard the town until they had hacked through the fishing boats the townspeople had sunk in the harbor to block the British fleet. That gave the patriots time to beg reinforcements from Williamsburg. Riding all night to cover thirty miles through heavy rain, riflemen of the 2nd Virginia Regiment, plus Culpeper Minutemen, were able to take position in Hampton's brick houses as the British began firing their cannons. Although much of the town crumpled, the brick houses were strong enough to withstand the four-pound cannon balls. Through the barrage, the Virginia marksmen picked off the British sailors on the ships' decks and riggings. Eventually manning their guns seemed like sure suicide, and the British ships withdrew.

Since the Hampton skirmish, the Williamsburg camp had been in an uproar to take the fight *to* the British, rather than waiting to see where Dunmore would strike next. Word was they would soon move out to secure the region's important river towns. The mission was critical.

Dunmore was already strongly entrenched in Norfolk, housed and aided by its loyalists and Scottish merchants. Just off the Chesapeake Bay, Norfolk was the largest seaport in Virginia, possessing warehouses and wharves useful to waging war. More importantly, the city gave Dunmore control of the York and James Rivers where they connected with the Chesapeake Bay and the bay opened to the Atlantic Ocean. If the patriots didn't dislodge Dunmore from Norfolk, all Virginia's towns and ports would be bottled up like Boston. The British would cut the colonies in half.

Nathaniel well remembered his ship of bondage sailing up the Chesapeake Bay. He had cursed its waters then and longed to return to England. Funny that he now wanted to defend it.

"Nathaniel Dunn!" a voice bellowed from the tents. "Drilling soon! Come here at once!"

Nathaniel winced, recognizing Jeremiah's bullying tone.

Maria blushed. "I'll not trouble you more, Nathaniel. But I wanted to give you something, before you left, in thanks for the poem on cursive." After Edan's fit, Nathaniel had recopied it and given it to her. Maria reached into her pocket and pulled out an envelope, neatly inscribed with his name. "I copied it from our newspaper."

As she held it up for him to take, Nathaniel took an awkward step forward and grasped her hand. "Maria . . ." He faltered, paused, and tried again, "Maria, I don't know when I will be coming back. But . . . but . . . well . . . I will be glad to see you then." He held onto her small, pale hand, crushing the envelope.

"Oh," she cried, hearing the stationery crumple.

"Sorry," said Nathaniel, realizing her distress.

He dropped her hand, dropped the letter, stooped to pick it up. Nathaniel tried again. "I hope to see you when I come home."

"Oh, Nathaniel, I just . . . I just don't know. . . ."

Nathaniel's spirits fell like lead in water. Doesn't know? Wouldn't she want to see him? He took a step back, hurt, embarrassed.

"Wait." She stopped him. "I meant I don't know if I will be here. Our printing business is doing worse. We've lost the position of Printer to the Public. It was awarded to Mr. Purdie instead. I might need to be bound out, to support my brothers."

That meant Maria would be entered into servitude akin to Nathaniel's indentureship. He shook his head. "Oh no, Maria, don't let them do that."

"I may have no choice." Maria choked a bit as she said it. "I just hope it can be with a family in Williamsburg so I can still see my brothers and . . . and . . ."—she looked up then, finally, into Nathaniel's eyes—"and you, Nathaniel."

Without warning, she kissed him on the cheek, curtseyed, and ran. Nathaniel's face burned where her lips had touched him. He opened the envelope to see slightly blotted but delicate, careful penmanship of the words:

Freedom's charms alike engage
Blooming youth and hoary age;
Time itself can ne'er destroy
Freedom's pure and lasting joy;
Love and friendship never give
Half their blessing to the slave;
None are happy but the free,
Bliss is born of Liberty.

Nathaniel tucked it into his shirt—just in time to keep Maria's gift from scattering in the wind. From behind, he was shoved—hard enough to hurl him to the ground.

"I called you!"

Nathaniel rolled over, spitting out dirt, to look up at Jeremiah, standing overtop him, his fists balled into threats. "Get up. I'll teach you to not come when I call. As a drummer, I am the more important."

Nathaniel fumed, tensed, felt himself ready to spring. Was he going to have to put up with blows from a boy now too? This boy who had constantly heckled Ben and who was responsible in a way for his maimed hand? How could he hold himself back?

"Get up!" Jeremiah kicked him. "You are such a

weird-eyed weakling. Figures you'd be sotted over that girl. The whole town knows what a failure her family is. Perfect company for you!"

The insult to Maria did it. Nathaniel dove at Jeremiah's knees and knocked him down. The two boys rolled over and over, flaying at each other, without really knowing how to hit their mark in the cloud of dust they kicked up.

"Here! Here now! Stop!" Two large hands took hold of the collar of each boy and hurled them apart.

Somehow Nathaniel and Jeremiah landed on their feet. They were about to go for each other again, but a tall man held up his hands and ordered, "Stand fast, boys, or so help me I will arrest you. Don't we have enough enemies to fight without you scrapping with each other?"

He was young and robust, twenty years or so in age. His fringed deerskin trousers and buck-tail hat marked him as one of the frontier marksmen. On his hunting shirt were embroidered the words "Liberty or Death." His belt held a tomahawk and scalping knife. His appearance was quite daunting. The boys stood fast indeed.

"He started it," Jeremiah whined, pointing at Nathaniel.

"Ah, lad, for shame," said the man. "You bear false

witness. I saw you knock him down from behind after the lass left."

"Did not. He called me a—"

The man shook his head and interrupted. "Save the stories, boy. I'm the eldest of fifteen brothers and sisters. I know hogwash when I hear it. Heed this: lies beget lies. Now be off with you." He waved Jeremiah away.

Nathaniel stood, dusting off his clothes. He knew he shouldn't feel so, but he felt rather proud of himself.

"Hmmm, dust that smirk off your face as well, lad. You must not spar in camp. 'Twill bring you trouble with the officers and with me. I am the drillmaster for my company of Culpeper Minutemen."

Despite the reprimand, the young man grinned at Nathaniel. "I like your pluck, though. That ill-tempered youth is an ox. I am glad to meet a David who would take on such a Goliath." He bowed and tipped his hat, sending the deer tail on it dancing. "Lieutenant John Marshall, of the Fauquier Rifles, is my name. And yours?"

"Nathaniel Dunn, sir."

He winked. "Best to your duty, Nathaniel."

"Aye, sir." Nathaniel rushed off, happy about his letter, happy to have found his courage. He was ready now, ready to fight for liberty. Mayhap Ben had been right about him.

Chapter Thirty-four

NATHANIEL WOULD NEED that fortitude a few days later when his regiment's battle against the British redcoats began.

"It's coming round again, lads. Steady."

Crouched behind a large rock on the riverbank, Nathaniel peeped over its top to watch the riflemen of the 2nd Regiment and the Culpeper Minutemen, lying flat in front of him, take aim at a British warship.

"Wait till you see the buttons on their red coats!" shouted a captain, speaking of the soldiers manning the vessel's cannon.

"Teach them to wear such an easy-to-see target," joked a man.

A chuckle rippled through the ranks as the shirtmen raised their rifles, resting the barrels on the logs or rocks littering the sandy shore. They waited, ready, like the coiled rattlesnake on their Culpeper banner that proclaimed: "Don't tread on me. Liberty or Death."

The patriots were pinned down at Burwell's Ferry, just southeast of Williamsburg. They'd marched there to cross the James River on their way to Norfolk. But just as the first group began rowing against the tide, the HMS *Kingfisher* warship rounded a bend in the river, its sails full, its brow beating up and down against the waves. Firing its six-pounder cannon, the British ship blew holes through the ferryman's house and wharf. The regiment scattered, the men dodging and shouting, hurling themselves behind trees, logs, banks.

Now, they were in a sort of stalemate. A tender boat from the warship kept tacking back and forth within a few hundred yards of shore, shooting at anyone who stood up straight or tried to advance toward the ferryboats. When the tender came close enough, the frontier riflemen shot back.

Stuck in between the American troops on shore and the British boats was a small barge. Its unlucky oysterman had been approaching the wharf to deliver his catch when the skirmish began. After their first volley, the British ordered him to come alongside the warship. Wanting to salvage all the boats that they could for their crossing, the Virginia riflemen shouted at him to stay where he was. Both sides made their point with gunfire. Now the poor oysterman had disappeared from view, probably lying flat in his boat, praying.

Of course, some of the rifleman had other plans for the boat. They wanted its catch. An officer lying atop a pile of crushed shells called out, "I don't know about you, boys, but I'd love oysters for dinner. Let's get on with this! This bed of mine is most uncomfortable!"

"Aye!" many shouted. They, too, were covered with sand and were lying atop rocks and sharp river debris.

"Here she comes," warned the officer. "Ready! Aim. . . ."

The men squinted, finding their mark.

"FIRE!"

CRAAAAACKK. Crack, crack, crack. Two dozen rifles fired.

British gunfire answered with cannon grapeshot.

Lead balls whizzed by—*ping . . . ping, ping, ping*—burrowing into the dirt around them, ricocheting off Nathaniel's rock, snapping off branches.

All around him, Nathaniel heard gasps, curses, and then laughter when the men checked themselves over and realized that they were still alive.

A minute passed as the riflemen reloaded. It was a painstaking process, compared to the muskets, which could be reset in fifteen seconds. First the marksman poured powder into the pan by the firelock, and then an exact charge amount of coarser powder down the rifle barrel. He covered the end of the barrel with a greased patch of cloth, onto which he placed the ball. Then he rammed both in and down, withdrew the ramrod, and aimed.

CRAAACK. Crack, crack, crack. The patriots fired again.

Ping, ping, ping. The British boats answered.

T-wang. A ball chipped a fist-sized splinter off Nathaniel's rock. He dove down, jostling Basil, who huddled beside him.

"Oooooh, the Lord is my shepherd. I'm walking through the valley of the shadow of death, Lord, help me . . ." Basil cried.

"Master." Nathaniel shook him a bit. "Courage." Armed with a musket that only had a fifty-yard range at best, Basil was not expected to be firing. But Nathaniel didn't want the other men to see him so fearful.

Basil kept praying. "I shall fear no evil, I shall fear no evil. . . ."

Nathaniel stared at the little quaking ball of man that was Basil. Nathaniel was afraid too, afraid but strangely exhilarated by each volley he survived. He glanced around at the nearby men. Some were hunkered down like Basil, but most were gritting their teeth, holding firm. No one else was facedown in the dirt.

But something seemed to be wrong with Basil

other than the gunfire. His panic had started on the river. He and Nathaniel had been in one of the first ferry rowboats when the cannonading began. Rocked by the concussion of a cannonball crashing into the water within inches of them, their boat had rammed another, hurtling Basil and several others into the water.

The water in the James was deep, the current murderous. Basil disappeared under the dark waves; surfaced, flailing and gasping; disappeared again; bobbed up; went under. Nathaniel shouted for help. But there was too much confusion. Basil popped up once more, but this time his struggling was far weaker. Nathaniel realized that if Basil went under again, he wouldn't come back up. He snatched up one of the long oars and shoved it toward Basil. "Take hold!"

His action tipped the boat wildly. Men yanked him back to balance it. "No! Help him!" screamed Nathaniel. But the men were concentrating on untangling the boats.

Thrashing and shouting, Nathaniel tried to clamber out of the boat. His hysteria finally alerted one of the men already in the water. The man swam for Basil, grabbed him up, and towed him to the boat. Hands held on to their shirt collars and dragged them along through the waves as the men in the boat rowed with all their might to regain land.

Nathaniel had half carried the old man to this rock while Basil shivered, coughed, spluttered, crying out, "Myra, Myra!"

During the past hour, he'd alternated between crying out for her—whoever she was—and praying in the sand.

CRAAACK. Crack, crack, crack.

Nathaniel braced himself for the Brits' answer.

No return fire.

The regiment waited, each man holding his breath.

Still silence.

A few dared to lift themselves up to survey the river. The British tender was heading back toward the *Kingfisher*. The autumn sun was going down quickly. The British preferred a daylight fight.

"Huzzah!" the men cheered.

"Let's to the oysters, men!" shouted the hungry officer.

That night the regiment threw up a makeshift camp further inland, away from the ferry, out of reach of British guns. In the cold moonlight, American sentries kept an eye on the warship, sleeping on the river. Everyone else slipped into a wary slumber. Everyone, that is, except Nathaniel. He kept watch over Basil.

The freezing waters and the November chill had thrown the old man into a kind of delirium. Nathaniel had tucked his and Basil's blanket around him, but still Basil shivered. He dreamed fitfully, crying out about a frozen-over river in Scotland, about ice skates, about Myra.

After many hours, Basil finally settled into a real sleep. Nathaniel dozed.

"Lad?" Basil's hoarse whisper awoke him in the morning.

"Aye, master?"

"Methinks you saved my life."

"Nay, master, not I."

Basil shook his head. "Aye, 'twas you, I think, sounded the alarm."

Nathaniel shrugged. "I am glad you are better." Then he added the thanks he'd always meant to say before but had not. "You saved me once, master."

Basil smiled weakly. "I made a promise to myself, long ago, Nathaniel, to save anyone I saw drowning before me. No matter what might happen to me. To make up for failing—failing horribly, God forgive me—once before."

He sighed and with a sadness so heavy, his voice

dropped so low Nathaniel could barely understand. "I . . . I had a wife. A beautiful, delicate lass, she was. I was a teacher at a school . . . oh, my life was so blessed. . . . Then the students wanted to try a new sport—skating on ice. We all went out onto the river. . . . The ice . . . the ice seemed so certain . . . but . . . but it was thin and . . ." Basil gasped and dropped his head into his hands. "I fell in trying to save Myra. I managed to pull the two of us out, half frozen, near death. . . . But I let two boys drown to save her. They sank under the ice, calling my name, begging me to help them. . . . I had to tell their parents . . . I had to . . ." He groaned. "My beautiful Myra died from pneumonia. The school dismissed me, the town threw garbage at me as I left." He lifted his head and stared into the darkness. "I ran away. And then I came here."

He turned to look at Nathaniel, pleading in his eyes. "Methought you were drowning when I first saw you, Nathaniel. That blacksmith was a river that could swallow you and drag you under."

"Aye, master, that he was."

Nathaniel's answer seemed to give Basil something he desperately needed. His face cleared a little. "You must really stop calling me 'master.' Basil will do."

"Aye . . . Basil." The name sounded odd on his tongue. Nathaniel knew that it was more likely he would continue to call the old tutor "master," but now it would be a term of affection rather than obligation.

Chapter Thirty-five

THE NEXT WEEK turned bitter cold. The men moaned as they slogged through frigid, slimy swamp waters and puddle-filled roads.

"Lord, my feet ache."

"I wish I had ice creepers."

"My toes are frozen stiff." Only those with good boots or shoes could attach the wrought-iron spikes of ice creepers that elevated their feet out of the cold mud and gave them traction. Most merely wrapped their feet in rags to protect toes that protruded through worn-out leather, to cover holes in their soles, to waterproof their moccasins.

The loudest complaints came from those with "iron bondage"—carrying the heavy cast-iron kettles that each mess of six men needed to cook their food. Whoever had the duty was bruised up and down from the wide, thick pot banging against his legs. His shoulders and arms ached.

"It's not as if we need the wretched thing," Basil mumbled the day he struggled with it. "They give us naught to cook in it."

It was true. On good days during a march, their diet consisted of beef cooked hurriedly on bayonets held over fire—burned and crusty—and fire cakes—a paste of flour and water. Many days, fire cakes were all they had.

Their forty-five-mile trek to Norfolk grew longer than it should have been. Repeatedly harassed at Burwell's Ferry by British ships, the regiment circled northwest—the opposite direction of Norfolk—to cross the James River. The American Colonel William Woodford was under strict orders to protect the troops' limited ammunition. So, rather than continue to spar with the British ships, he took his men to Sandy Point. It took several days to make up the distance that loop cost them.

The lost time also gave Dunmore a substantial victory. The weight of it spread through camp one night, rattling the regiment.

"Heard you the news from Kemp's Landing?" One of their tent mates plopped down beside Nathaniel and Basil.

Basil had just finished daubing a stone with flour

paste and setting it near the campfire to cook. Nathaniel was already eating his fire cake. Charred on the outside, cold and soggy on the inside, it was completely unappetizing. But shaky with hunger, Nathaniel gagged it down.

"Let us hope it is good," answered Basil.

"It's not," replied the man. "Dunmore marched out of Norfolk with a hundred fifty British regulars, loyalists, and runaway slaves. Waiting for them in the woods was our militia from Princess Anne County. We had twice the redcoats' number. We should have held. But we panicked. Our militia only fired once and then was driven back into a creek. A number drowned, the rest fled, deserting our officers, who were captured. The redcoats ransacked the hamlet, scaring the women half to death.

"Dunmore has declared martial law in Virginia, saying that anyone who does not support the crown is a traitor. He's also issued a proclamation offering freedom to any slave or indentured servant belonging to 'rebels' *if* they are capable of bearing arms and join His Majesty's troops. He's made a regiment called Lord Dunmore's Royal Ethiopian.

"Most of the inhabitants around there have signed an oath of loyalty to the king—the cowardly scoundrels. Even the mayor and aldermen of Norfolk signed! They hosted a feast for Dunmore when he paraded back into town. Loyalists wear a badge of red cloth. They say most everyone in the city sports one now. The worst of it is that several hundred of our colonial militia went over to Dunmore. They have been reorganized as the Queen's Own Loyal Virginia Regiment.

"Norfolk is fortified against us. Dunmore has built a fort at the Great Bridge, our only way to Norfolk by foot. We're marching straight into a loyalist lions' den. We're doomed, I tell you."

Everyone silenced. Only the fire crackled and spat as the men nervously looked from one to another.

"I'm thinking it's about time to go home to my missis," muttered one man.

"Aye," grumbled another.

"Oh, pshaw! Nonsense!" Out of the shadows stepped the tall frontiersman John Marshall. He squatted by the fire and held his hands up to its warmth, rubbing them. "Weak minds are easily led and easily changed. We will win the people of Norfolk back. Our cause is just. Know any of you the works of Alexander Pope?"

"Oh yes, sir, I most certainly do," said Basil, brightening. "I used his verse often to teach grammar and morals at the same time."

"Good man. My mother used it to tutor me in the

exact fashion. Master schoolmaster, tell our friends what Pope's main philosophy is."

"Well"—Basil puffed up a bit, preening at the chance to talk philosophy—"in his *Essay on Man*, Pope argues that reason separates and elevates us from the animals. Still, we are only part of the universe, not the focus of it. The point of his I like best is his optimistic belief that evil or what seems to be bad luck is actually part of some overall plan for good."

"Exactly!" applauded Marshall. "Well said, sir scholar. Here is a verse for us to remember tonight, my friends." He closed his eyes and recited:

"All Nature is but Art, unknown to thee;
All Chance, Direction, which thou canst not see;
All Discord, Harmony not understood;
All partial evil, universal Good:
And, spite of Pride, in erring Reason's spite:
One truth is clear, WHATEVER IS, IS RIGHT."

"That's right!" chirped Basil. "Pope believes things happen for a reason that we cannot understand until a future time."

"So we can hope that Dunmore's victory at Kemp's Landing will only increase his conceit and, therefore, his foolhardiness," said Marshall. "He's so contemptuous of us, he won't fear us. He'll act rashly, and then we'll have him."

"Hope, that's the word, hope," Basil replied. "Pope said, 'Hope springs eternal in the human breast.' It's one of mankind's most admirable qualities—his ability to hope and dream of better things."

"Very true," agreed Marshall. "Hope has led us to this fight, hope for independence and a better life, hope in ourselves. Let us remember that, gentlemen."

Encouraged, the crowd about the fire seemed to breathe a collective sigh of relief.

That is, until a rustic fellow, who had inched closer during the discussion, spoke up: "I had one season at school. Didn't learn much. Me wife was the one to always be reading in the Bible, God rest her. But I do remember one saying from Alexander Pope that the master learnt us: 'Fools rush in where angels fear to tread.'"

The man's sour comment squashed the uplift in spirits.

There was something familiar about the stranger's voice that made Nathaniel look at the man more carefully in the glow of the firelight. He wore the fringed shirt and motto of the Culpeper men. His face was badly pocked, making his natural features hard to distinguish. Obviously he'd survived a bad case of smallpox. There was also a long, jagged scar along his hairline that puckered and distorted the skin of his forehead. He had a kind of grotesque appearance. What nature had originally made him was no longer visible.

Nathaniel recognized nothing in his appearance. Perhaps it'd just been the voice that carried the accent of Yorkshire in it that caught his attention. But there was nothing extraordinary about that, really. Most Virginians still spoke with traces of the motherland in their voices.

Marshall laughed heartily. "Another fine quote from Mr. Pope. But you mustn't let your experiences with the Indians on our borders fill you with spite and bitterness about our fellow countrymen. And Providence obviously saved you, my friend, from a scalping for a reason. I think—"

"Stop! Thief!"

Jeremiah came crashing into the ring of men about the campfire. Confused and wild eyed, he tried to push his way back into the dark, but the men caught him.

A fat, red-faced sergeant major thundered into the firelight. "Give it up, boy. You've nowhere to hide now."

"What's he done?" Marshall asked.

"Nothing, that's what," whined Jeremiah. "Nothing at all."

"We caught him trying to slip past the sentinel to come back into camp, Lieutenant," said the sergeant, struggling to regain his breath.

"Was out scouting for loyalist Tories, that's what I was doing."

Marshall looked at Jeremiah and then at Nathaniel, clearly recognizing Jeremiah as the bully he had pulled off Nathaniel. "Tell the truth, lad."

"It is the truth! I was out looking for the enemy."

"You know there is an express order that no man is to leave this camp under the pretense of searching out Tories?" asked Marshall.

"But I had orders!"

"Really? Aren't you a drummer?"

"Yes, I am." Now Jeremiah puffed up like a rooster. "Very important my drum calls are!" he crowed.

"Indeed, they are. That's why you would never be ordered on a search party. First lie. Try telling the truth of it."

Jeremiah stood with his mouth hanging open, thinking. "I . . . I . . ." He started shuffling his feet, as if to run off. Nathaniel couldn't help being glad that Jeremiah was finally being caught in his balderdash. Recognizing that Jeremiah was about to bolt, he stood up and planted himself in the way.

Jeremiah whipped around to hurdle himself into the night and crashed right into Nathaniel. Out of his hunting shirt dropped a roasted mutton leg.

"Oh! Lovely!" Several men dove for the meat.

"Stand off." The sergeant pushed and kicked them away. "He stole that off the miller down the road. Went right into the house, asking for water, and then pinched their dinner." He grabbed Jeremiah by the collar. "You are under arrest, boy."

Marshall shook his head. "Plundering is a court martial offense, boy. You best plan on truthful testimony and begging the court's mercy. Lying will only make things worse for you."

The sergeant dragged Jeremiah, now silent and small looking, away into the shadows. The circle broke up, and Nathaniel pulled out his fife, preparing to play the tattoo—the call to send all men to their tents and to quiet until morning reveille.

"What does a court martial bring?" Nathaniel asked Basil, hoping that justice would finally come to Jeremiah—some public humiliation that would put him in his place.

"Most like a flogging, lad. 'Tis barbaric, but the way of it."

A flogging? Nathaniel had thought he'd be put in the

stocks for a day or two—uncomfortable and embarrassing but nothing like a flogging. A flogging tore flesh away. If Nathaniel hadn't stood in Jeremiah's way, he might have made his escape. Suddenly, Nathaniel felt sick inside.

Chapter Thirty-six

THIS WAS NATHANIEL'S chance, his chance to get even. Jeremiah stood whimpering, hands tied, stripped to his waist, shivering in the cold, helpless. The court martial had ordered twenty lashes for stealing and leaving camp without permission.

"Fifer," commanded the sergeant major. "Five lashes, well laid on."

Nathaniel's fingers tightened on the handle of the cat-o'-nine-tails. Its knotted cords were already wet with blood.

He had known this was a duty of the field musicians—to carry out whippings ordered by officers. Since they stood apart—not really officers, not really soldiers—the camp drummers and fifers could mete out physical punishment without fear of retribution during a battle. Or so was the thought. Others darkly joked that it was good drumming practice. All the musicians knew that if they refused to do the whipping, or did it lightly or half-heartedly, they would be punished by receiving the same amount of lashings as the condemned.

Two fifers had already dealt Jeremiah their five strokes. Now it was Nathaniel's turn.

The sight of Jeremiah's torn back nauseated him. And yet, he clung to his anger. Here was the chance to be revenged, and not just on his latest tormentor. Just once, wouldn't it feel good to be the one dealing out the blows rather than the one taking them? To no longer be the one swallowing the pain and the humiliation.

Nathaniel raised the whip and felt the lashes swing round his head. Jeremiah began sobbing.

"Blessed are the merciful: for they shall obtain mercy." His mother's voice whispered in Nathaniel's ear.

He took a deep breath and readied himself to strike.

But the voice came again, that sweet voice that had crept through the Bible, learning, teaching Nathaniel: *"What doth the Lord require, but to love mercy."*

His raised hand started to shake as he hesitated.

"Fifer," shouted the sergeant. "Five lashes or you will receive the same."

Nathaniel nodded. "Aye, sir." He wasn't about to take a lashing to save the hide of this cruel, arrogant boy. This boy who raised himself up by putting others down. Nathaniel closed his eyes against seeing his blow do its work.

"Let he who is without sin cast the first stone."

Nathaniel had stolen. And from the very person who had saved him from abuse. His mind raced.

What had Mistress Maguire said to him? That to be truly free of its pain, he had to leave the past in the past. It must not rule the way he chose to behave today. Jeremiah was not the merchant, the planter, the blacksmith, Edan Maguire, or even his father who had left him behind. He was just Jeremiah, a stupid, blubbering bully, who was terrified.

Nathaniel had felt similar terror. If he made someone else suffer that kind of agony, then he was just as bad as those who had done it to him. And it would be yet another instance of someone forcing Nathaniel to do something against his will, to do something he didn't believe in. He had changed. He had his own mind. This growing revolution promised that he could use it.

Nathaniel lowered his hand. He planted his feet firmly and looked directly at the sergeant major. "I will not, sir."

"Fifer, you will do as you are told or suffer the same sentence," barked the sergeant major.

"I understand." Nathaniel's voice sounded as if it came from someone else.

The sergeant motioned to two soldiers. Nathaniel was led to Jeremiah's side. As the men pulled down his hunting shirt and woolen scarf, Nathaniel realized that the linsey-woolsey shirt his mother had sewn and he still wore underneath would be bloodied. "Wait, please," he murmured, and pulled the shirt off, folding it carefully. He looked about to the men witnessing the court martial and found Basil's ashen face in the crowd. "Master, will you hold this, please?" he called.

Stumbling through the men, Basil came to him. "Lad," he whispered, his voice quaking, "you needn't take this scurrilous boy's lashings."

No, he needn't. But for some strange reason he couldn't explain, Nathaniel was going to.

The drum major called up the next two fifers—one for Jeremiah, one for Nathaniel. "Five lashes, well laid on!"

Jeremiah sobbed louder. Nathaniel heard the whistle of the lashes as the boy musicians snapped the whip back without a moment's hesitation. He sucked in his breath. He tried to adopt the same attitude that he had always had before—that it didn't matter, he wouldn't feel it, he was beneath caring or feeling anything, almost as if he didn't exist. But Nathaniel was no longer that subservient boy. He cared. He made do instead with sheer stubbornness and the memory of what

Moses had said about the whipping awaiting him—a lash might cut his skin, but it could not harm his mind now that it was free. Armed with that, Nathaniel braced himself.

There was a whine of the whip slicing the winter air as the blow landed. Nine lines of pain seared his back. Nathaniel gasped, staggered, as the earth spun in front of him. He vaguely saw Basil covering his face with his hands.

"Wait! Hold!" John Marshall stepped forward. He had been one of the twenty-four officers sitting in the military tribunal. "I wish to speak for this boy."

"Lieutenant Marshall," warned a senior officer, "you are out of line. This is the prescribed punishment for such insubordination. And the order of twenty lashes for stealing is merciful. Had the drummer been a full-grown man, it would have been forty."

"Yes, sir, I know. But how can we reward the courage of this fifer with a lashing? Isn't this exactly the kind of bravery and resolve we are asking of our soldiers in the face of a superior force?"

The colonel sighed and shook his head. "The consequence for not performing an ordered discipline is a long-standing prescription in the military."

"Yes, but in the *British* Army, sir. The very same army that makes its foot soldiers wear red coats so that when they are shot in battle, their blood will not show—that's how little regard they have for individual human life. I am fighting against such attitude, sir."

The crowd murmured and shuffled, agreeing.

"Marshall, you are spreading sedition. I will not have it."

Marshall put his hands on his hips and looked to the ground for a moment before continuing. "May I argue this boy's case instead? Is not this court martial still sitting?"

The colonel hesitated, and then nodded. "Yes, it is. Proceed."

"Aren't we fighting to allow a man to have a voice in his governance? We're asking our fellow Americans to stop blindly accepting; to speak up for their rights. Isn't the very heart of our struggle to abolish arbitrary judgments of arrogant aristocrats and laws that give no thought to individual liberties? We see that as tyranny. Why should we simply repeat the harsh rules of the British Army? These men are volunteers, choosing to risk themselves to free their country. Look at my shirt, sir. It calls for liberty or death. We risk all for liberty. This," he pointed at Nathaniel, "this is not liberty."

"Lieutenant Marshall, you make your point with eloquence, but you do not convince. If we are to defeat the British, we must have discipline. We cannot have our soldiers thinking for themselves in battle. We can worry about rewriting military law after we have won." He nodded to the sergeant to restart the lashing.

"No. Wait!" Marshall stood fast. "Then let me plead for leniency. For mercy. Let mercy be a check and a balance on our judgment. I have seen this boy"—he gestured to Jeremiah—"beat this one, fifer Nathaniel Dunn, for no reason other than for sport. The fact that Nathaniel will refuse to raise his hand against his enemy, when that enemy is already laid low, should be an example to all of us. Let us be different. Let us make our point swiftly and judiciously, without crushing a man's spirit. Both these boys bleed. I think they have learned well what we desire to teach."

A captain whispered in the colonel's ear. The colonel turned to another officer and talked with him. After a few more moments of excruciating waiting, the colonel said, "Release the drummer and fifer. Bring out the next prisoner and continue."

Back at their tent, Basil washed the welts on Nathaniel's back. "Some of these are broken open, lad. I wish I had not used up my salt ration. I need salt to cleanse these gashes."

"I can help." Nathaniel looked up to see the pock-faced man. His hands were cupped, holding something.

"My mess collected our salt for the boy."

"Thank you, sir. That is generous of you."

The man grunted and knelt. "This will burn, boy. But it will heal. Ready?"

Nathaniel nodded.

The man pressed the salt into the cuts. Nathaniel about screamed from the sting. He doubled over, shuddering, but he only shed a few tears.

"Ah, lad." Basil put his hand atop Nathaniel's head. "You amaze me." Gently he covered Nathaniel with a blanket before standing up. "Thank you for your help." He extended his hand to shake the man's and introduced himself.

"The boy's name is Nathaniel?" the man asked.

"Aye."

"Dunn?"

"Yes. And your name, sir? So that we may know our friend?"

"Smith," the man blurted. "I go by Smith." Abruptly, he turned and left.

Nathaniel paid no heed. Exhausted, he slipped into the deep sleep that comes after trouble is over, and with a clear conscience of having done the right thing.

PART TEN

December 1775

Torn from a world of Tyrants,
Beneath the western Sky,
We formed a new Dominion,
A Land of Liberty;
The world shall own we're freemen here,
And such will ever be,
Huzzah! Huzzah! Huzzah!
For love and Liberty. . . .

Lift up your Hearts, my heroes,
And swear, with proud disdain,
The wretch that would ensnare you
Shall spread his net in vain;

Should Europe empty all her Force,
We'd meet them in array,
And shout Huzzah! Huzzah! Huzzah!
For Brave America!

—"Free America," words attributed to Boston patriot Dr. Joseph Warren, set to the tune "The British Grenadiers"

Chapter Thirty-seven

NATHANIEL'S BACK ACHED. He rolled over, trying to get comfortable, but the marshy, damp ground and the frigid December night air wove a blanket of cold around him. Teeth chattering, he crawled out of the tent and stretched, wincing as the movement pulled taut the welts on his back. He might as well give up on sleep. He peered into the night, trying to find the figure of Basil, who had sentinel duty. There he was, pacing and stamping along the corner of the Great Bridge Chapel, around which the 2nd Regiment and Culpeper Minutemen, about seven hundred men total, had camped.

Great Bridge. Nathaniel snorted as he made his way across the high saw grass, slick and crunchy with frost. He didn't see what was so great about this place. Twelve miles south of Norfolk, the forty-yard-long wood bridge stretched over the Elizabeth River and was, indeed, one of the few in Virginia. But the places it connected! At each end were islands of land, thrown into the vast sea of the Dismal Swamp, with ink-black waters, rotted trees, vile-smelling mud, and tangles of vines. Walk into that, Nathaniel speculated, and leeches and water snakes would get you quick. Mosquitoes were sure to be vicious in the summer.

Still, the road was the only land approach from North Carolina, the only way for that colony's tar, pitch, turpentine, and lumber to go directly to Norfolk's shipbuilders. As a result, Great Bridge had become a decent-sized hamlet on the southern side of the bridge, with a church, a mill, and about twenty houses in between.

To hold the bridge, Dunmore built a log fort on the Norfolk side, studding it with four-pound cannons and swivel guns. Inside he posted elite British grenadiers plus turncoats of the Queen's Own Loyal Virginia Regiment and Lord Dunmore's Royal Ethiopians. Colonel Woodford estimated they numbered two hundred and fifty.

Despite the Americans' superior numbers, a direct attack on the fort would be sure death. The bridge was only about eight feet wide, the causeway approaching it little more than a narrow dike. Anyone approaching the fort that way would be easily gunned down, hemmed in by natural barriers.

So instead, Woodford prepared for a siege. He

ordered his men to cut logs and construct a barricade across the road, facing the bridge and the fort. Built in a sagging M shape, the breastwork was seven feet high and about one hundred and fifty feet in length. Off to the left, on a higher embankment, the Virginians piled dirt, mud, and logs as a battery for cannon—*if* the guns ever arrived with the North Carolina militiamen supposedly on their way to reinforce them.

The two armies settled into a stalemate of skirmishes. As the patriots worked, the British fired their cannon. Culpeper riflemen shot back, hiding behind the cluster of houses closest to the bridge.

As Nathaniel neared Basil, he could hear the old man moaning as he shivered, creating a kind of trembling hum. His breath made billows of smoky vapor in the frigid air, like a smoldering dragon. He heard Nathaniel coming and swung around, alarmed, dropping his musket with a clatter.

"Nathaniel! You frightened the life out of me."

"Forgive me, master." Nathaniel picked up the musket and handed it to Basil. He wondered what in the world the old schoolmaster would do if truly confronted by enemy soldiers. Perhaps Nathaniel should just sit Basil's watch with him.

"I've two more hours on my watch, lad. No need for you to stand out in the cold."

"It's all right," Nathaniel replied. "It's not as if it's warm in the tent. We've no straw. I was lying on mud. I might as well have been on a slab of ice. Besides, master, two pairs of eyes will keep a better watch."

It was a cloudy night, and the swamp coughed up a drifting fog. But in the splotches of moonlight, Nathaniel could see Basil's relief.

"I need to pace that way." Basil pointed toward the bridge. Nathaniel nodded and followed him, winding their way through the deserted houses.

He noted how stiffly Basil shuffled. His shoes worn thin, Basil had wrapped them in rags to protect his feet from the wet. But Nathaniel knew they were soaked. Just walking from the tent to the church had left his own toes damp, the wet from the grasses quickly saturating the thin leather of his shoes and seeping through his woolen stockings. Nathaniel was immensely grateful for the shoes Mistress Maguire had given him the previous year—tight and cracked as they were. Many of the men had none at all.

"Stop," Basil whispered. "There it is again. Listen, Nathaniel. What do you think that is?"

They stood rooted. In the cold night along the waters, sounds traveled far, couriers of nature's doings. Nathaniel could hear a slight breeze pushing bare branches about, rattling, the rhythmic lapping of the river along its banks as its tide meandered southward. He cupped his hand behind his ear and strained to capture more, but there was nothing. . . . Wait . . . that was odd . . . a *kerplunk,* as if a large fish had just jumped out of the water and splashed back in. But that was a sound of summer—no fish played about in frigid December waters.

Basil and Nathaniel eyed each other nervously.

"Back home in Scotland," Basil breathed, "there are many tales of monsters lurking in the lochs. In such an eerie place as this, it is easy to imagine such things."

Kerplunk. Kerplunk.

Clouds passed across the moon's face and blackened the earth. Basil disappeared from Nathaniel's view, even though he was mere steps away.

The world was silent again, nothing save the wind and water. Where had he heard something like that *kerplunk* before? Where? Nathaniel puzzled.

It came to him like a slap to the face—boats! That was an oar going into water.

Nathaniel gasped, turning into the night, trying to see Basil. "Master, we need to—"

But at that very moment, Nathaniel felt shadows brush past him. There was the muffled sound of something rushing through grasses.

Heart pounding, Nathaniel held his hands out and felt his way to the edge of a building. "Master?" he whispered, creeping along the wall. He sensed a body pressed up against the house just ahead of him and made his way toward it.

A flash of light. Nathaniel saw a ball of fire lurch up from the ground, somersaulting over and over itself until it crashed into the roof of a house. Immediately the thatching caught flame.

He heard more rustling. Another ball of flame jumped up. That roof flared. Torches. Someone was throwing torches onto the roofs to set the town ablaze!

He had to warn the camp! Hurry! Nathaniel reached into his pocket for his fife, desperately trying to remember the call to arms. Would his chilled fingers work the notes? Hands trembling he lifted the little wooden alarm to his lips. He blew, but his numb lips only spluttered. He tried again.

"No, you don't," hissed a deep voice in the darkness. Huge, strong hands grabbed Nathaniel's throat, knocking the breath out of him. The hands starting squeezing, shaking him. "No, you don't."

Choking, coughing, Nathaniel dropped his fife. He grabbed onto the hands, tore at the fingers locked around his throat. Tears of pain ran down his face. Needles of light pierced his vision as he fought passing out.

"No, you don't," the voice kept repeating.

Nathaniel felt his feet being lifted off the ground.

Kick! his mind screamed. *Kick, or you're going to die!*

Nathaniel flailed, feeling like his neck was about to snap. One of his kicks landed a blow. He felt himself topple over, the hands still wrapped around his throat like a hangman's noose. A knee was on his chest, pressing him to the ground.

Nathaniel gasped for air, but sucked in nothing. His chest felt like it was going to explode. He tried to scratch the hands around his throat, but he could no longer feel his own arms move. This was the end.

A ball of fire shot up over his head. Nathaniel felt the torch's burning brightness light up his face. But he could no longer see. He was dying.

Nathaniel!

He heard his name. Oh, so far away it sounded. Was his mother calling him? Suddenly the hands let go his throat. Nathaniel felt himself lifted and dragged.

He must be dead. These were either angels or devils carting him to heaven or hell. He tried to recite the Lord's Prayer. *Mother, speak for me,* he thought.

"Nathaniel!" The voice spoke again, but this time it sounded closer. He felt himself dropped and his shoulders being shaken. "Breathe, boy. Don't let me have killed you."

Nathaniel began to feel air coming . . . in . . . out . . .

in . . . out. He forced his eyes open. His eyelids felt as if they weighed a hundred pounds.

The clouds drifted away from the moon. Nathaniel could just barely see a face hovering over his.

"Thank God." The voice sighed. "Breathe, boy."

"Moses?"

The face smiled. "That's right. You be all right now. Lord, have mercy. I almost killed you, boy. I never would have forgiven myself. Never."

Nathaniel focused more clearly. Moses wore a simple, frocked uniform. On his shirt were painted the words "Liberty to Slaves."

"Moses?" Nathaniel was so confused.

"Ensign Moses! Look at me, Nathaniel, a soldier in the Royal Ethiopian. Now, rest a minute. I be back to take you."

"Where?"

"To liberty, boy. Across the river with the British. Ain't you heard? Lord Dunmore say indentured servants what fight for him go free, too. There's an indentured man run off from George Washington with us. He's good for information about that fellow. May lead us up the Chesapeake right to Washington's house to capture his wife as hostage. They be glad to hear what you know about the soldiers camped here." Moses stood up.

"But, Moses, I'm a fifer with Virginia's Second Regiment."

"That man you calling master sell you into his fight?"

"No, Moses. It's not like that. I'm free now. I chose to fight."

Moses crossed his arms in disgust. "You going to fight for people who whine for their own liberty and keep me in chains?"

"But . . . but," Nathaniel struggled. Moses was right. How could they justify that? "But Moses, Dunmore owns dozens of slaves. Has he freed them? Hasn't he sent back slaves who've run to him who belong to loyalists? Right back to God knows what punishment? Didn't he turn you away when you tried to help him at the palace? Don't trust him, Moses. He's deceitful. He set a trap in the magazine that near killed me. Don't fight for him."

"You want me to fight for slave masters?"

"Aw, Moses, it'll be different when we're done with this fight. How could it not be? You'll see. I'm sure that—"

A musket shot interrupted him. "To arms!" It was Basil's quavering, shrill voice. "To ar—"

There came an answering musket shot. Voices

began to shout around the tents. A fife began calling into the night.

"Moses!" Nathaniel struggled to his feet. "The camp is up."

Moses grabbed Nathaniel's arm. "Can you run, boy? Here. I'll carry you."

"No!" Nathaniel pushed him off. "I can't go with you. Join me, Moses. Join the patriots. Take off that British uniform before they see you." He held up his hands imploringly.

"No." Moses stepped back, shaking his head. "This shirt is my liberty. You come with me."

Stunned, baffled, the two friends stared at each other in bitter disappointment.

"There! Stop them!"

Nathaniel looked back and saw dozens of Virginians rushing to fight whatever was in the night. And there was Moses. All alone. None of his regiment in sight. No British grenadiers to stand for him.

Great God! He didn't want to think about what the regiment might do to him. Nathaniel shoved Moses. Shoved him into shadows. "Run, Moses. Run!"

His friend hesitated.

"Run!" Nathaniel pushed him again then turned and darted toward the oncoming Americans. "They went this way," he called, pointing in the opposite direction of Moses. "This way. Hurry! I saw more of them with torches! Dozens of them, I think!"

Believing, the men ran. Glancing over his shoulder as he followed, Nathaniel saw Moses had disappeared.

He slowed and stopped, winded, heartsick, wondering if he'd ever see his friend again. So many sudden, forced good-byes between them. And now their separate quests for liberty could make them enemies. How could that be?

Nathaniel covered his face. The world made no sense!

When he was indentured, he hadn't tried to understand anything, he just had to survive it. How was he going to be responsible for himself, how could he make the right choices, if he couldn't understand the workings of the world or the adults who ran it?

If ponies rode men and if grass ate the cows . . . then all of the world would be upside down. . . . Basil's song came to Nathaniel. Basil! Basil could explain it to him.

Then, like a kick to his stomach, Nathaniel remembered the sound of Basil's voice in the dark, cut short.

Where was Basil?

Chapter Thirty-eight

NATHANIEL FOUND BASIL sprawled on the ground, holding his head. Several men were huddled beside him.

"Lad! You're alive! Thank goodness! I was frantic with worry when I couldn't see you!" Basil's excited shouts completely echoed Nathaniel's thoughts. Basil tried to stand up, but toppled over, dazed. One of the men caught him. "Oh my," swooned Basil. It was then Nathaniel saw that blood flowed down his face.

"Master, are you hurt?" Nathaniel cried.

"A bit," Basil murmured. "Although I can't recall how exactly."

"Someone's cracked his skull open with the butt of a musket," the man holding him explained. "But your old friend is the hero of the night. Sounded the alarm, he did, and saved this town from burning—maybe even our camp from burning. I say three cheers for Mr. Wilkinson, eh, lads?" he sang out to the men who were beginning to gather around, back from their chase of redcoats, all of whom had disappeared back into the night.

"Huzzah!" the men crowed.

Looking completely perplexed, Basil modestly said, "Oh, it was nothing, my friends. Nothing at all. Nothing you wouldn't have done." He looked as if he would fall flat on his face.

Nathaniel rushed to help prop him up, and Basil grinned at him like a drunkard. "Me a hero. Imagine, lad! Oh, marvelous." His grin disappeared and he touched his fingertips to the steady trickle of blood coming down his face. "I say, though, Nathaniel, wicked headache. Do you suppose Mistress Maguire has something for this?" He fainted. Nathaniel buckled, trying to hold him aright.

"Here, lad." One of the burly frontiersmen scooped Basil up and carried him in his arms like a baby back to the camp hospital. Nathaniel skipped anxiously along behind. "Don't worry, lad," said the soldier. "He'll just have to sleep it off for a day or two."

While Basil recuperated, very proud of the twelve stitches in his head, the Americans and British continued to spar with one another.

Moses's raiding party had been small, sent by the

British to flatten the town's houses to provide their fort a clearer line of fire. They torched five buildings. But thanks to Basil, the rest remained standing. All the Ethiopians and loyalists had slipped back into the darkness without being caught. To retaliate, Colonel Woodford sent a scouting party across the river the next night. They burned a few buildings themselves and returned unharmed. Another evening, John Marshall led a quick hit-and-run raid across the causeway, returning safely fifteen minutes later.

During daylight hours, riflemen fired at any redcoated grenadier who appeared atop the fort's battlements. The British occasionally hurled a cannonball at the American breastworks. Neither side accomplished a thing in the standoff that seemed like it could go on forever.

It came to a point that a cannon being fired caused little reaction among the Virginians. One morning, at dawn, that became a mistake.

Nathaniel and the other musicians had just finished playing reveille.

KABOOM!

"There 'tis," muttered one of the drummers, "the redcoats' morning salute."

"Don't you think they could leave off and save it for

a proper battle?" complained another. Unimpressed, the musicians began to disperse.

Pop . . . pop . . . pop . . . pop.

Nathaniel paused. Another skirmish. Out of curiosity and nothing else to do, he trotted toward the bridge just to see what was up. Within ten steps, his mouth dropped in horror. Marching across it was an endless red surge of British grenadiers, six abreast, row after row of them, bayonets fixed and glinting in the dawning light.

BOOM!

A cannonball hit one of the houses near camp. Shingles and timbers flew. The house collapsed, exploding into a blaze.

How could it be? Somehow, in night's darkness, the British had pulled their four-pounder to the end of the bridge without being seen. Now everything in the camp—everybody—was in full range of its blast.

"Boys! Stand to your arms! To arms!"

Suddenly, the camp swarmed with men yanking on their breeches and scrambling to load their muskets as they ran to the barricades. Dodging, sprinting, knocked down by men hurrying, Nathaniel fought his way back to the musicians.

He careened to a halt beside the other fifers.

Fighting to keep the fife level against his shivering lips, Nathaniel played the oddly serene tune of eighth and quarter notes. Shouldn't he be blaring out a screaming run of sixteenth notes to reflect the terror, the urgency, the lunacy of facing down lifelong soldiers from the best-trained army in the world?

Pop-pop-pop-pop.

CRACK . . . crack, crack, crack.

BOOM!

The musicians played the music's repeat as billows of smoke began to collect along the bridge from the gunfire.

"All right, lads," shouted the drum major. "Find your company and stand your ground. Listen for my calls."

Nathaniel looked around, unsure of where to go. Everyone had scattered so quickly to take a position. He could see the tall figure of John Marshall and other Culpeper Minutemen dashing to the embankment to the left of the bridge. The 2nd Regiment must be at the breastwork facing the oncoming redcoats.

He joined the chaos of darting, shouting patriots. Grown men with long legs outran him. He slowed to give way. They were far more needed than he. And how much use would he be without Jeremiah? The drum and fife worked together in battle. And the drum was definitely more important if the troops needed to make a flanking movement. Like Basil, Jeremiah was in the camp's hospital, convalescing with the sick, his back still raw.

But when Nathaniel reached the breastwork and squeezed himself into the protection of its shadow, there was Jeremiah. His drum was in position, held with a strap across his back. He was obviously in pain. However, when he saw Nathaniel, he nodded in a kind of salute.

Startled, Nathaniel nodded back.

Peeping around the men and breastwork, Nathaniel saw that the situation was even worse than he had imagined. A vanguard of British was marching through the dense smoke from blazing buildings. Behind them came grenadiers, in perfect parade formation, marching to the cadence of two drums. Waiting on the far side of the bridge to follow were The Queen's Own loyalists.

Terrified, Nathaniel tried to steel himself by the shouts of the older men. But they were flustered, too.

"Why didn't we see them coming?"

"I can't believe they're coming straight across the causeway!"

"How did we miss their moving the cannon so close?"

"Can anyone tell their number?"

"Great God! There are hundreds of them. Could

they have marched here from Norfolk last night?"

The line began to waver. Some of the men lowered their muskets, gaping, terrified. Others began to instinctively inch backward, almost in a trance of fear. Nathaniel could feel the urge to flee tingling through them all.

"Steady, boys, steady." A calm voice broke the spell.

It was Basil, head bandaged, a tranquil smile on his face! He spoke in a soothing voice, much like the tone Nathaniel took with spooked horses: "They are hemmed in by the bridge and the swamp, poor fools. If we keep our heads, lads, we can knock them down like ninepins." There was something about his logic, something about an old man standing among them, wounded but confident, that reassured them.

The men took in deep breaths, swelling their chests, filling up the words embroidered on many of their shirts: *Liberty or Death*.

"Give me liberty or give me death." That was the stark choice Patrick Henry had laid before them, the stark reality of Dunmore pronouncing them traitors. It had to be their credo.

They held.

"Make ready!" a distant British voice shouted. The grenadiers stopped and aimed.

"Get down, boys! Get down!"

"FIRE!"

A hail of lead whistled toward them. Nathaniel crouched and gritted his teeth, hearing bark and wood fly as the balls met their shield of logs. He remembered too well what those little pieces of lead felt like when they hit.

The Virginians popped up, took aim, and fired back.

Crack, crack, crack, crack.

Smoke and the stench of gunpowder choked them all.

"Reload!" shouted a regiment lieutenant. "Reload!"

In flurried unison, voices muttering curses and prayers, the line of Virginians reached into boxes at their waists. They pulled out cartridges, bit off the tops—spitting them out in a shower. Shaking hands poured powder into their muskets' pans.

Scraaaaaaaaape. Dozens of ramrods scratched along musket barrels, cramming cartridges down into the explosive powder.

Click, click, click, click. Flintlocks cocked.

Within twenty seconds, the men were reloaded and took aim. Waiting, the overwhelming sound was of the men panting.

"Hold your fire! Hold your fire until they are within fifty yards!"

On the British redcoats came, drums beating. Their faces were beginning to be visible—perfectly shaved, determined faces, no emotion on them. In front of them marched a tall, lanky captain, his face set, grim.

"Fire!"

CRRRRRRACK . . . crack . . . crack . . . crack.

A thunderous echo of shots rang out. Redcoat after redcoat fell, grasping at their sides, their legs, their heads. The front ranks flattened into piles of groaning men. The British captain crumpled too, holding his knee.

The Americans paused. Surely, so bloodied, they'd stop.

But the English captain was not about to give up.

Stunned, the Americans watched him pull out a white handkerchief and wrap it around his knee. Almost instantly, it soaked through with blood. He straightened up, took off his hat, and waved it. "Remember our ancient glory, men!" the captain shouted. "The day is our own!"

The British grenadiers climbed over their wounded and marched on.

"Reload! Reload now!" shouted the Americans.

"Fire!"

"Fire!"

The barrage was deafening. Nathaniel looked to Basil, who was shouting something he couldn't hear.

The British kept dropping, kept coming, following their captain.

"Good God! They're almost on us!"

Crack . . . crack . . . crack . . . crack.

Finally, a mere fifteen feet from the barricade, the British captain fell, riddled with bullets.

Without him, the grenadiers broke. They scrambled backward, crushing one another in their rush and the confines of the narrow bridge.

From the left came a whooping onslaught of Culpeper riflemen, clambering over their embankment to take cover farther down, nearer the bridge. They opened up on the British. The British returned fire.

It was a fifer's duty to drag the wounded out of battle. With the gunfire now off to the side of them, Nathaniel remembered that job. Looking about, he saw that all the patriots seemed fine. Only one was nursing a wound to his hand. Basil was helping him.

Several other Virginians crawled from behind the barricade to pull wounded British to safety. Nathaniel wriggled out to help. Coming around the edge of the logs, Nathaniel staggered to a halt. Blood was everywhere. Bodies were broken and writhing. He doubled over and retched.

"Here, boy. Pull yourself together. Help me!" One of his company was dragging a young redcoat.

Nathaniel hesitated, still sickened.

"Quickly, lad! Before the firing starts again!"

The thought of being completely exposed to musket

balls kicked Nathaniel into action. He grabbed the redcoat's collar and pulled.

"Don't scalp me! Please, don't scalp me!" the redcoat screamed.

Settling him behind the barricade, the patriot answered, "What, man? I am no savage. Who told you we would scalp you?"

"Lord Dunmore told us to fight to our death because if any of us were captured, you would scalp us out of spite, like Indians."

The patriot laughed. "Well, we are warlike, man. We will stand against you. But don't believe everything you are told. I'd heard that you lobsterbacks all had horns, flesh-and-blood devils. I see none on you."

Crack-crack-crack-crack.

Nathaniel flattened himself to the ground. The battle's smoke enveloped him. He waited for more death to rain. He waited . . . waited.

Through the gunpowder fog came a muffled shout—"Cease firing! Cease firing!"—and the sound of a lone fife, singing out peace.

Awash in relief, Nathaniel stood to take up the cease-fire song. Here, there, there again across the line of battle, the high-pitched song of the fife called an end.

It was the most beautiful music Nathaniel had ever played.

Chapter Thirty-nine

WHEN THE BATTLE'S smoke drifted away across the swamp, the patriots found seventeen British grenadiers dead, forty-nine wounded. Every American—save the one with the slight wound to his hand—was completely unharmed.

Dunmore had called for such a foolhardy head-on assault because he was confident that the Virginians would turn tail and run. Well, the twenty-minute battle had proved him wrong. The patriots could stand their ground and stand it well. It was an astounding victory for the untrained little army.

The British abandoned the fort that night. The patriots' way to Norfolk was now clear.

Among the captured were two dozen escaped slaves of the Royal Ethiopian Regiment. Trying to be inconspicuous, Nathaniel anxiously walked through them as they sat on the ground. Moses was not there. Nor was he among the dead. Nathaniel could hope he was still a free man.

With sorrow he watched the Ethiopian soldiers as they were handcuffed together in a long chain that bound them with the loyalist prisoners. Once again slaves, they were to be marched back to Williamsburg to be reclaimed by their owners or to be sold in the West Indies.

Moses's words haunted him: *You going to fight for people who whine for their own liberty and keep me in chains?*

Nathaniel tried to think instead about the heroics of an African who'd fought with the Americans. A freeman named Billy Flora had been one of four sentries keeping watch that morning. While the other three fired once into the thick rows of British and then retreated, Billy loaded and fired eight times before running across a plank to the breastwork in a barrage of bullets aimed specifically at him. He even stopped and pulled the board up behind him, preventing the redcoats from using it, before taking cover.

Moses was brave like Billy Flora. Oh, if only Moses could join them! How Nathaniel wished he could make it so he could. Surely men like Patrick Henry or Thomas Jefferson—men who spoke so eloquently and heatedly about human dignity and rights—would see the injustice of keeping other people in slavery. The only answer Nathaniel could see was to win their fight against the British first. And then, surely, surely, patriot leaders would right that wrong.

Nathaniel turned his eyes away from the prisoners and hurried away, needing to clean himself up as best he could. The whole regiment had been ordered out to give the fallen British captain—who had led the grenadiers so valiantly—a full-honors funeral to pay homage to his courage.

A few days later, sitting by their tent, Basil elbowed Nathaniel. "Look at all these boys, lad." They were watching three newly arrived companies of Patrick Henry's 1st Virginia Regiment and several hundred North Carolinians try to find dry space for their tents. With their number now swelled to over a thousand fighters, the patriot army would march on Norfolk soon.

"As the twig is bent, so is the tree inclined," Basil quoted one of his many proverbs. "Now that we've shown we can actually survive a fight with British regulars, more men will join our ranks. We might actually have a chance, Nathaniel. We might actually."

Basil pulled out his precious copy of *Robinson Crusoe*. "Do you remember when Robinson takes on twenty cannibals with only himself, his man Friday, and a few pistols and muskets? Oh, the courage of it. Not unlike untrained farmers or old schoolmasters taking on the world's best-trained army, eh, Nathaniel?"

Nathaniel smiled to himself. No matter how much he wanted to claim himself as a soldier, Basil would forever and always be first a dreamer, second a teacher. Himself, what was Nathaniel?

"Nathaniel Dunn?"

Nathaniel looked up to see the pock-scarred man who'd laid the salt in his wounds from the whipping. "Aye?"

"A word?"

Nathaniel stood. The man grunted and pointed, walking a little distance away from Basil, who was flipping pages and muttering happily to himself.

"Your regiment will be leaving soon."

Nathaniel nodded.

"Some of the Culpeper men, meself included, are to stay behind to secure the fort."

"Aye?" Nathaniel wondered what the man wanted.

The man hesitated and scowled. "Are you the same Nathaniel Dunn what come across the Atlantic on *The Planter* in the year 1772?"

"Aye." How would he know, thought Nathaniel.

"Know you what happened to your father?"

Nathaniel felt his breath quicken. "No. Do you?"

The man nodded. "He was taken to the frontier, beaten to clear acres of dense forest for fields."

"Did he die there?"

"No."

"Well, what happened?" Why was this man being so mysterious? Nathaniel wanted to shake him. "Do you know where he is?"

"Aye," the man growled.

"Where?" Nathaniel nearly shouted.

"Here."

Nathaniel grabbed the man's arm. "Show me!" He pulled on him. But the man stayed rooted, motionless.

Suddenly Nathaniel realized that this man, masked with those horrendous scars, was his father. He dropped the man's sleeve and stepped back.

In silence, they stared at each other. Finally, his father spoke, "I'd always thought those eyes of yours weak, boy. I see steel in them now."

Anger overwhelmed Nathaniel. "Where were you? Why didn't you come for me?"

His father seemed surprised. He answered matter-of-factly: "My heart was dead, boy. Died when they poured your sweet mother into the sea. I wanted to die myself. I almost did. The work about broke me. Then I caught the pox. I was lying from that when the

Indians raided the frontier settlements. They killed everyone at our place and almost scalped me. I think the pox scared the savage off. Probably figured I was death itself."

"Why didn't you come for me then?"

"I didn't know where you were."

"Did you try to find out?"

"No."

"Why not?"

His father shrugged. "Was busy trying to survive. Set meself a cabin in the wilderness where no one could claim me. I only came out when I heard about the Culpeper Minutemen. Gave me the chance to kill Englishmen what done this to me."

Nathaniel reeled from the information. He didn't matter to his father at all then—certainly not enough to search for. His new, hard-won sense of self-worth wavered.

"Oh, oh, Nathaniel," Basil called out excitedly. "I've found it. Such a rousing passage! Come hear it, lad."

Nathaniel felt Basil's hand reach into the waters to pull him up, yet again. The moment of doubt passed. He mattered to Basil. Family didn't have to be blood relations, he reckoned.

Nathaniel called back over his shoulder to Basil: "In a moment, master."

"Does that old man own your time?"

"He did once. I am free of it now."

"So you can join the Culpeper. Then we can go back to the cabin. In the hills, it is, beautiful. I can use your help to clear it."

Nathaniel had oft imagined a reunion with his father. And this was about as good as he'd envisioned—an offer of a future together. And yet, now that it was here, it fell flat. He hardly remembered this man. And this man had left him adrift. It was only the war that had thrown them back together.

Nathaniel heard Basil, exclaiming behind him. "Yes, yes, oh, wonderful!" He was reading, as usual. "What a writer!"

Nathaniel smiled, listening to the old man's delight. Basil had found his courage, just as Nathaniel had. Still, he needed Nathaniel, if nothing else but to help him carry his books on the march.

Nathaniel glanced about at the men of the camp, shabby but determined. They needed him too. They needed his music. Their cause called him.

He looked at his father with renewed confidence. "I am sorry, Father. I cannot stay. I wish to go on with my regiment."

It was hard for Nathaniel to read any expression on his father's face; his scars were so deep and puckered.

But it seemed that he respected the decision. "After this fight is over with, then."

"Aye, Father. Perhaps then we can meet."

His father grunted. "Where would you be?"

Nathaniel hesitated. Where would he be? He thought a moment, not having imagined any "after." He had never before planned for a future. But after a moment, he thought on Basil's courtly good-bye with Mistress Maguire, and on Maria's poem. "I think we will be visiting in Williamsburg."

His father nodded. He held out his hand.

Nathaniel took it, firm, and shook good-bye. "Till then, sir."

"Aye."

Nathaniel watched his father disappear among the soldiers. He took in a deep breath of clean, cold air. He felt it fill him up, brace him, strong and straight. He looked to the sky, to the wispy clouds veiling a pale blue. The color of sky and mist mixed together as the world awoke, just as his mother had described the color of his eyes. It was a beginning, a new day for him, for his country.

Nathaniel had made a choice, no longer afraid of its responsibility, knowing full well that there were no guarantees of happiness or success, just possibilities.

The line about hope his mother so loved came to him, just as it had the day he was sold. The day he had wanted to die of sorrow. The day that Basil came into his life. The day he first heard of the cause of liberty.

Hopes all things? Aye, perhaps now he could.

Author's Note

Mark Twain, that witty American author who wrote both "truthful" journalism and "made-up" fiction, said this about the two: "Truth is stranger than fiction, but that is because fiction is obliged to stick to possibilities. Truth isn't. Fiction," said Twain, "has to make sense."

And there's the challenge of creating a story, not simply reporting it. As we know, real life can make no sense whatsoever! Fiction, on the other hand, has to be believable. Characters must react in ways that are in keeping with their personalities and the circumstances in which they find themselves. This is especially true in historical fiction in which the plot and its moral challenges grow out of the times. The setting, dialogue, and day-to-day details must be accurate.

That being said, history can present a writer with a wonderful and frustrating paradox: it can send the imagination soaring at the same time it hobbles it.

That's because the trick, as Twain so adroitly pointed out, is finding and then sticking to possibilities.

Let me tell you some of how this affected *Give Me Liberty*.

My editor suggested I write about the Revolutionary War. There are many masterworks on that conflict set in Boston and Massachusetts where the physical battles—the shots heard round the world—began. So I aimed my setting instead for Williamsburg and Virginia, where so many of the impassioned and catalyzing words of the Revolution were penned.

One of the first things I discovered was a brief but pivotal battle in December 1775 at Great Bridge, just outside Norfolk where the Chesapeake Bay opens onto the Atlantic Ocean. Some historians equate the battle in importance to Concord. Untrained, ill-fed, ragtag volunteers not only stood up to well-equipped, professional British grenadiers, they completely dominated the skirmish, winning it in a mere twenty minutes. As a result, the Virginians reclaimed the strategically important port town of Norfolk. They broke the momentum of Royal Governor Lord Dunmore and his fleet of warships. Within a few months, Dunmore left Virginia waters altogether. Had Dunmore succeeded in holding Norfolk, he would have cut the colonies in half, bottled up Virginia, and denied General Washington and the Continental Army of the men and food Virginia would supply throughout the war.

It was a perfect climatic ending to a book.

In that battle was another gem of a detail that ignited my imagination. Many runaway slaves fought at the Battle of Great Bridge, not for the Americans, but for Dunmore, as part of his Royal Ethiopian Regiment. They mocked Patrick Henry's slogan, "Liberty or Death"—which the Virginia regiments emblazoned on their hunting shirts—by wearing a sash that read: "Liberty to Slaves." The terrible irony of that insisted I create a slave character with the Ethiopians who had to face off with a close friend fighting with the patriots. So, history quickly provided the inspiration for an ending, two characters, and a moral dilemma. It also presented a theme—how people had to seek liberty in many different ways. It is a perplexing and disappointing reality that white Americans fought for their own freedom while continuing to deny African Americans theirs.

Here's how history boxed me in. I wanted my main character to be young and an indentured servant. There were many indentured servants in America, especially during the early years of the Jamestown settlement, when as many as 40 percent of those colonists were bound property. Many indentured servants were literally worked to death during that time. Those who survived were owed freedom dues as lucrative as fifty acres of land. Such possibilities kept the practice going. Scholars estimate that between 1700 and 1775, half the white European emigrants were free, while 33 percent were indentured and 17 percent were bound-out convicts.

Hoping to start anew, indentured servants sold themselves and their labor for four years or more in exchange for the price of Atlantic passage. Some of them, young boys in particular, did not come willingly. The term "kid-nap" was coined during the mid 1700s. A bank failure sent hordes of people to London, looking for jobs. Many vagrant boys were simply rounded up and put onto boats heading to America. Scores of poor families embarked together, only to find they could be separated and sold apart in the land of opportunity. These boats were mostly cargo ships, so the hold in which they made the six-week passage was dank and disease ridden. If a family member died past the voyage's halfway mark, a child might be responsible for paying off the deceased's passage—his or her time—as well as his own.

However, by the 1770s, slave labor was steadily replacing that of indentured servants in Virginia. So, to stick to possibilities, I spent hours reading ads in the *Virginia Gazettes* announcing the arrival of ships bringing indentured servants to Leedstown. I was looking for tradesmen who truly purchased them.

There I found carriage maker Elkanah Deane. Deane advertised for apprentices and journeymen. He also ran notices about his indentured servant, John Hunter, who ran away three weeks before one of his journeymen, Obadjah Puryer, also disappeared. Sound familiar? Edan Maguire is based directly on Elkanah Deane, who had in fact followed Lord Dunmore from New York to Williamsburg, thinking the association would guarantee him a prosperous business.

Deane purchased a lavish house on Palace Green and announced that he had many fine riding chairs, phaetons, and carriages to sell. He also advertised rooms to rent, fine liquors for sale, and that his wife would take orders for stays. He did spar in the papers with a competitor, who dubbed him "the Palace Street Puffer." His ads requesting payment progressed from respectful to anxious to belligerent, threatening his customers with public exposure of their debt if they did not pay. He clearly was an ill-tempered taskmaster.

As I wrote, I decided to use a fictional name because, as often happens, the character took on a personality and an opinion of his own. As his actions came to parallel the king's oppression of the colonies, the character grew more sinister and paranoid than what I could absolutely verify by his ads.

Still, there is something tragic about Edan and the real-life Elkanah. His decline and bitter disappointment represent how the Revolutionary War destroyed the fortunes of countless merchants. Many did nothing worse than simply try to remain neutral. Others were falsely accused of loyalist activities by rivals or disgruntled servants. A few were tarred and feathered; several were dragged into the woods outside Williamsburg, given mock trials, and scared into running groveling apologies for their opinions in one of the *Gazette* papers; others left what they had spent a lifetime building and fled to England.

In many ways, our revolution against the British king and his Parliament was a civil war. Not everyone wanted a break with England. In fact, had you told leaders such as Thomas Jefferson or George Washington as late as 1770 that within five years they would be fighting for independence, they would have been shocked. Americans were proud to be part of the British Empire. They simply wanted their rights as Englishmen respected and their colonial legislatures to have the same authority as Parliament. Taxation without representation violated those fundamental rights. Had the British Parliament heeded their petitions and been a little less patronizing, less brutal in their response to American protests, we might still happily belong to the United Kingdom. Once the British blockaded Boston and put Massachusetts under military rule, however, there was no turning back.

Even so, it took fourteen months of fighting before colonial leaders could bring themselves to declare independence from their mother country. Throughout the long seven years of the Revolutionary War, a third of the populace was actively loyalist. Another third remained neutral, desperately hoping the conflict would end. Only one in three Americans was a true patriot. They were gentlemen and yeomen, educated and illiterate, hardy, determined, plucky, idealistic—a new breed of man.

Here are the other true facts and people in *Give Me Liberty*.

All protests and confrontations—from the silent march supporting Boston to the marines stealing gunpowder to the patriots burying the British captain with such homage—happened when and where I described. My imagination provided *probable* conversations and characters, based on newspaper accounts, memoirs, and letters of the day. Patrick Henry, Thomas Jefferson, George Washington were in and out of Williamsburg at the times depicted. Patrick Henry's spellbinding oratory did rouse the country to action. After the Revolution, he was distrustful of a strong central (or "Federal") government. Instead he pushed for the Bill of Rights as protection against it and served Virginia several times as governor. Jefferson's interaction with Nathaniel is make-believe, but the third president's musical talents and romancing of his wife were well known.

George Washington, although a strong advocate for the Non-importation Agreements, was not seen initially as the critically important leader he would become. Without his undaunted courage, his steady and steadying commitment, the country clearly would have failed miserably in its quest for liberty.

At that time, Peyton Randolph—a name few know today—was called the father of our country. Speaker of the House of Burgesses, the first president of the Continental Congress, Randolph was the man most trusted to design persuasive policies to prod the king and stabilize the fledgling association of thirteen colonies. Sadly, he died of a stroke in October 1775, shortly after his loyalist brother, John, fled Virginia for England. John left his violin behind for his cousin, Thomas Jefferson. After he died, per his request, John Randolph's body was carried back to Virginia, the land he loved. He is buried beside his brother Peyton in the chapel of the College of William and Mary.

The Supreme Court Chief Justice of the United States, who molded the court into a truly powerful third branch of government, fought with the Culpeper Minutemen during the Battle of Great Bridge. He was a tall, commanding, well-read, enthusiastic nineteen-year-old. His name? John Marshall, the frontiersman I imagine befriending Nathaniel. He was indeed the eldest of fifteen children, known for his convivial nature, hearty laugh, and ability to negotiate squabbles. Alexander Pope was his favorite writer.

President James Monroe was a student at William and Mary in 1775. He was one of a handful of teenagers who stormed the governor's palace to make off with all Dunmore's guns and swords. Peter Pelham was both organist and jailer. Maria Rind; her mother, Clementina; and her cousin John Pinkney lived and championed liberty's cause in their paper. Maria's fate is not as happy as I would have wished. Her cousin died in 1776, and Maria was bound out as a servant to another family.

The character of Ben Blyth grew out of snippets of information about the patriot activities of Williamsburg youth. A number of them did break into the magazine in the early hours of Whitsunday, June 4, 1775. A spring-gun booby trap left by the British wounded two for sure. The only participant named in the newspapers was Beverly Dixon, and he may have been the mayor's son. In a deposition made in 1833, when he was seventy-three years old, Robert Greenhow, son of the Williamsburg merchant, told how he had been part of a company of boys led by a then fourteen-year-old Henry Nicholson. He said the boys raided the magazine and made off with blue-painted stock guns. I included the Guy Fawkes bonfire after seeing an ad run by "an association of protestant boys" stating their plans to host one. I had been looking for something else entirely. See what a surprising and pivotal treasure hunt research can be?

Basil is a mixture of influences, partially found in journals kept by two schoolmasters: John Harrower, an indentured Scotsman, and Philip Fithian, who left New Jersey to tutor Robert Carter's children in the Northern Neck of Virginia. Teachers and musicians were, indeed, jacks-of-all-trades. There was a "surgeon" in Williamsburg who also purchased teeth, taught swordplay, and repaired harpsichords! Basil evolved according to his own demands. He came to represent the palpable excitement of the Age of Enlightenment, the ideas that inspired men to dare all.

Much of Basil and Nathaniel's friendship blossomed from the mechanics of getting fourteen-year-old Nathaniel into the Virginia 2nd Regiment. To join, given his age, he would need to be a fifer. The importance of music within Nathaniel's odyssey, therefore, grew and prompted me to include the many songs patriots wrote to rally the country. Playing or singing in an ensemble can coax shy children like Nathaniel—too reticent to join playground games—into communicating and bonding with their peers. It's like magic. Music speeds Nathaniel's journey to spiritual liberty, much as fife "calls" bring men to duty.

I leave it to you to determine Moses's fate after Great Bridge. Here are the facts that can guide your imagination: five thousand African Americans fought in the colonial patriot forces, with the minutemen, militia, and the Continental Army. There were two famous black regiments: the 7th Massachusetts Regiment and the Rhode Island Regiment. But most African Americans, whether freemen or slaves purchased to be soldiers or substituting for their masters, fought side by side with whites, including forces from Virginia. Toward the end of the war, one fifth of our Northern regiments were African American, making the Continental Army the most racially integrated American force until the twentieth century.

Some of Dunmore's Royal Ethiopians lived to gain their freedom. Eventually five hundred more runaways joined the three hundred who belonged to Dunmore's forces at the time the Battle of Great Bridge took place. But many died of an epidemic of smallpox and fever.

Only three hundred were still alive when Dunmore left Virginia for New York in 1776. Once in New York, the regiment was dissolved.

Tragically, it would take another war to grant African Americans the freedom and equality proclaimed by the immortal words of the Declaration of Independence: "We hold these truths to be self-evident: that all men are created equal; that they are endowed by their Creator with certain inalienable rights; that among these are life, liberty, and the pursuit of happiness." (Despite Abigail Adams's plea to her husband, John, our second president, to "not forget the ladies," it would take even longer before women were considered equal and afforded the right to vote in 1920.)

How could men fight for their own liberty while holding others in chains? Moses raises this with heart-wrenching incomprehension. More specifically, how is it that Thomas Jefferson—the man who penned the eloquent, persuasive words that changed the world—and George Washington—the man who led a people through bloodbaths, starvation, and killing winters to forge a new nation—could be slave owners? It is a baffling and deeply distressing question.

Both Jefferson and Washington professed to abhor slavery. Washington called it "a wicked, cruel, and unnatural trade." He did help create legislation that banned the importation of new slaves and longed for a plan that would abolish slavery altogether "by slow, sure, and imperceptible degrees." In 1789, as president, he signed an ordinance prohibiting slavery in the new Northwest Territories, which eventually became Ohio, Indiana, Illinois, Michigan, Minnesota, and Wisconsin. Hampered by Virginia laws that made it extremely difficult for an owner to release his slaves while he was alive, Washington did free all his servants at his death.

Probably the most moving words Jefferson wrote in his Declaration of Independence condemned slavery. He railed against King George, saying he had "waged cruel war against human nature" by "captivating and carrying" a "distant people who had never offended him" into "slavery in another hemisphere, or to incur miserable death in their transportation thither."

The Continental Congress crossed out those words.

The paragraph was extremely controversial with Southern owners and New Englander shippers who profited from the trade. The delegates wanted a unanimous passage of the Declaration. South Carolina and Georgia refused to sign anything that stated slavery violated "the most sacred rights of life and liberty." So what could have been the beginning of the end for slavery during the Revolution was removed.

Although he never freed his own slaves, Jefferson tried to outlaw the horrific practice again in 1784. He introduced legislation to Congress that would abolish slavery in every state by the year 1800. The motion lost by a single vote.

Just months before his death, the eighty-two-year-old Jefferson acknowledged that he had left the task of freeing a race of people to the next generation. "The abolition of the evil is not impossible," he wrote a young friend. "It ought never therefore to be despaired of."

New ideas and the power of words to spread them spawned the Revolution and our country. It was truly a radical, remarkable notion that every person had the ability and the right to govern himself. It was a hope, a leap of faith in ordinary people that turned the world upside down.

This, of course, is a theme I hope resounds throughout *Give Me Liberty*. I had planned to strike it like a bell at the conclusion, by having Basil read Thomas Paine's *Common Sense*, a fifty-page pamphlet that was published shortly after the Battle of Great Bridge. It was an instant bestseller, read on the street, read to the troops, read to and by all who could get their hands on a copy. In direct, easy-to-understand language, at a time Americans were hesitating about what step to take next, *Common Sense* called for a declaration of independence.

Paine's words ennobled and spurred a nation of people.

But the facts of history stopped me. Given the time it took for news to travel in colonial America, copies of *Common Sense* didn't make it from Philadelphia to Virginia until early February, two months after Nathaniel's story, as I could best tell it, was done.

So instead I will conclude now with some of Paine's stirring words:

"Nothing will clear up our situation so quickly, so efficiently, than that of an open and determined declaration for independence. . . . the blood of those already killed cries out for it. It is time to part. . . .

"Remember that virtue and ability are not hereditary. . . . We have it in our power to begin the world anew. . . .

"Oh, ye that love mankind. Ye that dare oppose not only the tyranny but the tyrant, stand forth. America shall make a stand not for herself alone, but for the world."

Prelude to Revolution

1764–1773

1764 Parliament passes the Sugar Act to raise money to pay for the costs of the French and Indian War. It taxes sugar, textiles, coffee, wines, and indigo dye.

1765 The Stamp Act, the first direct tax of Americans in the 150-year history of the colonies, is passed. All printed goods—newspapers, legal documents, playing cards—must carry a fee-stamp. The Quartering Act requires Americans to house and feed British troops. Outraged, colonists ban together to defy the law. They boycott British goods. In Boston, a radical organization called the Sons of Liberty, is formed. Mobs intimidate stamp collectors.

1766 The Stamp Act is repealed. The Declaratory Acts state that Britain still has the right to pass any laws regarding the American colonies.

1767 The Townshend Revenue Acts impose taxes on paper, tea, lead, and paints.

1768 Massachusetts sends a "circular letter" to all colonies, urging them to boycott British goods. British troops occupy Boston.

1769 The Virginia House of Burgesses passes a resolution opposing "taxation without representation" and the British government's plans to put American protestors on trial in England. The resolution also bans further slave importation.

MARCH 5, 1770 The Boston Massacre. A mob harasses British soldiers with snowballs. The soldiers fire into the crowd, killing five and injuring six.

APRIL 1770 The Townshend Acts are repealed except for duties on tea. The Quartering Act is not renewed.

NOVEMBER 1772 A Boston town meeting sets up a committee of correspondence to communicate with other nearby towns and endorses the concept of self-rule.

March 1773 The Virginia House of Burgesses appoints a committee of correspondence to communicate with other colonies regarding British actions. New Hampshire, Rhode Island, Connecticut, and South Carolina follow suit.

May 1773 The threepenny-per-pound tea tax takes affect. Colonists must buy their tea from the British East India Company, cutting out American merchants.

December 16, 1773 The Boston Tea Party. Colonists disguised as Mohawk Indians dump 342 chests of tea into the Boston Harbor.

1774

Spring Parliament closes the port of Boston until the tea is paid for. It passes the Coercive Acts, ending self-rule in Massachusetts. It occupies Boston with troops.

June 1 Williamsburg observes a day of fasting, humiliation, and prayer in support of Boston. Royal Governor Dunmore dissolves the House of Burgesses.

September 5 to October 26 The First Continental Congress meets in Philadelphia with delegates from every colony except Georgia. Congress passes the Non-importation Agreement to boycott British imports and discontinue the importation of slaves. It promotes the formation of local militia groups.

1775

March 23 Patrick Henry pushes Virginia to create an army, delivering his rousing "Give me liberty, or give me death" speech.

April 18–19 Lexington and Concord. Ordered to suppress rebellion in Massachusetts, General Gage marches seven hundred redcoats to Concord to destroy the colonists' weapons depot. Warned by Paul Revere and other riders, seventy Massachusetts militiamen face them. A "shot heard round the world" begins a skirmish. Eight Americans are killed and ten wounded. Colonists attack the redcoats at Concord and harass them all the way back to Boston, killing or wounding 250.

April 21 In the pre-dawn hours, British marines—acting on the orders of Virginia's Royal Governor, Lord Dunmore—empty Williamsburg's magazine of most of its gunpowder.

April 23 Massachusetts Provincial Congress calls 13,600 American soldiers to surround Boston, beginning a year-long siege of the British-held port.

May 10 American volunteers led by Ethan Allen and Benedict Arnold capture Fort Ticonderoga in New York. The Second Continental Congress convenes in Philadelphia. In June, it unanimously appoints George Washington commander in chief of the Continental Army.

June 17 The Battle of Bunker Hill. In the first major battle of the war, two thousand redcoats storm a Boston hill held by Americans, ordered to not fire until they see "the whites of their eyes." By the third assault, Americans run out of ammunition and flee. The British lose half their number, the Americans four hundred, including an important leader, Dr. Joseph Warren.

JULY 5 The Continental Congress sends "the Olive Branch Petition," once more expressing loyalty to the king and the hope for reconciliation. The next day, Congress also adopts a declaration on the causes and necessity of taking up arms against the British. King George refuses to read the petition and instead declares the Americans to be in a state of open rebellion.

DECEMBER 9 The Battle of Great Bridge. British and Virginia troops clash near Norfolk. The British suffer 40 percent casualties while no American is harmed. The twenty-minute battle prevents the British from controlling the Chesapeake Bay.

1776

JANUARY 5 New Hampshire adopts the first American state constitution.

JANUARY 9 *Common Sense* by Thomas Paine is published in Philadelphia.

MARCH 4–17 American troops capture Dorchester Heights

overlooking Boston. The British evacuate to invade New York.

JUNE 28 South Carolinians deflect a British naval attack at Charleston.

JUNE-JULY New York harbor is occupied by thirty British warships with twelve hundred cannon, thirty thousand soldiers, ten thousand sailors, and three hundred supply ships.

JULY 4 A new United States of America boldly declares its independence through the stirring words: "We hold these Truths to be self evident, that all Men are created equal, that they are endowed by their Creator with certain inalienable Rights, that among these are Life, Liberty, and the Pursuit of Happiness."

It will be another seven long years before the British give up their fight to rule America and the peace treaty ending the Revolutionary War is signed on September 3, 1783.

Bibliography

Histories and Biographies

—Boorstin, Daniel J. *The Americans: The Colonial Experience.* New York: Random House, 1958.

—Coffman, Suzanne E. *Official Guide to Colonial Williamsburg.* Williamsburg, Va: Colonial Williamsburg Foundation, 1998.

—Holbrook, Jay Mack. "Virginia's Colonial Schoolmasters, 1660–1776." Ph.D. diss. Georgetown University, 1966.

—Holton, Woody. *Forced Founders: Indians, Debtors, Slaves & the Making of the American Revolution in Virginia.* Chapel Hill: University of North Carolina Press, 1999.

—Hume, Ivor Noel. *1775: Another Part of the Field.* New York: Alfred A. Knopf, 1966.

—Malone, Dumas. *Jefferson the Virginian.* Boston: Little, Brown, 1948.

—Mayer, Henry. *A Son of Thunder: Patrick Henry and the American Republic*. New York: Grove Press, 1991.

—McCullough, David. *1776*. New York: Simon & Schuster, 2005.

—Morgan, Kenneth. *Slavery and Servitude in Colonial North America*. New York: New York University Press, 2001.

—Selby, John E. *The Revolution in Virginia, 1775–1783*. Williamsburg, Va.: Colonial Williamsburg Foundation, 1988.

—Smith, Jean Edward. *John Marshall: Definer of a Nation*. New York: Henry Holt, 1996.

—Van Der Zee, John. *Bound Over: Indentured Servitude & American Conscience*. New York: Simon & Schuster, 1985.

18th-century Journals

—Dewees, Samuel. *A History of the Life and Services of Captain Samuel Dewees, a Native of Pennsylvania, and Soldier of the Revolutionary and Last Wars*. Baltimore: Robert Neilson, 1844.

—Farish, Hunter Dickinson, ed. *The Journal and Letters of Philip Vickers Fithian, a Plantation Tutor of the Old Dominion, 1773–1774*. Charlottesville: University Press of Virginia, 1957.

—Mays, David John, ed. *The Letters and Papers of Edmund Pendleton, 1734–1803*. Charlottesville: University Press of Virginia, 1967.

—Riley, Edward Miles, ed. *The Journal of John Harrower: An Indentured Servant in the Colony of Virginia, 1773–1776*. Williamsburg, Va: Colonial Williamsburg Foundation, 1963.

—Tarter, Brent, ed. *The Orderly Book of the Second Virginia Regiment*, September 27, 1775–April 15, 1776.

Music

—Camus, Raoul F. *Military Music of the American Revolution*. Westerville, Ohio: Integrity Press, 1975.

—Keller, Kate Van Winkle. *Fife Tunes from the American Revolution*. Sandy Hook, Conn.: Hendrickson Group, 1997.

———. *George Washington: Music for the First President, a companion music book to the recording by David and Ginger Hildebrand*. Sandy Hook, Conn.: Hendrickson Group, 1999.

—Keller, Kate Van Winkle, Mary Jane Corry, and Robert M. Keller. *The Performing Arts in Colonial American Newspapers, 1690–1783 Text Database and Index*. New York: University Music Editions, 1997, CD-ROM.

—Maurer, Maurer. "The Library of a Colonial Musician, 1755." *William and Mary Quarterly* 3 (October 1950): 39–52.

———. "The Professor of Musick in Colonial America." *Musical Quarterly* 36 (1950) 511.

—McNeil, Keith and Rusty. *Colonial and Revolution Songbook*. Riverside, Calif.: WEM Records, 1996.

Everyday Colonial Life

—Bullock, Helen. *The Williamsburg Art of Cookery or, Accomplish'd Gentlewoman's Companion*. Richmond, Va: Dietz Press, 1938.

—Cotner, Sharon; Kris Drippe, Robin Kipps, Susan Pryor. *Physick: the Professional Practice of Medicine in Williamsburg, Virginia, 1740–1775*. Williamsburg, Va.: Colonial Williamsburg Foundation, 2003.

—Gilgun, Beth. *Tidings from the 18th Century: Colonial American How-to and Living History*. Texarkana, Texas: Scurlock Publishing, 1993.

—Flynn, Norma Twilley. *Puttin' on the Dog: A Potpourri of Colonial Sayings and Customs.* Sold in Colonial Williamsburg stores.

Specifically for Young Readers

—Brenner, Barbara. *If You Were There in 1776*. New York: Simon & Schuster, 1994.

———. *If You Lived in Williamsburg in Colonial Days*. New York: Scholastic, 2000.

—Cox, Clinton. *Come All You Brave Soldiers: Blacks in the Revolutionary War.* New York: Scholastic, 1999.

—Egger-Bovet, Howard, and Marlene Smith-Baranzini. *Brown Paper School: U.S. Kids History; Book of the American Revolution*. New York: Little, Brown, 1994.

—Moore, Kay. *If You Lived at the Time of the American Revolution*. New York: Scholastic, 1997.

—Nixon, Joan Lowery. *Maria's Story: 1773*. New York: Delacorte Press, 2001.

—Taylor, Theodore. *Rebellion Town: Williamsburg, 1776*. New York: Thomas Y. Crowell, 1973.

—Wilbur, C. Keith. *The Revolutionary Soldier, 1775–1783*. Guilford, Conn.: Globe Pequot Press, 1969.

Acknowledgments

I AM GREATLY indebted to the many historians who have written such thorough, painstakingly researched accounts of the American Revolution and the thoughts, doubts, hopes, and people who built it. Their books taught me and fueled my imagination.

Re-enactors are "amateur" historians who bring distant times vividly to life. I owe a large thanks to several who spent hours answering my questions, demonstrating their crafts, or guiding me to other sources. Fife major John Glover, of the 1st Virginia Regiment, repeatedly played duty calls and explained the daily life of a Revolutionary camp musician. Todd Post, founder and president of the 2nd Virginia Regiment, generously guided me at the beginning of my research, pointing me to several important primary documents, such as the *Orderly Book of the 2d Virginia Regiment*, kept during the Battle of Great Bridge. The details I gained from them so enlivened Nathaniel's story. Dr. David Hildebrand, of the Colonial Music Institute, also offered advice about sources and the reality of musicians' lives.

There were many with the Colonial Williamsburg Foundation who graciously shared their knowledge: Tim Sutphin, manager of the Williamsburg Fifes and Drums, explained the teaching and customs of fife players and drummers, verified historical elements, and provided costuming for reference. Others who provided valuable information include historians Linda Rowe and Kevin Kelly; Dale Smoot of the gunpowder magazine; wheelwright Chris Wright; and Pete Wrike, an expert on the Ethiopian Regiment who shared information from his pending book, *Slave Soldiers, Gentleman Officers.* My deepest gratitude goes to Juleigh Clark, public service librarian at the John D. Rockefeller Library who patiently and thoroughly answered countless e-mail inquiries from me, helped me negotiate the foundation's astounding digital archive of the *Virginia Gazette* (www.pastportal.com), and located wonderfully rich articles or long-ago testimonials.

As always, my editor, Katherine Tegen pushed me to ask better questions of my characters. If you find value in these pages, thank her.

My children, Peter and Megan, and my husband,

John, are my muses, my devoted and diplomatic fans, my first editors. This book started percolating during our many family trips to Williamsburg as I witnessed my children's delight in the governor's maze, in listening to Patrick Henry and Thomas Jefferson interpreters, and in trying to play instruments and games of the period. Their constant wonderment about the human race and how we have become who we are inspires me to try to understand it myself through writing.

ALSO AVAILABLE

Annie, Between the States

IRA/CBC Teachers' Choice
New York Public Library Book for the Teen Age

"Part Ken Burns' *The Civil War*, part *Gone With the Wind*, Elliott's novel will be devoured by fans of historical fiction."—ALA *Booklist*

"So powerfully drawn that readers will be engaged from chapter one."—*Kirkus Reviews*

"A strong and memorable heroine, romance, and an understanding of both sides of the conflict."
—*School Library Journal*

Praise for *Married Lovers*

"The fabulous *Married Lovers* has plenty of Hollywood women kicking-ass with a trio of new heroes." —*New York Post*

"Sexier, steamier, and more scandalous than ever. Love and lust, where the good get what they deserve and the bad get their comeuppance." —*Daily Express* (London)

"Nothing says summer like lathering on the sunblock, laying on a lounge chair, and pulling a very steamy novel from the queen of romance from your beach bag—Jackie Collins's latest romance, *Married Lovers.*" —NBC's *The Today Show*

Praise for *Lovers & Players*

"Collins is back with another sexy page-turner." —*New York Post*

"A decadent concoction sure to appeal . . . a fast-lane take on the lives of the rich and fabulous." —*Kirkus Reviews*

"A fast-paced, glamour-heavy Collins extravaganza . . . packed with intrigue, revenge, and romance." —*Publishers Weekly*

Praise for *Drop Dead Beautiful*

"Delicious!" —*Cosmopolitan*

"[*Drop Dead*] *Beautiful* may be the best novel starring Lucky Santangelo yet." —*Entertainment Weekly*

"[Collins's] can't-put-it-down style and feisty drop-dead glamorous characters transport us to a beyond-fabulous world. Yet with Jackie as our guide, we feel right at home." —*Glamour*

"[F]euding families and simmering vendettas, punctuated by lusty liaisons. One for fans of *The Sopranos* and *Desperate Housewives.*" —*The Daily Telegraph*

Lucky Santangelo Novels by Jackie Collins

Drop Dead Beautiful

Dangerous Kiss

Vendetta: Lucky's Revenge

Lady Boss

Lucky

Chances

Also by Jackie Collins

Married Lovers

Lovers & Players

Hollywood Divorces

Deadly Embrace

Hollywood Wives—The New Generation

Lethal Seduction

L.A. Connections—Power, Obsession, Murder, Revenge

Thrill!

Hollywood Kids

American Star

Rock Star

Hollywood Husbands

Lovers & Gamblers

Hollywood Wives

The World Is Full of Divorced Women

The Love Killers

Sinners

The Bitch

The Stud

The World Is Full of Married Men

POOR LITTLE **BITCH GIRL**

Jackie Collins

ST. MARTIN'S GRIFFIN ☙ NEW YORK

This is a work of fiction. All of the characters, organizations, and events portrayed in this novel are either products of the author's imagination or are used fictitiously.

www.stmartins.com

The Library of Congress has cataloged the hardcover edition as follows:

Collins, Jackie.
Poor little bitch girl / Jackie Collins.—1st ed.
p. cm.
ISBN 978-0-312-56745-3
1. Upper class—California—Beverly Hills—Fiction. 2. Murder—California—Beverly Hills—Fiction. 3. Beverly Hills (Calif.)—Fiction. I. Title.
PR6053.O425P66 2010
823'.914—dc22

2009039570

ISBN 978-0-312-54882-7 (trade paperback)

10 9 8 7 6 5 4 3 2

For family and friends.

You are the best!

&

For my three incredible,

amazing daughters.

Talented, smart, and caring.

I love you all so much.

1

Annabelle

Belle Svetlana surveyed her nude image in a full-length mirror, readying herself for a thirty-thousand-dollar-an-hour sexual encounter with the fifteen-year-old son of an Arab oil tycoon.

Belle knew she was a beauty. What the hell, enough money had been spent along the way to make sure she was beautiful. A nose job ordered by her mother when she was a mere fourteen, a boob job shortly after—that was *her* decision. And then later, liposuction when needed, lip enhancement, regular facials, and skin-lasering treatments to make certain her skin remained the milky white she'd worked so hard to achieve (getting rid of her freckles had been a bitch, but she'd done it). Ever since her teenage years Belle had strived for perfection, and now she'd gotten pretty damn close. Her hair was a pale golden red, shoulder length and wavy. Her eyes were a spectacular emerald green. Her body—a playground of delights.

Yes, she thought, staring intently at her unabashed nakedness, *I am worth every cent of the thirty thousand dollars cash already neatly stashed in my safe.*

Usually she did not go out on "dates" herself, but Sharif Rani, the oil tycoon, had insisted that it was she who should teach his youngest son the joys of the flesh. So, for a princely sum, she'd finally agreed.

Carefully, she stepped into a peach slip of a dress—powdered, perfumed, and ready for action.

Thirty thousand an hour. Not bad for a job that would probably take her no more than fifteen minutes to complete.

Of course, she could have turned the job down and suggested one of her twenty-thousand-an-hour girls, but sometimes it was fun to play, especially as she could pick and choose among her roster of rich, powerful, and famous clients—which included everyone from Hollywood's biggest stars to several princes, more than one captain of industry, a few superstar rappers, dozens of sports heroes, and too many politicians to count.

Yes, Belle Svetlana, née Annabelle Maestro, ran *the* most exclusive, expensive call girl business in town—the town being New York, as opposed to Los Angeles, the city she'd grown up in, surrounded by luxury and all the opulence two movie-star parents could buy.

Thank God she'd escaped those two egomaniacs—Mom, the ethereal queen of quality independents; and Dad, the macho king of big-budget schlock. What a horror show having *them* as parents.

When she'd dropped out of college in Boston and settled in New York, neither of her loving parents had given a rat's ass. Admitting to a grown daughter did nothing to enhance their public images, so they'd arranged to send her a monthly allowance, blithely told her to follow her dreams, and left her to her own devices.

Annabelle was no slouch when it came to following her dreams; she'd soon found herself caught up in the club-and-party scene—a lifestyle that had satisfied her for a while. Then one night she'd been introduced to Frankie Romano, a popular deejay who worked private parties and the occasional hot club. One look at Frankie and it was lust at first sight.

Originally from Chicago, Frankie was quirky and attractive in a Michael Imperioli kind of way. Fast-talking and edgy, he had longish dark hair, icechip blue eyes, and sharp features.

The trouble with Frankie was that he was usually broke—he was a dedicated cokehead, so whatever money came his way went straight up his nose.

Annabelle fell hard, for in spite of Frankie's drug use, it turned out that he was a star in bed, whenever he wasn't too coked-out to perform. She didn't know anything about his background, and she didn't care. As far as she was concerned, they were soul mates.

After a few weeks of crazy togetherness, Frankie had moved into her SoHo loft, a move she hadn't objected to. The only downer was that eventually she'd found herself spending her entire allowance keeping him in drugs, so it wasn't long before—at Frankie's urging—she'd called her dad in L.A. and requested that her allowance be increased.

Ralph Maestro—the self-made son of a Brooklyn butcher who'd gotten shot by a robber when Ralph was twelve—told her no way. "I made it on my own without two cents to rub together," Ralph had informed her sternly. "We've already given you a head start. If you want more money, I suggest you go out and find yourself a job."

Annabelle was furious. Her parents raked in millions, and Daddy Movie Star was telling her to get a job! Screw them! It was increasingly obvious that they didn't give a damn about her.

A couple of weeks later, she and Frankie had come up with a master plan. They'd been lying in bed reading the lurid headlines about a married politician who'd recently gotten caught having sex with a series of high-priced call girls.

"How stupid is he?" Frankie had ruminated, scratching his skinny butt. "The dumb asshole should've paid cash. That way nobody gets busted, an' everyone goes home happy."

"Cash is good," Annabelle had agreed. "For special girls only."

"Yeah," Frankie had said half-jokingly. "Not some mouthy skank who's gonna sell her story, but *very* special girls. Y'know the kinda babes I mean. Models, actresses—they're always on the lookout for an extra score. An' here's the sweet part of the deal: We know 'em all."

"We sure do."

"So . . ." Frankie had said after a thoughtful few minutes. "You thinkin' what *I'm* thinkin'?"

She was indeed. And so their adventure had begun.

At first they'd both considered it a lark, but after a few months it had turned into one of the most successful call girl businesses in town.

Flushed with success, Annabelle had soon created two identities for herself. One was Annabelle Maestro, a girl struggling to make it in the fashion industry as a sometime designer. And the second was Belle Svetlana (she got off on the exotic sound of the Russian surname), a woman of mystery who was able to supply the right girl to satisfy any man's fantasy.

For a price.

A hefty price, depending on what was required.

Annabelle's girls were not hookers. They were stylish, good-looking career women who enjoyed the extra income. Models, actresses, singers, designers, all classy, smart, and discreet, some of them quite well-known.

It was Annabelle's idea that the girls they recruited should wear masks when they went on jobs, to hide their identities. She was sure the men would get off on the mystery, and the girls were happy, too, imagining that wearing masks would conceal their true identities.

Finding the right girls was no problem. Frankie, a major cocksman before hooking up with Annabelle, knew them all, and he used his considerable way with words to talk them into anything. A shitload of untaxable cash income was the big temptation, and as Frankie pointed out, since most of the girls were fucking for nothing, what was the big deal if they did it and got handsomely paid? Especially if they were able to remain anonymous.

Frankie vetted all their would-be clients, while Annabelle liaised with the girls and arranged the appointments. Between them they pocketed sixty percent of every assignation, and it didn't take long before they were rolling in cash. It was always cash, no paper trails involved.

Now they'd been doing it for almost a year, and what a sweet money-making business it had turned out to be. Neither Annabelle nor Frankie had any complaints—that is, until they both realized they needed help.

After thinking about it for a while, Frankie had recruited Janey Bonafacio, one of his many cousins, who lived in Brooklyn and worked as a bookkeeper. He'd asked her if she'd be interested in working for him, and since she'd always harbored a huge crush on her cousin Frankie, she'd immediately quit her job, and he'd hired her to take care of the phones and schedule the girls' appointments.

Janey, a 275-pound unmarried mother with a nineteen-year-old-son, Chip, was delighted to get the job. Worshipping her cousin from afar was one thing, but actually working for him was a dream come true, even if the business he ran with his snooty girlfriend was fairly dubious.

Annabelle kind of trusted Janey, but she wasn't so trusting when it came to Chip—a surly slacker with way too much attitude and a complaining disposition. Annabelle regarded him as a not-so-charming Frankie-in-training. They used him to run errands and drive the car.

"At least they're family," Frankie had assured her. "They'll never screw us."

"Don't be so naive," she'd retorted. "When it comes to money, everyone has an agenda."

"Hey," Frankie had said, "we're payin' Janey plenty to make *sure* they stay discreet. An' remember this—Janey's got a thing for me, she'd never do anythin' to hurt me."

Annabelle was not so sure.

~ ~ ~

After making certain that she looked her most seductive, Annabelle buzzed downstairs to check that her car was waiting. Her main residence was a Park Avenue penthouse where she and Frankie spent most of their time, but she still kept the SoHo loft; it was the place her parents and old friends could contact her. Not that her parents ever did—she heard from them maybe once every few weeks. And she wasn't really interested in her old friends. She had a new life now, and in her new life very few people knew who her parents were and where she came from. That's the way she liked it.

Earlier in the day, Frankie had driven to Atlantic City to spend the weekend with a couple of his guy friends, Bobby Santangelo Stanislopoulos and Bobby's business partner, M.J. Annabelle knew both Bobby and M.J. from way back when they'd all attended the same high school in Beverly Hills. Yeah, fun times. She'd never forgotten the infamous prom night when the three of them had hung out, gotten totally high, and on a dare she'd ended up making out with the two of them.

Hmm . . . just one of those crazy out-of-control teenage escapades, although it was quite a memorable experience. None of them had ever mentioned it again. It was a no-go zone.

Then one night, years later after she'd moved to New York, she'd walked into Mood, and there they were—Bobby and M.J. At first it was a shock seeing them, but they'd soon got to talking and catching up on old times. In fact, it was M.J. who'd introduced her to Frankie.

She'd never told Frankie about her one night of lust with his two best friends; some things were better left in the past. Besides, she didn't imagine he'd be too thrilled if he ever found out, and when pushed, Frankie had a vicious temper.

Since gambling seemed to be Frankie's new passion, she hadn't objected to him taking off. Her live-in boyfriend was a handful and then some, so she didn't mind the occasional night on her own. Chilling out without Frankie would allow her a pleasant break.

The concierge informed her that her driver was parked outside. She picked up her Chanel purse and headed for the door.

As she stepped out into the hallway, the phone began to ring, but she chose to ignore it. She had a thing about phones, hated answering them. Whoever it was could leave a message.

She left the apartment and descended in the elevator, quite psyched about the prospect of inducting an innocent young man into the joys of sex. His father, Sharif Rani, was one of their best customers. Sharif required a different girl several times a week, and he always came back for more. Annabelle considered Sharif Rani to be a primo client, along with the Hollywood movie star who was an insatiable pussy-hound and the Hall of Fame rock 'n' roller with the nine-inch cock and a penchant for girls who would agree to indulge in bathroom activities all over his craggy face.

"Good afternoon, Miss Svetlana," the concierge said, moving out from behind the long marble counter, rubbing his palms together in anticipation of a large tip.

Annabelle discreetly slipped him a twenty. She'd learned early on that it was smart to keep everyone happy.

The concierge tried not to stare at her. She was a beauty, with her pale red hair and slinky body. She was also quite mysterious. Nobody in the building knew what she or her boyfriend did, just that they were young and rich and that they had plenty of good-looking friends.

Annabelle walked outside, slid onto the backseat of the Mercedes they'd recently purchased, and settled back against the plush leather. She was glad this was an afternoon assignation, because after educating the boy, she wanted to pop into Saks and buy herself the new patent-leather Prada purse she'd seen in the catalog. And since Frankie was not big on buying her gifts, maybe she'd even treat herself to a David Yurman piece of jewelry.

Yes, that's what I'll do, she thought dreamily. *I'll reward myself for five minutes of not-so-hard work. I deserve it.*

"Hey there," Chip said, glancing in the rearview mirror, his narrow eyes busily checking her out. "How's it goin'?"

"I'm not in the mood for conversation, Chip," she said crisply, tuning him out because he bothered her. There was just something about him. . . .

"'Scuse me for existing," he muttered.

Damn! She decided then and there that Chip had to go. And the sooner the better.

2

Denver

My name is Denver Jones, and I am a twenty-five-year-old so-called hotshot attorney, summoned to be part of the defense team being put together to save Ralph Maestro—a mega-famous action movie star—from a murder rap, should he be arrested.

His beautiful wife, Gemma Summer Maestro—also a movie star—is dead. Shot in the face, her ethereal beauty no more.

It is early December, and in spite of the blazing California sun, the fake snow is already stacked neatly along the Maestro driveway as I make my way up it. It doesn't surprise me, as I have been here before, many years ago when I was a scrawny twelve-year-old attempting to curry favor with the most popular girl in school, Annabelle Maestro.

"Fake snow!" I remember exclaiming the first time I'd visited the Maestro mansion. "You mean your parents have fake snow brought in and pile it all along your driveway?" I'd stared at my new best friend in disbelief.

Twelve-year-old Annabelle Maestro had stared back at me defiantly. "Denver Jones," she'd said, wrinkling her freckled nose, the braces on her teeth catching the afternoon sunlight. "You are *sooo* dumb! This is Beverly Hills, stupid. We don't *have* real snow in Beverly Hills."

"You don't?" I'd mumbled, fresh out of Chicago with my not-so-normal parents: Dad, a maverick lawyer; Mom, a political activist and sometime homemaker.

"No way!" Annabella had huffed, as if I were the town idiot. "You're so dense!"

"Sorry," I'd muttered, although I'd had no clue what I was supposed to be apologizing for.

Annabelle had picked up a fist full of fake snow and pitched it forcefully into my face. It felt like cotton candy.

"Come on," she'd said, her long legs racing up the snow-covered driveway. "I'm starving!"

I'd trailed behind her, brushing the fake snow off my face and out of my hair.

That was then, and this is now, and I am no longer that naive twelve-year-old girl, but I'll never forget Annabelle and her freckles and the way she used to wrinkle her nose. I haven't seen her in years. We lost touch right after high school, then later I heard she'd left L.A. to attend college in Boston. After dropping out, she'd apparently moved to New York, where she was doing something involving fashion.

I wondered where Annabelle was now and if I'd run into her. We hadn't stayed friends for long. I was never cool enough for her—too work-oriented and different for her tastes. Her deal was trolling up and down Melrose and Robertson searching for the new hot bag or the latest cool jeans, and that was hardly my scene. Even if I'd wanted to, I certainly wouldn't have been able to afford the Maestro princess lifestyle. In fact, it was a relief when Annabelle had started ignoring me and hanging out with a group of similar rich girls with equally famous parents.

Losing Annabelle's friendship was no big deal. My mom was relieved; she'd never much liked Annabelle or all the things her family represented. Fame. Vast wealth. The full Beverly Hills scene. Mom was happier when I teamed up with Carolyn Henderson, a brainy kid whose father was a plastic surgeon and whose mother worked in real estate. As soon as Carolyn graduated college, she scored a job as an intern in Washington. She is currently personal assistant to Senator Gregory Stoneman. We are still close friends, even though we live in different cities. We keep in touch on a regular basis, although it isn't always easy as we're both majorly busy. Thank God for e-mailing and texting.

This year, Carolyn has promised to make it out to L.A. for Christmas, in spite of a workload that makes *me* look like a slacker, and believe me, I am no slouch.

I can't wait to spend time with her, especially as we both recently broke up with our significant others, which means we'll have plenty to talk about. Carolyn dumped her boyfriend, Matt, because she caught him cheating, which came as no surprise to anyone. Matt was an up-and-coming political journalist who everyone (except apparently Carolyn) knew had a major zipper problem.

My breakup was a different story. Josh, a successful sports doctor, left *me*. He complained that I put work first and that he'd had it with always coming second.

On reflection I have to admit that he was right, or maybe I simply didn't love him enough.

Josh and I were together three years, so the breakup came as kind of a jolt, but I'm not heartbroken. I do miss our Sundays devouring the newspapers in our sweats, taking long, vigorous hikes up Malibu Canyon, watching *Entourage* and *Dexter* on TV, and gorging on my favorite Chinese food straight from the cartons.

I do *not* miss the sex; it wasn't that great to begin with. Like most relationships, ours started off with incredibly raunchy and hot sex, but after six months it had become kind of boring and comfortable.

Where did all the passion go? Hey, I'm no expert, but I did experience a couple of sizzling affairs in college—one with a married professor and one with a major jock. Both times the sex was mind-blowing, so I certainly know the difference. Although sleeping with a married man on the side is not for me. Too many lies and complications.

Sometimes I think our dog, Amy Winehouse, misses Josh more than I do. We came across Amy, a mixed breed, wandering lost and filthy on Venice Beach, so we took her home and named her after my favorite singer because of her throaty growl that emulated Amy's low-down, sexy voice.

When Josh left I inherited Amy. "No visitation rights," I informed him coldly. Although what I really wanted to say was, *Piss off, asshole*, you're *dumping* me.

Josh gave me attitude about the dog—but, hey, if he wanted out, that's exactly what he'd get. Out. Gone. History. I don't believe in dragging things out. When something's over, it's best to make a clean break.

This time my mom was not happy. She was fond of Josh, as was the rest of my family, especially my three older brothers.

Too bad. Josh was likable as a friend, but he certainly wasn't the man I planned on spending the rest of my life with.

And who might that man be? Truth is I haven't found him yet, and the prospects in L.A. are hardly promising. The only men I meet are clients, and they're usually married or gay. Then there's the slick lawyers who drive gleaming Porsches or the latest Mercedes, and favor twenty-year-old nubile blond models or actresses with all the attributes.

Not that I'm a dud looks-wise. If I didn't live in L.A., I guess I'd be considered extremely attractive. I have long chestnut brown hair with natural golden highlights, wide hazel eyes, I'm five feet seven, and I take a size eight dress (large by Beverly Hills standards, small for the rest of the country!).

Okay, so I'm no Pamela Anderson, and believe me, I have no desire to be. Fake anything grosses me out—lips, breasts, cheekbones, and chins. Ugh! What are these women *thinking*?!

The truth is that if Josh hadn't broken up with me, I would have eventually dumped *him,* because comfortable is great for a while, but passion is definitely lurking out there somewhere, and I *do* intend to find it. That's when I have time, 'cause as I might have mentioned before, I'm a dedicated workaholic.

This all happened three months ago, and word is that Josh has hooked up with a new girlfriend, some blond anorexic stylist to the stars that he picked up in a club.

Hmm . . . talk about not waiting around. Anyway, good luck to him. I couldn't care less.

I myself am a little more discerning. Right now I'm not interested in anything permanent. I've decided that I should have some fun while I'm waiting for Mister Right to put in an appearance.

"You're late," my boss scolded, greeting me at the door to the Maestro mansion.

My boss, Felix Saunders—or Mr. Shark Teeth, as he has become known around the office since he had his teeth recrowned and they shine like a row of dazzling white beacons—is ready for action. He is an imposing man with a sharp Roman nose and a shock of crazy silver hair that stands on end; he kind of resembles a white Don King. He also has a penchant for light-colored Brioni suits, colorful shirts, and pointy-toed lizard shoes dyed in a variety of outrageous colors. Most people regard him as quite a character.

Saunders, Fields, Simmons & Johnson is the name of the law firm I work for. I started out clerking for them while still in law school; and after I passed the bar, they hired me as an associate. Within three years, I was promoted to senior associate.

I hate to sound immodest . . . well, not really! But I am good, very good, and I think that Mr. Shark Teeth loves me. Not as a woman, but as his right hand—a hand he knows he can always depend on. The man is a brilliant lawyer with a killer mind, so over the years I studiously ignored the whiter-than-white teeth, the out-of-control hair, and the overly expensive suits and learned everything I could from him. He is an excellent teacher and I'm a quick study, so it's turned out aces for both of us. Soon I expect to be promoted to junior partner.

I guess Josh is correct: I do put work first. And right now I have no reason not to.

I consulted my watch—Cartier, a birthday present from Mr. Shark Teeth. Personally I'm not into labels, but other people seem to hold them in high regard, especially in Beverly Hills.

"Two minutes hardly counts as late," I said crisply.

Felix Saunders raised a bushy eyebrow. "Always an argument," he said, verging on irritable.

"Facts are facts," I responded.

"The girl who always sees things in black and white," he said dryly, tapping his chin with his slightly crooked index finger.

"Nothing wrong with *that*," I countered. Getting in the last word is one of my habits that drives people crazy. I don't give a crap, I *enjoy* having the last word. Besides, I don't wish to sound immodest, but I'm usually right.

"Follow me," he said. "We have work to do."

I am considered a hotshot attorney because in the past eighteen months I have defended two high-profile men with great success. Client number one was a well-known studio executive accused of rape by a TV star whose career was on the downslide. The upcoming trial hit the front pages for months, culminating in a fast five days in court.

The actress was not a popular woman; she'd portrayed a bitch on TV for several years. It wasn't difficult for me to convince the jury that her role on TV came naturally to her, while also playing up the studio executive's happy family angle. I pointed out that as far as he was concerned, the one night of sex was consensual, he loved his wife and family, and he deeply regretted the entire incident. Then I emphasized how much the actress needed—in fact *craved*—the headlines of her past stellar career. And how she'd gone after Mr. Big Studio Executive with a vengeance. "You saw the Beyoncé movie *Obsessed*," I stated dramatically in my closing argument, fixing the jurors with my wide hazel eyes, which I've been told can be quite hypnotic. "Then may I suggest that you consider this as the real-life version. Put yourselves in this man's position." A long pause for effect. "Yes, it's true, my client cheated on his wife, but he's never claimed to be a saint. And that's *all* he did. One night of weakness with a seductive actress determined to get her career back on track. So . . . because of one lapse, and a fading actress who feels she's been rejected, is this innocent man supposed to lose everything?" Another long, pregnant pause. More deep eye contact. "I don't think so. Do *you*?"

The jury was sold.

Result: a big victory.

Everyone at the firm was more than pleased with the way I handled myself in court, and within six months I was handed another big newsworthy case. This time, it was a beloved comedian accused of exposing himself to children in public places. I painted him as squeaky clean. He had a family who was dear to his heart. A wife he doted on. Children of his own that he adored.

Then I gave the impassioned closing argument about how this man—this *gentle* man who had raised so much money for children's charities—would *never* harm a child or even think of doing so.

Once again, we won.

Now this. A murder case. Although nobody had actually accused Ralph Maestro of killing his wife.

Yet.

"I think you'd better fill me in," I said to Mr. Shark Teeth as I followed him inside the imposing mansion.

Felix stopped and patted me on the shoulder while whispering confidentially in my ear, "Ralph Maestro is a very big movie star." He paused a moment to reconsider his words. "I mean he *was* the biggest. Not so much today. But once a movie star, it sticks, whether you're still pulling in the big bucks or not."

"And is he?" I asked curiously.

"Is he what?"

"Still pulling in the big bucks?"

"That's irrelevant," Felix said testily.

I wondered if now was the time to tell him that I knew the Maestro family, had indeed attended school with their daughter. Then I decided it wasn't necessary; they wouldn't remember me anyway.

Felix proceeded to tell me what had taken place. Apparently, the Maestros had attended a major fund-raiser the previous evening at the Beverly Wilshire Hotel, returning to their home at eleven. Gemma Summer Maestro had gone straight upstairs to her bedroom, while Ralph had stayed downstairs to watch TV, enjoying one of his expensive and most likely illegal Cuban cigars. Later, he'd walked outside to visit with his dogs—two fierce pit bulls who were not allowed inside the mansion.

Around one A.M., he'd gone upstairs to his bedroom—the Maestros kept separate bedrooms, not unusual among affluent celebrity couples. There he'd watched more TV, until finally he'd fallen asleep around three. When he'd awoken at six in the morning, he'd gone straight to his private gym in the back of the house. It wasn't until their Guatemalan housekeeper, Lupe, discovered Gemma's body—shot while lying in her bed—that Ralph realized anything was amiss.

I quickly fired off a few relevant questions. "Have the police found the murder weapon?"

"No."

"Any sign of a break-in?"

"No."

"Were the Maestros getting along?"

Felix shook his head. "Who knows? But once I shift the detectives out of here, we'll soon find out."

There were two investigating detectives and a legion of cops crawling all over the house.

The housekeeper, Lupe, was in the kitchen making wailing noises.

Gemma Summer's body was still upstairs in her bed, while the police photographer was on his way downstairs.

I started talking to one of the detectives, an African-American guy with an older Will Smith look. My imagination told me that he'd come to Hollywood hoping to be discovered and ended up becoming a detective. That seems to be most people's story. He was Detective Preston, and his partner, an Asian-American woman, was Detective Lee.

I wondered if either of them had called Annabelle and told her the devastating news.

Suddenly, I felt a sick feeling in the pit of my stomach. How does anyone make that call?

Good afternoon, Miss Maestro. This is the Beverly Hills Police Department. Your mother's dead, shot in the head. Your father is the prime suspect. Oh yes, and may I take this opportunity to wish you a Merry Christmas.

"What's the matter?" Felix growled. He expected my full attention at all times; a wandering mind didn't do it for him.

"Has their daughter been notified?" I asked.

Felix narrowed his eyes. "How do you know they have a daughter?"

"It's general knowledge," I answered quickly, still not prepared to reveal my connection to the Maestro family.

"As far as I know, nobody's been notified yet," Felix said, groping for a packet of extra strong breath mints in his jacket pocket. Without offering me one, he popped a couple in his mouth before putting the packet away. "Do you have any idea how the press are going to bite into this one?" he said, minty breath wafting in the air. "It'll make the Phil Spector and Robert Blake cases look like goddamn picnics."

"Do you think the police are planning on arresting Ralph Maestro?" I asked curiously.

"Not if *I* have anything to do with it," he answered, full of his usual unshakable confidence. "There is absolutely no evidence Ralph did it, none at all."

Did he? I was dying to ask. But I refrained from doing so. Sometimes you learn more by saying nothing.

3

Carolyn

"You told me you were going to leave your wife," Carolyn Henderson said, her pale blue eyes filling with tears as she confronted her boss, her lover, the man who had promised her everything and delivered nothing. "You faithfully promised it would happen before Christmas."

Senator Gregory Stoneman paced around his office, unable to look at the pretty girl with the honey-colored bob and the tears in her eyes. He was a tall man of fifty, with a thick head of graying hair, a sharp aquiline profile, and a politician's ready smile.

"Listen to me, sweetie," he cajoled. "You must—"

"I've *been* listening to you," Carolyn interrupted. "I've listened to you nonstop for the last two years." She stared at him accusingly. "You swore to me that we'd be together this Christmas. You promised you'd leave her."

"I know, but—"

"You lied to me, Gregory," she continued, her voice rising. "You *still* haven't told her about us, have you?"

Tears began to course down her cheeks in an uncontrollable torrent.

Gregory Stoneman frowned. There was nothing more irritating than a crying female. Bad enough that he had to put up with it from his wife on occasion, now this one was starting to become extremely demanding. He didn't need this kind of nonsense. Besides, he'd recently met a British journalist, the London correspondent for an upmarket U.K. newspaper. The girl was young and fresh, and lookswise she put Carolyn to shame, although he had to admit that Carolyn did have a sensational body—great tits—which was one of the reasons he'd strung her along with all the false proclamations that one day he was definitely going to divorce his wife.

As if.

There was a game in Washington. And the game had stringent rules. An affair is an affair, and it *never* interfered with a marriage. Everyone who cared to play should learn to abide by the rules.

"Hush," he said soothingly.

"Screw hush," she shouted.

"After Christmas—" he began.

"No!" she shrieked. "You promised. And I expect you to keep that promise, or . . ."

"Or what?" he said ominously.

"Or *I'm* telling your wife about us, since you can't seem to do it."

Her words hung between them like a dark curtain.

Gregory's frown deepened. If only her boyfriend, Matt, had stayed around, this wouldn't be happening. But no—Matt had made an abrupt exit. And where did that leave him? Stuck with a clinging girl who was starting to make demands he had no intention of meeting. And if that wasn't bad enough, now she was making threats. Threatening *him*, Senator Gregory Stoneman, an upstanding member of the Senate with an unsullied reputation and a solid twenty-year marriage.

Her behavior was unacceptable, and he was not about to stand for it.

"Kindly do not do this in my office," he said, glancing agitatedly at the closed door.

"Why not?" she demanded, her face reddening. "Everyone will know soon enough."

"No, they won't."

"Oh yes, they will."

He was getting severely fed up with her attitude. Who the hell did she think she was?

"And how's that?" he asked coldly.

"Because *I'm* going to tell them," she replied, eyes flashing. "Your wife first, and then everyone else."

He caught hold of her arm in a viselike grip. "No, you are not," he said, his voice turning to steel. "Do not even think about it."

"Try stopping me," she countered defiantly.

"Why?" he asked, making a stringent effort to control his anger. "Why, after all this time, are you doing this to me now?"

Carolyn stared at him, her lower lip quivering, hands shaking. She hadn't wanted it to come out like this, but he had to know.

Her words were slow and halting. "I'm pregnant," she said at last.

"*What?*" he said, blanching visibly as he took a step back.

"Pregnant," she repeated, delighted that she finally had his full attention.

"That's impossible," he snapped, refusing to entertain the idea. "You're on the Pill."

"Mistakes happen," she muttered.

"What *are* you talking about?" he said brusquely.

"The Pill doesn't always work," she explained. "It happens, you know."

"Christ!" he exploded.

"So, you see," she said, beginning to feel a lot calmer now that she'd told him, "it's time for us to come out in the open. We have to."

He paced up and down for a moment or two before turning toward her with an accusatory expression. "What makes you think it's mine?" he said harshly.

She'd known he'd say something like that. It pained her, but she understood Gregory's weaknesses only too well. When it came to confrontations, he always tried to dodge the blame, exactly as he did in his political career.

And yet . . . she loved him. Couldn't help herself.

Now she had his child growing inside her, and she wanted to be with him more than ever.

"It's definitely yours," she said quietly. "There's no doubt."

"It could be Matt's," he argued, furious that he was caught in the oldest trap known to man.

"It's yours," she repeated.

"How can you be so sure?" he insisted.

Oh God! He was making her feel like such a loser. And it simply wasn't fair. She loved him so much; she always had.

"Because I haven't slept with Matt in over three months," she said in a low voice. "This baby is yours, Gregory, face up to it."

"Christ!" he exclaimed for the second time. "Why did you do this?"

"Why did *I* do this?" she responded with a sudden flash of anger. "If I remember correctly, it's *you* who comes to my apartment twice a week all ready to fuck my brains out."

"Don't be so damn crude," he said, throwing her a disgusted look. "It doesn't suit you."

This wasn't turning out the way she'd planned. She'd wanted him to say, *You're right. This is wonderful news. We should be together. I'll divorce my wife immediately.*

Yeah. Sure. In her dreams.

Deep down, she'd had a hunch his reaction would be pure crap.

She sighed and wished she had someone to confide in. But right from the beginning of their affair he'd sworn her to secrecy, so she hadn't even told Denver, her best friend, who lived in L.A. As far as Denver knew, she'd been in a loving relationship with Matt until they broke up.

Ah, Matt. Even *he* had never suspected what was going on. They'd kept separate apartments, and he'd rarely stayed over at hers, so she'd been able to keep her affair with Gregory secret.

Now all she wanted to do was tell the world, and she especially wanted to tell Gregory Stoneman's wife, Evelyn, who according to Gregory was a cold, domineering woman who refused to give him any sex. It was one of the reasons Carolyn had never felt guilty about sleeping with a married man. He needed her. She needed him. They shared an extremely close bond.

Gregory walked over to the window and stared out, his back to her.

"So . . ." she ventured, hoping his attitude was about to change and soften. "I think this means you have no choice. Either you tell your wife, or I do."

He turned around, a strange look in his eyes. "Is that what you think will happen?" he said, his tone icy.

"Yes, Greg," she answered bravely. "This time I really mean it."

"Do you?"

"Yes."

His expression was thoughtful. She took this as a positive sign; it was better than listening to him rant.

There was a long silence, and then he said, "You shouldn't've told me here. This is something we need to talk about in private."

"I agree," she said, relieved that it seemed he was finally accepting the news.

"And you have to give me a couple of weeks to work this out," he added, staring at her intently. "I cannot perform miracles overnight."

"I can do that," she said quickly.

"As you know only too well," he continued, biting on his lower lip, "it's very, very complicated. There's my wife, and my children to consider. . . ."

"Yes, Greg," she said obediently. "I understand that it won't be easy."

"You bet it won't," he said, a sharp edge to his voice.

"But the thing is, we can do it together," she added soothingly. "It'll all work out, and then we'll have each other."

He shot her a wary look. "You haven't told anyone, have you?" he demanded.

"Of course not," she assured him.

"You're absolutely certain?"

"Why would I? It's our secret."

"People tell secrets."

"Not me."

He began pacing, not looking at her.

She took a deep breath and waited for his next words.

"How pregnant are you?" he asked.

"Seven or eight weeks. I'm not sure."

"Have you seen a doctor?"

"I made an appointment with my gyno for next week," she answered, encouraged that he was taking an interest.

"Cancel it," he stated abruptly. "I want only the best for our baby. I'll arrange for you to see someone."

Our baby. How intoxicating were those words coming from Gregory. *Her* Gregory.

She thought about the time two months ago when his wife and children were out of town and he'd taken her to his house. They'd spent a magical few hours together. He'd been so loving, and so had she. That must have been the day she'd become pregnant.

Filled with a sudden rush of affection, she moved toward him, impulsively throwing her arms around his neck. "I'm so sorry, Greg," she whispered, nuzzling close and inhaling his masculine smell. "I didn't mean for this to happen. But now that it has, I think it was meant to be. You do know how much I love you, and how I'll always be here for you."

"I know," he said, his mind racing in a hundred different directions, none of them pleasant.

"It'll be such a relief when we can come out in the open," she said, imagining herself accompanying him to important Washington events and glittering dinner parties. "You'll see."

"Yes," he said slowly. "Only you must allow me to handle things my way."

"I will," she said quickly.

"You cannot say a word to anyone," he continued. "That's imperative. Do you understand?"

"Yes, of course I do," she said, kissing him, her tongue darting in and out of his mouth.

In spite of himself, he was aware of a familiar stirring in his pants. He felt angry, cornered, and threatened, yet the conniving bitch could still give him a hard-on. Hands on her breasts, he began tweaking her nipples through her blouse.

"Lock the door," he muttered after a few moments, his voice suddenly thick with lust. "Then take off your top, get down on your knees, and do that thing with your tongue you do so well. We'll call it a celebration."

"Yes, Greg," she murmured, thoroughly grateful that everything was going to be all right. "Whatever you want."

4

Bobby

When Bobby Santangelo Stanislopoulos walked into a room, women took notice. Not only was he over six feet tall, in his mid-twenties, and undeniably hot, he possessed great style. With his longish jet hair, intense black-as-night eyes, Greek nose, and strong jawline, he drove women a little crazy. And it wasn't about being incredibly good-looking, which he was. And it wasn't about being the heir to a major fortune, which he was. No, it was just a certain something. A hint of the young John Kennedy Jr., a touch of the Ashton Kutcher edge, and the mysterious allure of a Robert Pattinson.

Bobby's Greek billionaire father, the late Dimitri Stanislopoulos, had been a powerful man, a true force in the business world of shipping and commerce. Bobby had never harbored any desire to follow in his father's footsteps; that kind of business was not for him. Nor did he wish to emulate his mother's successes: The wildly beautiful Lucky Santangelo, a woman who had always done things her way, had made a fortune building several Las Vegas luxury hotels and then running and owning Panther Movie Studios for several years. Bobby had always been surrounded by high achievers. Apart from his parents, there was his stepfather, Lennie Golden, a former comedian/movie star who now wrote and directed highly successful independent films. And his maternal grandfather, the inimitable Gino Santangelo.

So . . . what was a young college guy supposed to do to make his own mark in the world?

Fortunately, Bobby had big ideas of his own. Without asking anyone's permission or opinion, he'd dropped out of college and headed for New York with his best friend, M.J., the son of a renowned African-American neurosurgeon. The two of them had put together a group of investors, enabling them to open Mood, a private club, which after a few months had taken off and become *the* late-night place of choice.

Bobby was a hybrid of both parents. He'd inherited Dimitri's dominant personality along with his acute business savvy, and he possessed Lucky's addictive charm, stubborn ways, and strength of character. Not a bad combination.

Everyone wanted to be Bobby's friend, but Lucky had taught him at an early age that when it came to friends and acquaintances, he had to be extremely discerning. "People will want things from you because of who you are," she'd warned him. "Money always manages to attract the wrong people. Look at Brigette and the series of losers who've latched on to her along the way. She's fortunate to have survived."

Brigette Stanislopoulos was Bobby's niece, even though she was almost a decade older than him. Brigette was the daughter of Olympia, Bobby's deceased half sister, and the granddaughter of the long-dead Dimitri.

It seemed there were a lot of deaths on the Stanislopoulos side of the family. Bobby always kept the belief that he was more of a Santangelo.

He was extremely fond of Brigette, but from the stories he'd heard, it seemed that she'd always fallen for the wrong men, and as a result she'd paid the price over and over again.

Because of Brigette's example, Bobby trod a wary path, especially with women. He'd had many girlfriends, not one of them serious, all of them incredibly beautiful. Society girls, models, actresses. They came, they went. He enjoyed himself. Why wouldn't he?

But none of them had meant anything apart from Serenity, a woman he'd been hung up on eighteen months ago until she'd dumped him, had a one-nighter with his friend Frankie Romano, then mysteriously vanished with her Russian husband to God knew where.

And then along came Zeena, a singing star known by one name. Zeena was the wrong side of forty, with a body like Madonna, a bad-girl attitude, and a cultlike following.

The woman was something else, an exotic beauty—half Brazilian, half Native American. She sashayed into Mood with her adoring entourage at least twice a week, always with a different young guy in tow, yet somehow or other—much to Bobby's extreme irritation—she usually managed to either flirt with or totally ignore him.

Zeena's switches in temperament were driving him a little nuts. It was a miracle that he was keeping his infatuation to himself and not confiding in M.J. or Frankie—especially Frankie, who deejayed at the club and was Annabelle Maestro's boyfriend.

There were times Bobby couldn't help wondering why he and Frankie were such close friends; they were so different that it was ridiculous.

Frankie was into doing coke and getting high.

Bobby wasn't.

Frankie was into cheating on Annabelle.

Bobby believed in monogamous relationships.

Frankie had an aversion to real work.

Bobby got off on making deals. Together with M.J., he was currently planning a franchise to open branches of Mood in Miami, London, and maybe Moscow.

Yet despite their differences, Bobby liked to think that Frankie would always have his back and vice versa. Besides, they had a history together, and that would be Serenity—the beautiful Slovakian model who'd slept with both of them and then taken off.

Bobby still felt the sting of Serenity's rejection.

Wisely, he chose not to trust either M.J. or Frankie with his latest obsession. If he told them about his thing for Zeena, they'd plague him to death with smart-ass remarks and sarcastic gibes. Better he stay silent.

That didn't mean he couldn't have an urge to talk to someone about her, get an unbiased take on the situation.

Was she into him? Or did she get off on torturing him? Because she sure as hell knew how to do that.

He often wondered why the women he was most attracted to were the ones who rejected him. Lucky's best friend, Venus, who'd treated him like a kid. Serenity, who'd treated him like an annoying lapdog. And now Zeena . . . what did *she* have in store for him? And why did he want her so much?

A shrink could go to town on *that* one.

To get his mind off Miz Superstar, he decided to take the weekend off and go to Atlantic City with Frankie and M.J. Frankie had been bugging him about it for weeks, so why not indulge in a little R&R?

Perhaps Zeena would miss not having him around, although being the woman she was, she probably wouldn't even notice he was gone.

~ ~ ~

The drive to Atlantic City went by quickly. Frankie had been desperate to take his new red Ferrari, but as M.J. had rightfully pointed out, there was hardly room for two, let alone three. So they'd ended up taking Bobby's black BMW sedan instead. Bobby could've easily bought himself the latest Lamborghini or Porsche, but keeping a low profile was more his style, especially since on his twenty-fifth birthday he'd inherited the lion's share of his late father's estate, making him even richer.

He and Frankie never discussed money. It was one of those taboo subjects that neither ventured near ever since Frankie had requested a loan early on in their friendship and Bobby had turned him down flat—there was no way he was financing Frankie's coke habit. Besides, Lucky had taught him it was a big mistake to lend money. "You'll lose a friend who'll end up resenting you," she'd explained. "So either give them the money and expect nothing back, or simply say no." It was excellent advice.

Apart from deejaying, Frankie had recently gotten what he claimed was an investment business going on the side, something that he and Annabelle had gone into together.

Bobby and M.J. knew exactly what Frankie was up to—girls talked. But they'd decided to wait until he told them himself. Business must be booming, because Frankie's latest acquisition, the red Ferrari, spelled out that whatever he was into was making him big bucks.

Before they left, Bobby got on the phone to Lucky. She divided her time between Vegas, L.A., and wherever her husband, Lennie, happened to be on location shooting one of his movies.

He reached her in Vegas, where she was keeping a sharp eye on the Keys, her latest creation—a magnificent hotel/apartment complex. Open only a couple of years, the Keys was already a major success.

No surprise there—everything Lucky did always turned to gold. Being her son, Bobby had a lot to live up to, and didn't he know it. It was one of the reasons he'd taken off for New York and done his own thing. No competition.

Thank God it had all worked out. He had a successful club, with more on the way. A great apartment on the West Side. Friends. A crazy social life. And a mom, stepfather, two half siblings, and various other family members he loved. Especially as they lived mostly in California and he was settled firmly in New York.

As far as his inheritance was concerned, it was a huge responsibility—and instead of dipping into it, he'd decided not to touch it until he was older and wiser. Right now he was almost twenty-six and making it on his own. That was enough for him to feel damn good about himself. His inheritance could just sit there earning interest. It was far more rewarding and a hell of a lot better for his ego to live off the money he made himself.

"Hey," Lucky said over the phone, sounding delighted to hear from him. "What's going on with my number-one son?"

"Number-one son is on his way to Atlantic City for twenty-four hours of debauchery and sex," he answered lightly.

"Just like your grandfather!" Lucky responded. And he could imagine her smiling when she said it.

"Seriously," he added. "I'm taking off with M.J. and Frankie. Turning my phone to dead."

"I wish you wouldn't," Lucky said. "I hate it when I can't reach you."

"Twenty-four hours, Mom."

"Fine," she said with a dramatic sigh. "I won't worry."

"Yeah, like *you* worry. Not!"

Lucky laughed. "The only one I worry about is Brigette. Have you seen her lately?"

"Spoke to her a while ago. She seems okay."

"You're her uncle," Lucky scolded. "I wish you'd stay in touch."

"Yeah, an uncle who happens to be ten years younger than her," Bobby pointed out. "It's not like we have a lot in common."

"Doesn't matter. You know she's a magnet for losers. Someone has to watch out for her, and I'm not there."

"Got it," Bobby said, scrawling Brigette's name on a pad by the phone so he wouldn't forget. "I'll call her when I get back."

"Thank you," Lucky said briskly. "Oh, and give my love to M.J. When are you two coming to spend a weekend at the hotel? I'm very fond of M.J."

"Yeah, M.J.'s cool," Bobby agreed, thinking how far back they went. High school. College. Opening Mood together. They shared many a fine memory. And since they both came from money, they'd never wanted anything from each other, only friendship.

"Speaking of the hotel, how's everything going?" Bobby asked, glancing at his watch. It was almost time to hit the road.

"Thriving. We're completely booked out. Even Gino gets off on visiting, so I've allotted him his own special suite. You should see him, Bobby, that man is king of the pool, everyone loves him. Men, women—*especially* women. He's such a dog."

Grandfather Gino Santangelo. A notorious figure in Las Vegas back in the Meyer Lansky/Bugsy Siegel days when Vegas was just beginning. Gino, who'd built major hotels, fought off vicious rivals, bedded hundreds of women, and created an empire. Now he was ninety-seven years old and still active, with a much younger wife (his fourth) and a true zest for living.

"Tell him hi from me," Bobby said. He was in awe of his amazing grandfather. Gino Santangelo was a force of nature.

"Tell him yourself," Lucky responded. "The old man's planning a trip to New York."

"No kidding? Jeez, I'd better start lining up a shitload of action. Strippers . . . hookers . . ."

"Paige will be thrilled to hear how excited you are," Lucky said dryly, referring to Gino's current wife.

They both laughed.

"By the way," Lucky added, "Max is desperate to talk to you."

"Where is little sis?"

"Max is not so little anymore, Bobby."

"Yeah, I can believe that."

"And right now she's probably out with yet another horny boyfriend."

"How many horny boyfriends does she have?" he asked, amused.

"As many as she can get," Lucky replied with a resigned sigh.

"Okay, so I'll give her a call later."

"Do that. I have a feeling she's ready to take off on her own, and there's no way I can stop her. She's saying a flat-out no to college and anything else we suggest."

"Face it, Mom, she's a wild one, exactly like you."

"I had to fight for *my* survival," Lucky said pointedly.

"Heard it all before. I'll definitely call Max. You stay out of trouble."

"Shouldn't I be saying that to you?"

"Yeah, yeah. Stay cool, Mom."

"Yes, Bobby," Lucky drawled sarcastically. "Whatever you say."

Bobby grinned. His mom was something else. Still insanely beautiful and ready to take on anybody and anything. Lucky walked through life her way, and woe betide anyone who tried to stop her.

Max, his nearly eighteen-year-old half sister, was the mirror image of Lucky. A straight-talking beauty unafraid of anything, she was bold, sassy, and kind of street-smart. Even though Lucky and Lennie had tried to protect her, she'd never allowed herself to be fenced in, not even after a life-changing kidnapping when she was only sixteen. Like Lucky, Max took no prisoners.

Bobby knew that she was desperate to come back to New York and move in with him; she'd dropped enough hints. But he wasn't looking for a roommate. And he certainly had no intention of being responsible for her. Little sis was too much like hard work.

She'd visited him a year earlier, a few weeks after graduating high school. She'd arrived all set to party, a total wild thing. He shuddered at the memories. Every guy in the club had started checking her out, especially Frankie. Bobby had soon found himself desperate to ship her back to L.A. before she got herself into real trouble.

Yeah, a repeat performance was not on his agenda. Babysitting a teenager was hardly his thing.

Still . . . Max was an extraordinary girl, very special. And he had to admit that he did miss her. On occasion.

5

Annabelle

Assignation: Teenage boy.

Time: 4:00 P.M.

Place: The Four Seasons.

Room: Penthouse suite.

Boy's name: Omar.

On the way up in the elevator, Annabelle smoothed down the bottom half of her silk dress. The material felt sensuous and rich against her skin. She wore no undergarments, just the slip of a dress, her honey-colored fox-fur coat, and spike-heeled Christian Louboutin short boots.

Before arriving at the door to the boy's suite, she slipped on a satin eye mask, the trademark move of all her girls. Not that she was a recognizable face, as were most of the girls who worked for her, but she'd soon realized that mystery was everything.

The moment she slipped the mask over her eyes, it transported her to another zone, an exciting place where she became Belle Svetlana—a woman with no history, light-years away from Annabelle Maestro, the unknown and unnoticed daughter of two famous movie stars.

The door to the suite was flung open by a twenty-something fat creature wearing baggy rapper clothes with multiple gold-and-diamond chains hanging from his neck, sinister oblique wraparound shades, diamond stud earrings, and an elaborate tattoo of a dragon covering his forearm.

Annabelle was thrown. There was not supposed to be anyone else present; she'd made that perfectly clear to Sharif Rani.

"Omar is expecting me," she said, imagining that this creature must be the boy's bodyguard.

"I know," the man cackled. "I *am* Omar."

"That's impossible," she said. "There's no way you're fifteen."

Letting forth another manic cackle, he reached forward, grabbed her wrist, and hauled her into the suite, almost knocking her off balance. "Fifteen an' way ready for some hot, steamy action," he guffawed, kicking the door shut with his Nike-clad foot. "We're gonna get it on, *beeitch*. I bin waitin' all day."

~ ~ ~

If there was one thing Frankie Romano knew about his girlfriend, Annabelle, it was that she hated cell phones, always had. In fact, she hated phones altogether. It bothered her that with a phone in her purse anyone could reach her at any time. Frankie often told her that she was crazy—he was never without his iPhone and his BlackBerry, both of which he used constantly. But Annabelle was adamant: No cell phone for her. She preferred voice mail on her home phone, which she hardly ever checked.

"What if there's an emergency?" Frankie often asked.

"Then I'll deal with it when I get home," she always replied.

So after Frankie checked into the hotel and caught the news of Gemma Summer's murder on TV, there was no way he could reach Annabelle. She was locked away somewhere with a fifteen-year-old Arab kid, teaching him the joys of sex. Meanwhile, her mother had been shot to death in L.A.

This was obviously the emergency he'd always worried about.

Damn Annabelle for refusing to carry a phone. She was a stubborn one, always insisting that she wanted things her way. Usually he didn't object, but today was something else.

He tried to remember if she'd mentioned where the assignation was taking place, but they'd both been joking about it so much that he couldn't recall. All he could remember was that they were pocketing thirty thousand dollars for her to have a quick sex romp with a teenager that would probably last all of three minutes.

"Find out if he's got a sister," Frankie had quipped. "I'll do her for the same price."

"You will *so* not!" Annabelle had retaliated, exhibiting her fiery jealous streak. As far as she was concerned, it was okay for her to service a client or two if they paid enough, but Frankie with another woman—no way.

Frankie was well aware of the house rules, so he never pushed it. Why rock the latest Ferrari he'd recently purchased?

"Shit!" he muttered. What exactly was he supposed to do? He was in Atlantic City with the guys, and he knew that if he reached Annabelle with the news, she'd expect him to rush right home.

Not that he wasn't into her—she was the greatest. How many other women would embrace the business they'd embarked on with such unbridled enthusiasm? *And* participate when the money was right?

But he was on a fun trip, and it wasn't as if Annabelle was close to her mom. In fact, from the few times she'd mentioned her famous mother, it was quite the opposite.

It occurred to him that since Gemma Summer's untimely death was all over the TV, he didn't have to be the one to tell her. She'd find out soon enough, and when she finally called him, he could make out that he hadn't heard.

Yeah, that would work. Especially if he turned off his phone for a while so that he could enjoy at least a few hours of freedom.

Frankie always had an answer for everything.

Determined to put the news from L.A. out of his mind, he rejoined M.J. and Bobby in the casino.

"Where were you, man?" M.J. asked, indicating an empty seat at the blackjack table.

With his shaved head, dazzling white teeth, and friendly brown eyes, M.J. was irresistible to women, even though he was on the short side. They all wanted to mother him, although once he got them into bed, mothering him was the last thing on their minds. M.J. had hidden talents.

"Takin' a crap," Frankie announced, eliciting a disapproving glare from an elderly woman at the far end of the table.

"I'm losing my ass, while Bobby's cleanin' up," M.J. griped.

"Bobby always cleans up," Frankie grumbled, sitting at the table. "It's in his genes."

Taking his eyes off the dealer's cards for one swift moment, Bobby shot Frankie a devastating grin. "Sit. Play," he commanded. "I need someone at this table who knows what he's doing."

"Jeez!" M.J. complained, rolling his eyes. "I'm tryin' to work it here, an' that's the thanks I get?"

Frankie passed money to the dealer in exchange for chips. "I'm in," he muttered.

Bobby shot him another look. "Wipe your nose," he said sotto voce. "You look like you fell into a vat of baby powder. I don't get why you're so into that shit."

Automatically, Frankie ran his hand across his nose. It pissed him off big-time that Bobby refused to indulge. Without the coke to keep him elevated, he simply couldn't function.

He'd started hanging out with Bobby and M.J. when he'd deejayed at their club over a year ago. M.J. had hired him to work several private parties, and it didn't take long before Frankie and Bobby discovered they happened to be sleeping with the same girl—Serenity, a sleek and overly confident bitch. She'd thought she was playing them, but when they'd discovered they were both in bed with her, they'd bonded, even though they hailed from totally different backgrounds.

Bobby came from money, money, money, while Frankie was the son of a timid mother and a tough Italian Chicago union boss who used to beat the crap out of both of them, until at age fifteen he'd tried to defend his mom, and his dad had beaten him so badly that he'd had to be taken to the hospital. Two weeks later, he'd said good-bye to his mother, made a midnight run for freedom with seventy bucks in his pocket, and headed straight for New York. He'd never looked back, although he often fantasized about returning home and putting a bullet right between his dad's eyes. Frankie might seem cool on the outside, but within there lurked a simmering deadly anger.

"This game is shit," Frankie complained after losing four times in a row.

M.J. agreed. He wasn't doing well, either, while Bobby was continuing to rake it in.

"Hey," Bobby said, tossing the dealer a generous hundred-dollar chip, "if you guys aren't into it, let's split. I got no problem with that."

"Finally!" Frankie exclaimed, pushing his chair away from the table, feeling only vaguely guilty that he wasn't on a fast track back to New York to be by Annabelle's side.

What the hell, he wasn't about to give up a night out with the guys. And maybe a girl or two. Because when Annabelle wasn't around . . . who knew what the evening would bring?

~ ~ ~

Annabelle was overcome with feelings of deep apprehension. This huge, sweating hulk in the would-be rap-star outfit and insane tattoo was hardly the innocent young Arab boy she'd been expecting. He wasn't Middle Eastern, he was all-American. And he *certainly* wasn't fifteen.

She did not appreciate the way he hauled her into the suite and almost threw her down onto a large couch.

"You can't possibly be Sharif Rani's son," she said, gathering her composure, while in her mind she was busy planning a fast exit. *No sex with this big lout. No sirree.*

"You doubtin' me, *beeitch?*" he shot back belligerently, planting himself in front of her, massive legs widely spread. "My old man paid you up front, an' he din't pay you to ask no dumb questions. So get your fuckin' clothes off an' let's get it on."

"There's been a very big mistake," she said, managing to keep her cool.

"What fuckin' mistake would that be?" he snarled, folding his arms across his burly chest. "You got your money, din'tcha?"

Yes, she had gotten the stacks of cash delivered early that morning by one of Sharif Rani's minions. The money was even now inside her safe.

"I said there's been a mistake," she repeated. "I need to speak to your . . . uh . . . father."

"Y'know what?" he said, smirking lustfully. "Soon's we get it on, *beeitch*, y' can talk all ya want."

And with those words he dropped his pants, revealing multiple rolls of dimpled white fat around his middle and, lower down, a small, angry, uncircumcised penis pointed in her direction.

Annabelle had never been caught in a situation like this before, although sometimes she'd heard stories of bad behavior from her girls. There was the family TV star who was into strangulation and nearly went all the way with one unfortunate girl. There was the rock star with a sudden urge to inflict extreme pain. There was the soul singer who attempted to involve a child before his "date" walked out on him. Oh yes, she'd heard many things, but she'd never personally experienced a difficult situation.

Now that situation was here, and how was she supposed to handle it?

"Suck my dick," Omar commanded, thrusting his penis toward her. "Suck it hard."

"Oh no," she said firmly, struggling to get up from the couch. "This is *not* going to happen."

"That's what *you* think," he roared. And before she could get to her feet, he fell on top of her, jamming his penis into her mouth, at the same time ripping the front of her dress and exposing her breasts.

She would've screamed if it were possible. But it wasn't.

Omar was on a roll, and he obviously had no intention of backing off.

6

Denver

Shaking hands with Ralph Maestro was not a pleasant experience. His hand was big, meaty, and slick with sweat.

Not a flicker of recognition crossed his bland face as he shook my hand. But why should it? There's no reason he'd remember me. After all, why would a big movie star like Ralph Maestro remember a scrawny little kid from Chicago who'd hung out with his daughter many years ago?

"Sorry for your loss," I murmured respectfully. Hey, whether he'd done it or not, as part of his future defense team I had to hope he was innocent.

"Thanks," he muttered, practically ignoring me as he turned quickly to Felix. "Is this your secretary?" he asked, cracking his knuckles.

"No," Felix answered patiently. "Denver is my colleague. She's an excellent and accomplished associate, and I can personally assure you that she's a brilliant girl who has done some outstanding work for our firm."

Brilliant, outstanding! I preened a little. This was the first time I'd heard such a positive statement of my talents coming from my boss, although I'm not thrilled that he referred to me as "girl." Surely "woman" is more appropriate?

Ralph Maestro was unimpressed. "She looks awfully young," he grumbled, hardly a man bent double with grief. "And what kind of name is Denver?"

It's my name, asshole. So don't even go there.

He didn't, nor did Felix, who knew better than to do so. We'd had the name discussion a few months after I joined the firm. "Maybe you should change your name to something less strange," Felix had suggested.

Strange? I'd never considered Denver strange. In fact, I was very fond of my name. According to my parents, I'd been named for the city I was conceived in, and Denver suited me just fine.

The two detectives had left the room, but they remained in the house, huddling in the front hallway, no doubt trying to decide their next move. To arrest or not to arrest, that was the question on their minds.

No weapon. No apparent motive. No witnesses.

My guess is that they won't risk it. Ralph Maestro is famous. He has clout. He knows all the right people. And in Beverly Hills, having connections means everything.

"Nothing wrong with being young," I said brightly. It was probably the wrong thing to say, because after that Mr. Maestro froze me out and spoke only to Felix, even when *I* asked the questions.

If there's one thing I can't stand, it's a big fat chauvinist. And even though Ralph Maestro is not fat—still surprisingly buff, actually—he's an obvious chauvinist.

I started wondering if he'd done it. Shot his beautiful wife in the face. Killed her beauty and her future.

Bang. Bang. You're dead.

He'd always had a thing about guns. I can recall Annabelle dragging me down to the basement one day, where there was a locked room dedicated to his gun collection. Naturally Annabelle was adept at picking the flimsy lock; she was one of those girls who did anything she wanted and always got away with it. And on that particular day, she'd been intent on showing off her famous dad's gun collection.

I decided it was time to jog Mr. Maestro's memory. What the hell, *I* certainly had nothing to lose.

"Uh, Mr. Maestro," I ventured. "Or do you mind if I call you Ralph?"

He threw me a baleful glance. Yes, he minded, it was written all over his movie-star face.

"Do you still have your gun room downstairs?" I continued.

"Huh?" Felix said, startled.

"Excuse me?" said Ralph, also somewhat surprised.

"Your gun room," I repeated.

"What gun room?" interrupted Felix, almost spitting out a mint.

"How do you know about that room?" Ralph demanded, shooting me an action movie star's suspicious look.

At least I finally had his attention. "Your daughter, Annabelle, and I used to be friends," I volunteered. "We were at school together."

Now it was Felix's turn to shoot me a look, one that said, *How come I'm only just finding this out?*

"You and Anna were friends?" Ralph asked, as if to say, *How is that possible?*

"Yes, we hung out for a short time."

"And you came to my house?"

I noticed he said "my house," not "our house." Interesting.

"That's right," I said, feeling that *I* was the one being questioned.

"So you're saying that my daughter took you into my private gun room?" he said, his tone verging on outraged that she would do such a thing.

"She was probably showing off on your behalf," I answered. "You know how kids are."

Ralph shook his head as if he still couldn't quite believe it.

I took the time to study his face. It was definitely a face meant for the big screen. Larger than life and craggy, with a strong jawline and enormous white teeth. Ralph Maestro was handsome in that older action movie star kind of way. He possessed a Harrison Ford/Bruce Willis vibe. Kind of sexy if you're into older dudes. Actually I'm not. I prefer them young and way hotter than this old movie star.

"Showing off on my behalf, huh?" Ralph said at last.

"Well . . ." I ventured. "Like I said, you know how kids are."

"No, I don't," he sneered, curling his lip. "How are they?"

Ralph Maestro was being facetious. His beautiful wife was lying dead upstairs, and he was behaving like a major asshole without anything on his mind except being pissed at a couple of kids who'd invaded his privacy years ago.

I shut up, because I knew if I said anything more, I'd be history. And I wanted to be involved in this case; it had major potential.

Later in the day, the press descended. Not that they could get in the house or even up the long, winding, fake-snow-decorated driveway. But the security cameras showed that they were out on the street with a vengeance. TV camera trucks, on-air talent with handheld microphones and plenty of pissy attitude, paparazzi darting around like a trail of furtive ants, with their long-lens cameras at the ready.

Bad news travels fast, and this happened to be a juicy piece. The brutal shooting of a beautiful woman. Two mega–movie stars. Money. Fame. Hollywood. Oh yeah—this one's a surefire headline grabber.

I'd better remember to call my parents. There is nothing they like less than catching a glimpse of me on the TV news without fair warning. My dad was horrified when I became a highly paid defense attorney. He thinks I should have followed the path of righteous prosecutor and eventually become a D.A.

I obviously didn't agree with him. Defending people is a challenge, and I always get off on challenges. Besides, my dad is a civil prosecutor, an excellent one, so when I decided to study law, I did not want the comparison. There is nothing more soul destroying than attempting to follow a member of one's family into the same profession.

The thing is, I love my dad, but doing the same thing . . . no way.

As we walked down the winding driveway on our way out, Felix gave me one of his long, penetrating looks. "Well?" he asked, clearing his throat. "I always rely on your intuition. What do you think, Denver? Did he do it or did he not?"

I took my time answering because I honestly wasn't sure. And whether Ralph Maestro had killed his wife really didn't matter. We were the defense team, we had a job to do, and that was to protect Ralph Maestro at all costs.

"I'm not sure," I answered hesitantly. "He certainly doesn't seem at all broken up."

Felix popped another mint, still not bothering to offer me one. "They won't arrest him," he said knowingly. "Too many connections."

"*She* must've had connections, too," I pointed out.

"Ah, but *she's* dead."

Oh really, who would've guessed?

"We'll keep a sharp watch on this one," Felix added. "Be on alert. I gave Ralph your cell phone number. Told him he can reach you at any time of the day or night."

Thanks a lot! Why am I on call? What's wrong with your cell phone?

"The press'll go to town on this one," Felix continued. "But I can guarantee that Ralph won't be arrested."

Note to self: If I ever decide to murder someone, I must first become famous, then make sure to commit the crime in Beverly Hills. Movie stars can get away with anything. Or so it seems.

The crowd of press people jumped when they spotted us emerging through the imposing wrought-iron gates. Felix is well-known to the media, and since my two high-profile cases, I like to think that I am, too. However, I always follow my boss's lead, and his lead is to hold up a firm hand and announce in sonorous tones, "No comment, people. Kindly back up."

I know it's shallow, but I kind of get off on seeing my photo in the newspapers.

"Hey, Denver," one of the on-air reporters called out. "What's *your* opinion on this?"

I did a fast double take. I'd been checking this guy out on TV for the past few weeks. He was new to the L.A. job from a popular news show in San Diego. Now here he was in the flesh. And I have to admit that the flesh was quite tempting for a girl who's been on a sex-starvation diet. He's Latino, with a buff bod, smoky eyes, and a cocksure grin. Even better—he felt comfortable enough to use my name, and that boosted my ever-needy ego.

I decided that he's probably great in bed. Latino men usually are, or so I've heard.

Hmm . . . perhaps the time has come to put it to the test.

"Sorry, I don't have a take yet," I replied, incurring a disapproving glance from Felix, who would prefer me to stay silent.

"When you do, how about giving me a call?" suggested Mr. Latino, swiftly handing me his card.

We'd reached Felix's car, a conservative black Bentley. My boss got in, and with a terse, "See you back at the office," he took off.

I turned around and headed for my four-year-old silver Camaro, a twenty-first-birthday present from my parents.

"Nice wheels," Mr. Latino murmured, trailing me curbside.

I took a surreptitious glance at his card. Mario Riviera. Quite a memorable name.

I couldn't help wondering if there was anything else about him that was memorable, what with sex being on the missing list and all.

I think I need it. In fact, I damn well *know* I do.

"Thanks," I said casually, aware that he smelled of grass and sweat, a potent combination. I imagined that he must've been running or lifting weights when he was called to work, and he hadn't taken the time to shower.

The very thought turned me on.

"How about we get together for a drink later," Mario suggested, moving closer. Obviously he was as into me as I was into him.

Hmm . . . a drink—isn't that a euphemism for sex and let's get it on?

Of course it was, so why not? Because I am certainly ready, especially as Josh has moved on like a freaking express train, and here *I* am fast becoming a nun!

Enough is enough. I'm ready for action, and plenty of it. So bring it on, Mr. Reporter.

"Sure," I answered casually, thinking, *He's way hot, I'm horny, and we're both available.*

Or are we?

I quickly checked his hand. No ring.

Okay, then. As far as I'm concerned, it's a done deal.

7

Carolyn

Carolyn drove to her apartment in a happy daze. She'd told him! She'd actually told him!

It was such a relief. And the greatest news of all was that Gregory had agreed with her that it was for the best and that he would finally inform his wife of their affair—an affair that would eventually culminate in marriage!

Well . . . he hadn't actually mentioned marriage, but she was sure that when his divorce came through, and he was a free man, and their baby was born . . . that yes, marriage was definitely in their future.

She smiled to herself, almost running a red light.

God! She was so excited. She'd been sleeping with this man for two years, and during that time he'd made countless promises to leave his wife. Soon it was about to happen, and she was dizzy with anticipation.

Of course, she wasn't naive. There was always the possibility that he could break his promise yet again.

But this time, she was positive he wouldn't. This time, there was a baby to consider . . . and the fact that she was carrying his child made all the difference.

This time she was home-free.

~ ~ ~

"Fucking devious cunt!" Gregory Stoneman muttered as he got into his dark blue Lexus and set off on his drive home. Did Carolyn honestly believe he would leave a woman like Evelyn for a snip of a girl like her? She might possess a great set of tits, but Carolyn Henderson was a nobody, a nothing—whereas Evelyn was cultured, a woman of great style, a well-established Washington hostess, and even more important, she hailed from a powerful and extremely affluent family.

Evelyn's father was a judge, and her mother was heiress to a textile fortune. The Bamberry family represented old money and excellent breeding.

Gregory would never give that up, especially as he came from more modest stock. His father was a car salesman, and his mother was a former nurse. Quite frankly, he regarded his family as an embarrassment, and the less he saw of them, the better.

Meeting and marrying Evelyn had boosted his political career no end, allowing him to move into social circles that before Evelyn had been beyond his reach.

Apart from that, he had his children to consider, eleven-year-old Clarence and seven-year-old Miranda. Two shining stars in his otherwise complicated life.

Well . . . complicated only because of his needy assistant pulling the oldest stunt in the business. "I'm pregnant," she'd said—the words no man wants to hear from a woman he's banging on the side.

What to do now?

Offer her money for an abortion?

No, he understood Carolyn well enough to know that she would never agree to an abortion.

Set her up in an apartment, wait until she gave birth, and have the baby adopted?

No way would she accept adoption.

What, then?

Carolyn Henderson wanted him to leave Evelyn and marry *her.* He had no doubt that was exactly what she expected him to do.

She'd maneuvered him into a corner, and now there was no escape.

Or was there. . . .

~ ~ ~

"Hi," Kerri Tyson called out as Carolyn passed by on the way to her apartment.

Carolyn stopped short, so caught up in her thoughts that she hadn't noticed her neighbor emerging from the apartment opposite hers.

Kerri was half African-American and half Asian. Plump and pretty, with short curly hair and an appealing personality, she was a legal secretary who went through boyfriends at an alarming rate, most of them found online.

"You look as if you just won the lottery," Kerri remarked. "Either that or you're getting royally laid."

Carolyn considered her answer. She wished she could tell Kerri everything. They were friends—not close, but they'd been out to dinner a few times, hit a couple of bars, exchanged ex-boyfriend horror stories.

"Wouldn't *that* be nice." Carolyn sighed. "But unfortunately it's not true."

Kerri raised an eyebrow. "No new stud on the horizon?" she inquired. "'Cause you got the glow goin'."

"It must be my new makeup," Carolyn answered modestly. "NARS blush. It's called Orgasm. It's obviously working."

"You bet your ass it is." Kerri giggled. "Got to grab me some of that. If you're free tomorrow, maybe we can hit the mall. Whaddya think?"

"I'll have to let you know," Carolyn replied, stalling. Now that she'd told Gregory she was carrying his baby, she expected things to change. Even if he didn't tell his wife immediately, he would probably want to spend more time with her.

"Call me," Kerri said, heading for the stairs to the street. "I'll be home later."

"I will," Carolyn said as she unlocked the door to her apartment.

God! She was so excited, she had to tell *someone*. But who could she trust? Perhaps her parents? No way. They were wonderful and supportive, but sleeping with a married man—especially as that married man happened to be her boss—would not fly at all. Her mother, Clare, would certainly not approve. And George, her handsome plastic surgeon father, would be shocked and disappointed in his little girl.

She didn't want to let them down, they meant everything to her.

Then how about telling Denver, her best friend since school?

Unlike most people, Denver could keep a secret. And she'd be totally thrilled, although she'd also be majorly surprised, since Carolyn had never mentioned that she was involved in a hot and heavy affair with the senator.

Oh my God! Carolyn thought excitedly. *I cannot keep it to myself any longer! I'm going to tell Denver. I'll call her tonight.*

~ ~ ~

"Daddy! Daddy! Daddy!" Miranda squealed, hurling herself against her father's legs.

"How's my girl?" Gregory said, bending down to sweep his cute little daughter into his arms.

"I had a fun day at school," Miranda announced, stroking his cheek with stubby, slightly sticky fingers. "Did *you* have a fun day, Daddy? *Didju? Didju? Didju?*"

No, I didn't, he wanted to scream. *I had an impossible day. The worst.* Although he couldn't discount the world-class blow job Carolyn had managed to bestow on him. It had been satisfying at the time, but now he regretted allowing her to touch him, because as far as he was concerned, the affair was over.

Evelyn floated out of the living room into the front hallway of their well-appointed house. She always appeared immaculate, not a white-blond hair out of place, not a wrinkle in the chic Valentino black cocktail dress on her slim, toned body. At forty, Evelyn was a handsome woman. The problem was that she wasn't twenty-something, and that's what Gregory required for sex—a twenty-something girl who worshipped him. A girl who'd put his cock in her mouth and suck him dry. The same girl he'd married twenty years ago, except now that girl was a woman who wouldn't dream of indulging in oral sex.

"How was your day?" Evelyn murmured, and without waiting for an answer, she announced that they had a fund-raiser to attend and he'd better shower and dress.

The interaction between him and Evelyn was never personal. They were hardly ever intimate, as he imagined most married couples might be. The sex was becoming less and less frequent, perhaps once every two months. And it was always the same: Evelyn flat on her back with a pained expression on her face, while he did all the work.

Evelyn never reached orgasm.

Evelyn thought oral sex was perverted.

Evelyn considered penises ugly and disgusting and never cared to touch him down there.

The truth was that Evelyn hated sex, so who could blame him for getting his kicks elsewhere?

Nobody, that's who.

~ ~ ~

Carolyn practically danced around her apartment, she was so elated. Fantasy names spun around her in head. *Senator Stoneman and his lovely wife, Carolyn. Mrs. Gregory Stoneman. Carolyn Stoneman.* They all sounded so perfect. She was ecstatic.

Today is a magical day, she thought. *Today is the beginning of my new life. I love Gregory so much, and we will be so happy together.*

Punching in the numbers on her cell phone, she called Denver in L.A.

No answer. Voice mail requested that she leave a message.

Hmm . . . this was not any kind of news to announce on voice mail.

"It's me, Carolyn," she said at last. "And I have something major to share with you. If you want to hear what it is, call me back. I can't wait to talk to you, so hurry!"

She clicked off the phone, a big smile on her face. Gregory couldn't get mad at her for telling one person.

Besides, he'd never find out.

8

Bobby

Frankie had an urge to visit a strip club. Bobby didn't. M.J. was prepared to go either way. He was a people-pleaser.

"Why'd you want to go see a bunch of fours in Atlantic City when you've got a ten at home?" Bobby said, thinking of Annabelle and how much she was into Frankie.

Frankie was *not* thinking of Annabelle. He had banned all thoughts of Annabelle and her dead mother. Fuck it, he was out to have a blast. "Jeez, Bobby, sometimes you sound like you're fifty years old!" he complained.

"Yeah," Bobby retaliated. "Maybe it's 'cause I'm smart."

"Says who?" Frankie said, pulling a face.

"Says me," Bobby replied, throwing a playful fake punch at Frankie's stomach.

"Can you two pull it together an' decide what's happenin'?" M.J. insisted. "I'm freakin' starvin' here. Let's go Asian."

"Good thinkin', 'cause I'm really into Asian pussy," Frankie said with a leer. "Didja know that Asian girls are screamers? I likee!"

"You likee if it has a pulse," Bobby tossed back, deadpan.

"And you don't?" Frankie countered.

"Got a hunch I'm more discerning than you," Bobby said, grinning.

"Yeah, so discerning you only go for the ones you can't have. What's *that* about?"

Bobby decided to ignore Frankie's veiled comment.

"You're such a privileged prick," Frankie muttered, only half joking.

"Go fuck yourself," Bobby responded good-naturedly.

"Yeah, yeah . . ." Frankie sighed, taking no offense. "If only I could, it'd make life so much easier."

"C'mon, guys, we're in a casino," M.J. said. "You got a choice—gambling or food. So somebody make up their freakin' mind."

"Steak," Bobby decided. "I need my strength if I'm spending the rest of the night with this asshole."

Frankie rolled his eyes. "It takes one to know one."

"You think?" Bobby said, checking out a sleek blonde walking past with a much older man.

"I *know*," Frankie responded, his eyes swiveling to take in the blonde's ass.

They finally ended up in Morton's Steakhouse, where the waitress was no slouch when it came to spotting three sexy, obviously single young guys. She zeroed in on Frankie, who threw off that bad-boy vibe she'd always found irresistible.

Frankie flirted back. Waitresses weren't his usual style, but this one had an amazing rack, and he wasn't about to waste a night away from Annabelle. Besides, Annabelle was enjoying a little something on the side, so why shouldn't he?

"What's your name, beautiful?" he asked after ordering a steak, fries, and his favorite onion rings.

Running her tongue along her lower lip in a most provocative way, she leaned into the table. "Patricia," she said. "But my friends call me Tree."

"An unusual name for an unusual girl," Frankie said, turning on the bullshit charm that always worked so well for him. "You're too fine to be slaving away at a job like this. How come?"

"I'm actually an actress," she explained, her expression serious. "Doing this to make the rent until I can afford a move to New York."

Bobby and M.J. exchanged looks. They knew exactly what Frankie would say next.

He didn't disappoint. "Maybe I can help," he offered in his best sincere voice.

Bobby raised a cynical eyebrow. M.J. stifled a laugh.

"Really?" Tree said, wondering if this guy was as full of crap as most of them were.

"Yeah, really," Frankie continued. "I know people. I got connections."

M.J. rolled his eyes.

"What time you get off tonight?" Frankie persisted.

Tree hesitated. This guy *was* cute enough, with his long hair and bedroom eyes. And maybe—just maybe—he could help her.

"Eleven," she said, licking her lip again.

"Then eleven it is."

"Y'know," Bobby said after the waitress had moved on to another table, "you should get yourself some new lines."

"Yeah," M.J. snickered. "It's way beyond time, man. 'I got connections' simply don't cut it."

"It's not a line," Frankie protested, feeling boastful. "I can make that girl a lot of money."

"Doing what?" Bobby inquired.

"Something that comes naturally," Frankie replied. "I'll give her a test run an' let you know."

"Let us know *what?*" M.J. persisted, exchanging another knowing glance with Bobby.

Frankie paused for a moment. Should he tell them about his and

Annabelle's moneymaking venture or should he not? He'd been dying to show off about pulling in the big bucks, but he knew that somewhere within Bobby there lurked a strong moral streak, and he had a feeling that Bobby might not approve of his new business.

On the other hand, fuck it. Bobby ran a club where booze, drugs, and getting laid took center stage every night, so who was he to object?

Frankie decided to go for it and reveal the truth. "I've been meaning to tell you guys something," he began.

"If it's about the hookers, we know," Bobby said matter-of-factly.

Frankie was thrown. "Huh?" he said, his forehead wrinkling.

"What?" M.J. guffawed. "You thought it was a secret?"

"Are you shitting me?" Frankie said. Now his left eye was twitching, a sure sign he was disturbed.

"Who would shit the king of the bullshitters?" Bobby said, laughing.

"You bet your ass we know," M.J. added.

"We were kind of waiting to see how long it took before you summoned up the balls to tell us," Bobby said, winking at M.J.

"Jeez!" Frankie grumbled. "I didn't expect it to be public knowledge."

"It's not," Bobby said. "But girls got big mouths, and now that word is around, you'd better be way careful."

"Careful?" Frankie said, his left eye still twitching. "Like why?"

"Like you could get your ass arrested for pandering," M.J. offered.

"What the fuck is pandering?" Frankie snapped.

"Selling pussy," M.J. said.

"We're not selling anything," Frankie insisted. "We're arranging meetings between two consenting adults."

"And pocketing a commission, right?" Bobby said.

"That's pandering," M.J. pointed out.

"Well, shit, nobody can prove anything," Frankie said, getting defensive. "It's a cash-only business, no credit cards, no paper trails. We're not dumb."

"That sounds very organized, only don't ask *me* to come bail you out when you make it all the way to the front page of the *New York Post*," Bobby warned. "You've made enough bucks to buy yourself a Ferrari, so my advice would be to get out while you can."

"Are you fuckin' *crazy*?" Frankie said, eyebrows shooting up. "This is the sweetest deal ever. It's a no-hassle, no-break-your-balls walk in the park."

"Yeah, an' you're gonna walk your way right into a jail cell," M.J. interjected. "C'mon, man, you're a freakin' pimp. That kinda shit's against the law."

"When did *you* turn into Mr. D.A.?" Frankie snarled, not pleased with the way this was going. He'd expected compliments, not criticism.

"Hey," M.J. muttered, "it's your deal, it's sure as shit not mine."

"I'm taking a walk," Frankie said, abruptly rising from the table. "I'll catch up with you later."

"That went well," Bobby said dryly as soon as Frankie was out of sight.

"Frankie's an asshole," M.J. remarked. "We both know it, so how come we hang with him?"

"'Cause he's *our* asshole," Bobby said, forever loyal. "And that means we gotta look out for him."

"Gettin' him off coke would be a start," M.J. said. "Then maybe he'd take things more seriously. This sellin' pussy deal is a big mistake."

"You know Frankie, there's no way he'd listen," Bobby stated.

"Then how about Annabelle?" M.J. suggested. "Maybe we should talk to her."

"Oh, c'*mon*. Annabelle? Are you kidding me? She's worse than Frankie," Bobby said. "And when it comes to our boy, in her eyes he can do no wrong. You *know* that."

Tree headed back to their table, balancing various dishes. She glanced around for Frankie and was disappointed to see he was gone. "Where's your friend?" she asked boldly, placing the plates of food on the table.

"I wouldn't sweat it," M.J. said. "He'll be back."

Tree hesitated for a moment. "Can I ask you guys something?" she said, lowering her voice.

"Go ahead," Bobby said, digging into his steak.

"Well . . . it's just that working here, I get a lot of horny guys coming on to me. Y'know how it is. They're in town without their wives or girlfriends, and it's like open season on waitresses."

"What do you wanna know?" M.J. asked, hungrily picking up French fries with his fingers.

"Well . . . uh . . . can your friend really help me, or is he handing me a line?"

"You're a smart girl," Bobby said. "Figure it out."

Tree managed a disappointed look. "So he's full of it?" she said.

"Depends on what you expect from him."

"Okay, thanks," Tree said hesitantly. "Then I guess I can trust him."

Trust him to do what? Bobby thought. *Get you in the sack and bang the crap outta you? Yeah, sure, you can certainly trust him to do that.*

Later, Tree returned with the check. Bobby threw down his credit card, and a few minutes later Tree came back with the receipt for him to sign.

"Isn't it awful about Gemma Summer," she remarked, deciding they were now friends and it was perfectly okay to make conversation. As a matter of fact, she was beginning to think that she might have picked the wrong one to flirt with. The black dude with the big brown eyes and sexy shaved head was certainly cute. And the other one was a total babe. "They're saying that Ralph Maestro might've done it," she continued. "What do *you* think?"

"Might've done what?" Bobby asked, just about to sign the check after adding a more-than-generous tip.

"Shot his wife in the face," Tree said, keeping an eye out for the manager, who didn't approve of his waitresses lingering at tables.

"*Whaat?*" M.J. exclaimed.

"Arc you saying Gemma Summer got shot?" Bobby asked, shocked. "How do you know this?"

"'Cause it's everywhere," Tree said, surprised they hadn't heard about a newsworthy event like a famous movie star getting shot in her own bed. "It's on TV, the Internet—it's everyplace."

"Holy shit!" Bobby said. "We'd better go find Frankie right now. He needs to get back to Annabelle pronto."

"Who's Annabelle?" Tree asked.

"It doesn't matter," Bobby said, hurriedly scribbling his signature on the bill and jumping to his feet. "We gotta go."

"So you think it's okay if I hook up with your friend?" Tree inquired hopefully.

"I wouldn't bet on it," M.J. said, sliding out of the booth. "Gotta strong hunch he's not gonna show."

And with that, the two of them took off, leaving a somewhat bemused waitress full of hopes and dreams that were certainly not reaching fruition anytime soon.

9

Annabelle

Clutching her coat around her to conceal her ripped dress, Annabelle finally managed to leave the hotel suite where Omar Rani—if that was indeed his name—had kept her captive for the last two hours. What had happened to her was unthinkable. She'd been more or less raped and brutalized, treated like an object to be used for one man's pleasure. Omar had been more than rough with her, exhibiting no respect at all. As far as he was concerned, she was bought and paid for, which in his eyes allowed him to do anything he wanted. Her pleas of "Stop! No! This isn't going to happen!" affected him not one bit. She'd struggled, but to no avail. He was relentless. The bastard had treated her like a cheap street whore.

With shaking hands, she reached into her purse, retrieved the cell phone she used only when going on an "appointment," and speed-dialed Chip.

"I'm coming out now," she said, stepping into the elevator. "Are you outside?"

"The friggin' doorman moved me on," Chip complained in his usual whiny voice. "I thought you said you wouldn't be more than half an hour."

"Never mind what I said," she hissed as the elevator made a fast descent. "Get here *now*!"

The elevator doors opened and she stepped out into the grand lobby, praying that she would not run into anyone she knew.

She stood still for a moment, shuddering at the memory of Omar's sweaty hands all over her body, invading her most private places, fondling and handling her as if she were a piece of meat.

Well, screw the fat bastard. There was no way she was allowing him to get away with it. Wait until Sharif Rani heard what had taken place—then the shit would really fly.

Outside the hotel, there was no Chip to be seen. Swearing under her breath, she decided to tell the doorman to hail her a cab.

Chip pulled up in the Mercedes just as she was about to enter the cab. For a moment she hesitated, wondering whether to stick with the cab or go with Chip.

Chip honked the horn.

Moron. The last thing she needed was attention. After thrusting money at the cabdriver, she turned and headed for the Mercedes.

"Where exactly were you?" she demanded imperiously, sliding onto the backseat.

"Traffic," Chip whined. "It's a miracle I got here as fast as I did."

"You're fired," she snapped, taking out her frustration on her erstwhile driver.

"No way," Chip said, glancing at her in the rearview mirror. "S'not my fault this city has more traffic than a nest fulla ants."

She was silent.

"You don't look so good," Chip ventured, narrowly avoiding a meandering jaywalker. "You feelin' okay?"

"Just be quiet," she muttered, seething with anger. "I pay you to drive, not talk."

Chip swallowed a smart reply. She'd fired him once; if she did it a second time, she might actually mean it. And he didn't want to lose his job, it was some cushy setup.

~ ~ ~

Sharif Rani was in the middle of an important business meeting when one of his many cell phones began to vibrate in his jacket pocket. After excusing himself from the conference table, he took out the vibrating phone and realized it was his sex phone—the one he used to arrange all his liaisons. Sharif Rani had a very jealous, very young fourth wife, not to mention a slew of business acquaintances who would love to get something on him. Hence the sex phone. Listed under one of his minion's names and used only to set up his "special" appointments. The caller ID identified Belle Svetlana.

Goddamn it, why was *she* calling him? Belle was supposed to use this line only to confirm his "appointments." And the rest of the week was all taken care of—a different woman every other day, women hand-picked for him by Belle. She knew what he liked.

He contemplated not answering the phone, then decided it was probably wiser to do so in case Belle had to change one of his "appointments."

"Yes?" he said, lowering his voice as he moved toward the door of the conference room.

"Sharif?" Annabelle questioned, her voice quivering with the fury she would soon unleash on him.

"What do you want?" he snapped.

Annabelle was in no mood for a sharp retort. Surely Sharif Rani knew exactly what she wanted. He'd set her up with a sex-mad teenage monster—certainly not a virgin. Now he had to accept the consequences.

"I . . . can't believe what you did to me," she said, almost tripping over her words, she was so angry.

"What do you want?" he repeated, his tone getting icier by the second.

"I want . . . I want . . ." Trailing off, Annabelle realized that she didn't know *what* she wanted. An apology, yes, that was it—an apology for setting her up with such an uncouth piece of crap, Sharif's so-called son. And another thing—she wanted the boy to apologize, too! Boy! Ha!

"Your son is a pig!" she blurted. "He treated me badly. He was rough and rude and disrespectful. You told me he was a fifteen-year-old virgin, and you know that's not true. I want—"

Annabelle was so busy complaining that she didn't hear the click on the other end of the line.

When she discovered he was no longer there, she was enraged. Sharif Rani had hung up on her! The man's manners were appalling. Just who exactly did he imagine he was dealing with?

A little voice in her head whispered, *Hooker. Whore. Prostitute.*

These were words she did not wish to contemplate. She was none of those things. She was a stylish, rich New Yorker who'd succeeded on her own without any help from her movie-star parents.

Tears of frustration filled her eyes. Where was Frankie when she needed him?

~ ~ ~

Frankie was in a strip club getting a lap dance from a sulky redhead with huge fake breasts and a very active tongue. The stripper was busy licking his neck when it suddenly occurred to him that getting pissed at Bobby and M.J. was a waste of time. They were merely jealous that he'd made a success of such a sweet business. And who could blame them? After all, he couldn't stay a deejay forever; he had to move on. And if moving on meant raking in the big bucks, then more power to him. Bobby and M.J. came from wealthy families—what did they know about having to make it on your own with no help from anyone?

Frankie regarded himself as a true survivor. He'd come up the hard way and made it all the way to the top.

There were a few things he regretted along the way. Some dark and ominous memories he did not care to revisit. Some very dark memories he pushed to the back of his mind whenever they came up.

The coke helped him forget the bad things. The coke always put him in a mellow mood, made it easy for him to achieve anything he set his mind to, made him feel like a winner.

Who would have thought that snorting a flurry of white powder could have such a life-affirming effect?

His habit was expensive, but he considered it worth every dime. It wasn't as if he was into crack or heroin or any of the hard stuff.

He liked cocaine. Big fucking deal.

The stripper was becoming restless. She was executing her best moves, but he wasn't responding. She was dangling her pastie-covered nipples dangerously close to his mouth, while thrusting her pelvis against his crotch. Her tongue was still working hard on his neck, heading toward his left ear, although actually touching the customer was not allowed. But she didn't care. This was one stripper who was working all the way toward a hefty tip.

Frankie suddenly got up, sending her flying.

Sprawled on the floor, she was about to spew a tirade of insults when he groped in his pocket, took out several twenty-dollar bills, and threw them at her.

"Another time," he muttered. "Not in the mood."

~ ~ ~

Since Frankie was not answering his cell, an upset Annabelle texted him and then called up Bethany, one of the girls who sometimes worked for her. "Can you come over?" she asked, feeling in need of company. "Frankie's in Atlantic City and I'm by myself."

Bethany, a lounge singer who'd been around a couple of years too long, was happy to oblige. She arrived half an hour later, carrying a bottle of champagne—Cristal, of course—and a carton of orange juice.

"I thought I'd make us mimosas," Bethany announced, and headed for the kitchen.

"Fantastic idea," Annabelle said, putting on a brave face, although she still felt used and abused and furious.

"Is everything all right, Belle?" Bethany asked curiously.

"No. It's not," Annabelle said, following Bethany into the pristine kitchen, which never got used because Annabelle didn't cook. She'd been raised in a household where they had people to do the cooking and anything else that needed doing.

"Is it Frankie?" Bethany asked, full of sympathy but ready for some juicy gossip all the same. "Have you two had a fight? I mean, he's a hot guy, but I'm sure he's not the easiest—"

"Why would it be Frankie?" Annabelle interrupted, immediately switching to defensive mode.

Bethany opened the freezer and scooped out an ice tray. "'Cause it's usually a man," she said, selecting two tall glasses from the kitchen cabinet and popping out a couple of ice cubes. "Men are all such bastards, I can never understand why we put up with their shit. They eat, fart, sleep, and snore. And let me assure you, my vibrator gives me better sex."

Obviously she's never slept with Frankie, Annabelle thought.

"Actually, I've sworn off men," Bethany continued. "Unless they're paying. Now I'm all about my career—*that's* what's important to me."

"Well . . ." Annabelle said, heading back to the living room. "Talking of paying, have you ever experienced . . . uh . . . a client who . . . uh . . . treated you badly?"

"Don't call them clients," Bethany said sharply, sitting on the couch. "The word *clients* makes us sound like whores, and we're not. We're professional career women making a lot of money doing something other women do for free."

"That doesn't answer my question," Annabelle said, not interested in Bethany's analysis of the call girl business.

"Your question, hmm . . ." Bethany said, giving her a piercing look. "I didn't think you went out on jobs."

"I don't," Annabelle answered quickly. "I'm asking for one of the other girls. She got . . . abused."

"Abused how?" Bethany asked, raising a penciled eyebrow.

"The, uh . . . guy was very rough with her. He practically raped her."

"Had he paid?" Bethany inquired, all business.

"Yes."

"Then it's not rape, is it?" Bethany said, sipping her mimosa. "It's a done deal."

Annabelle was getting more aggravated by the minute. Why couldn't Bethany understand? "But let's say she didn't want it," she said, pressing on. "How about she changed her mind, wasn't happy with the look of him?"

"The real question is," Bethany said wisely, "did she take the money?"

"I told you—yes."

"Then as I said, it's a done deal, no rape involved. Closed case. Now," Bethany continued brightly, "do you have any peach schnapps? If we add it to our mimosas, you'll be one very relaxed cookie. And then you can tell me all about who pissed you off."

An hour later, still upset and verging on slightly drunk, Annabelle managed to get rid of Bethany. It wasn't easy because Bethany was on her third mimosa, and although Annabelle had thought she needed company, she'd realized she was better off alone.

Nursing a pounding headache, she made it into her bedroom and flopped down on the bed.

What if Sharif's no doubt illegitimate fat slob of a son had given her a disease? Or even worse, gotten her pregnant?

She'd carried condoms in her purse, but the horny little bastard had prevented her from reaching them.

She could sue. Yes, sue Sharif Rani and his whole fucking family. He probably had a slew of sons from different women. White, black, Arab, American, Asian.

Yes, but how could she sue without giving the game away? Her game. . . .

She could just imagine Mommy's and Daddy's movie-star faces if they ever found out what kind of business their dear little daughter was running. . . .

After a while, she fell into a half-sleep.

Frankie would solve everything.

Frankie always did.

10

Denver

Mario is a total all that I could ask for and then some. He's way hot, from the tip of his beautifully shaped toes to his deep olive skin. And about his abs . . . well, all I can say is gimme more! They are world-class!

I have a thing about abs. I guess I feel about them the way most men feel about boobs. Kind of obsessed.

Maybe I shouldn't have jumped into bed with Mario the night of our first drink together, an occasion I can hardly classify as a date. But what the hey—two cosmos and it's all bets are gone with the wind!

And yes, we were wild. We headed back to his place pronto. Leaped into bed with a feverish discarding of clothes. Thankfully he made a grab for a handy condom, because I certainly wasn't thinking in a rational fashion. Then we were hitting it all the way and then some. It was *sooo* good that I wanted it never to stop. Guess I'm kind of sex-starved at the moment, and Mario had all the moves down. First his hands were everywhere—long, tapered fingers moving like lightning, exploring all the right places. He was fast but sleek, obviously majorly experienced at locating all the key spots.

I opened up to him like a flower thirsting for water. I was hungry for the feel of a man inside me, a real man. And Mario definitely scored on all levels.

Now he's asleep, and I'm checking out his body first, his house next.

You can find out a lot about a person from the way they live, and since Mario wasn't expecting me to come back to his small house on Fountain, I'm impressed that it's so clean and tidy. Not much mess at all, just a couple of dirty dishes in the sink and a crumpled shirt scrunched up on the bathroom floor. Everything else is kind of neat.

Too neat?

I can only observe that he's a hell of a lot neater than Josh, who was a basic slob when it came to cleaning up after himself.

As for the bed activity . . . double, triple *wow*! Not to mention *bingo*!

Naturally Mario made me come on the first try, and that's not always a given. Sometimes it could take weeks before Josh got me to the point where I scored the big O.

Hmm . . . maybe that was one of the reasons we both got in such a rut. Boredom ruled. And when boredom enters a relationship . . .

The absolute truth is that Josh might have ended it, but believe me, I was more than ready.

"Hey," Mario called out from the bedroom. "Where are you?"

"Robbing your apartment," I called back. "Only I can't find anything worth taking other than two Santana CDs and a signed photo of Derek Jeter. What are you doing with a signed—"

"It's a long story," he said, chuckling, emerging from his bedroom unabashedly naked.

I was glad that I had prudently commandeered his terry-cloth bathrobe, obviously stolen from a *Vanity Fair* event because it had *Vanity Fair: The Hollywood Issue* emblazoned on the back.

Yes, forcing him to walk around naked was an excellent move.

My eyes checked out his delightful buff bod. It was quite a sight.

"C'mere, you," he said, reaching out lazily. "Back to bed immediately."

I liked the way his mind worked. Back to bed, and it was only one hour previously that we were at it like a couple of randy high schoolers on prom night. But who am I to argue? Mario Riviera was exactly the distraction I've been looking for.

Well, hardly looking—"hoping" might be a better description.

He's athletic.

I tried not to disappoint.

He's adventurous.

So am I.

He's insatiable.

Unfortunately, I'm getting slightly exhausted. It's been an extremely long day, and I'm not used to all this wild and wonderful sexual activity. My thighs ache, my nipples are becoming overly sensitive, and a night's sleep in my own bed was beginning to sound like an excellent idea.

But oh . . . my . . . God! Before I can even think about it, we're back in bed and Mario is making me come again with all his smooth moves in full action.

I tingle and vibrate all over—the sex is *that* satisfying, with a raunchy edge that I must admit turns me on.

"You're easy," he said, grinning down at me with a self-satisfied look on his face because he *knows* he's good.

I noticed his teeth, perfect and exceptionally white. They reminded me of Mark Consuelos's teeth. In case you're wondering, Mark Consuelos is the extremely handsome husband of Kelly Ripa. And in case you're wondering, Kelly Ripa is the on-air partner of the ageless TV star Regis Philbin.

"Easy?" I replied, grinning back. "Is that an insult?"

"Nope," he said lightly. "You're into sex as much as I am. And here's what I like about you: You're not one of those girls who's got that 'playing games' thing goin' on."

Was this a positive or a negative?

I didn't bother asking because I was feeling quite comfortable with this man I hardly knew. And it's ridiculous, because he could be a rapist, a serial killer, a thief, or—

Stop that thought. I've always had a very active imagination; sometimes it gets me into big trouble.

"I think I should be going," I ventured. "It's way past my bedtime."

"We've *had* bedtime," Mario pointed out with a lascivious grin. "Now I'm starving. How about we go grab a burger?"

Yummy! Food! I have to admit that I was hungry, too. Great sex always gives me an appetite.

Before I could say yes, my cell started playing Beyoncé's "If I Were a Boy" from the confines of my purse.

I reached for it and answered.

Mistake.

It was Ralph Maestro. And it was two A.M.

Crap! Why did I pick up?

Because it's my job. And Mr. Shark Teeth makes himself unavailable after ten P.M.

"Hi," I said somewhat gingerly. "Is everything okay?"

"I have to speak with you," Ralph said, sounding brusque as usual.

"It's two in the morning," I pointed out, although surely he must know.

"I need you to come over right now," he said before clicking off.

"Who was that?" Mario asked, slipping into nosy reporter mode.

"A jealous lover," I answered vaguely. Grabbing my jeans, I scanned the floor for my thong, which was nowhere to be found.

"I don't believe you."

"Of course you don't," I responded, deciding I had no choice but to go commando. "And nor should you."

Mario threw me a long, quizzical look. "You're different from most of the girls I come across," he said.

"We live in L.A., so thank God for that," I replied crisply.

"You're direct," he said. "An' I kinda think I like it."

"In that case," I answered succinctly, "thank you for the memorable sex, but I'm afraid I must be on my way."

He burst out laughing. I joined him.

Then he leaned forward and kissed me on the lips, a long, juicy kiss—*sooo* nice.

"I'll call you," he promised.

"Sounds like a plan," I replied, slipping on my shoes. "Don't wait too long."

And then I was out of there, in my car, and on my way to the Maestro estate.

~ ~ ~

Ralph Maestro was smoking a very large cigar, puffing on it and blowing thick smoke throughout the living room.

He was wearing a heavy silk maroon bathrobe with black piping. On his feet were matching slippers. Once again, I did not think that he looked like a man in mourning.

This must be my night for men in bathrobes, only I prefer the more simple white version on Mario. And I certainly prefer what's underneath.

"Hi," I said, holding back an "I hate cigar smoke" cough.

"You look as if you just got fucked," Ralph remarked. Not a man who thinks before he speaks.

I decided to take the high road and ignore his sexist comment.

"What can I do for you, Mr. Maestro?" I asked, attempting to maintain a professional client/lawyer relationship while wondering if I looked as glowing as I felt. Apparently so.

"You can get on a plane and fly to New York," he answered matter-of-factly.

"And why would I be doing that?" I responded. I've learned never to be surprised by the things clients request, although flying to New York at two A.M. is a new one.

"Because," Ralph said, speaking slowly, "you know my daughter, and I can't reach her. So it's up to you to go get her and bring her back here."

"It's up to me to do *what*?" I asked, frowning, because it was a ridiculous request.

"You're not deaf, are you?"

"Excuse me?" I said. What a rude pig! Maybe he *had* shot his beautiful wife.

"For crissakes, girl. I'm not asking you to fly to the moon," he said irritably. "Annabelle should be here with me, and you're the only person I can think of to bring her back."

"Mr. Maestro—Ralph," I said hesitantly. "I haven't seen or spoken to Annabelle in years, so I hardly think she'll—"

"I've already discussed this with Felix," he said, interrupting me as if anything I had to say didn't matter. "And he agrees that Annabelle should be here. He also agrees that you're the one person who can persuade her to come."

"But—" I started to say.

Ralph was not in a listening mood. "There's an e-ticket on your laptop," he said, all business. "United. Seven A.M." He handed me a computer printout. "This is her address and phone number. I've left a message on her answering machine that you're on your way."

And with those words, he blew a plume of vile cigar smoke in my face and waved a dismissive hand in my direction. "Good night," he said, putting an end to any further discussion.

Beyond furious, I left the Maestro estate. Who the hell does Ralph think I am—an errand girl?

This is total bullshit, and I cannot believe that Felix agreed I should do this.

Screw Mr. Ralph Movie Star Maestro. And screw Mr. Shark Teeth. I'm a lawyer, not a freaking escort service.

Why should I fly to New York to bring Annabelle Maestro home for her mother's funeral?

Why does it have to be me?

11

Carolyn

After calling Denver and connecting with her voice mail, Carolyn wished that she'd asked Kerri where she was going and maybe tagged along. Her adrenaline was surging, and she didn't feel like spending Saturday night alone in her small apartment.

What was Gregory doing? Was he thinking of her? Was he thinking about their baby and their future together? Was he as happy as she was?

She simply couldn't wait for them to be together out in the open for everyone to see. She imagined his wife's face when he told her. Evelyn was a cold fish and obviously didn't love him, so why would *she* care?

Gregory had told her many times that he and Evelyn never made love, that they had no shared interests, and that he would have divorced her long ago if it weren't for the children.

Carolyn knew it was a clichéd situation—married man with a wife who didn't understand him—but she believed him all the same. Gregory was different, he had integrity, and she loved him with all her heart.

Thinking about it, she wished it hadn't been necessary for her to yell and threaten in the office earlier. But being pregnant was not something to be taken lightly. She'd been forced to jolt him into understanding that now their situation had to change dramatically.

He got it. He finally got it.

Now all she had to do was wait a little longer.

~ ~ ~

"Jesus, Evelyn, who *are* these people?" Gregory hissed in his wife's ear.

Evelyn adjusted a ruby-and-diamond Cartier earring and responded sotto voce, "These *people* are reformed criminals who are making our city a much safer place."

"What the hell does *that* mean?" he growled, none too pleased that she'd dragged him to yet another of her boring do-good events.

"You see that man over there?" She pointed out a bearded Latino in an ill-fitting suit, with a fierce tattoo on his neck and a single gold stud earring.

"Yes. I see him. So what?"

"He's a former gang member who has come over to our side. He currently counsels young boys about how *not* to get trapped into gang life."

Listening to Evelyn speak, Gregory was struck by how incongruous she sounded. What the hell did she know about gang life? His wife, the do-gooder. She always had a cause. She always regarded herself as holier-than-thou.

"Come," Evelyn said, gripping his arm. "I'll introduce you to him."

Gregory had no desire to be introduced to a former gang member. He had other things on his mind, like what was he supposed to do about Carolyn? Whiny, pregnant, cock-sucking Carolyn.

Evelyn steered him across the room and in her best lady-of-the-manor voice said, "Ramirez, I'd like you to meet my husband, Senator Gregory Stoneman."

Ramirez threw him a stony look.

Gregory recognized the look. It was a "Fuck you, white asshole" look. This guy was no reformed gangbanger. He was a smart criminal forging connections.

"It's a pleasure to meet you," Gregory said, pasting a politician's smile on his face. "My wife tells me you're doing very worthwhile work for our city."

"I'm tryin'," Ramirez responded, his eyes darting around the room. "It ain't easy, but I'm tryin'."

"Excellent," Gregory said, waving over a waiter. He needed another drink.

"Yes," Evelyn said, twisting a thin diamond bracelet on her delicate wrist. "We need more funding for the centers Ramirez plans to open across the city. Right now we only have one, and it's such important work, keeping young boys off the street. I'm hoping to put together a special concert to raise money. Ramirez seems to think we can get some of those rapper people involved."

Rapper people! Evelyn existed in another world. Even *he* knew the correct term was rap artists.

"Anythin' you can do to help," Ramirez said. "Maybe you can drop by tomorrow, see for yourself the work we're doin'."

Yes, Gregory thought, *that's exactly how I plan on spending my Sunday.*

"I might do that," he said. *And then again I might not.*

Ramirez had his eye on Evelyn's bracelet.

Damn! Gregory thought. *I hope he doesn't know where we live.*

~ ~ ~

Nellie Fortuna resided in the apartment next to Carolyn's. Nellie was in her late eighties, and apparently she had no one left. No relatives. No friends. No one. Everyone had died on her.

Long ago and far away, Nellie Fortuna had been a beautiful eighteen-year-old movie starlet living in a Hollywood mansion with a withered old producer who happened to be a millionaire. Way back in the 1930s, millionaires meant something, whereas today you had to be a billionaire to be relevant. Anyway, that's what Nellie said; she was very talkative and quite a character.

Carolyn tried to stop by at least once every couple of days to make sure the old dear was still alive and to feed her rather mangy cat, Gable. Apparently, back when Nellie was at the peak of her career, she'd been the lover of many silver-screen icons—including Clark Gable, whose faded picture sat proudly in a silver art deco photo frame on her mantelpiece. The photo was inscribed, "To Dear Nellie, Love from Clark."

It could have been a fan photo, or it could have been the real thing.

Nellie assured Carolyn it was the real thing.

"Every tomcat I ever owned I named Gable," Nellie would often say. And then she'd smile and become all dreamy-eyed. "He was quite the man. . . . I'll never forget *that* one."

When she had the time, Carolyn enjoyed listening to Nellie's stories of old Hollywood. They were filled with all the sparkle and glamour of yesteryear, and Nellie spun her tales with such relish.

"These gals today, they all look the same," Nellie would grumble. "And their outfits! Downright disgusting! Now, in *my* day . . ."

With Gregory on her mind, Carolyn knocked on Nellie's door and was relieved, as she always was, to find the old lady alive and well, sitting in front of her TV watching the E! Channel, her favorite.

"Just checking on you," Carolyn called out. "Can't stay."

"Hello, dear, you look so pretty today," Nellie said, as always, alert and astute. "You've got quite a gleam in your eye. Could we have a new boyfriend?"

Carolyn couldn't stop smiling. "Well . . . not exactly new," she said softly. "More like . . . I don't know . . . committed."

Gable padded over and began rubbing himself languorously against her leg. She bent down to stroke him, and he purred loudly.

"I think I know," Nellie said, nodding wisely. "It's that nice young man, your boyfriend—what's his name? Ah yes, Matt. He's asked you to marry him, hasn't he?"

"No," Carolyn said, shaking her head. "Matt's history."

"There *is* someone, though, isn't there?" Nellie persisted. "Who is he?"

Carolyn wished she could tell her. Wished that she could sing it from the rooftops. *I'm pregnant with Gregory Stoneman's baby! I'm pregnant pregnant pregnant!*

"Just an old friend," she said.

"Ah . . . old friends," Nellie mused. "I had plenty of those. Old costars. Old lovers. Old married men who couldn't keep it in their trousers. Ah yes, old friends. . . ."

"Have you fed Gable?" Carolyn asked. Nellie loved to ramble on about her many affairs, and she wasn't in the mood to listen.

"Yes, dear, all done," Nellie said. "But thanks for dropping by anyway. You know how much I appreciate it."

"My pleasure," Carolyn said, making a quick exit. On her way out, she decided it would be a nice gesture to invite Nellie Fortuna to their wedding.

Senator Gregory Stoneman

&

Ms. Carolyn Henderson

Invite you to witness their joining in matrimony.

Yes! Yes! Yes!

~ ~ ~

"No!" Gregory said sharply as he and Evelyn were in the car on their way home. "I will not visit some rat-infested center filled with gangbangers because *you* think it's a good idea."

Evelyn remained calm, as she always did. "Gregory, dear," she said, her voice smooth as silk, "visiting Ramirez at his center will enhance your reputation. The voters will appreciate such a goodwill gesture, they always do. Have your little assistant alert the press. It's an excellent photo opportunity."

Why did she always refer to Carolyn as his "little" assistant? Carolyn was at least five feet eight, hardly little. It was Evelyn's way of putting her down. Not that she suspected anything, but Evelyn was less than flattering about any other female. At a White House dinner party, he'd been seated next to Gwyneth Paltrow, and later Evelyn had called her a skinny little nothing. Again her use of the word *little*. It was Evelyn's ultimate put-down. What she really meant was that they were less than her, small and unimportant.

Evelyn was a snob. She'd married him only because politically he was destined to go places, especially with Evelyn and her powerful family behind him.

Had she ever loved him?

Probably not.

But they had two fine, healthy children, and his career was progressing in the right direction, and generally life was on track.

Now "little" Carolyn Henderson was determined to screw everything up. And what was he supposed to do about *that*?

One thing was patently clear: He had to do something, and fast.

12

Bobby

Back in their hotel suite, M.J. ran around packing their overnight bags while Bobby had Frankie paged. He'd tried reaching Frankie on his cell phone, to no avail; he'd also attempted to contact Annabelle so that he could alert her that they were on their way back to the city. She didn't answer her phone, either.

By this time, M.J. had switched on the TV and they'd gotten the full gruesome story of Gemma Summer's murder.

"I can't believe we didn't hear about it earlier," Bobby said, perplexed. "I feel so bad for Annabelle, she must be frantic."

"You think it's possible her old man did it?" M.J. asked. "He always scared the crap outta me."

"He might be movie-star dumb, but not dumb enough to shoot her in their own house," Bobby mused. "Like who would do that?"

"Yeah," M.J. ruminated. "Dumb, or maybe he's so arrogant he thinks he can get away with it."

"The media's gonna get off on this one," Bobby said. "It's their dream scenario. Two movie stars and a murder."

Should he call Lucky? He seemed to remember that when she'd owned Panther Studios, Ralph Maestro and Gemma Summer had both appeared in movies her studio had produced. She must've known Gemma, maybe even been friends with her.

Frankie burst into the suite, looking disheveled. "You had me paged?" he questioned, long hair flopping in his eyes. "What the fuck is *that* about? I was all set to make a killing at the craps table."

"I guess you haven't heard the news," Bobby said, his tone somber.

"What news?" Frankie questioned, thinking, *Oh, shit. They've found out. Good-bye, weekend of freedom with the guys. Too fuckin' bad.*

"Annabelle's mother's been shot," Bobby said flatly. "We just heard about it."

"Jeez!" Frankie said, striving to put a shocked expression on his face. "What the fuck happened? When? How? Is she dead?"

"Yes, she's dead all right," Bobby said. "Take a look at the TV. You should call Annabelle right away."

"Yeah, man," M.J. said, joining in. "We gotta get your ass back to New York."

"You know Annabelle doesn't carry a phone," Frankie said, pissed that this definitely meant a fast exit.

"Then try your apartment," Bobby said. "I bet she's there."

"Yeah, yeah," Frankie said. He made a show of moving toward the TV and pretending to catch the news for the first time.

"There's a buzz goin' around that her old man could've done it," M.J. interjected. "The whole scene is way brutal. Whaddya think?"

"Never met her parents," Frankie said. "An' believe me, Annabelle wasn't close to them. They hardly ever spoke."

"You need to be with her," Bobby said. "We're packed up and ready to go, so I suggest we hit the road."

"Sure," Frankie said, albeit reluctantly.

Bye-bye, rendezvous with the sexy waitress from Morton's. Too bad. I could've fucked her, then recruited her.

~ ~ ~

A few hours later, Bobby pulled his BMW up outside the building where Frankie and Annabelle resided.

Frankie took his time getting out of the car. It was late, past midnight, and the last thing he felt like doing was listening to Annabelle bitch about her parents. He knew that's exactly what she'd do. Bitching about Mommy and Daddy was one of her favorite rants. It was always about how self-absorbed they were and how they'd never taken any notice of her when she was growing up. Usually he told her to quit complaining, but tonight the circumstances were different. With the tragedy and all, he would be forced to sit and listen for hours. It was sympathetic boyfriend time, of that he was sure.

"You want us to come up with you?" Bobby asked, not really meaning it but making the effort all the same.

"Yeah, man, maybe we should," M.J. said, equally halfhearted. They both knew what a drama queen Annabelle could be, and tonight she'd be out of control, probably hysterical.

Frankie decided it wasn't necessary. "I can take care of her."

"Well . . ." Bobby said. "Be sure to give her our love, and tell her how sorry we are. We'll check in with you first thing."

"Got it," Frankie said, finally moving away from the car.

Once Frankie had vanished into the building, Bobby said, "Maybe we should stop by the club, surprise everyone."

"Right," M.J. agreed. "I wouldn't mind checkin' on how many waiters we got runnin' out the back with a shitload of steaks stuffed down their pants."

M.J. had a thing about the staff stealing. If he had his way, he'd install hidden cameras everywhere from the kitchen to the workers' restroom.

Bobby's attitude was more laid-back. He'd learned from Lucky that in the hotel and club business you had to make allowances; it was a fact of life that the barmen would replace Grey Goose vodka with a cheaper brand, the waiters would steal, and the kitchen workers would take home whatever they could. As long as the stealing was not excessive, it was better to live with it and not stress out.

Bobby wondered if Zeena would be in the club, surrounded by her usual group of sycophants.

He hoped she was, then he immediately hoped she wasn't.

Dammit, the crush he had on her was ridiculous. She might be a famous, talented superstar, but she treated him as if he didn't exist. And he wasn't used to being ignored.

After all, he was a Stanislopoulos, and his mother was Lucky Santangelo. He deserved respect. And he planned on getting it.

~ ~ ~

"Another Bellini," Zeena ordered in her slightly accented, deep-down husky voice.

The boy toy on her left jumped to attention. He was a Peruvian model, all of nineteen, and he was Zeena's latest plaything. She paraded him around like a trophy, and the boy was quite beautiful with his sleepy bedroom eyes, pouty lips, and flushed cheeks.

Zeena called him Puppy. She called all of them Puppy, and she came up with a new one every month.

Out of the corners of her exotically made-up eyes, she noticed Bobby Santangelo Stanislopoulos enter the club.

So good-looking. So trying hard to play it cool. So longing to get into her pants.

She wondered how surprised he'd be to discover that twenty-five years ago, when she was a mere fifteen, his father, the great Dimitri, had deflowered her on his magnificent yacht in the South of France.

A smile played around her scarlet lips. Ah . . . Dimitri . . . what a man, what a lover. . . .

Like father, like son?

Should she take the time to find out?

Perhaps. It might amuse her. Then again, it might not.

Bobby was fast approaching her table. He was late tonight; usually he was around much earlier. Watching him, she had to admit that he had a certain style, although style wasn't everything. Seasoning was preferable. If they weren't nineteen, then Zeena liked them to be older and extraordinarily powerful. Extreme youth and excessive power—in Zeena's world, those were the two most important aphrodisiacs.

She continued to observe as Bobby slowly made his way over, stopping at each table. She watched as every female in the club clung to his arm, trying to persuade him to sit at their table. She watched as he extracted himself with a polite shake of his head and a few kind words.

Finally he presented himself at her table.

"Zeena," he said, playing the perfect host. "Nice to see you. Anything you need? Anything I can get you?"

"If Zeena needs anything, Bobby," she drawled, toying with the back of Puppy's long hair, "Zeena will ask a waiter."

Bobby nodded. At least she remembered his name tonight. That wasn't always the case. "Yeah. Sure," he said. "But I'd like to send over a bottle of Cristal for you and your party."

"Only *one* bottle, Bobby?" she said with a sly tilt of her head.

Christ! She reminded him so much of Serenity, even though she was at least twenty years older. She had the same pissy attitude.

"Or two," he said, determined to stand up to her.

Puppy smirked.

Yeah, Bobby thought, *keep on smirking, dude, you'll soon be last month's model.*

Zeena gave him a very direct, challenging stare before flipping back her sheet of glossy black hair, which fell below her waist. "Five bottles, Bobby," she said, indicating the group of hangers-on surrounding her. "Zeena's friends are thirsty."

Bobby kept his cool, trying not to think about how spectacular she looked tonight in some kind of chocolate brown spidery dress that barely covered her breasts. He could see her nipples. Yes, he could definitely see her nipples. "Two bottles on the house," he said evenly. "The rest I'm afraid we'll have to charge you for."

She arched a painted eyebrow. "You can't possibly be serious?"

He stood his ground. He might be suffering from some kind of insane crush, but business was business. "House rules," he said pleasantly.

"Ah, Bobby . . ." She sighed. "Are you aware that Zeena can go anywhere in the world and get everything for free?"

"Lucky you," he said, testing her.

Would she get up and leave? Or would she stay? What did he want her to do?

He honestly didn't know.

"Yes," she murmured with a sarcastic twist. "Zeena is extraordinarily lucky." A long beat. "How about you, Bobby? Are *you* lucky?"

This was the longest exchange of words they'd ever had, and since it was obvious she was staying, he thought about making his move, even though she still had one hand caressing the back of Puppy's neck.

Puppy was glaring at him, yet in spite of the glare he was giving off quite a gay vibe. What was *that* about?

"I . . . uh . . . like to think a person makes their own luck," Bobby said, clearing his throat.

"Keep on thinking that way," Zeena replied. "Naïveté is *such* a special quality."

And without further ado, she pulled Puppy's face toward hers and indulged in a long, tongues-down-each-other's-throats, intimate kiss.

Bobby backed away from the table. Screw Zeena and her full entourage of hangers-on. She was playing with him, and he didn't like it.

Or was that exactly what he did like?

13

Annabelle

"Wake up, babe," Frankie crooned. "C'mon, sweetie, open up those sexy eyes."

Annabelle rolled over in bed. Someone was shaking her shoulder, someone was pulling her away from *the* most delightful dream she'd ever experienced. In her dream, she was lying on a bed in a luxurious hotel room overlooking the ocean. With her were Chace Crawford and Brad Pitt. Chace was busily kissing her neck, while Brad was patiently awaiting his turn. But Brad was beginning to get antsy . . . he started roughly shaking her shoulder . . . and—

"Oh my God!" Annabelle exclaimed, waking with a start and seeing Frankie standing over her. "What are *you* doing here? You're supposed to be in Atlantic City."

"I came back as soon as I heard," he lied, sitting on the side of the bed. "You didn't think I was gonna let you go through this alone, did you?"

Annabelle rubbed her eyes, reluctant to leave her dream but happy that Frankie was concerned enough about her degrading experience with Sharif Rani's son to forgo his weekend with the boys and race to her side. "Frankie," she murmured, reaching up to touch his cheek with her fingers, "it was so awful. . . ."

"I know, baby," he said soothingly. "It's a terrible thing, but let's be honest about this—it wasn't as if you were close."

"Close!" she exclaimed, struggling to sit up. "Close! I was in the same room, goddamn it. How much closer could I get?"

"Calm down," Frankie said, realizing that she was in shock and had no idea what she was saying.

"What time is it?" Annabelle demanded, glaring at him. "'Cause whatever time it is, I want you to get on the phone to that son of a bitch and ream him a new asshole. Did I tell you he hung up on me? He actually clicked off his phone. Can you believe it?"

So . . . Ralph Maestro had hung up on his own daughter. Maybe Ralph *had* shot his wife and was now filled with guilt. After all, they were Hollywood people—who knew what kinds of brutal acts they were capable of?

Frankie's mind went into overdrive. If Ralph Maestro *had* murdered his wife, was convicted and eventually sent to jail—who would inherit everything?

As their only child, Annabelle, of course. This whole murder thing could end up having a silver lining.

Frankie immediately imagined himself living in L.A., residing in a mansion, throwing wild parties by the pool, and mixing with big-time superstars. Movies, sports, the music biz—he'd get to know them all.

It bugged him that whenever he'd suggested taking a trip to L.A., Annabelle had always shut him down. "I don't ever want to go there again," she'd informed him many times. "Living in L.A. was the unhappiest time of my life."

Now everything had changed.

"Well?" Annabelle asked, a determined look in her eyes. "Are you going to phone him or not?"

"Hey," Frankie said, shrugging. "The thing is, I don't even *know* the dude, so what would I say?"

"For God's sake!" Annabelle snapped, green eyes blazing. "Of course you know him. Just tell him that we're *never* doing business with him again."

"Huh?" Frankie said, confused.

"I . . . hate . . . him," Annabelle said through clenched teeth. "And for your information, I don't care how much money we'll lose, it's no big deal, we'll make it up elsewhere. There are plenty of other billionaires in the sea—we'll put out a fishing net and haul in a few."

She was delirious; that much was obvious.

"Listen, babe," he began, "I know this is hard—"

"Hard!" she exploded. "How about taking a look at my bruises? I'm covered in them."

"Huh?" He was getting more confused by the minute.

"Bruises, Frankie," she said, narrowing her eyes. "Bruises from a big fat moron who was *no way* fifteen. And bites—he bit me on my thigh! Sharif Rani should be ashamed of himself setting me up with his so-called son. Illegitimate, I'm sure, 'cause he sure as hell wasn't the innocent young Arab boy Sharif led us to believe I was meeting. He was a big fat hairy American rapist!"

Oh, shit! Annabelle wasn't even talking about her mother's murder. She was carrying on about her meeting with Sharif Rani's son. Jesus Christ! Did she even *know* her mother was dead? Hadn't anyone told her?

"Have you heard the news?" he ventured.

"Didn't you read the text message I left on your phone?" she said shortly. "'Cause you don't seem to care that I got beat up and *raped*! What's the matter with you?"

"I'm here, aren't I?" Now he was sorry that he hadn't checked his messages. He'd been too busy losing at blackjack, picking up a pretty waitress, and almost enjoying a lap dance.

"Babe," he said, finally realizing that *he* was the one who had to tell her, "there's something you should know."

"What?" she said, furious that he wasn't reacting in a stronger fashion.

"It's your, uh . . . mother."

"What about her?"

"Jesus, I don't know how I'm supposed to tell you this," he muttered. "So I guess there's no other way but to give it to you straight." He stopped and took a deep breath. "Your mother was murdered earlier today. Shot in the face."

There was an eerie silence.

"I . . . uh . . . thought you knew," he added, watching her closely to see how she reacted.

Annabelle stared at him in disbelief. What was he saying? What was he talking about? Was she still dreaming? Had her dream turned into some ridiculous nightmare?

"I'm so sorry, babe," he said. "It's a total bummer, I know."

"When?" she said at last, catching her breath. "When did this happen?"

"Sometime this morning in L.A. I dunno much, only what I saw on TV. Soon as I heard the news, I got in the car an' came racing home."

"This morning," she repeated dully, her expression blank. "How come nobody contacted me?"

"I'm sure somebody must've. You checked your messages?"

She shook her head. Suddenly everything seemed surreal. Her mother had been murdered. Her mother, the world-class beauty. The woman everyone loved. The heroine of countless movies. The Oscar-winning actress with the undeniable talent.

Her mother. The untouchable Gemma Summer. A woman she'd never been close to. A woman who'd allowed her only child to be raised by a series of disinterested nannies. A woman who'd spent most of her daughter's childhood away on location shoots—unless there was the need for a *People* or *Vanity Fair* cover story, in which case a cute little five-year-old added to the appeal of the picture. Then, after Annabelle turned eight, there were no more photo sessions. Eight was too old to be considered cute anymore, although sometimes her father took her to Lakers games and they were photographed sitting courtside. But even he stopped doing that when she hit puberty.

Ah yes, puberty. Her South African nanny had taught her the facts of life. Her mother had decided she needed a nose job at fourteen. And a young Mexican gardener who worked on their estate had taught her how to give head.

At school she'd perfected the art of the blow job, becoming the most popular girl in her class. Sex was her way of getting plenty of attention. She excelled at it.

There was also shopping, for her parents didn't stint when it came to giving her money. They handed her a bunch of credit cards and gifted her with a Porsche on her sixteenth birthday. Anything to keep her out of their way.

So there she was, a popular girl, a rich girl, a spoiled girl, with nobody around to stop her from doing anything she wanted.

And what she wanted was to get away from her self-absorbed movie-star parents. Fly the coop and lose the hated tag: *This is Annabelle. Her mother is Gemma Summer and her father's Ralph Maestro.*

Moving to New York was the best thing she'd ever done. Very few people knew who her parents were and who she really was. That's the way she liked it.

Gemma Summer. Mother. Dead. And she'd never even got to know her.

"Check the messages on the phone at the SoHo apartment," she said, her throat constricted. "That's the only number Ralph's got."

Frankie did so, and sure enough there were a slew of messages, including a terse one from Ralph himself, saying that he was sending one of his lawyers to New York to bring her home.

Frankie informed Annabelle, who shook her head stubbornly. "I refuse to go back to L.A.," she said flatly. "Why should I?"

"'Cause it's about your mom," Frankie said, reasoning with her. "You gotta do it, babe. There'll be a funeral, an' you have to be there. I'll come with you. Don't you worry about it, I'll be beside you all the way."

14

Denver

My flight to New York was uneventful apart from the fact that I spotted Denis Leary pacing up and down, waiting to board the plane. Since I'm such a huge *Rescue Me* fan, I contemplated going up to him and telling him what a clever and entertaining show it was. But then I realized he already knew that, and I would probably come across like some half-baked starry-eyed fan—or even worse, a stalker. So I controlled myself and instead studied the L.A. edition of the *New York Post* and *USA Today*, both of which featured screaming headlines about Gemma Summer Maestro's brutal demise.

It made me realize that by the time I reached Annabelle, she would already know the shocking news; in fact, she might even be on a plane heading for L.A. We could be crossing in the air, which would mean that my trip to New York would be pointless.

I wondered how Annabelle would take the news of her mother's murder. It was such a shattering and terrible event. To be shot in the face in your own bed . . .

For a second, I tried to put myself in Annabelle's place. What if it was my mom? Thank God that was impossible. Or was it? Who knew what lurked just around the corner? We all understand that fate has a way of playing unexpected tricks.

My thoughts moved on to Mario. Should I have called or texted to tell him I was heading out of town? Or would he perceive that as coming on too strong too soon?

Crap. I shouldn't be thinking such thoughts. It's not as if it's a relationship. Mario is not my boyfriend, nor do I want him to be. I am happy on my own. Quite content, thank you very much.

Although . . . sometimes I do miss that spooning thing in bed, the kind of deal you get only when you're with a proper boyfriend.

Once off the plane, I checked my BlackBerry. There were several messages and texts. My dad, saying he'd read my name in the papers and what was happening with the case. I'd not had a moment to call him. Felix, reiterating that I should bring Annabelle back ASAP, per Ralph's instructions. And yippee—a call from Carolyn informing me that she had something major to tell me.

Carolyn has been my best friend forever. I hope that her news is good, like she's gotten back together with Matt and they're planning on getting married. Carolyn should be married, she's that kind of girl: smart and sensible and nurturing. Any man would be lucky to have her.

I myself am not the marrying kind. I have no desire to be tied down to one man forever. I possess no maternal instinct, although I do love kids—other people's, that is. And the last thing I am is nurturing. No, I have to admit that career is all-important to me, and right now it definitely comes first. Which is why I'm in New York and not languishing in bed with Mario, experiencing even more exceptional sex.

Carolyn and I haven't seen each other in ages, and I miss her. I am so looking forward to her upcoming trip to L.A. She's promised to stay for ten days, and I have all kinds of plans. I'm thinking we could sneak off to Vegas for a couple of days and maybe visit a spa retreat. We both work so hard that her visit will be a great excuse to do nothing else except chill out. I've already warned Felix I will be adding to the Christmas vacation time with a few leftover vacation days I've been saving up. He didn't take it well.

As I stood outside the airport, shivering while I searched for a cab, I wondered if sex with Mario was as exceptional as I'd thought. Maybe it *seemed* great because I hadn't had it in a while. Or maybe Josh was *really* bad in bed.

Poor Josh . . . not my problem anymore.

I finally spotted a cab and grabbed it before someone else did.

"Where to?" asked the driver, a surly white man with incongruous dreadlocks and a missing front tooth.

Good question. I hadn't booked a hotel because all I planned on doing was meeting Annabelle, persuading her to fly to L.A. with me, and catching the next flight back.

I checked my BlackBerry for the address in SoHo that Ralph had given me and instructed the driver to take me there. Then I tried the phone number Ralph had also given me and connected with voice mail, which seemed reasonable, as I'm sure Annabelle wouldn't be answering her phone at a time like this.

I left a message: "Hi, this is Denver Jones. I don't know if you remember me, but I'm now an associate at your father's law firm, and I'm here to assist you back to L.A. for the funeral." Lamely I added, "I'm very sorry for your loss."

I wondered if she *would* remember me. After all, Denver Jones is not exactly an everyday name. We'd shared some fun times until she'd dropped me. But that was a long time ago. We were kids then, and I'm sure she's nicer now.

On impulse, I called Mario. Didn't mean to, but somehow my phone decided to go there.

"Hey," he said.

"Hey," I responded. "Guess where I am?"

"I know where you *should* be," he said, sounding pleased to hear from me.

"And where would that be?" I answered coyly, horrified at myself, for I am not a coy girl. There's just something about Mario that brings out the girl in me. Maybe it's those world-class abs. More likely his world-class cock.

"In my bed, next to me," he said.

Giggle. Giggle. Oh crap, I'm falling to pieces before my very eyes!

"I'm in New York," I managed, slightly breathless.

That piece of news aroused his interest. "You are? What are you doing there?"

Should I tell him?

No. He's a TV reporter, can't let him know too much.

"A couple of personal things I have to take care of," I answered vaguely.

"I thought you were on the Ralph Maestro case," he said suspiciously.

Was he fishing?

Probably. He's a journalist, after all. He has to be curious.

"I am," I answered carefully. "I mean, my firm is. But right now there's nothing to do."

"Unless Ralph Maestro is arrested," he stated.

"And why would they arrest Ralph Maestro?" I asked, my tone becoming a tad frosty, since I had planned on having an intimate conversation about our amazing night of sex, not a discussion about the Maestro case.

"Word is they got nobody else in mind," Mario said. "You should take a look at the blogs, they're all over it."

"That's ridiculous!" I exclaimed, jumping to my client's defense.

"Yeah?" Mario took a long, steady beat. "You sure?"

"I have to go," I said, suddenly eager to get off the phone.

"When you coming back?"

"Maybe later. Maybe tomorrow."

"Quick trip."

"It is."

"So . . . Denver," he said, his voice turning sexy and seductive. "Dinner the instant you return? Yes?"

I loved the way he said my name. I managed a casual, "Sure," and quickly clicked off.

Mario Riviera could be trouble. I'd spent only one night with him, and already I was thinking about him far too much.

~ ~ ~

After an hour of horrendous traffic jams and death-defying driving, my cabdriver deposited me outside a building in SoHo.

I checked my watch: It was almost four-thirty New York time and bitterly cold. Pulling my not nearly warm enough jacket around me, I checked the row of push buttons by the door and spotted "A. Maestro." After pressing the buzzer, I waited . . . and waited . . . and waited . . .

No answer.

I'm sure my instincts are right and Annabelle is already on a flight to L.A.

Damn Ralph Maestro and his stupid instructions. I could be in my sunny office in Century City right now instead of freezing my ass off in front of a locked building in SoHo.

As I was contemplating my next move, a tall, youngish man emerged from the building all bundled up in a long khaki army coat, striped scarf, and one of those knit caps that Jake Gyllenhaal's always photographed in.

I felt like ripping the cap off his head, I was that cold. Nobody had prepared me for a New York winter, and I was not dressed for the part.

"Excuse me," I said, jumping right in. "Do you happen to know an Annabelle Maestro?"

"Who?" he said, stopping for a moment.

"A. Maestro." I indicated the row of bell pushes. "She lives here."

"Oh," he said, wrinkling his forehead. "You must mean the redhead on the top floor. Seen her a couple of times in the last year. She doesn't come here much."

"I thought she lived here."

"Nah. From what I hear, she has a boyfriend uptown. I guess she bunks with him."

"Would you happen to know where?" I asked, rubbing my hands together with the hope of generating some well-needed heat.

"Sorry, can't help you." He veered around me and began to stride briskly down the street.

Before the main door closed, I slipped inside. At least it was warmer in the vestibule, and I could figure out what my next move should be.

I was standing by a row of mailboxes, and I did a quick check to see what A. Maestro's held. The guy in the army coat was right: Annabelle obviously didn't spend much time here. Her mailbox was overflowing, and since it wasn't locked, I shuffled through her mail to see if I could spot anything with the boyfriend's name on it.

Nothing except junk mail, bills, and several magazine subscriptions. *Vogue, InStyle, Harper's.* Yes, this was definitely Annabelle's mailbox. And then, right at the bottom of the pile, I discovered a copy of *Rolling Stone.* It was addressed to Frankie Romano at Annabelle's address. Bingo! Must be the boyfriend.

What to do next?

I decided to call Ralph Maestro. Mr. Friendly.

Naturally, I was informed by a snippy-sounding assistant that Mr. Maestro was taking no calls, and when I assured her it was important and concerned his daughter, she came back with a sharp, "No exceptions," and hung up on me.

Very pleasant.

Next I called Felix and told him what I knew.

"Stick around," Felix said. "I'll find out where she is and get back to you."

Ha! *Stick around.* Apparently he didn't realize the weather in New York was below freezing.

Reluctantly I left the building, trudged down the block, and discovered a grungy little coffee shop. When I say grungy, I mean it wasn't all clean and sparkly like a Starbucks or a Coffee Bean. This place had character—it also had the guy in the army coat, sitting at a table drinking a mug of coffee while tapping away on his laptop.

"Hi," I said on my way to the counter.

He barely glanced up.

So much for my powers of attraction. Well, I suppose I wasn't looking my best, with unwashed hair pulled back into a messy ponytail, bloodshot, sleep-deprived eyes, and a red nose.

I'd almost gone from Mario's bed to the airport, and sleeping on the plane is not my fave thing. I prefer to stay alert, just in case.

I walked up to the counter and ordered a cappuccino and a piece of appetizing apple pie from a heavyset, middle-aged man who appeared to have strayed out of a scene from *The Sopranos.* He was unshaven, with badly dyed black hair poufed into a Donald Trump–style bouffant, a pallid complexion, and heavy-lidded eyes.

On impulse, I asked him if he happened to know a Frankie Romano. After all, this was a small local coffee shop, so it was possible.

The man thought for a moment, then said, "Yeah, I remember Frankie. He was quite a character, but he don't come around no more."

What a lucky break. I'd scored with my first question!

"Do you know where I might find him?" I asked.

"Dunno. He was some kinda deejay—played records for a livin'. Used to be in here every mornin'."

"So do you know if there's any way I can locate him?" I asked, probably sounding too much like a lawyer.

"Why? You pregnant?" The man burst out laughing at his incredibly sexist remark.

Army Coat glanced up from his laptop. He'd removed his knit cap, revealing a mop of blondish curly hair.

"Actually," I said, clinging to my dignity, "Frankie's inherited money. That's why I need to find him, so I can make sure he gets what's coming to him."

Mr. Shark Teeth—aka Felix Saunders—had taught me to always mention money when tracking someone down. The word had a magical way of opening doors.

"The kid's gonna be happy 'bout that," said the man behind the counter, scratching his chin. "I think we got a card or sompin'. Yo, Mara!" he bellowed. "Get your fat ass out here."

Mara appeared from the back, an illicit cigarette dangling from her lips. She was obviously the man's wife, and she looked the part. Scads of heavy makeup, ample hips, and a sour expression. HBO would cast her in an instant. "What?" she snapped.

"This girl's lookin' for Frankie Romano. Remember the deejay kid—used to be in here all the time? Din't he give you his card 'cause you was thinkin' of using him for your cousin's weddin'?"

"Too expensive," Mara sniffed. "What did the little pissant think, that we was made of money?"

"Yeah, yeah," the man agreed. "But ya still got his card, don'cha?"

"Chucked it," Mara said, shooting me a flinty glare—like how dare I even ask.

"Sorry, girlie," my Mafia don said. "The pie's on me. Enjoy."

I took my pie and cappuccino and retreated to a table in the corner. Two minutes later, the guy in the army coat leaned over—as I said before, the place was tiny—and handed me a slip of paper.

"What's this?" I asked, noticing that he had very appealing brown eyes fringed with long, thick lashes.

"Frankie Romano's number," he said.

"How did you—"

"Overheard your conversation, so I Googled him. Frankie Romano, deejay. Parties. Events."

"Oh . . . wow, thanks," I said appreciatively. "I really need to get in touch with him."

"You're not a New Yorker, are you."

"How can you tell?"

"I dunno, kind of the way you're dressed."

"What's the giveaway?" I asked curiously.

"Thin jacket. No boots. No scarf. No gloves. You must be freezing."

"I am," I confessed, noting that the brown eyes went nicely with the curly blondish hair. "In fact, the moment I saw you I wanted to rip that warm-looking cap right off your head," I added jokingly.

Army Coat grinned. He had crooked teeth, not perfect like every guy in L.A., but just crooked enough to work.

"It's yours," he said, gallantly handing me his cap.

"No, I can't accept it," I protested.

"Sure you can. It's not as if I'm giving you a diamond. Besides, your hair looks like it's in dire need of rescue. Bad night?"

"Actually it was a great night," I said, thinking of Mario. "But then I had to get on a seven A.M. flight and come straight here."

"From?"

"L.A. Can't you tell?"

"No," he said, shaking his head.

"Really?"

"Yeah."

"How?"

"No fake tan, among other things." He grinned again and offered his hand. "Sam. And you are . . . ?"

"Denver."

"Interesting name. Different."

"My parents thought so."

"What are you really here for, Denver?" he asked, adding more sugar to his coffee and stirring vigorously.

"Business."

"What kind of business?"

"Wow! You're curious."

"Yeah, I've been told that before," he said with a wry smile. "It's 'cause I'm a writer—makes me want to know everything."

Alarm signals went off in my head. Writer or journalist? Nosy reporter lurking around Annabelle's building or merely a neighbor?

"What kinds of things do you write?" I inquired.

"Screenplays," he said, and took a gulp of coffee. "And you—what's your gig?"

"I'm an associate at an L.A. law firm," I replied, toying with my apple pie. I couldn't help thinking that the poor guy should move to L.A., where everyone and their brother is attempting to write a screenplay. He had no chance of getting anything off the ground in New York.

"And why are you really looking for Frankie Romano?" he asked, leaning forward.

I did not feel inclined to change my story. "He's inherited money," I answered vaguely. "I'm here to see he knows about it."

"Hmm . . ." Sam said, looking skeptical.

"I need to find a bathroom," I said, deciding to end this line of conversation.

I got up and approached my Mafia don at the counter. "Is there a ladies' room I can use?" I asked sweetly. After all, he had given me a free slice of pie.

"For you, honey, anythin'," the man said, having apparently taken a shine to me the minute I'd mentioned money. "Mara!" he yelled, turning his head. "Female customer comin' back to use the john."

He opened a partition on the counter and ushered me through. I thought for a moment he was going to pat me on the ass, but fortunately he restrained himself.

I didn't need to pee. What I did need to do was call this Frankie Romano guy and find out if he knew where Annabelle was so I could get her back to L.A.

Mara greeted me in the back hallway with a scowl and cigarette breath.

"In there," she muttered, directing me toward a tiny, dark toilet. "An' don't go throwin' nothin' down the toilet bowl," she warned. "I don't want no clogged system."

And with those sweet words, she shut the door on me.

I took out my phone and punched in Frankie Romano's number.

15

Carolyn

Sunday morning, Carolyn got up late. Usually her alarm woke her at six A.M., but today was different. Today was Sunday, and she could luxuriate in her bed for as long as she felt like it. Too bad that Gregory couldn't luxuriate next to her. But soon . . .

She tried to imagine what their Sundays would be like when they were together. Long and leisurely. She'd cook breakfast while Greg read the newspapers and checked out the political shows on TV. She knew he enjoyed doing that, because a few months ago he'd arranged for her to accompany him on a business trip to New York, and they'd spent the entire weekend together. Total bliss—although if she was honest with herself, sometimes his sexual appetite veered toward the selfish. He loved getting oral sex from her, claimed it was the best he'd ever had. But the sad thing was that he never reciprocated, which was a big disappointment.

She was sure that once they were living together, things would change. She'd tell him in the nicest possible way what she required in bed, and of course he would comply. Why wouldn't he?

Now, lying under the covers, she wished she could phone him, if only to say good morning and hear his voice.

But no, he'd given her strict instructions never to call him at home on Sundays. "I spend all day with the children," he'd told her. "No interruptions, not unless there's a worldwide emergency."

Respecting his request, she curbed the urge to contact him and called Kerri instead, saying that she could indeed go to the mall. They arranged to meet at noon.

Finally she got up, took a shower, studied her stomach in the bathroom mirror from all angles to see if she was showing yet, and realized it was far too early to notice anything.

Pregnant! She was embarking on an exciting journey.

~ ~ ~

Anything to get out of the house and away from Evelyn's cloying presence. The woman was stifling him; Gregory felt it more and more each day.

Sitting behind his sturdy mahogany desk in his study, he contemplated calling Katy, the British journalist he'd recently met at a press conference. Katy was young and full of ambition, and she'd definitely thrown out all the right signals.

Then he thought that calling her on a Sunday might seem too eager. Perhaps it was best to wait a day or two, then have Muriel set up a lunch for next week. Katy had said she wanted to interview him. So be it.

He still had the problem of a long, boring Sunday ahead of him. Both his children were staying with their maternal grandparents for the weekend, and that left Evelyn.

Within minutes, his problem was solved when Ramirez Ortego called on his private line.

How the *hell* had Ramirez gotten his private number?

Evelyn, of course.

"Senator," Ramirez said. "Thought I'd follow up on last night's conversation. If you can make it today, my people would be most happy to see you."

Before he could think of a reason to say he couldn't make it, Ramirez gave him the details of where to go.

He wasn't that angry, because at least it was a legitimate excuse to get away from Evelyn. He was sure his dear wife would have no wish to accompany him, and he was right about that. After telling him she was too busy to go anywhere, Evelyn said, "Did you call your little secretary and tell her to alert the press?"

"I do not plan on bothering my *assistant* on a Sunday," he replied pointedly.

"Too bad," Evelyn said, elegant in a cream pantsuit and daytime pearls. "It's such an excellent photo opportunity."

"Yes," he answered dryly. "Me hanging out with a bunch of gangbangers. What a photo!"

"No, dear," Evelyn corrected. "You helping out at a community center, making sure our fine city stays safe."

God, his wife was so full of shit.

It occurred to him that now he had a legitimate reason for calling Katy, the British journalist. He could ask her if she'd like an exclusive on his visit to the community center, because he was in desperate need of a diversion. He couldn't get his mind off Carolyn's baby announcement, and how was he supposed to take care of *that* problem? He sure as hell wasn't allowing her to ruin everything he held dear. If Evelyn found out, she'd make certain he was punished in every possible way. She'd immediately take away his children, she'd attempt to ruin his reputation, and the ensuing scandal would no doubt put paid to his career.

He needed to get Carolyn out of his life, and that had to be done soon. But how? That was the question.

Damn Carolyn, and damn Evelyn, too. Bitches of a different caliber, but bitches all the same.

~ ~ ~

Kerri was an avid shopper with a passion for malls. Carolyn hated shopping and loathed large shopping malls.

Kerri raced from store to store with all the enthusiasm of a new puppy. Carolyn trailed behind.

"I *sooo* love this," Kerri cried out, happily trying on a selection of high-heeled pumps in myriad colors. "What do you think?" she asked Carolyn while tottering around the shoe store in a pair of yellow stilettos that made her legs appear even shorter than they were.

"Beige might be a more useful color," Carolyn suggested, trying to be diplomatic. "Beige goes with everything. Or maybe black."

"Boring!" Kerri squealed. "That's one thing nobody's ever accused me of being. Boring? Nooo!"

Carolyn could believe it, since Kerri never stopped talking and always had something to say. Lately it was all about her adventures on the Internet.

"There's some unbelievable sites," Kerri assured her with a knowing wink. "All you have to do is post your photo and a brief description of yourself. Then before you know it—just like the song—it's raining men!"

Carolyn nodded, feigning interest, although she could imagine nothing worse than trolling for a man on the Internet. Besides, she had her man now, and Gregory Stoneman was all the man she could ever want.

~ ~ ~

The street where Ramirez's community center was located was smack in the middle of a slum. As Gregory searched for somewhere to park his expensive car, he regretted that he had not called his driver. The least Evelyn could've done was warn him. Although knowing Evelyn, he was pretty sure she'd never visited the neighborhood. She talked a good game, but she probably had no idea where she was forcing him to go.

At least Katy was on her way. Katy with the British accent, trim figure, and small but appealing tits. He'd called her, told her where he would be, and she'd jumped at the opportunity to cover his visit.

"Can I bring my photographer?" she'd asked.

"Why not?" he'd said.

He had plans for Katy once Carolyn was out of the picture. A man could not live with just Evelyn for his sexual gratification. He had to have more, and Katy seemed to be a likely candidate.

After finding a parking space next to an empty lot, he reluctantly left his car, hoping it would still be there when he returned.

Walking back to the center half a block away, he passed a couple of grizzled old winos slumped against the wall of a crumbling building, swigging from a shared bottle of cheap booze. A Mexican woman scurried past, pushing a battered stroller with two babies inside, while a toddler trailed behind her, sucking his thumb. A couple of suspicious-looking Latino youths lounged on the steps of the center. They scowled at Gregory as he made his way past them and entered the building, which was actually an old abandoned warehouse.

He entered into a cavernous room filled with groups of people of all colors. Hurriedly he looked around, spotted Ramirez, and marched purposefully toward him.

Ramirez extracted himself from conversation with an obese woman in full African dress, a white preacher, and a jumpy-looking teenager and stepped forward to greet him.

"You came," Ramirez said.

"You didn't think I would?" Gregory replied, noting that the place smelled of rotting garbage with faint overtones of urine.

"Politicians," Ramirez said flatly. "They promise a lot and do nothing."

"What is it that you expect us to do?" Gregory asked, a fake concerned expression stuck firmly on his face.

"Money," Ramirez said, gesturing around. "This place is a shithole. We need all the funding we can get to make it better, put in heating, get some chairs for people to sit on and a fridge that works. Make it a place that kids want to come to an' hang out. We gotta get 'em off the street, it's the only way to bring about change."

"Evelyn's the fund-raiser in the family," Gregory said smoothly. "You should talk to her."

"You can help us," Ramirez said, ignoring the reference to Evelyn. "A word in the right place would go a long way to getting us a grant."

"I'll see what I can do," Gregory promised, wondering when Katy would show up. It better be soon, because he wasn't hanging around.

"But *you're* the man who can make *sure* it happens," Ramirez continued. "Come with me. You should meet some of my helpers, see how hard everyone works."

"Fine," Gregory said, realizing there was no immediate escape.

~ ~ ~

Carolyn was sitting in the Food Court, eating Panda Express from cardboard cartons with Kerri. As usual, Kerri was talking nonstop. "I went out with this one guy," she announced, nibbling on a greasy sparerib. "And like at first he seemed perfectly normal. I mean, he wasn't exactly Zac Efron, but he could've been a contender."

Carolyn nodded, trying desperately to appear interested in yet another of Kerri's dating misadventures.

"We went on a couple of dates," Kerri continued, licking barbecue sauce off her fingers. "Then he informed me that since we'd been on two dates and he'd paid, it was time we had sex. Can you imagine? Just like that he comes out with it."

"Shocking," Carolyn murmured, taking a sip of water.

"No!" Kerri exclaimed. "I haven't *gotten* to the shocking bit yet."

"Go on," Carolyn said, managing a surreptitious glance at her watch.

"He wanted sex with me *and* his former girlfriend! Apparently she was waiting at his apartment all ready to party!" Kerri rolled her expressive eyes. "Can you imagine! How gross is *that*!"

"I presume you said no."

"Like . . . duh! Do I look like an idiot?"

Carolyn glanced at her watch again. "I should be getting home," she said, starting to fidget. "Do you mind if we leave soon?"

"Really?" Kerri said, her face registering disappointment. "We haven't covered half the stores."

"I've got some work to finish up, and I promised to look in on Nellie," Carolyn explained. "She's all alone. It must be hard for her with no friends or family."

"You're so good to do that." Kerri sighed, then stuffed a piece of sweet-and-sour chicken in her mouth. "I always mean to drop by and see how she's doing, but I never find the time, although I do pick up her meds every month."

"I expect your dating schedule keeps you on the go," Carolyn said, slightly tongue-in-cheek. "*How* many dating sites did you say you're on?"

"A lot," Kerri answered with a cheery grin. "And you know what? We've got to sign you up, too. You'll enjoy it! It's *sooo* much fun."

No, Carolyn thought. *I will not enjoy it at all. I have found the love of my life, and soon he will be all mine.*

16

Bobby

There was a group of guys who met up and played softball in the park on Sunday mornings. They had a set routine: Nine or ten guys would assemble, and each week after the game, one of them would host the rest of the day at his apartment. Hosting meant getting in plenty of deli food, making sure there was an abundance of snacks, a full supply of European beer, and, most important of all, every sports package on the latest wide-screen Blu-ray high-def TV.

They called themselves the "Sunday in the Park" gang. Bobby and M.J. were the founders.

Bobby treasured his time with the guys. No women were allowed—it was strictly a males-only day. Frankie was not a member of the club. Bonding with the guys was out of his comfort zone; he preferred hanging out with Annabelle, catching the latest action movie, playing pool, and dropping into a card game or two.

Bobby was relieved, because although he and M.J. reluctantly accepted Frankie's drug use, he knew the others wouldn't be so understanding. In their book, doing coke on a permanent basis was for losers. It was okay for a party once in a while, but snorting it numerous times a day was a definite negative. There were times Bobby tried to talk to Frankie about his excessive use of cocaine, but Frankie was never in a listening mood, so every time their conversation ended up going nowhere.

The Sunday in the Park gang consisted of two hedge fund guys, a computer genius, a drummer with a rock band, an investment banker, a well-known chef, a tennis pro, and an actor who starred on a daytime soap. The camaraderie among them was special. The youngest member was twenty-three—that would be the chef. And the oldest was thirty—the investment banker. Everyone left their troubles at home and enjoyed a relaxed, no-pressure day. No one was married, and no one was close to doing the big deed, although the subject of women was always up for discussion. One of them always had a dating story to tell, and the other guys felt free to offer advice. "Didja fuck her?" was the most popular question on their agenda.

This Sunday was Bobby's day to host, but he was concerned about Frankie and Annabelle. He kept on wondering if he should drop out and spend some time with them. Annabelle was a pain, but he'd known her since high school, and he kind of felt sorry for her, especially now.

He called Frankie, who mumbled something about being asleep and said he would check in later.

"How's Annabelle doing?" Bobby wanted to know.

"Later, man," Frankie answered with a big fat yawn.

So much for spending time with them. Frankie obviously had everything under control.

Outside in the park it was crisp and icy, but the freezing weather spurred Bobby to play his hardest. By the time he got back to his apartment, he was feeling invigorated and ready for anything.

For a moment, as he was laying out cold cuts and cartons of potato salad and coleslaw on the kitchen counter, it crossed his mind that it might be nice to have a girlfriend around to help out. There'd never been anyone special, never anyone who'd lasted more than a couple of months. He simply wasn't that interested in the girls he came across—the beautiful models and actresses, the party girls and young society girls, most of them searching for a rich husband. Oh yeah, great for a few weeks or months of fun sex, but that was it.

Not that he was concerned. He was just about to hit twenty-six, too young to even think about getting married. But would a steady girlfriend really be such a bad thing?

Frankie had a steady girlfriend, Annabelle, and all Frankie wanted to do was cheat on her—so come to think of it, what was the point?

Bobby considered Lucky and Lennie a shining example of what a great relationship should be. Both were extremely independent, but they were also loving and volatile, passionate and crazy—and after years of marriage still madly in love. *That's* what he wanted. A relationship filled with fire.

Zeena had fire. She might be years older than him, but he knew that if he was with her, things would never be dull.

What did age matter, anyway? Madonna was over fifty and smokin' hot. Demi Moore was with some dude a good ten years younger than her. Not to mention his mom's best friend, the very sexy and gorgeous Venus—married to Billy Melina, a movie star many years her junior.

Fuck it! He promised himself that the next time he saw Zeena, he was definitely going for it.

~ ~ ~

The next time came sooner than he thought. Stacking dishes in the kitchen after all the guys had departed, including M.J., he was just about to check in with Frankie again when his doorbell buzzed.

Thinking that one of the guys had left something behind, he flung open the door, and there she stood, Zeena herself.

"Bobby," she drawled, wandering past him into his apartment as if she'd visited a dozen times before. "Zeena was in the neighborhood. Decided to see for myself how the heir to a shipping fortune lives."

Shocked and startled, he was also instantly pissed off that she knew about his background. He kept a low profile, stayed out of gossip columns, never discussed his heritage with anyone except M.J. So how exactly had she found out? And what was she doing in his apartment?

Not that he minded.

How could he mind when the object of all his most recent fantasies was standing in his living room clad from head to toe in black leather? She had on a tiny leather miniskirt, fishnet stockings, thigh-high boots, and a black turtleneck cashmere sweater, paired with a slouchy leather silver-studded motorcycle jacket. Her coal black hair fell in a straight curtain way below her waist, and her exotic eye makeup emphasized her almond-shaped eyes.

There was a whiff of dominatrix in the air, but Bobby didn't care. She was here, in his apartment, and it was up to him to make a move.

What did she expect from him? That was the question. He was so used to being the one in control that this was a whole new experience.

After extracting a pack of Gauloises from her oversize Prada crocodile purse, she shook out a cigarette and proceeded to light up with an art deco silver cigarette lighter.

The way she touched the flame to the tip of the cigarette was extremely sexual. Bobby decided against telling her that there was a no-smoking rule in his apartment.

She inhaled deeply, and then, watching him closely with her catlike eyes, she exhaled slowly.

"Here we are," she finally said, a plume of strong-smelling smoke drifting in the air between them. "Alone together. Isn't that what you've been waiting for, Bobby?"

"No young studs today?" he asked, trying to keep it light. "No entourage hanging on your every word? What's up with that?"

"Disappointed?" she murmured, her tone mocking him. "Were you hoping for a threesome? Or perhaps you're gay." A long, drawn-out sigh. "Ah . . . such beauty." Another long beat. "*Are* you gay, Bobby?"

God! She reminded him of Serenity, all sarcasm and bitchery spewing forth from a mouth he was desperate to kiss.

Was that what turned him on?

Apparently so, because he could feel himself growing hard, and he had the strongest desire to grab her and simply go for it.

He should do it. Because that's why she was here, no other reason.

Miz Superstar had come visiting to see exactly what he had to offer. And he had no intention of turning her down.

17

Annabelle

Annabelle was in total shock. The fact that she was probably one of the last people to hear of her mother's murder made her feel sick. Why hadn't she answered her phone earlier? Or even switched on the TV?

She hated the fact that it had to be Frankie who'd given her the devastating news. Damn Frankie!

Somehow or other, they'd become embroiled in a huge fight. Frankie had been insisting that she call her father back and make arrangements for them to fly to L.A. Annabelle hadn't wanted to talk to Ralph, so in retaliation she'd screamed that he should be getting on the phone and reaming Sharif Rani a new asshole instead of insisting that she call Ralph.

In the midst of their fight, Annabelle had picked up a bottle of vodka and begun purposefully swigging from it. She was too upset to think straight, and since she had a low tolerance level, it didn't take long before she was totally drunk.

Frankie then laid out several lines of coke and snorted them right in front of her. He didn't usually indulge with her watching, because she didn't do any kind of drugs, preferring the lure of alcohol. But he'd felt like getting high, so fuck it.

Their fight had escalated. She'd called him a useless druggie with no balls.

He'd called her a fucking princess with no conscience.

She'd yelled that he was nothing more than a pimp and had no idea how to handle anything.

He'd yelled back that she was a selfish, coldhearted bitch with no emotions, and all she cared about was herself.

Those were just a few of the insults exchanged.

Eventually, Annabelle had staggered into the bedroom, still clutching the now half-empty bottle of vodka. After slamming the door in Frankie's face, she'd fallen on the bed and lain awake, tossing and turning, before finally falling asleep in the early hours of Sunday morning.

Frankie had resisted a strong urge to walk out, but since he had nowhere to walk, he'd ended up trying to sleep on the couch.

They'd both slept their way into Sunday afternoon, and it wasn't until four o'clock that Annabelle finally surfaced with a killer hangover.

She lay in her bed quite still for a moment, mulling over the events of the previous day, whereupon the enormity and horror of what had taken place in Los Angeles suddenly overcame her. She began to sob, deep, body-racking sobs that enveloped her whole being.

Her cries woke Frankie, and forgetting about their ferocious fight, he hurried into the bedroom. Because if there was one thing that really got to him, it was the sight and sound of a crying female. The very thought evoked bad memories. His brute of a father used to beat the crap out of his mom on a weekly basis, and from as far back as he could remember, it was up to him to comfort her.

He'd always felt guilty about taking off, because who was left behind to console her when he was gone?

No one.

Frankie had moved on. He was busy chasing a new life, and there was no going back.

"Hey, babe," he soothed, holding her close. "It's okay, everything's gonna be cool."

"No, it's not," she said, sniffling. "My mother's dead. And you know something, Frankie? I barely knew her."

"Not your fault," he said, handing her a tissue.

"Maybe it is." She sat up and dabbed her eyes. "Maybe I should've stayed and *forced* her to take notice of me."

"There's no way you could've done that," he assured her. "According to you, she was always on a movie set or posing for pictures in magazines. She was a very busy woman."

"I should've tried harder," Annabelle lamented, filled with a cold, empty feeling of loss and sorrow.

"No, babe," Frankie said, playing good boyfriend to the hilt. "You did the best you could."

"Do you really think so?" she asked tremulously. "Are you *sure*?"

"No doubt, babe, none at all."

Annabelle spent the rest of the afternoon watching all the coverage and stories on TV about her mother's demise. It was as if she'd finally realized what had actually taken place, and now she couldn't get enough details.

A couple of times Frankie tried to suggest that she call Ralph, but she waved him away and remained sitting in front of the TV.

Frankie was relieved that at least she seemed to have forgotten about her bad experience with Sharif Rani's son, which was excellent news because Sharif was their star customer, and losing him as a client would be a disaster.

As soon as he'd calmed Annabelle down, made her a cup of green tea, fed her a couple of Advil, and persuaded her to stay in bed until she felt better, he'd called his cousin Janey to check on everything.

Janey did not come in on weekends; she worked from home on the computer he'd bought her.

"I'm so sorry," Janey wailed over the phone. "How is Annabelle holding up? Even more important—how are *you*?"

Janey was one of the few people in their lives who actually knew who Annabelle's parents were. Frankie had sworn her to secrecy, warning her that if she revealed anything to anyone about Annabelle or the business they ran, she would be out of a job. Since Janey would allow nothing to come between her and her beloved cousin, she'd agreed. Her son, Chip, however, had not.

Frankie had never considered Chip a threat. As far as he was concerned, Janey's son was around simply to do everyone's bidding. At least he could drive a car and was family—that had to count for something. Besides, Chip would never dare defy his mother.

Frankie instructed Janey to double-check on everyone's "appointments" and make sure that things were on the right track. "Annabelle's gonna need a few days off," he informed her. "We might hav'ta fly to L.A., so it's up to you to make sure you got it all under control. No fuckups. There'll be a hefty bonus in it, Janey, so make Frankie proud."

"Should I come in today?" Janey asked, desperate to get as close to Frankie as possible. "I could be there in an hour."

"Not necessary," he said, anxious to get her off the phone. "I'll get back to you later. Gotta go now—my other line's buzzing."

~ ~ ~

Chip Bonafacio aspired to far greater things than driving a car for a bunch of whores, picking up second cousin Frankie's dry cleaning, and generally doing whatever that snooty bitch Annabelle Maestro requested.

Oh yes, he knew who she was all right. He'd made it his job to find out as soon as he'd started working for them, even though his mom had attempted to tell him as little as possible about the business Annabelle and Frankie were running.

What did she think? That he was a total moron?

Yeah. Apparently so.

Janey thinking he was dumb worked for him. He still lived at home—too lazy to move out, and his mom did everything for him. She cooked and cleaned and did his laundry, handed him money whenever he needed it, and kept her nagging under control, although sometimes she begged him to show an interest in something—anything. *Yeah. Right.*

When he wasn't running his ass off for Frankie—a man he envied and hated at the same time—he preferred to slack off, watch TV, download porn, bet on football, screw whatever girl he could get his hands on, and drink as much beer as humanly possible.

It never occurred to his mom that he knew everything that was going on, including the identities of some of the better-known women he ferried to their dirty little assignations. Everyone acted as if he were invisible, but he was smarter than they thought. He was keeping his own black book filled with all the info he'd gleaned.

Gemma Summer Maestro's murder struck him as the break he'd been waiting for. The gruesome story was splashed across the front page of every newspaper and every Internet site in the country.

Chip was sure that he was dangerously close to scoring some major bucks.

Chip Bonafacio had big plans for his future. And they did not include his fat, addicted-to-Frankie, dumb-ass, annoying mom.

No fucking way.

18

Denver

"Hi," I said, relieved because I was finally getting an answer from Annabelle's boyfriend's phone. "Is this Frankie Romano?"

"Who wants to know?" said a suspicious-sounding male.

"My name's Denver Jones," I said quickly, pressing on regardless. "I'm a lawyer working for Ralph Macstro, and I'm here in New York trying to contact his daughter, Annabelle."

"Why?" he asked guardedly.

"Well . . . I'm sure you heard about the tragedy—"

"Who hasn't?"

"So you can understand that I do need to speak with Annabelle. It's quite urgent. Can you give me a number where I can reach her?"

"Where'd you get *my* number?"

"You're listed," I answered shortly. "Frankie Romano. Deejay. Right? Annabelle's boyfriend."

"What makes you think I'm her boyfriend?"

For God's sake! He was more cagey than the CIA! I was cold and tired, and I'd been trying to reach her for hours. Thank goodness for Sam, because he'd taken pity on me and let me come back to his apartment and hang out while I tried to reach Annabelle's boyfriend, who was now behaving in a most irritating fashion. Why had I ever left Mario's bed? 'Cause that's exactly where I wanted to be right now, cuddly and warm and having great sex. Instead of which I'm in a strange man's apartment—well, not so strange, actually; kind of very attractive in an Owen Wilson kind of way—freezing my ass off and wondering how late the planes continue to take off for L.A.

"Can you help me find her or not?" I said, fast losing patience.

"Is Ralph sending a private jet?"

"Excuse me?" I said. Not only was this guy an asshole, he was a pushy asshole.

"The man's gotta have his own plane," Frankie insisted.

"He doesn't," I said firmly, although I had no idea whether Ralph did or not. And if he did have a plane, he certainly hadn't volunteered it. "Is it possible to speak to Annabelle? I've left several messages, none of which she's responded to."

"Annabelle's unavailable."

I played what I hoped was my trump card. "I *do* know her," I explained. "We went to school together in L.A. Tell her it's Denver Jones, I'm sure she'll remember me."

"Y'know what," Frankie said, unimpressed. "I'm gonna hav'ta call you back."

Damn! I need to get home. This trip is not working for me. And how come Felix hasn't called me?

I gave Frankie the number of my cell and said, "Please make it soon." Then I clicked off, frustrated.

"Problems?" Sam asked, strolling into the room carrying a mug of something hot.

"Annabelle's boyfriend sounds like a total jerk," I muttered.

By this time, I'd told Sam why I was in New York. After my first attempt to reach Frankie when we were still in the coffee shop, I'd slumped back at my corner table, wondering what I was supposed to do next. Completely at a loss, I'd finally told Sam the truth about why I was there and how I couldn't return to L.A. without Annabelle in tow.

Sam had turned out to be an extremely sympathetic listener. After an hour, he'd suggested that I might like to sit it out at his place while I continued to try to reach either Annabelle or Frankie, whoever answered their phone first.

Gratefully I'd accepted his offer, and now here I was, seething with frustration, sitting on the couch in his very nice, roomy apartment, waiting for Annabelle's asshole boyfriend to call me back.

"Drink this," Sam said, handing me the mug he was carrying.

"What is it?" I asked, wondering if he was planning on slipping me a roofie and ravishing my poor cold body. Not that anyone would want to ravish me the way I look. I bet my nose is redder than Rudolph's!

"It's hot chocolate with a side of the rape drug," he said with a straight face.

Wow! It's as if he can read my mind.

"I *am* a lawyer," I reminded him sternly.

"I know," he said. "That's why I'm giving you all the info up front." He paused and smiled slightly. "You *know* that's what you were thinking."

"No, I wasn't," I replied, stifling an embarrassed grin.

"Yes." Now he gave me a full-on knowing smile. "That's exactly what you were thinking."

I smiled back at him. Suddenly I felt very comfortable in the apartment of a man I'd met only two hours earlier.

I sat on his couch and sipped hot chocolate, praying that Frankie Romano would call me back soon and put Annabelle on the line so that I could get the hell out of here and back to L.A.

Although . . . things weren't so bad. Sam was quite attractive in a lean and lanky way, and I had to admit that we were definitely on the road to a major flirtation.

Was I being unfaithful to Mario?

Hell, no! It's not as if Mario is my boyfriend, and it's not as if I'm about to jump into bed with Sam.

Although . . . the thought had crossed my mind.

From a total dry patch to a couple of hot contenders, and all in the course of two fun-filled, insane days. This was kind of crazy.

"You hungry?" Sam asked, moving over to an open-plan kitchen. "I could fix us some eggs, or if you're really starving, there's a spaghetti joint around the corner."

"Why are you being so nice to me?" I jumped off the couch and followed him across the room.

"Oh," he said vaguely. "Could be 'cause you're smart and appealing and I took an instant like. You're also gorgeous."

Gorgeous?! Is he talking to me, with my bed-head, red nose, and shivering body?

"Hmm . . ." I said. "Have you recently returned from a desert island where you were deprived of female company?"

"Can't take a compliment, huh?" he said, teasing me.

"Never been adept at that."

"Well, you *are* gorgeous," he said. "You've got that Julia Roberts thing going for you."

"*Pretty Woman* or *Erin Brockovich*?" I asked caustically.

"The hooker or the smart babe," he mused. "Now, that's what I'd call a great combination."

"Will you *stop*," I said, although I couldn't help smiling.

He laughed and leaned his elbows on the countertop. "I recently got disengaged from a total bitch."

"You did?" I asked, perching on the edge of a high stool, relieved that the conversation was taking a new direction.

"Right on I did. Caught her screwing my best friend. How cliché is that?" He shook his head as if he couldn't quite believe it had happened to him. "If I wrote it," he added wryly, "I'd get laughed off the page."

"I wouldn't laugh."

"How's that?"

"'Cause it's always the best friend," I said airily, "never fails."

He gave me a look. "Personal experience?"

"Absolutely not," I said firmly.

"How about you?" he asked, striving to keep it casual. "Are you in a relationship right now?"

"Absolutely not," I repeated. And after a meaningful pause, I couldn't help asking, "Are you?"

"Absolutely not," he said, mimicking my voice. Then he burst out laughing.

I think I could like this guy. Infectious laugh. Owen Wilson looks, a writer, *and* he has a sense of humor. Quite a lethal combination.

Of course, I suspect that he doesn't possess killer abs like Mario, but are abs *really* that important?

No. They just look nice on the page.

"So," Sam said, flexing his long, tapered fingers, "what did we decide? Spaghetti or eggs?"

He'd just used the *we* word, as if we were a couple, which we most definitely are not.

"If spaghetti means venturing outside," I said, pantomiming a mock shiver, "then my vote is for eggs."

"A fine choice." He opened a cabinet door and took out a frying pan. "Forgive my ego, but I'm a master chef with eggs."

"You are?"

"Oh yeah. Scrambled? Over easy? Poached? Or how about an omelet?"

I glanced at my watch: It was almost eight. Was there any chance of finding Annabelle and getting her on a plane tonight? Hardly likely.

"Scrambled's great," I said.

"Soft? Hard?"

"Excuse me?"

"The eggs."

We both grinned. I felt as if I'd known him for at least a week.

"Soft," I murmured, all thoughts of Mario definitely leaning toward the back burner.

"That's the way I like 'em, too," he said, opening the fridge and removing a cardboard carton of organic eggs.

"Y'know," I ventured, "as soon as we've eaten, I should start finding a hotel."

With his back to me, he said casually, "You can stay here if you like."

Oh, crap! I'd probably sounded as if I were hinting. How pathetic!

"That's okay," I answered quickly. "I, uh, love staying in hotels."

"Really?" he said skeptically.

Was I sounding even more pathetic by the minute or what? *I love staying in hotels.* Truth is I hate hotels, ever since I was bitten by bedbugs in a hotel in Phoenix when I was tracking down some information on a cheating wife for Felix.

The sound of Beyoncé's "If I Were a Boy" filled the room. My BlackBerry was in action, so I hurriedly groped in my pocket and extracted it.

"Tomorrow morning," Frankie Romano said, all business. "Ten A.M. at our apartment in SoHo. Do you know where that is?"

Duh . . . yes.

"Book two first-class tickets on the two o'clock United flight to L.A. An' make sure you have a limo to take us to the airport, and one on the other end. We'll need a suite at the Beverly Hills Hotel, and a car and driver on twenty-four-hour alert. See you at the apartment." And without waiting for me to say a word, he hung up.

Mission accomplished.

Or so I thought.

19

Carolyn

Since Carolyn was playing the kindly neighbor, Kerri felt that she should at least make an effort and go with her to Nellie's apartment.

Carolyn had not intended to visit Nellie again so soon, but as she'd used her as an excuse to leave the shopping mall, she'd had no choice since Kerri had opted to accompany her.

Once there, the two of them sat around making idle conversation with the garrulous old woman for over an hour. Nellie was all agog about the murder of famous movie star Gemma Summer Maestro. She had all sorts of theories about what could have happened. And when she'd exhausted the various scenarios she'd conjured up, she began delving back in time and reminiscing about the Fatty Arbuckle scandal that had taken place in Hollywood many decades earlier. Next she started speaking about Marilyn Monroe and her connection to John and Bobby Kennedy.

"I knew Marilyn," Nellie revealed with a secretive smile, indicating that they might have been close. "She was such a luminous beauty. Big-boned, though. It didn't matter. Every man she ever met fell in lust with her. It was a sight to see."

After ten minutes of Marilyn and the Kennedys, Nellie returned to the subject of Gemma Summer's murder.

At that point, Carolyn decided it was best not to mention that when she was a kid she'd attended several birthday parties given for Gemma's daughter, Annabelle, at the Maestro mansion. For some misguided reason, her mom had forced her to go, claiming it was the polite thing to do since the entire class was invited. She was ten—how could she argue?

At every party, she'd hovered awkwardly in the background, watching while circus clowns performed, live elephants paraded across the manicured lawns, and a line of ponies ferried the children around in circles. There was also a huge party tent shading tables loaded with hot dogs, hamburgers, pizza, cookies, and cakes. Carolyn remembered there being enough food to feed the homeless for a year.

Gemma Summer had appeared only when cameras were rolling. Carolyn recalled thinking that she had not seemed like a very hands-on mother, but then Annabelle was hardly the easiest of daughters. Annabelle was always boasting and showing off, flaunting her privileged life in front of all the other kids.

Fortunately for Carolyn, when Annabelle turned thirteen, the parties stopped. Or, at least to Carolyn's relief, the invitations stopped coming. It was then that she'd palled up with Denver, and they'd formed an unbreakable friendship.

Denver had not called her back, which was surprising in view of the cryptic message she'd left on her voice mail.

God! She had to tell someone her exciting news soon or she'd burst!

~ ~ ~

"In every way we can, we gotta break the cycle of fatherless kids gettin' caught up in gangs," Ramirez lectured, his long, pockmarked face a stern mask, his tone loud and harsh. "When there's no father in the house, an' the mother's strung out on drugs or mebbe she's taken two jobs to keep the family goin', *that's* when these boys choose a new family—the family that operates on the streets. An' I should know. I was one of them."

The group of people standing around him verbalized their approval.

"The street gangs have a *need* to keep their army goin'," Ramirez continued, raising his voice. "So they start recruitin' kids as young as eleven an' twelve. By the time they're sixteen, those *children* are hardened criminals with no future. We all have to help stop this. It's our civic duty. An' we can do it, people."

"Hear, hear," piped up Katy, the British journalist who'd turned up just when Gregory was contemplating a fast exit.

Gregory had already noticed that she looked petite and quite fuckable in a pair of knee-high Ugg boots, tight jeans, and a fuzzy blue top. But she came with an unfortunate appendage: her husband, who also happened to be the photographer.

Gregory was aggravated; he could not believe his luck. One pregnant assistant, and now the girl he had in mind for his personal pleasure turned out to be married!

On second thought, he decided she wasn't so hot. Too young and chirpy. Her high, excited voice with the clipped British accent would soon become annoying. And she obviously bit her nails, a disgusting habit.

Ramirez droned on, while Gregory reconciled himself to the fact that there was no escape until this lecture on gang life reached its conclusion.

Katy seemed fascinated, while her husband—a tall, skinny jerk in even tighter jeans than his wife's—snapped away.

Gregory endeavored to keep a concerned expression on his face. Not easy. Was Ramirez ever going to shut up?

~ ~ ~

It's me again, where are you? Carolyn texted to Denver. *Call me as soon as you get this. I have major news.*

She checked her message machine one more time to make certain that Gregory had not tried to contact her.

It was a wasted effort. Of course he would not phone her, Sunday was family day. Although in view of her condition, she'd hoped for at least a short message. Surely that wasn't asking too much?

Yes, it was. He was most likely busy with his kids and oblivious to all else. Gregory was a wonderful father, and one of these days he'd be a wonderful father to the baby she was carrying.

Escaping from Nellie's apartment had not been easy. The old woman loved to talk, so between her and Kerri's nonstop chatter, it had been an exhausting day. She couldn't wait for Monday, when she would be back in the office with Gregory a mere few yards away. Meanwhile, she had little to do except daydream about their future together.

Nothing wrong with that.

~ ~ ~

After Ramirez's never-ending lecture, rescue finally appeared in the form of two Latino males in their early twenties who marched straight up to Ramirez—shoving people out of the way—and began harassing him in Spanish, yelling and waving their arms around in a threatening fashion.

Although it was apparent that Ramirez was attempting to keep his cool, after a few moments he snapped and began yelling back.

Jesus Christ! Gregory thought. *What the hell is going on?*

He took a quick look toward the entrance, wondering if he should just go. Get out before this escalated. He didn't speak Spanish, but the anger taking place between Ramirez and the two men was palpable.

Katy was openmouthed, while her husband continued to snap photos, until one of the men flashed him the universal *Fuck you* sign and spat out,

"Quit with the mothafuckin' camera or I'll shove it up yo' mothafuckin' white ass."

Nice to know they spoke English.

The agitated man returned his attention to Ramirez, and the argument continued.

Katy moved toward Gregory. "Do you speak Spanish, Senator?" she whispered.

"No, I don't," he responded, getting a pleasant whiff of her floral scent. "Do you?"

"They're fighting about some kind of drug deal," she said in a low voice. "They're claiming Ramirez owes them money and that he should pay up or else."

"How is he responding?"

"He's telling them to get out."

"But they're not listening."

"No." She shook her head. "I think the one with the red bandanna might be his brother."

Gregory took a second look at the man with the red bandanna tied across his forehead. He was clad in the usual uniform of oversize T-shirt, baggy pants sitting so low they looked ready to fall off, and untied yellow, black, and silver sneakers. A large gold medallion hung from a long chain around his neck, while his forearms were covered in various tattoos. He did indeed resemble a younger version of Ramirez, but where Ramirez radiated a certain amount of calm, this young male was vibrating with bitter anger.

Katy's husband had packed away his camera, and now he grabbed his wife's arm. "Let's go," he said abruptly. "Who knows where this is heading."

"Senator Stoneman," Katy said, wide-eyed, "you should leave with us."

"Yes, yes, I think that's an excellent idea," Gregory agreed. Silently he cursed Evelyn for allowing him to get trapped in such a potentially volatile situation. "Lead on, I'll follow."

The moment they got outside, Katy's husband bundled her into his truck, which was conveniently double-parked. He barely gave her a chance to bid Gregory good-bye before taking off, leaving a bemused and somewhat annoyed senator standing alone on the overgrown sidewalk. Gregory was not at all pleased. What a waste of a perfectly good Sunday.

As he started off down the street, hoping his car was still parked where he'd left it, a commotion erupted from the front of the center. The two Latino males who'd been arguing with Ramirez came racing out and began running down the street. A beaten-up old car roared into view.

Gregory turned to look. Suddenly shots rang out. He felt something graze past his head, knocking him backward.

Then he was falling . . . falling . . . and everything turned to black.

20

Bobby

"I'm getting a strong vibe that this is all a game for you," Bobby said, coming to the realization that he'd fallen right into Zeena's cleverly planned trap.

She'd arrived at his apartment with every intention of luring him into bed, and naturally he'd gone for it. Why wouldn't he? She was major hot, and he had a thing for her. It was a no-brainer. Except why, after the act, did he feel like a girl who'd given it up on the first date? Gotten fucked way too fast?

Man, he was so mad at himself.

"A game?" Zeena questioned, casually propping herself up on one elbow, long dark hair draped around her broad shoulders. Totally naked and beyond fit, she was all sleek, burnished skin, sinewy muscles, and lean, loose limbs.

"Yeah, a game," he repeated. Then, determined to make a point, he added, "But you know what, Zeena? I'm not one of your boy toys—the kind of guy you can have your fun with and then shove aside."

"Did I say you were, Bobby?" she drawled, arching a perfectly plucked and penciled eyebrow. "And *I* should point out," she added succinctly, "there is nothing *little* about you. But I'm sure many women have told you that."

"I'm serious," he said, trying to shake the feeling that she'd used him for her own pleasure and amusement.

"So young . . ." She sighed, slowly licking her lips. "Sad that Zeena always gravitates toward the young ones."

"How come you're pulling the age card?" he said, irritated. Her cavalier attitude was beyond annoying. "What are you, fifteen years older than me? Today that's nothing."

"Actually," she opined, leaning across him to reach her crocodile purse, which she'd placed on the floor beside the bed, her exceptionally large, hard nipples brushing against his chest, "you're more mature than my usual conquests."

Conquests! Was she referring to him as a conquest? Goddamn it! Who exactly did she think she was dealing with? He was a Santangelo. He'd better start acting like one.

Removing a pack of Gauloises from her purse, she let forth a low, throaty chuckle. "Poor Bobby," she said mockingly. "So handsome, so rich, but you need to work on your self-esteem, and maybe your lovemaking technique could use some improvement."

Shaking his head in wonderment, he realized she was Serenity all over again—a dismissive bitch on wheels trying to screw with his self-confidence. Nobody had ever complained about his lovemaking technique before. As far as he knew, he was an accomplished lover, considerate, not too fast, and he was pretty certain he made all the right moves.

What kind of head trip was she trying to pull?

"I thought you came," he said shortly.

"Zeena always comes, Bobby," she said, lighting up her cigarette. "I make sure of it."

Now he was really pissed. "What're you saying? That you don't need me? That you can do it all by yourself?"

"Any woman who depends on a man to give her an orgasm is either a fool or in love," she responded, blowing lazy smoke rings in his direction. "Zeena discovered that a long time ago."

Great, just great. He'd performed to the best of his ability, and she was putting him down. Was this her idea of afterplay? Most women opted for a smooch and a few kind words. Zeena preferred to go for the jugular.

He should've known.

"I guess we're done here," he said, staunchly refusing to let her get to him any more than she already had.

She stretched like a particularly athletic cat, throwing her muscled arms high above her head and making a purring sound. "Zeena is in no hurry," she assured him. "Whenever you're ready, perhaps we should try again."

And with that she stubbed out her cigarette on his glass-topped bedside table, turned to him, trailed her long fingers down his chest, and murmured, "How long do you think that will be, Bobby? Zeena can get very impatient."

~ ~ ~

Later, when he awoke, he had no idea when Zeena had left, because it was now early Monday morning and there was no sign of her.

Although when he sat up and took a look around, he discovered a few signs. The cigarette stubs on his bedside table; the brandy glass half-filled with cognac, the imprint of her blood-red lipstick still on the glass, her musky scent wafting in the air like some kind of olfactory reminder.

Was he surprised?

No. He should've guessed she would leave silently in the middle of the night without so much as a good-bye.

She was the man.

He was the woman.

Fuck! It was an infuriating situation.

Every time she'd suggested that they make love, he'd complied. Well, it wasn't happening again. He was about to man-up, stop with the girlish infatuation, and redeem his balls.

The second time they'd fucked, she'd made him feel as if he were auditioning for the role of the perfect lover. Any moment he had the feeling that she was about to call out, "Sorry. Not good enough. Next!"

Zeena. What a frigging ball breaker!

And yet . . .

No! He was not signing up for a second round. No way.

His phone rang, and he jumped to answer it. Maybe it was Zeena calling to tell him that she'd had a fantastic and unforgettable time, that he was the best lover she'd ever had, and when could they do it again?

It was M.J.

"Wassup?" Bobby mumbled, once again surveying the pile of cigarette butts on his glass-topped table. Miz Superstar could've at least requested an ashtray. But, no, that wasn't her style. Zeena lived to screw with people, was into testing them—just to see exactly what she could get away with.

"We got an eleven o'clock with the Russian investors for the Miami deal," M.J. reminded him. "Don't tell me you forgot?"

Bobby squinted at his watch. "It's not even eight, M.J. What's with the panic?"

"No panic, man. I was thinking that before the meeting we should drop by an' see Annabelle, pay our respects."

"Yeah, you're totally right," Bobby agreed. "I'll call Frankie, give him a heads-up we're coming over."

"Do that, an' while we're talkin' . . . what happened to you last night? I thought you were joining us at Nobu?"

"Got hung up."

"Anyone I know?"

"An old girlfriend stopped by."

"Didja—"

"Don't even ask," Bobby said quickly. "Let's just say it was a very long night."

After clicking off the phone, he made his way to the kitchen. He grabbed a bunch of paper towels, then returned to the bedroom and cleaned up Zeena's mess of stubbed-out cigarettes.

Who *did* that kind of thing? It was gross. Once again, he wondered why she hadn't requested an ashtray. She certainly hadn't been shy about asking him to go down on her. Actually not so much asking, more like an imperious command.

"Let Zeena see what your tongue can do, Bobby," she'd murmured, as if his cock were a nonstarter.

Jesus! She'd made him feel so damn inadequate.

He'd gone down on her for almost half an hour, and she hadn't come. She'd been holding back purposely, he knew it.

Then they'd started to fuck again. He was no slouch, but this woman's energy was endless. She was one unstoppable bundle of yoga moves and impossible positions. By the time they were finished, he felt as if he'd gone several rounds with Mike Tyson at his peak.

She'd requested handcuffs.

He didn't have any.

She'd requested a vibrator.

He didn't have that, either.

She'd told him she enjoyed being spanked with leather gloves.

Too bad. Leather gloves were not his thing. Come to think of it, neither was spanking or vibrators or handcuffs. Weren't they dirty-old-man fetishes?

"Next time Zeena will come prepared," she'd said with a dismissive sniff.

What made her think there would be a next time?

After the sex marathon, he'd fallen asleep.

Now it was morning, and she was gone.

Get over it, he told himself. *Forget about Miz Kinky Superstar. She's a bad drug, and you know it.*

He was over her.

Oh yes, he was definitely over her.

21

Annabelle

"We're flying to L.A. tomorrow," Frankie informed Annabelle. "We're headin' over to the SoHo apartment first thing an' meetin' your dad's lawyer. How about that?"

Annabelle threw him a baleful look. "I thought I told you—"

"No!" he interrupted sharply. "You gotta be there for your mom's funeral. You'd never forgive yourself if you weren't. So that's it, babe. I made the decision, an' we're goin'. The lawyer's put together all the arrangements for us to travel in style."

Annabelle was about to argue further, but then she decided against it. Frankie was right, she should go to her mother's funeral. Besides, after watching the devastating story unfold on TV, she was eager to learn the real truth.

Could it be possible that her father *was* a suspect?

No. Impossible. Movie Star Daddy would never harm Gemma; he'd loved and adored his beautiful wife to the exclusion of everyone else, including his own daughter.

Annabelle had often reflected on the few times she'd been alone with her movie-star dad. He'd never complimented her or asked about her life. It was always about how exquisite and talented Gemma was and how loyal and sweet-natured his wife was. "You should try to be more like your mother," he'd once said in a gruff voice. "Your mother is the perfect woman."

Annabelle had immediately taken that to mean that she was the imperfect daughter.

No wonder she couldn't wait to get away. Far, far away.

Now she was going back, because Frankie was right—she'd always have something to regret if she didn't.

California, here I come, she thought sourly.

"Why are we going to the SoHo apartment?" she asked, trying to make up her mind what outfits she should pack.

"'Cause that's where your family thinks you live," Frankie explained. "And if they find out about Park Avenue, that could open up a shithole of questions 'bout how you can afford it."

"Perhaps I should tell Daddy Dearest about our highly successful business," she said, a spiteful gleam in her eyes. "That way he might finally notice me."

"C'mon, babe," Frankie groaned. "Ralph can't be *that* bad."

"Wait until you meet him. Mr. Movie Star is not easy, you'll see for yourself."

"Yeah, but you're forgettin' that I get along with everyone," Frankie boasted. "Mr. Movie Star Daddy's gonna like me plenty."

"We'll put it to the test," Annabelle said, opening up her jewelry drawer and selecting a few choice pieces to take with her. "And I'm telling you now," she added, "I am absolutely *not* staying at the house."

"All taken care of," Frankie said triumphantly. "Suite at the Beverly Hills Hotel. Twenty-four-hour limo on tap. Am I a comer or what?"

"Ralph agreed to everything?" She turned to look at him, surprised that her controlling father hadn't insisted they stay at the house.

"He wants you in L.A., doesn't he?"

"I guess so," she said, dreading the fact that she would have to spend time with her father. "By the way, what about our business? We can't just take off."

"I got it all under control, babe. Janey's steppin' in to make sure everything runs smooth as syrup."

"Oh, that's just great," Annabelle sneered.

"She's practically doin' that anyway," Frankie said.

"Not really," Annabelle argued. "It's you who recruits the girls, and it's me who usually deals with the clients."

"I'm gonna have Janey move in here while we're away."

"Guess I'd better lock my closet," Annabelle said caustically. "I'm sure she'd love nothing better than to play dress-up."

"Why're you always so down on her?" Frankie said, his left eye starting to twitch. "She's doin' an okay job."

Annabelle had her doubts. She didn't care for Janey, and it showed. She and Frankie had a thriving business going on, they were raking in big bucks, and she didn't want anyone screwing things up. Leaving Frankie's cousin in charge could be a major mistake.

"Maybe you should stay here with Janey," she suggested. "Y'know, just in case any problems come up."

"No way," Frankie said, frowning. He had no intention of missing out on a trip to L.A. "Janey can handle everything. Besides," he added, sidling close and stroking her arm, "my best girl ain't goin' nowhere without me, an' that's a Frankie Romano promise."

~ ~ ~

"I wanna speak to the person in charge," Chip Bonafacio insisted, his shifty eyes darting this way and that.

It was early Monday morning, and he was standing at the reception desk of a huge glass-and-chrome building, home to one of the biggest tabloids around—*Truth & Fact*.

The girl sitting behind the desk—a trashy bleached blonde with straw-like hair extensions and badly applied fake eyelashes—was giving him a hard time, even though he'd told her he had a major story to sell.

"Do you have an appointment?" she asked for the third time.

"I keep on tellin' you, I don't *need* an appointment," he said impatiently, well aware that the acne he so dreaded was sprouting all over his chin. Aggravation always accelerated his condition, and this skank giving him such a hard time was the last thing he needed.

"Yes, you *do*," she said, glaring at him. "Everyone does."

"Even George Clooney?" he said, challenging the douche.

"You're not George Clooney," she answered scornfully, wondering if she was going to have to call Security to get rid of this loser.

"What's your name?" he snapped.

"My name? Why do you want *my* name?"

"'Cause when they buy my story for a million bucks, I'm gonna make sure your skinny ass gets fired."

"Oh yeah," she said in full sneer. "Like *you* got a story worth selling."

Chip took a step back. "Gonna risk it?" he asked, giving her what he considered his most effective stink-eye. "I drove up in a Mercedes. I'm not some bum off the street, y'know. I got connections, I know important people."

The girl tapped her talonlike nails on the glass-topped reception counter. Like her eyelashes, they were fake, and last night at a party with her wannabe rapper boyfriend, one of them had fallen off. Her head was pounding from too many appletinis the night before, and she was not enjoying this exchange. She was certainly not enjoying this jerk's threats about getting her fired. What if he was legit and *did* have a hot story? Would she get the blame for not letting him through?

Deciding not to risk it, she made a snap decision. "Mr. Waitrose isn't in today, but his right hand is," she said, avoiding eye contact. "You can go on up, sixth floor. Someone'll meet you at the elevator."

Chip was elated. That shit about taking down an employee's name actually worked! He'd watched Frankie do it a dozen times, and it had always worked for him. Now he, Chip Bonafacio, was also the man.

Good freakin' goin'.

~ ~ ~

Before leaving their apartment in the morning for the SoHo loft, Annabelle got on the phone with several of the girls who worked for them on occasion. She wanted to make sure they all knew that dealing with Janey was only a temporary measure while she was away on a quick business trip to L.A.

Next she called Janey and gave her explicit instructions on how to behave toward the girls when they came by the apartment. "No gossiping," she warned. "No driving them crazy with inane chatter. And *no* asking for autographs. Understood?"

"As if," Janey whined, conveniently forgetting the time she'd asked a fairly well-known lingerie model to sign her center spread in *Playboy*. Janey hated dealing with Annabelle; Frankie was her main guy.

"As long as we've got that straight," Annabelle said. She thought back to Frankie's suggestion the previous night that he give Janey the combination to their safe. She'd told him absolutely no way.

"C'mon, babe," he'd said, trying to persuade her to give in. "What's she supposed to do with all the cash the girls deliver?"

"She can hide it under her fat ass," Annabelle had said with no intention of budging on this one. "I'm sure she's got plenty of room."

Frankie's cash-only policy was well in place. Sometimes the clients paid ahead of time, like Sharif Rani, but usually it was the girls who collected the cash, and then later they dropped off the commission. It wasn't the best way of doing business, but Frankie adhered to his no-paper-trail policy. That way, he figured they could never get caught.

His naïveté was impressive.

22

Denver

I am not a tramp, and I am certainly not a slut—words men like to use to put women down. I simply happen to enjoy sex, and quite frankly, why the hell shouldn't I? If one takes the proper precautions, there is nothing wrong with a fast one-nighter.

Okay, so my bad—*two* fast one-nighters. And not so fast at that.

Hey—if I were a guy, nobody would blink.

As I've mentioned countless times, I'm coming off a major dry spell, and I happen to have met two interesting, sexy guys. Mario of the fab abs. And Sam, who's a little quirky and seems like a really nice guy. The abs might not be quite as fab as Mario's, but everything else is in primo working order. And yes, the sex was once again memorable.

I can't recall exactly how it happened. Well, yes, actually I can. After I'd gotten on the phone and made all the arrangements for Annabelle and Frankie's forthcoming trip, Sam decided I needed to chill out. So he'd cracked open a bottle of red wine, and we'd giggled that wine and scrambled eggs didn't exactly go together.

No, I did not get drunk, just slightly happy. And when he started to kiss me, it was mutual and warm and nice.

We kissed for quite a long time before he ventured further, which was okay because Sam was a good kisser. Hey—we're both adults, so when the kissing progressed to a place where neither of us cared to stop, we didn't.

Sam had moves that reminded me of that ode to awesome lovemaking by the Pointer Sisters: "Slow Hand." Adele or Duffy should definitely rush into the studio and remake that one—they'd score a megahit.

Anyway, I digress. Let me put it this way: Sam was also a winner in bed. Totally different style from Mario's, but a winner all the same. Sam's touch was measured, more tactile, in a way more loving. Now, I understand that might sound ridiculous since I've known him only a few hours, but I felt the connection big-time.

Am I out of control?

No way. I'm a normal, healthy American female, acting like a normal, healthy American male. Good for me!

He undressed me slowly, taking his time. And I let him. No feverish discarding of clothes on my part, like I had done with Mario. No, this was different. He smelled good, and that was a turn-on. His abs were by no means perfect, but that was to be expected. He was a pale New Yorker, not a bronzed L.A. sun god.

I liked that he took his time, kissing me everywhere—and I do mean everywhere. I liked that he waited for me to climax before he did. I liked that he didn't move off me when he'd finished. Yeah, sex with Sam was a satisfying experience.

Now it's Monday morning, and I'm psyched. Today I get to accompany Annabelle and her pushy boyfriend to L.A.

Sam is in the shower. I considered joining him, but since we're not exactly a couple, I squashed the thought.

Josh and I used to shower together. It saved on energy, and we probably had our best sex with cascades of water raining down on us. Josh loved it when I gave him head in the shower; it was his favorite thing.

I wondered if he showers with Miss Stylist-to-the-Stars. Probably not. I was the one who always instigated it.

Now, why was I thinking about Josh?

I do occasionally. No reason.

Jumping out of Sam's comfortable, cozy bed, I headed straight for my BlackBerry. There were numerous messages, but none that required urgent attention. I smiled at a cryptic text from Carolyn and immediately texted her back: *In New York. Back to L.A. today. Can't wait to hear your news.*

Sam came strolling in fresh from the shower, a towel knotted casually around his waist. "It's all yours," he said.

Did he mean the shower or what I knew was lurking under the towel?

I mentally slapped myself. I was having too much fun when I should be concentrating on work. Besides, I was eager to get back to L.A. and find out exactly what was going on. *Was* Ralph a suspect in his wife's murder? Or was the media simply conjuring up a series of meaningless headlines to sell papers, magazines, and TV shows? I had to know. It was my job, and it's imperative that I dig deep for the real story. It was too early to call Felix, but I couldn't wait. Ralph Maestro was on my mind, and I needed information.

"Thanks," I said to Sam. Funny, but I wasn't feeling at all awkward about the previous evening's activities, even though I was wrapped in a bedsheet with nothing but yesterday's clothes to put back on.

I went into the bathroom and closed the door. Sam had laid out a toothbrush still in its package and a small travel tube of Crest. I added thoughtful to his list of attributes.

Wow! I couldn't wait to tell Carolyn about my two guys. Superstud Mario—all hot, passionate Latino sex. And Sam—laid-back, smart, and considerate.

Standing under a torrent of soothing warm water felt delightful. I was anticipating my meeting with Annabelle. What would she be like now? Still the same spoiled, entitled human being? Or maybe she'd evolved. And how about Frankie Romano? On the phone he'd sounded way cocky with his list of demands. Would I hate him on sight? I had a thing about men who considered themselves superior beings. Frankie sounded like that kind of guy.

I peered at my reflection in the bathroom mirror. Not good. Julia Roberts indeed. Ha! More like Julia Child! Anyway, I did the best I could to make myself look presentable for my upcoming escort duties.

After I was dressed, I emerged from the bathroom to find Sam busying himself in the kitchen, making pancakes.

"Are you sure you're a writer and not a chef?" I quipped, thinking how fine he looked in a faded denim shirt and jeans. He was barefoot, and his curly hair—still damp from the shower—was ruffled and quite sexy.

"Yesterday was a big surprise." He threw me an appreciative look. "I wasn't expecting a beautiful woman to fall into my local coffee shop."

I felt myself blushing. And I am *so* not the kind of girl who blushes.

"I wasn't exactly expecting to spend the night with such an . . . uh . . . interesting man," I managed.

He raised an eyebrow and half smiled. "'Interesting'? Is that all you can come up with?"

"It's short notice, give me time."

"You can have all the time you want."

"Thanks," I said, slightly flustered, "but I've got to get two people on a plane to L.A., so you'll have to give me a rain check."

"It's only nine," he said, handing me a glass of what looked suspiciously like freshly squeezed orange juice. "Sit down and enjoy your pancakes."

"You sound like my mom."

"Gee, thanks," he said wryly. "My life's ambition has always been to sound like someone's mom."

It suddenly occurred to me that I should definitely have breakfast with this man I'd spent the night with, because I'd probably never see him again. And I liked him. Besides, I had nowhere else to go. I could hardly stand outside Annabelle's front door for an hour.

"Can I get syrup with my pancakes?" I asked. "The real thing, not some low-fat substitute?"

"Do I look like a guy who'd give you a substitute?"

"No," I said, sitting on a stool, watching him flip a pancake.

"Then relax and enjoy." He transferred the pancake to a plate and handed it to me, following up with a glass bottle of organic maple syrup—the expensive kind. No Aunt Jemima for him.

I poured on the syrup and took a bite. "Delicious!" I exclaimed. "Who taught you to be such a whiz in the kitchen?"

"Remember the bitch fiancée I was telling you about?"

"You're kidding."

"She was—*is*—a professional chef."

"Well, at least she left you with something."

"That's a matter of opinion."

"You sound bitter."

"Not at all," he said easily. "I'm a great believer in things happening for a reason, and if I was still with her, I wouldn't be spending the morning with a refreshingly bright and beautiful L.A.-based attorney."

Hmm . . . that's the second time he's called me beautiful. Flattery will definitely get him wherever he wants to go.

"You're pretty free with the compliments," I remarked, gulping down my orange juice, which was indeed freshly squeezed.

"Only when they're deserved." He flipped a second pancake onto my plate.

"Are you trying to make me fat?" I joked. "I'm already enormous by L.A. standards."

"You have an incredible body," he said.

Wow! The compliments were coming fast and furious. Enough already.

"Do you mind if we put on the TV?" I said quickly. "I need to see what's happening with the Maestro case."

He handed me the clicker. "Go ahead."

The *Today* show was all over it. Matt, Meredith, Al, and Ann were in the middle of one of their group discussions. The theme was Hollywood justice. The question was, How come celebrities always manage to walk? They didn't mention Ralph by name, but the implication was that it was a big possibility he could've done it.

"Give me your cell phone," Sam said, leaning over me.

"Excuse me?"

"I'm putting all my information in it so you'll have no excuse not to stay in touch."

I couldn't think of a good reason to object. Besides, I wanted all his various forms of communication—address, cell, home phone, e-mail. I'd just spent the night with the guy, so why not?

Obediently I handed him my phone, and in return he handed me his. Obviously, it's the latest form of intimacy—downloading all your information into someone else's cell phone.

"So . . ." I ventured. "I'll be going soon."

"I have something for you," he said.

Oh, dear me, I hope it's not payment for our night of lust. How humiliating would that be if he thought I was a hooker masquerading as a lawyer!

Did I mention that I have a very active imagination?

"What is it?" I asked tentatively.

"No arguments," he said. He reached down and handed me his knit cap and striped scarf.

"Wow!" I managed, graciously accepting his gift.

"At least it'll keep you warm on your way to the airport."

"Thanks, Sam," I said, quite touched that he was concerned about my welfare. "That's very thoughtful of you."

He grinned, crooked teeth fully on display. "Don't mention it," he said, then he leaned over again and gave me a warm hug.

I reached up and hugged him back, inhaling his masculine scent and loving it.

What a shame he doesn't live in L.A. This could be the start of something . . .

Or not.

23

Carolyn

Waking up lying on an unmade bed in an unfamiliar room, Senator Gregory Stoneman struggled to remember where he was and what exactly had taken place. His mind was a jumble of thoughts. Jesus Christ! Had he been *shot*? Shouldn't he be in a hospital? What the *hell* was going on?

His head was throbbing as he attempted to sit up and get his bearings.

A scowling but pretty young girl in cutoff jeans and a tight orange tank top loomed into view, gazed down at him, and yelled over her shoulder, "Yo, Benito—the old dude's awake."

Benito, the energetic Latino male with the red bandanna cutting a swath across his forehead, sprang into the room.

"Yo, man," Benito muttered, wild eyes darting around. "You had some kinda shit-ass fall. We took you in so's we could help."

"What are you talking about?" Gregory reached up to examine the side of his head with his hand. His temple felt sore, rough to the touch, and extremely tender. "I didn't fall," he said, filled with a sudden flash of anger. "If I recall correctly, somebody took a shot at me."

"Accident, man," Benito said, shifting on his colorful sneakers. "Bullet skimmed past. You got nothin' but a dumb-ass graze."

"Excuse me?" Gregory said, his fury building.

"Listen, man—nobody want trouble, an' you don't want no bad publicity up in yo' shit. That's why we help you."

"You didn't *help* me," Gregory said, outraged, sitting up all the way. "It was no doubt *you* who shot me. I'm calling the police."

"Told ya," the scowling girl brayed triumphantly. "He gonna turn yo' mothafuckin' ass in."

"Shut the fuck up," Benito snarled, turning on her. "He ain't callin' no fuckhead cops."

"Why am I here?" Gregory demanded. "Why didn't you take me straight to the emergency room?"

"'Cause I tol' ya—you ain't got nothin' but a scratch," Benito explained. "You one lucky sombitch. Gun went off by accident. But if the cops get a smell—I go back inside, an' I ain't goin' back again 'cause a some dumbfuck accident. You unnerstan'?"

"No," Gregory said grimly. "I certainly do not understand."

Benito bounced around on the balls of his feet. The large gold medallion sitting on his chest began flying across his baggy T-shirt. "*Accident*, man," he repeated, taking a reassuring grope of his crotch. "Ya gotta unnerstan'. I did you bad, now you be here, an' I be puttin' it t'you like I'm sorry, that kinda shit. An' anythin' you want me t'do—anythin'—then we gonna be even."

Suddenly Gregory felt everything fall into place. He understood. He got it.

God had heard his pleas for help and handed him the solution to his biggest problem of all.

Benito was standing before him. His savior.

~ ~ ~

Most people dreaded going to work on a Monday morning since it signaled the end of the weekend, and five long working days loomed ahead. Carolyn, however, couldn't wait. To her, Monday morning meant five exciting days working in close proximity to Senator Gregory Stoneman. *Her* Senator Gregory Stoneman, because soon he would be all hers.

She couldn't help wondering if he'd told Evelyn yet. Had the opportunity arisen? And if not, why not? The time had come for him to quit with the weak excuses. The time had come for him to be strong and stand up to Evelyn once and for all. That's exactly what he'd promised to do.

She was smiling as she entered the office. She greeted Gregory's newest male intern and nodded at his other executive assistant, Muriel, an older woman who took care of arranging his speaking engagements and social events.

"Morning, everyone," she said brightly. "Isn't it a gorgeous day?"

Muriel, drab in a sludge brown pantsuit that emphasized her pear-shaped figure, glanced at her as if she were out of her mind. "It's actually extremely cold," she said, tight-lipped. "And this afternoon the weather forecast calls for rain and maybe even snow."

"Ah, yes," Carolyn answered cheerily. "But right now the sun is peeking through the clouds, and later, if we're lucky, we might see a rainbow."

"Always the optimist," Muriel said, making "optimist" sound like a dirty word.

There was not much love lost between the two women. Muriel had worked with the senator for ten years, and when Carolyn had come aboard, she'd felt slighted. Muriel had always resented Carolyn, especially when she'd begun to suspect that there was more than a professional relationship between "the new girl," as she always referred to Carolyn, and her boss, the esteemed senator.

"Senator Stoneman will not be in this morning," Muriel said, delighted that it was *she* imparting the information and not Carolyn telling her.

"What do you mean, he won't be in?" Carolyn asked, the smile slipping from her face. "How do you know?"

"Mrs. Stoneman called me at home."

"And said what?" Carolyn asked, her mind racing in all directions.

"She told me that he won't be in until this afternoon."

"Why did she call *you*?"

"Is there a problem with that?" Muriel snapped, stretching her scrawny neck.

"Uh . . . no," Carolyn said. "I simply wondered why she didn't call me."

"I've known the senator's wife for many years," Muriel replied with a superior smirk. "We often speak on the phone."

"That's . . . uh, fine," Carolyn said, determined not to show that she was ruffled. "Did she give you a reason why the senator is coming in late?"

"No," Muriel said, satisfied that she'd ruined "the new girl's" day. "I've already canceled all his morning and noon appointments, no need for you to bother."

Furious that Muriel had taken it upon herself to cancel appointments that she should have been dealing with, Carolyn retreated to her small but pleasant office.

Had Gregory told Evelyn, and that's why he wasn't coming in until later? It was a possibility. Evelyn might be hysterical, so it stood to reason that he was busy handling the situation. Perhaps they were already meeting with a divorce lawyer.

Experiencing a shiver of excitement, Carolyn decided that Gregory had finally done it. After their talk on Saturday when she'd revealed that she was pregnant, he'd obviously realized that it was time to take action; there could be no more stalling.

Good for Gregory. She couldn't wait to see him.

~ ~ ~

Late Sunday afternoon, Gregory had returned home with a Band-Aid covering his grazed temple and a raging headache. Evelyn was in the living room, entertaining several of her women friends with a game of canasta, and she'd hardly looked up when Gregory walked into the house. Later on, she'd noticed the Band-Aid and with an extreme lack of interest had asked him what had happened.

"Ran into a door at that damn slum you sent me to," he'd said shortly, and that was that. She hadn't even bothered to inquire what had transpired between him and Ramirez.

That night, he'd hardly slept. His mind was on high alert, wondering if the scenario he'd arranged with Ramirez's brother, Benito, would work. It was a crazy plan that he'd come up with, and he knew it. But had Carolyn given him any choice?

No.

Carolyn was determined to ruin his life, and she'd forced him to fight back. It wasn't his fault, it was all hers.

Benito. A young Latino with criminal tendencies. A drug dealer who'd been in and out of juvenile hall and then prison from the age of fourteen. A desperate man—for if Benito was accused of shooting at a senator, they would surely throw the book at him, lock him away for a long, long time. There was the matter of kidnapping, too. Instead of taking him to a hospital or the emergency room, Benito had bundled him into his wreck of a car and transported him to the run-down condemned house he called home.

Yes, that was kidnapping all right, a federal offense.

The truth was that Benito had not been shooting at him at all. As Benito was leaving the community center, a car full of rival gang members had driven by, spotted him, and started shooting. Benito had immediately retaliated, hence the stray bullet that had whizzed past Gregory's head.

Gregory was well aware that had it been a direct hit, he would've been killed. Just like that. Gone in seconds.

But it wasn't a direct hit. As it turned out, it was a fortuitous happening. A happening he planned on taking full advantage of.

~ ~ ~

For over an hour, Carolyn debated with herself whether she should call Gregory's home. After all, she *was* his assistant, and it *was* a workday. Surely she was allowed to call his house?

Unless Evelyn knew about her. Then it wouldn't be such a clever move. No. Not clever at all.

But still . . . she was, as always, anxious to speak to him, if only to hear his voice.

Reluctantly, she ventured into Muriel's office. The room smelled of lilac and stale cigarette smoke. Yes, Muriel had a bad habit: She smoked, although she always pretended that she'd given it up. The overpowering smell of lilacs concealed nothing.

"Did Mrs. Stoneman give any indication of what time the senator might come in today?" Carolyn asked.

Muriel glanced up from her desk, brow furrowed. "No, dear, she didn't."

"I see," Carolyn said, adding a cheerful, "Well, I'm sure he'll be in soon."

"Or not," Muriel said tartly.

"Excuse me?"

"Perhaps he's taking the day off," Muriel suggested with a sly smirk. "Perhaps he and Mrs. Stoneman are spending some quality time together while the children are at school."

Carolyn couldn't help herself. "Why would he want to do that?" she blurted.

"Their wedding anniversary is coming up next week," Muriel said, the sly smirk still hovering on her thin lips. "I would imagine he might be taking her shopping at her favorite jewelry store."

Carolyn backed out of the room. That was *so* not happening. He'd be in soon, and everything would be fine.

24

Bobby and Annabelle

While Bobby waited for M.J. to pick him up, Frankie called to tell him that if they wanted to see Annabelle, they should come to the SoHo apartment. "We'll be there," Bobby said.

Try as he might, he could not seem to put Zeena on the back burner. She was on his mind big-time. And how dumb was that? The woman was famous, a freaking superstar, and he didn't even have her phone number.

He hadn't asked.

She hadn't offered.

Which meant that if he wanted to reach her, how was he supposed to do that?

It didn't matter, because he had no desire to contact her, did he?

A warning voice in his head stated, *No way.*

Another voice said, *Sure. Why not? It's one helluva crazy ride. Why not take it?*

Obviously his emotions were conflicted. His hunch was that whenever Zeena decided, she would simply turn up at his apartment unannounced, just as she had the first time. And knowing Zeena, he was sure she'd expect an instant replay.

He realized this was not a healthy situation. The woman was messing with his head, and if he was smart, he'd get out now before she appeared at his door armed with handcuffs, vibrators, and God knew what else.

Was he strong enough to turn her away?

He would have to put that one to the test.

~ ~ ~

Annabelle fidgeted on the backseat of the Mercedes. She was all packed and ready to go to L.A., but as they headed for the SoHo apartment to meet the lawyer her father had sent, she couldn't help feeling scared. What would it be like facing Ralph? She hadn't seen him in over a year. In fact, she hadn't seen either of her esteemed parents in that amount of time. Now she would never see her mother again, unless Ralph opted for an open casket. And she suspected he wouldn't go for that, not since Gemma had been shot in the face, her ethereal beauty obliterated for all time.

Annabelle remembered their last meeting. Ralph's latest over-the-top movie was premiering in New York, and they'd invited her to attend the grand opening. She hadn't wanted to go, so she'd claimed she was too busy with her design business, and instead she'd dropped by the Four Seasons, where they were staying.

The three of them had sat down for breakfast in their luxurious VIP suite. As usual, Annabelle had thought that they were the most beautiful couple she'd ever seen, so physically perfect in every way. Ralph, tall and craggy faced, resplendent in silk pajamas, a burgundy robe, and fancy monogrammed slippers. Gemma, a fairy princess in a pale pink negligee, golden curls surrounding her exquisite face, small diamond stud earrings affixed to her delicate earlobes.

They'd seemed pleased to see her.

"You look lovely," Gemma had said with a faint note of surprise.

"Yes." Ralph had nodded his large superhero head. "New York obviously agrees with you."

She'd taken their words to mean that they would prefer she stayed in New York—out of sight and out of mind, away from the dazzling stardom of her illustrious parents.

Ralph had slipped her a check for ten thousand dollars. "A little extra something," he'd said with a jaunty wink. "Spend it wisely."

Yes, Daddy, she'd thought. *I promise I'll spend it wisely and not return to L.A. to disturb your idyllic life together.*

That was then, and this was now. Soon she'd be on a plane back to L.A., her most unfavorite place.

"You okay?" Frankie asked, patting her on the knee.

"I'm fine," she replied coolly. "Why wouldn't I be?"

Frankie shrugged. One moment she was hysterical about Sharif Rani's rough son—an incident she seemed, thankfully, to have forgotten about. And the next she was all together and composed, planning what outfits she would take to L.A. Her mother's murder didn't seem to factor into anything. He'd never really understood Annabelle and her mood swings. But who cared? He was too busy trying to be blasé about the trip, although he was definitely psyched that they were going. The circumstances might not be ideal, but hey—he was heading for L.A. And he couldn't wait.

~ ~ ~

Both Bobby and M.J. felt right about stopping by to pay their respects to Annabelle. The three of them went back to their high school days, and although they'd never been that close, there were a few shared memories—especially the infamous prom night when the three of them had gotten way beyond wasted and ended up having a threesome in a suite at the Beverly Hills Hotel. The kicker was that the suite had been thoughtfully reserved for Annabelle by her loving parents, who'd wanted their girl to have a memorable prom night with her friends. Oh yes, it had turned out to be memorable all right, although everyone's memories of it were somewhat fuddled owing to the amount of alcohol consumed.

Frankie greeted the guys at the door to the SoHo apartment.

"Why're you here and not at the Park Avenue place?" M.J. wanted to know.

"'Cause this is where Ralph thinks Annabelle lives," Frankie explained. "He's sending his lawyer to escort us to L.A. Gotta stay cool."

"Right," Bobby agreed.

"We're travelin' first-class all the way," Frankie boasted. "I got it all arranged."

"Wouldn't doubt it," Bobby said.

Annabelle appeared, wearing a sleek Valentino jumpsuit, thigh-high Jimmy Choo boots, and a short, stylish fox-fur jacket. Her pale red hair was half pulled back, and large blackout Chanel sunglasses concealed her eyes. "Hey, guys," she said in a world-weary voice.

They took turns hugging her while letting forth the usual words of sympathy: "Sorry for your loss."

"And *I'm* sorry for dragging you to this place. It's such a dump," Annabelle grumbled, staring around the light and airy space, which was by no means a dump.

"We're only here for fifteen minutes," Frankie said sharply. "Stop bitchin'."

Annabelle raised her sunglasses and threw him a dirty look. Frankie was starting to get on her nerves. Why couldn't she have hooked up with someone like Bobby? He was way hot and so good-looking. The two of them would make a dynamite combination. Plus he was rich. Megarich. If she was with Bobby, she could stop running hookers and live a life of luxury.

Hmm . . . problem was that after the threesome incident, Bobby had never pursued her, as if he regretted their history. Besides, he was one of Frankie's best friends, so while she and Frankie remained a couple, things could never progress.

"Anyway, thanks for coming by, guys," she said. "It's nice of you to make it all the way down here."

"No problem," Bobby said, thinking that she didn't seem at all upset by the tragedy that had recently taken place in L.A. Her attitude was one of remarkable calm. Frankie was the edgy one, darting around the apartment with an overabundance of restless energy, coked out to the eyeballs.

Bobby tried to imagine how he would react if anything ever happened to *his* mom, the dangerously beautiful and vivacious Lucky Santangelo. He would surely kill, set out to wreak vengeance, do *something*—for he was a Santangelo, after all. He would certainly not sit around in any kind of calm state like Annabelle. One thing was for sure: No Italian blood ran through *her* veins.

"Where's the lawyer?" Annabelle asked, glancing impatiently at her watch. "Shouldn't he be here? It's almost ten."

"I forgot to mention," Frankie said. "The lawyer's a she—says she knows you."

"Knows me?" Annabelle questioned. "How can she possibly know me?"

"Dunno," Frankie said, cracking his knuckles. "It doesn't matter, she'll be here soon. All we need to know is that she sounds like she's on top of everythin'."

"Great!" Annabelle complained, her mouth turning down into a petulant pout. "Now we'll have to contend with one of Ralph's uptight watchdog bitches. Can't wait!"

"I guess we'll take off," Bobby said. He wasn't about to hang around listening to Annabelle and Frankie bicker.

"I wish you were coming with us." Annabelle sighed. "I'm going to need all the support I can get, and you've always been such a supportive friend to me, Bobby."

"You're a strong girl, you'll get through it," he assured her. "All you gotta do is keep it together. Don't let anyone or anything get to you."

"Right," M.J. agreed. "You'll be back here before you know it."

"I suppose . . ." she managed, her voice trailing off as she reached out to touch Bobby's arm.

He jerked away automatically, sensing that Frankie would not approve of the way she seemed to be drawing close. Body language was a dead giveaway, and Annabelle was definitely leaning in his direction.

"We'd better get goin'," M.J. announced. "Big meeting with a group of Russian investors. Mood, Moscow—I can see it now!"

"Sounds exciting," Annabelle murmured. "If it all comes off, I'll fly in for the big launch. All of us in Russia together, what a trip that would be!"

"Yeah, go hit it out the park, guys," Frankie said, joining in. "We'll both be in Moscow to celebrate with you. Caviar, vodka—gotta feelin' Moscow's my kinda town."

"You got a feelin' everywhere's your kinda town," Bobby joked as he and M.J. headed for the door. Annabelle waved them a reluctant good-bye.

Frankie opened the front door to let them out, and as he did so, Denver appeared.

The sight of her brought all three of them to an abrupt stop.

25

Denver

"Bobby!" His name slipped out of my mouth before I could stop myself. "Bobby Santangelo?" I pretended to be confused, although I wasn't, not at all. I was transported back in time to the gawky, overgrown thirteen-year-old with the biggest crush on a boy who had no idea I even existed.

Bobby Santangelo Stanislopoulos was every prepubescent girl's big crush. Handsome, charismatic, a basketball champ who also excelled at football, he hailed from an exciting and glamorous family. Along with his best friend, the very handsome M.J., Bobby was a true star who could get any girl he wanted. And he did, oh yes, he did. Over the years, he went through girls at an alarming rate, including one drunken prom night where legend had it that he and M.J. had gotten involved in some kind of insane sex romp with Annabelle. It was the talk of the school for weeks. Annabelle had walked around with a knowing smile, although I remember taking note that she was never one of the lucky ones who actually got to date Bobby. I think it must have pissed her off big-time.

Now here I was, on my way into Annabelle's apartment. And here *he* was, the childhood crush of my dreams—Bobby Santangelo Stanislopoulos. Crazy that I even remember his full name.

"Do I know you?" he asked, giving me a puzzled smile. It was glaringly obvious that he had no idea who I was.

Recovering my composure, I rallied to the occasion. "Uh, actually, not really," I managed, striving for a cool vibe. "I'm representing Ralph Maestro."

"Annabelle's dad?"

"Right. I'm here to escort Annabelle to L.A. And, uh, well, strangely enough, I went to school with Annabelle, and you were at the same high school. So . . . I guess I do know you, but not really."

His smile widened. Perfect teeth. Of course. Would I have expected anything less? I wondered what his abs were like.

"You've got a fantastic memory," he said pleasantly. "I'm a dud at remembering anything."

"I guess it's 'cause I'm a lawyer," I retorted. "It's a trick of the trade. I never forget a face." *Especially yours.*

"A lawyer, huh?" he said, dark eyes checking me out. "You look too young to be a lawyer."

If that's a compliment, I'll take it.

"I do?" I said, noting that he looked even better than he had back in high school.

"It's not a bad thing," he said. "I'd be kinda flattered if I was you."

We exchanged a long look. Y'know, one of those looks that last a few seconds too long—but in a good way.

"Well . . ." I began. And just as we were about to continue our mildly flirtatious conversation, the skinny guy with the longish hair and sharp features interrupted. "You *are* the lawyer Ralph sent? Right?" he questioned. "You're here to take care of everything."

"You must be Frankie Romano," I replied, my ever alert eyes noticing a thin residue of white powder under Frankie's left nostril. *Wonderful. I got me a druggie to hike back to* L.A.

"Right," Frankie said, giving me a second once-over with his ice-chip blue eyes.

Obviously this was a morning for full inspection. I was so glad I'd washed my hair and made an effort to look half-decent. Of course, I also had that just-got-laid-two-nights-in-a-row glow, so I felt confident that I looked kind of okay, in spite of wearing the wrong clothes for a New York winter.

M.J. threw me a curious glance. "Hey," he said.

"Hi," I answered with a brief nod.

This was all too surreal. A total jolt from the past.

"Come on in," Frankie said. "These guys are on their way out."

"Short but sweet," Bobby said, throwing me a friendly wink.

"Right," I answered, adding a hasty, "By the way, if you ever need a lawyer—young but killer—look me up. Denver Jones. I'm with Saunders, Fields, Simmons and Johnson." And then, before I could stop myself, I slipped him my card.

What am I doing? I am so *embarrassed! It's so unlike me to troll for business. Oh God! The cold weather is turning my brain to pure mush!*

Bobby and M.J. drifted off, and I followed Frankie into a large, light, but strangely unlived-in-looking space.

Annabelle was sprawled on a lime green couch, sipping Diet Coke from the can. The TV was tuned to *The View*, and Elisabeth Hasselbeck and Joy Behar were picking at each other, arguing about something political.

Annabelle appeared ready for a fast getaway. She was dressed all in black, expensive black—*very* expensive black. Her sleek, pale red hair was smoothed back, and her eyes were covered with oversize blackout shades. Glamour personified. Would I have expected anything else?

She gave me a look and then did a fast double take. A surprised, actually kind of shocked expression crossed her face—or what I could see of her face, considering the enormous shades.

"Denver?" she questioned, her voice rising. "Oh . . . my . . . God! It *is* you."

I had not expected her to recognize me, let alone remember my name. We hadn't seen each other in years, and I was sure I looked totally different from the rather serious teenager with the drab brown hair, several extra pounds, and braces on her teeth. Or at least I hoped I did.

Suddenly I was fifteen again, the plain, smart girl, as opposed to one of the in crowd. "Yes, it's me," I said, trying to gather myself. "Long time no see."

"Damn right," Annabelle said, jumping to her feet. "How about you—you're lookin' great. Some transformation."

The last thing I expected to come out of Annabelle Maestro's mouth was a compliment. For a moment, I was totally thrown. Annabelle had *never* said anything nice to me in all the years I'd known her.

"Uh, so do you," I managed. Suddenly I was remembering the last shopping expedition we'd gone on together, when she'd informed me I was way too fat to get into any of the designer jeans sold at Fred Segal, the mecca of one-stop shopping for rich Beverly Hills girls with money to burn.

At the time I was a healthy size eight, while Annabelle was an unhealthy size zero.

"Are you really a lawyer?" Annabelle asked, actually sounding vaguely interested.

I nodded.

"That's amazing!" she exclaimed. She sat down again and placed her Diet Coke on the coffee table. "I'm so proud of you."

Now, why would she be proud of me? After our brief year of one-sided friendship, she'd barely acknowledged my existence.

"Your father's very happy you're coming home," I said, sounding horribly phony. "And may I take this opportunity to say how sorry I am about your mom."

Annabelle lowered her shades and threw me a stony stare. "So," she said flatly. "Did the old bastard do it? Did Mr. Movie Star finally crack and blow away all that fucking perfection?"

I was stunned into silence. The venom in her voice was palpable.

Frankie saved the day. Quickly he took hold of my arm and dragged me over to the window. "Take no notice of anythin' she says," he muttered. "She's in deep denial, doesn't know what she's talking about. Ignore her."

Concerned boyfriend had spoken. A piece of work if ever I'd seen one.

I wished he would wipe his nose; the residue of white powder was such a giveaway.

Glancing out the window, I noticed Sam trudging down the street, laptop under one arm. He was probably on his way to the coffee shop, which he'd revealed was his favorite place to write. I wondered what he would make of this scene.

Annabelle shifted off the couch once more. "Are we leaving or what?" she asked irritably. "The sooner I get this over with, the better I'll feel."

Frankie shot me a look. "Is the limo downstairs?"

"Ready and waiting," I replied, totally on top of the situation.

"You wanna tell the driver to come get our luggage?"

"Sure," I answered pleasantly.

From lawyer to assistant in one fell swoop. I couldn't wait to deliver these two.

Annabelle and Frankie. A match made in heaven.

Or not?

I guess that's up to me to find out on our long trek west.

~ ~ ~

It didn't take me a great deal of time to realize Annabelle had not changed one bit. She might be older, but she certainly wasn't any wiser. She had no clue about how to treat people, starting with our limo driver. The moment she got in the limousine, she began complaining about his driving skills.

According to Annabelle, he drove too fast; his stops were jerky; the heating in the car was overpowering; the TV did not function properly.

Bitch. Bitch. Bitch. All the way to the airport.

I was amazed that she had no questions about her mother's murder, how Ralph was doing, funeral details—nothing.

Frankie seemed used to the constant stream of complaints. He chose to more or less agree and then ignore.

Clever strategy.

At the airport, I'd arranged for special services to meet us curbside. Annabelle handed the woman her heavy Louis Vuitton carry-on bag, then proceeded to act as if the woman didn't exist.

Fortunately, checking in was swift, although when we got to security, Annabelle managed to create an annoying drama.

"Do I *have* to take my boots off?" she whined. "The ground is filthy."

"Everyone has to," I explained. Who the hell did she think she was? "And you've also got to remove your belt and take off your jacket," I added, annoying her even further.

"Shit!" snapped Annabelle as a line of pissed-off travelers waited impatiently for her to wriggle out of her thigh-high boots, an act that seemed to take forever.

Frankie had already shot ahead of her, leaving me to manage the situation.

Thanks, Frankie, I love you, too. She's your girlfriend, you should be dealing with her crap.

By the time I got them to the VIP lounge, I'd had enough. I left them in the hands of our escort and ducked out to make a few quick calls.

First Felix, my boss. I didn't care that it was early in the morning in L.A. I merely wished to report that we were on our way.

"Good girl," Felix said.

I hated it when he called me "girl"—so damn patronizing. Maybe it was time to change law firms, move on. I don't like to sound immodest, but I have managed to earn myself a stellar reputation, and sometimes I don't think Felix treats me with the respect I deserve.

Next I called my dad. I knew my family must be wondering what the hell had happened to me, because part of our family tradition is a phone call a day.

"Why did they send *you* to New York?" Dad wanted to know. "They should've sent an assistant."

I heartily agreed and informed him I'd be there for our usual Thursday night dinner.

"You'd better be," he said.

Thursday night dinner is a family tradition. Everyone gathers at my parents' house. It's quite a mob scene, what with my three brothers, their various wives and girlfriends, and several nieces and nephews. Actually it's great, because with all the craziness of working in L.A., Thursday night represents stability and a safe haven. Josh and I used to love our Thursday nights with the family.

Thinking of Josh took me straight to thoughts of Sam and Mario. I really hadn't taken the time to go over the recent events in my personal life. The last couple of days had been quite something. Sex with two totally different guys. Hmm . . . adventurous little me!

On impulse I texted Mario: *Getting on a plane. How about dinner tonight?*

Then I texted Carolyn: *Keep on missing you. On my way back to L.A. Will call when I arrive.*

Done with my phone calls, I returned to the lounge, where Annabelle had spread herself across a couch and was downing what looked to be her third vodka on the rocks.

Lovely. A coke addict and a drunk. What a perfect start to the day.

26

Carolyn

"Where are you?" Carolyn asked, relieved that Gregory had finally called. "I've been frantic. Is everything all right?"

Since he'd failed to come into the office all day, she'd started to become concerned. It wasn't like Gregory to take a day off.

"Everything's fine," he assured her. "Why wouldn't it be?"

"You know why," she replied, keeping her voice low as she spoke into her cell phone.

"Yes, of course," he said, clearing his throat. "But surely you must realize that I have to tread slowly?"

Tread slowly? What did *that* mean?

She couldn't resist getting in a dig. "Muriel said she thought you'd gone jewelry shopping with your wife."

"Oh, for God's sake!" he exclaimed. "Please don't tell me that you actually believed her."

"I wasn't sure what to think."

"You know me better than that."

"Yes, but when you didn't come in today . . ."

"Stop speaking nonsense," he said irritably.

"It's not nonsense," she said, holding her phone tightly. "I was concerned."

There was a brief silence. "Does anybody know we're talking?" he said at last.

"Excuse me?"

"You didn't say my name aloud, did you?"

"No."

"You're alone in your office?"

"Yes," she said, slightly puzzled. "And I don't understand why you're calling on my cell. How come you didn't call the office line?"

"Because from now on everything between us has to remain private." He cleared his throat again. "There's no reason for anyone to know anything. I'm cementing our future, Carolyn. Remember that."

"Does this mean—"

"It means I'm taking care of everything my way, so start trusting me, and stop asking so many questions."

She experienced yet another shiver of excitement. The man she loved was taking care of everything. Before very long their secret would be out in the open, and everyone would know—including Muriel with her tight-assed, disapproving attitude.

"I do trust you," she said softly. "But I couldn't help worrying."

"I have a surprise for you," he said.

"You do?"

"Something you deserve."

Her smile returned with a vengeance. "What is it?" she whispered excitedly.

"Listen to me very carefully," he said, his voice tense. "Then I want you to follow my instructions to the letter."

"Sounds mysterious," she said.

"It's not mysterious. It's exactly as I said before: we have to be diligent and tread extremely carefully."

"I know that—you keep on telling me."

"Then I hope you're listening."

"I am."

"Okay, Carolyn, please listen once again, for this is exactly what I want you to do. . . ."

27

Bobby

"Is it just me or are the two of 'em the weirdest fuckin' couple in the world?" M.J. asked as he and Bobby headed for the meeting with their potential Russian investors, a meeting they were anticipating would lead to a major expansion of their club business.

"Hey—whatever turns you on," Bobby answered, still thinking about Zeena.

"Annabelle's like cold as a fuckin' ice truck," M.J. muttered. "Doesn't she get that her mom's been freakin' *murdered*? How about showin' an inch of emotion?"

"She's always been like that," Bobby remarked. "Remember high school?"

"Remember an' regret," M.J. said, grimacing.

"Regret what?"

"Y'know, that prom night deal."

"Nobody was scoring off anyone," Bobby pointed out. "It was mutual, we were all so out of it."

"Yeah, but the way I remember it, I'd sooner it never happened."

"Too late now eight years later," Bobby said, reaching for his vibrating cell. He paused for a moment before answering, wondering if it might be Zeena requesting a repeat performance.

Was he even into a repeat performance?

Maybe.

Maybe not.

One thing was for sure, he was definitely confused.

Fortunately, or not so fortunately, it wasn't Zeena. It was Lucky.

"You're up early," he said.

"What else is new?" Lucky replied briskly.

"What can I do for you, Mom?"

"Come back to live in L.A."

"Huh?"

"Just messing with you," Lucky said lightly. "But I do have a proposition I think will interest you."

"You do?"

"Something you've been ragging me about."

"What?" he asked, interest piqued.

"Last night I threw out the son of a bitch who runs the main night spot at the Keys. He's been getting sloppy. Yesterday I found out for sure that he's been running drugs *and* laundering money. Can you believe it? *So not* a brilliant move to do that kind of crap on *my* property."

"Right."

"I told the asshole if he didn't want his balls served up for breakfast along with two fried eggs and a rasher of bacon, he'd better get the fuck out. Instantly."

Bobby began to laugh. Lucky had such a way with words.

"What did the asshole say?"

"You honestly think I gave him a chance to say anything, Bobby? You know me, I abide by the rules: Never fuck with a Santangelo."

"Oh yeah, Mom, I know the rules."

"The moron should've taken note of my rules," Lucky said. "He's gone."

"Just like that?"

"Yes," Lucky said firmly. "Just like that."

"An' now . . ."

"Now I finally might require your services to take over the club. Something you've been begging to do ever since I opened the Keys."

"Hey, not begging, Mom," Bobby corrected. "I'm a Santangelo, remember? Santangelos do not beg."

"Then how about asking?"

"That was a couple of years ago. We'll be gettin' off the ground in Miami soon. M.J. an' me, we got a cool franchise thing in place for Mood. We're meeting with a syndicate of Russian investors this morning, so I'm not sure—"

"Yes or no, Bobby?" Lucky said impatiently. "You want in or not? Do not play games with me, because we both know who's gonna end up winning."

"I gotta talk to M.J."

"Do it. And if your answer is yes, I'll expect you here tomorrow to cut a deal."

"Tomorrow? In Vegas? Isn't that kinda soon?"

"This is business, Bobby. And this is a onetime offer. Call me back within the hour."

Then she was gone. Lucky Santangelo. Businesswoman. World-class beauty. Ball breaker. Unstoppable force of nature. Mom.

"Wassup?" M.J. wanted to know.

"You're never gonna believe this," Bobby said, slowly shaking his head.

"Try me."

"The Keys. If we want to take over the club concession, could be that it's ours."

~ ~ ~

The Russians were a cagey group of billionaires. Three men and one of the men's wives, an older woman with sinister slit eyes, a Botoxed face, bright red lips, and a sneering attitude.

The men were all bald, with protruding guts, yellow teeth, and disagreeable personalities. Bobby hated every one of them on sight. He'd inherited Lucky's immediate judgment and Dimitri's acute business sense.

The Russians proposed a deal so ridiculously one-sided that Bobby and M.J. couldn't wait to walk out of their overdecorated offices.

"Y'know," Bobby said as they hit the elevators after the disappointing meeting, "Lucky always told me that when one door closes, another is bound to open. An' I think we're lookin' at an open door all the way to Vegas. What's your take on it?"

"I think if you can get together on a deal with Lucky, then we're sure as shit gettin' on a plane," M.J. said, full of enthusiasm. "You know me, I love L.A. An' as for Vegas . . . yeah, we can definitely make it work."

Bobby nodded. He'd always wanted Vegas; after all, it was his heritage. His grandfather Gino was one of the pioneers, along with Bugsy Siegel, way back in the late forties. Gino had built one of the first big Vegas hotels, and Lucky had followed suit, building two magnificent hotels of her own.

For once, Bobby thought about using the Stanislopoulos plane, although he didn't usually take advantage of such a luxurious perk. But it was Vegas, and if using the plane made it easier to get there fast, so be it.

M.J. loved the idea. "Never been on the Stanislopoulos plane," he remarked.

"That's 'cause I never use it," Bobby replied.

"Man, if I had a plane at my disposal—"

"It's a company plane. It's for the board of directors."

"And you," M.J. pointed out.

"And Brigette," Bobby said quickly. "She can use it whenever she wants."

"How is Brigette?" M.J. asked. "She never comes by the club anymore. I miss seein' her."

Bobby experienced a twinge of guilt. He'd promised Lucky he'd watch out for his niece, yet he hadn't called her in weeks. Last time he'd spoken to her, she'd mentioned something about getting together with someone new. Bobby knew he should've followed up the way Lucky would have, but what the heck—he had other things on his mind. And Brigette was a big girl, she could look after herself. Or could she?

No. Everyone knew that Brigette attracted losers. They flocked in her direction like ants racing toward a bowl of honey.

"I'm calling Brigette," Bobby decided, "see if she's into makin' the trip with us. Business plus fun. May as well make the most of it."

"Cool," M.J. responded. "An' since we're takin' your plane, how about I bring my girlfriend?"

"*What* girlfriend?" Bobby asked with a note of surprise.

"A girl I've been seein'," M.J. answered casually.

"For real?"

"What?" M.J. quipped. "You think I'm makin' her up?"

"You've never mentioned you're seein' someone."

"You've never asked. An' if you'd turned up at dinner last night, you would've met her."

"Who is she?" Bobby asked, curious.

"Someone kinda special," M.J. replied with a self-satisfied smile. "I think I might've finally found the one."

Bobby raised a cynical eyebrow. "*Now* you're telling me."

"Wanted to be sure, man. Nothin' wrong with that."

"Bring her," Bobby said. "I'll let you know what I think."

"All due respect, bro, but when it comes to this one—I don't give a shit *what* you think."

~ ~ ~

"Yes," Brigette said.

"Yes?" Bobby repeated.

"Why not? It sounds like a fun trip," Brigette said. "And we haven't used the plane in ages. I'll bring Kris."

"Who's Kris?"

"My new friend."

"You're sure you want to—"

"Yes, Bobby, you'll get along. I faithfully promise you that Kris is not one of my losers."

Sure. He'd heard that before. But at least he'd get a chance to judge for himself, and no doubt Lucky would want to meet the new man in Brigette's life.

So . . . the trip was a go. The plane would be ready to take off at eight A.M. the next morning. M.J. was bringing his new girlfriend. Brigette was bringing her latest love. And Bobby . . . well, Bobby was flying solo.

28

Annabelle

Returning to L.A. brought back a rush of memories for Annabelle. As she stepped off the plane, she stood still for a moment and inhaled the still-familiar L.A. smell—a mixture of smog and jasmine. Taking a deep breath, she braced herself for the homecoming, such as it was.

Fortunately, they would not be staying at the family house. Frankie had been smart enough to arrange for them to have a suite at the Beverly Hills Hotel.

Ahh . . . the Pink Palace, as the luxurious hotel was called back in the day. Many's the time Annabelle had skipped school and hung out at the downstairs snack bar in the hotel, scoffing hamburgers and milk shakes and the hotel's famous Neil McCarthy chopped salad. She'd often hit on a random male who was into spending time with a fifteen-year-old truant, and that had been a blast, especially when she'd eventually revealed who she was.

One old producer she'd hit on had practically crapped himself when she'd told him her dad was Ralph Maestro. She'd been blowing him at the time in his poolside suite, and his cock had all but vanished up his own asshole.

Good times!

Now she was returning to the Pink Palace with her boyfriend, Frankie, and who knew what surprises lay ahead.

Denver checked them both in and accompanied them to their suite. "Your father is expecting you at the house for an early dinner," she informed Annabelle.

"With you?" Annabelle asked.

"No, not with me."

"But you must be there," Annabelle wailed, clinging to Denver's arm. "I can't go unless you come, too. You're my support system. I need you."

"I'm not invited," Denver explained.

Frankie threw her a piercing look. "*She's* inviting you," he said, putting his hand on her arm and guiding her toward the door. "Don't we all want this to go as smoothly as possible?"

"I'm one of Mr. Maestro's lawyers, not a babysitter," Denver argued.

"Do this for her," Frankie insisted. "She's vulnerable right now, needs all the help she can get. An' you're one of her oldest friends."

"Bullshit I am!" Denver said hotly.

"It doesn't matter. Just do it," Frankie said, and gave her a gentle exit shove through the door.

Annabelle was busy exploring the suite. Fortunately, it was to her liking. After testing the bed, she ordered a dozen more pillows and a fresh duvet. Then she inspected the marble bathroom and ordered three dozen large bath towels and extra toweling robes. After that, she made an appointment at La Prairie spa.

Meanwhile, Frankie took a walk around the hotel. It surpassed his wildest dreams. The grounds were a magnificent tangle of bougainvillea, wild roses, and exotic palms of all varieties. He'd never seen anything like it. The weather was balmy and clear, with a slight cooling breeze. The pool in all its Olympic glory was surrounded by private cabanas. He immediately booked one, charging it to the room. Then he made his way to the famous

Polo Lounge and checked that out. He thought he spotted Justin Timberlake sitting in a booth with a delicious-looking blonde.

Shit! This was his kind of town, his kind of action. Frankie could definitely see himself setting up shop in this town. Frankie Romano, purveyor of grade-A flesh princesses to a parade of horny guys who preferred paying for it rather than playing the dating game. Horny, *famous* guys who would soon become his asshole buddies. Frankie imagined Cruise, Clooney, Snoop Dogg . . . yeah, maybe even Timberlake.

Frankie grinned to himself. L.A. was where he belonged. And with a little help from Annabelle, he was going to make sure they were here to stay.

~ ~ ~

Simon Waitrose leaned back in his beaten-up leather swivel chair situated behind a crowded desk and stared at the shifty-looking youth who'd recently slunk into his office. "Whaddya got for us, Chip?" he said.

Chip Bonafacio blinked several times in quick succession. This Simon Waitrose man with the British accent and shrewd eyes made him uneasy. He reminded Chip of the infamous Simon Cowell on TV. Direct, challenging, and rude. But Chip wasn't visiting Simon's office to make friends. No. He had a story to sell, and he'd already made a tentative deal to get paid a shitload of money. All he had to do was produce proof that the story he was selling was the truth and nothing but.

He'd already had two meetings at *Truth & Fact*. The first was with Simon's right hand, an abrasive woman with buckteeth and an unfortunate squint. And the second meeting was with Simon himself, who'd informed him that if he could produce solid proof that Annabelle Maestro was involved in running call girls, then he'd get his payout.

Solid proof. What constituted solid proof?

Well, for one thing, his timing couldn't be better. With Frankie and

Annabelle out of town, and his mom staying at their Park Avenue apartment, he'd had a perfect opportunity to search out whatever he could find. First he'd had to put his mom out of action. She was a nosy one, always butting into his business.

No problem. He had a plan, and late Monday afternoon he'd activated it: slipping two Ambien into her tea, a move that soon sent her to the land of Nod, leaving him free to roam around the damn apartment, searching for anything he could find to corroborate his story.

And search he did—starting in the master bedroom, where he found nothing but designer clothes, shoes, and handbags. Annabelle Maestro obviously spent money as if it were going out of style.

He'd moved on to Frankie's crap—discovering two-hundred-and-fifty-dollar ties with the price tag still affixed, Hugo Boss jackets, Brioni suits, expensive sports clothes, and a dozen matching black cashmere long-sleeved sweaters.

Between the two of them, they must've blown a fortune.

Chip felt distinct twinges of envy. He did all the goddamn work driving the whores wherever they needed to go, while Miss Nose-in-the-Air Maestro and her coked-out boyfriend reaped all the benefits.

Well, fuck 'em both. Chip was exposing their twisted game, and to hell with the consequences. Soon he'd have his own big bucks to splash around.

The locked drawers in the library gave up all the proof and photos he'd ever need.

"Here's your proof," he said, trying to sound macho as he thrust a manila envelope across Simon's messy desk.

"And what exactly do we have here?" Simon said, opening the envelope and tipping the contents onto his desktop.

"Plenty," Chip boasted. "All juicy stuff."

"Juicy, huh?" Simon questioned. "It better be, 'cause wasting my time pisses me off."

"Wouldn't want to do that," Chip responded with a feeble chuckle.

"No, mate, you wouldn't," Simon said as he sorted through the items from Chip's envelope. He held up a photo of Annabelle with her famous parents and scrutinized it. She was about fifteen at the time the photo was taken. "Pretty girl," he remarked. "Got something more recent?"

"Keep lookin'," Chip said.

Simon picked up another photo. This one was of Annabelle with Frankie and two of the girls who occasionally worked for them—one a fairly well-known singer, one an actress on a weekly series—both of them recognizable faces.

"Those two are workin' girls," Chip said. "I've driven them to many appointments."

"You have?"

"Yeah. They're into scorin' extra bucks. They get ten grand a pop."

"Proof?" Simon said.

"You'll see," Chip replied. "I got photos of 'em with their masks on. I got hotel receipts. I got dates, times, client names. Everything's there."

"Okay, then," Simon said, leafing through more photos. "Looks like we got ourselves a big kick-ass story. An' here's the good news—if I rush it through, we'll make it for the front page of Wednesday's edition, just in time for Thursday's funeral."

29

Denver

My freaking luck, Annabelle has decided that I am her best friend in the world, and Felix seems to think that this is excellent news. Anything to keep his number-one client, Mr. Ralph Maestro, happy—including sacrificing me for the benefit of the case.

Not that there is a case as such, because while I was freezing my ass off in New York, two suspects were pulled into the mix. Swift work by the Beverly Hills Police Department. I was impressed.

Suspect number one—usurping that prime position from Ralph—a stalker/fan who apparently had done all his stalking (letters, gifts, threats, declarations of love/hate) from New Orleans, so nobody had taken the threats seriously. But after Gemma's highly publicized murder, the stalker/fan's sister had come forward to reveal that said stalker/fan had set off for L.A. two days earlier, intent on meeting the woman of his dreams/nightmares.

Suspect number two—dropping Ralph even farther down the ladder—was a mysterious man the paparazzi had caught Gemma lunching with at a secluded restaurant in the hills above Malibu. The photos were taken the day before her murder, and nobody—including Ralph—knew who the man was.

Was Gemma having a secret affair? Was she cheating on Ralph? Was the perfect movie-star couple not so perfect after all? The Internet gossip sites were in overdrive.

But back to me and my new best friend, Annabelle Maestro.

"I have a life," I informed Felix. "Why do you think it's so important that I go to this dinner tonight with Annabelle? Ralph doesn't even like me, he treats me as if I'm your assistant. I'm an excellent lawyer, Felix, I deserve respect."

Felix Saunders, aka Mr. Shark Teeth, talked me down in his slightly supercilious fashion. It was all about how important client/lawyer relationships were, how the client depends on his lawyer not only as legal counsel, but as a loyal friend and confidant.

Eventually I caved, because the truth is I wouldn't mind observing the interaction between Annabelle and her famous dad. As a keen watcher of human behavior, I was sort of looking forward to it, in a perverse kind of way. One of the things I do in court is keep a sharp eye on the jury and their reactions to even the smallest piece of information. I find that when it comes to the crunch, it always pays off.

Mario had texted me back: *Dinner on. Can't wait!*

I contemplated phoning him, then decided against it. Another text would do. Brief and to the point: *Sorry. Dinner off due to work. How about tomorrow night?*

I didn't really care that much. Mario was a diversion, certainly not the start of something meaningful.

Carolyn had sent me another text while I was on the plane: *We must talk!! So much happening!!*

She was due to arrive in L.A. for the Christmas vacation, and once again. I began thinking about all the girly things that I never seem to find the time to do on my own. I envisioned a lazy and relaxing day at the Korean spa. A mindless shop at the Grove. Plenty of movies. Maybe even a long weekend in Palm Springs with my main gay—Teddy, hairstylist supreme. Carolyn was a true friend, the kind of person who would always be there for me no matter what. I could tell she was really psyched about something, and I couldn't wait to hear her news.

~ ~ ~

While we were waiting at the entrance to the hotel for the limo, Annabelle grabbed my hand and said, "Thanks for doing this, Denver. I do know it's not part of your job description, and I truly appreciate it."

Annabelle. Appreciating something. Definitely out of character.

Then she added, further confusing me, "Did you know that at school I always used to envy you? Your life seemed so normal compared to mine. You had parents that actually came to school events, and they seemed to *care* about you. I was majorly jealous."

Was she freaking kidding me? Annabelle Maestro jealous of me! Absolutely no way.

Before she could say anything more, Frankie loped over, having just introduced himself to a famous basketball player who was standing by the entrance waiting for his car.

"Jeez!" Frankie exclaimed, pleased with himself for having spotted another celebrity. "That Rick Fox is one tall motherfucker. I invited him to stop by Mood next time he's in New York. Gave him my card."

"Who's Rick Fox?" Annabelle asked blankly.

"Who's Rick Fox!" Frankie chortled. "A former Lakers great! Everyone knows who Rick Fox is. He used t'be married to Vanessa Williams, a total babe."

Just as Annabelle was about to ask who Vanessa Williams was—and I would've explained because I'm a huge *Ugly Betty* fan the limo pulled up and we all piled in.

Ten minutes later we arrived at the house, and a stony-faced Ralph Maestro greeted us at the door to his imposing mansion. He gave me a brief nod, shook Frankie's hand, and leaned forward to honor Annabelle with an awkward hug. No words were exchanged as we followed him into the house.

I glanced at Annabelle. Her perfectly made-up face gave nothing away.

Ralph led us into the enormous living room, where a huge portrait of Ralph and Gemma dominated over the mantelpiece, a fake log fire burned brightly, and a waiter hovered behind an exceptionally long bar.

"Order your drinks," Ralph said in a strained voice. "Have whatever you want."

I noted that his tan had faded since our last meeting. Perhaps visiting a tanning salon was not the best idea during these difficult times. But surely Ralph had people who came to him?

While I was pondering the disappearing tan, Annabelle requested a martini, and Frankie went for a Jack on the rocks. Frankie was obviously under the impression that Jack (note: Jack, as opposed to Jack Daniel's) was *the* hot Hollywood drink. And it seemed he was right, because Ralph ordered the same thing.

I opted for a glass of white wine. Wimpy drink, but at least I could make it last while everyone around me got wasted. And getting wasted was definitely on the agenda, for Annabelle downed her martini in three fast gulps, then immediately requested a second one.

Oh, wow! Here we go. Hold on tight, 'cause I've got a strong suspicion it's going to be a bumpy night.

~ ~ ~

Imagine being at a dinner where it is apparent that everyone hates everyone else, but for the sake of appearances, politeness rules.

One would think Ralph was hosting a dinner for several avid fans who'd won an evening to be spent with the great Ralph Maestro. He was stiff, uncomfortable, and distant.

Frankie, on the other hand, did not shut up. On his usual coke-fueled high (oh yes, it hadn't taken me long to figure out his numerous visits to the bathroom were not to pee), he carried on about the hotel, the city, the weather, and what an honor it was to finally meet the amazing Ralph Maestro.

"I've seen every movie you ever made," Frankie enthused, eliciting a glare from Annabelle, who'd had no idea he was such a fan. "*Brain-Dead, The Great American Train Wreck, Jolt, Finding Mr. Lee.* I grew up watchin' your movies. You and Bruce Willis, you guys kicked it like nobody else."

I had a strong feeling that Ralph had been prepared to dislike Annabelle's boyfriend, but the accolades were coming so fast and furious that Ralph's enormous ego couldn't resist. He nodded, accepting the praise as if it were his due.

Annabelle and I listened in stunned silence as Frankie proceeded to talk about every one of Ralph's movies in detail.

After a while, it seemed Annabelle couldn't take it any longer. "Excuse us," she said, standing up and throwing me a pointed look. "We'll be right back."

Hmm . . . I guess that means I'm going with her, leaving Frankie to shove his nose all the way up Ralph's ass, an act he's obviously enjoying.

Annabelle led me into an ornate guest powder room decorated in over-the-top shades of turquoise and gold. "I'm in dire need of a cigarette," she muttered, groping in her Balenciaga purse for a pack of Marlboros. "Isn't this torture?"

"I imagine your dad is still in shock," I said lamely. "Besides, Frankie is kind of monopolizing the conversation."

"Frankie can be such a dick," Annabelle said, dismissing her boyfriend with an abrupt wave of her hand. "Who knew he worshipped Ralph? I certainly didn't."

"You had no clue?"

"Nothing. Nada. We never even talked about my family, and now this show of worship. Quite frankly I'm pissed."

"Don't blame you."

"Oh, Denver," Annabelle said, suddenly clutching my arm, "I'm so grateful you're here. I honestly couldn't go through this if you weren't around to support me."

"That's nonsense," I said, swallowing fast. "You'd be fine."

"No, I wouldn't."

"Yes, you would," I insisted.

What was going on here? Why was I Miss Indispensable all of a sudden?

"Anyway," Annabelle continued, "you *are* here, and as long as we stay together I'll be able to cope. The funeral's on Thursday, and right after I want to be on a plane back to New York. Can you arrange it?"

Crap! So add travel agent to my job description.

Back at the dining table, Frankie was quoting lines from *Brain-Dead*, and Ralph was finally looking bored. Ignoring Frankie in full quote, Ralph fixed Annabelle with one of his steely stares and said, "I expect you to go through your mother's things while you're here. The housekeepers will help you. Be sure they don't try to take anything."

"You want *me* to do it?" Annabelle stared at him in disbelief.

"*Yes*, you," Ralph said sharply. "There's nobody else that's family, therefore it's your responsibility. Be here at ten in the morning."

"But—"

"Annabelle," Ralph said, his voice cold. "You're her daughter. It's what she would have wanted."

"I don't think so," Annabelle mumbled.

"Well, I do," Ralph said, big movie-star face staring her down.

End of discussion.

We finally got out of there at nine-thirty.

"Time to party," Frankie said, rubbing his hands together in anticipation of a wild Hollywood night. "Where's *the* place to hang?"

I had definitely had enough of Frankie Romano for one night. "Beats me," I said with a quick shrug. "I'm going home to bed."

"No way!" Frankie exclaimed. "We're hittin' it tonight. I gotta know what's goin' on in this town. Gotta catch the vibe."

"Sorry," I said, not sorry at all. "You're on your own."

"Yes," said Annabelle, agreeing with me. "You're on your own, Frankie. After dinner and all that tension, I'm exhausted."

"Jesus Christ!" Frankie complained. "What's *wrong* with you two?"

"The driver will steer you in the right direction," I offered. "Right after he's dropped us at the hotel, where I'll pick up my car and Annabelle can go get a good night's sleep."

"What are you guys, like fifty?" Frankie sneered.

"Twenty-five, actually," I said, loathing him more every minute. "But don't sweat it, I'm sure you're capable of having fun on your own."

Annabelle stifled a giggle. It wasn't often Frankie didn't get his way.

Back at the hotel, Annabelle and I scooted out of the limo and Frankie took off to go God knew where.

Annabelle didn't seem to mind. "You're right, he can look after himself," she said. "I'll see you in the morning, Denver."

"You will?"

"Ten o'clock. We'll drive over to the house together and deal with my mother's things."

"Look, Annabelle," I said, feeling awkward, "I'd really like to help you out, but here's the thing—I have to be at my office tomorrow. I'm way behind on everything. Got a thousand things to take care of."

"Not to worry," Annabelle said with an airy wave of her hand. "I'll have Ralph fix it with your boss. Just remember this—while I'm in L.A., you're all mine."

Talk about getting caught in a trap. It seemed I had no choice in the matter.

30

Carolyn

Tuesday morning, Carolyn awoke early but was too revved up to fall back to sleep. Gregory had promised her a surprise, and the thought of what it might be was driving her crazy. She was sure it was something she'd like, something to do with their future together, something amazing.

Humming softly to herself, she decided she had time for a run before work. She slipped into a pale blue tracksuit and her Puma sneakers, grabbed her keys, and left the apartment. Out in the hall, she bumped straight into Kerri.

"Am I glad to see you," Kerri exclaimed. "Got a big favor to ask."

"Ask away," Carolyn replied.

"Well, you know how I always pick up Nellie's meds once a month."

"I know you do, and she really appreciates it. It's so thoughtful of you."

Kerri gave a modest shrug. "Guess it's my twelve good deeds for the year. But here comes the favor. I can't do it today—got a way hot date, an' he's meeting me from work. So since Nellie is out of her sleeping pills *and* her heart meds, can you pick them up for me an' drop them off at her apartment?"

"Of course I can," Carolyn said. "No problem."

"Everything's prepaid," Kerri explained. "I gave the prescriptions to the pharmacy yesterday, they'll be ready after five."

"Done," Carolyn said.

"You're such a doll," Kerri said, leaning forward to give her a quick hug.

"We should take turns doing it anyway."

"I'm down with that."

"I should've thought of it before."

"Hey, you're doin' your bit, always lookin' in on the old dear, makin' sure she's breathin'."

"We both do what we can."

"How about an early breakfast tomorrow?" Kerri suggested. "I can give you all the filthy details from what I hope is gonna be a night of crazy mad lust!"

"Sounds good," Carolyn said. Then she couldn't help adding, "I might have some exciting news of my own."

"Awesome!" Kerri said. "Are you seein' someone?"

"I could be . . ." Carolyn replied, almost tempted to spill everything.

"That's my girl. You can tell me all about him tomorrow. Same time, same place. My treat."

Carolyn nodded. "Make sure to take note of every single detail."

"Oh, I will," Kerri said, beaming. "Don'cha you worry 'bout *that*!"

~ ~ ~

Later in the day, Carolyn breezed into Muriel's office and said, "I'm leaving early today."

"Why is that?" Muriel inquired, tightly wound as she sat ramrod straight behind her desk.

"The senator knows," Carolyn continued. "I mentioned it to him last week."

"He didn't tell me."

"Does he tell you everything?"

"Where are you going?" Muriel asked, tapping her pen on her desktop.

None of your business, Carolyn was tempted to say. But she remained cool. "Dentist," she said shortly.

"In the middle of the day?"

Carolyn shrugged. "The senator said it was okay, and since it seems he's not coming in again, my timing appears to be right on."

"Personal appointments are supposed to take place after office hours," Muriel said primly. "Surely you're aware of that?"

"Yes, I am aware of it," Carolyn replied. "But exceptions happen."

"For *some* people," Muriel sniffed.

Carolyn couldn't help going for the comment she knew would get to Muriel. "Well," she said, "I guess I'm *some* people. See you later, Muriel."

Escaping from the office without further interrogation, she made her way to the underground parking lot. Things were about to change; it was exciting, and she couldn't wait.

She got into her 2006 Pontiac and sat quietly for a few moments, contemplating her future. She was filled with all kinds of anticipation. Gregory *had* been mysterious, but extremely firm. He'd said he had a surprise for her. What could it possibly be?

When they'd spoken on the phone the previous day, he'd given her strict instructions and told her to follow them without question. "Do not tell anyone anything," he'd warned. "If you do, it will ruin everything."

As if she would. She was hardly likely to confide in disapproving Muriel or the new male intern, who wore patent-leather shoes a size too large and an ill-fitting button-down Oxford shirt.

Gregory's words echoed in her head. *Take the main highway over the bridge and follow Route 105. Turn off at exit 10, and drive approximately fifteen minutes until you reach the abandoned Shell station. Wait there until I contact you.*

She had a hunch she knew exactly what he had planned. He was arranging to meet her somewhere quiet, out of sight of prying eyes, and then he was taking her to view a house.

Yes! What else could the surprise be?

It was a no-brainer. Gregory was putting into motion the seeds of their new life together.

She was sure of it.

31

Bobby

M.J.'s new girlfriend, Cassie, was a miniature version of a younger Janet Jackson. Heartbreakingly pretty with a pocket Venus figure, she was only eighteen and trying hard to crash the music business.

Bobby took M.J. to one side while they waited for Brigette to arrive at the private airport. "Holy shit! She's a baby!" he exclaimed. "Jeez, M.J., she's almost the same age as Max. What're you thinking?"

"I'm thinkin' that I've finally found the one," M.J. responded. "Nothin' wrong with that—you should try it sometime."

"We're taking her across state lines," Bobby pointed out. "Is it even legal?"

"Hey, bro, she's eighteen, not twelve," M.J. snapped. "An' I'd kinda appreciate it if you'd quit with the comments an' get with the program."

"Fine," Bobby grumbled. "Baby snatch, what do I care?"

He and M.J. had been friends since eighth grade. M.J. had always been a player, and girls loved him, but as far as Bobby was concerned, his friend was way too young to start settling down. It wasn't cool. Still, Bobby had to admit that M.J. and Cassie made a great-looking couple, and Cassie seemed sweet. Although sweet wasn't usually M.J.'s type—he liked them sassy and sexy.

Brigette arrived late, as usual, a trait she'd inherited from Olympia, her deceased mother. Olympia had been Bobby's half sister, and even though Brigette was ten years older than him, he was indeed her uncle, a fact they laughed about a lot.

"You're late," he said.

"I know," she said with a big unapologetic grin.

Bobby was pleased to note that Brigette seemed happy. It must be the new boyfriend's influence.

A tall, athletic blonde emerged from Brigette's limo. She had short-cropped hair, broad shoulders, a healthy tan, and a wide smile.

Brigette grabbed the woman's hand. "Bobby," she announced, beaming, "I want you to meet Kris. She's the woman who put a smile back on my face. Isn't she amazing?"

~ ~ ~

All the way on the flight to Vegas, Bobby kept thinking about what Lucky would have to say about this unexpected turn of events. Brigette changing tracks was quite a surprise, although when he thought about it, he wasn't that shocked. After all, Brigette had experienced quite a parade of losers and psychos, all of them men, so maybe she'd have more luck with a woman. She was certainly happy enough, and she looked fantastic. She and Kris were joking around like a couple of teenagers.

Kris was a pro tennis player and very successful. "We met in the Hamptons at the P. Diddy All White Party," Brigette revealed. "I was with an out-of-work actor who'd decided I was just the ticket to pay all his bills, including his ex-wife's alimony. And Kris had recently broken up with her longtime girlfriend."

"We'd been together eight years," Kris chimed in. "She wanted a marriage license and a baby. All I wanted was out."

"Neither of us were looking—"

"Until we looked in each other's direction," Kris interrupted.

"And then," Brigette added with a shy giggle, "it was a lightning strike. I knew immediately that Kris would change my life. And although we've only been together since the summer, she has."

Kris squeezed Brigette's hand and then concentrated on Bobby for a moment. "I'm so happy to finally meet you," she said. "I know her family means a lot to Brigette, so when the opportunity came up to make this trip together, we both said a resounding yes! I can't wait to meet the rest of the family."

"You will," Bobby said, glancing over at M.J. and Cassie, who were all over each other.

It seemed he was the odd one out. By himself. No significant other.

All he had was the hots for a famous superstar who'd used him for stud service. Nice.

~ ~ ~

The last thing Bobby expected to see as the eight-passenger extra-long silver limo took them from the airport to the Keys complex was a huge billboard of Zeena on the strip, heralding a one-night-only appearance at the Cavendish Hotel. She was due to appear the following night.

Jeez! Was there no escape?

The Cavendish, a successful boutique hotel, was located right next to the Keys, and the owners—a lesbian couple—were good friends of Lucky and Lennie.

It occurred to Bobby that tomorrow night, he and his group would be sitting ringside at the Cavendish, watching Zeena perform. It was a hunch, but if he knew Lucky, she'd already set it up as a fun thing to do. When guests visited Vegas, Lucky always made sure they were treated to the best entertainment going.

So . . . if that was the case, what was he planning on doing?

He'd go, of course. Watch Zeena perform. No big deal. She wouldn't even know he was there; he'd be sitting in the audience like any other fan.

"Oh, look!" Cassie exclaimed, leaning out the window and checking the billboard. "Zeena's appearing here tomorrow night. I love her! M.J., can we go?"

She could have asked him to strip naked and run down the street, for M.J. was in the land of the besotted.

"Sure, sweetie, I'll try to get tickets," M.J. promised.

"Lucky's probably already got 'em," Bobby remarked.

"Or if she hasn't, why don't *you* call Zeena?" M.J. suggested. "She's always eyeballin' you like you're her next steak dinner."

It threw Bobby that M.J. had noticed and not mentioned a word until now.

"You think?" he said, playing it major cool.

"C'mon, bro," M.J. said, riding him. "You know as well as I do Zeena's got a thing for you. She wants your body, man. She wanna ravish your fine ass."

"Didn't notice."

"Yeah, sure," M.J. said, winking at Cassie. "*You* didn't notice, but everyone else in the club did."

"Wow!" Cassie clapped her hands together. "Zeena is awesome!"

"And bisexual," Kris added, joining in the conversation. "I must say, I do like a woman who can't quite make up her mind."

If they only knew, Bobby thought.

Before he could think about it further, their limo began pulling into the Keys complex.

32

Annabelle

Breakfast in the Polo Lounge with a hungover Frankie took care of Annabelle's morning. She pushed eggs Benedict around her plate while tapping her foot impatiently on the floor.

"Can't wait to get back to New York," she muttered.

Frankie raised his retro Ray-Bans, revealing bloodshot eyes. "*C'mon*, this place rocks, babe," he said, full of enthusiasm. "You shoulda come with last night. I'm tellin' you, it was a major scene. You missed out."

"I'm sure I did," Annabelle answered primly, clearly forgetting about her own crazed teenage years. "I'm well aware of the L.A. scene. Decrepit old dudes on the make with Viagra fever, and moronic underage girls flashing their lack of underwear. Lovely!"

"Sounds like our kinda town t'me," Frankie quipped, and gulped down a glass of fresh-squeezed orange juice. "Y'know, babe, we could clean up here. Far as I can tell, it's ours for the taking."

"Why would we want L.A. when we've got New York?" Annabelle said, frowning.

"Expansion, babe. That's what business is all about."

"But, Frankie," she argued, "surely you understand that we need to be hands-on? We can't run our business from another city."

"Then we should consider spending more time in L.A.," he said, getting off on the thought. "We'll bring in someone like Janey to run things when we're *not* here."

"Sure," Annabelle murmured sarcastically. "There's a Janey lurking around every corner."

"I'll find someone," Frankie insisted. "You know me, I can sniff 'em out."

"I don't understand why you can't be satisfied with what we've got going," Annabelle said, wishing he weren't so damn stubborn.

"'Cause I want more, babe," he explained. "Nothin' wrong with that."

Annabelle pushed her plate away. Frankie was starting to bug her again. Why was he so set on L.A. when he knew she hated it?

She glanced at her watch. Where was Denver? Thank God she had someone she could depend on to get her through this mess.

Annabelle's memories of Denver at school were fuzzy. She vaguely remembered that they'd hung out for a while, but Denver hadn't been up for clubbing and shopping. She'd always put schoolwork and her family first, plus she'd never had money to burn. Come to think of it, Denver had been a total drudge.

It didn't matter. She was here now, and Annabelle needed her for support since it was becoming painfully obvious that Frankie could not be depended on.

"Isn't that Mel Gibson?" Frankie asked, lowering his voice as the famous actor strode past their table. "Jeez! The dude looks great."

"Who cares?" Annabelle said, tossing her hair back. "And what was all that fan crap going on with you and Ralph last night? Have you any idea how dumb you sounded?"

The word *dumb* did not sit well with Frankie. "What's crawled up *your* ass this morning?" he said irritably.

"Apparently not you," Annabelle responded.

"What does *that* mean?"

"It means we seem to be growing apart," she said, refusing to look at him.

Frankie was silent for a moment while his mind computed what was going on. His girlfriend was getting all snarky on him, and he didn't appreciate it. He realized she was upset about her mother, even though *she* didn't seem to know it, but that was no reason to take it out on him. They were finally in L.A., and they should be enjoying every minute; instead they were at each other's throats.

He decided to save the day, turn on the Frankie Romano charm, lure her back into the best relationship she was ever likely to experience.

"Y'know what?" he said. "We're both tense, it's been a helluva few days. But you do know how much I love you, right, babe?" Leaning over, he nuzzled her neck exactly the way he knew turned her on. "Tonight I'm takin' you for dinner, just the two of us. An' then—"

"Frankie . . ." she said, making a halfhearted attempt to push him away.

"Don't even bother arguing," he said firmly. "You're right, we need some alone time. Leave it to me, babe, I'm gonna arrange everything."

~ ~ ~

"Do you have a boyfriend?" Annabelle asked as the limo whisked them toward the Maestro mansion.

"Uh, not exactly a live-in," Denver replied, unwilling to reveal any details of her love life to Annabelle.

"Very wise." Annabelle nodded as she lit a cigarette. "But then you always were the smart one. Who needs a man cluttering up your apartment, or do you have a house?"

"No house."

"Apartments are better."

"I suppose so," Denver said, hating this conversation that was going nowhere.

"I have a fantastic apartment in New York," Annabelle boasted.

"I know, I saw it."

Annabelle shut up. She was talking about her stunning Park Avenue spread, not the SoHo dump. Denver probably wouldn't even understand the difference.

They rode the rest of the way in silence until they reached the Maestro estate. As they waited for the gate to open at the end of the driveway, a couple of stray paparazzi fell out of the shrubbery and began snapping away.

Annabelle immediately covered her face with her hands. "Oh God!" she cried. "I can't be photographed. People in New York have no idea who I am. This is impossible."

Denver decided not to point out that at the funeral they'd be inundated with TV crews, photographers, and press. It would be a media frenzy.

Once they reached the house, Lupe, the Maestros' housekeeper, answered the door. She escorted them up the main staircase to Gemma's sumptuous dressing room, which was almost as big as Denver's entire apartment.

Annabelle plopped herself down on a fancy pink love seat and said with an exhausted sigh, "I simply can't do this, you'll have to do it for me."

Suddenly, Denver was overwhelmed with a rush of bad memories. Annabelle whining to her in high school, "I can't do this history test, you'll have to do it for me," and "I can't make it to the cafeteria today, you'll have to get lunch for me," and "I can't go to Carolyn's party, you'll have to tell her for me."

Denver found herself in bad memory hell, and she didn't like it. Once upon a time, she'd been desperate to be one of the cool girls—so desperate that she'd done everything Annabelle had asked. But things were different now. All she wanted to do was get back to her office and resume her burgeoning career.

"Guess what," she exclaimed, tapping her watch. "I forgot a very important meeting I'm supposed to be at this morning. I'm so sorry, I have to go."

"But I need you!" Annabelle wailed. "You can't leave!"

"Don't worry, I'll send my assistant, Megan, over. Megan is supercompetent, she'll handle everything. You'll love her." And before Annabelle could object further, she was heading for the door.

Annabelle was livid. She could not believe she'd been deserted in her time of need. Denver Jones should be kissing her ass, not running out on her. Fine friend she'd turned out to be.

~ ~ ~

Sitting in a private cabana at the Beverly Hills Hotel, Frankie surveyed the action. There was not much going on, but it was still early; there was plenty of time for a parade of movie stars to appear and hang out. Preferably Jessica Alba and Megan Fox in the smallest Brazilian bikinis.

A lounger had been laid out for him by the pool, so after slathering on some sun protection and ordering a Bloody Mary, he took himself outside the cabana.

Last night, he'd gotten caught up in quite a scene. Talk about pussy heaven—L.A. was it. Girls galore. Girls in backless, almost topless, short, skimpy outfits. Girls with long blond hair and obvious fake tits. Girls with long dark hair and obvious fake lips, all trying desperately to emulate their goddess Angelina. Too bad none of them succeeded.

Frankie had hit a couple of happening clubs. At the second club, he'd taken a seat at the bar and surveyed the action. After slipping the barman his card, he'd inquired if there were any owners around.

Eventually Rick Greco, the guy who ran the club and was also a part owner, had appeared and introduced himself.

Frankie thought there was something vaguely familiar about Rick, but he couldn't quite place him.

"Sorry, dude, we're not lookin' for any deejays," Rick said, giving him a friendly pat on the back.

"Don't sweat it, 'cause I'm not lookin' for a job," Frankie responded. "I'm in town for my girlfriend's mother's funeral. Gemma Summer. You probably read about it. Big case."

"Shit," Rick said, duly impressed. "That's some bummer." A short pause, and then, "Her daughter really your girlfriend?"

What did the jerk think, that he'd made it up?

"S'right," he said, surveying the room casually. "Annabelle Maestro. We live together in New York."

Rick snapped his fingers for the barman. "Can I buy you another drink?"

"Sure," Frankie said amiably. "Why not?"

So they'd got to talking, and Frankie had decided that Rick might be an excellent connection, especially when Rick revealed he was a former teen idol who'd been big on TV in the nineties.

"Y'know, I thought I recognized you," Frankie said, flashing back to his early teen years. "Weren't you on that show with the smokin'-hot mom an' the two obnoxious asswipe kids?"

"That was me," Rick said proudly. "We had a three-year run. It's something I'll never forget."

Frankie took a second look at the man perched on the bar stool next to him: Rick was in his late thirties now, but there were still traces of the former teen idol. Cowlike brown eyes hidden behind wire-rimmed glasses. Sandy brown hair groomed into a semblance of style. And clothes that certainly favored the nineties—a button-down pink shirt, skintight Levi's, and pointy-toed cowboy boots.

What a douche, Frankie thought. *This town is ripe for a takeover, and I am just the man to do it. But I need help, and this schmuck could be it.*

"So . . . Rick," he ventured. "You an' I should get together."

"Yeah, really," Rick said, nodding. "I'd like that."

"How about tomorrow?" Frankie suggested. "We could do lunch around the pool at the Beverly Hills Hotel. I got a business proposition you might find interesting."

"Why not?" Rick said. "I'm always open for new ideas."

Frankie smiled. He was king of the freaking connections. He'd been in town less than twenty-four hours and already he was in action.

Life was good.

Life was very good.

33

Denver

I received a text from Sam and read it on my way to the office.

Miss my red-nosed Los Angeleno. Our time together was special. You're special. Who am I supposed to make pancakes for now?

A smile spread across my face. I couldn't help liking that he missed me. Well, he must to send a text like that.

I contemplated my reply. Had to hit exactly the right note, couldn't sound wimpy. I finally came up with, *Hmm . . . memories of special pancakes. I'm certainly in the mood for more.*

Ambiguous. Just right.

I was still smiling when I entered the office.

Mr. Shark Teeth soon wiped the smile off my face with a tart lecture about the importance of client/lawyer relationships.

I stood firm. Told him enough was enough and that I was no trained babysitter.

He finally accepted the fact that I was done, then informed me that we would both be attending the funeral on Thursday as a show of respect. I agreed.

I finally made it into my office and summoned Megan, my personal intern, who unfortunately was not the competent assistant I had promised

Annabelle. Megan was the daughter of a business associate of Mr. Shark Teeth, and she was about as dense as they come. I'd tried to teach her a thing or two, but getting through to her was like slogging through the desert at noon in ski clothes.

Megan was a Valley Girl with nothing but shopping, clubbing, and boyfriends on her mind. Her heroes were Lindsay Lohan and Paris Hilton. She worshipped Zac Efron and considered George Clooney and Brad Pitt to be two very old men.

Actually, after thinking about it, I decided she was probably the perfect person to hang out with Annabelle. Two spoiled brats together.

I sent her off to the Maestro mansion with a brisk warning to behave herself and try to represent the firm in a suitable fashion.

Megan was thrilled to escape boring office duties.

After she'd left, I sat at my desk and reviewed the work I had piling up. A shoplifting case involving a TV has-been and a small boutique. And an aggravated assault case between a rapper and a fine upstanding member of the paparazzi. Nothing too exciting, but since both cases involved fairly well-known people, I would try to make the most of them.

In a way, I regretted the fact that Ralph had not been accused of his wife's murder. It would've been one hell of a case to help defend. Felix would have done an excellent job, and I'd've been right there beside him, watching and learning.

After a while, I called the vet to inquire about my dog, Amy Winehouse. Amy did not take kindly to being boarded at a kennel, so whenever I traveled I boarded her at my vet, because they treated her like the queen she thought she was.

"I'll pick Amy up later today," I informed the receptionist.

"Uh, Miss Jones, your friend came in with his cat yesterday morning, and when he spotted Amy he said he'd take her. He told me you knew about it and everything was arranged."

"My friend?"

"Mr. Meyer."

For a moment, shock and fury overcame me. Mr. Meyer. *Josh* Meyer. My ex–live-in.

"What?" I managed.

"Amy seemed pleased to see him," the receptionist said. "Her tail was wagging like crazy. Is it okay that I released her?"

No, it's not okay, you stupid cow. Josh always wanted to keep Amy, *and I told him not a chance in hell. Hanging on to Amy was my way of punishing Josh, letting him know that he couldn't always get his own way. And now he's just taken her. Well, screw him. This is war.*

"Uh . . . actually, in the future, please do not release my dog to anyone but me," I said, trying not to lose my temper.

"I'm so sorry," the receptionist wailed. "I do hope—"

"It doesn't matter," I cut in. "I'll deal with it."

After slamming down the phone, I called Josh on his cell. Fortunately he had not changed numbers, but unfortunately I didn't get him, I got his damn voice mail.

"This is Denver," I said, employing my best ice-cold voice. "You took Amy, and I do not appreciate it. You know we agreed the dog would stay with me—so what the fuck, Josh. Call me as soon as you get this."

I clicked off, steaming. How dare he kidnap *my* dog!

~ ~ ~

By five o'clock, Josh had still not called back.

Son of a bitch!

Dognapper!

Major asshole!

I realized a confrontation was in order if I wished to retrieve Amy. I knew where Josh worked, taking care of the limbs of some of the biggest sports stars in the city, but I figured going to his home would be a better bet to get my dog back. So a few minutes after five, I took off and drove to his house in Hancock Park. Yes, after we split, Josh had purchased a house, something he'd never considered doing while we were together.

I hadn't visited his house before, although I have to admit that after I found out he'd bought it, I did do a couple of drive-bys.

Josh's house was set back from the street, with a well-kept green lawn and plenty of trees. The old colonial-style architecture was impressive.

I parked on the street, marched up to the front door, and rang the bell.

A frighteningly skinny short woman with long golden curls and a tough expression opened the door. In her late twenties, with the obligatory fake L.A. tan, she was dressed designer casual from head to toe.

"Yes?" she asked, one hand on her bony hip. Her tone was as friendly as a bucket full of shit.

"Hi," I said, attempting to peer past her. "Is Josh around?"

She narrowed her flinty, overmascaraed eyes. "Who wants to know?"

"I do, actually."

"And you are . . . ?"

"Denver." No sign of recognition crossed her pinched face. "Denver Jones," I added, because I was sure he must have told her about me. Still nothing. "Josh's ex."

The information finally hit her pea-brain. Am I being unfair? I don't think so. She's an idiot, I can just tell.

"He has my dog," I said evenly. "I want her back."

"That's a relief," said Miss Skinny. "I can't stand the mangy creature. Dogs bring out all my worst allergies."

As if to prove she was telling the truth, she sneezed twice and glared at me as if it were my fault.

Lucky Josh, he'd found himself a winner.

"Where is Amy?" I asked, tightly wound.

"Amy?" she questioned vaguely.

"My dog."

"Oh, that thing. I locked it in the shed at the back."

I wanted to smack her. "Why did you do that?"

"I told you. Allergies," Miss Skinny said, stifling a yawn. "Plus the stupid dog never stops barking. How do you stand it?"

"Amy is barking because you've locked her up," I said. "Where's Josh?"

"On his way home, I guess."

"Then I'll take my dog and leave."

"Does Josh know you're taking the dog?"

"Yes," I said shortly. "It's all arranged."

"Well then," she said, "you'd better come in, 'cause I'm not opening the shed door, the dumb dog'll probably bite me."

I wish!

I stepped into the interior of the house, which was one big mess. Racks of clothes stood around the living room, and various piles of accessories littered every table. Miss Skinny Stylist-to-the-Stars had certainly marked her territory. The only sign that Josh lived there was a huge flat-screen TV and his comfortable old chair, the chair I'd never been able to persuade him to dump.

Ha! He'd never dumped the chair, but he'd had no problem dumping me.

Not that I cared. Honestly, I couldn't care less.

In the distance, I could hear Amy barking. Suddenly Josh came bounding into the house.

Josh Meyer. My ex. The man I'd once spent several precious years with.

I looked at him. He looked at me. For a moment, it was as if time stood still and we were back together and nothing had changed.

"What's going on here?" Josh asked, breaking the spell. "What are you doing here, Denver?"

I gave him a cold stare. How dare he thieve my dog and then have the nerve to ask me what I was doing in his house?

I observed that he'd put on weight, at least ten pounds, and I couldn't help feeling pleased. I knew that I looked good, although I probably looked like a giant standing next to Miss Skinny, who wasn't an inch past five feet.

"You took my dog," I said accusingly.

"Our dog," he snapped back.

"No. *My* dog."

"You left Amy at the vet. I could see she wasn't happy, so I took her out of there."

"You had no right to do that."

"I had every right. We found Amy together, remember?"

"Your little girlfriend doesn't even like dogs, so why would you take her?"

"There you go, always trying to control everything," Josh sneered. "Amy was *our* dog, I'm *entitled* to take her."

"No. You are not."

"Yes, I am."

"Pul-ease!" said Miss Skinny, inserting her nonexistent body between us. "Take your dog and go. The two of you are giving me a migraine."

Allergies, migraines . . . Josh had found himself a real prize.

"Yes, Josh," I said, weary of fighting. "Give me my dog."

Josh's mouth thinned to a straight line, a sure sign he was majorly pissed.

Had I ever really loved this man?

I guess so, but not anymore.

"Fine," he said, still tight-lipped.

"Fine," I responded, staring him down.

A few minutes later, I was out of there with Amy Winehouse, both of us happy to be on our way.

I had to make a quick stop at the office, and then after that I had a late dinner with Mario planned; he'd already texted me confirming we should meet at Ago. I would just have time to go home and change into something suitable for our evening out, which would probably end at his place.

Hmm . . . After my Josh confrontation I needed a little loving care, and Mario was the guy to supply it.

I drove straight to the office, left Amy with my favorite parking attendant, and took the elevator all the way to the forty-second floor.

Megan was back and beaming. "I had the *best* time," she enthused. "Annabelle is awesome!"

Ah yes, there's nothing like going through a murdered movie star's clothes with the star's daughter to put a smile on a girl's face.

"Mr. Saunders asked for you to take a look at these photos," Megan added, handing me an eight-by-ten manila envelope.

"What are they?"

"He didn't say. Can I leave now?"

"Sure," I said, ripping open the envelope.

Felix had enclosed a short note: "Denver. View these photos of Gemma Summer. Any thoughts? Ralph is eager to know who the man is."

Of course Ralph was eager to know. His beautiful wife had been photographed with another man the day before her murder.

I took a long look at the photos. There were four of them. Gemma looking beautiful, obviously enjoying herself, clinking glasses with the stranger—a man barely visible, just his profile on show. They were taken at a secluded restaurant high in the hills above Malibu. The photographer must have followed Gemma there, then hidden in the bushes to get his shots.

I looked once, twice, three times, and then it struck me.

Mystery Man was Carolyn's father.

34

Carolyn

The last thing Carolyn remembered was stopping her car outside the deserted Shell station—long since shut down—and waiting patiently for Gregory to arrive. She couldn't recall what had taken place next, although she had faint memories of a girl knocking on her window, a young Hispanic girl who'd seemed agitated and maybe in some kind of trouble. Being the Good Samaritan that she was, Carolyn had rolled down her window to see if she could help, and that was it—no more memory.

Now she found herself waking up in the dusty trunk of a moving car, her hands and ankles bound, a filthy rag stuffed in her mouth.

Panic immediately overcame her. Was this a nightmare? Surely she would wake up any minute. But no. She was trussed up in the trunk of a car, and the vehicle was on the move.

Bile filled her throat, but she swallowed it down, fearful that she might choke.

She attempted to move. Impossible. Her hands were tied behind her back with electrical cord. The cord was cutting into her wrists, hurting her.

Please, God, help me.

She was desperate to say the words out loud, but that was impossible, too. So she chanted them in her head like a comforting mantra and hoped that somehow He would hear her.

~ ~ ~

"You sure she ain't gonna *die* on us?" asked Rosa, Benito's sixteen-year-old girlfriend. Rosa was a pretty girl, although her prettiness was marred by a thin white scar running the full length of her left cheek, the result of an all-girl gang fight. Her mama had punished her for that one, kept her locked in the house for two whole weeks.

"How many times I gotta tell ya," Benito answered with a vicious scowl. "We just puttin' a scare in the *puta* so she lose the mothafuckin' baby."

"All she hadda do was get the dude to pull out," Rosa offered. "Works every time."

"An' that's why *you* got a ten-month-old baby livin' with your mama," Benito said, his expression sour. "'Sides, *she* don' wanna dump her baby, it's what the senator prick wants."

"Some asswipe," Rosa mumbled, swigging from a can of Red Bull, then wiping her mouth with the back of her hand. "Why's you doin' it for him, anyway?"

"I be doin' it 'cause I ain't gettin' my ass thrown back in t'joint," Benito said impatiently.

"What you supposed t'do with her?" Rosa opened her purse and took out a CoverGirl powder compact she'd recently swiped from the drugstore.

"Ya think *I* know?" Benito said, blinking rapidly. "How long it take t'lose a fuckin' baby?"

Rosa shrugged, then began carefully examining her face in the compact mirror. "Dunno," she said at last, discovering a zit that needed squeezing. "But a girl in school went to some Irish dude—she got an abortion for fifty bucks. Whyn't we take her there?"

"'Cause it gotta look like a accident," Benito insisted, wishing Rosa would keep her mouth shut for once.

"Why?" Rosa asked, running her tongue over her lips.

"Quit with the fuckin' questions," Benito growled.

He'd been seeing Rosa on and off since she was fifteen, almost six months—a record for him. She was obliging, didn't nag *too* much, and sucked him off like a seasoned trouper.

The downside was she'd had a baby with a rival gang member, and any time the opportunity arose, the fucker attempted to blast his ass from here to the White House. It was an ongoing feud, and Benito was seriously thinking about dumping Rosa because of it.

But not now, not with the senator's pregnant bitch trussed up in the trunk of his car. That wouldn't be smart.

~ ~ ~

"It's black-tie tonight," Evelyn Stoneman reminded her husband over the house intercom.

Another black-tie event was the last thing Gregory needed. But he was well aware of how prudent it was for him to attend, because while Carolyn was on the missing list, he had to make certain that every move he made was accounted for.

Not that anyone had reported Carolyn missing. Considering she lived by herself, that could take days, and by that time she would no doubt be back with no baby growing in her belly. Upon her return, Gregory would commiserate with her, make noises about how there should be tougher laws to combat crime. And then—when the time was right—he'd break up with her.

If luck was with him, the shock of being abducted should make her lose the baby fast, perhaps within hours. And when that happened, she would be set free, and Gregory would also be set free. It was the perfect plan.

He'd instructed Benito not to harm her, merely to shake her up. Not that Benito was the most trusted human being on the planet, but Gregory had been given no choice. The baby had to go, and Benito seemed to be his only way out.

Evelyn appeared at the door to his dressing room clad in a long white Carolina Herrera gown and tasteful diamonds. "You're not ready," she admonished, wagging a beringed finger at him.

"Give me five minutes," Gregory said gruffly, reaching for a crisp white dress shirt on a nearby hanger. "That's all I need."

~ ~ ~

Once again Carolyn felt the bile rise in her throat, and once more she managed to swallow it down.

The car was traveling over rough terrain, and she was unable to protect herself from being thrown around in all directions.

She attempted to calm down and think rationally. When Gregory arrived to meet her and realized she was missing, surely he would report her disappearance to the police.

Or would he? Knowing Gregory, he might be too cagey to do so—he was always so worried about his precious reputation.

But if her car was still outside the abandoned gas station, then Gregory would know that something was wrong, and of course he'd report it. His conscience would force him to do so.

But what if whoever had her locked in the trunk of their car had stolen her Pontiac and driven it off? Then how would Gregory know she'd been taken?

Tears filled her eyes and began sliding slowly down her cheeks.

How would Gregory know? That was the question.

And who would rescue her?

35

Bobby

Surveying the club location at the Keys with M.J. and Lucky, Bobby experienced a full-on flash of triumph. Finally he would be taking over the place, changing the name to Mood, and creating the most successful late-night venue in Vegas. It was something he'd dreamed of doing ever since Lucky had built the Keys. He'd always nagged her about allowing him to get the club concession, but she'd resisted, saying he had to prove he could do it first. Well, he'd sure as hell proved it: After being open for almost three years, Mood in New York was raking in big bucks. Soon he'd be making a deal to open Mood in Miami, and now he had Vegas to look forward to.

"Y'know we're gonna be making major changes," he informed Lucky.

"Wow," she drawled, "I'm *so* surprised."

"You want our stamp on it, don't you?" he said, noting that his mom never changed. With her long dark curls, deep olive skin, and blacker-than-night eyes, she was still the most beautiful woman he'd ever seen. And the smartest.

"That's why I called you, Bobby."

"No," he argued. "You called me because I'm the only one you can trust not to set up my own deal on your premises."

"Hardly true," Lucky objected. "There are plenty of reputable club owners I could've brought in. Rande Gerber, Brent Bolthouse—"

"Keep going, Mom," he said confidently. "You *know* you need me."

"I do?"

"Yeah, say it," he urged. "Go on—say it."

"I need you!" Lucky said in a mock dramatic fashion. "You too, M.J."

"Thanks, Mrs. Gol—"

"Lucky."

"Uh, thanks, Lucky," M.J. muttered. Bobby's incredible mom always managed to make him feel like a kid again.

"Do you realize, M.J., that I've known you and your family since you were twelve?" Lucky said, smiling at M.J. "Your father looked after Gino when he had that aneurysm problem. And your mom is *the* most delightful woman."

"Yeah, an' I bet you didn't know that M.J.'s *still* got a crush on you," Bobby quipped. "Only now he has a girlfriend, so I got a hunch you're probably safe."

"Who wants to be safe?" Lucky teased, mildly flirting.

M.J. glared at Bobby; he was beyond embarrassed. "Whyn't you tell your mom who's got a thing for *you*?" he said.

"And who would that be?" Lucky asked, faintly amused.

"Zeena," M.J. blurted. "She's got the hots for Bobby, big-time."

Bobby threw M.J. a dirty look. "Bullshit," he muttered.

"That's quite a coincidence," Lucky said. "Because tomorrow night we're seeing her show. I hear it's amazing, so I got us all tickets."

"Never mind about Zeena's show," Bobby said, determined to get off the subject of the predatory superstar. "Aren't you interested in hearing what *kind* of changes I'm gonna make?"

"I have a strong suspicion I can guess," Lucky said, smiling. "But go ahead, tell me anyway."

Bobby launched into his plans for Mood in Vegas. He had many ideas, and the first order of business was to do away with the illuminated staircase, indoor fountains, and expensive art. His plan was to create a replica of Mood in New York. "It's gotta have a cooler, more laid-back vibe," he insisted. "Right now it's screaming Vegas."

"Business has always been good," Lucky pointed out. "Getting people into the club was never the problem."

"It's not about how much money you rake in," Bobby insisted. "It's more about the crowd."

"And the crowd should be . . . ?" Lucky questioned.

"No tourists, unless they're young an' way hot. No fat asses. Like I told you when you first opened—you gotta make the club a happening place for the locals to hang after they get off work. So . . . sexy girls in sexy outfits. Rich dudes with their Ferraris and Bentleys parked outside. Visiting celebs. Everyone with a cool attitude. *That's* the vibe we'll be going for."

"Okay, guys," Lucky said, readily agreeing. "I think I get the picture."

"You do?" Bobby said, surprised that she wasn't putting up a fight about the changes he intended to make.

"Sure I do. So how about we go work out a deal? Then we can relax and have some fun."

Bobby grinned. "You got *my* attention."

~ ~ ~

Later it was his half sister, Max, who really got his attention. Surprising him, she simply showed up without warning—hammered on the door to his room at the Keys and burst inside.

Bobby hadn't seen Max in a few months, and at seventeen she'd blossomed into a beauty. But she still hadn't lost her wild streak. Max was the mirror image of Lucky at the same age: tall and lithe, with a mass of unruly black curls, sun-burnished olive skin, full lips, and plenty of attitude. The only difference was their eyes. Lucky's were dark and intense, Max's were a brilliant emerald green.

The moment he opened the door, she threw herself at him, wrapping her long legs around his waist and hugging him tight.

"Whoa!" he said, laughing as he attempted to disentangle himself. "Not appropriate, you're way too old."

"Ha!" Max exploded with a wild giggle. "I flew here for the day just to see you. The least I expect is a decent greeting."

"Brat!" he said affectionately.

"Womanizer!" she responded, green eyes sparkling. "You're like *so* totally lame, Bobby. Why didn't you tell me you were coming? I had to hear it from Mom. So I jumped a plane, an' here I am."

"Nice to see you, too," he said, still laughing.

"But I love you anyway, big bro," she added with an infectious grin.

"You love me, huh?"

"Yup."

"Nice to know."

"And you love me, right?"

"Sometimes," he teased. "When you're not pissing me off."

"C'mon, Bobby," she said, mock frowning. "Stop jerking me around."

"Who's jerking you around?"

"You! You! You!" she yelled.

"Calm down."

"Where's M.J.?" she asked, switching moods and opening the minibar. "I'm supposed to haul his rockin' ass back to L.A."

"An' why's that?"

"'Cause my BFF, Cookie, is desperado to jump his sexy bones."

"Your friend Cookie is way too young to jump anyone's bones."

"Pu-*lease*!" Max said, rolling her eyes. "What century were *you* born?"

"S'great to see you, too, kiddo," Bobby said, grinning. "Still with the same smart mouth."

"Anyone ever tell you you're beginning to sound like Grandfather Gino?" She extracted a packet of M&M's from the minibar.

"An' that's a bad thing?"

"Here's the deal, Bobby," she said as she stuffed a handful of M&M's into her mouth. "I think it's way time I came to New York an' moved in with you. Cool plan?"

"No," he said, shaking his head. "Not a plan at all."

"Why?" she demanded. "You just announced that you loved me. And I'd behave myself. Honestly, Bobby—you can do your thing an' I'll do mine."

"Thanks," he said dryly. "Does that mean I have your permission?"

"Ha-ha! *Pu-lease*, Bobby."

"Sorry. The answer is no."

"Why? Why? Why?"

"'Cause you've got to go to college," he lectured. "You know that's what Lucky and Lennie are expecting you to do."

"Not gonna do that," she said stubbornly.

"And your reason is?"

"'Cause Mom didn't go, an' then you went for two minutes an' like immediately dropped out. So why *I* gotta suffer? It's not fair."

"A proper education means a lot, Max."

"Crap!" she muttered, flinging herself onto the couch, long bronzed legs stretched out in the shortest of skirts.

"No," he said crisply. "Fact of life."

"Man!" she complained. "You're getting as lame as Mom. I guess I'll hav'ta take off on my own with no help from you."

"And go where?"

"You'll see," she said airily. "No college for this girl. I crave Adventure with a capital A. And for your information, nobody—an' I mean nobody—can stop me."

Bobby shook his head. He felt sorry for Lucky and Lennie. They had big trouble on their hands.

"What kind of adventures did you have in mind?" he asked.

"Oh, y'know," she answered vaguely. "Screwing a lot of guys—my choice. Kind of living on the edge."

"The edge of *what*?" he asked, trying not to laugh.

"You just don't get it, do you?" she said, throwing him a dirty look. "I'm my own person, I'm not Lucky's little girl or your baby sister or Lennie Golden's kid. I'm *me*."

"Nobody's arguing with *that* sentiment."

"Cool, 'cause I'm totally unique, and I plan on doing my own thing."

"And when's this gonna happen?"

"Sooner than anyone thinks," she said mysteriously.

"Yeah?"

"Bet on it, big brother," she said, green eyes flashing danger signals.

"Now you sound like Lucky."

"An' that's a bad thing?" she said, mimicking him.

"C'mon, baby sis," he said, reaching for her hands and pulling her off the couch. "We got a big dinner to get to. Brigette and her new friend, M.J. and his girl. So you'd better behave yourself. There'll be plenty of time to talk about your future later."

"Believe me, Bobby," she threatened, "we will. And I'm gonna win on this one—you'll see."

36

Annabelle

"Pack everything up and have it all put into storage," Annabelle instructed Lupe. "I'm too upset to deal with anything now, I'll get into it another time."

"Yes, Miss Anna," Lupe said obediently. Somehow she'd never been able to master saying Annabelle's full name. "Miss Gemma's jewelry?" she added, full of concern. "What I do with it?"

Annabelle assumed that all of her mother's expensive jewelry was secure at the bank or tucked away in a safe hidden in the house. Frankly, she didn't care. Gemma's jewelry wasn't to her taste.

"Leave it," she answered vaguely. "I'll go through it tomorrow."

Right now she was eager to get out of there. Being back in the house was a total downer, it was making her feel physically sick. All the bad memories of her teenage years had come flooding back with a vengeance. She needed to escape from her childhood home and do something to take her mind off the upcoming funeral.

By the time she got downstairs, Megan was standing just inside the front door. "Denver sent me," Megan announced. "Your housekeeper let me in. I'm Megan, and I'm here to help out."

Annabelle took a quick look around. Fortunately, Ralph was nowhere in sight.

"Come," she said, quickly sizing the girl up and deciding she seemed a likely candidate for a fun day of retail activity. "We're going shopping."

~ ~ ~

Frankie made sure he was seated at a prime table near the pool, where he could see everyone. It occurred to him that he could've ordered lunch in the cabana, but an excellent table right at the front was more impressive. Besides, who needed to be hidden away? Frankie had an urge to be seen.

He'd already spied a girl just perfect for their L.A. operation, were they to get it off the ground. The girl was tall and stacked, with a kick-ass body that made him think of Ursula Andress stepping out of the sea in an early Bond movie he'd watched on TV countless times. He could easily recall getting off on the fact that Bond was such a bad-ass—his kind of guy. And as for Ursula . . . well, she was the fantasy woman who'd guided him through many a lonely teenage night. He'd experienced his first orgasm with the delectable Ursula.

The girl in question was with a decrepit old dude who looked ready to croak any minute. The dude had white hair—surprisingly, a full head of it—and a shaggy white beard. The girl wore a bikini so small that she might as well not have bothered. Occasionally, Frankie caught her glancing in his direction. He sensed she was dying to get laid; the old fart did not look capable of managing a sneeze, let alone anything else. Frankie had his card at the ready should she come over.

Rick Greco arrived ten minutes late, wearing all white. "Thought you mentioned we were meeting in the Polo Lounge," he said, obviously put out. "I was waiting around upstairs."

"Nope," Frankie answered, not getting up, a power move. "It was always by the pool. I'm a New Yorker, gotta catch the rays."

"Yeah," Rick said. He pulled out a chair and sat down. "How about our weather? This is December. Not bad, huh?"

"That's exactly why I wouldn't mind movin' here," Frankie allowed, chewing on a breadstick.

"Really?"

"I get off on the climate," Frankie said. "Not t'mention the scenery." He indicated the girl in the bikini, who was now sitting by the edge of the pool, dangling her long legs in the water.

"You can do a lot better than her," Rick said with a ribald chuckle. "You've already seen the pussy that hangs at my club."

"Right on!" Frankie said.

"But let's not forget you've got a girlfriend, right?" Rick reminded him.

"Yeah, Annabelle." Frankie signaled for the waiter, a man he'd tipped handsomely earlier to make sure he got nonstop service. "But I'm here to tell you, Rick, my lady is *very* understanding. She's into lettin' me do my own thing."

"Now, *that's* the kind of girlfriend to have," Rick said, rubbing his palms together.

"You got that right," Frankie agreed. He ordered himself a mimosa, while Rick settled for a vodka on the rocks.

He's a daytime drinker, Frankie thought. *All the easier to manipulate. I'm gonna make my mark with this one. I'm gonna take over this freaking town. Everyone's gonna know who Frankie Romano is.*

~ ~ ~

Annabelle had a satisfying time spending the day shopping with Megan. They hit all the best places, including Annabelle's favorite, Fred Segal, and Megan's not-to-be-missed Kitson on Robertson. Then they covered all the large department stores—Neiman's, Barney's, and Saks—ending up at Maxfield on Melrose, where Annabelle dropped a cool eight thousand on a couple of hot outfits.

By the time she got back to the hotel, she was loaded down with shopping bags and feeling pretty damn pleased with herself. Shopping always gave her an incredible high.

Frankie had his coke. She had her black AmEx. A fair exchange.

Just as she was about to phone Janey to check that everything was running smoothly, the hotel spa called the suite to remind her of her afternoon appointment.

Abandoning her call to Janey, she took off, prepared to be deliciously pampered.

~ ~ ~

In the middle of lunch, Frankie received a call from Bobby. "'Scuse me," he said to Rick as he turned away to take the call.

"Guess where we are," Bobby said, sounding hyper.

"Atlantic City, gettin' it on with my waitress," Frankie joked. "What was her name again?"

"No, man, we're in Vegas," Bobby said, laughing.

"You *gotta* be shittin' me."

"I'm here with M.J. and his girlfriend."

"M.J. has a girlfriend?" Frankie said, surprised. "What's she like?"

"Young, black, and pretty. He's in love."

But Frankie wasn't interested in hearing about M.J.'s love life; he had bigger things on his mind. "How come you're there?" he said. "I just saw you in New York, didn't look like you were goin' anywhere."

"Got a call from Lucky asking if we wanted to take over the club concession at the Keys."

"That's some surprise, but it's what you always wanted, right?"

"Sure is. And I was thinkin' that you an' Annabelle might be up to takin' a twenty-four-hour Vegas break. I can send the plane for you."

"You're finally using your plane?" Frankie said, shocked. "What's got into you?"

"I needed to get here fast."

"Jeez," Frankie said, mind racing as usual. "Vegas sounds like a plan."

"Doesn't it."

"Yeah, but the drag is we gotta be here for the funeral on Thursday."

"No problem. We'll all fly back to L.A. together early Thursday. Lennie's away, so Lucky's asked me to escort her."

"Lucky's goin' to the funeral?"

"It seems Gemma did a couple of movies for Panther when Lucky ran the studio. She liked her."

"I'll talk to Annabelle," Frankie said, all revved up. "But you can bet your ass *I'll* be there, with or without her."

"Then I'll go ahead and make the arrangements. Check in with me later."

"For sure," Frankie said, and snapped his phone shut.

Rick was looking at him expectantly.

"My best friend, Bobby Santangelo Stanislopoulos." Frankie explained, keeping it casual while thinking that Bobby couldn't have called at a better time. Rick was already impressed; this should nudge him right over the edge. "He's, uh, sending his plane to fly me to Vegas."

"Is that *the* Bobby Santangelo?" Rick asked. "Lucky Santangelo's son? The dude who owns Mood in New York?"

"Bobby's my closest friend. We're thinkin' of partnerin' up."

"Nice."

"Isn't it," Frankie said with a self-satisfied smirk. And then, after a long beat, "So, Rick, how about you an' me talk a little business. I wouldn't mind openin' up a place in L.A."

~ ~ ~

"How was your day?" Frankie asked when he and Annabelle finally met up in the suite around five.

"Shitty," Annabelle complained, deciding not to mention the shopping spree and her relaxing time at the spa.

"It must've been tough, sorting through your mom's things," Frankie said, going for the sympathy vibe. "I feel for you, babe."

"It was," Annabelle agreed with a put-upon sigh. "You can't even imagine."

"Not to worry, 'cause tonight I've planned a romantic dinner. An' tomorrow I'm flyin' you to Vegas for the day. Decided you needed a break."

Annabelle's eyebrows shot up. "Vegas?" she questioned. "What's in Vegas?"

"Bobby, for starters. An' I managed to convince him to send his plane for us."

"What's Bobby doing in Vegas?" she asked, thinking that things were looking up.

"Takin' over a club. An' he'll be at your mom's funeral with *his* mom, so we'll all fly back together early Thursday. How cool is that?"

"Yes," Annabelle said, secretly delighted. "You're so right, I do need a break."

"Sure you do," Frankie agreed, not certain if he was pleased or disappointed that she was coming to Vegas.

Before they left for dinner, Ralph called. Annabelle was busy putting the finishing touches to her makeup in the bathroom, so Frankie picked up the phone.

"I'm expecting you both for dinner at the house," Ralph said brusquely.

"You are?" Frankie said, almost speechless for once. "Didn't realize that. We were just on our way to grab a bite at Spago."

"Fine," Ralph said. "I'll meet you there." He clicked off before Frankie could object.

Not that Frankie would object. He was in awe of Ralph Maestro, although he was certain that Ralph joining them at Spago would not fly with Annabelle. In fact, she'd be majorly pissed.

After thinking about it for a few minutes, he decided the smart thing was not to mention that Ralph had called. Play it dumb, and when Ralph showed up, look surprised.

Annabelle emerged from the bathroom wearing one of her new outfits.

"You look like a star, babe," Frankie commented. "Hot an' sexy. Now, *that's* my kinda girl."

"I stopped on my way back to the hotel and shopped," Annabelle confessed, pirouetting in her Dolce & Gabbana sleek bronze leather dress. "You like?"

"I'm into the dress," Frankie said, reaching out and grabbing her around the waist. "But what I'm *really* into is the body that's in it."

Annabelle gave a slow smile. Sometimes Frankie knew exactly what to say.

37

Denver

The first thing on my mind was trying to reach Carolyn. I had no idea what I was going to say to her, I only knew that we had to speak before I told anyone else of my discovery.

Carolyn did not pick up, so I sent her a text: *Call me immediately. Urgent!* I figured that would get her attention.

Then I started thinking about her parents, Clare and George Henderson. I hadn't seen them in a while, but Carolyn always talked about the two of them with love and affection, and whenever I'd gone over to her house when we were younger and Carolyn was living at home, they'd both seemed perfectly in tune with each other.

George Henderson was a well-respected plastic surgeon. I wondered if that was how he'd met Gemma.

Clare Henderson, once George's assistant, worked in real estate. I remembered Clare as a pleasant woman—pretty, but no great beauty.

George, on the other hand, was a very attractive man, tall and lanky with an easygoing charm. All of Carolyn's teenage friends had harbored a big crush on him.

I hadn't seen the Hendersons in at least two years, but Carolyn often mentioned that they were both doing well, George especially. He kept an extremely low profile, never courted publicity, but according to Carolyn had worked on some of the most famous faces in Hollywood. He also did pro bono work at a children's hospital and twice a year visited poorer countries around the world to use his skills to help people with horrible disfigurements. Carolyn often mentioned how proud she was of him.

George Henderson was hardly a likely candidate to be conducting an affair with one of the most beautiful women in the world. But there he was, photographed with Gemma, and any fool could see just by looking at the photos that these two people were totally into each other.

Why was I the only one to have recognized him?

Because his famous clients were hardly likely to step forward. According to almost every actress in Hollywood, their beauty was God-given, untouched by a plastic surgeon's scalpel.

Hmm . . . George Henderson. Should I call Felix and tell him that I'd identified the man with Gemma? Or should I wait until I'd spoken to Carolyn and found out exactly what was going on?

I decided to wait. I didn't want to start something without checking with her.

In the meantime, Mario was expecting me at Ago. I could certainly do with some well-deserved R&R, not to mention a decent meal followed by some Mario-style sex.

Wow! Was I turning into a sex maniac?!

No. Simply releasing the tension.

Seeing Josh ensconced in his new life with Miss Skinny Stylist was not my favorite way of spending an afternoon. On the plus side, Mario made Josh look like an out-of-shape slacker.

I hurried home, fed Amy, took a quick shower, touched up my makeup, slid into a low-cut top and silk pants sans underwear, then jumped in my car and headed for Ago.

Mario was waiting. Well, not exactly waiting. More like sitting at what I presumed was our table, engaged in intimate conversation with a Hollywood Blonde. That's the term I use for a certain group of women who look exactly alike. Hollywood Blondes all have long, thick, glossy blond hair (extensions help the style to stay just so). Smooth, faintly tanned, unlined faces (a mixture of Botox, self-tan cream, and weekly facials). Long, lean bodies (Pilates, yoga, spinning). And exactly the right size fake breasts.

This one in her tighter-than-tight True Religion jeans and lacy loose top, with dangling earrings and a dozen Me&Ro bracelets—including the red Kabbalah string—fit the mold perfectly.

Mario spotted me approaching and quickly stood up, but the Hollywood Blonde had no intention of shifting her finely tuned ass. She stayed firmly in her seat and attempted to ignore me as if *I* were the intruder.

"Hi," I said. Better to be friendly than bitchy.

The Hollywood Blonde threw me a disinterested look, while Mario wrapped his arms around me and greeted me with a warm hug. "Welcome back," he whispered in my ear. "I missed you."

"You did?" I said, falling into his extraordinarily addictive dimples.

"You'd better believe it," he responded.

The Blonde glared at me, then finally realized she was a third wheel and reluctantly stood up. "I guess I should be getting back to my friends," she ventured, obviously hoping Mario would ask her to stay.

He didn't. But that didn't stop her from grabbing his hand, leaning into him, and whispering something into *his* ear.

To his credit, Mario immediately backed off. "Great running into you, Lisa," he said. "See you around."

"Call me," she purred, once again ignoring my existence—which was basically Mario's fault, because shouldn't he have at least introduced us?

Finally she was gone, and I quickly sat down. The seat was still warm from Lisa's True Religion–clad ass.

Mario also sat down, a sheepish grin spread across his face.

I decided not to ask any questions; playing jealous girlfriend was not my MO. After all, we'd had only one date, it wasn't as if I possessed any proprietary rights.

"Lisa's an old friend," he volunteered.

"Not so old," I retorted, unable to help myself.

Leaning across the table, he took my hand in his. "Jealous?" he asked, still with the sheepish grin.

I might be. But I just had sex with a very attractive stranger in New York. So, jealous? I hardly think so.

"Maybe," I countered. No harm in fluffing his ego.

"You don't have to be," he assured me. "Lisa an' I are ancient news."

Too much information. I did not wish to imagine Mario in the sack with Lisa, whoever she was. It wasn't conducive to a night of unbridled lust, and I was anticipating a very lustful night.

"Thanks for the info," I said crisply. "I'll store it away for future reference."

Flashing his whiter-than-white teeth, he said, "That's what I like about you."

"Do tell."

"You're acerbic."

"I am?"

"Makes a refreshing change. A lot of beautiful women don't have much to say."

Was he calling me beautiful?

Yes, he was.

Mario was definitely going to get major lucky tonight.

~ ~ ~

There's something totally addictive about sex. When you haven't had it in a while, you can definitely live without it. But when you're back in action—watch out!

And I was back in action big-time.

After dinner at Ago—delicious sole for me, pasta primavera for him, and a bottle of red wine between us—we headed back to his place in a hurry. I followed him in my car, anticipating what was to come.

I would've invited him back to my apartment, but I figured Amy Winehouse had experienced enough trauma for one day; she didn't need the added stress of me and Mario making out.

No sooner were we inside his front door than we both went at it like a couple of sex-starved teenagers. Clothes began falling off at an alarming rate. First his, then mine, until we were both standing naked in the small living room of his modest house. He pulled me close so that my breasts were against his chest and his hard-on was pressing against my thigh.

"Put your legs around my waist," he ordered, grabbing my ass to assist.

Oh yes, no problem.

But wait a minute—where was the foreplay he'd been so adept at last time? I might be horny (again?!), but a little attention to turning me on even more might be nice.

And just as I was thinking this, his doorbell rang.

It was past midnight, and straddling him in his living room with no clothes on was suddenly making me feel quite vulnerable.

"Uh, are you expecting anyone?" I asked, unwrapping my legs from around his waist.

"Me? No," he said, equally startled.

"Should we ignore it?"

"It might be important," he decided. "Go wait in the bedroom, I'll deal with it."

He didn't need to tell me twice. I hurried into his bedroom and slid between the sheets. Then I realized I'd left my purse in the other room, and I wished I hadn't because I needed to check my phone to see if Carolyn had tried to reach me. It was imperative that I reveal George Henderson's identity first thing in the morning, and I so needed to speak to Carolyn first.

Suddenly, sex with Mario didn't seem so urgent. Whoever had rung his doorbell had put a damper on things. I had a strong desire to get dressed and go home. But I couldn't, given the fact that my clothes were strewn all over the floor in his living room.

Mario returned. Still naked. Still with an impressive hard-on.

I decided to stay until we finished what we'd started and then take off.

"Who was that?" I asked. "And don't tell me you answered the door with no clothes on?"

"Protected my modesty with a cushion," he quipped. "A very large cushion."

"I thought size didn't matter," I said lightly.

"You're kidding, right?" he said, leaping into bed beside me and starting to lick my nipples.

Ah . . . now we get foreplay.

"You're adventurous, right?" he said, his voice low and husky. "Ready to try anything?"

"Why?" I asked breathlessly, totally turned on again.

"'Cause *I* am. It's my thing to always embrace the unexpected. It can turn out to be a real trip."

And with those words he threw off the sheet and began moving his magical tongue down my body, spreading my thighs with his strong hands, licking his way to between my legs.

I gave a deep sigh and threw up my arms, covering my eyes. A man who *really* knows how to give head is a gem indeed. And Mario knew a thing or two about how to please a woman. Suddenly all thoughts of taking off were gone with the wind as I lay back and enjoyed the ministrations of his talented tongue.

He paused for a moment. I urged him not to stop. "Whatever you're doing, it's *sooo* good," I murmured. "I'm almost there. . . ."

And his tongue returned to giving me serious pleasure.

I couldn't hold back any longer, it was just too damn hot. I let myself go and experienced an all-consuming, everlasting orgasm of mammoth proportions. "Oh . . . my . . . God," I gasped, my body quivering with delight. "That was . . . orgiastic!"

"She has such a way with words," Mario whispered, nibbling on my ear.

Wait a minute—how could he be attending to my ear when his head was still between my legs?

And then it dawned on me. There was a third party in the bedroom.

38

Carolyn

"Under no circumstances contact me," Gregory had warned Benito. "I will contact you if necessary."

Benito didn't care. He'd been given a job to do, and once the job was completed he and the senator had no reason to ever speak again. Unless he got into trouble and needed help, in which case he'd have no problem asking for the senator's assistance. One thing Benito knew for sure was that he would *never* allow himself to be carted off to the big house again. *Never.* Dead and buried was the only sane alternative to jail.

Meanwhile, this job of taking the senator's bitch and shaking her up so that she lost her baby was lasting too long. He'd thought it would all be over fast. Grab the *puta*, ride her around in the trunk of his car for a few hours, and bingo—baby gone.

But, no—he'd driven around for endless hours outside the city, over the bumpiest roads he could find, until eventually Rosa—sitting next to him in the passenger seat—had started moaning that she was tired and hungry and that they'd better stop and see if they'd achieved what they'd set out to do.

"I'm openin' the trunk," Benito growled, pulling over to a deserted side street. By now it was nighttime, and come to think of it, he could go for a burger himself. "You go take a look at her," he commanded.

"Why *I* gotta do it?" Rosa objected, argumentative as usual.

"'Cause I ain't lookin' between her legs," Benito steamed. "That ain't no man's work."

"It's *your* shit-ass deal," Rosa said belligerently. "You got us into this."

"Shut your mouth an' *help*," Benito ordered, grabbing a flashlight and jumping out of the car. He ran around to the back, popped open the trunk, and shone the flashlight on Carolyn. She was lying there, still trussed up, and now she was motionless, which scared the crap out of him. The first thought that went through his head was, What if the *puta* went and died on him? If that happened, it meant he'd be heading back to lockup, or even worse—the executioner's chair.

Immediately he slammed the trunk shut, and without saying a word, he got back in the car and drove to his dump of a house, borrowed from a drug-dealer cousin who was doing time. Once there, he parked the car among the rotting garbage in the alley at the back, and with some reluctant help from a complaining Rosa, he half dragged and half carried the senator's pregnant girlfriend inside before dropping her down on the bed and untying her.

The good news was that she was still breathing. The bad news was that there was no blood in sight, and even he knew that when she lost the baby there had to be blood. Rosa had assured him of that. "'Course," his sixteen-year-old girlfriend had said, as if she were some kind of expert, "we dunno how knocked-up she is. If the baby's big, we're gonna see it when it come out. My cousin lost her baby, an' that stupid baby was so huge she couldn't even flush it down the shitter."

Benito didn't care to listen. What did Rosa know? Exactly nothing.

After securing the woman's wrist to the bed frame with strong electrical cord, he slunk into the other room, switched on the TV, threw himself into a chair, and stared blankly at the screen.

His gut told him this was not a healthy scene.

His gut told him that he had to get rid of the woman. She was bad luck, bad karma.

Fortunately she hadn't seen him, but she *had* seen Rosa.

So what? There were a million girls who looked like Rosa, with their short skirts, platform shoes, too much makeup, and teased hair. Their captive would never pick out Rosa in a lineup, and even if she did, Rosa would not risk opening her mouth and involving him.

One thing he knew for sure: He had to come up with a new plan, because keeping the senator's pregnant bitch in his house was no longer an option.

~ ~ ~

With Benito settled in front of the TV, Rosa seized the opportunity to slip out to the alley and open the back passenger door of his car. She was looking for the woman's purse. When they'd taken her, first smothering her face with a chloroformed pad, Rosa had grabbed the purse and thrown it on the backseat. Benito hadn't noticed, he'd been too busy trussing up his unconscious victim and attempting to jam her in the trunk of his car.

Sometimes Benito could be so dumb. This taking the woman thing was dumb, but Rosa went along with whatever Benito wanted because he was her boyfriend, and it wasn't easy finding a boyfriend once you had a crying baby at home. Besides, having an older boyfriend like Benito gave her power in school when she bothered to attend. Nobody dared mess with Benito's girlfriend; everyone knew she was his property and therefore untouchable.

Rosa had decided that grabbing the purse was her bonus for helping out. She wasn't walking away empty-handed, why should she?

After recovering the purse from the car, she scurried back into the house and stashed it under the kitchen sink. Later, when Benito was asleep, she'd take a look and see what was in it. Hopefully money, 'cause Benito gave her nothing. She had to steal from his pockets when he was sleeping.

"Yo!" he yelled from his seat in front of the TV. "Get me another beer, an' slide your ass in here."

Rosa obliged. She knew what he wanted. Beer followed by a solid blow job.

It was never wise to fight with Benito.

~ ~ ~

Gaining consciousness, Carolyn realized she must have passed out, for when she came to she was no longer tied up in the trunk of a car. She was lying on a narrow, sagging bed in a dark room with her right wrist tightly affixed to the bed frame.

Little did she know that this was the same room Gregory had woken up in only a couple of days earlier.

Waves of fear overcame her as she attempted to sit up. She was desperate to use the bathroom, her stomach ached, and she began to shiver uncontrollably.

The room was small, cold, and damp. There was the smell of cigarette smoke and onions in the air, no carpet on the bare floorboards, and a tattered covering tacked up with nails over the one window. Through the walls she could hear the noise of a TV, and overhead there was the faint drone of a helicopter.

Where was she?

What was happening to her?

She wasn't rich or famous, so why would anyone want to kidnap her?

Panicking, she tried to determine how much time had passed since she'd been taken. A few hours? A day? She had no idea, but it seemed to be nighttime, and her growling stomach informed her she was hungry, while her dry mouth craved water.

Overcome with feelings of fear and confusion, she could only pray that any minute she would wake up and this would turn out to have been some insane nightmare.

Then a thought came to her. Gregory would race to her rescue. He had to.

After all, she was carrying his baby.

39

Bobby

The dinner with Brigette and Kris, M.J. and Cassie, Lucky, Max, and the two female owners of the Cavendish Hotel, Renee and Susie, went well. As usual, Bobby found himself impressed with the way Lucky had a knack for making everyone feel comfortable, even though Max spent most of the evening needling her.

Max Santangelo Golden was on a roll, and she did not appear to be quitting anytime soon.

Lucky seemed delighted with Brigette's choice of lover, while Kris was totally enamored of Lucky. Renee and Susie were in lesbian heaven. Meanwhile, Cassie and Max were hitting it off big-time.

Why not? Bobby thought, watching the two girls chat nonstop. *They're almost the same age. M.J. is definitely cradle snatching.*

Finally he got a chance to talk to Lucky alone, just the two of them. "What's up with Miss Wild Thing?" he asked, referring to his little sister.

"Max is driving us crazy," Lucky confessed. "But what can we do?"

"How about letting her make her own decisions?" Bobby suggested. "She's almost eighteen, she's smart enough."

"Not as smart as *you* were at eighteen, and she's still only seventeen,"

Lucky responded. "It would drive me insane to see her go through the kind of experiences Brigette endured."

"What makes you think that might happen?" he asked.

"*C'mon,*" Lucky said, shaking her head. "Max is young and gorgeous, plus she comes from a megarich family. You and I both know that every asshole searching out a major score will be after her, which is why I want her safely stashed in college until she's older."

"No chance, Mom," Bobby told her.

"Why do you say that?"

" 'Cause little sis is ready to roll—with or without your permission."

"You think?"

"She's already told me she's not going to do the college thing."

"Too bad, 'cause there's certainly no way I'm letting her run wild. That's not an option."

"Could be you got no choice."

"There's always a choice," Lucky said, her face clouding over. She took a long beat before continuing. "You know what the main problem is, Bobby? She takes after me when I was her age, and trust me, I never listened to anyone."

"Shouldn't that make you understand where she's coming from?"

"Believe me, I try."

"If I remember, didn't Gino marry you off at sixteen?"

"Oh yeah, he sure did," Lucky said with a dry laugh. "Gino did it 'cause he thought that way he could control me. Naturally it didn't work. I outsmarted him all the way."

"But you turned out a winner, Mom. You've achieved so much. *And* you did it all by yourself."

"Thanks, Bobby, but you still don't get it. Nothing's simple anymore. We live in dangerous times."

"Back in the day, wasn't your mom murdered? And your brother, *and* the guy you were engaged to? Are you telling me things weren't dangerous then? Jeez, Mom, gimme a break."

"Sure they were, but like I said—it's a different world now. Besides, I was major street smart. I knew how to look after myself in any situation."

"Max is smart. She got herself out of that whole kidnapping scam a couple of years ago."

"Pure luck."

"I guess you know she wants to move to New York."

"Oh yes, I've heard all about that. She's conjured up this fantasy about living with you."

"No way," he said, shaking his head vigorously. "I love little sis, but I'm not about to be responsible for her."

"Believe me, I get it, Bobby."

"Hey—you and Lennie will work it out. You always do."

"We'll sure as hell try."

"Lotsa luck with that," Bobby said, grinning. "You're gonna need it."

Lucky smiled ruefully. "Enough about Max. What's going on with my number one son?"

"I'm taking over your club, that's enough to keep me busy."

"I mean relationshipwise, Bobby. What's the deal? Any girl I should know about?"

"Nobody special," he answered casually. A pause, another grin. "I'll just have to keep looking."

Early the next morning, Max flew back to L.A. Bobby drove her to the airport. Once again he urged her to think about giving college a try, then he left it at that. There was no point in arguing with her. Max wanted her freedom, and as far as she was concerned, nobody was going to stop her.

Later, he spent the day at the club with M.J. They brought in an architect, a designer, and a building contractor. It was all systems go.

Although he immersed himself in the meeting, Bobby also kept a sharp eye on his watch so he'd be around to welcome Frankie and Annabelle when they arrived at the hotel. He wasn't sure why he'd invited them; it was a spur-of-the-moment decision he was starting to regret. On reflection, he realized that he might've thought he needed a wall of people around him to protect him from Zeena, the man-eater. Not that he planned on getting sucked in again, but perhaps it was inevitable.

Where were all the nice girls? The smart, intelligent, age-appropriate girls? They certainly weren't hanging out at Mood. He'd had it with the models and the party girls and the rich heiresses.

For a moment his thoughts turned to Denver, the lawyer he'd run into at Annabelle's in New York. She'd mentioned they'd attended the same high school. He hadn't remembered her from then, but he'd liked her style, even though their meeting was brief. She'd given him her card, and it occurred to him that maybe he should call her. She'd seemed normal enough. She'd had a kind of appealing glow about her, and she wasn't stick thin; she looked as if she might enjoy a steak or two. He should've told Frankie to bring her.

Well, too late now. What was he thinking, anyway? He was simply trying to protect himself from Zeena.

Or was he? *Bring it on, Miz Superstar. I can deal with anything you got.*

~ ~ ~

Like most megastars who are known by only one name, Zeena expected everything—and then more. Her demands were calculated and bizarre, and nobody dared argue with her. She strolled through life secure in the knowledge that most people would bow down to her, and she could get away with anything she wanted.

Zeena had a penchant for using people. She got off on seeing how far she could push them. It was all a game, and if she happened to destroy someone along the way, too bad.

Men intrigued Zeena, although she was not averse to a woman or two when the occasion arose.

Bobby Santangelo Stanislopoulos intrigued her. He was different from the usual younger men she was attracted to. He had style, he had money, he had presence. And . . . even though she'd criticized him in bed, he certainly knew what he was doing.

So when Zeena discovered Bobby would be in Vegas the one night she was appearing there, she considered it serendipity.

Renee, the owner of the Cavendish, let it drop that Lucky Santangelo and a group—including Lucky's hot son—would be attending Zeena's one-night charity event.

Zeena feigned disinterest. "Would Zeena find them interesting people?" she asked.

"You mean you've never met Lucky?" Renee responded. "Oh my God! Lucky is *the* most amazing woman. The two of you should get together, you'll love her."

"Zeena is very particular about who she loves and doesn't love," Zeena purred. "However, I trust your judgment, Renee. So after my show, arrange for this Lucky woman and her group to attend a private dinner with us."

"Done!" Renee said, clapping her hands together. "You won't regret it."

"Hmm . . ." Zeena drawled, reaching for her trademark Gauloises. "I sincerely hope not, because Zeena hates to be bored. Being bored is a mortal sin."

~ ~ ~

By the time their meeting was over, Bobby found himself alone. M.J. had taken off with Cassie; Brigette and Kris were at the spa; and Lucky was on the phone in her palatial office, dealing with business.

He wondered if he could get out of attending Zeena's concert that night. Then he remembered he'd invited Frankie and Annabelle along with everyone else, so there was no escape.

Zeena would be up onstage doing her thing. It wasn't as if he'd have to see her or spend any intimate time with her.

On impulse, he decided to make the limo trip to the airport and meet Frankie and Annabelle himself. It was better than sitting around doing nothing, and maybe they'd all stop off at the Wynn and play a few rounds of blackjack before hitting the Keys.

On his way through the lobby to the front of the hotel, he passed the magazine and newspaper stand. A headline caught his eye. A headline that stopped him in his tracks.

Holy shit! This was not going to be pretty.

40

Annabelle

There were two flight attendants on the Stanislopoulos plane—Gitta, an attractive Dutch woman; and Hani, a Hawaiian beauty. Both women were pleasant and competent, and both knew how to deal with any situation. They'd been working for Stanislopoulos Shipping and Industries for over ten years—Gitta since she was twenty-five and Hani since a day before her nineteenth birthday. But today they had a problem, and both were mulling over different ideas about how it should be handled.

Frankie Romano was aboard the plane with his girlfriend, Annabelle Maestro. They were on their way to Las Vegas, and therein lay the problem. To tell the loving couple about what could be lying in wait for them the moment they stepped off the plane or to maintain a discreet silence?

Gitta opted for silence. Hani thought it best to forewarn the couple.

At loggerheads, they consulted one of the two pilots, an older married man who harbored a secret crush on Hani.

"You should do what feels right for you," the pilot said, gazing at Hani, the woman he could never have on account of a wife and three small children at home.

"Then we tell them," Hani said firmly. "It is better they are forewarned."

"Not them, *him*," Gitta said, always the diplomat. "*He* should be the one to inform her. Less embarrassing."

"Maybe I could take a peek at this magazine" the pilot suggested.

"We don't have a copy," Gitta answered.

"Gitta thought it best if we didn't bring it aboard," Hani explained.

The pilot shrugged. "If it's one of those tabloids, then it's probably a story based on lies," he said. "Could be best if you *don't* mention it." Hani threw him a stony look, which forced him hurriedly to backpedal. "Although," he added quickly, "you could take this Romano guy to one side and warn him."

"I'll do it," Gitta said firmly. "It'll be better coming from me."

"Why?" Hani argued. "Are you not sure I can handle it?"

"I know you can," Gitta said soothingly. "But should he get excited, I'm an expert at calming people down."

"And I'm not?"

"We both are," Gitta allowed. "Why don't I bring him to the galley, and we'll tell him together."

"Problem solved," the pilot said, relieved that he was off the hook. "Let me know how it turns out."

~ ~ ~

"I have a lurking suspicion that I might've been molested as a child," Annabelle mused, picking at a dish of nuts as Bobby's plane zoomed them toward Vegas.

"An' you're remembering it *now*?" Frankie said incredulously. "You're so full of it."

"Obviously I buried the memory," Annabelle persisted. "But now that you've dragged me back to L.A.—"

"I haven't dragged you anywhere," Frankie said, narrowing his eyes. Jesus! She was in a pissy mood.

"May I remind you that it was your brilliant idea that we fly to L.A. for the funeral, leaving a perfectly excellent business in New York, which Janey and her moron son are probably screwing up as we speak."

"Janey's not screwin' up anything," he snapped.

"Have you spoken to her?" Annabelle demanded, removing her sunglasses and glaring at him. "Checked in?"

"Jesus Christ, babe, we just got here," he groaned. "Isn't it time you stopped breakin' my balls?"

"I thought you left your balls with Daddy," Annabelle sniped. "All tied up with a pink satin ribbon and the credits of his latest movie."

"You can be such a bitch," Frankie said, shaking his head.

"Ralph Maestro. Your hero," Annabelle taunted. "And possibly *my* molester."

"Gimme a fuckin' break," Frankie said shortly. "When did you decide to invent *that* story?"

"Oh, you think it's a story, do you?" Annabelle said, bristling with annoyance that he didn't immediately believe her. After all, it *could* be true. Frowning, she decided she needed to go to one of those regression shrinks who would dig deep into her murky childhood and find out everything.

"It's not that I don't believe you, babe," Frankie said, figuring that he should at least humor her. Once she got into one of her impossible moods, it could easily turn into an outrageous knock-down fight about nothing. "It's just that I think your mom's murder is affectin' you emotionally."

Unexpectedly, Annabelle's eyes filled with tears. Yes, of course it was. That and Sharif Rani's big fat son attacking her—about which Frankie had done exactly nothing.

There and then, she made a life-changing decision: She had to lose her boyfriend. Frankie was a toxic son of a bitch who thought about nothing except snorting coke, scoring money, and looking out for himself. Plus she couldn't stand the fact that he'd sucked up to Ralph as if he were the fucking president of America.

The thrill was definitely gone.

Should she tell him now, on the plane, leaving her free to run to Bobby?

Hmm . . . interesting thought. But probably wiser to wait until they got back to New York and things calmed down.

Bobby was definitely a future prospect, but since he was a friend of Frankie's, she had to make sure her timing was right. If she dumped Frankie, she was certain Bobby would offer a sympathetic shoulder to cry on.

And from there . . . who knew what could happen.

~ ~ ~

"Excuse me, Mr. Romano," Gitta said, tapping him lightly on his shoulder. "Might I have a word with you?"

"Huh?" Frankie said, looking up. Something in the attendant's tone of voice made him immediately wary. Had he left a residue of coke on the bathroom counter or something? Was this woman in her smart pink-and-green uniform about to tell him it was against federal rules to snort coke on a plane?

Shit! What could she do? Arrest him?

No way. He was being paranoid.

"Is there a problem?" he asked, automatically swiping his hand beneath his nose to obliterate any telltale signs of white powder.

"There's something you should be aware of," Gitta said. "I don't think we should disturb Miss Maestro at this time, so perhaps if you can come with me . . ."

They both glanced over at Annabelle, who had fallen into a light sleep, a copy of *Us Weekly* almost slipping off her lap.

It occurred to Frankie that maybe the plane was in trouble. A faulty engine, a locked landing gear, a fire. Jesus Christ! It could be anything.

Leaving his seat, he followed the flight attendant to the galley, where the second flight attendant, a pretty Hawaiian girl, was standing with her arms crossed. She didn't look panicked, she looked altogether too calm for there to be anything wrong with the plane.

"What's up, ladies?" he asked, thinking that the younger flight attendant was kind of hot in an exotic kind of way.

"This is quite awkward, Mr. Romano," Gitta said. "But we've decided that it will be better for all concerned if we advise you of the situation."

The goddamn plane *was* going down. His fucking luck.

"What situation?" he managed. *And where's the fucking pilot?*

"There's a headline story in one of the tabloids," Hani said, crisp and to the point. "It's about you and Miss Maestro."

So . . . their relationship had finally made the rags. What was so awkward about that? Annabelle had never courted publicity, but he didn't mind at all. He imagined the headlines:

FRANKIE ROMANO—STUD AT LARGE

HANDSOME BOYFRIEND OF
MURDERED MOVIE STAR'S DAUGHTER
TAKES OVER HOLLYWOOD

The truth was that being famous had always appealed to him.

"I'm afraid it's not a very reputable story," Gitta continued, bursting his bubble. "The truth of the matter is that it's quite scandalous, which is why we thought we should warn you before you de-planed."

"Not very reputable how?" he questioned, wondering if he'd done anything to rock the boat.

"Well," Hani said hesitantly, "they're calling Miss Maestro a notorious madam, and they're also saying that you are a drug addict, and that you procure girls for the prostitution business the two of you run."

"Naturally we understand that none of this is true," Gitta said, hastily joining in. "But we thought it best to tell you before the paparazzi descend."

"I do hope we've done the right thing," Hani added.

Frankie stood quite still. He was in total shock. A headline story in the tabloids about their private business venture. Calling Annabelle a notorious madam and him a drug addict and a procurer. How could this be?

Annabelle would go fucking nuts. And she'd blame him, because according to his lovely girlfriend, everything was always his fault.

"Where is this lying piece-of-crap rag?" he demanded, his voice an angry growl.

"I'm sorry, Mr. Romano," Gitta said, "we didn't bring a copy aboard."

"Why the fuck not?" he said, suddenly losing it. "You feed me this shit story, an' now you got nothin' to show me. What the fuck is wrong with you?"

"Mr. Romano—" Gitta began.

"Don't Mr. Romano me," he raged. "I'll tell you what you can do for me. You can keep your dumb fuckin' mouths shut, an' not mention a word about this made-up crap to my girlfriend. You understand?"

"Whatever you say," Gitta said, throwing an "I told you so" look in Hani's direction.

Hani was not happy with Frankie's reaction. How dare he speak to them in such a rude fashion! The tabloid story was probably true. Then she started to wonder how someone as nice and low-key as Bobby Stanislopoulos could be friends with such an uncouth man.

Frankie Romano was a pig. As usual, Gitta was right. They should have not said a word, merely allowed him to find out on his own time.

~ ~ ~

Annabelle slept right through the landing. Frankie did not bother waking her; the longer he kept her away from the two bigmouthed flight attendants, the better.

His mind was in overdrive, but he realized there was nothing he could do until he got a look at the offending tabloid and read every word.

Bastards! He'd sue the shit out of them and then some. He'd hire the sharpest fucking lawyer in New York. Ralph would pay. Ralph would be as outraged as he was that his daughter's reputation was at stake.

Where the fuck had the tabloid gotten its information?

Christ! He needed to know exactly what they'd printed. The timing couldn't be worse, what with the funeral coming up the next day. Ralph would shit himself.

He had to phone Janey, see if she knew anything. But right now his main thrust was to get Annabelle off the plane, stash her in the limo Bobby was sending to the airport, and go pick up a copy of the tabloid.

It couldn't be that bad.

Or could it?

41

Denver

To say I was furious would be putting it mildly. More humiliated, mortified, and degraded. How could I have allowed myself to be caught in such a shocking trap?

I am no prude, but a threesome, without my knowledge? *No! No! No!* Another woman sneaked into the bedroom by Mario, my knight in very tarnished armor? *I think not.*

What a douche! What an asshole! How could I have ever liked him? And here I'd always considered myself such an excellent judge of character.

And guess who the third wheel was?

Yes, you guessed right: the Hollywood Blonde herself, sans True Religion jeans and lacy top. Lots of blond hair on her head and nothing down below. Men like them fully shaved in Hollywood—that way they can pretend they're screwing a twelve-year-old!

Once I realized the situation, I was out of there in a flash. Racing from the bedroom, grabbing my clothes and purse off the living room floor, and dashing out the front door, with a naked Mario in full pursuit, yelling, "Come back. What's up, baby? I thought you'd be into some harmless fun."

Harmless fun! Was he kidding me?

Harmless fun with a Hollywood Blonde—or any other female, for that matter—was simply not my scene.

I made it to my car and drove off with a still naked Mario running alongside, hammering on the passenger window. Once home, I stood under the shower for a good ten minutes, trying to wash away all memories of Mario's trickery.

Now it's Wednesday morning, and I am still pissed. I feel as if I've been made a fool of—and I also feel violated and superdumb for allowing it to happen. The clue should've been Mario coming back to bed without telling me who was at the door. And silly me—for some reason, I didn't press him to find out. God! How stupid could I get?

After taking another long shower, I threw on a comfortable tracksuit, pulled my hair into a ponytail, and, sans makeup, ran an eager-for-activity Amy Winehouse around the block a couple of times.

Amy's tail began wagging as soon as we headed back to my apartment.

I soon discovered there was a reason: My loving ex, Josh, was lurking outside. Exactly the person I *didn't* need to see, especially as I was not dressed for an old boyfriend confrontation.

Josh was balancing two Starbucks containers of coffee and what had to be a bag of bagels, obviously with every intention of coming in.

Amy Winehouse leapt on him, full of doggie excitement. I threw him a stony look.

"Hi," he said.

"What are you doing here?" I responded curtly, deciding I didn't even care that he was seeing me in my makeupless state.

He handed me a coffee. "Peace offering," he said, going for the friendly approach. "I was out of line taking Amy, and I wanted to apologize."

Josh always had perfect timing. *Not.*

"Can I come in?" he asked, bending down to pet Amy.

"Actually"—I made a show of consulting my watch—"I need to get ready. I'm running late."

"Five minutes," he implored. "That's all I ask."

I weakened. Not that I wanted Josh to come in, but I have this stupid thing about hurting people's feelings, and he *had* brought me coffee. Besides, a toasted bagel before facing the rest of the day sounds good.

"Fine . . ." I sighed. "Five minutes only."

"She's a hard woman," Josh said, going for his jokey voice, which did not impress me.

We headed into my apartment—once *our* apartment.

I indicated the paper bag. "Bagels?" I questioned.

"From your favorite place," he said, obviously pleased with himself. "Shall I do the toasting honors?"

"Go ahead." Suddenly I was feeling tired and weary. I had no clue why Josh was visiting, and frankly I didn't care.

Josh went behind the counter that divided my living room from the kitchen area and popped two bagels into the toaster.

"You bought a house," I stated blankly, sitting at the counter.

"What did you think of it?" he asked cheerfully, as if we were the best of friends.

"Very nice. Lucky you," I said, unable to keep the venom out of my tone. What I really wanted to say was, *You bought a house without me, and that's not fair.*

"It's a sound investment," Josh remarked. "Especially in this economy."

"Why? Are you getting married?" I asked in full bitchy mode.

"No way," he said vehemently. "Tori and I, we're merely temporary."

Tori. Of course!

"Does *she* know that?" I asked, mildly curious to find out if he was stringing her along.

Josh decided to ignore my question. Typical Josh. He extracted the bagels from the toaster, slightly burned, exactly the way he knew I liked them. After spreading butter on mine, he put it on a plate and handed it to me.

This was just like old times. If it were Sunday, we'd be reaching for *The New York Times* by now and settling in for a long, leisurely read.

But it's not Sunday, it's Wednesday, and I have a ton of stuff to get done. Besides, Josh and I are no longer together, so what the hell is he doing in my apartment?

"You look great," he said, scratching his chin while he eyed me up and down. "Have you lost weight?"

Was he saying that last time he saw me I was *fat*? *Son of a bitch!*

"No," I answered shortly, thinking that he'd definitely put on a few pounds. "Still the same old me."

"The same old *beautiful* you," he said with a strong emphasis on the *beautiful*.

Man, what was it with the compliments lately? Getting laid definitely sends out mad signals.

I munched my bagel, sipped my coffee, then said, "Thanks for coming by, Josh, but I really do have to get going."

"Yes, sure," he said obligingly, then added a slightly tentative, "We should do this again, right?"

Wrong! But I nodded anyway.

Later, at the office, I wished I'd told him to screw off. He had a lot of nerve dropping by my apartment without an invitation. Who exactly did he think he was?

Megan knocked on my office door and entered bearing a huge vase of red roses.

"Somebody likes you," she said cheerily, placing the roses on my desk. "And Mr. Saunders has requested your presence, pronto."

I grabbed the note attached to the roses: "Sorry seems to be the hardest word. Mario."

Yeah, right.

Then I checked my cell for the fifth time to see if Carolyn had replied to my text. She hadn't. She also wasn't answering her phone, and when I'd tried her office earlier, they'd informed me she had not come in. I wondered if she knew about George and Gemma. She'd always been close to her father; maybe he'd confided in her.

Hmm . . . I had to give Mr. Shark Teeth the name of the man in the photo with Gemma. No more holding back, it was full-disclosure time.

~ ~ ~

Felix was sitting behind his massive desk, a grim expression on his pointy face, lizardskin-clad feet up on his desk. Today the lizard shoes were dyed a bright shocking pink, so wrong for the workplace.

Before I could say a word, he tossed a tabloid magazine across his desk and said, "Have you seen this?"

I picked up the magazine and took a look. The headline was enough to horrify me:

MURDERED MOVIE STAR'S DAUGHTER
RUNNING PROSTITUTION RING
WITH DRUG ADDICT BOYFRIEND

And next to the headline was a rather glamorous photo of Annabelle wearing a slinky evening dress and a seductive expression.

My mouth must have dropped open, because Mr. Shark Teeth said, "I presume you did not know about this?"

He presumed right. I was in total shock.

"Uh . . . no," I managed.

"Weren't you with them in New York?" he asked accusingly, as though in the short time I'd spent with them, I should have found out everything. I mean, I'm smart, but not *that* smart.

"Yes, in time to pick them up and take them to the airport," I explained. "I hardly spent a week or two hanging out with them, so how on earth would I know about their so-called business?"

"A good lawyer knows everything," Felix said, shooting me a critical look.

A good lawyer should not wear shocking pink lizardskin shoes. It's totally wrong. Besides, the color hurts my eyes.

"Sorry, my private detective skills are not quite up to par," I said snippily. "However, I do have the name of the man in the Malibu photos with Gemma Maestro."

This piqued Mr. Shark Teeth's interest. "You do?" he said, tapping his gleaming front teeth with a long, thin index finger.

"His name is George Henderson," I continued. "He's a plastic surgeon."

"Are you sure?"

"Quite sure," I answered confidently. "Actually, he's the father of a friend of mine, Carolyn Henderson. Carolyn, Annabelle, and I all went to the same high school together."

"Seems you know everyone," Felix said, his tone caustic.

"Well, I've lived here since I'm twelve."

"Anyway," Felix said, removing his feet from the desk, "Ralph is expecting us. He'll want damage control on this tabloid nonsense. And let's see exactly how much he knows about George Henderson."

"Are you thinking that I should come with you?" I asked, willing him to say no.

Naturally he didn't. My damn luck.

So, Maestro mansion, here I come again!

All I needed was Mario hanging around outside, and once again my day would be perfect.

42

Carolyn

After enduring a long and restless night listening to the pouring rain outside, and feeling desperate about the situation she was caught in, Carolyn wasn't sure whether she'd actually slept or not. Her stomach ached badly, and she was beginning to be concerned for the welfare of her baby.

Light was peeking through the torn covering on the window, so she assumed it must be morning.

She started thinking about the girl who'd brought her the bread and water the night before. The girl wasn't doing this alone; there was a man involved, a man who didn't want her to see his face. After the girl had blindfolded her, the man had taken her to the bathroom and stood there while she'd urinated. Another humiliation.

Who were these people? And even more important, what did they want with her?

Awash with waves of despair, she attempted to think more clearly and work out a timeline. She knew she'd been taken early afternoon on Tuesday, and after that she'd been driven around stuffed in the trunk of a car for endless hours. A couple of times she must have passed out, for when she awoke she was lying on this filthy bed, with her right wrist tied to the bed frame with strong electrical cord.

Now it had to be Wednesday, so people should be missing her. Kerri would know something was wrong when she'd failed to pick up Nellie's meds and then not met her for breakfast. Muriel would surely be suspicious when she didn't come into the office. And as for Gregory . . .

She wondered what he was doing, thinking.

When he'd turned up to meet her at the deserted gas station and she wasn't there, what was his reaction?

It all depended on whether her car was still there. If they'd abandoned her car, and she wasn't in it, then he had to know something was horribly wrong, and surely he would have immediately called the police?

Or would he?

~ ~ ~

Benito spent Tuesday night sleeping in his chair in front of the TV, while Rosa curled up on a beaten-up old couch. She'd tried to go home, but Benito was having none of it. "Yo! You're stayin' here," he'd yelled at her in a threatening fashion. "An' don' go givin' me no shit."

Before going to sleep, he'd made her take a peek at their captive to make sure she was still breathing.

Shackled to the bed frame, the woman had stared up at her with fear-filled eyes and begged for water.

For a moment, Rosa had felt sorry for her. She'd fetched her a mug of water and a couple of slices of stale bread.

After gulping down the water and devouring the bread, the woman had requested to use the bathroom.

Rosa had run to Benito and asked him what she was supposed to do.

"Don' want her pissin' in my bed," he'd grumbled. "Blindfold her, we'll take her."

Why did he keep saying "we"? It pissed Rosa off, but she'd reluctantly done as he asked. When she was finished, Benito had come into the room, untied the woman, and half dragged her to the toilet.

As soon as he got her back in the bedroom, he'd secured her wrist to the bed frame once again and made a fast exit.

Rosa had realized she was as trapped as the woman on the bed. Why did she have to be involved in Benito's business? It wasn't her shit, it was his.

After ripping the blindfold from their captive's eyes, she'd taken off before the woman could say anything and joined Benito in front of the TV.

Now it was morning, and Rosa decided she'd better take the woman more bread and water. Didn't want her dying on them; that wouldn't be cool. And because of Benito, she could end up getting half the blame.

~ ~ ~

With her mind veering off in all different directions, Carolyn didn't know what to think. One moment she was panicked, the next she somehow or other forced herself to remain calm.

When the young girl came back with a couple of slices of stale bread and a half bottle of tepid water, she decided that she'd better try to forge some kind of communication between them. She'd read somewhere that if ever you found yourself in a hostage situation, you had to attempt to bond with your captors, make them realize that you were a human being.

"Thanks," she muttered, gratefully swigging the water. "My name's Carolyn."

The girl stood there watching her, a blank expression on her face.

"If it's money you're after," Carolyn said, attempting to speak slowly so the girl would understand, "my father will pay. I can tell you how to contact him." She paused for a moment. "Or my boss. My boss is a senator, a very important man. He'll pay to get me back."

The girl still didn't say a word.

"I don't know if you're aware of what you're doing," Carolyn said, making sure to keep her voice low and even. "But you and your friend have kidnapped me. Kidnapping's a federal offense. The punishment is extremely severe, and I, uh . . . think I should tell you that I'm pregnant, so you're not just kidnapping me, you're—"

The girl suddenly came to life. "I know you're fuckin' knocked-up," she blurted. "'Cause that's t'reason you here." Then, realizing she'd probably said too much, she rushed out of the room.

Carolyn felt waves of sickness overcome her. The only person who knew she was pregnant was Gregory. So how did this girl know?

Then a thought entered her head, a thought so twisted and evil that she immediately tried to dismiss it.

Did Gregory have anything to do with this?

Was it possible?

No.

Yes.

Maybe.

~ ~ ~

"No way I'm keepin' the bitch around," Benito announced the moment he awoke, a scowl crossing his face. "This mo'fuckin' shit get me jail time for sure," he added, vigorously scratching his balls. "Gonna cut her loose."

"What about the senator?" Rosa inquired, in her mind planning how she could get out of the house. She had a very bad feeling about what was going down, especially after the woman's chilling words about kidnapping and severe punishment. She wasn't responsible for any of this, it was all Benito. She was just doing what he ordered her to do. Besides, she'd already explored the contents of the woman's purse, and there were prime pickings, including a cell phone and eighty bucks in cash. She couldn't wait to get her hands on everything.

"The asswipe don't know how t'find me," Benito said, full of bravado. "Prick can't do nothin'."

"When you plannin' on gettin' her outta here?" Rosa asked.

"We're gonna dump her on the street tonight," Benito said, stretching his heavily tattooed arms. "Soon's it get dark."

"If she lasts that long," Rosa muttered. She wished he'd stop including her in his plans.

"What?"

"She ain't lookin' too healthy."

"Bitch lose the kid yet?"

"No."

"Fuck!"

"I gotta go home," Rosa ventured. "Spoke to my mama last night. My baby's sick, an' Mama's gotta get to her job. Day care won't take the baby when she's sick, so I gotta go."

"Ya ain't goin' nowhere," Benito said, still in full scowl. "Not till we get the *puta* outta here."

"You don' understand, I *gotta* go, Benito," she whined. "My mama's gonna kill me if I don't take the baby."

"Whyn't ya stop with yo' fuckin' whining an' start doin' what I tell ya for once?" he demanded.

"But my baby's sick," she repeated, trying to squeeze out a tear or two, almost believing her own lie.

"Don' give a shit."

"What I gonna tell my mama?"

"You ain't tellin' her nothin'," he said, still scowling. "An' why ya always gotta gimme such a hard time?"

"Sorry," she said sulkily, backing off.

"Y'know," he said with a sly smirk, "I got plenty wimmin chasin' me. I can pick any *puta* I want, so's ya better watch it."

"They gonna do you like I do?" Rosa said, standing up for herself.

"It don't take no degree t'suck me off," he boasted with a self-satisfied chuckle. "It be their pleasure."

"*Hijo de puta,*" Rosa muttered. It was the one Spanish insult she knew.

Fortunately, Benito didn't hear her.

43

Annabelle and Bobby

Had Frankie seen a copy of *Truth & Fact*? That was the question on Bobby's mind. And if Frankie *had* seen it, he must be going ape-shit.

Just in case, Bobby stashed a copy of the offending tabloid under his jacket and waited impatiently to greet Annabelle and Frankie at the airport.

The moment the two of them alighted from the Stanislopoulos private plane, Bobby could tell Annabelle knew nothing. She was all smiles and full of enthusiasm about spending the night in Vegas, hardly the picture of a grieving daughter.

"I cannot wait to see Zeena's show," she said, giving Bobby a warm hug. "Zeena is *such* an amazing performer. I saw her show last year in Miami. She's a true superstar, like Madonna."

Was it his imagination, or did Annabelle purposely rub her breasts against him?

Frankie, on the other hand, definitely looked as if he knew something was up.

"Gotta take a piss," Frankie said as they approached the limo.

"Why didn't you go on the plane?" Annabelle asked, turning to him with a frown.

"'Cause I didn't hav'ta go then," he said, left eye twitching. "Is it all right with the queen of everythin' if I go take a piss?"

"I'll come with," Bobby offered.

"How cozy," Annabelle drawled. "All boys together."

"We'll be right back," Frankie said.

"There's champagne in the limo," Bobby offered. "Make yourself comfortable."

The two of them took off, away from the limo and into the airport building.

"I guess you know," Frankie stated.

"Of course I fucking know," Bobby replied. "It's a screaming headline on every newsstand. They all carry *Truth and Fact*."

"Jesus!" Frankie exclaimed as they headed into the men's room. "For real?"

"You've seen it, right?" Bobby asked.

"Not yet. Your two flight attendants warned me it was out there, but they didn't bring a copy on board."

"Prepare yourself," Bobby warned. "It's rough."

"No shit," Frankie said glumly.

"Here." Bobby extracted the copy of *Truth & Fact* he'd kept under his jacket. "Read it and go slit your throat."

Frankie snatched the magazine and began reading. The headline was brutal enough, but he could not believe what was in the story. Times, dates, scribbled monetary transactions, names of alleged clients, and the identities of several girls who worked for them. And even worse were the private photos he and Annabelle had taken just for fun. Photos from their personal collection. *Stolen* photographs. Annabelle joking it up with some of the girls holding up their masks. Intimate photos of them lounging in bed together. Photos from Annabelle's childhood, with Gemma and Ralph front and center.

How the fuck had the stinking tabloid gotten hold of them?

There was only one answer. Someone must have broken into their Park Avenue apartment and stolen them.

Frankie could feel the fury building inside him like a volcano about to blow. Why the hell hadn't Janey informed him there'd been a break-in at the apartment? What the fuck, he paid her enough, so how come she hadn't called and warned him?

Another dumb douche bag. Annabelle was right, he should never have hired her.

"Gotta make a call," he said to Bobby.

"To your lawyer?"

"No. To my half-witted cousin who's supposed to be looking after things for me."

"May I say she's doing a fine job."

"Fuck you," Frankie said, thrusting the magazine at Bobby. "Y'see these photos? They're all filched from our apartment. Annabelle's gonna go freakin' nuts."

"There's nothing you can do, it's out there now," Bobby said, attempting to calm him. "Next week it'll be old news."

"Fuck that shit," Frankie said, burning with anger. "I'm gonna sue the ass off everyone involved."

"It'll cost you," Bobby pointed out. "Once you put yourself in the hands of lawyers—"

"I've got the money," Frankie responded, thinking of the stash in their safe in New York. "I'm takin' this all the way."

"Yeah, but if you ignore it, it'll go away."

"They've crapped all over my reputation, Bobby, an' that kinda garbage stays around an' stinks up my world. So fuckin' ignore it—no way."

"I'm sorry, bro, this is a bad situation."

"Listen," Frankie said, "do me a big one—go with Annabelle to the hotel while I try an' work out my next move. Tell her I got the runs or somethin'."

"Nice."

"Maybe she won't even see it. Right?"

"C'mon, Frankie, get real. Someone's bound to mention it—her father, for starters. And don't kid yourself—there'll be a ton of press at the funeral."

"Thanks. You're makin' me feel a whole lot better."

"I'm just saying the way it is. You want the truth."

"Yeah. Right."

"Okay, then, take it easy. I'll escort your girlfriend to the hotel. And remember, next week this'll be yesterday's news."

~ ~ ~

Annabelle lounged in the back of the limo, sipping champagne while she considered her options. Bobby had certainly been happy enough to see her. His greeting had been overly friendly, and she liked that. She smiled to herself. Once she was rid of Frankie, Bobby would be easy pickings. And why not? Without Frankie hanging around, she was a total catch. She'd give up the business and hand it over to her ex as compensation, because ever since the incident with Sharif Rani's son, she was totally over it. Bobby would certainly be able to keep her in style; she wouldn't have to run a stupid call girl business. He was—or would be when he inherited everything—a freaking billionaire.

Yes, as soon as they got back to New York, she'd tell Frankie to move out. They'd split the cash in the safe, and then they could both get on with their lives.

Thursday was the funeral. Friday they'd be on a plane back to New York. And Saturday she'd give her coke-addicted boyfriend the news.

It's over, Frankie. Have a nice life.

~ ~ ~

"Hey," Bobby said, jumping in the back of the limo and settling himself next to Annabelle.

"Hey yourself," she replied, thinking how handsome he was and what a smart decision she was making about her future. "Where's Frankie?"

"He's got an upset stomach, so he's sitting tight in the bathroom. He'll meet us at the hotel."

Annabelle couldn't believe her luck. Alone with Bobby so soon—it seemed the perfect time to start planting the seeds of their future together.

"Y'know," she ventured, lowering her voice so the driver couldn't hear, "Frankie's coke habit is veering out of control. I'm not sure how much longer I can take it."

"He seems okay to me," Bobby said. He was determined to stay neutral, especially in view of what Annabelle was about to discover. Now was not the time for her to start worrying about Frankie's coke addiction; she had bigger problems ready to slap her in the face.

"*You* don't have to live with him," she said bitterly. "*You* don't have to walk in on him snorting that disgusting white powder up his nose, and then swearing he hardly ever does it when I know it's a constant thing."

"Yeah, that must be a drag," Bobby said, trying to sound sympathetic.

"It's more than a drag," she said vehemently. "You know what, Bobby? I can't deal with it anymore. I want out."

Damn! This was something he didn't wish to hear right now. Annabelle and Frankie had a shit-storm to face, and the best way to deal with it was to present a united front.

"Have you talked to him, told him it upsets you?" he said.

"Frankie's not responsible like you, Bobby." She reached over and covered his hand with hers. "Have *you* ever tried talking sense into him?"

"He's not *my* boyfriend," Bobby remarked, wondering how he could get his hand out from under hers without it looking obvious.

"Y'know," she mused, "Frankie isn't one of us, he never was. You, me, and M.J., we've always been tight. Remember high school? We were like the Three Musketeers. Everyone wanted to be part of our group."

Bobby had no idea what she was talking about. He and M.J. had never hung out with Annabelle, only on that one fateful prom night. After that they'd gone out of their way to avoid her and the group of privileged princesses she spent all her time with.

He slipped his hand out from under hers on the pretext of reaching for a bottle of Evian.

"No champagne?" she said coyly, holding up her glass for a refill.

"Can't drink during the day," he said, pouring her more champagne. "Gives me a hangover."

"Poor baby," she crooned. "You'll have to catch up tonight. Oh, and by the way, make sure I'm sitting next to you, I might need your moral support."

Jeez! What was up with Annabelle? Suddenly the prospect of spending the evening with Zeena seemed quite inviting. Anything was better than getting trapped with a needy Annabelle Maestro on the eve of her murdered mother's funeral. Even another sex romp with the man-eater.

44

Denver

Wow! Ralph Maestro in a fury was a sight to behold. Big movie-star face all red and wrinkled. Eyes flashing venom. Voice a rough, tough growl. Huge frame overpowering and quite threatening.

He was pacing around his living room, and he was not a happy man. His longtime publicist, Pip—a small, middle-aged man wearing a white suit and a jaunty fedora—sat silently in an oversize armchair. Everything except Pip was oversize in the Maestro mansion, including Ralph.

Ignoring me as usual, he pounced on Felix like a black panther trapping its prey.

"I am outraged and horrified," he bellowed. "This filth is purely a ploy to embarrass me. What are you doing about it?"

"We're hitting them with an injunction to stop next week's issue," Felix said, calm as usual.

"Next week's issue," Ralph roared. "Are you telling me there's more?" He turned angrily on Pip. "Did you know this?"

Pip nodded his head, his expression hangdog.

"'Fraid so," Felix said apologetically. "Once these rags get ahold of a story, they hang on until all the blood is drained from the body."

Even I was surprised that there was more to come. I'd read the offending headline story on the way over, and it was pretty tawdry. How much worse could it get? And why hadn't Felix mentioned to me that there was more? It pisses me off when he leaves me out of the loop.

"Have you *seen* next week's story?" I asked.

Ralph's heavy-lidded movie-star eyes swiveled to take me in. "You," he boomed. "Weren't you with my daughter in New York? Surely you knew what was going on?"

"I, uh, merely escorted them back to L.A.," I explained.

"It's her goddamn drug-addicted boyfriend," Ralph thundered. "He's the one that got her into this. I should put a hit out on the cocky bastard."

Pip huddled deeper into his chair. Felix and I exchanged shocked glances. Had Ralph really just said that?

Yes. Unfortunately, he had.

Pip cleared his throat. "Be careful what you say, Ralph. Walls have ears, and if Annabelle's boyfriend should end up on a slab in the morgue . . ."

He didn't have to say any more, the implication was quite clear.

"Where are they?" Ralph yelled. "I called the Beverly Hills Hotel and was informed that they won't be back until tomorrow."

I remembered the text I'd received from Annabelle saying they were off to Vegas to see Zeena's one-night show and would be back in time for the funeral. Annabelle had added a cryptic P.S. stating that she expected me to accompany them to the funeral. Seems I'm a popular funeral date. First Felix wanted me to accompany him, and now Annabelle was insisting that I go with her and Frankie.

Ah . . . choices, choices.

I relayed the information about Vegas to Ralph.

"Vegas!" he steamed. "For what? To pick up more dirty little tramps for their degrading business? How do you think this garbage reflects on *me*? I'm a big star, not the father of some goddamn whore. This could ruin my career."

Talk about exaggeration! Ralph was obviously a master.

"They'll be back early tomorrow," I offered, hoping to defuse the situation.

"That's not soon enough," Ralph announced ominously. Once again, he turned to Pip. "Get me a plane," he commanded as if he were requesting a cup of coffee. "We're going to Vegas."

~ ~ ~

One private plane later and we're all on our way to Vegas. No time to go home and change. No time to do anything except call my neighbor, a martial arts expert, and ask him to walk Amy.

Felix wasn't pleased. I had a strong suspicion he too would've appreciated changing clothes, maybe put on a less colorful pair of shoes.

Pip had arranged for Ralph to have use of a studio plane, but once Ralph was aboard he acted as if he owned it.

As soon as we were airborne, Felix brought up the subject of George Henderson.

"Of course I knew she was seeing him," Ralph said, loud and abrasive.

"You mean you were aware it was him in the tabloid photos?" Felix asked, put out. "Why didn't you tell the police? Or at least you should've mentioned it to me. I *am* your lawyer."

"Gemma cherished her privacy," Ralph replied, lighting up a foul-smelling cigar. "She didn't want anyone knowing that she might be considering a few nips and tucks."

So *that's* how she'd explained the intimate photos to her husband. Very clever.

"The detectives need to know," Felix said a tad sharply. He was a stickler for always doing the correct thing.

"They're detectives, let them find out for themselves," Ralph said, puffing on his cigar and blowing noxious fumes throughout the cabin.

In the end, both men decided it should be my job to discover where Annabelle and Frankie were staying in Vegas.

Who's the detective now?

As soon as we landed, I called Annabelle's cell. No answer. Next I tried Frankie. He picked up immediately, as if he were expecting my call.

"Frankie?" I questioned.

"Who is this?" he asked suspiciously.

"It's Denver."

"What do you want?"

Charming! Such a lovely greeting.

I decided not to mention the tabloid. Too risky. He might lose it, if he even knew about it.

"Just checking in about tomorrow," I said casually. "Annabelle told me you're in Vegas for the night. What time will you be returning to L.A.?"

"Dunno," he said. "You'll hav'ta ask Bobby, we're flying back on his plane."

So Bobby had a plane. What was *that* about?

"Where can I find Bobby?" I asked, keeping it light.

"At the Keys."

"Are you all staying there?"

"Gotta go," Frankie said abruptly.

I had my answer.

Yes, I think I would've made an excellent detective.

~ ~ ~

On the way from the airport in a white ultrastretch limousine that could've comfortably accommodated fifteen people, I checked my texts and voice mails while Pip called the Keys and instructed them to have a suite available for Ralph Maestro's use.

There were still no texts from Carolyn, and I was starting to get worried about not hearing from her. Taking off without a word to anyone was not Carolyn's style, so why wasn't she answering me? How often did I say urgent in a text?

I made up my mind that once we reached the hotel, I would find a quiet corner and call her office again. If she was away, surely they'd know where she'd gone?

In the meantime, I sent her another text.

I had several voice mails to get through, most of them business related, plus two calls from Mario asking if I got his flowers and when could we get together again.

Uh, how about never?

Then came the surprise—a call from Carolyn's dad, George. Wow! Had he somehow or other found out that I knew he was the man in the photo with Gemma? This was crazy. I quickly listened to his message.

"Denver, it's George Henderson. I'm sorry to bother you, but Clare and I received a very disturbing call from the Washington, D.C., police. Apparently Carolyn's car, which is registered in my name, has been found abandoned. I can't seem to reach her, and since I know you two are close, I wondered if you have any idea where she is. Please call us as soon as you get this message."

My heart did a skip and a jump. Intuition told me that this was not good news. I slid along the endless leather side seat and finally got near enough to the driver to ask how long it would be before we reached the hotel.

"Five minutes or fifty," the driver announced, flashing me an annoying smirk. "It all depends on our Vegas traffic."

"See if you can make the five work," I said, curt and to the point. "Mr. Maestro is in a hurry."

"Sure thing, miss."

Did I look like a miss? Shouldn't I be addressed as a Ms. or at least ma'am?

My mind was wandering, as it always does when I'm stressed. I needed to call Carolyn's dad back, and I didn't want to do it from the limo. Therefore I'd just have to wait, frustrating as that was.

I attempted to think about other things. Bobby Santangelo Stanislopoulos drifted into my head. So . . . he had his own plane. How did *that* happen?

Then I remembered. Not only was his mother the infamous Lucky Santangelo, but apparently the word around school had been that his father was some kind of billionaire Greek shipping tycoon who'd died when Bobby was young and that Bobby and his niece were destined to inherit everything when they reached a certain age.

Hmm . . . I guess the plane is part of everything.

"Are we almost there?" Ralph growled, sounding more like an angry dog than a worldwide movie star.

"Five minutes or fifty," I replied, trying not to breathe in too much cigar smoke. "It all depends on the Vegas traffic."

"Fuck Vegas traffic," Ralph thundered. He turned to his browbeaten publicist, who seemed to be aging by the minute. "Pip," he commanded, "call someone and get me a police escort. I need to be there *now*!"

45

Carolyn

Senator Gregory Stoneman carried on as normal. To the outside world he was his efficient, hardworking self, dealing with business as usual. However, inside he was a stone-cold mess, hoping that an unpregnant Carolyn would soon put in an appearance and everything would return to the way it was. Well . . . almost to the way it was, minus one baby—not even a baby, a fetus growing inside Carolyn.

She'd given him no choice except to do something about it before it was too late. He'd had no alternative but to think of some way to stop her from destroying his career and ruining the lives of his family—especially his two precious children, who deserved to be protected at all costs.

Hiring a drug-dealing gangbanger was hardly the perfect way to deal with the situation, but it was the only solution that had presented itself to him. And at the time, it had seemed so easy.

Now he was starting to get worried that he might have gone too far. Thank God he'd warned Benito not to hurt her, simply shake her up enough to lose the baby and then set her free.

But surely it couldn't be taking so much time?

She'd been snatched just after noon on Tuesday, and now it was late Wednesday afternoon. So where was she?

He had a cell number for Benito, but he didn't dare use it. Cell calls could be traced, and it was imperative that he not be connected to Carolyn's disappearance in any way.

As Gregory was mulling this over, Muriel entered his office. "Senator," she said, a worried expression on her face, "there is a police detective who wishes to have a word with you. Is it all right if I show him in?"

~ ~ ~

Rosa managed to get out of the house on the pretext of going to the market and buying food. Benito had a voracious appetite for junk food; he always had a yen for Twinkies and doughnuts and packets of salty chips, which he dipped into tubs of spicy salsa. Prison had taught him nothing about healthy eating.

Rosa didn't care. She too existed on junk food, which was satisfying and cheap.

Before leaving the house, she'd transferred the contents of Carolyn's leather purse into her fake Louis Vuitton bag, purchased from a street vendor for fifteen bucks. The pickings were excellent, the prize being the woman's iPhone. A freakin' iPhone with music and photos and all kinds of other shit. Rosa was in heaven. She already possessed a cheap cell that did exactly nothing. Now she had her own iPhone!

The drag was figuring out how to work the stupid thing. It seemed complicated. She managed to turn it on and pressed the iTunes icon. So cool! Lists of songs came up, so she tapped "Boom Boom Pow" by the Black Eyed Peas.

Listening to the song with a smile on her face, she danced her way toward the corner market, oblivious to what was going on around her. So oblivious, in fact, that she didn't notice the three teenage girls who surrounded her out of nowhere, snatched her purse, grabbed the iPhone out of her hands, knocked her down, kicked her in the face, head, and stomach, and took off.

The last thing Rosa remembered thinking was, *Benito is going to kill me.* Then everything faded to black.

46

Bobby and Annabelle

"Hey, kiddo, you're on your own," Lucky informed Bobby. "I'm handing over the tickets for Zeena's show, and please don't forget that Renee and Susie are throwing a private dinner after the event, so be sure to make it. Renee is expecting all of you."

"Jeez, Mom, they're *your* friends," Bobby complained. "An' now you're running out on us. What's *that* about?"

"Lennie is stopping off in L.A. for exactly three hours en route to his New Zealand location," Lucky explained. "And I plan on spending all three hours with him. Okay with you, number one son?"

"I guess that's why you've got the greatest marriage in town," Bobby said, wondering if he'd ever have a relationship that good.

Lucky flashed him her brilliant smile. "Yes, Bobby, that's exactly why. Lennie comes first."

Which meant that he was stuck. Concert. Private dinner. *Zeena. Zeena. Zeena.*

All his guests couldn't wait to see her show. Brigette and Kris, M.J. and Cassie, and Annabelle and Frankie. What a group!

Why couldn't he fly back to L.A. with Lucky and leave them all to it?

Because he'd invited them, and that would be rude and inconsiderate.

So . . . there was no escape.

He wondered how Frankie was doing. Had he found out who gave the tabloid the story? Had he told Annabelle? Would he have the *balls* to tell her? And when he did so, would he have any balls left? Annabelle was already muttering about splitting with him, and the *Truth & Fact* story could seal the deal.

Deciding to find out what everyone was up to, he called Brigette, who told him that she and Kris were just about to hit the casino floor. "Kris has never gambled before," Brigette said excitedly. "I'm going to teach her blackjack."

Bobby hoped she wasn't bankrolling her girlfriend's gambling fling; that wouldn't be cool.

Next he reached M.J., who informed him that he and Cassie were going to hang out in the suite until showtime.

"I'll meet you in the lobby at seven," Bobby said. "Don't be late."

"Yeah, man, we'll be on time," M.J. assured him. "Cassie's real excited."

I bet she is, Bobby thought. M.J. was a total catch.

When Lucky had first built the Keys, he'd considered buying an apartment in the luxury condominium building attached to the hotel. Now he was glad that he hadn't done so. Vegas was for bachelor parties, getting married in either a lovesick haze or a drunken stupor, and losing money at the tables. Lucky loved Las Vegas, but he wasn't such a fan, although the challenge of making Mood the hot club in town was appealing. He'd already made the decision that he'd commute for the first few months, get the club up and running, then put in a manager he could trust to run things his way.

Bored with his own company, he thought he'd make his way downstairs and join up with Brigette and Kris. It was a better prospect than doing nothing.

~ ~ ~

By the time Frankie reached Janey on the phone, he'd developed strong misgivings about her involvement in the tabloid story. She *had* to know about it, so why hadn't *she* called *him*? Even worse, she wasn't picking up the phone at the Park Avenue apartment, where she was supposed to be looking after things. It was only after three attempts that she finally answered her cell.

"What the fuck, Janey?" he screamed down the phone. "Who did this?" And even as he said the words, it suddenly came to him. Janey's lazy, good-for-nothing, devious, motherfucking son.

"It's Chip, isn't it?" he yelled. "That moron sold us out."

"It's nothing to do with me. I didn't know anything about it," Janey said, immediately defensive.

"Don't fuck with me, Janey," Frankie warned. "You know you don't wanna do that."

"Well," Janey said reluctantly, "if it *was* Chip, then he must've gone behind my back an' done it."

"Stop feedin' me shit," Frankie said, his left eye twitching with anger. "How'd he get the photos if you didn't help him? There's no way. You're the one with the run of the apartment. You must've helped him."

"He stole them," Janey admitted, starting to snivel. "He had to have gone through everything while I was passed out." A pregnant pause. "Frankie"—sob sob—"I got a horrible feeling he drugged me, his own mother! How could he do such a thing?"

"Where is the prick?" Frankie said, imagining exactly what he would do to Chip when he got hold of him. "An' you'd better find out, 'cause when I get back I'm gonna snap his scrawny neck in two."

"Oh, Frankie," Janey wailed in desperation, "please don't say things like that. Chip is family, you know he's a good boy at heart."

"Bullshit! He's a born loser."

"Somebody must've gotten to him, offered him lots of money. He's young, he doesn't understand."

"Do you honestly think I give a fast crap in hell? When I get hold of your demented baby boy, he's gonna understand good. In fact, he's gonna be sorry he was born."

"No, Frankie," Janey pleaded. "Please don't do anything rash. I beg you."

"Shut the fuck up, Janey. I suggest you shift your fat ass an' go find him. Chip is gonna pay for this. Our fuckin' business is ruined, not to mention my reputation."

"I'm so sorry, Frankie," she sniveled.

"You should be, for givin' birth to the little bastard," Frankie said, then snapped his phone shut.

He was still in the airport men's room, and several men going about their business were staring at him.

Shoving the phone in his pocket, he stared back.

"Bad day?" one man ventured.

"Fuck off," Frankie muttered, and marched outside, where the first thing he saw was a newsstand with copies of the offending tabloid, *Truth & Fact*, piled high.

With one big sweeping gesture, he knocked them to the ground, scattering them everywhere.

Muttering, he set off to find a cab.

~ ~ ~

The suite Bobby had gotten them in the Keys was pure luxury, even more so than their rooms at the Beverly Hills Hotel, which was a touch too traditional for Annabelle's taste.

The Keys suite featured an enormous circular bed covered in fur throws (fake, of course; Lucky was a strong supporter of PETA), a giant flat-screen TV, and a full shelf of the latest DVDs, CDs, and best-selling books.

The bathroom was all pale green marble, with a TV in the ceiling above the tub so that guests could lie back comfortably, soak, and watch their favorite programs.

Annabelle wished they were staying longer. She also wished that she were sharing the bed with Bobby, not Frankie.

Soon . . . yes, soon, she was sure of it.

Where the hell was Frankie, anyway? He was taking his time coming from the airport, and she didn't appreciate being kept waiting.

She thought about creating a big fight when he finally arrived and getting it over with. Or was it wiser to wait until after the funeral?

Probably. But Annabelle was into instant gratification, and instant gratification meant dumping his sorry ass the moment he hit the suite.

No, she had to do the smart thing and wait until they returned to New York. If she did it now, he was perfectly capable of running back to New York without her and clearing out the safe. She wouldn't put that kind of move past him, and there was a lot of cash in their safe—a few hundred thousand, at least.

Then another thought occurred to her: Why was she even considering splitting it with him? She was the brains behind the business. Why shouldn't she keep everything for herself?

It was an excellent thought. Before dumping him, she'd remove the cash and put it in a safe-deposit box at the bank, registered in her name only. Frankie would go nutzoid, but there would be nothing he could do about it. *Too bad, Frankie.*

Annabelle realized that she had plenty to think about before making any rash moves.

~ ~ ~

Testing his luck, Frankie stopped by a roulette table on his way up to the suite and placed a two-thousand-dollar bet on black. It came up. He let the four thousand dollars ride, and black came up again. Six thousand dollars profit in a matter of minutes—not bad for a two-thousand-dollar initial bet. Maybe his luck was changing and this whole tabloid thing would blow over without anyone noticing.

Yeah, sure, and roses would grow out of President Obama's ass.

Still testing himself, he let the full eight thousand ride once again. And to his shock and amazement, black hit again!

Clutching his sixteen thousand dollars in thousand-dollar chips, he headed for the cashier's station. On the way, he spotted Brigette Stanislopoulos sitting at one of the blackjack tables. Next to her was a statuesque blonde.

Never one to miss an opportunity, he made his way toward them. "'Scuse me," he said, tapping Brigette on the shoulder. "Brigette, right? We met at Mood in New York a few times. I'm Frankie Romano, close friend of Bobby's. We're all gettin' together tonight."

"Of course. Frankie," Brigette said with a polite smile. "Bobby told me, and I do remember you. You're the superdeejay."

Jeez, she was so damn pretty. A little older than he would've liked—thirty-something—but she was megarich like Bobby. He'd heard so many stories about Brigette Stanislopoulos and her fatal attraction to losers. If he weren't with Annabelle, a woman like Brigette, with her startlingly bright blue eyes, cascades of blond hair, and extreme megabucks, might be exactly what he needed. There was nothing wrong with a little older woman action. Yes, he could definitely go for the voluptuous heiress.

"This is my partner, Kris," Brigette said, introducing him to the blonde sitting next to her, another stunner.

Bummer! The heiress had turned dyke. Too bad. Although . . . the potential for a threesome flashed before his eyes, and he was major into what he saw.

Bobby interrupted his fantasy by coming up behind him and saying, "You're back."

"Yeah, I'm back," Frankie said.

"And I see you've met Brigette."

"Listen, guys," Brigette said with a good-natured smile, "much as I'd love to sit around and chat, I'm trying to teach Kris to play blackjack, so can we catch up later?"

"You got it," Bobby said, grabbing Frankie's arm. "Let's go, bro."

They walked across the casino.

"I just won a shitload of money," Frankie said, still slightly dazed by his big win. "Gotta cash in."

"Have you told Annabelle yet?" Bobby asked as they headed for the cashier.

"About my big win?" Frankie said flippantly.

"No. About the story, asshole."

"I'm figuring she's not gonna find out," Frankie said as he plunked down his chips at the cashier's counter.

"Then you're a bigger asshole than I thought," Bobby said, shaking his head in wonderment at Frankie's thick skin. "Of course she'll find out. Believe me, it'll go a lot smoother if she hears it from you."

"You don't know Annabelle," Frankie said glumly.

"Yeah, I think I do. So take my advice and tell her."

"Later," Frankie said, stuffing wads of cash in his pockets. "Right now I'm on a roll. An' nothin' stops Frankie when he's hittin' a hot streak."

47

Denver

Ralph Maestro actually got a police escort. I couldn't believe it! Two motorcycle cops (very studly motorcycle cops) appeared out of nowhere, and with sirens screaming, the heavy traffic opened up. Within eight minutes, we were arriving at the hotel.

And what a hotel! The Keys—a magnificent structure. Unlike most Vegas hotels, the Keys screamed class and style.

I hadn't been to Vegas since Josh and I spent a weekend at the Hard Rock when he attended a college reunion and insisted I accompany him. Total nightmare. Although for some strange reason, the sex was outstanding. I guess Vegas turned Josh on.

Valets, porters, bellboys, and a couple of guys in dark suits surrounded our limo, and when Ralph emerged everyone went into "Let's kiss the big movie star's ass" mode. It was a sight to behold, although Ralph was obviously used to it. He practically ignored everyone as they escorted him through the lobby to a private elevator and then up to a magnificent four-bedroom suite with a pool table, a full bar, and a white piano in the living room. Outside the suite, a gleaming turquoise lap pool shimmered in the middle of an exquisitely landscaped terrace.

We were staying, what—two hours at the most? But only the best for Ralph Maestro, Mr. Movie Star Supreme.

I needed to call George Henderson back, and I didn't want to do it from the suite, so I made a quick excuse that I had to buy something in the pharmacy and ducked out.

Mention the word *pharmacy* to a man and he'll immediately back off. Felix was no exception, although he did tell me to make it fast.

Downstairs, I searched out a quiet corner near a side entrance and pulled out my phone. But before I could use it, who did I see walking toward me but Bobby and Frankie.

I had nowhere to run, and it was too late anyway. Frankie had seen me, and the two of them were heading full force in my direction.

"What the hell are *you* doin' here?" Frankie demanded, left eye in full twitch. "Didn't you just call me from L.A.?"

"I never said I was in L.A.," I answered defensively.

"What the fuck is goin' on?" Frankie wanted to know, moving closer, invading my personal space.

Oh, crap. What was I supposed to say? That I'd flown in with Ralph, who was ready to kill him? And that if he was smart, he'd run for the hills without passing go.

"Leave the girl alone," Bobby said, throwing me a dazzling smile. "You're questioning her as if you're the D.A."

"I'm not into people playin' mind games with me," Frankie grumbled. "Why was she pretendin' to be in L.A.? Somethin's wrong, I can smell it."

Bobby gave me a sympathetic look. My eyes couldn't resist focusing on his lips. Was it possible for a man to have such kissable lips? I guess so, 'cause he sure as hell had them.

"Look," I said, deciding to come clean. "If you must know, I flew in with Ralph Maestro. He's major pissed about the story in *Truth and*

Fact, and he's come here to find Annabelle and take her home with him."

Frankie looked as if he'd been socked in the face with a wet fish.

"Ralph Maestro is here?" he managed to splutter. "Here, in Vegas?"

" 'Fraid so," I answered calmly, sneaking another look at Bobby's lips.

"Fuck!" Frankie exclaimed, completely deflated. "He didn't believe that shit, did he?"

"I rather think he did. Y'know, there are photos, details . . ." I trailed off.

Frankie seemed ready for a total meltdown.

"What's the deal?" Bobby asked. "Should Frankie go see him, try to explain that it's all a big mistake?"

I admired Bobby for trying to help his friend out. On the other hand, what kind of mistake could it possibly be?

"I think if Frankie can manage to stay out of his way, that might be the smartest thing for him to do," I said. "You've got to understand that Ralph is furious. He's out for blood, and it might be Frankie's."

"Annabelle hasn't seen the story," Frankie said, left eye now twitching out of control. "I need to get to her before Ralph."

Bobby leaned in and took my arm. "Maybe you can do us a favor and not tell Ralph you've seen Frankie," he said. "Give Frankie time to figure things out."

"I guess I can do that," I replied, not minding Bobby invading my personal space at all.

"Gotta go," Frankie suddenly said. And before either of us could say a word, he took off like a rocket ship, leaving me alone with Bobby.

"Jeez!" Bobby sighed. "What a crappy situation. I think I need a drink. How about you?"

"Now, *that* sounds like a plan." I decided not to worry about returning to Felix and Ralph and the obsequious Pip. They would just have to manage without me.

"We'll go over to the Cavendish," Bobby said, taking charge. "It's quieter."

Who was I to argue? I was on my way to having a drink with my teenage crush, Bobby Santangelo Stanislopoulos, and nothing was going to stop me.

~ ~ ~

An hour later I realized I still hadn't called George Henderson, let alone reported back to Felix, who was no doubt livid. But sometimes in life you gotta go with the flow, and this was one of those times.

We were sitting out on the terrace bar at the Cavendish, sipping mojitos. Well, that's not strictly true—I was sipping a mojito, while Bobby was drinking beer from the bottle. "Tastes better that way," he'd informed me.

We were talking nonstop, and I found him to be so interesting, not shallow at all. In school, I'd convinced myself that he might be the best-looking thing on two legs, but because he was a rich kid he was probably boring and full of himself.

Not so. Not so at all.

He was telling me about his club in New York and how he planned on taking over the club concession at the Keys. He was full of terrific ideas and loads of enthusiasm. Then he started asking me about myself and what aspirations *I* had for the future.

Wow! This was a two-way conversation—unusual, to say the least. Most men got off on talking about themselves on a first date, and that was it. Not that this was a date, merely a friendly drink to discuss Frankie's plight. Not that I cared about Frankie, but Bobby, being a loyal friend, seemed concerned.

Ah yes, a date would be a whole different ball game. And maybe . . .

No! What was I thinking? Bobby probably dated models and actresses, true beauties with stick-thin bodies and a penchant for throwing up.

"Why are you smiling?" he suddenly asked.

"Um . . . I didn't realize I was."

"Yeah, you had a real Cheshire cat grin on your face."

"I did?" I said, innocence personified.

"You sure did."

"I must've been thinking of work," I said vaguely.

"Huh?" He gave me a full-on quizzical look. "Well, that's flattering," he said teasingly. "And why would thinking of work make you smile?"

"Mr. Shark Teeth. My boss. He always makes me smile."

"And she has a nickname for her boss," he said, shaking his head. "Y'know, you're funny."

"I try to amuse," I said as I felt my phone vibrating for maybe the sixth time. "Do you mind if I check my messages and make a quick call?"

"Go ahead." He took a beat. "Any need for privacy?"

"That's okay. It's just that I have a friend in Washington who seems to be on the missing list, and I should call her father back, see if he's found out where she is."

Bobby nodded. He had the greatest eyes, dark and intense. I imagine he's a killer in bed.

George Henderson had left another message for me to call him, but when I did he failed to pick up. So I left *him* a message to say that I didn't know where Carolyn was, and would he please try *me* back again.

Meanwhile, Bobby's cell rang. He stood up and walked away from our table. Apparently he *did* require privacy.

When he returned, he had a thoughtful expression on his handsome face.

"Everything okay?" I asked, sipping my mojito.

"I'm guessing I can tell you 'cause I do believe you're on our side," he said. He picked up his bottle of beer and took another healthy swig.

"Tell me what?" I said, delighted that he seemed to trust me.

"Annabelle and Frankie are heading back to L.A. They're being smart and getting out while they can."

"Wow!" I exclaimed. "Ralph will be even more major pissed."

"You can't tell him," Bobby warned. "This stays between us."

"Scout's honor," I answered without even thinking about where my loyalty should lie.

"You don't look like a Scout to me," he said, grinning.

"I don't?" I said, being all flirty and girlish.

"No, you don't," he said, flirting back.

Oh God! I was enjoying this far too much.

"By the way," Bobby said, "I'm now stuck with a couple of extra seats for Zeena's show tonight. You want to come? You can bring someone if you like."

"Uh, it's just me," I said, adding a quick, "There is no special someone right now."

He gave me a long, lingering look. "Join the club," he said.

And as our eyes locked, there was a major commotion and the very famous superstar Zeena and her five-man entourage made a splashy entrance into the bar.

Bobby jerked to an upright position, while I inspected the woman with curious eyes. I'd seen Madonna once in person, and she'd seemed so much smaller than she appeared in performance. Zeena was quite the opposite. A tall, swanlike creature with coal black hair hanging below her waist, heavily shadowed cat's eyes, and deep ruby red lips. As she swept by us, the scent of her perfume was overpowering.

Bobby glanced at his watch and immediately called for the check. "I'll take you back to your hotel," he said. "And remember, you know nothing about Annabelle and Frankie taking off."

"I know nothing," I repeated, formulating a story to tell Felix that would keep me in Vegas overnight.

The check came, Bobby threw down cash, and we got up to leave. As we moved toward the entrance, a deep, throaty voice called out his name.

Bobby stopped short and turned around. "Zeena," he said as if he hadn't noticed her before. Like how could he miss her? "This is a surprise."

"A surprise, Bobby," she drawled, her tapered fingers playing with the stem of her wineglass in a most suggestive way. "How can it be a surprise when you're coming to my show tonight?"

"Yeah," he said curtly. "We're looking forward to that."

And without another word, he gripped my arm and steered me out of there.

~ ~ ~

Felix was steely-eyed and irate, exactly as I'd expected.

"Where have you been?" he hissed in my ear, so close that I could smell his peppermint breath.

"Funny thing," I replied, made-up story at the ready. "I ran into my mom's sister and family. They live in Detroit, and I haven't seen them in five years."

"We are here on business," Felix reminded me sternly. "This is not family reunion time."

"I understand," I replied, refusing to be intimidated. "Which is why as soon as I could get away, I did. But here's the thing—I had to promise to stay over. Not to worry," I added quickly, giving him no time to object. "I'll catch an early flight to L.A. in the morning. I'll be back in time for the Maestro funeral."

Felix was lost for a snappy reply, not something that happened to him very often.

"Ralph cannot reach his daughter," he said at last. "Since there is no answer from their suite, Ralph wants you to locate her and bring her here without the boyfriend. He'll deal with Frankie Romano later."

"How am I supposed to do that?" I asked, nonplussed. "She could be anywhere. Besides, she never goes anywhere without Frankie."

"Annabelle trusts you," Felix said.

"I know she does," I replied, thinking, *What does that have to do with anything?* "This place is huge," I added. "How will I find her?"

"Figure it out," Felix said shortly. "You have one hour. After that we're flying back to L.A. And you, young lady, are making a mistake not coming with us." He waved his index finger at me and threw me an extra-stern look. "A very *big* mistake."

48

Carolyn

Nobody knew who she was, the Latina girl in the cheap bloodstained top and the tight little miniskirt. She'd been lying in the street in the pouring rain for a while before a passerby had finally called 911 and the paramedics had come to get her.

The attending doctor in the ER figured she was very young, although after a thorough examination to see if she'd been raped before being beaten, the female doctor ascertained that she'd given birth not that long ago.

The girl was unconscious, with serious head injuries and damage to her face, especially her right eye. The doctor wasn't sure they could save the eye; it was not her field of expertise. They were waiting for the eye specialist to come and examine her.

In the meantime the girl remained unconscious, and until she woke up, nobody knew who she was.

~ ~ ~

"Not another damn charity event," Gregory Stoneman said, his face darkening with annoyance. "Night after night, Evelyn, you drag me to these things, and yet you know how much I hate them."

"The people who attend events such as this one tonight are the people who keep you in office," Evelyn said, giving him one of her disapproving frowns. "They are the ones who vote for you, Gregory, and you would do well to remember that."

Christ! Evelyn was so sanctimonious.

He could do with a blow job right now. His cock itched for the feel of Carolyn's tight mouth, the way she held the shaft of his cock with her hands when he came, the way she never said no *and* allowed him to come in her mouth.

"Are you listening to me, Gregory?" Evelyn said in her imperious queen voice. "You have one hour to be dressed and ready. It's not black-tie, a suit will do. Wear your new blue shirt and the gold cuff links my father gave you last Christmas."

Was she actually telling him how to dress now? God! The woman was insufferable.

Idly, he wondered what she'd do if he bent her over his desk and took her from behind, jammed his itching cock right into her uptight backside and let her have it.

She'd scream, that's what she'd do.

Oh, Carolyn, Carolyn. What have I done? Where are you?

A detective had come to his office earlier in the day. The police had found Carolyn's car abandoned with the driver's door wide open. The detective wanted to know if he had any idea where she might be.

He'd shaken his head and managed a worried expression. Then Muriel had volunteered that Carolyn had left to go to the dentist the previous day, and nobody had seen or heard from her since.

"It's nothing serious, is it?" he'd asked, faking major concern.

The detective had maintained a noncommittal demeanor. "Please contact us if you hear anything, Senator."

"Certainly," Gregory had said.

Of course it was serious. A missing woman. An abandoned car in the middle of nowhere. It was dead serious.

Why hadn't Benito hidden the car?

But then again, why would he? He was a gangbanger, not a person with any brains.

Gregory experienced a sudden flash of extreme guilt.

"By the way," Evelyn said, toying with one of her cabochon ruby earrings, "I heard from Ramirez earlier today. He requested that you call him or drop by the center. There is something he wishes to discuss with you."

A leaden weight lodged itself in the pit of Gregory's stomach. What the hell did Ramirez want?

~ ~ ~

Benito could not believe that Rosa was disrespecting him by not coming back to the house after he'd allowed her out to go to the market to buy food. He knew exactly where she was: She'd run home to her baby, a baby fathered by another man, an enemy—member of a rival gang.

Swearing under his breath, he vowed to punish Rosa for doing such a thing. No female disrespected him and got away with it. How dare she put her baby before him! It was an insult. She was lucky he kept her around, the ungrateful *puta*.

Now he was faced with the problem of getting the senator's pregnant bitch out of his house without Rosa's help. Who had time for this shit? He had things to do, people to see. His lucrative street-corner drug business did not run itself.

~ ~ ~

Rigid with fear, Carolyn feverishly began working on the electrical cord securing her right wrist. Something her captors hadn't reckoned on was that she was left-handed, so even though the knots were tough to undo, she was making progress.

If only she had a knife or something to cut the damn cord with, it would be so much easier. The noise of the TV coming from the other room was relentless.

Several hours had passed and no one had come anywhere near her. Was their plan to keep her shackled to the bed like a dog until she starved to death?

Her fear was mixed with a mounting anger. She was no fool, and she was beginning to understand that perhaps love had blinded her to the man Gregory Stoneman really was.

Why had he asked her to meet him in such a deserted spot?

What was his obsession with her telling no one of her pregnancy?

And the worst thought of all: Had Gregory arranged to have her taken because she was pregnant with his child?

The more she thought about it, the more convinced she became that Gregory could be involved.

It sickened her. What a disgusting human being he must be to have come up with this plan. And what exactly did he expect the result to be?

Were these people supposed to kill her and the baby she was carrying? Was that it?

Systematically, she continued to work on freeing herself.

49

Bobby and Denver

Seeing Zeena at the Cavendish hotel bar had done nothing for Bobby. In fact, he was pleased to note that observing Zeena in the harsh light of day was quite a shocker. She came across as hard-looking, with her heavy dramatic makeup and long sweep of coal black hair. Truth was she might be athletic in bed, but out of bed her famous toned body was downright masculine. She had muscles like a man and long, sinewy arms. There was nothing feminine about her.

And here he was, sitting with a normal, extremely attractive woman with soft curves, full natural lips, and the most inviting hazel eyes. Denver. Pretty, smart . . . and he was rapidly falling in like.

After he left her, he returned to his suite feeling elated. Maybe this could be the start of something. She'd mentioned she was unattached, and since he was, too, who knew what could happen?

Zeena. An adventure. An experience. Been there, done that.

With a sudden flash of insight, he realized he was over his infatuation.

A shower seemed like a plan. After stripping off his clothes, he padded into the bathroom and switched the ceiling TV to a sports channel. Then he stood under the six powerful showerheads, giving himself up to the cascades of water beating down on him. The cold water was invigorating.

He wondered how his wild and wonderful mom would get along with Denver. Lucky would like her, because Denver was smart and independent—Lucky's kind of woman. Max would hate her, because little sis was insanely jealous of any female he dated. In Max's eyes he was her big brother, and woe betide any woman who came before her in his affections.

The volume on the TV was so loud that Bobby didn't hear the bathroom door open. When someone slid into the shower beside him, it took him completely by surprise.

"Hi, Bobby," drawled a totally naked Zeena in her low-down, husky voice. Then, cupping his balls, she added, "Have you missed me?"

Surprising him in the shower . . . the move was pure Zeena.

"How the hell did you get in here?" he asked, dumbfounded. He tried to back away, but she had his balls in a disturbingly firm grip.

A throaty laugh. "Surely you know that Zeena can go anywhere she wants? And Zeena can *get* anything she wants. And right this moment Zeena wants your cock in her mouth. So do not fight it, simply enjoy."

And before he could move or do anything, the superstar was on her knees sucking his dick—which had a mind of its own, because out of nowhere it was ramrod hard. He had no say in the matter.

Zeena did nothing halfheartedly. She was what the guys would describe as a "master cocksucker." Although "mistress of the blow job" might be more apt.

She sucked him dry and then some, and he put up no defense—or rather, his dick didn't. When she was finished, she announced she had a show to prepare for, and leaving him dripping in the shower, she was gone as stealthily as she'd appeared.

Holy shit! Thank God he didn't have to explain what just happened to a girlfriend, because if he *did* have a girlfriend, she'd never believe him.

Feeling used and angry at himself, he made it out of the shower and dressed quickly.

Basically Zeena had molested him, and his dick had happily gone along with it.

Goddamn it! Why hadn't he locked the bathroom door? Or at least the hotel room door?

But then again, knowing Zeena, he was sure that locks would present no deterrent. Miz Superstar could probably spring a lock with her snatch!

Still pissed, he left the suite and went downstairs.

~ ~ ~

So here I was stranded in Vegas with nowhere to hang out until my date (yes, I'm calling it a date) with Bobby.

It was almost five, so I had two hours to kill before meeting him. When Ralph and entourage departed, the luxury suite became unavailable, so I was on my own. I quickly made up my mind that a change of clothes was in order and maybe a blow-dry at a hair salon. Plus I'd better book myself a room for the night, unless . . . No! Too soon! Bobby wasn't just another guy. He was special.

I hit the shopping mall, searching for something suitable to wear. Nothing too sexy—that would be obvious. More subtle sexy.

Hmm . . . I was in Vegas. Subtle sexy was a whole world away.

After traipsing through several stores, I finally came across the perfect dress. A one-shouldered Donna Karan number in soft red silk jersey. Too expensive by far, but hey—I was in a reckless mood, so what if it cost almost two weeks' salary?

The problem was that once I had the dress, I knew I had to buy shoes to go with it.

Here's the deal: I am not usually an extravagant person, but for tonight's adventure I am planning—obviously—to go all out. And yet . . . I don't understand why.

Yes, actually I do understand. This so-called date with Bobby is taking me back to my awkward teenage years. It's validating the fact that the boy everyone craved back in the day is paying attention to *me*!

This entire episode was so juvenile. I have actually blown off my boss, not to mention an important client of the firm, to indulge myself for once. Crazy behavior! What happened to work always comes first?

I was beginning to get mad at myself. This was so totally unlike me.

Then I spotted the perfect shoes: strappy gold sandals with ultrahigh heels and an ultrahigh price tag.

Should I? Shouldn't I?

Oh, man! I was turning into a *Sex and the City* kind of girl, and that wasn't like me at all.

I purchased the shoes and headed for the beauty salon, where they washed and blow-dried my hair into soft curls, then talked me into having a professional makeup. More crazy behavior!

After the makeup artist and hairstylist were done, I changed into my new dress in the ladies' room and inspected my image in a full-length mirror. It was the superglam version of me. Quite a radical change.

Did I like the way I looked? I wasn't certain. But I *was* certain that with the minimakeover, I was sure to be more Bobby's type, false eyelashes and all.

~ ~ ~

M.J. and Cassie both had dizzy smiles on their faces when Bobby met them in the bar downstairs.

"You look happy," he remarked, ordering a beer.

"Yeah, we do," M.J. responded, exchanging an intimate grin with his young girlfriend.

"What?" Bobby said. "You won at blackjack?"

"Better than that," M.J. responded. His grin getting was wider by the minute.

"Spill," Bobby said.

"We got married!" Cassie squeaked, her pretty little face all aglow. "Isn't it awesome?"

"You did *what*?"

"Married, dude," M.J. said excitedly. "Would've liked you as a witness, but it was an off-the-wall kinda 'let's go ahead an' do it' deal."

"Holy shit, M.J.," Bobby said, shaking his head. "Your mom's gonna kill you."

"Not when she meets Cassie, she won't," M.J. said confidently. "She's gonna love her."

"You're sure about that?"

"Yeah, man. Can you try to look happy for us?"

"I can't wait to see Zeena," Cassie piped up. "Will we get to see her after the show?"

"Sure," Bobby promised her, smiling. Inside, though, he was mourning the loss of his best friend, for he had no doubt that after M.J.'s announcement, there would be no chance of a one-on-one conversation.

"Where's Annabelle and Frankie?" M.J. asked. "They need to hear our news. We got some major celebrating to do later."

"An emergency came up," Bobby explained. "The two of them had to turn around an' fly back to L.A."

"Too bad," M.J. said. "They never got to meet my bride."

Bobby wasn't prepared to deal with M.J.'s craziness right now. Getting married in Vegas indeed. What a cliché! No prenup. No proper wedding. M.J.'s parents were going to flip out.

Soon Brigette and Kris appeared, and they too were all smiles.

It seemed everyone was having a great time except him. Bobby knew that he'd be having fun too if it weren't for the Zeena incident. In retrospect, he realized he should've pushed her out of the shower and told her to get the hell away from him.

But no, he hadn't done that, because his goddamn dick had been too busy getting off on the attention.

Damn! A little control would have been nice.

~ ~ ~

Maneuvering my way through the casino in heels much higher than I was used to, I realized that with the clinging red dress, the new hairstyle, and the superslick makeup, I had taken myself totally out of my comfort zone.

Men were paying me a lot of attention, and I didn't like it. The attention was making me feel exposed and vulnerable. And speaking of feeling vulnerable, the red dress did not allow for a bra, so the girls were out there for all to see.

What was wrong with me? Why this sudden need to get all glammed up?

Because obviously I was competing with the legions of women who I imagined were constantly chasing after Bobby.

Irrationally, I started to feel angry. At him! It was all *his* fault. Why had I put myself in this position? It was ridiculous. I should've flown back to L.A. with Mr. Shark Teeth and Ralph the movie star. I'm a professional lawyer, not some lovesick girl attempting to get noticed.

By the time I reached the bar where we'd arranged to meet, I was ready to tell Bobby that unfortunately I couldn't stay, so sorry.

But all bets were off the moment he stood up to greet me. He had on a blue shirt open at the neck, dark jeans, and a thin leather belt, and his black hair was slightly damp and curling over his collar.

Mario, with his dimples and fine abs, was not even close to looking this good.

"Wow!" Bobby said, pulling me in for a small but intimate hug. "Look at you!"

Was that a compliment? Please let it be a compliment.

"Wow!" I retaliated. "And look at *you*."

"I guess we both clean up pretty good," he said with a wide and irresistible grin on his face.

"I guess so," I replied, slightly breathless.

He introduced me to his friends, and after that I was lost in his dark, sexy eyes.

I knew without a doubt that it was destined to be a memorable evening.

50

Annabelle

Not only were they flying back to L.A. before Ralph was able to find and confront them, they were suffering the indignity of making the trip back on a commercial flight.

Annabelle was apoplectic with fury. Frankie had ruined her life; her well-thought-out plans for a delightfully uncomplicated future with Bobby were shattered.

The problem was that her drug-addict boyfriend had screwed them both by hiring his asinine cousin and her dim-witted son. What a pathetic pair! She'd warned Frankie time and time again that the two of them were useless, but he'd refused to listen. Now their story was splashed across the front page of the cheapest tabloid around, and she was being painted as a madam! A madam—how ridiculous was that?

When Frankie had appeared in the suite earlier, she'd been all ready to blast him for taking his time getting there. But before she could say a word, he'd handed her a tastefully gift-wrapped package and urged her to open it.

Annabelle needed no encouragement when it came to opening presents. She'd ripped off the wrapping paper, revealing a black leather box. In the box nestled a pair of sparkling diamond earrings.

Hmm, she'd thought. M*aybe Frankie isn't such a loser after all.*

The earrings were expensive and quite exquisite. For once, Annabelle was impressed.

After putting them on and admiring herself in the bathroom mirror, she'd wandered back into the bedroom, where Frankie was in a lustful mood. She'd responded, because when Frankie was on his best behavior, the sex could be outstanding, and lately they'd not been connecting.

He'd undressed her slowly until all she had on were the diamond earrings and her strappy Jimmy Choos. Then he'd sat her on the side of the bed, spread her legs, gotten on his knees, and gone down on her.

Giving oral was not Frankie's thing at all, so she'd been delighted. The result was an amazing orgasm.

But then, in true Frankie fashion, he'd ruined everything by telling her about their headline story in *Truth & Fact*. And on top of that, he'd informed her that Ralph was in Vegas intent on splitting them up, dragging her back to L.A. with him, locking her up, and probably throwing away the key forever.

Frankie was exaggerating, but Annabelle did not know that.

When he'd finally gotten up the nerve to show her a copy of *Truth & Fact,* she'd gone berserk. To see herself depicted as a madam and sometime call girl was shocking. She was appalled.

"We gotta get outta here," Frankie had said, sweating and agitated. "Pack up an' let's hit the road."

"But what about Zeena's concert?" she'd asked. *And Bobby?* she'd wanted to add but didn't.

"Fuck the concert. You want Ralph to find us? We gotta split like half an hour ago."

Annabelle had done as she was told, but not without a litany of objections along the way.

They were now at the airport, and horror of all horrors, they were boarding a commercial jet that didn't have first class! Even worse, their seats were located in the back of the plane.

Annabelle voiced her objections to the African-American flight attendant, who couldn't have given a rat's ass.

"Sorry," said the flight attendant, not sorry at all. "This flight is completely booked out. You're lucky to get seats at all."

"Lucky?" Annabelle sneered. "I think not."

The flight attendant moved away. She'd had a tough day and was in no mood to deal with a difficult passenger.

"I hate this!" Annabelle complained in a loud voice. "Who are all these ugly people dragging so much crap aboard?"

"It's called hand luggage," Frankie said, wishing she'd be quiet. He was trying to figure out their next move, and it wasn't easy. Should they run back to New York? Or should they stick it out and stay around for the funeral?

"Hand luggage!" Annabelle sniffed. "More like the entire contents of their miserable houses."

"Excuse me," said a middle-aged woman with a bad perm sitting across the aisle. "Aren't you that movie star's daughter turned hooker?"

Annabelle blanched visibly. Was some fat old hag calling her a hooker?! How could that possibly be?

"You got the wrong person, lady," Frankie said quickly, leaning forward to shield Annabelle from the woman's prying gaze.

"No," the woman insisted in a shrill voice, "I don't. I was reading about you two this morning in the hotel coffee shop." She wagged her finger at them. "Naughty! Naughty!"

"You got it wrong," Frankie said gruffly, willing her to butt out.

Their annoying fellow passenger had no intention of doing so. "It's you. I *know* it's you." She nudged her husband, who was slumped in the seat next to her, trying to pretend he had no idea what was happening. "It's them, Fred," she shrieked. "I told you so! Should I get their autograph?"

"Leave it be, Gladys," Fred said irritably.

"Why should I?" the woman argued. "Their autograph could be worth a few bucks on eBay, you never know."

"I doubt it," Fred said, burying his head in the airline magazine.

"Oh," she said dismissively. "*You* doubt everything I say. But I'm telling you, it's them, and I should get them to sign *something*."

Frankie tuned the couple out. He had too much going on to care about the likes of a loudmouthed old bag who wouldn't quit bothering them.

Annabelle hunkered down in her seat and ordered Frankie to get her a glass of champagne.

"Not on this flight," he said, thinking that she lived in a dreamworld. "You'll have to wait until we get to the hotel."

In his mind, he was formulating a plan. What if he was able to use this story to their advantage? Milk it for free publicity. Turn up at Gemma Summer Maestro's funeral and brazen it out. Annabelle would be the one garnering all the attention. Annabelle would be the star, making Ralph an also-ran. The media got off on big juicy scandals, and this was a huge one. Beautiful daughter of two megafamous parents—one of them recently murdered—caught peddling the flesh of New York's most elite women.

If Annabelle was the star, then there had to be a villain. He could play the villain, why not? It hadn't gone too badly for that couple from *The Hills* reality show. Heidi and Spencer. Or Speidi, as the press had christened them.

Yeah. This story could launch them into the fame stratosphere he'd always dreamed of. So what if it was a fame based on scandal? They'd still be famous.

What they needed to point them in the right direction was a smart manager, a savvy person who would guide and protect them. A person who would get them out there in the right way.

No *Howard Stern Show* or *Access Hollywood* for Annabelle. Her first interview should be with Barbara Walters or Diane Sawyer. After that exclusive, the couch on *The View,* Annabelle explaining her story to the women. Her story would be all about poor little rich girl—or in Annabelle's case, poor little bitch girl! The women of *The View* would eat it up.

This would lead to an appearance on *Oprah* and after that a multimillion-dollar book deal. If it all fell into place, they'd be sitting on top of everything they'd ever dreamed of.

Frankie's adrenaline was fast surging into overdrive. This was an opportunity not to be missed.

Now all he had to do was convince Annabelle.

51

Carolyn

One or two more swigs of cheap Scotch from the bottle, and glancing outside, Benito was satisfied that it would soon be dark enough to smuggle the senator's bitch out of the house and dump her somewhere—anywhere far away from him.

He'd been sitting around drinking all day, brooding about Rosa running out on him, leaving him with nothing to eat except a few stale crackers and half a jar of rancid peanut butter.

He couldn't believe she'd had the stones to treat him this way. Little whore. They were all dirty little whores, including the one taking up space in his bedroom. The sooner he got rid of her, the better off he'd be.

He'd had it with being trapped in the house, unable to take care of business, stuck in front of the TV watching all kinds of dumb shit. The boredom was getting to him. What he needed was some porno to change things up.

He moved over to a rickety table standing next to the TV and rifled through his cousin's collection of DVDs stacked on the floor.

Sure enough, between *Rambo: First Blood* and *First Blood Part II* and a pile of wrestling DVDs, he came up with a promising title: *Fat Black Pussies.*

Not that he was into black bitches, but this was no time to be particular.

After slotting the DVD into the player, he took another swig of Scotch and sat back, ready for some satisfaction.

~ ~ ~

"Any identification on her at all?" Detective Lennox asked the female doctor, a petite brunette.

They were both standing next to Rosa's bed in the hospital. The detective was a tall man with sparse gray hair and sharp features. In a strange way, he reminded the doctor of Clint Eastwood; he had that reassuring take-charge quality about him.

Dr. Glass shook her head. "Nothing," she said. "Whoever beat this poor girl even took her shoes. All she had on was her top and skirt."

"Gotta tell ya, the street violence in that particular neighborhood is out of control," Detective Lennox remarked, jotting something in his notebook. "Gangs, addicts, thieves, hookers. The *real* lowlifes. They're out there in force, an' they prey on anyone they can. Nobody's safe."

As she nodded in agreement, Dr. Glass found herself wondering if he was married.

"Y'know something?" Detective Lennox continued. "Even *I* wouldn't walk around there after dark. It's that bad of a cesspit."

"This didn't happen when it was dark," Dr. Glass pointed out. "It was daylight when they brought her in."

"Poor kid," said Detective Lennox. He handed the doctor his card, thinking she was an extremely attractive woman. "Do me a favor an' have someone call me when she starts talking."

"You mean *if* she starts talking," Dr. Glass said.

"Yeah," Detective Lennox said with a weary shake of his head. "Can't hurt to hope for the best."

~ ~ ~

Keeping a watch on the fading light behind the tacked-up curtain covering the window, Carolyn had almost freed herself from the ties binding her wrist. But the fear was building. Her heart was pounding, and so many new questions kept running through her head.

Did she have an escape plan? Not really, and there were so many unknowns to contend with. Even if she did manage to get out, what was she supposed to do then? Especially as she had no idea what part of the city she was in.

She had no money, no phone, and her clothes were filthy and covered in sticky grease, the result of being locked in the trunk of a car. On top of everything else, she was starving, thirsty, exhausted, and worried for her baby.

But most of all, she was determined.

Determined to somehow or other get out of this degrading trap and confront Gregory, for now she was almost sure that he *had* to be responsible.

If he was, she would make him pay for his betrayal of what she had imagined was their mutual love.

She would make him pay with his career, because she finally understood that his damn career was the only thing he really cared about.

Senator Gregory Stoneman, you are in for a nasty shock.

52

Bobby and Denver

Bobby was hardly surprised that everyone warmed toward Denver. She was smart and engaging, and damn, she looked hot! A little too hot—not only was M.J. ogling her cleavage, but Kris had eyes for her, too. Brigette didn't seem to notice, nor did Cassie; they were both so psyched to be on their way to Zeena's show.

Bobby was not psyched. The last thing he wanted was to sit and watch Zeena perform for two hours. But how to get out of it?

No suitable excuse came to mind.

Renee and Susie, the owners of the Cavendish, met them in the lobby of their hotel when they arrived.

"Zeena's looking forward to seeing all of you after the show," Renee said. "I'm sad Lucky won't be joining us."

"Yeah," Bobby said. "Lucky sends everyone her love."

"Oh my God! I can't wait to see Zeena onstage," Cassie exclaimed, full of girlish enthusiasm. "She's *such* an icon. I've been listening to her music and watching her on TV and in the movies since I was five!"

"Don't tell *her* that," Renee warned. "No artist needs to be reminded of how old they are, especially coming from a pretty little thing like you."

"Hands off my wife," M.J. said sotto voce to Bobby.

"You're safe," Bobby replied. Then, remembering something Lucky had told him, he added, "Susie might look mild, but if Renee even thinks about straying, watch out!"

"Good to know," M.J. said.

~ ~ ~

Bobby's friends seemed nice. I remembered M.J. from high school—he was always the cool dresser with the hot car. His new wife was very young but sweet, and she was in a high state of excitement about seeing Zeena's show.

I have to admit, I'm not that into Zeena's kind of music; it's a little too dance-techno for me. I'm more of a John Mayer, Jason Mraz, kind of girl. Also I'm very into old eighties soul.

I wondered what kind of music Bobby liked. Rock? Rap? Soul? A combo? There was so much about him I didn't know.

"Hey," he said, holding on to my arm as we headed for our seats, which happened to be front and center. "If you don't like the show, we can always duck out and catch up with everybody later."

"No, we can't," I replied, enjoying the feel of his hand on my bare arm. "We're right in Zeena's eye line."

"She'll never notice," he said as Brigette settled into the seat next to him.

"Of course she will."

"So . . . uh, tell me," he said with a half smile. "Did you pull that sexy dress out of your purse?"

"Excuse me?" I said, curbing a strong desire to reach up and touch the slight stubble on his chin.

"You flew here for the day, right?"

"Correct."

"Were you expecting to stay?"

"Actually," I confessed, "if you must know, I went out and bought this dress after we had drinks together. I got it especially to wear tonight. For you," I added boldly.

"For me?" he said, raising an eyebrow.

"Most popular boy in high school, who never even knew I existed," I said lightly. "So I figured tonight I'd make sure you noticed."

"Oh, I'm noticing all right," he responded, his half smile turning into a full-on grin.

"Excellent," I said crisply. "That means I haven't wasted two weeks' salary."

"Ah, Denver . . ." He sighed. "Don't you know—the dress doesn't make the woman, the woman makes the dress."

I blushed. I swear I did. And I *do not* blush.

Oh crap, why hadn't I flown back to L.A. with Felix?

This might be the start of something that could quite possibly rock my world.

Did I want that?

Yes, right now I really did.

~ ~ ~

Before Zeena appeared, a female Asian announcer in an electric blue tie and tails outfit, with whip in hand, took to the stage and sternly warned the audience there could be no taking of pictures and to please turn off all cell phones.

Denver wasn't happy about that. "I'm expecting an important call," she whispered to Bobby.

"Put it on vibrate," he advised. "And if it's a horny boyfriend, you can tell him he's too late."

"I'm not expecting any calls from horny boyfriends. And trust me, if they were my boyfriend, they wouldn't be horny, they'd be perfectly content and satisfied."

"Whoa!" Bobby said, and burst out laughing. "High opinion of your skills."

They exchanged a smile as the lights dimmed to complete darkness and a center spot highlighted a golden cage descending from the ceiling, containing Zeena and two live white tigers. The audience gasped as the music rose to a crescendo, playing the superstar's current number one hit single, "Power."

Clad in a smoky see-through catsuit that emphasized every curve of her sinewy body, the tigers lounging on either side of her, Zeena milked the adoring audience like the true professional she was.

Stepping out from the cage, she left the tigers behind and launched into an elaborate song-and-dance routine with six African-American male backup dancers clad in leopard-print leotards, which culminated in them picking her up and holding her aloft like a pharaoh queen.

The audience went nuts. Zeena *was* their pharaoh queen in the flesh. And they were worshipping at the altar.

Two elaborate production numbers later, Zeena sauntered to the microphone to indulge in some light repartee with her adoring audience. Every word she said was met with sighs and applause and an edgy expectation about what would come out of her mouth next. Zeena was known for saying the most outrageous things.

As usual, she had the audience exactly where she wanted them, and that always encouraged her to stretch the boundaries.

Watching her, Bobby was beginning to feel uncomfortable. He wished he could blank out the earlier sex romp in the shower. Hardly a romp—more like Zeena getting exactly what she wanted, as usual. He promised himself he would never allow it to happen again.

Sneaking a sideways glance at Denver, he saw that she was checking a text message on her phone. Obviously she was as unimpressed with Zeena and her gaudy theatrics as he was.

"If I sound particularly smooth tonight, I'd like to give a shout-out to my special lover, Bobby Stanislopoulos," Zeena crooned into the microphone. "Bobby is a man who knows *exactly* what Zeena needs to make all the sweet sounds you appreciate."

The audience roared its approval.

Bobby could not believe what she'd just said. Lover? Was she freaking *kidding*?!

M.J. leaned across Brigette with a big grin and gave him a thumbs-up.

Denver stopped checking her phone and concentrated on the woman standing on the stage.

"You see," Zeena drawled, savoring every moment of her bizarre announcement, "when Zeena wants her voice to soar, then Zeena has need for a certain male nectar . . ." A long, suggestive pause. "So, Bobby . . . may I take this moment to thank you for the late-afternoon shower and the delicious nectar of love that works *sooo* good."

The audience screamed.

Only the incredible Zeena would dare go there.

~ ~ ~

I was attempting to read an urgent text from George Henderson when out of nowhere Zeena mentioned Bobby's name. And she didn't just mention his name, she called him her lover. *Lover?* Wow! She sure as hell had *my* attention.

Miz Superstar then went on to spew forth a slew of euphemisms.

I am not slow, but believe me, I got the picture. So did everyone else in the damn place.

What a full-on drama queen! The thought of her with Bobby made me feel nauseated. Oh crap, I sure could pick 'em!

Bobby started pulling on my arm, a distraught expression on his face. "It's not what you think," he half whispered, losing his cool and almost stuttering. "She's crazy."

When caught, why do men always say, "It's not what you think"? Isn't that even lamer than "It's not you, it's me"?

I made a swift recovery. *Never let them see you care.* My mom had taught me that. *Thanks, Mom!*

"Listen," I said, managing to sound collected, "I promise it has nothing to do with what Zeena announced to the world, but I have to get out of here. I received a text telling me there's an emergency situation going on in Washington concerning my best friend. I should head straight for the airport right now."

Of course he didn't believe me. Why would he?

Zeena had launched into another production number. I had no intention of staying around, so as quietly as I could, I stood up, squeezed past his friends, and made a fast exit.

Bobby jumped to his feet and followed me. I had a feeling he would, but it wasn't going to do him any good. No damn good at all.

53

Annabelle

Frankie was never happier than when he was in action, and seizing control of a no-win situation invited major action. He refused to allow *Truth & Fact* to besmirch his reputation and walk away the victors. Oh no, he would turn it around as only he could.

When their plane landed at LAX, he informed Annabelle that they were not checking back into the Beverly Hills Hotel. "Not a smart move," he told her. "Ralph will track us down, an' that's exactly what we don't want to happen. So here's my plan. . . ."

Annabelle listened as he laid out what he had in mind. He informed her that he was looking into hiring a manager who would handle everything, including damage control regarding the *Truth & Fact* story. "I'm gonna make us famous, babe," he assured her. "TV appearances, a reality show, the works. We'll be rollin' around in big bucks."

In theory it sounded fine, but who knew if Frankie was capable of pulling it off?

"Don't you worry about a thing," he said as he checked them into a suite under an assumed name at the Sunset Marquis, a hotel where Ralph would not be likely to look for them.

"What about my things?" she demanded, still playing the Hollywood princess. “All my stuff is at the Beverly Hills Hotel. I need my stuff, my clothes, my makeup.”

“I'm taking care of it,” he said. “You sit tight an' let me handle everything.”

“Oh God, Frankie,” she wailed, suddenly seeming quite vulnerable. “We are so fucked.”

“No way, babe. We're coming out on top. I'm never gonna let you down.”

Annabelle decided he wasn't so bad after all. At least he was there for her all the way, and that was something.

Frankie ran around trying to make his girlfriend comfortable. As soon as he'd settled her in front of the TV with a bottle of Cristal and a Leonardo DiCaprio movie on pay-per-view, he made his first call.

One call was all he needed to get connected.

~ ~ ~

Fanny Bernstein had a reputation. Fanny Bernstein was not a woman many people dared argue with. Fiftyish, she was big and brash, with a mass of frizzed dyed orange hair, enormous boobs that she had no objection to flashing when the occasion arose, diamanté-rimmed eyeglasses, and a cavern of a mouth. She called everyone “honey” or “dollface,” and if you were on her shit list, she called you “cuntface.”

Nobody wanted to be on Fanny's shit list—especially Rick Greco, who had remained close to his former manager even though she had never landed him another job after the demise of his successful nineties sitcom.

When Frankie called Rick—who knew all about the story in *Truth & Fact*, as did everyone else in Hollywood—and asked him who he should meet with, Rick didn't hesitate. “My onetime manager, Fanny Bernstein. Fanny's kicked more ass than you've had hot pussy. There's nobody she doesn't know.”

"Can you set up a meeting for me right away?" Frankie said. "And by right away, I mean today."

"Sure," Rick said agreeably. "And if the two of you do business, I'll expect a finder's fee for putting you together. Are we down with that?"

"Put us together in the next couple of hours and you got it."

Exactly an hour later, Frankie was sitting in Fanny's garishly decorated office, taking in the framed photos of Fanny with everyone from President Clinton to John Travolta hanging on her walls. Rick Greco was also present, stinking of a particularly strong aftershave and once again dressed all in white. The two of them were waiting for Fanny to put in an appearance.

Frankie kept glancing at his watch. Rick had said an hour, so where was this woman who, according to Rick, was about to turn everything around?

"Fanny gets off on making a grand entrance," Rick remarked. "She's eccentric, but I swear to you she's the one person you want in your corner. She's got all the power and clout you'll ever need. Like I told you, Fanny's a dynamo."

The dynamo made her grand entrance twenty minutes later. She swanned into her office clad in a purple caftan that clashed with her orange hair, spangly flip-flops, large cartwheel earrings, and dozens of jangling gold bracelets. Under her arm she clutched a miniature poodle, its fur dyed the same color as her hair.

"Boys," she announced, plopping her considerable ass down in the leopard-print chair behind her mirrored desk, "I'm here, I'm not queer, so what's your fuckin' problem that I had to forgo a session with my acupuncturist?"

"Meet Frankie Romano," Rick said. "You might've seen him on the cover of *Truth and Fact* this week."

"Seen him! I've fucked him!" Fanny cackled, breaking up at her attempt at humor. "No, kiddies, I haven't," she continued. "That must've been the water delivery guy. You've seen one little prick, you've seen 'em all!"

Frankie shot Rick a dirty look. *This* was the woman he was about to trust with his and Annabelle's future? No way.

He started to get up.

"Sit your ass down," Fanny commanded, taking off her diamanté glasses and twirling them in a circle. "Learn to take a joke, an' you an' I will be tight as an ant's crack."

For once in his life, Frankie was speechless.

"I've read the story," Fanny continued. "So tell me, Mr. Pimp Man, whaddya want outta this? Fame? Money? Glory? 'Cause I can get you all of it."

"You're sure about that?"

"Oh, dollface, I'm sure as a shitload of sailors on shore leave headin' for a whorehouse."

And Frankie didn't know why, but suddenly he was convinced.

~ ~ ~

The Leonardo DiCaprio movie finished, and Annabelle was bored. Frankie had told her not to go anywhere, but being holed up in a hotel was not to her liking. She sat in the middle of the king-size bed, propped herself up with multiple pillows, and clicked TV channels, coming across *Entertainment Tonight*, a program she sometimes watched, probably because Mark Steines was so damn cute.

Mary Hart was sitting outside on a location shoot with Shia LaBeouf, questioning the young actor about his love life.

Idly, Annabelle watched them interact until a slew of commercials hit the screen.

Back from commercials, a somber-faced Mark Steines announced that he had a breaking news story. As he launched into it, Annabelle realized that he was speaking about her mother's murder: There had been an arrest.

Sitting up straight, she immediately called for Frankie. Then she remembered he was out, securing their future.

Damn. She needed to speak with him. And she needed to speak with him now.

~ ~ ~

"Simon, you limey son of a bitch," Fanny roared into her old-fashioned pink phone perched atop her mirrored desk. Her words carried a mixture of cheery affection and thinly veiled venom. "What's kickin' between *your* big balls today?"

"Fanny Bernstein," declared Simon Waitrose, editor of *Truth & Fact*. "*My* balls are doing fine. How about *yours*, luv? Still big and bouncy?"

"That's my tits, you horny bastard," Fanny cackled.

"How could I ever forget?"

"You got that right, sleazebag. Once seen, never forgotten."

This entire conversation was being played out on speakerphone. Frankie and Rick were Fanny's attentive audience.

Frankie was impressed that she knew exactly who to call and that she had the man's home number, because it was three hours later in New York.

"I presume I must've insulted one of your clients," Simon Waitrose said. "Right, luv? 'Cause why else would the lady herself be calling, interrupting my dinner with a lovely young thing?"

"A date with another hooker, Simon?" Fanny said caustically, winking at her captive audience. "Is she one of Frankie Romano's girls?"

"Oh, Jesus! Don't tell me Frankie Romano is your client," Simon groaned.

"Yes, dear. So I wanna know two things. Who gave you the story? And you'd better e-mail me part two, otherwise there'll be a big fat juicy lawsuit writhing its way up your skinny English ass."

"Goddamn it, Fanny," Simon objected. "Every word we printed is the truth."

"Sure it is, dollface," Fanny warbled. "An' *you* don't use Viagra."

"What?"

"E-mail me part two, then we'll talk."

She hung up with a satisfied smirk, opened her desk drawer, and removed a stack of faxes, which she passed across the desk to Frankie. "Part two," she said. "Read it, then get down on your knees an' thank me."

"But didn't you just ask him to send you part two?" Rick said, sweating, because Fanny refused to put on the air-conditioning. She insisted her office remain eighty-five degrees at all times.

"Simon's main assistant resides in my back pocket, if y'know what I mean," she said with another knowing wink. "Soon as you told me why we were having this meeting, I got on to it. Simon Waitrose deserves to shift his ass for the deal I'm about to offer him."

Frankie was busy reading part two. All of a sudden, he had relatives and friends he never knew existed, and there were photos of him as a kid and quotes from his dad—the fucking loser who used to beat the crap out of him and never came looking when he took off at fifteen. "I don't believe this shit," he said, angrily throwing the faxes back on her desk. "I've never heard of any of these assholes claimin' they were at school with me. As for my dad, we haven't spoken in ten years."

"Not to worry, dollface," Fanny said. "I'll get it stopped. Simon owes me a big one. And in return, after the exclusives with the respectable media—and I use the word *respectable* loosely—we'll throw him a bone. A one-on-one sit-down with Annabelle. So tell me, dollface, where *is* your partner in the selling-flesh business?"

"At the hotel," Frankie said. "We're hiding out so Ralph doesn't get ahold of her. We've heard he's in a raging fury and wants to bury my ass."

"Ah . . . Ralphie." Fanny sighed, a faraway gleam in her eyes. "Had him when I was fifteen and a virgin. It was a one-night stand. He spotted me at a party, sent his stand-in over to see if my tits were real, then took me upstairs and had his way with me." She guffawed at the memory. "Nice cock. Not big enough for me, though."

Once again, Frankie was speechless.

54

Carolyn

Fat Black Pussies wasn't his favorite porno, but it was still turning Benito on. He started thinking about jacking off since Rosa wasn't around to service him.

No food. No pussy. What the fuck was a man supposed to do to keep himself entertained?

Then it occurred to him that there was a perfectly workable pussy lying on his bed. A pussy that was good enough for a senator. And if he jammed his big fat dick into that pussy, maybe it would shift the baby she was carrying, and everyone could go home happy.

Yeah. He'd blindfold her, fuck her, give her a whiff of chloroform, stick her in the trunk of his car, and drop her off on a street corner far enough away that she could never lead anyone back to his cousin's house.

Screw Rosa. He didn't need her. He'd solved the problem all on his own.

He moved toward the door of the bedroom and opened it an inch. The room was dark enough, but he could make out his victim moving around on the bed.

Then just as he was about to fling the door wide open and take his hard-on into the bedroom, the phone rang.

Shit! Bad timing! But in case it was business, he closed the door and picked up the phone.

It was big brother Ramirez.

~ ~ ~

For a moment, Carolyn was paralyzed. Fear crept over her like a shroud of fog, and she found herself unable to move. She'd almost freed herself, then the door had begun to open. But fortunately a phone rang, and whoever was there closed the door and went away.

She was almost too scared to run.

Get it together, her inner voice cried. *At least make an attempt to find a way out of this hellhole. Do it! Do it now!*

After breaking the final tie, she forced her feet to the floor. Her shoes were gone; they must've fallen off when she was first taken. But having no shoes was the least of her problems.

Shaking, she got off the bed and ran to the window, then dragged aside the torn covering.

Outside it was pitch black. She could see nothing.

Her heart was pounding, but she persevered.

The window itself opened outward with a rusty handle. There was no lock and she knew it would be tight, but with a little luck she could squeeze through the limited space. She had to.

Random thoughts flooded her brain.

What if her captors came in the room and pulled her back inside when she was halfway through the window?

What if they were so mad they beat her up, or even *killed* her?

As frightened as she was, there was no going back.

Somehow or other, she began her escape.

~ ~ ~

"Fuck you!" Benito screamed into the phone. "I ain't listenin' to anything ya gotta say."

"Calm down, my brother," Ramirez replied. "All I'm asking is that you come to the center tomorrow and speak with me."

"Why t'fuck I wanna do that?" Benito yelled.

"Word on the street is that you're a target," Ramirez said calmly. "And I can help you."

"Don' fuck wit' me just cuz ya think ya king of the fuckin' do-gooders," Benito sneered. "I got news—anybody get near me, they seein' a war on their mo'fuckin' hands. I got an army behind me."

"What good an army do you if someone put a bullet in your head?" said Ramirez, the voice of reason. "No army gonna save you then."

"Fuck you!" Benito screamed again, then slammed down the phone.

His brother drove him loco, always trying to persuade him to come to the center and repent his ways. Last time he'd gone there, he'd almost gotten shot leaving the place. Rosa's fuckin' baby daddy again. He knew it was time he reversed the situation and blew the mo'fuckin' prick away.

He began going over his conversation with his brother. It wouldn't surprise him if Ramirez was trying to set him up. Get rid of him, so that under the guise of Mister Clean, Ramirez could move in and take over his lucrative drug-running business.

Yeah, that was it. Ramirez was jealous—he wanted what was his.

Too bad. Big brother was getting nothing.

55

Bobby and Denver

We were on our way to the Vegas airport, Bobby and I. When I'd told him about my emergency, he'd insisted on flying me to Washington in his plane in spite of my objections. Then he'd decided he'd better come with me in case I required his assistance in any way.

What was I supposed to do? The text from George Henderson was a desperate cry for help, and although George wasn't asking me to head for Washington, where he and his wife already were, I knew that I had to go. And if the fastest way to get there was on Bobby's plane, so be it.

Carolyn was missing, and not in a "gone away for a few days" kind of way. In a sinister "she's been abducted" kind of way. And everybody who's ever watched the news knew exactly what that meant.

Missing girl more often than not equals rape and murder.

According to George, the police had found Carolyn's car abandoned in a remote spot with the driver's door open, one of her shoes lying on the ground. She had not turned up at work, had missed an arranged breakfast with a neighbor, and had not been seen since noon on Tuesday, when she'd left the office for a supposed dentist appointment. When contacted, her dentist said there *was* no appointment.

I had no idea what I could do to help, but Carolyn was my best friend, and I knew I had to be there, if only to lend moral support to her parents.

I called Felix on my way to the airport to give him a heads-up.

"I don't understand what's the matter with you lately," Felix snapped, his usual charming self. "Do you not care about your job?"

This hurt coming from Felix. Of course I cared. In all the time I'd worked at Saunders, Fields, Simmons & Johnson, I'd always put my job first. Just ask Josh.

Once again, I wondered if the time had come to think about moving on. I was sure I could score an excellent position elsewhere.

Next I phoned my next-door neighbor to let him know I would not be back for a few days, and could he keep Amy Winehouse for me. "She's fine," he assured me. "Not to worry." Then I called my parents.

As soon as I was off the phone, Bobby jumped on my case. "Everything okay?" he asked, being annoyingly solicitous—like *that* was going to make me forget Zeena's revealing little speech, something neither of us had mentioned.

The not-mentioned speech was standing between us like an elephant in the room. Except we weren't in a room—we were in a limo on our way to the airport and Bobby's private plane.

He is *so* not me. What was I thinking?

~ ~ ~

Ever since Bobby realized that he had a certain power because of his heritage, he'd managed to gain control over most situations. He'd learned from both his parents, and even though he was a child when Dimitri passed, he'd studied his late father in photos and on videos and noted the way he acted. Dimitri had always conducted himself with immense charm, compassion, and unwavering control. The three C's.

Lucky had her own way of handling things, and it always seemed to work for her.

Both his parents were tough, loyal, and driven, they both knew what they wanted, and they'd always come out on top.

Bobby desired the same for himself. He realized he'd been born into great privilege, but he'd never allowed himself to get carried away by all the trappings of enormous wealth, and he'd certainly never traded on his exceptional good looks. He'd made a concentrated effort to make it on his own, and he'd succeeded.

One of the things he prided himself on was that he'd always treated women well, making sure to let them down easy when things didn't work out. He'd endeavored to be a good guy.

Now Zeena had managed to make him look like her dumb-ass little plaything. And he was furious. At Zeena. But most of all at himself.

From the moment the words had slipped from Zeena's scarlet lips, Denver had begun to treat him like a vague acquaintance whom she was being forced to spend time with. Sure, she'd agreed to a ride on his plane, but that was out of an urgency to get to Washington, not because she wished to be with him.

He didn't know what to say to her. Should he try explaining? *Uh, Denver, here's the deal: Zeena came into my shower unexpectedly. I never invited her, and, uh, yeah, she did give me head, but uh . . .*

Shit! Where could he possibly go with this?

The first girl he'd liked in a long time, and Zeena had crushed any hope he had of taking it further.

The limo pulled up at the airport, and a special services escort smoothed their path to the plane.

Once aboard, Denver noted where Bobby was sitting and deliberately chose a seat across the aisle. Gitta, one of the attractive flight attendants, asked her if she needed anything. "I'm fine," she said. "Thanks anyway."

"You know," Bobby said, leaning across the aisle, "there's a bedroom aboard, so if you feel like sleeping . . ." He trailed off. Mentioning a bedroom sounded suggestive in a ridiculous kind of way, almost as if he were coming on to her. Which he wasn't. Not at all.

But he'd like to. Oh yes, he'd definitely like to.

The problem was that Zeena had put paid to any chance of that.

~ ~ ~

It's strange. When something dramatic happens in your life, everything else seems unimportant. Two hours ago, I'd been kind of obsessed with Bobby, and right now I couldn't care less. Had I *really* been running around spending all my salary on a sexy designer dress and shoes? Getting my hair done? Enduring the discomfort of stupid false eyelashes and too much makeup? Silly me. I must have lost my mind.

Now all I could think about was Carolyn. Where was she? Had she been abducted, as George Henderson seemed to believe? How did one even begin to search for her?

I didn't have any answers, and for someone who needs to be on top of things, that's frustrating.

Pulling out my phone, I decided to go over the recent texts I'd received from her. Fortunately, I store everything in memory, just in case. Was there a clue somewhere?

The last text I'd received from her was on Monday: *We must talk!! So much happening!!* What did *that* mean? Was she back with Matt, her ex? Had she met someone new?

It had to be about a man; I was sure of it.

I glanced over at Bobby. He was slumped in his seat, probably exhausted after his late-afternoon blow job from the scary-looking superstar. Zeena reminded me of Vampira—a superwoman from another planet.

Still clad in my far too revealing red dress and uncomfortable heels, I grabbed the shopping bag that contained my original clothes, undid my seat belt, and stood up.

A pretty Hawaiian flight attendant who'd introduced herself as Hani rushed to see what I needed. "I'd like to change clothes, Hani," I said. "Is that possible?"

"Certainly," Hani replied with a polite smile. "Follow me."

I followed her into a fully decorated bedroom. A bedroom! On a plane!

There was a queen-size bed, a flat-screen TV, a closet, and a full en suite bathroom complete with a walk-in shower!

I wondered if Bobby had given Zeena a ride on his plane.

No, she probably had her own 747. Megarich people lived in a different world.

I didn't care. All I cared about was finding Carolyn.

~ ~ ~

Denver shut herself in the bedroom and emerged fifteen minutes later dressed in the clothes she'd worn earlier in the day: loose-fitting beige pants, a crisp white shirt, and a slouchy jacket. Her hair was back in a ponytail, and she'd removed most of her makeup.

Bobby thought she looked glowingly beautiful. This girl was a natural beauty, she didn't need all the trimmings. He recalled the great time they'd had in the bar at the Cavendish earlier. The two of them had experienced such a strong connection. He knew it wasn't his imagination; they'd really had major chemistry.

Damn! Why did Zeena have to come along and screw everything up?

"Uh, did you find everything you needed?" he asked, feeling totally off his game.

"I wasn't looking," Denver answered coolly. "Is there a phone I can use?"

Bobby summoned Gitta and asked her to show Denver where the phone was located.

Denver picked up the phone and turned her back on him.

He was dying to know who she was calling. She'd said she didn't have a current boyfriend, but who knew?

He tried reversing the situation in his head. Male singing star announcing to the world that he'd just gone down on Denver. Not a happy thought. It was no surprise she'd closed ranks on him.

He made an attempt to look at the positive side. At least she'd accepted a ride on his plane. Maybe there was some way he could make amends.

Then he thought, *No chance in hell.*

He had a strong hunch that Denver was not the kind of girl who forgave easily.

56

Carolyn

The fear was so overpowering that Carolyn found it hard to breathe. Taking short, desperate gasps of air, she attempted to pace herself and stay focused, for she knew that whatever distress she was in, it was not going to stop her from doing what she had to do. And what she had to do was get the hell out.

She was determined to run from this loathsome place where she'd been treated as subhuman.

Yanking open the window as far as it would go, she was hit with a heavy sheet of rain. But she summoned all the strength she had left, climbed onto the sill, and squeezed her body through the small window. At one point she almost got stuck, but with a supreme effort she forced herself out.

As she hit the ground outside, her bare feet sank into thick mud, and the heavy rain that had been falling all day began to pound her body, soaking her within seconds.

She had no idea where she was. There were no streetlights, and the night was deadly black. Somewhere in the distance she could hear a dog howling and the incessant drone of a helicopter.

Forcing herself into survival mode, she began to run.

~ ~ ~

Muttering and cursing, Benito tried to shake off Ramirez's phone call and return his attention to the porno taking place on the TV screen.

His fuckhead brother had always tormented him, ever since they were kids living in a one-bedroom slum house with a drugged-out mother and no father in sight. It was Ramirez who'd forced him into gang life at the age of twelve, and by the time he was thirteen, Ramirez had him out on the street selling drugs.

Ramirez was a hard-core bad-ass who'd suddenly changed tracks and turned into a self-righteous, hypocritical son of a mo'fuckin' *bitch*. Benito hated his guts.

Staring at the TV screen, he tried to block out memories of when he was a kid.

It took a while, but eventually *Fat Black Pussies* had the desired effect, and his dick began to get hard again—a combination of the raunchy sex he was watching and the hatred and anger he felt toward his brother.

Soon he decided it was time to show the senator's bitch who was really boss.

Abruptly he got up and strode purposefully toward the bedroom door.

57

Annabelle

"What do you mean, they've made an arrest?" Frankie said, scratching his forehead.

Annabelle had jumped on him the moment he'd arrived back at the hotel, not giving him a chance to tell her about Fanny Bernstein and how full of innovative ideas their new manager was.

"Switch on the TV. It's on every channel," Annabelle announced excitedly.

"Who'd they arrest?" Frankie asked. "The stalker?"

"What stalker?" Annabelle stared at him blankly.

Annabelle Maestro was something else. Apparently, she hadn't been following her own mother's murder case.

"There was mention of a stalker," Frankie said. "Some overzealous fan from New Orleans who came to town to worship at Gemma's feet. The cops had him pegged as a person of interest."

"This time they're not saying who it is. All they're saying is that an arrest has been made."

"You must be relieved," Frankie said, pulling a Diet 7Up from the minibar.

"Maybe it's Daddy Dearest," Annabelle suggested with a wicked chuckle.

"Jeez, Annabelle, if it *was* Ralph, we'd all know about it," Frankie said, disgusted that she was not taking this seriously. "And if you're interested in hearin' *my* take on it—even *thinkin'* that Ralph could've done it is pretty sick." A beat. "You might wanna see a shrink about that."

"And *you* might want to see a shrink about your vile coke habit," Annabelle retaliated.

"Listen, babe," he said, backing down from a fight, "there's someone you've got to meet. The woman's a freakin' powerhouse, an' she's the one who's gonna get us out of this mess."

"Exactly *how* is she going to do that?" Annabelle asked with a look of disbelief.

"She'll tell you how when you meet her," Frankie said, holding on to his patience. "Fanny will explain every move we're gonna make."

"And when am I supposed to meet this so-called powerhouse?" Annabelle asked, faking a bored yawn.

"Tonight. Ten o'clock in the garden restaurant at the Chateau Marmont."

"Ten is too late," Annabelle said irritably. "We've been on and off planes all day. I'm exhausted."

"We gotta eat, don't we?" Frankie said, exasperated.

"I suppose so."

"Okay, so let's do it."

"I guess," Annabelle said, less than enthusiastic.

"An' babe, I should warn you," Frankie said, thinking it was best to prepare her for the ball of energy that was Fanny. "This woman is some crazy character. But you gotta believe me, Fanny Bernstein is gonna get us everythin' we want."

~ ~ ~

One look at Fanny, and Annabelle shifted into her snobby, Beverly Hills "I'm better than you" mode.

Fanny got her number immediately. Rich girl. Bitch girl. Movie star's daughter with all the privileges and none of the attention and love. During her long and illustrious reign in Hollywood as a top manager, Fanny had met plenty of girls like Annabelle.

Calm down, she was tempted to say. *You chose to hook up with a coke addict from the wrong side of the tracks. So get off your high horse, honey, and let's discuss your future.*

Annabelle offered a limp handshake, appalled that Frankie was even thinking of doing business with this hot mess of a woman.

Fanny rejected the handshake and moved in for a hug, repulsing Annabelle even more as she found herself enveloped in Poison, her most unfavorite scent.

"Fanny Bernstein," Frankie said, "meet Annabelle Maestro, the love of my life."

Fanny winked at Annabelle as they settled at an outdoor table. "Doesn't that corny bullshit make you wanna throw up?" she cackled.

Annabelle couldn't help agreeing.

"It's men, dollface," Fanny continued. "They all spew forth the same tired old lines. Y'know what I'm sayin'?" And then, affecting a deep male voice, she said, "Damn, you look beautiful tonight. No, your ass doesn't look big in that dress. Sure I'll buy you a new car. How about sucking my pee-pee, darlin'? I promise not to cum in your mouth."

Unable to help herself, Annabelle broke up laughing. This woman in the outrageous purple caftan with the huge earrings, orange hair, and loud mouth was hilarious.

"I slipped that one to the prez," Fanny confided. "The horny bastard ate it up. The truth always gets a big haw-haw."

Annabelle didn't like to ask which president she was referring to. Probably Clinton. Not Bush, and certainly not Obama.

Frankie relaxed. He'd been nervous about putting Annabelle together with Fanny, but now he could see why Fanny was so successful. She knew how to play it, and before long she had Annabelle completely under the Fanny Bernstein spell.

~ ~ ~

Back in New York, Janey Bonafacio was in a state of deep panic. Not only had her son run off with what she was sure was a formidable payment for selling the story of Annabelle and Frankie's business venture to a tabloid, but she was left to deal with the fallout—and there was considerable fallout. The phones hadn't stopped ringing. Reporters and paparazzi were staked outside the swanky apartment house, much to the fury of Annabelle's snooty neighbors. Clients were threatening that if their names were revealed, there would be major lawsuits. And some of the so-called celebrity girls, their identities disclosed, had actually turned up at the front door ready to kill Frankie and Annabelle or whoever else was available.

Janey was a nervous wreck. But even though Frankie had spoken to her in such a harsh way over the phone, she still harbored a soft spot for him. He was still *her* Frankie, and because it was Chip who'd done such a reprehensible thing, she felt that in a way she was responsible.

According to one of her neighbors who had a key to her apartment in Queens, Chip had vanished. Packed up all his stuff and taken a midnight run. Which was just as well, because when pushed, Janey had a formidable temper, and she would have felt no guilt taking it out on her good-for-nothing son.

Anyone else would've abandoned the Park Avenue apartment and run for the hills. But Janey remained loyal, hoping that when Frankie got back to New York, he would forgive her.

~ ~ ~

"It's settled, then," Fanny said, attacking the shared dessert plate set in the middle of the table. "We all know what we have to do?"

Annabelle nodded. She felt a lot more secure now that Fanny had taken over.

"Outfit?" Fanny questioned, just to make sure Annabelle had absorbed her instructions for tomorrow's funeral.

"Black," Annabelle said obediently. "Not pants, a skirt—"

"Of a decent length," Fanny interrupted.

"No jewelry except my Maltese cross. Very little makeup. Dark shades."

"Perfect," Fanny said, her fork heading for another scoop of chocolate cake. "And you, Frankie?"

"Yeah, yeah, I got it," he said restlessly. "Nothin' flashy, keep my mouth shut whatever happens."

"Don't worry. I'll be there to make sure Ralph doesn't turn on you. Which is unlikely because the press'll be out in force, and Ralph's an actor, so he'll never risk besmirching his movie-star reputation by doing anything stupid in front of the cameras."

"How about after?" Annabelle questioned. "Do we go back to the house?"

"We'll play that one by ear," Fanny said, a dribble of chocolate trickling down her chin.

"Done deal," Frankie said.

"Yes, it is," Fanny agreed, reaching for a forkful of cheesecake. "Oh, and Frankie, we'll be doing the *People* magazine interview in the afternoon, so keep your coke intake to a minimum, and no telltale white powder decorating your nose."

"Hey—" Frankie began to say.

"Don't bother," Fanny stopped him. "I've heard every excuse in the book, and I couldn't give a monkey's left ball about what you do on your own time. But when we're working, no drugs. Got it?"

Annabelle smiled. Finally someone who could control Frankie. What a bonus!

58

Carolyn

Grabbing his crotch as he once again approached the door to the bedroom, Benito turned the handle. He was good and hard, which meant that the senator's bitch was in for a treat now. She was about to get the real deal, not some old dude's limp dick. Benito Ortego was a man to be reckoned with.

The bedroom was in darkness, but he planned on blindfolding his victim anyway—a security measure in case she ever tried to identify him. Yeah, he'd blindfold her, then put on the light so he could see exactly what kind of pussy he was getting.

As he entered the room, he was hit with a freezing rush of cold air coming from the window. Rosa, the stupid douche, must've opened it for some reason. The place was like a mo'fuckin' iceberg.

Then, as he groped his way over to the bed, he realized with a combination of shock and disbelief that his captive was no longer there.

Shit! The fuckin' bitch had escaped!

~ ~ ~

Rosa's eyes flickered open. One eye, actually—because her right eye was throbbing and covered with a heavy dressing.

She attempted to speak, but she couldn't do more than let out a croak since her mouth was so dry.

"Where am I?" she tried to say.

A nurse appeared. "Stay quiet, dear," she said in a soothing voice. "I'll let the doctor know you're awake."

"I want my mama," Rosa whimpered, reverting to the scared teenager she was.

The nurse paged Dr. Glass, who appeared fifteen minutes later.

As soon as the doctor saw that the girl was conscious and talking, she called Detective Lennox.

"Something came up, I'm on another case," the detective said, not sounding too pleased about it. "I'm goin' to send someone else to take her statement."

"You're not coming yourself?" asked Dr. Glass, strangely disappointed.

"Missing woman. Senator's assistant," Detective Lennox explained. "By tomorrow the press'll be all over it. The chief already is."

"I understand," Dr. Glass said.

"If things clear up, maybe I'll stop by tomorrow, speak to the girl myself." A pause. "You on duty tomorrow?"

"All day."

"See you then."

Dr. Glass returned her attention to her patient.

"I want my mama," Rosa repeated, tears streaming down her cheek. "I want her to come here *now*."

~ ~ ~

"What can I do for you, Ramirez?" Gregory asked over the phone, keeping his voice neutral. He'd made up his mind that it was wise to get the phone call over with, find out what Ramirez wanted.

"It's about my brother," Ramirez said.

"Your brother?" Gregory questioned, swallowing hard. Had Ramirez found out what was going on? Was it possible that Benito had ratted him out?

Jesus Christ! The shit was about to fly.

"I need to speak with you about him," Ramirez continued. "Can you come by the center early tomorrow? It's urgent."

Ramirez might as well have said, *Bring plenty of money, 'cause I'm about to blackmail your dumb white ass.*

Gregory bit down hard on his lower lip. Yes, he was dumb, for what he'd put into motion was unforgivable.

"I'll be there," he said gruffly.

~ ~ ~

Stepping on something sharp caused an excruciating pain to shoot through Carolyn's foot. She let out a cry. God! Wasn't it enough that she was drenched, freezing, and running for her life? Now this.

As her eyes became acclimated to the dark, she began to get her bearings and realized she was running down an alley filled with overflowing garbage cans, overgrown weeds, abandoned cars, old furniture, and rotting mattresses.

A rat scurried across her path. Stifling a scream, she kept going. She had to get as far away from the house as fast as possible. If her captors discovered she was gone and came looking for her, what then?

It wasn't something she cared to think about.

59

Denver

Bobby had suddenly become like one of those annoying big dogs that one is constantly tripping over.

He didn't know how to back off. It was apparent he'd never had to.

Go back to Vegas and let Zeena blow you from here to the next Lakers game, I had a yen to say. But of course I didn't. That's the "not into hurting people's feelings" side of me.

Sometimes I can be such a wimp. Or a bit of a hypocrite, depending on how you look at it. I'd gone off Bobby because he'd gotten head from some scary superstar who'd announced their sex tryst from the stage. But in the last few days I've had excellent sex with two different men, so I'm hardly a vestal virgin!

Still . . . when Bobby and I had drinks together, I'd definitely felt the spark of something special happening. So having him run straight off to get blown by Queen Vampira was a bit of a downer to my ego.

But hey—it wasn't as if we'd slept together, or even kissed. So maybe I was making too big a thing of it.

I settled back in my seat and tried to catch a few hours' sleep. I'd need all the energy I could muster when we arrived.

It was late by the time we landed in Washington—three A.M. on Thursday morning Vegas time, six A.M. local Washington time. I didn't care about the time; I had every intention of meeting up with Carolyn's parents to find out what was happening.

"They'll probably be asleep," Bobby said.

"Are you kidding me?" I gave him a withering look. "Would *your* mom be asleep if *you* were on the missing list?"

"You've got a point," he said, nodding his handsome head.

I might have gone off him, but that didn't mean I couldn't still appreciate his spectacular looks. *Dammit!*

While we were winging our way to Washington, Bobby had made arrangements; he was obviously a master at that. A car to meet us at the airport. God, I hoped it wasn't another limo. A two-bedroom suite in the same hotel as the Hendersons. That didn't bother me because I had no intention of sleeping, and at least it would serve as a base.

A few minutes before the plane landed, Bobby felt it necessary to say something about the Zeena incident. He'd obviously been building up to the great explanation.

"Uh, Denver, there's something I should explain about Zeena," he said, sounding mighty uncomfortable. "Y'see, she's uh . . . a very demanding woman, goes for what she wants whenever she wants it. And, uh . . . yesterday, what she wanted happened to be me."

"I kind of get that," I said, refusing to help out.

"Yeah, well, I was taking a shower, and she suddenly appeared out of nowhere. Now, I know I should've told her to get out, but—"

"Hey—" I said, quickly stopping him from making any more excuses. "You don't have to account for anything to me. We hardly know each other, Bobby. It's none of my business."

"But it is," he insisted. "We spent time together earlier, and it was so great." He took a long beat. "You've got to understand that the Zeena thing meant nothing to me."

"Apparently it meant something to her," I said, still refusing to let him down easy.

"I've come up with this crazy idea," he said.

"What?"

"Why don't we forget about what happened, and consider returning to square one?" he suggested, dark eyes locked sincerely on mine. "How does that sound to you, Denver? 'Cause it sounds real good to me."

God! The man was irresistible. Any other time I probably would've forgiven him in a flash. But right now my mind was on Carolyn, and getting involved was nowhere near the top of my agenda.

"Look, I get it," I said, weakening. "No hard feelings." Suddenly I found myself grinning stupidly. "Did that sound like a pun?"

He grinned back at me. "Yeah, as a matter of fact it did."

We exchanged a long, meaningful look. Then he said something very special. "Right now we should concentrate all our energy on finding your friend. I'm here for you, Denver, and I'll do everything I can to help you. But after that, it's a new beginning for us. Right?"

And like a lovesick fool, I found myself murmuring, "Right."

60

Carolyn

Alarm and fury propelled Benito into action.

His alarm was about the woman remembering the location of his house and fingering him as her kidnapper.

His fury was about her getting away in the first place.

How long had the senator's bitch been gone? He didn't know. It couldn't have been that long.

Had Rosa helped her? Was that why she'd run out on him? Had she left the window open and untied their prisoner?

Shit! Shit! Shit!

She could've already reached the cops and told them where he lived.

He was not going back to jail. No fucking way. If the cops arrested him, he'd spill everything in exchange for a deal. Senator Stoneman would be the one taking the rap for this fucked-up mess, not him.

Maybe he wasn't too late, he thought, grabbing his gun on the way out to his car. Maybe he could catch her and drag her back to the house.

The only way she was leaving was when *he* said so.

~ ~ ~

By the time Carolyn ran out of the alley and reached the street, she was soaked to the skin, her foot was bleeding, and she knew she had to get help.

Looking up and down the run-down street, she realized she was in a bad part of the city, most likely somewhere in the southeast quarter, a notorious, crime-ridden area.

There was no one around, most of the streetlights were broken, and the only place open was a bar on the corner.

She limped toward it, the pain in her foot excruciating.

If only she could get to a phone . . . that's all she needed to be safe. One phone call to the police, and they'd come get her.

Outside the bar, she pushed the wooden door to gain entry.

A big man stood inside the doorway, blocking her way. Arms crossed against a massive chest, he yelled, "Get the fuck outta here, ya filthy, stinkin' cunt! How many times I gotta tell ya vagrants that ya ain't gotta come around here."

"But I've—"

He wasn't having it. Red in the face and angry, he was not prepared to listen. In one fell swoop, he grabbed her around the waist and propelled her outside, shoving her so hard that she fell in the gutter.

"An' don't come back!" he shouted, slamming the door.

This was impossible. She'd escaped a devastating kidnapping, and now she was being treated like a piece of garbage.

Slowly, she picked herself up.

A homeless man walked by, pushing a shopping cart. Dressed in rags, he had an American flag wrapped around his head and a mangy dog trailing behind him.

She ran over to him and begged for help.

"Wanna get a feel?" he guffawed, exposing himself to her. "You're gonna cream over my piece of meat, girly. C'mon, help yourself, gimme a lickin'. No charge."

She turned and started running down the street again, avoiding a drunk who spat at her and two transvestites who ignored her when she tried to ask for help.

She passed two public phone booths, both with broken phones dangling by the cords.

Finally she realized that until it was light, it was too dangerous to be out on the street.

She ducked inside the covered doorway of a pawnshop and huddled in the litter-filled corner, exhausted and scared.

All she could do was wait for daylight and pray that she would survive the night.

~ ~ ~

When his car wouldn't start, Benito flew into a rage. This was no time for his piece-of-shit car to break down! And the pissing rain didn't help.

He tried to start the car again, with no success. The battery spluttered for a second, then died.

He had to get moving and search for the senator's bitch, but how was he supposed to do that with no car?

Then he remembered that Rosa's mother had an old Buick. It sat outside her house doing nothing. So fuck it, he'd take it. Too bad.

Pulling up his hoodie to ward off the rain, he set off to cover the ten blocks to Rosa's mother's house.

His taking her precious mama's car would be Rosa's punishment for running out on him. *Puta!* She would pay for her behavior.

61

Bobby

Bobby was convinced he'd made some headway with Denver regarding the Zeena debacle. He'd tried to explain exactly what had taken place, and to his relief, after ignoring him for most of the flight, she'd seemed pretty cool about it. She'd even ended up smiling at him—a *most* positive sign.

He was glad he'd been able to provide his plane to take her to Washington. There were some perks of his multimillion-dollar heritage he could choose to take advantage of.

He was also pleased that he'd decided to accompany her. Although he was sure M.J. and his bride and Brigette and her girlfriend would hardly be thrilled to discover their absence. Not to mention the absence of the plane. They were probably all bitching that he'd deserted them.

Too bad. He was in pursuit of a girl he wanted, and for once he was throwing caution out the window. Lucky would definitely approve of his actions. She was a staunch proponent of going after what you wanted.

The bottom line was that Denver was special. And if he had his way, they'd end up being special together.

Meanwhile, he had every intention of helping her find her missing friend, and since Lucky had connections across the board, he'd called her from the plane and asked if there was anything she could do to help.

After asking a few relevant questions, Lucky was her usual brilliant self. She promised to make a few phone calls. Naturally she knew people in Washington, including the chief of police. Lucky's intervention didn't mean they would automatically find Carolyn, but it did mean that everyone concerned would be putting in their best effort.

He decided against telling Denver. It was probably better that way.

62

Denver

Tentatively, I knocked on the door of the Hendersons' hotel room. I'd asked Bobby not to come with me. This was no time for introductions. Reluctantly, he'd stayed in the suite.

George Henderson answered the door. A tall man with salt-and-pepper hair and an easy charm, he looked totally drained. I could see the pain in his eyes. And for a moment, I wondered about the source of that anguish: Was it because Carolyn was missing, or did it have something to do with Gemma Summer's murder?

Whatever. The man was in a distressed state.

Even though I hadn't seen him in a couple of years, we embraced, and in a choked-up voice he said, "Thanks for coming, Denver. It means a lot to me and Clare."

Clare, his wife, emerged from the bathroom. Once a very attractive woman, she was now thin and gaunt, with dark shadows under her eyes and a mass of tangled graying hair. I was shocked at her appearance.

It occurred to me that this deterioration in her appearance could not have taken place just in the last twenty-four hours. This was a disturbed woman. Whatever she was going through, Carolyn's disappearance had only added to the mix.

"Hi," I said, taking a firm step toward her, ready to hug her, too.

She backed away like a nervous filly. After an awkward moment, she said, "Where do *you* think my daughter is?"

There was almost an accusatory note in her voice, as if I *should* know, and if I didn't, I was of no use to her.

"I'm so sorry, Mrs. Henderson," I said quietly. "I don't know where Carolyn could be."

"But you girls talk all the time, I know you do," Clare said, a hostile gleam in her weary, red-rimmed eyes.

"No, we don't," I said, shocked at this bitter, angry woman who in no way resembled the soft-spoken woman I remembered from my youth. Carolyn and I used to hang out at the Hendersons' house, and sometimes Clare Henderson baked us cookies and drove us to the mall. That woman with the softly styled hair and kindly demeanor was gone.

"Perhaps you can bring me up-to-date on everything," I said, turning to George.

"Oh, he can bring you up-to-date all right," Clare said, her voice rising. "He can tell you all about the affair he was having with his murdered movie-star girlfriend." She paused to glare at him. "*That's* why Carolyn is missing. It's karma. George's punishment. And mine."

Finished with her rant, Clare collapsed on the end of the unmade bed, sobbing hysterically.

George looked at me despairingly—a look that said, *What's done is done. I can't take anything back.*

"I'm sorry," I said in a low voice. "But shouldn't we be concentrating on finding Carolyn?"

"Of course," George said. "I received a call from a Detective Lennox. He'd like us to come over to the precinct as soon as possible. From the sound of him, he certainly seems more cooperative than yesterday when we arrived. I'm hoping they'll have good news for us."

Being summoned to the precinct didn't sound like good news to me. Had they found Carolyn's body? Was *that* the good news?

Suddenly, the enormity of what was going on washed over me. My best friend was missing. And there was a strong possibility she was dead.

63

Hank Montero—The Wild Card

The recession had hit everyone hard, especially Hank Montero—former actor, stunt double, property master, mechanic, and finally housepainter. Hank, a good-looking guy in a rough-and-ready way, had always managed to pull down a steady income. First as an actor—not successful. Second as a stunt double—until he got badly injured and was on Social Security disability benefits for a year. Next, he'd gotten himself a job as property master for a TV commercial company, but cash went missing, and unfortunately, Hank got the blame. He'd tried being a mechanic, but after he'd taken some rich dude's Ferrari on a joyride and smashed the car against a brick wall, breaking a leg in the process, he'd gotten fired. Finally, an old acquaintance from a short spell he'd done in prison for grievous bodily harm (he'd beaten the schmuck with the Ferrari—long story) offered him a part-time job housepainting. That job lasted until he screwed the woman whose house he was painting, and the woman's husband came home unexpectedly and caught him rear-ending his devout Christian wife.

Jobless, he'd jumped on anything that came his way.

Meanwhile, his third wife was pissed, his two teenage kids (a goth and a slut) were pissed, and his house was in foreclosure.

Hank Montero was a desperate man when he got an offer that was to change his life.

And change his life it did.

But that was before his insane nineteen-year-old ex-stripper current wife tried to shoot him in the nuts with his own unlicensed stolen handgun. A nosy neighbor reported the incident to the cops, and since they had nothing better to do, two cops had turned up at his house. After ascertaining he had no permit for his gun—and noticing the hefty stash of cocaine his wife had left in full view on the kitchen table—they'd hauled him down to the precinct.

Which would've been fine. *If the gun hadn't been the same one that shot the big movie star Gemma Summer.*

Hank Montero was fucked.

64

Carolyn

Benito hit the street fast, his anger propelling him through the driving rain until he reached the run-down house where Rosa's mama lived.

Sure enough, her beat-up old Buick was parked right outside. He tried the handle. The lock was broken, so the door swung open easily.

The interior of the car smelled like old cabbage and sweat, and one of the side windows was shattered. But what did he care? He had only one purpose in mind, and that was finding the senator's bitch.

After hot-wiring the car, he eased out of the parking space and took off, soon realizing that the Buick was an even worse piece of shit than his own car.

Sticking to the curb, he crawled along, keeping a sharp watch for the senator's bitch. She couldn't have gotten far. Besides, he was feeling lucky, and when Benito felt lucky, nothing stopped him.

~ ~ ~

Shutting her eyes tightly, Carolyn tried to pretend she was safely home, but the noise of cars roaring past kept her on alert. Down the street, a bunch of gangbangers had appeared, and there was some sort of drag race going on. Men were screaming and yelling at one another as their souped-up cars raced up and down the street. She could hear glass breaking and girls shouting their encouragement in shrill, drunken voices.

The more noise the gangbangers made, the tighter she squeezed into her corner, terrified that one of them would spot her. She'd often read stories about homeless people being tortured, then set on fire simply for sport. And she was well aware that's exactly what she must look like, a homeless person with nowhere to go.

Would they help her?

No. She didn't think so. Self-preservation told her it was safer to stay exactly where she was until it started to get light.

~ ~ ~

Rosa's mother, Florita, got to the hospital way beyond visiting hours. But after she'd explained to the night-duty nurse that she'd had to find someone to sit with her daughter's baby, and then discovered her car had been stolen, the nurse let her through.

Rosa sobbed when she saw her mama, genuine tears of regret that she'd never listened to anything her mama had to say, that she'd always thought she knew better.

Florita, a small, compact woman with a ruddy complexion and work-worn hands, hugged her only daughter, tears filling her eyes. "*Mi chiquita,*" Florita crooned, rocking Rosa back and forth in her arms. "*Mi amorcita.*"

Then she'd begun a rant in Spanish all about how Benito was the lowest of the low. He must be the one responsible for this terrible thing. She should never have allowed Rosa to spend so much time with such a *bastardo*.

Rosa was too beaten up to argue. She wasn't fluent in Spanish, although she got the gist of what her mama was saying, and she was inclined to agree with her.

In Rosa's heart, she knew that what Benito had done was criminal and bad. Kidnapping the senator's woman was wrong, and lying in a hospital bed, Rosa realized she had to tell someone, explain that it wasn't *her* doing.

"Mama," she whispered, "I have something to tell you . . ."

~ ~ ~

Keeping a sharp lookout, Benito continued to hug the curb, driving as slowly as possible without the crappy car stalling. She couldn't've got far, he kept telling himself. He'd seen her lying on the bed less than an hour before she'd vanished.

He should've kept the bitch trussed up like a chicken, but Rosa had said securing her wrist would do.

Rosa—another dumb bitch. He would surely punish her for running out on him.

As he drove down the main street, he noticed activity ahead—a group of dudes drag racing. Then, with a flash of realization, it dawned on him that he'd ventured out of his comfort zone into a part of town Rosa's baby daddy and his cohorts ruled.

It was *their* territory. *Their* street.

Shit! It wasn't as if he were in his own car.

No, but he was in Rosa's mama's Buick.

Fuck! Better get out of here before they saw him. Better get out fast.

~ ~ ~

Carolyn heard the sound of tires squealing on the wet street. The noise, the yelling. And then to her horror she heard gunshots somewhere in the distance.

She covered her ears. This had to be her worst nightmare.

Huddling deep into her corner, she prayed for morning.

65

Bobby

Prowling restlessly around the suite, Bobby felt helpless. He wasn't used to being sidelined, and it pissed him off. He would've preferred going with Denver to see the Hendersons, but she'd decided it wasn't a good idea. And since he hadn't wanted to push it, he'd stayed behind.

After ordering coffee from room service, he switched on the TV. The *Today* show was in progress, Matt Lauer interviewing yet another politician accused of cheating on his wife with a hooker.

Recognizing the guy's name, Bobby realized the man had been outed in the tabloid piece on Annabelle and Frankie. The poor ill-advised bastard was actually on TV attempting to defend himself. What a dumb-ass move.

The interview with the politician ended, and on came the news. The lead story was all about the arrest of a suspect in the Gemma Summer murder case. The newscaster stated that the police were not revealing the name of the person who'd been arrested.

Bobby immediately thought of Denver. Was she aware that an arrest had been made? Probably not.

Well, one thing he knew for sure: She'd want to hear the news at once. Especially as her boss was Ralph Maestro's attorney.

Checking with the front desk, he got the number of the Hendersons' room. He now had an excellent excuse to go there.

Fuck it. Denver was not getting rid of him that easily. He was there to help her find her friend, and help her he would. No more sitting around in the background. That wasn't his style.

66

Denver

I must say that I was kind of delighted when Bobby arrived in time to accompany us to the police station. Yes, I'll admit it: I'm relieved that he's here with me. Usually I'm superconfident that I'm able to deal with any situation, but imagining what could've happened to Carolyn was making me queasy.

I'm not a very religious person, but all I could think was, *Please, God, let her be alive.*

Horrific scenarios kept running through my head. I remembered reading about the girl who was buried alive and found three months later. Another shocking case was the serial killer who'd dismembered his victims—including several young women—and buried them under his house. Then there was the famous case of Washington intern Chandra Levy, whose remains were discovered in a park thirteen months after her disappearance.

Chandra had worked for a politician with whom she'd been having an affair.

For a moment I thought about Carolyn's boss, Senator Gregory Stoneman. Carolyn had often spoken about him in glowing terms. I'd once accused her of having a crush on him, and she'd become most defensive instead of laughing it off.

I thought about her last text: *We must talk!! So much happening!!* And her text before that: *Call me as soon as you get this. I have major news.*

What was her major news? And what did *So much happening!!* mean?

I wondered if the police had spoken to the senator. If they hadn't, I decided to suggest that they should.

As soon as he arrived, I introduced Bobby to the Hendersons. By this time, Clare was a tad calmer.

Bobby, who did not know about George's involvement with Gemma Summer, filled me in on the Gemma Summer arrest.

I noticed George go on major alert. He was obviously desperate to ask questions, but he refrained from doing so.

At least *he* wasn't the shooter, merely the lover.

Bobby had a car and a driver waiting downstairs. Thank goodness it was a low-key sedan and not a flashy limousine.

"We'll all ride together," I suggested to the Hendersons. They agreed.

It was too early in L.A. for me to call Felix and hear the news about who'd been arrested. My money was on the stalker, but believe me, I couldn't wait to find out everything.

67

Hank Montero—The Wild Card

Hank Montero was no virgin when it came to police questioning, but the two Beverly Hills cops who'd arrested him were relentless. They'd kept him in a room all night, asking him the same questions over and over. His head was reeling, it was so intense. And Hank Montero did not do well with intense.

It was all his damn wife's fault. Pinky, the nineteen-year-old ex-stripper with the foreign accent and huge bouncy boobs. She'd been after a green card, and he'd been cross-eyed at the thought of spending leisurely nights playing with those boobs. But it all turned sour as soon as he married her, what with the house going into foreclosure and his two appalling kids—the goth and the slut—both of whom flatly refused to leave home.

After they were married, Pinky had stopped stripping, turned into a nagging shrew, and announced that her boobs were off-limits.

Damn! What was a man supposed to do?

He'd taken a bad-ass job he'd known was wrong, collected the money, stashed it in a safe-deposit box in his name only, and celebrated by screwing their next-door neighbor—a flat-chested Southern bleached blonde who made up for her lack of boobs by behaving like a maniac in bed.

Unfortunately, Pinky had come home early from her latest job at Hooters, caught him at it, gone for his gun, and made a dangerously close pass at shooting him in the balls.

The Southern blonde had run from their house, a neighbor had called the cops, and all would've been fine if Pinky hadn't left a pound of coke on the kitchen table. Yeah, as a sideline she dealt coke for a neighborhood thug. Lovely girl.

The cops had hauled everyone down to the station.

Later, when they'd checked out his gun, they'd discovered it was the same weapon used to kill Gemma Summer.

Big whoopee.

Hank was well aware that they had him in their clutches and they weren't letting go anytime soon.

Unless . . . he could make a deal.

68

Annabelle

Following Fanny's orders, Annabelle dressed down, all in black. With her pale red hair, her favorite diamond Maltese cross nestled at her neck, and a more subtle makeup, the effect was startling. She looked a little like her famous mother.

Staring at herself in the mirror, she was conflicted. Half of her wanted to run back to New York, hide away in her apartment, and not speak to anyone. The other half wanted to face the world and fuck 'em all, as Frankie was prone to say.

But could she maintain that attitude?

She wasn't as strong as everyone seemed to imagine. And the thought of facing Ralph—Big Daddy—at the funeral was making her stomach cramp up.

Ralph in a fury was a frightening sight to behold. She remembered that as a child, she would run and hide in a closet whenever her father lost his temper.

Annabelle decided she needed more than Frankie and Fanny to bolster her confidence. She needed Denver by her side. Her old school friend was so together, always exuding total confidence. That's what Annabelle needed, a positive person who had nothing to gain by being there for her.

Denver had promised to accompany her to the funeral. But that was before the embarrassing headline story in *Truth & Fact*. Denver probably wanted nothing to do with her now that she'd been painted as a goddamn madam! Besides, Denver was on Ralph's side; she worked for his lawyer.

All the same, she knew that Denver was a good person, and perhaps if she contacted her, they could work something out.

~ ~ ~

Frankie had a lot going on. Contrary to backing off, Rick Greco was hot to get into business with him. They'd started talking about creating a new club situation, maybe involving Bobby and M.J. if they were interested.

Fanny Bernstein had turned out to be a star. She knew everyone and was proceeding full speed ahead. He and Annabelle had already signed a letter of agreement giving Fanny twenty-five percent of future earnings. Fanny wasn't one to sit around.

"I'll be talking to Bravo, E!, and MTV about a reality TV show next week," she'd informed him. "You'll hang out in L.A. until we go to New York for Annabelle to appear on *The View.* Stick with the big picture, Frankie. You'll be shifting to L.A. permanently, so get your skinny ass moving."

Frankie hadn't revealed that golden nugget of news to Annabelle. Right now she was agitated, so he had to handle her with care. Hopefully after the funeral she'd return to her usual self, then they could both start enjoying their upcoming success.

Frankie Romano, media star. It had a winning ring.

Yeah! Finally! Frankie Romano was going to be famous!

~ ~ ~

Fanny Bernstein didn't just enjoy funerals, she reveled in them. Funerals to Fanny were not a place to mourn the dead, they were a place to cement old connections and forge new ones, a place to see and be seen; to talk about future projects and make lunch arrangements. Fanny had never come across an opportunity she didn't embrace, and funerals were full of opportunities—especially if the deceased was a famous person.

The Gemma Summer funeral should be a hotbed of new and interesting connections. And Fanny was certain she'd have an excellent seat, because she'd be walking in with her two new clients.

Surprise, surprise, Ralph Maestro. Let's observe your reaction to this little play.

Fanny selected a black ruffled dress, enormous earrings, sparkling silver slippers (high heels hurt her feet), and many silver bracelets.

Eventually she was good to go.

~ ~ ~

Preparing for his wife's funeral, Ralph Maestro chose what clothes he would wear.

Gemma was dead. *He* would be the center of attention; every eye would be on *him*. And not all of them for the right reasons, thanks to his dear daughter, Annabelle.

Annabelle Maestro. A rebellious child, an impossible teenager . . . and now, as an adult, she'd brought disgrace to the Maestro name, humiliating him beyond redemption.

His first instinct had been to separate her from her sleazy boyfriend, drag her back to the house, and shake some sense into her—hence his fast trip to Vegas. But when he couldn't find her in Vegas—no doubt she'd fled back to New York—he'd changed his mind.

The solution to Annabelle was to cut her off, disown her, allow her to bury herself in her own filthy profession. He was through.

Lupe buzzed his dressing room. "Meester Saunders ees here," she announced. "An' Meester Peep."

"Tell them I'll be right down," Ralph said, fixing his tie. A recent purchase. Black silk. Six hundred and fifty dollars.

Every eye would be on him.

69

Carolyn

At first light, Carolyn awoke from a half-sleep with a start. She was freezing, every bone in her body ached, her mouth was parched, and her foot was still throbbing. Yet she felt elated because she'd managed to survive the night, and now she was certain she'd find someone on the street who'd help her, or at least call the police on her behalf.

Gingerly she stood up, barely able to feel her feet. The rain had finally stopped, but it was still bitterly cold.

Was it safe to venture out of her hiding place?

She wasn't sure.

She peered down the street. The neighborhood she was in seemed derelict. There were several vacant lots littered with garbage, rusting half-finished buildings protected by broken construction fencing, packs of stray dogs, and one small market that was closed.

At least it was daylight and she was still alive. So was her baby. She patted her stomach and set off down the street. There had to be a police station or a post office, someplace official where she could get help.

~ ~ ~

Florita swore her daughter to silence when Rosa had confessed how she'd helped Benito kidnap the senator's woman. Florita crossed herself, sank to her knees, then in Spanish begged the Lord for her daughter's redemption.

"You will never see that *cabrón desgraciado* again," she wailed when she was finished praying. "The moment you leave the hospital, I send you to your cousin in Guatemala."

"No, Mama, no," Rosa protested. "What about my baby?"

"For your protection," Florita admonished, wringing her hands, "I look after baby. You stay away. This a very bad thing you have done, Rosa. *Estúpido*. But God will watch over you, *mi amorcita*. He will be your Savior."

Rosa nodded. Mama was right. God had punished her for doing a bad thing. Now God would protect her.

~ ~ ~

Senator Gregory Stoneman left his house early on Thursday. He'd spent a restless night contemplating why Ramirez wanted to see him. Ramirez had said it was urgent and that it was something concerning his brother, so as Gregory approached the community center, he was prepared for the worst.

If it was blackmail, he'd pay up. He had no damn choice.

Carolyn was also on his mind.

Where was she? What had Benito done with her? He was supposed to have taken her for a few hours, shaken her up until she lost the baby, and then let her loose. It was now two days and there was no sign of her.

What if they'd harmed her? Could he be held responsible?

Jesus Christ! *What had he done?*

70

Denver

On the way to the precinct, I opted to sit up front with the driver, leaving Bobby in the back with the Hendersons.

It was already eight A.M. in Washington, which meant it was five A.M. on the West Coast. I didn't dare disturb Felix, but I had no qualms about waking my intern, Megan. Pulling out my cell from my purse, I decided to do just that.

What a surprise, the girl was awake!

Thinking she was an early riser, I said, "Megan, getting up early is a very positive way to start the day. You'll get so much extra work accomplished."

"Actually," Megan replied with a most unbusinesslike giggle, "I'm just getting home."

Oh, great! Was she drunk? I couldn't tell.

"I need a report on the Maestro case," I said briskly. "I understand there's been an arrest. Who is it?"

"Who's what?" Megan asked, her words followed by a couple of random hiccups.

Ah yes, unfortunately my brainy little intern was totally wasted.

"Does the firm know who's been arrested?" I said, all business.

"Dunno," she replied.

"Find out and call me back," I said tersely. "I'm on my cell."

"Will do," Megan said. This was followed by a series of muffled giggles.

Megan was not alone.

Half of me wished I were in L.A., finding out for myself what was going on. The other half knew I was exactly where I should be, trying to discover the truth about Carolyn's disappearance.

71

Bobby

Detective Lennox was a tall man, lean and weathered, with terse features, knowing eyes, and a deep voice.

Bobby thought he looked like a man who knew what he was doing, and Denver's initial reaction toward him was positive. To both of them, he seemed like a man in charge.

"Mr. and Mrs. Henderson," Detective Lennox said, ushering the distressed couple toward his office. "Please follow me."

Bobby and Denver were right behind them.

Detective Lennox stopped for a moment and held up an authoritative hand. "And you are . . . ?"

"Friends," Denver said quickly. "I'm a lawyer, Carolyn's closest friend."

"We have no need for a lawyer," Detective Lennox said, dismissing her with a wave of his hand. It was a move that did not go down well with Bobby.

"Ms. Jones is not here in an official capacity," Bobby interrupted, asserting himself. Denver threw him an appreciative glance. "I'm Bobby Santangelo," he continued. "We're ready to assist in any way we can, and we'd appreciate all the cooperation you can give us. We all have the same goal—and that's to find Carolyn as quickly as possible. Right?"

The detective nodded. When word had filtered down from the chief to treat this case as a high priority, he'd heard the name Santangelo mentioned somewhere along the way.

"Well," Detective Lennox said uncertainly, "if it's okay with the Hendersons."

"It is," George said.

They all crowded into the detective's cramped office. There were not enough chairs to go around, so Bobby took up a position by the door.

Denver glanced over at him. He had an authoritative air about him, and she felt secure having him around.

George Henderson spoke up. "Can you please bring us up-to-date," he said in a strained voice.

"Of course," Detective Lennox said, linking his fingers together and making an ark. "Since yesterday there has been some progress."

"Progress?" Clare Henderson said, her face lighting up. "Have you found my little girl? Is she all right?"

Detective Lennox cleared his throat. "I'm sorry, Mrs. Henderson, we haven't found her, but we do have an excellent lead. We've managed to trace several calls made from her cell phone. They're all coming from the same area."

"What area would that be?" Bobby asked.

"Not a very salubrious part of town, I'm afraid. We suspect that the calls are not being made by Carolyn. Right now we have people checking on the recipients of the calls."

"Have you spoken to Senator Stoneman? And Carolyn's coworkers?" Denver asked, thinking that for a cop he sure used a lot of fancy words.

"We have," replied Detective Lennox. He was mildly annoyed that this beautiful young woman who claimed to be a lawyer was speaking to him as if he were an amateur. Of course he'd interviewed everyone the missing girl had worked with. And her neighbors.

"How about her ex-boyfriend?" Denver asked.

"Nobody's mentioned an ex-boyfriend."

"His name is Matt London. I'm sure he's listed."

"Thank you, Ms. Jones," Detective Lennox said, his voice tinged with sarcasm. "Always a bonus to get help on the job."

Bobby took a quick look at Denver. He had a strong feeling she was going to lose it, and that wouldn't do them any good at all. Attempting to defuse the situation, he asked the detective to pinpoint the area the cell calls were coming from.

Detective Lennox said he could not divulge that information, but he would keep them up-to-date on everything. The best thing they could all do for now was go back to their hotel and wait.

Bobby suspected that sitting and waiting was not about to fly with Denver, so as soon as they were outside the precinct, he walked to the corner and called Lucky again.

One thing about his mom, she was a real sport. Even though he was waking her, she promised to call him back once she had the information he needed. "Make it soon," he urged.

"It's me you're talking to Bobby," Lucky responded dryly.

Back at the hotel, the Hendersons went straight to their room. Bobby turned to Denver and suggested breakfast.

"I'm not hungry," she said listlessly.

"You've got to eat."

"Why?"

" 'Cause you should stay strong."

"For what?" she said with a helpless shrug. "So I can identify her body when they find it?"

"Don't think like that," he said, placing his arm around her shoulders. "You're not the kind of girl who gives up."

"How do you know?"

Bobby gave her a long, slow look. "I just do."

72

Hank Montero—The Wild Card

The public attorney assigned to Hank Montero was short, fat, and bald. His name was Dewey Find, and he was in the middle of a personal crisis—an acrimonious divorce that was costing him everything he had.

Dewey had loser clients up the wazoo, and frankly he didn't give a fast fuck about any of them. His plan was to opt out of the rat race as soon as he'd saved enough money and flee to Hawaii, where he planned on finding himself an innocent native girl and living in a hut on the beach for next to nothing.

Dewey existed in a dreamworld of his own making.

He hated Hank Montero on sight. Hank was all the things he wasn't: tall, well built, with a full head of hair.

"Make me a deal," Hank implored.

Yeah, Dewey thought. *You did a bad, bad thing, so I'll make you a deal that'll guarantee you at least ten years behind bars getting butt-fucked by all the guys who used to jerk off to Gemma Summer's movies.*

"Write a confession," Dewey advised his latest client. "Full disclosure. It'll go a long way to helping you receive a much lighter sentence."

So Hank, not the smartest pebble on the beach, did just that.

73

Annabelle

There is nothing the media likes better than a good old-fashioned funeral with all the trimmings. Gemma Summer's funeral promised to provide everything and more. A church service, followed by an outdoor burial service, with stars and top executives galore. Plus—bonus time—the exquisite Gemma's celebrated movie-star husband. And her daughter, Annabelle—notorious since her exposure (twenty-four hours ago) as a top New York madam who wasn't averse to turning a trick or two herself.

This all was nirvana to the hordes of press assembled at Forest Lawn Memorial Park, a burial place for megastars. Especially as they'd gotten word through an anonymous source (Fanny Bernstein) that Annabelle Maestro would indeed be attending.

The excitement level was high.

Standing slightly apart from the throng was Mario Riviera, who hoped he might get a glimpse of Denver. He'd certainly blown it on their last date, and he'd been trying to make amends ever since, without much success.

Denver could be privy to some inside scoop she might share with him. It was always a coup getting one over on the rival entertainment shows with information they didn't have, and since he'd recently been promoted to coanchor on the new show *Hollywood Word*, he was out to prove himself. Why not make use of any connections he could muster?

Mario Riviera was not just another pretty face.

~ ~ ~

Leaning toward her new client, Fanny grasped Annabelle's hand. "Stay strong, dollface," she said, full of good cheer. "It'll be over before you know it."

"I'm not on my way to the dentist!" Annabelle said tartly, thinking that sometimes Fanny could be quite irritating.

Along with Frankie, they were sitting in a low-key black town car on their way to Forest Lawn Memorial Park in the Hollywood Hills.

Annabelle was apprehensive about facing Ralph. Her father was such a frightening figure, so much larger than life. When she was a child, she'd sometimes experienced nightmares starring his massive face. It had been very disturbing.

Even thinking about it now brought back creepy memories. That larger-than-life face looming over her . . . it was not a pleasant recollection.

Unfortunately, Ralph now knew all about the business she was running with Frankie. She was well aware how furious he must be.

But then she had to believe that Fanny was right: There was nothing he could do or say to her in front of everyone, especially since there would be a huge media turnout observing his every move.

Fanny, clad in a black ruffled dress that made her look twice her size, reached for the bottle of champagne she'd thoughtfully brought with her. She handed it to Frankie along with some plastic glasses. "Open," she ordered. "Then pour, dollface. We are in dire need of a tipple to take the edge off." She turned to Annabelle. "Am I speaking for both of us, princess?"

Annabelle nodded her agreement. A glass of champagne was exactly what she needed to get through the upcoming ordeal. Maybe two or three glasses. Slightly buzzed seemed like a grand alternative to stone cold sober.

~ ~ ~

Accompanied by his lawyer and Pip, his trusty PR flack, Ralph Maestro left his house prepared for the circus that was to follow.

There had been much speculation over the past week about Gemma's murder, but now thankfully all the gossip and innuendo had been put to rest. An arrest had been made, and that was that.

The police had not revealed any details, but the general assumption was that the stalker from New Orleans who'd been tracking Gemma was the person arrested. Even Felix didn't know for sure.

Ralph was still steaming about the recent revelations concerning his daughter. Annabelle was not a smart girl, and she'd always been jealous of the relationship between him and Gemma. She'd barely been able to hide the resentment she'd felt toward both of them.

It was sad, but now he was done with her. Annabelle would never receive another penny from him.

~ ~ ~

The funeral procession was small and dignified. Gemma had no immediate family; she was an only child, and her parents were deceased. Ralph had invited only a few of their friends to be part of the line of black limousines following the hearse containing Gemma's flower-bedecked coffin.

Actually, not so much friends as heads of studios and important executives. Ralph, like Fanny, was never one to let a career-enhancing opportunity pass by.

Several helicopters containing news crews hovered over the procession. Even in death, Gemma Summer could still make headlines.

74

Hank Montero—The Wild Card

As confessions go, Hank Montero's was a winner. With the help of his attorney, he'd worked on it all night. Put in every detail he could recall. One thing about Hank, he had a pretty good memory for details.

Nobody was locking up Hank Montero for a murder he'd been hired to commit. No freaking way.

Yeah. That's right. He was a paid assassin.

An outside contractor.

Not responsible.

And Hank Montero had no compunction about pointing the finger at the person who'd hired him.

No compunction at all.

75

Denver

Under different circumstances, I would be falling madly, crazily in love with Bobby. Believe me, I am not a romantic, but there is something about him that is so damn irresistible. Not only is he totally drop-dead gorgeous in a very manly way, he's actually thoughtful and kind and, most of all, *nice*!

What I should be doing is backing away big-time, because he's actually too good to be true. But then I remembered Zeena and the blow job incident, so maybe he's not *that* perfect. Hmm . . .

Actually, I shouldn't be thinking about him at all. My concentration should be on Carolyn, my vanished friend, most probably the victim of foul play. She could've been raped and killed and left for dead, and here I am falling in love with a man I'll probably never see again after we part ways.

He lives in New York.

I live in L.A.

No chance of anything happening here.

Besides, I'm sure he has an army of beautiful women falling at his feet, because apart from all his other attributes, he's megarich.

Not that I care about money; I don't. It's the person who counts.

"Breakfast is the most important meal of the day," Bobby lectured, guiding me through the lobby into the hotel dining room.

"You sound like my mother," I murmured.

He threw me a quizzical look. "I'll let you off the hook with that remark because you're under stress."

A hostess led us to a booth, giving Bobby an extra-special smile along the way.

Seconds later, a waitress came over to the table and handed out menus. Once again, Bobby received a special smile.

That's what it would be like with a man like Bobby—women coming on to him all the time.

Why do I always pick the handsome ones? Mario, a classic example with his three-in-a-bed plan.

Sam, the screenwriter I'd left in New York, was a better fit for me. And Josh, when he was interesting. Not now with the ten extra pounds and the "I think we made a mistake breaking up" attitude.

Men! Life would be much simpler without them. But not as much fun!

"I'm ordering for you," Bobby said, taking control.

"And why's that?" I asked.

"'Cause you're staring at the menu like it's written in a foreign language."

"Sorry. I can't concentrate."

"I know." He gave me a long, sympathetic look. "It must be tough."

"Carolyn and I have been best friends since high school," I said, my eyes welling up with unexpected tears. "She's like the sister I never had."

"You can't give up hope," Bobby said, moving nearer and sliding his arm around my shoulders. "The police have found her phone. That's a positive."

"Is it?"

"Yeah, Denver, it is."

I managed to down a glass of apple juice, a few sips of coffee, and half a piece of toast.

Bobby went through a plateful of eggs, bacon, and sausages like a starving man. Then we both took out our phones and started checking messages.

I had quite a few, several of them from Mario saying things like *I miss you. Where are you? Why aren't you returning my calls?*

Hey, Mario—it's 'cause you're an asshole.

There was a crisp text from Annabelle: *I know things are different now. But I wish you would come to the funeral with me. I really need you.*

Annabelle Maestro needed me! Wow! Never thought I'd hear that coming from the princess of Beverly Hills.

There was a terse message from Felix, obviously sent by his assistant, because anyone over the age of fifty has no clue how to text: *I am very disappointed in you, Denver. Work should always come first.*

Screw you, Mr. Shark Teeth. As far as I'm concerned, personal emergencies will always take first place.

I contemplated sending him that message. Then I thought, *Why bother?* I'd definitely decided it was time to move on.

Bobby's phone vibrated, and he hurriedly answered the call. After talking for a few moments, he clicked his fingers for the check. "Let's go," he said. "Instead of sitting around waiting, I have a plan."

76

Carolyn

Carolyn soon discovered that if you had the look of a homeless person, you were regarded as invisible. The few people on the street scurrying about their business went out of their way to avoid her. They either crossed the road or hurried on by, pretending she didn't exist.

She knew she must be a frightening sight, filthy, with matted hair, her clothes coated with mud, no shoes. She presented a pathetic figure limping barefoot along the street like a crazy woman.

A couple of drunks sitting against a graffiti-decorated wall shouted lewd insults at her as she passed by. A gaggle of kids heading for school jeered and laughed in her face. One of the boys picked up a large stone and threw it. It hit her on the forehead, drawing blood.

She quickly ducked into another doorway and took refuge.

After a while, she emerged from the doorway. Now the streets were filling up, people hurrying to work, every one of them avoiding her as if she had a communicable disease.

Her pleas for help went unanswered.

When was somebody—anybody—going to help her?

~ ~ ~

"Good morning," Gregory said, entering the community center. He was disgusted at what he was being forced to deal with. Most of all, he didn't want to be here. He didn't want to hear what Ramirez had to say. He already knew that whatever it was, he wasn't going to like it.

Ramirez was sitting at an old wooden table, scribbling notes with a pencil in a dime-store notebook. He glanced up. "You're early, Senator," he remarked.

"Got a lot to do today," Gregory answered, thinking, *Let's get right to it, you blackmailing son of a bitch.*

"Pull up a chair," Ramirez said. "Sorry the coffee machine is broken. Nothin' to offer you. That's the way it goes around here."

"Perfectly all right," Gregory said. He sat down and stared at Ramirez. "What exactly can I do for you?"

"It's about my brother," Ramirez began, putting down his pencil.

Yes, Gregory thought, *I'm sure it is.* Then he waited for Ramirez to tell him that unfortunately Benito had gone too far with Carolyn, and now that she was dead, he'd better be prepared to pay up, because it was all due to his devious plan.

"He's in big trouble," Ramirez continued, his long, pockmarked face quite somber.

"And how exactly can I help?" Gregory asked, playing along.

"My brother is a target," Ramirez said. "He refuses to listen to me. But you . . . a senator . . . I was thinking if you offered him a job. Maybe you need a gardener, a pool man, someone to do odd jobs. If he could live on the premises, get off the street . . ."

Gregory kept his face expressionless. This was insane. Did Ramirez honestly think he would hire his brother for no good reason? Why would he do that?

"It would only be for a few weeks, a temporary situation, while I take care of the threat."

"What threat?" Gregory asked hoarsely.

"It's the usual story," Ramirez said. "You'd probably call it gang warfare. My brother, Benito, has a girlfriend who had a baby with a member of a rival gang. This *cholo* wishes Benito dead. It's as simple as that. And if I don't intervene . . ." Ramirez trailed off.

Benito. Dead. Would that be such a terrible thing? Especially as he'd harmed or maybe even killed Carolyn.

Gregory shook his head. "I'm sorry, Ramirez. I can't help you with this."

Ramirez's eyes were like two steely slits. "Can't?" he questioned. "Or won't?"

Gregory felt hostility in the air. He stood up. Now that he was not about to be blackmailed, he needed to get away from this depressing place and forget all about Ramirez and his goddamn brother.

"Can't, Ramirez," he said in a tone that invited no response.

Ramirez also stood. "I see," he said. "But, Senator, I must tell you this—if it was a member of *your* family in peril, perhaps one of your lovely children, I would do everything in my power to help you."

Was there a threat behind Ramirez's words? Was he threatening Gregory's children?

Goddamn it. Why had Evelyn introduced him to this man? These people were toxic. Evelyn should have known better.

"I'm sorry I cannot assist you," he said, walking firmly toward the door. He had to get away from Ramirez and this place as quickly as possible, especially as the threat of blackmail was no longer looming over him.

Ramirez followed him to the door. "You are a disappointment to me, Senator," he said. "I thought, like me, you were prepared to help get these kids off the street."

"Your brother's not a kid," Gregory snapped.

Ramirez blinked several times. "And how would you know that?"

Gregory shrugged. "I simply assumed." He opened the door and walked outside.

It had started to rain again, and Gregory was annoyed that he'd left his umbrella in the car. He had on his new gray suit, and raindrops would ruin it.

As he started to leave, an unmarked police car pulled up outside and a plainclothes detective emerged.

Gregory immediately recognized the man as the same detective who'd been at his office asking questions about Carolyn.

What was this all about?

Once more, he was filled with a sense of foreboding.

77

Denver

Bobby was a take-charge kind of guy, and since I'm a take-charge kind of girl, it could've developed into a battle of who's going to make the decisions. But I was in a weakened state, so whatever Bobby suggested I went along with.

Apparently, he'd obtained information about the area where the calls from Carolyn's cell were coming from. His decision was that we drive around the streets in that part of town, simply to check things out.

Normally I would've said, *What's the point?* But since it was a better plan than sitting in a hotel room waiting for news, I went along with it.

Our driver, a friendly guy from Sierra Leone, informed us we were venturing into foreign territory. "You don't want to leave the car," he said, puzzled as to why we would consider going there in the first place.

"Not planning to," Bobby assured him.

But when we were in the thick of the dilapidated and supposedly dangerous neighborhoods, I kept on spotting vacant lots full of overgrown brush and abandoned buildings surrounded by broken fences, and I thought, *Oh my God. What if Carolyn's dead body is lying out there somewhere? We have to do something.*

"Shouldn't we get out of the car and search?" I said to Bobby.

He looked at me as if I were certifiable. "Search where?" he asked as we drove by a graffiti-covered wall, a bunch of derelicts huddled against it, hiding from the rain under a makeshift awning of old cardboard boxes.

"I . . . I don't know. Anywhere, somewhere. There's all those empty lots. Why aren't the police here with tracker dogs? Shouldn't there be search parties out looking for her?"

"They can't start searching with nothing to go on," Bobby said gently.

"Then *we* should do it," I burst out.

"Hey," Bobby said, "I know you want to do everything possible, but this is a big city, she could be anywhere."

I slumped back against the leather seat. "I know," I said softly. "But doing nothing makes me feel so helpless."

"You want to go back to the hotel?" Bobby asked, reaching for my hand and squeezing.

I'm not psychic or anything like that, but something told me we should keep looking.

"No," I said. "Let's drive around some more."

"That's my girl," he said.

Was I his girl? Not yet. But there was a strong possibility.

78

Annabelle

Several people gave eulogies at Gemma's funeral. Her longtime agent. A studio head. Her most recent costar. A celebrated director she'd worked with many times. Her best friend, an older woman who could barely contain her tears. And finally Ralph Maestro himself.

Ralph made an imposing figure standing at the podium—larger than life in every respect, cleverly concealing his anger over the fact that his daughter had dared to put in an appearance with her low-rent boyfriend. The two of them had balls of steel. He was outraged that they'd had the nerve to turn up.

Common sense prevailed. The press were out in force, so he'd said nothing to Annabelle. At Pip's urging, he had not ignored her. He'd greeted her with a distant kiss on each cheek, Hollywood style, and walked away to mingle with other mourners.

Ralph spoke about his beautiful wife with great sincerity. His eulogy was touching and gentle. The audience of friends sitting in the neoclassical Hall of Liberty at Forest Lawn Memorial Park were filled with compassion for this bereaved movie star, destined to be a lonely man.

But of course, this being Hollywood, everyone knew that Ralph Maestro would not be lonely for long. Women were already musing about who would have first shot at him. Ralph Maestro was a major get.

~ ~ ~

"This is an excellent start," Fanny Bernstein whispered in Frankie's ear. "Annabelle's a natural. Did you *see* how our little dollface handled the press?"

Frankie nodded, none too pleased. Yes, he'd seen all right. Who would've guessed that Annabelle possessed acting talent? She'd done a fine job of portraying the inconsolable daughter. She'd expertly deflected any questions about the piece in *Truth & Fact*. And the assembled media had fallen in love with her.

Frankie, on the other hand, found himself ignored. He wasn't important enough for the press. They couldn't care less about him, it was Annabelle all the way.

Frankie's considerable ego had taken a major nosedive.

Fanny appeared to know everyone, but she didn't bother introducing him, another irritant. Goddamn it, she was supposed to be representing both of them, not just Annabelle.

After the funeral, he planned on having a serious heart-to-heart with Fanny Bernstein. It was about time she treated him with the respect he deserved.

~ ~ ~

After the private service, everyone trooped out to the cemetery to watch as the coffin was lowered into the ground.

Several helicopters swirled overhead. It was a perfect California December day, no clouds in the sky, a warm but slight breeze.

Annabelle wondered if they should go back to the house with all the other mourners.

Fanny said they should.

In a strange way, Annabelle was elated. People were being so nice to her; they were talking to her about how she resembled her mother and how lovely she was. They were asking whether she'd ever consider a career in the movies. Nobody—not one person—mentioned the damn tabloid.

The studio head handed her his card and suggested she call him. Her mother's best friend said they must have lunch. Gemma's most recent co-star, a handsome actor with a Johnny Depp swagger, inquired if she was single.

"Yes," she answered quickly, hoping that Frankie wasn't lurking anywhere nearby.

Hollywood. Beverly Hills. Los Angeles. Suddenly Annabelle felt she was finally home.

Good-bye, New York. L.A. was her future.

79

Bobby

They'd been driving up and down for over an hour.

"Maybe we should head back to the hotel," Bobby suggested. "This wasn't such a brilliant idea."

"How about ten more minutes?" Denver said hopefully, her eyes glued to the side window, scanning the street. "I can't explain, I've just got kind of a feeling."

"No." Bobby shook his head. "I'm sorry, Denver. This is a useless exercise. I don't know why I suggested it."

She nodded, eyes still watching the street. "I guess you're right." She sighed.

"Hotel?" their driver asked, thinking that his passengers had to be from out of state. They obviously didn't realize how dangerous these streets could be.

"Yeah," Bobby said, reluctant to give up but realizing it was for the best. "The hotel."

The driver put his foot down, a happy man.

Suddenly, Denver let out a cry to stop the car.

"What?" Bobby said, startled.

"Stop the goddamn car!" Denver yelled at the driver. "Right now!"

The poor man didn't know what to do. One passenger wanted to return to the hotel, but now the pretty woman wanted him to stop. He tried to explain that even though it was daylight, it still wasn't safe, but she was having none of it.

"Stop this car," she commanded. "Now!"

"What did you see?" Bobby asked. "What is it?"

"I . . . I'm not sure," Denver stammered as the driver reluctantly pulled the car to the curb. "It's crazy, I know. But back half a block, there was a person on the street . . ."

"A person?" Bobby repeated blankly. "What kind of person?"

"No, really . . ."

"What person, Denver? Someone you know?"

"I . . . yes . . . I . . . I think it was Carolyn."

80

Carolyn

"What are you doing here, Senator?" Detective Lennox inquired.

Gregory stepped back out of the rain into the entrance of the community center.

Slumming. What else would I be doing here? "I am concerned about the welfare of the youth in this city," Gregory said, launching into smooth politician talk. "Ramirez Ortego and I often meet to see what I can do to help. Getting these kids off the street is of major importance."

Ramirez shot him a look.

Detective Lennox sighed. "Can we go inside? I'd appreciate it if you would come, too, Senator."

Gregory experienced a leaden feeling in his stomach. What now? Had the detective discovered Carolyn's body and somehow linked it to him and the Ortego family?

Stay calm, he told himself. *Do not panic.*

Ramirez and Detective Lennox obviously knew each other, for as the three men walked inside, Detective Lennox placed his hand on Ramirez's shoulder in a familiar fashion. "I came here to tell you myself, Ramirez," he said with a heavy sigh. "I didn't want you hearing it on the street."

Ramirez's face was a frozen mask. "Is it Benito?" he said at last. "Is it my brother?"

Detective Lennox nodded. "I'm sorry," he said. "It happened last night. I'm really sorry."

~ ~ ~

Carolyn did not think she could make it any farther. Every street she turned onto was another desolate row of broken and empty buildings. And every person she attempted to approach turned his back on her. This was America, yet nobody was prepared to help her. It didn't seem possible, yet it was.

She was cold and alone. Her foot was swelling up, and in spite of the freezing cold she felt feverish and dizzy. If someone didn't help her soon, she'd just give up, find a corner, and curl into a ball. No food. No water. A sharp pain in her lower abdomen.

Was she losing the baby? Was that blood she felt trickling down her leg?

She couldn't go on. It was too much.

She leaned against the wall of a boarded-up shop and gasped for breath.

A car drove past. A decent-looking car.

Would they stop for her? Feebly, she waved.

No. They wouldn't stop. Nobody would.

She crumpled to the ground on the wet pavement and closed her eyes.

"Carolyn?"

It was the voice of an angel.

"Oh my God, Carolyn!" the voice said. "It *is* you!"

81

The Shocker

In Hollywood, expecting the unexpected is an everyday occurrence. Scandals take place on a daily basis.

Phil Spector shoots a woman in the face. O. J. Simpson slashes up his wife and her male friend. Britney has a public meltdown. Lindsay Lohan runs around smashing up cars and wearing no panties. Heath Ledger overdoses. Jessica and Jennifer and Cameron break up with yet another boyfriend. Michael Jackson dies amid much speculation.

There is always something going on. The Hollywood community is rarely shocked.

But once in a while, something happens that is so off the chart that people are actually stunned.

The Gemma Summer funeral presented such an event.

Everything went off smoothly. The ride to Forest Lawn Memorial Park. The heartfelt eulogies. The lowering of the coffin.

And then came the big finale, witnessed by everyone present.

Several police cars. A scattering of cops. And two detectives. Detective Preston, a tall African-American man, and Detective Lee, a younger Asian-American woman.

The two detectives approached Ralph Maestro as he walked away from the grave site, their expressions determined.

Immediately alarmed, Pip, loyal PR flack that he was, stepped in front of his important client.

"Move," said Detective Lee in a surprisingly deep voice.

"Ralph Maestro," Detective Preston said, "you are under arrest for your involvement in the murder of your wife, Gemma Summer Maestro. You have the right to remain silent. Anything you say can and will be used against you in a court of law. You have—"

"This is an outrage!" Felix Saunders exploded as the detective finished reading Ralph Maestro his rights.

Ralph remained stoic, his larger-than-life movie-star face devoid of any emotion. After all, this was Hollywood, and he was a star.

Nothing was going to happen to a big celebrity such as himself.

Nothing at all.

82

Denver

Wow! So much happened in such a short period of time that I'm kind of dazed.

Discovering Carolyn wandering the streets was a total fluke. Amazing!

I have to thank Bobby for working behind the scenes and finding out everything he could. Guess it's pretty useful coming from a family who can pick up a phone and call the chief of police.

We rushed Carolyn to the emergency room, with me holding her in my arms all the way there and Bobby taking care of reaching the Hendersons and Detective Lennox.

A Dr. Glass met us at the ER and whisked Carolyn off, while I hugged the Hendersons and tried to make sense of the whole thing.

Bobby was there for me all the way, fielding everyone's questions, getting me coffee, watching over me. It's kind of a strange feeling having someone look after me. I've always been so independent, sure I could handle any situation. But right now I realized that having Bobby around was pretty damn comforting.

When we picked up Carolyn and bundled her into the car, she looked so pathetic and wrecked, and she was hysterical. God knows what kind of ordeal she'd suffered through.

Detective Lennox was waiting to question her, but Dr. Glass had not given him the go-ahead, which I think kind of pissed him off. He paced up and down, drinking endless cups of coffee out of Styrofoam cups.

Finally, Dr. Glass appeared in the waiting area. "Carolyn's going to be fine," the doctor assured us, paying special attention to Mrs. Henderson, who looked kind of wrecked herself. "She's suffering from exhaustion and severe dehydration, and she has a nasty cut on her foot that will need stitches. We're giving her a tetanus shot just to be safe. However, you will all be happy to hear that the baby is fine."

"Baby?" Mrs. Henderson said, confused.

"Baby!" I gasped, equally confused.

"Carolyn is almost two months pregnant," Dr. Glass revealed. "I thought you all knew."

So *that* was Carolyn's exciting news. Finally!

Bobby took my hand and squeezed it.

Hmm . . . who knew that mere hand-holding could send chills down a girl's spine?

"You surprised?" Bobby asked.

"You bet!" I replied. "Now I need to find out who the father is."

He gave me a slow smile.

Oh, man! Those whiter-than-white teeth. Those lips. Those dark, intense eyes.

Should I be getting turned on at a time like this?

I think not.

But screw it. Carolyn's safe. So what was wrong with concentrating on Bobby?

Nothing.

"Why?" he said sensibly. "Isn't it up to her to tell you when she wants you to know?"

Smart, too. Questioning her right now was not a good idea.

I suddenly realized how tired I was. Emotionally drained and ready to go home and crawl into bed with Amy Winehouse beside me.

There was nothing more I could do here. The Hendersons needed time with their daughter. I would just be in the way. Besides, if all was okay, Carolyn would be coming out to stay with me in a week or so.

I asked if I could see her. Dr. Glass said no, only family for now.

Bobby kind of read my mind. "How about I fly you home?" he suggested. "Your friend is safe, there's nothing more you can do here."

"But you live in New York," I murmured. "I can easily catch a commercial flight."

His dark eyes bored into mine. "I'm taking you home," he said, his tone inviting no argument.

I said my good-byes to the Hendersons, wished them well, and made them promise to have Carolyn call me as soon as she was up to it.

We both shook Detective Lennox's hand and then took off, me and Bobby Santangelo Stanislopoulos.

Sitting in a car on the way to the airport, I felt a shyness overcome me, and that's not me at all.

Oh God! In the midst of all the drama, was I falling in—

No! No! No!

"Whereabouts do you live in L.A.?" Bobby asked.

"Why? You planning to have your plane land on my street?" I answered flippantly.

"Maybe," he said, grinning. "That way I can get rid of you sooner."

"Get rid of me! How dare you!" I joked.

"Y'know," he said, giving me a long, lingering look, "you're even prettier when you're mock angry."

I swallowed hard. Usually I would come up with a smart retort, but Bobby had me flummoxed.

The plane was waiting. Naturally. It seemed Bobby snapped his fingers and things happened.

Hani and Gitta were on board to greet us, clad in their smart uniforms.

Hmm . . . I think I could easily get used to this style of travel.

I glanced at my watch. It was almost noon Washington time. Three hours earlier in L.A. The Maestro funeral would soon be under way, and I would not be there to participate.

Too bad.

Or not.

The moment the plane took off, I fell into a deep sleep curled into a tight ball. Someone—I think it was Bobby—put a blanket over me and a pillow behind my head, but nothing was about to wake me. I was totally beat.

When I did surface a couple of hours later, Bobby had news.

Apparently, Ralph Maestro had been arrested for ordering his wife's murder. It was all over the Internet.

Unfortunately, or fortunately, I'd missed the whole thing.

I couldn't wait to get home and find out everything.

As soon as we landed, Bobby had a car waiting—of course—and we set off for my apartment.

I was major conflicted. Was I going to invite him in? What kind of state had I left my apartment in? Where were we headed? Could this possibly turn into something?

Yes! Yes! Yes!

But fate always has a crazy way of intervening. Standing outside my apartment was Sam, the screenwriter I'd spent one night with in New York.

"Hey there," Sam exclaimed, full of enthusiasm. "I just sold my screenplay to Universal, so here I am!"

And yes, there he was—complete with overnight bag.

Awkward.

Very awkward.

Especially as Sam was acting as if we were a couple. Or at least that's what Bobby seemed to think, for he gave me a quick peck on the cheek and took off fast. There was nothing I could say to stop him.

Bye-bye, Bobby, nice knowing you.

Completely thrown, I invited Sam in, gave him a drink and hearty congratulations, and then told him he couldn't stay.

Sam got the message; he wasn't slow.

Over the next few days, I found out a lot. I discovered that Ralph Maestro was not merely a movie star, he was a man with major connections. Important and powerful connections. So although he was arrested and charged with hiring Hank Montero to murder his wife, Ralph was released within hours. Felix Saunders saw to that. A five-million-dollar bond, and the big movie star was back in his enormous mansion, a confident man. Confident that when the case finally came to trial—perhaps in four years, the same amount of time it had taken to get famous record producer Phil Spector into court for trial number one—he would walk free. For in Ralph's mind, he was guilty of no crime.

The beautiful, ethereal Gemma Summer, his loving wife, had screwed around on him, and to Ralph that was an unforgivable sin. He revealed to Felix and the investigating detectives that one day, while sharing a beer with his former stunt double Hank Montero, he'd happened to mention that any woman who cheated on her husband deserved to be shot.

How was he to know that Hank, a man who'd fallen upon hard times, would take him literally?

"It was a stupid joke," Ralph informed them all. "A careless remark seized upon by an unbalanced psychopath."

Felix nodded. He understood. Felix understood everything.

Later, there were questions about the money Hank claimed Ralph had paid him.

"The man was down on his luck," Ralph said without a flicker of guilt. "I gave him a few thousand dollars to tide him over. If you can't help your fellow man, what use are you to anybody?"

I had looked into his face and seen raw evil in Ralph Maestro's piercing eyes.

But Felix was a master. He knew he would have no trouble getting Ralph exonerated from all charges.

Felix was a killer lawyer.

And Ralph was a killer client.

Shortly after, I quit the firm of Saunders, Fields, Simmons & Johnson.

Perhaps my dad was the one with the right idea. Suddenly, prosecuting criminals instead of defending them seemed a lot more palatable.

Carolyn was on her way to stay with me for Christmas, and hopefully she'd tell me everything—for so far, her kidnapping remained a mystery. I was also dying to find out who the father of her baby was. We had a lot of catching up to do.

I wasn't sure what my future held, but one thing I did know for sure: I planned on making all the right choices.

As for Bobby . . . well, harking back to high school, he was the handsome jock, and I was the studious girl he never noticed. I'd always known it couldn't possibly work out.

Now I could get back to concentrating on my career.

I was free. I could do absolutely anything I wanted.

The Epilogue: Six Months Later

At first Annabelle was dazed—not even shocked, because instinctively she'd sensed her father was guilty all along. Oh yes, she'd joked about it, but deep down she'd always harbored a gut feeling that somehow or other Ralph was responsible for her mother's brutal demise.

Ralph Maestro and Gemma Summer.

The perfect couple.

Perfect no more.

Of course, she was sure that Ralph would be acquitted, if he ever went to trial. This was Hollywood, after all. Movie stars could and did get away with murder.

~ ~ ~

Janey Bonafacio was never able to track down Chip, nor could Frankie. Janey was relieved that Frankie had finally forgiven her for allowing Chip to run riot in their New York apartment, stealing photos, documents, and all the cash from their safe.

Frankie had not discovered the money was gone until he and Annabelle had returned to New York for Annabelle's appearance on the *Today* show. When he'd found out they'd been robbed, he'd gone crazy.

Annabelle was more pragmatic. "There's nothing we can do," she'd said. "We're lucky Bobby fixed it so we didn't get arrested for running call girls."

This was true. Bobby and his family's connections had saved the day. Bobby was a true friend.

~ ~ ~

Chip Bonafacio relocated to Tucson and managed to stay out of sight. Neither Frankie nor his mom had any idea where he'd gone.

He changed his name, rented a penthouse apartment, hooked up with a pole dancer named Daisy, and bought himself a brand-new motorcycle. Man, he was rolling in cash, and he loved it.

However, his newfound affluence was not to bring him lasting joy. Three months after the *Truth & Fact* article ran, he was killed in a head-on collision with a delivery truck.

Daisy quickly gathered up all Chip's remaining cash, which was quite substantial, and ran out of town.

~ ~ ~

Annabelle refused to allow her father's newfound notoriety to slow her down. Oh no, not at all. Fanny was in charge, and anything Fanny suggested was right on the money.

The top shows wanted her: *Oprah*, *Larry King Live*, even *The Jay Leno Show*. She appeared on them all.

It turned out—exactly as Fanny had predicted—that in front of the camera, Annabelle was a natural. Charming. Sweet when she wanted to be, wicked when she didn't. Amusing. Literate. She was a talk show host's dream guest.

Then, exactly as Fanny had also predicted, along came the offers to put her name to a book. It was a multimillion-dollar deal: *My Life—A Hollywood Princess Tells All.*

A fast publication. A phenomenal rise to the top of the best-seller lists. And soon Annabelle Maestro was a bona fide star in her own right.

~ ~ ~

Frankie finally called it quits on their relationship. He did not appreciate Annabelle's shitty attitude, lording it over him as if she were the Second Coming of Angelina Jolie. One thing he knew for sure: Frankie Romano was not cut out to be background material.

Fanny was pissing him off, too. Everything she did was for Annabelle to shine—nothing for him. The reality show featuring the two of them as a couple never happened. Instead Annabelle was offered her own show based on her dumb book.

That was it for Frankie; he didn't give a fast crap. He had other things to get off the ground. Besides, he and Annabelle had grown apart months ago.

When Frankie said good-bye, Annabelle said good riddance. She blamed him for the stolen money and anything else she could think of.

Both of them had moved to L.A. The Hollywood lifestyle suited Frankie just fine. He and Rick Greco had gone into business together—a business Frankie knew only too well. Persuading out-of-work actresses to sell their perky little bodies on the side for mucho bucks was easy pickings.

After a while he sent for Janey, and she headed to L.A., anxious to be near her beloved cousin.

"What Chip did wasn't your fault," Frankie informed her. "You may as well come work for me. I need someone I can trust."

Janey was only too happy to oblige.

So far, business was booming. Frankie was one very happy Hollywood pimp.

~ ~ ~

Carolyn recovered in record time. Determined to put her ordeal behind her as quickly as possible, she decided to leave Washington and return to L.A. with her parents.

Evelyn and Gregory Stoneman visited her in the hospital. What a treat *that* was. Carolyn could hardly believe that Gregory had the balls to turn up with his wife.

"We're so sorry, dear," Evelyn had crooned, thrusting a box of expensive chocolates at her. "Poor Gregory was worried sick."

Worried sick, was he? Carolyn thought. *I bet he was.*

She did not know for certain if Gregory was involved in her kidnapping, but he sure as hell couldn't look her in the eye.

The love she'd once felt for him was long gone.

"Have the police found out who did this terrible thing to you?" Evelyn continued, while Gregory studied the floor and didn't utter a word.

What a coward! Carolyn thought. In case she suspected something, he'd turned up with his uptight wife to protect him. Someone he could hide behind.

Carolyn was sickened. Senator Gregory Stoneman was not the man she'd thought he was. In fact, now she realized that he'd never had any intention of leaving his wife and starting a new life with her. The man was a lying, cheating *married* son of a bitch.

But still—in spite of everything—when questioned, she'd been unable to implicate him in her kidnapping.

Detective Lennox had asked her what she was doing outside an abandoned gas station in the middle of nowhere, and she'd stated she was lost.

No word that it was the place where Gregory had instructed her to meet him.

What a coincidence it all was. And how strange that the girl who'd shoved a chloroformed-soaked pad in her face had known she was pregnant.

The girl's words continued to haunt Carolyn.

She was released from the hospital within twenty-four hours, none the worse from her terrifying ordeal but for several stitches in her wounded foot.

She left Washington with Gregory's baby growing inside her and no regrets. She would have his baby, and that would be his punishment, for there was no way she'd ever allow him in her baby's life.

Senator Gregory Stoneman was dead to her. And that's the way it would always be.

~ ~ ~

Zeena's illustrious career continued to soar, as did her collection of young men. She'd recently appeared at the Maracanã Stadium in Rio, and along the way she'd discovered nineteen-year-old twins—male underwear models—who played as a team in more ways than one. Then along came Minda and Miranda, two stunning Brazilian supermodels.

Zeena was quick to realize that mixed doubles was perhaps the most daring and exciting game of all.

Satisfaction guaranteed. That was for sure.

Once in a while, Zeena's thoughts drifted back to Bobby Santangelo Stanislopoulos, whom she considered to be the one who got away. Yes, sometime in the future she was sure that they were destined to reconnnect, and when they did, maybe she'd tell him about her teenage adventure with his father, the great Dimitri.

Maybe.

Maybe not.

Zeena never planned ahead.

~ ~ ~

Dr. Glass and Detective Lennox tentatively began dating. The two of them were extremely busy people who did not have time for romance. Both divorced, they were taken by surprise when their casual relationship developed into something more.

~ ~ ~

Mario Riviera received a welcome promotion. From cohost of the half-hour daily show *Hollywood Word*, he was upped to weekend host, anchoring a solid hour on Saturday and Sunday by himself. Apparently the viewers appreciated his flirty and audacious attitude, not to mention his spectacular abs and appealing dimples.

Obviously Denver Jones did not appreciate any of it, for she failed to reply to his numerous texts and never even thanked him for the flowers he'd sent her.

Too bad.

Ms. Jones was missing out.

~ ~ ~

Rosa returned from Guatemala a changed girl. Spending time in a not-so-affluent country with her impoverished cousins had taught her a thing or two.

While she was away she missed her baby, and she determined to be a better mother. She also missed her mama and promised herself she would stay home more, help out, and stop cutting school. Sleeping around was over for Rosa; she'd learned a serious lesson when she'd heard that Benito had been shot to death. His demise sent shivers down her spine, and even more bad news was that the shooter, now incarcerated, was her baby daddy.

Rosa was still only sixteen, but the realization that she had to change her lifestyle was strong within her.

She often thought about the woman Benito had kidnapped, and after checking through old newspaper stories on the school computer, she found out who the woman was and that she'd been rescued.

The news filled her with relief, but she still felt guilty about her involvement. Her mama had sworn her to secrecy, warned her she was never to tell anyone. But the information was too much for her to keep to herself. She had to tell someone.

One day after school, she went to see Ramirez at the community center he ran. She had never met him before, but she knew he was Benito's brother and, according to reputation, a good man.

Nervously, she told him the whole story. He listened intently to every word.

When she was finished, Ramirez hugged her tightly and assured her she had done the right thing.

Rosa felt cleansed at last.

~ ~ ~

Ramirez thought long and hard about Rosa's revelations.

He could go to the police, Detective Lennox in particular, because they'd known each other for some time and shared a mutual respect.

Or . . . he could keep his silence and use Rosa's story to his own advantage.

Ramirez had a choice, and it wasn't long before he decided which way to go.

Once more he called the senator and requested a meeting. Senator Stoneman informed him he was too busy to meet at the present time.

Ramirez told the senator that of course he understood, and perhaps he would call the senator's wife to discuss all the improvements he wished to put in place at the community center.

Gregory Stoneman sensed an implied threat and agreed to another meeting with Ramirez.

Within weeks, work was begun to completely renovate the community center. The money Ramirez had been begging for suddenly began to flow.

As far as Ramirez was concerned, it was an extremely satisfying solution.

~ ~ ~

As for Senator Stoneman, he lived in abject fear that one day the truth would be revealed about his involvement in Carolyn's kidnapping. There was no doubt in his mind that before Benito got himself shot, he'd confided in his brother, for although Ramirez had not said it in so many words, it was obvious that he knew.

And Carolyn seemed to know, too. The look of disgust and disappointment in her eyes when he'd visited her in the hospital was not something he'd forget in a hurry. If she ever talked, his career would be over.

However, Gregory was a survivor *and* a politician, so with a bland smile on his face, he kept on going with the ever-perfect Evelyn by his side. And when Ramirez wanted something more from him, he obliged.

Senator Gregory Stoneman definitely knew what was best for his survival.

~ ~ ~

M.J. moved to Vegas with his new bride to oversee the relaunch of Mood Las Vegas. Cassie landed a gig singing in the lounge at the Cavendish. M.J. was delighted. He wanted her to get a shot at stardom if that was her dream, and since she was so young, experience was everything.

It might have been a quickie Vegas wedding, but after six months of being together every day, they were both convinced they were in it for the long run.

~ ~ ~

Hank Montero had not led a charmed life. He'd had the looks to become a movie star like his old pal Ralph Maestro. Way back, they'd attended an acting class together on Hollywood Boulevard. The class was run by a tightly wound Englishwoman who'd ended up sleeping with Ralph. Naturally, because she and Ralph were sleeping together, she'd given him all the best roles in the student productions—the shows that casting directors got to see.

Because he was front and center, Ralph was soon discovered, and Hank was left behind.

A couple of years later, when Ralph was a known name, he'd had the studio hire Hank as his stunt double. Not a bad gig, until Hank had fallen off a goddamn building and broken nearly every bone in his body.

After that, things started to slide downhill, and when many years later Hank had finally looked up his old pal Ralph Maestro and begged for a loan, Ralph had said he'd think about it.

Think about it, for crissakes! Ralph was a freakin' movie star with money comin' out his ass. Hank was major pissed.

But two months later, to his surprise, Ralph had called him. They'd met at a bar on Hollywood Boulevard, a place they'd used to frequent back in the day.

Ralph had a proposition. It wasn't a proposition that Hank particularly embraced, but he was desperate for money, and what the hell—the way Ralph explained it, the bitch had it coming.

Ralph set everything up. Gave him the place of entry to his house, assured him there would be no alarm on the side door he told him to enter by and the dogs would be secured. Ralph issued instructions on where to go and exactly what to do once he got in. Ralph laid it out so there could be no mistakes.

Except nobody had taken into consideration Hank's third wife, the coked-out Pinky, and her out-of-control jealous streak.

Who would've thought she'd grab his gun (the same weapon Ralph had told him to dump in the Los Angeles River immediately after shooting Gemma—which of course he hadn't done) and attempt to blow his ass off? And who would've thought the goddamn nosy neighbor would call the cops? And who would've thought Ralph Maestro would walk away clean, while *he*, Hank Montero, received a minimum sentence of nineteen years in prison, because the jury of his so-called peers did not believe that Ralph Maestro had hired him to take care of business?

Yes indeed, Hank Montero had not led a charmed life.

~ ~ ~

The opening of the revamped Mood in Vegas was destined to be a lavish affair. Bobby wasn't into organizing a huge party, but Lucky was, and so was M.J. Between the two of them, they planned to make it the grand club opening of the year.

Invitations were sent out.

Bobby personally mailed one to Denver. He wasn't sure if she'd respond; after all, he hadn't heard from her since he'd left her in L.A. with an obvious boyfriend lurking on her doorstep.

Damn! He'd been looking forward to getting to know her, spending time with her, taking it slow and easy.

She'd told him she didn't have a boyfriend. Apparently she did.

He decided to phone her and see if she was coming to the opening, with or without her boyfriend. Preferably without.

Over the last few months he'd taken out a few girls, and they were always lacking that certain something Denver possessed. He'd thought about her a lot.

She picked up on the third ring.

"Hey," he said. "It's Bobby."

Without taking a beat, she said, "The same Bobby who ran off and left me with an ex-boyfriend on my doorstep? Not even an ex—a one-nighter from my past. Thanks a lot."

"I was being respectful," he said, feeling an immediate connection.

"And not even a phone call," Denver chided.

"Hey, whaddya mean, a one-nighter?" he said lightly. "I didn't tag you as a one-nighter kind of girl."

"You didn't tag me at all," she said boldly, delighted to hear from him.

When she'd received the invitation to the opening of Mood, she'd hoped he would call. But then she'd thought, *Why would he?* Over the last few months, she'd been busy getting her new career off the ground, and she hadn't thought about Bobby that much.

Well . . . sometimes . . . when she was out on a boring date and started remembering their camaraderie and the closeness they'd felt.

Christmas had come and gone, and so had Carolyn, her pregnant friend, who flatly refused to reveal who the father was. Carolyn had given up her job in Washington and moved back to L.A. to spend time with her mother. Clare Henderson was in the throes of divorcing Carolyn's dad.

Denver had a new job working for the city. She was an assistant D.A., and she loved it. Prosecuting the bad guys was far more satisfying than defending fat-cat movie stars with friends in high places.

"So," Bobby said. "If that guy was a one-night-only, does that mean you're free?"

"Well, I'm certainly not charging for it," Denver quipped.

"Nice," Bobby said, laughing.

"Where are you?" she added.

"In a plane on my way to Vegas."

"Your plane?"

"It's not my plane," he said patiently. "It's the Stanislopoulos company plane."

"But aren't you Bobby Stanislopoulos?" she teased.

"I guess so, Ms. District Attorney."

"How'd you know about my new job?" she asked curiously.

"You think I haven't been keeping tabs on you?"

"Hmm . . ." she said, experiencing a warm shiver of delight. "Really?"

"What's it gonna be?" Bobby said. "Am I stopping in L.A. or are you jumping a flight to Vegas?"

"Well . . ."

"Hey, Denver, I've heard of foreplay, but this is ridiculous."

"Yeah," she said softly. "It sure is."

"So . . . I guess I'm coming to L.A., right?"

"Looks like I can't stop you."

"Looks like you don't want to."

Denver clicked off her phone, unable to wipe the smile off her face.

Beyond the Epilogue: Denver

Four hours after Bobby's phone call, we were in bed together and it turned out to be everything I'd ever dreamed of.

Okay, so here's my checklist.

Abs: Perfect.

Technique: Perfect.

Lovemaking: Beyond.

Overall performance: I don't *think*—I *am* crazy in love. And yes, Bobby Santangelo Stanislopoulos is exactly as I'd imagined him to be.

After his phone call, which somehow or other I'd been expecting, he turned up at the door to my apartment, and it was pretty incredible to see him again.

He stood outside, tall, dark, and major sexy.

I reached forward, took his hand, and pulled him inside.

He moved toward me, slammed the door shut with his foot, and immediately began kissing me. Long, slow tongue kisses that took kissing to a whole new level.

"I haven't stopped thinking about you," he said, his voice deep and husky.

"Me too," I managed, touching his face.

"What?" he teased. "You haven't stopped thinking about you either?"

"Hey . . ." I said, giggling.

Oh God! I am *so* not a giggler.

Then his hands were pulling my T-shirt over my head, and I began to unbutton his shirt, because we both craved flesh and I wanted him more than I'd ever wanted anyone.

Bobby was king of foreplay—unfastening the front clip on my bra, brushing my nipples with his fingertips, nudging my breasts together and working on them both at once.

I was breathless with the anticipation of what was to come—half wishing he would move faster and yet at the same time wishing he would never stop caressing my breasts.

I felt him hard against my thigh, and I slid my hand down to feel him. Then I knew I had to taste him, make that intimate contact I didn't do with just anyone—in fact, no one since Josh, because call me old-fashioned, but giving oral sex should be saved for someone special. And Bobby was special.

Oh yes. . . .

Finally we made it to the bedroom, threw off the rest of our clothes, and started to make love in a leisurely fashion, because we both knew there was more to come, so there was absolutely no reason to rush.

I have no idea what will happen next.

Bobby lives in New York.

I live in L.A.

But one thing I know for sure: Some things are meant to be—and this is only the beginning.